I0627319

Carte Blanche

Carte Blanche

Confession: Book Four

COZY DUBOIS

Copyright © 2025 by Cozy DuBois

All rights reserved.

No part of this publication may be reproduced, distributed, or transmitted in any form or by any means, including photocopying, recording, or other electronic or mechanical methods, without the prior written permission of the publisher, except as permitted by U.S. copyright law. For permission requests, contact Heartwood Forest Publishing LLC.

The story, all names, characters, and incidents portrayed in this production are fictitious. No identification with actual persons (living or deceased), places, buildings, and products is intended or should be inferred.

Book Cover by Marta Susic.

Interior Formatting by Cozy DuBois.

Paperback ISBN: 978-1-964386-03-4

E-book ISBN: 978-1-964386-07-2

No generative Artificial Intelligence was used in the process of developing, writing, or designing this publication.

First edition 2025

To the dreamers and disasters.

Author's Note

Hello and welcome back to the final installment of the *Confession* series! I so deeply appreciate everyone following along this journey, and I hope Blanche's story brings you a full heart as their journey comes to a happy ending.

If you have not yet read the rest of the Confession series, I strongly recommend it before staring *Carte Blanche*. Many contemporary romance series feature interconnected standalones, where each couple has a book and past/future couples may make cameos, but they can be read in any particular order. The *Confession* series is **not** like that. This is an ensemble romance series that goes in chronological order, so while Lee and Antonio found their Happy Ending together in *Loving Lee*, that's not the end of their story. Likewise, Sunny, Tara, and Blanche started their character arcs in Lee's book.

The *Confession* series is the story of Lee and Antonio's chosen families as they come-of-age a little later in life (as many queer people do), growing together and falling in love along the way. A central theme of this series is that queer love is more than just who we love romantically—our relationships don't necessarily follow heteronormative milestones; our family ties are not always bonded through blood or law, and friendships are powerful influences in our lives. Trauma isn't cured through the power of ~~dick~~ love, and people don't remain in stasis while their bestie gets their heart broken. Character arcs don't wait for someone else's happy ending before they begin, nor do they end with an "I love you." Their journeys continue together as their family changes and grows, even after they've found their happily ever after.

This series is an ode to the queer community I love and the people in it. LGBTQ people of color are the heart and soul of what it means to be queer in America and have always driven our community forward. My goal as a writer is to put more books with happy endings for queer people out into the world, that represent all walks of queer life. As such, my lived experience as a white, queer, non-binary person is not reflected in this series. Through reading #ownvoices books, many conversations with trans and queer people of color from all backgrounds, and thoughtful reflection about my writing choices, I hope to have represented the spectrum of LGBTQ+ people from all walks of life in the series with dignity, admiration, and respect.

The series is *not* intended to depict a textbook perfect representation of anyone's experience—though the amazing sensitivity readers I worked with helped shape this into something that (hopefully) isn't horribly offensive and out of touch. Both Jazz and Blanche come from authoritarian religious backgrounds and have experienced more trauma than anyone should have to. Jazz's childhood of living with an abusive parent, her identity as a Black lesbian, and Blanche's background as an adoptee, cult survivor, sex trafficking survivor, sex worker, and intersex person, are outside of my own lived experience. I will never be the person who can write their authentic stories, so I encourage everyone to read works by authors who can. For recommendations, check out my Bookshop.org storefront: bookshop.org/shop/cozydubois (note: any and all affiliate earnings will be donated to the ACLU).

CONTENT ADVISORY

I have a more detailed explanation that includes spoilers on my website: CozyDuBois.com.

- Transphobia and homophobia, including sexual harassment, microaggressions, and deadnaming by unsupportive parents.

- A brief encounter with a past abuser.

- Difficulties managing mental health, including depictions of panic attacks, dissociation, flashbacks, and substance use to cope with emotions. This book explores recovery from sexual trauma.

- Sexual content between people of all genders to varying intensity, including: a professional BDSM arrangement; BDSM/kink within an established relationship; sex during pregnancy (including an off-page threesome); a significant age gap between a 21 year old and a 35 year old that is consent-centered but could be perceived as problematic.

- The main characters come in a wide range of body types and appearances. This book takes a body-neutral approach, however some characters have biases and insecurities. In particular, Gabe experiences more body dysmorphia than other characters, and Tara experiences some struggles with her changing body during pregnancy.

- References to past traumatic events occur off-page but may be heavy for some readers, including trafficking, child abuse, abusive relationships, addiction, self-harm, and assault.

SATURDAY, AUGUST TWENTY-EIGHTH

Chapter One

Blanche

Shoving a half-empty moving box into the hall closet, Blanche turned around, and around, and around in the entryway, wondering what to do next. Strange how a space could look both cluttered and empty. Each footstep echoed against the bare walls, save for a stack of storage bins that didn't fit anywhere else. In a stroke of genius, Jazz had covered them with a tablecloth to create a makeshift entry table. Given that they'd moved in mere weeks ago, their new home was as ready as it could be for a housewarming party.

The hardwood floors were scratched, but shiny and lemon-scented. Dust still scented the air like all old houses, despite Blanche and Lee meticulously wiping every flat surface several times over. Plant pots lined the floor of the sunniest rooms, waiting for the macrame hangers Blanche hadn't gotten around to buying yet. Furniture was sparse throughout. The small apartment Blanche had never felt quite at home in hadn't even had a dining area. They'd only brought their favorite chair, the small sofa, and the coffee table with them; their friends had promised to bring folding chairs.

As Blanche closed the closet door to hide the mess, a hole in the baseboards behind it caught their eye. One of the wrought iron grates from the ancient furnace was missing. With a sigh, Blanche shoved the makeshift entry table over to cover it for now, adding a replacement grate to the never-ending list of things to fix. The windows of the atrium had shattered long ago. The chimney above the fireplace had bats roosting in it. The floorboards on the porch were rotted through near the railings, and the kitchen cabinets were barely hanging on by the squeaky hinges.

None of that diminished the pride, excitement—the sheer relief—that fluttered in Blanche's chest anytime they remembered that this ancient money pit was *theirs*. They'd find a replacement grate from some salvage store to match the rest, because they were going to do their new home justice. The pink Victorian might be worn out, but so was Blanche. This house was supposed to give Blanche a fresh start, and they were going to do the same for it. If that meant spending weeks scouring flea markets for—Blanche roamed the ground level for another grate, finally finding one in the circular tower room—a cast-iron furnace grate with flower patterns, so be it.

Blanche was taking a photo as a reminder, when a knock at the door made them jump. They were supposed to be panic-cleaning before their guests came, but they kept getting distracted by the little details in their house that they'd never noticed before. The already extensive to-do list had tripled this morning alone.

Thankfully, no one expected anything close to perfection, especially from Blanche. Brushing dust from their bedazzled denim sundress, Blanche opened the door to find Freddy and Chas, their oldest friends, on their front porch. "I should have known you two would be the first to arrive."

"Well, if you had let us come over and see your new house *before* now, maybe we could have been fashionably late!" Chas teased in her irrepressible Texas accent. She held out her arms, her yellow wrap dress fluttering around her massive baby bump.

"Chas, you are eight months pregnant. I literally just hid a gaping hole in the floor mere seconds ago so no one would step in it." Blanche bent down to hug her, ducking to avoid the brim of Chas's cowboy hat. "No kids today?"

Wordlessly greeting Blanche with a peck on the cheek, Freddy handed them a bouquet of daisies and a bottle of scotch. Chest tight, Blanche murmured their thanks, burying their face in the blooms.

"Just number five." Chas patted her stomach as Blanche ushered them in. "God, I can't wait to wear pants again."

Leading them through the house, Blanche opened the heavy swinging door to the kitchen, stopping short at the sight of Jazz practically climbing the cabinets. Her thigh was perched up on the counter to give her leverage, reaching for the high shelf. The warm brown skin of her thigh strained against her cutoff shorts.

Blanche blinked, dragging their eyes up to where Jazz's fingers, short nails painted orange, grasped for a serving platter. "Need a chair?" they offered, mentally adding a step stool to the shopping list. They didn't want to gut the vintage kitchen, but the cabinets were so impractical. The lower cabinets were too low to be functional, while the upper cabinets crowded out any useful space, soaring too high to reach the top shelves.

"Almost got it." Jazz's fingertips nudged the serving platter just far enough to grab the edge. The cabinet door squeaked when she bumped it. "Why is this up so high?"

Worried Jazz might fall, Blanche hovered their hand over her back, keeping away from the bare strip of skin between her shorts and her tight orange tank top. "Your brother helped me unpack. I think he forgot I'm not as tall as him. Or you."

Chas snorted. "Don't act like you're not a giant, too."

With a squeak of surprise, Jazz whirled around as she climbed down, the platter banging against the countertop. Her brown eyes widened at the sight of Chas and Freddy in the small kitchen.

"Everyone is a giant compared to you." Blanche patted Chas's head, who swatted their hand away with a laugh.

With a polite smile, Jazz set the tray down and held out her hand. "Chas and Freddy, right? We met during the wedding rehearsal."

Blanche mentally kicked themself for forgetting introductions. Chas and Freddy had been such a big part of their life—and frankly, Lee's too—that they forgot Jazz might not know them. "Jazz is Lee's sister. She moved in last week, to keep me from going insane living here all by myself."

"Yeah, we pieced that together from Lee's clone makin' herself at home in your kitchen." Chas grinned, shaking Jazz's hand. "Pleasure to see you again, darlin'."

"Oh, let me get a vase for those flowers! I thought I saw one some-where." Jazz bent over to dig through the cabinet next to the sink, her wide hip bumping against Blanche's in the cramped kitchen. "Here! Why is this down here?"

Blanche winced as Jazz's head veered too close to the open cabinets above. Snaking a hand between her locs and the sharp corner, they closed it before she could crack her skull. "I didn't know I had one, let alone how it ended up there."

Thumbs tucked into his jean pockets, Freddy's mustache twitched as Blanche snipped the ends from the bouquet to put in the vase. They narrowed their eyes, pointing the scissors at him threateningly. They didn't know what he'd imagined he saw, but knowing Freddy, he should keep it to himself.

Freddy merely raised an eyebrow and pretended to pick lint off his blue checkered shirt.

Jazz's phone chimed from her back pocket. "Oh, my partners are here!"

"Partners? Plural?" Chas asked quietly once Jazz ran out of the room. "Does Lee know?"

"Not my business." Blanche snorted. "Apparently 'ethical non-monogamy' is all the rage among the young queers of today. Practically needed a diagram to follow the polycule."

They ushered Chas and Freddy into the dining room, where a solid wood door (which they'd found leaning against a wall in the basement) lay across some rusty sawhorses from the shed. It made do for a table, covered in a bedsheet laden with appetizers. The vase of daisies in the middle made a lovely centerpiece.

Jazz returned, dragging two women and a young man behind her. "Meet Blanche! This is Teddy and Mimi!" She gestured to the curvy white woman around Blanche's height in denim shorteralls with curly brown hair and hoop earrings, and a petite Asian woman with glasses and a loose black shift dress. "And Teddy's boyfriend, Ed!"

The gangly young Latino man standing behind Teddy waved, braces gleaming with a shy smile. His long hair pulled into a low pony. His black button-down hung open, revealing a t-shirt with a wizard on it that Sunny would probably recognize.

"Oh my god! We've heard so much about you!" Teddy gushed, hands shoved into her pockets as she rocked back and forth on her heels. "You're even more gorg than Jazz said!"

"Teddy, seriously?" Jazz huffed, covering her face.

Mimi pursed her lips to blow her long hair out of her eyes with a huff.

"Oh! Thank you!" Blanche's cheeks burned. They should be used to exaggerated compliments, considering they paid for their house in cash courtesy of their SubParty channel. But when a pretty woman complimented them to their face, they always got flustered. Even if she was a decade and a half younger than Blanche. And dating their new roommate.

"Anyway..." Jazz gestured to Chas and Freddy, who waved from across the table, filling a plate with appetizers. "This is Chas and Freddy—they work with my brother at Confession."

Freddy and Blanche exchanged an amused look. The description was an understatement, but that was how Jazz would see it.

Blanche smiled at the newcomers. "I was about to give a tour. You're welcome to join."

Teddy grinned and opened her mouth to accept, but Mimi interrupted with, "No thanks." The downward purse of her lips deepened into a frown. "Jazz can show us around later. Alone."

"Oh. Okay!" Blanche smiled tightly, wondering what they'd done to get off on the wrong foot with Jazz's girlfriend already. "If you're sure!" Turning to make sure Freddy and Chas were following, they led the way out of the dining area. "Let's start upstairs. I'll show you my recording studio."

"What was that about?" Chas muttered as they climbed the grand staircase.

"No idea." Blanche shrugged, the solid wood banister smooth under their hand. Obviously, Mimi was less than impressed. Perhaps jealousy that Jazz had moved in with Blanche, instead of her and Teddy? Jazz could fill them in later if it needed smoothing out. Relationships these days sounded exhausting.

JAZZ

MAYBE JAZZ SHOULDN'T HAVE invited her partners to this. Sitting cross-legged on the floor next to Ed, in the room Blanche had taken to calling the parlor, Jazz was stuck on how to break the ice with Blanche's friends. A draft wafted from the fireplace behind her, making her skin prickle despite the stuffy summer air. Her pointer finger twitched against her knee in a quick and silent *tap tap tap.*

The two groups had been having separate conversations while they waited for the rest of the guests to arrive. Mimi had claimed Blanche's chair, Teddy sitting on the arm, while Blanche and their friends took the couch. Maybe she'd been overconfident with her invitations. Would Blanche think she was too demanding, adding three guests who couldn't even bring their own chairs? *Tap tap tap.*

Jazz had been so sure it would go well, but if she couldn't even bridge the conversation between birthing plans and tabletop board games, how could she convince Lee to take the stick out of his ass and stop being a dick about her having a love life? She'd been so excited to introduce her partners to the one person in her family who she trusted with her real life. Eight months together, and one casual housewarming party was proving just how fragile this relationship might be. *Tap tap tap.*

With a sigh to let out all of the negative energy that had been growing in her chest, Jazz put on a smile. "So how long have you been married?" she asked Chas, who was stretched across the whole couch, feet on her husband's thighs so he could rub them. Blanche played with her hair in their lap, pinning a daisy chain from the bouquet into Chas's short-cropped hair. For someone who had come across so masc at the wedding, it was strange seeing her in a yellow dress with flowers in her hair.

Freddy made the first sound he'd made since he'd arrived: a raspy laugh.

"Oh, sorry, are you not married?" Jazz blurted out, mentally kicking herself for sticking her foot in her mouth. "I shouldn't have assumed."

"Nah, he just thinks he's funny!" Chas nudged Freddy's thigh in a flirty reprimand. "We have a runnin' joke that we conceived Confession out of wedlock, and had a shotgun weddin' so the financial paperwork could go through."

"I don't know why anyone would get married, let alone combine their finances," Mimi said, blunt as always when she was anxious. Her small hands were in fists around the hem of her shift dress; Mimi was probably too in her head to realize how she sounded. At least, Jazz *hoped* she wasn't being incredibly rude on purpose.

With a tight smile, Blanche exchanged a look with Chas. "Well, it's good then that people can make that choice for themselves."

Mimi only grunted in reply, not even looking up.

"Oh!" Ed wiggled back and forth next to Jazz as he perked up. "I brought a board game. Dungeon of Doom! It just came out! Should I go get it? It's in the car!"

While Jazz appreciated his attempt to break the tension, one of Ed's games would last for hours and have four million rules to learn. But he was obviously trying to escape the tension with a run to the car. Jazz smiled brightly. "If—"

"Isn't that the one with a two hour play time?" Mimi cut in with an unusually bitchy sneer.

Ed's face fell, and Jazz had to smother the flare of anger. *Tap tap tap* went her finger on her knee again. Why was Mimi such a piece of work today? She probably wouldn't be such a bitch if *Julissa* was here. Jazz barely fought her eye roll. *Tap tap tap.* And where the hell were Lee and Antonio? This was supposed to go smoothly—

"Maybe we can play later?" Teddy offered gently, her apologetic wince carefully hidden from Mimi. "Mimi's right, this probably isn't the best time to start such a long game. Not everyone is here yet."

Jazz let out the sigh building in her chest with one last *tap tap tap.* Lee would get here when he got here, even though it was highly unusual for him to be so late. She would have let her partners be fashionably late, if she'd known Lee wasn't going to show up fifteen minutes early.

"You go to the U, right?" Chas asked, thankfully ignoring Mimi's rudeness.

"Yup!" Jazz's smile was going to hurt by the end of this party. She fiddled with her necklace; the amethyst was cold in her hand compared to the stuffy room. "We're all about to start our junior year."

"What's yer major?"

"Plant magic," Blanche cut in with a teasing grin, adding another daisy to Chas's hair.

"It's not magic. It's science," Mimi interrupted, her voice far more terse than was polite. "Jazz is majoring in botany and ecology, I'm biochem, which are *sciences*."

Jazz chuckled to smooth over the awkwardness she was hoping was all in her head. But nope, Blanche and Chas exchanged another look. "Not magic, unfortunately. Not officially anyway."

"Or at all." Mimi cocked her head with a frown, pushing her glasses up her nose to shoot a confused glare at Jazz.

Jazz bit back the snarky comeback bubbling under her smile. Mimi wasn't *intending* to make Jazz feel two inches tall. She was just never aware of how bitchy she came across.

Though, Jazz really should get around to telling her polycule about the anthropology minor she was adding, to make her a stronger candidate for the ethnobotany PhD program she hoped to apply for next year. Something else she should also tell her partners. But making sure she wouldn't let her dad talk her out of it had to come first. It would jinx the plan to let her partners get excited for her too early.

Leaning far enough back against the chair so that Mimi wouldn't see, Teddy rolled her eyes. If *she* was over Mimi's attitude, then this wasn't all in Jazz's head. But Teddy's exasperation disappeared behind her contagious grin as she sat forward. "I'm a poli-sci and film double major, and Ed's doing social work."

"Film, huh?" Blanche beamed. "I don't suppose you know anyone who might enjoy editing BDSM porn, do you? I may need some more help starting next year."

Teddy perked up. "Not me, but maybe Jules? She's a cinematography major—"

"Jules would *not* be interested," Mimi interrupted. For once, Jazz agreed. She would rather not have Mimi's new girlfriend get involved with Blanche's SubParty. Julissa was already everywhere as it was.

The front door opened with a bang that made everyone jump. "We come bearing gifts!" Sunny called from the entrance. "Like, more than we can carry, if anyone wants to help!"

With a pang of disappointment that Lee still wasn't here, Jazz jumped up to lend a hand, Teddy and Ed on her heels. In the foyer, Sunny passed her two flat pack boxes, disappearing back out the door with a swirl of her red and black plaid dress. She called over her shoulder, "Put those somewhere, we've got way more than this."

Ed and Teddy followed Sunny out. Jazz cringed as their bare feet crossed the porch to the sidewalk. But with so many people in and out of the house today, dirt was inevitable. She'd have to mop again tomorrow, anyway. Doing her best to let the worry go with a soft exhale, Jazz brought the boxes to the living room.

"What is it?" Blanche asked, peering over the couch. The strap of their bedazzled sundress caught the light, shining against the bronze of their skin.

With a swallow, Jazz held one up as she put them on the floor, where she and Ed had been sitting. "Plant stands, it looks like."

Blanche beamed, and Jazz couldn't help but beam back. "Oh, that's actually a sweet gift. I'm surprised."

"It was Sunny's idea," Richard said dryly, shuffling sideways with two dining chairs tucked under his arms. The sleeves of his plain black t-shirt were rolled up to reveal two tattoos—much edgier than Jazz had expected; her earlier impressions of Richard was someone a bit straightlaced and uptight. "Where do you want these?"

"Wherever you want to sit!" Blanche waved him in.

"No, these are part of your new dining set." Like always, Richard's impassive expression was impossible for Jazz to read. "Do you want these in the dining room, or in here for people to sit?"

"You bought me a dining set?" Blanche helped Chas sit up so they could stand. "I just said bring chairs to sit on!"

"We found it at an estate sale!" Sunny chimed in, carrying two more chairs. "This looks like a dining room." She nodded toward the back of the house, where the makeshift table was visible from the foyer. Ed and Teddy, each carrying more chairs, followed her.

Jazz and Blanche hurried to make room, easing the heavy door and sawhorses closer to the wall. Richard, Sunny, Ed, and Teddy came back with massive pedestals, and then again with a solid oak tabletop.

"Maybe we should have waited for Gabe and Lee to do the heavy lifting for us," Richard huffed, his face red with strain as Freddy (who had gotten up to help, along with Mimi and Chas) and Blanche aligned the pedestals underneath.

Jazz snorted, her fingers aching under the weight of the tabletop. She hadn't exactly planned to get this sweaty or dusty at their housewarming party either. But at least now the rusty sawhorses could disappear back into the basement.

With the table finally secured, Jazz went to wash her hands and wet a washcloth, wiping the table as everyone transferred the food over from the door. As exhausted as everyone looked from the unexpected manual labor, it seemed to have broken the ice. Sunny and Ed were chatting about the wizard on his shirt, and Mimi offered to bring a dining chair to the living room for Chas, if that'd be more comfortable for her than the couch.

While everyone settled back into the parlor, Sunny and Teddy tore open the plant stand boxes. Sunny carefully arranged the dowels and screws around her, ignoring the conversation as she methodically assembled the structure. Teddy and Ed's workspace was like a tornado. Luckily, Mimi came to their rescue, pointing out where each piece was that they were looking for, collecting loose screws in her skirt, and telling them when they were doing something wrong. Her bad mood seemed to have passed. Or at least the plant stand gave her an outlet.

But Jazz was more anxious than ever; Lee was still not here.

Finally the door burst open, and Antonio sang out, "Sorry we're late, we've just been busy screaming, crying, and throwing up!" He practically skipped into the parlor, carrying a milk crate with a bow on it, wearing an orange tank top and cutoff shorts. When Jazz could breathe again, she would tease her new brother-in-law for copying her outfit. But that would have to wait for...

Lee followed him in, carrying another box. "But we can't tell you why, so please don't ask him any questions!"

"Oh shit!" Antonio winced with a guilty smile. "We're late because we were getting busy! No other reason! Forget I said anything else!"

Jazz sat up straight, her stomach swooping with anticipation. This was it. Any second now, Lee would notice her partners, and she'd finally be able to introduce them.

But Lee merely nodded at her in greeting, his gaze passing right back to Blanche. "Here!" He held up a box with another bow for Blanche. "We got you a record player. Where should we put it?"

"And vinyl!" Antonio held up the milk crate.

Jazz's stomach dropped. Maybe he wanted to do this away from everyone else? Lee hated being put on the spot. But really, *she* was the one on the spot.

"Seriously, what part of 'no gifts' was hard to understand?" Blanche huffed in faux-exasperation. "You didn't have to! But thank you."

Lee shrugged, adjusting his teal button-down to fix an invisible wrinkle. "We were going to get you a full sound system, but I figured you wouldn't know how to work it. This has a Bluetooth speaker too, if you ever figure out what that is."

"Should have known you'd find a way to call me old," Blanche laughed. "Here, let's put it in the den, I guess?"

Lee and Antonio followed Blanche into the back to deposit the record player and records on the built-in bookshelves in a small office-like room. Jazz sat up. This was as good a time as any. Lee could be in relative privacy, and she could rip this damn Band-Aid off. She nudged Mimi's leg with her knee, and poked Teddy's thigh with her toe. "Hey, let's go."

"Now?" Teddy pouted at the screwdriver in her hand. "No. Yeah, you're right. Ed, time to do the thing."

"Can I know what you're not supposed to talk about?" Blanche was asking as Jazz hovered at the door, her chest tightening as the reality of her plan hit her. She tugged the hem of her cutoff shorts down. A hand—Mimi's by the size of it—rubbed her hip encouragingly.

"Nope!" Antonio replied. "We signed an NDA."

Lee sighed. "We're not supposed to tell anyone that, either, babe."

"Shit. Forget I said anything."

"Lee?" Jazz rapped on the doorframe three times before she could talk herself out of this; the pressure of her partners and Ed waiting behind her was more than enough encouragement. "I have some someones I'd like you to meet!"

"Okay?" Lee asked carefully.

Jazz led her polycule in, touching each one in turn as she introduced them. "This is Teddy and Mimi, my partners. And Ed, Teddy's boyfriend."

Lee pushed his glasses up. "You're dating *three* people?"

"Well, two." Jazz crossed her arms, her finger on her elbow making a quiet *tap, tap tap*. "Ed isn't dating Mimi or I."

"Still bros though," Ed grinned, holding up a fist to Jazz.

She grinned back as she dapped him up. Ed was the only guy Jazz had ever liked enough to consider romantic possibilities with. Except when they'd attempted to go on a date, the whole experience had confirmed that Jazz was definitely a lesbian. Ed hadn't taken it personally, shifting back to platonic metamours like they had never tried for anything more. He was "poly-content," as he'd put it, with Teddy alone.

"And I have another partner, Julissa." Mimi piped up.

"Right." Jazz smiled tightly. *Can't forget Julissa.* "Two partners. Two metamours." Though she was far closer with Ed than Julissa; that friendship was nonexistent. Not for lack of trying on Jazz's part.

"Huh. Guess that 's' in your text wasn't a typo." Lee frowned at the three young people awkwardly standing in front of him, a spot-on imitation of Dad's glower. He tugged on the hem of his teal shirt, smoothing out yet another wrinkle that only he could see. "I assume all of this is a secret from Mom and Dad?"

"Really, Lee?" Jazz huffed. "That's all you can say?"

"It's so lovely to meet you all!" Antonio rolled his eyes, stepping around Lee to hug them all. "I'm Antonio, Lee's husband! We are so happy that Jazz has so much love and support in her life!" He ended with Jazz, giving her a long squeeze around her waist that made her eyes burn.

Jazz rubbed her forehead. "Thanks, Tonio."

Lee muttered, "What he said."

Blanche snickered at Lee's reluctant agreement, giving Jazz a sympathetic smile. Jazz's heart leapt as she returned it gratefully.

Clearing her throat, Mimi stared daggers at Blanche. With a raise of their eyebrows, Blanche edged out of the room, murmuring something about Tara and Gabe pulling up.

Jazz mouthed a "what is your problem?" to Mimi, who pretended she hadn't seen it. *Tap tap tap,* went Jazz's finger against her hip. While she'd had low expectations for Lee, this hadn't exactly gone great. *Tap, tap, tap.* And now Mimi was making Blanche feel awkward, in their own home? Jazz was lucky to be living here, and here her girlfriend was being incredibly rude for no reason! Mimi was almost acting jealous. But as far as Blanche was concerned, Jazz was merely their friend's little sister. And that's all Jazz would be. *Tap, tap, tap.*

Jazz exhaled gently, touching the amethyst pendant around her neck. This could be worse. She hadn't had to yell at Lee, thanks to Antonio stepping in. And Blanche was an understanding person; Jazz could explain later that Mimi could be socially awkward when she was anxious.

Letting this negativity simmer wouldn't be the good vibes she wanted to start off her new chapter, the freedom she'd been longing for her whole life. The universe had been working in Jazz's favor lately, and she wasn't going to let any chance pass her by. Blanche was giving her an opportunity to take charge of her future, right at the exact perfect time. And she'd be damned if she would let it slip away.

CHAPTER TWO

GABE

"I'M NOT AN INVALID, Coop," Tara muttered, narrowing her eyes as she picked up the slats for the daybed from the back of his station wagon.

Hefting the mattress onto his shoulder, Gabe tried to scoff, but his grin was irrepressible whenever he looked at her. Especially now, when she was wearing one of his shirts. Her running shorts hidden underneath made it look like that was all she wore. "I didn't say anything!"

"You didn't need to!" Tara snorted, nodding for him to head inside. "I could see your skeptical-ass face. I'm perfectly capable of carrying this. The fatigue hasn't been as bad lately."

"That's why I didn't say anything!" Gabe teased, leading the way up the porch, relieved to get out of the summer heat. Not that the inside of Blanche's non-air-conditioned house was much cooler, but at least it was shady and the ceiling fans whirled on high speed.

"What is this?" Blanche stamped their foot when they saw Gabe walk in with a mattress over his shoulder. "You already gave me a bed! Two of them!"

"Those were for sleeping! This is a daybed, for relaxing!" Gabe shrugged, the mattress growing heavier by the second, already sweating through his heather gray t-shirt. At least he was wearing shorts today. "Where should this go?"

"Fine." Blanche threw up their hands in defeat. "Let's see if it fits in the den."

"You're honestly doing us a favor," Gabe reassured them, amused as always by how grumpy Blanche got whenever anyone did anything nice for them. They were much like Tara that way. "We needed to clear out the room."

"Why?" Richard followed Tara into the small room, carrying the wooden frame of the daybed.

Gabe jumped. "Where did you come from?"

Richard set the frame carefully against the wall, looking unusually casual in linen slacks and a black t-shirt. But Gabe supposed he had no reason to hide his tattoos anymore, especially not in the summer heat. "You looked like you needed help. Why did you need to clear out the room?"

"For me to use as an office." Tara stared at the floor to hide the awkward grimace she always made when she lied. "If there's anything close to a bed in there, I'll sleep instead of work."

With a raised eyebrow, Richard hummed noncommittally.

Gabe's insides churned with guilt as he dipped out to grab the rest of the daybed; despite being in the second trimester, they still hadn't told Richard and Sunny about Tara's pregnancy. While he was fairly confident Richard had already guessed (he'd been suspiciously nosy, but hadn't been prying, thankfully), they certainly weren't going to make any announcements at Blanche's housewarming party.

Not when Tara *still* hadn't met his parents, who were being strangely flaky about any plans to meet her. At this point, they'd have to spring the baby news on them during their first meeting. Luckily Tara's bump was still small. Barely noticeable under her usual baggy athleisure, it became completely invisible when she wore his clothes. Which was often. Gabe's chest warmed, guilt forgotten when Tara looked up at him. Her cheeks pinkened with a smile.

"This will be quite nice, I think," Blanche murmured once the daybed was assembled in the corner of the small room. Their denim sundress swirled as they looked around. "If I ever learn how to decorate, it'd make a nice smoking room."

"I can decorate!" Jazz offered eagerly, wiping down the wooden frame. "Some books, a couple candles, this will be a nice little nest for you!"

"Oh, you don't—" Blanche started to protest.

But Tara wrapped her arms around them. "The words you're looking for are 'Thank you. That would be lovely.'"

Blanche growled. "Thank you, that would be lovely."

"You can say no, you know. I just like decorating." Jazz laughed. "Or at least, I think I will. I've never gotten to decorate anything before."

"I know. And I'm saying yes. I am accepting help, even though I don't need it," Blanche scoffed. "I hate my therapist."

Gabe snorted, slipping out of the room to get some snacks for Tara. And himself, but Tara would end up eating most of them. Balancing two plates of everything Tara had been craving, he found her in the living room, sitting on the couch. Despite her protests that she wasn't fatigued, Tara melted into the couch, her eyes heavy.

"Here," he murmured, handing Tara a plate stacked with pinwheels that Blanche had made—pickles wrapped in cream cheese and tortillas, instead of ham as Tara wasn't supposed to have cold cuts.

"Yes, pickles!" She shoved one in her mouth with a moan as he perched on the arm next to her.

Gabe smiled at her with a mix of adoration and revulsion, before greeting everyone in the room. Richard was sitting near Sunny, who was focused on assembling plant stands on the floor, along with some younger people Gabe didn't know. Presumably Jazz's significant others that Lee had been muttering about in the kitchen.

"Phin coming?" Gabe asked Richard. Blanche had invited him, but he hadn't heard if Phineas had accepted. They'd been an hour late, but compared to Phineas, they were still early.

Richard shrugged. "Blanche said he said he'd do his best, so probably not."

Gabe huffed; he had some things to ask Phineas about his trust. But Blanche's housewarming party was probably not the venue for that conversation, especially since his mom would be pissed if Phineas found out before her.

With a smile, he greeted Chas, who sat on Tara's other side on the couch, her feet on the coffee table. They'd gotten off on the wrong foot; no matter how much he and Blanche insisted that Gabe was not interested in Freddy, Chas still didn't like him. Chas's frown and the lines between her eyebrows, instead of a responding "hello," told Gabe nothing had changed. Even though Chas had reluctantly accepted that Gabe could help out at Confession on his mom's behalf when Chas and Freddy's baby was born.

Gabe played with the ends of his long hair. "So, you're genderfluid, right?"

Chas narrowed her eyes. "Yes. Why?"

"Can I ask what your kids call you?" Gabe leaned back to cross one leg over the other, attempting to be nonchalant. "Tonio said your pronouns change, depending on your expression. Just wondering if that changes at home, too."

Chas folded her hands over her belly. "They call me Mom. It's easier for them to understand that Mom isn't always a woman, than to explain why the rest of the world says I'm their Mom even on masc days."

"Ah. I see. Thank you." Gabe tried to ignore his disappointment. That might work for Chas, but no matter how long he sat with it, being a "dad" simply didn't fit him. He'd been hoping Chas would have some magical answer that his extensive queer parenting research hadn't turned up yet.

"Why?" Richard cut in, leaning back in his folding chair to cross his ankle over his knee. Silently, Sunny held up a hand, and Richard handed her a screw.

"Just curious." To avoid Richard's close inspection, Gabe's gaze latched onto Sunny, who was busy working on the new plant stands. "Want any help, Sunny?"

"No."

"Ah." Gabe rubbed his hands on his shorts.

Sunny looked up from the shelf she was assembling with a wince. "Nothing personal. I'm just in the zone. This is so relaxing."

Gabe sat back, still avoiding Richard's eye because he could feel Richard analyzing him and Tara—her outfit over his oversized clothes, the way she was noisily inhaling pickles with happy moans and rubbing her belly, even the question he'd just asked Chas. Despite taking after his mom in personality, Gabe could never direct a conversation the way she could. Right now, that skill would come in handy. The best he could come up with was, "So, work, huh?"

Richard merely blinked.

"Has it been sucking extra hard lately for you? Or is that just me?" Gabe scoffed. "Probably my boss, isn't it?"

Tara scoffed. "I keep telling you to find a new job."

He sighed, longing for the day when a new job would be a feasible option. But that would require figuring out what he wanted his new job to be first. Besides, he wasn't about to risk not having health insurance, not when Tara's OB was already concerned about her losing weight in the first trimester. "You know this isn't a good time."

"Why?" Richard asked again.

Gabe tugged at his hair, utterly failing at being nonchalant. "Just health insurance stuff."

Richard's eyes somehow narrowed further as he tilted his head. "Why?"

Unsure how to answer, Gabe gaped, exchanging a helpless look with Tara. Keeping this from Richard was grating, especially since a handful of his work friends—people he didn't actually like that much—had already found out. But at this point, he was determined that his parents would be the next to know. It'd already been two months since Antonio and Lee's wedding; how much longer could his mom resist meeting his new partner?

Luckily, Blanche poked their head around the door from the kitchen. "Gabe, want to help me pass out champagne for a toast?"

"Of course!" Gabe practically bolted out of the room, relieved for the escape. Until he saw the platter of champagne flutes. "Really?"

Blanche exchanged a look with Antonio as he poured a glass of sparkling grape juice and set it down next to the rest of the flutes, already fizzing with the Clicquot in Blanche's hand. The pink color stood out like a sore thumb.

"I am so sorry. I did not think through the decision to buy faux-sé." Antonio winced apologetically. "Pink sounded tastier than yellow."

Blanche emptied their bottle, counting the glasses before peeling the foil off another. "Maybe no one will notice? Tara isn't the only one drinking it. If enough people drink the juice, people might think there's rosé, too."

"Or maybe I suck at keeping secrets," Antonio laughed nervously, taking a glass of pink sparkling juice for himself. "Jesus, the next few months are going to be torture."

Gabe scoffed. "Few months? I hope it's a week, at most!"

"Oh, I meant the secret Lee and I—" Antonio paused, humming to himself. "Yup, just a week! Hopefully no one notices the pink?"

Gabe sighed, carefully picking up four of the glasses to pass around, doing his best to hide the bright pink behind his hands. "Too late to do anything about it now. We'll just hope no one says anything."

Blanche followed him with their own tray. Gabe handed Chas a pink glass, giving the other champagne glass to Freddy, who winked at Gabe as he took it. Chas smacked his leg.

Tara raised an eyebrow as she took the other pink glass, hiding as much of it as she could behind her hand. "Really?"

Gabe shrugged in exasperation; hopefully, Richard would keep observing without question the way he had been. "That's what I said."

Once all the glasses were handed out, Blanche raised their flute. "I'm not one for speeches, but thank you all, even those who brought a gift after I explicitly told you not to, for coming to my—*our*—housewarming party." They exchanged a smile with Jazz. "To new beginnings and fresh starts!"

With murmurs of cheers, everyone clinked glasses and drank.

"Tara, why aren't you drinking?" Sunny asked, already back on the floor to finish the plant stand.

Tara froze mid-sip. "I am."

"Yeah, but that's the same one that Tonio and Chas are drinking. It's nonalcoholic."

"Juice sounded good." Tara shrugged, her lying-wince starting to make an appearance as she exchanged a loaded look with Gabe. He hid his own in his glass. Why couldn't one of them be better at this?

"It's Saturday." Sunny narrowed her eyes.

"Yeah, but it's the middle of the afternoon."

"Oh my god! You *are* pregnant?!" Sunny gasped. "Dicky, you totally called it!"

"What? No!" Tara forced a laugh, that grimacy smile visible even behind her glass. "You're so funny!"

Sunny scoffed. "And *you're* shit at lying."

Tara and Gabe exchanged a wordless conversation, before Gabe threw back the rest of his champagne. "Okay, fuck it!" No point in pretending the cat wasn't out of the bag. His mom couldn't blame him for telling his parents last; he'd done what he could. Relief blooming with warmth in his chest, he exchanged a hesitant smile with Tara. "We are expecting our own...new beginning in early February." He wrapped an arm around her to gently touch her barely rounded stomach over her oversized t-shirt.

"Yes! A fellow Aquarius!" Sunny cheered.

"Coop, that was so corny." Tara rolled her eyes as everyone who wasn't in on the secret, other than Richard, exclaimed their congratulations.

"You like that I'm corny." Gabe kissed the top of her head.

Richard sipped his champagne and crossed his arms, index finger tapping against his seahorse tattoo. "Why are Sunny and I the last to know?"

"You're not." Gabe ran a hand through his hair, already dreading this conversation.

"Blanche obviously knew. As did Tonio and Lee based on their reactions. And if I had to hazard a guess, Jazz knew, too. And feels guilty about it for some reason." Richard's jaw flared. "Sounds like everyone but us. And Phin."

"Yeah. Sorry," Jazz winced apologetically to Tara. "Blanche told me so my tea blends wouldn't indirectly cause any more unwanted pregnancies."

"Unplanned, not unwanted," Tara corrected. Gabe smiled with her; they'd been working on reframing her thinking whenever she spiraled about the sudden turn their relationship had taken. It was a relief that the more optimistic perspective came so easily from her lips with other people. "Don't worry about it."

"Should I apologize for dragging the cat out of the bag?" Sunny looked up at Tara.

With a shrug, Tara picked up the second plate of snacks Gabe had been picking at, shoving another pinwheel in her mouth. "Eh. It was going to come out anyway."

Planting a kiss in her hair, Gabe disappeared into the kitchen, trusting she could handle the onslaught of questions, while he dealt with the person he'd been more worried about.

"Just so you know, you're not the last!" Gabe said, leaning against the counter. He ignored the ominous creak under his hip.

As predicted, Richard had followed him, arms still crossed. Expression impassive other than the tightness in his jaw, Richard waited silently, blocking the door.

"I was going to tell you after we finally told my parents," Gabe sighed, tugging on his braid. "They keep flaking on our plans. Like, we're thirteen weeks in, and it's getting weird that we still haven't told them." He scoffed, resenting how nice it felt to finally get this off his chest with Richard; Antonio always told him to just show up at his parent's house, but his mom did not do well with surprises. "And it's even weirder that they haven't met Tara. I keep telling her not to take it personally, but at this point, it's starting to seem kind of personal!"

"Oh." Richard's cheeks reddened. "That might be my fault. I told them they didn't have to worry about her, and to give you two some time and privacy. Though if I'd known *why* you wanted them to meet her, I wouldn't have reassured them so hard."

"Thanks, I guess?" Gabe huffed a laugh. "And for the record, sorry you had to find out like this. I was going to tell you privately so you could...y'know, process it."

Richard scowled, pulling out his phone. "I already suspected since Jaida let it slip that you added Tara to your health insurance. Everything else has been evidence, and this is simply confirmation. While I may be a little offended it took you so long to tell me, I don't need to process."

"Don't you?" Gabe teased gently, a pang of guilt tightening his throat. "Still happy to donate sperm—"

"Sunny would castrate you," Richard put his phone away with a smirk. "When we talked about you being the donor a decade ago, we didn't exactly anticipate that we'd end up dating close friends. Given the change in circumstances, it might be weird for all of us, I think, if our kids were genetically half-siblings. Besides, Sunny has, and I quote, 'enough sperm frozen to populate a small country.'"

Gabe's phone chimed with a string of texts from his mom, inviting him and Tara over for lunch the next day. He snorted. "Of course."

At least Tara wouldn't have that much time to stress herself out into a ball of panic about it. He was thrilled to be the person she turned to to bring her back to center, but she was almost as bad as him at overthinking herself into self-doubt.

"I didn't tell them *why*. I just gave them the green light." Richard turned on his heel, heading back through to the parlor. "I'm happy for you, genuinely. You're going to be a great dad."

"Parent." Tara and Gabe corrected together. She got up, gesturing for Gabe to sit on the couch so she could sit in his lap. "Excited for the kid, scared shitless about being a 'mom.'"

"And deeply uncomfortable with being called 'dad.'" Gabe kissed her shoulder as she settled into his lap. Yet another reason they'd been keeping it quiet: giving them time to process the increasingly complicated feelings of imminent parenthood. Yes, there was joy, and love, and excitement in abundance. But also an overwhelming sense of imposter syndrome, among other complicated feelings. They were both prone to overthinking, and they'd discovered the pregnancy so early on that they now had eight months to catastrophize. "We're still figuring out the labels."

"That explains a lot," Chas teased. "And here I thought you might have a mommy kink, what with all the questions you were askin'."

The rest of the room burst out laughing, as Gabe buried his face into Tara's shoulder.

JAZZ

"SO DUNGEON OF DOOM is a co-op heist game." Ed handed the rulebook to Mimi without prompting. Mimi liked to read it while Ed explained the game to Jazz and Teddy—well, to Jazz; Teddy would pick up the rules as she went. Probably why Mimi won most of the games they played.

Teddy wasn't even attempting to pay attention, watching the trailer for some vampire movie coming out in October for the eighth time, instead of listening to her boyfriend. Considering the film had a mostly queer and Black cast, Jazz was having trouble listening, too. She peered over Teddy's shoulder, half listening to Ed as she admired just how sapphic the trailer was.

"Our goal is to get into the inner chamber of the dungeon, steal the Moonstone," Ed intoned dramatically, pointing to the room in the middle of the board with a shiny faux pearl, "before midnight strikes, and get everyone out safely before dawn."

"I assume something will try to kill us?" Jazz asked, smiling at Ed's enthusiasm; his dramatic aura was slightly undercut by the lisp of his braces.

They'd settled around one end of Blanche's new dining table to play Ed's newest overly complicated board game. Everyone else had gone home from the party hours ago, other than Jazz's triad and Ed. Jazz's stomach tightened in guilt. She still had company over after Blanche's guests had left, and Blanche was cleaning up in the kitchen, while Jazz was just sitting here relaxing. Had her partners overstayed their welcome? The past week, Jazz had tried to be a good houseguest; she should be helping Blanche clean.

Except Lee had already done most of the cleaning—until Blanche had finally noticed Antonio was intentionally causing a diversion by showing them how to use the record player—and sent them both home. After ushering her brother out, Blanche had insisted Jazz hang out with her partners. They'd even reminded her that she was allowed to host whatever company she wanted, whenever she wanted—as long as they stayed out of the attic. As uncomfortable as it was, Jazz simply had to take Blanche at their word.

"Yeah, vampires and ghosts. If we don't get the diamond before midnight strikes, the world falls into eternal darkness. And if we don't get it out by dawn, the doors lock and we're stuck in the dungeon, presumably to die."

Her phone chimed with an incoming text from her mom: "just checking in." The way she had a dozen times the past week.

"Fun." Turning her phone on silent, Jazz flipped through the character cards, picking the redhead femme fatale assassin. Part of her wished Blanche had taken her up on the offer to join them. *Hard to relax when the person letting me stay here for free is cleaning. Especially when they're as messy as Blanche.*

A clatter rang from the kitchen, followed by a curse from Blanche. Probably making a mess of the floors Lee had mopped.

Jazz smiled to herself. To describe Blanche as chaotic was an understatement. Lee had warned her that Blanche wasn't the most focused person, but he'd undersold it. Since she'd moved in a week ago, she'd found the sink running twice because Blanche had wandered away in the middle of doing dishes. She'd have to deep clean in the morning anyway; if Blanche wanted to "clean" tonight, there was no harm in letting them.

"Your turn, Jazzy." Teddy elbowed her.

Jazz looked up. "Oh shit. Sorry, what did you do for your move?"

"No table talk," Mimi said, tapping the rulebook. "We need to find the power source before we can communicate with each other."

"Oh, sorry." Jazz looked at her options. "I guess I'll check the closet to see what items are in it?"

"You need a key." Mimi didn't bother with the rulebook this time, instead narrowing her brown eyes at Jazz from behind her glasses.

Jazz barely kept herself from rolling her eyes. Mimi's snotty tone had been grating on her nerves all day, but Jazz had no idea what she'd done to warrant the passive-aggressive ice queen treatment. "Can't I pick the lock? That's one of the skills I have."

"Hell yeah, bro!" Ed grinned, his lips catching on his braces. "Good catch! By picking the lock, you get three bonus items."

Mimi looked like she wanted to argue, but she put the rulebook down with a shrug. "I guess."

"Isn't this supposed to be cooperative?" Jazz muttered.

Teddy snorted into her beer. "You know how Mimi is about the rules."

"It's more fun when we play the game the right way." Mimi took the dice as Jazz finished up her turn.

"Any time with the polycule is fun." Teddy grinned, fiddling with the strap of her shorteralls.

"The whole polycule isn't here." Mimi's mouth thinned. "Don't forget Julissa."

"Yeah, can't forget Julissa." Jazz took a sip of the beer Teddy had brought, hiding her wince as she forced the stale, hoppy drink down. She did not understand the appeal of beer, but after a year and a half of Ed's frat parties, she no longer gagged when she drank it. Would Blanche mind if she helped herself to their liquor cabinet for the gin? Probably, though they'd probably never say anything. Best not to push boundaries so soon. Or ever.

It wasn't that Jazz didn't like Julissa, she just didn't know her newest metamour the way she did Ed. Ed was a sweetheart and one of the few straight men she enjoyed spending time with. He was a good friend who had made an effort to get to know Mimi and Jazz, even before he and Teddy opened their relationship.

Julissa—whom Mimi had been dating for all of two months—had made no effort. Jazz had tried to talk to her during their biology class over the summer, but Julissa barely engaged. And whenever Jules hung out with them, she'd glower at Jazz and Teddy anytime they interacted with Mimi.

Sure, she was new to the polyamory thing, but they all were. Their triad had only been together for eight months. As sheltered as she was, Jazz was certainly no expert in relationships or jealousy or possessiveness by any means. But Julissa could afford to lighten up.

"Hey, Beautiful?" Blanche poked their head around the kitchen door. "Any idea where the garbage bags might have moved to? I thought they were on top of the fridge."

"Did you look under the sink behind the garbage can?" Jazz asked with a grin, wondering why on earth the garbage bags would be on top of the fridge to begin with. That space should be used to display pretty but rarely used dishes, like vases or jars.

Blanche tapped their temple. "Good idea. I'll check."

As soon as the kitchen door swung shut, Mimi rounded on her. "Beautiful?"

Jazz shrugged. "Blanche likes nicknames."

"Sure." Mimi raised an eyebrow.

"What?" Jazz huffed. "You got something to say, get it off your chest."

"Should we get back to the game?" Ed asked, eyes flicking between them as he fiddled with the buttons on his shirt. Teddy sighed, blowing her bangs up.

"I was just wondering why you've been living here for a whole week, but didn't invite us over until now." Mimi tapped the table. "Now I see why."

"Do you? Enlighten me, please." Jazz rested her chin in her hand, forefinger *tap tap tapping* her jaw. She didn't like arguing, but clearing the air was better than suffering in silence, like she did with her parents. And she'd reached her limit of Mimi's huffiness.

After eight months of dating and a year of friendship before that, Jazz knew how this conversation would go. They'd say their piece and bicker, until Teddy stepped in with some humorous deflection to lighten the mood, because they were making the conflict-avoidant Ed uncomfortable. Then they'd have a hushed private conversation, where Mimi would be her usual sweet, affirming, and encouraging self. She'd talk Jazz through an orgasm or six, and call her baby, and things would go back to normal. Until Mimi started building up steam over something else that she'd let fester instead of being direct, and the cycle would start again.

Was it a little toxic? Maybe. But they were twenty-one, polyamorous lesbians, and this was both Jazz and Mimi's first relationship. They were figuring it out.

Mimi pursed her lips, mulling over her words before finally saying, "You're frustrated with Julissa because she likes to keep our relationship separate from us. Seems to me like you want to do the same thing with Blanche."

Jazz scoffed. "First of all, I didn't have you over because the house is a mess."

Over the past week, Blanche, Jazz, and Lee had cleaned every room in turn. But it was so disorganized, Jazz's brain itched. Things should have places, and Blanche's belongings were scattered haphazardly everywhere.

Even now from her spot at the dining table, Jazz could see the drill Blanche had been looking for in the built-in hutch, and a roll of paper towels under the liquor cabinet that should be in the kitchen.

"Now, it's at least clean, so you're welcome to come over anytime." Jazz forced a smile that Mimi didn't return, shaking the dice that Ed passed three times in her hand before rolling them. "Second, Julissa pretending we're not in the room when she's hanging out with us feels a little disrespectful. Especially since you promised me that you would talk to her about it, and it hasn't gotten better. She acts like you're not part of our triad—"

"That's not what she's—"

"Not done." Jazz held up a finger, fighting past the guilt of interrupting her girlfriend, even though Mimi had interrupted her first. "And frankly, I don't care how she sees it, because the impact still feels the same. But most importantly, Blanche is my friend and roommate. Not your metamour. Not involved in our polycule in any way shape or form, other than the fact that I'm living in their house. If you're having some feelings of jealousy, they're completely unfounded."

As Jazz *tap tap tapped* her game piece on the board and flipped over some useless potion card, Mimi's face clouded. "Really? You have absolutely no feelings for Blanche? All that gushing in the group chat this week was just friendly admiration? The way you look at them constantly and get that smile on your face when you're thinking about them is just a coincidence? You're gonna tell me I'm making this up?"

Her chest tightened as Jazz wrapped her hand around her pendant. She hadn't realized she'd been looking at Blanche in any type of way. "Yup. Pure friendship."

"Not from me." Teddy sighed dreamily. "God, they're so hot. Blanche can step on me whenever they want. You really undersold how gorgeous they are, Jazzy."

Jazz laughed, relieved that Teddy had finally stepped in; Ed looked like he was about to cry. "You're just thirsty."

"What? It's a compliment!" Teddy grinned, pinching Jazz's thigh under the table.

With a yelp, Jazz caught Teddy's hand and pressed a kiss to her wrist. She waited until Mimi finally met her eyes across the table. "We good?"

"Sure." Mimi shrugged.

Her nonchalance made Jazz's chest tighten. That wasn't anything close to sweet and affirming.

Ed's phone buzzed. He smacked his forehead when he read it. "Oh shit. I forgot my frat's having a party tonight. Gotta go!"

He kissed Teddy briefly as he stood up to leave.

"Can you drop me off on your way?" Mimi rose too.

Jazz's jaw clenched. That wasn't supposed to happen. They hadn't kissed and made up yet. Her finger *tap tap tapped* on the tabletop. "You're not staying?"

The plan had been for Teddy and Mimi to stay the night with Jazz. It was the first time she'd be able to actually spend the night with her partners, now that she wasn't living with her parents who would start calling at ten if she wasn't home yet. *Tap tap tap.*

"I feel like going home." Mimi looped her arm through Ed's.

He shot Teddy a panicked look. "Uh, yeah, sure. I'll get the game back at some point."

"I'll bring it to brunch tomorrow," Teddy reassured him.

Knowing Teddy, she would forget long before she left for brunch. Jazz would bring it to him during their shift at the science library next week. And ask him if Mimi had complained about her on the way home. *Tap tap tap.*

Jazz touched the cool amethyst around her neck with a soft exhale. She and Mimi butted heads, but they loved each other, and Teddy. They'd figure this out. And Jazz would learn to hide her lingering teenage crush on Blanche better. They were so similar to Mimi in many ways. Namely how perceptive they were. It was embarrassing enough that Mimi had picked up on her lingering childhood crush on her brother's friend. If Blanche found out, she'd have to move home from pure humiliation.

SUNDAY, AUGUST TWENTY-NINTH

Chapter Three

BLANCHE

Jolting awake, Blanche gasped. Darkness was irrepressibly thick as they struggled to catch their breath and place where they were. Only the black and white brick fourplex that Daisy had adored existed. The pool of blood. The brown eyes staring lifelessly into nothing.

Rolling over to feel around the bedside table, Blanche sighed with relief when they found a lamp, illuminating the room with a warm glow. They weren't in that run-down studio apartment. Like with every recurring nightmare, they'd known it was a dream. But they always awoke feeling like they'd been transported back to the darkest time of their life all over again.

It took a moment to remember where they were, trying to place the thick curtains over the window, the too-comfortable mattress that didn't sag under their body yet, the crystal doorknob of the closet door. Their new bedroom. With the rose pink walls they'd chosen for their sanctuary, as if a fresh coat of paint could fix anything.

The stale scent of dust filled their nose as they breathed deep to calm themself down. Better than the sharp iron tang they expected. The scent of blood always came to them unprompted after that nightmare, as if their brain was trying to be helpful and supplying all of the sensory inputs from their memory.

The night was too quiet. All Blanche could hear was their ragged breath, and the echoes of screams still ringing in their head. The nightmares weren't new, but the silence was. In their old apartment, the sounds of the city always lulled them back to sleep. That was something they missed about living in Eastside: the bustle of city life was relentless, drowning out any resonance in Blanche's memories. There was always a siren or a "firework", or people arguing, or horns honking at all hours of the night.

Here, the silence was oppressive. The weeks they'd spent staying at Gabe's house, in quiet residential South Bellamy, had been bad enough. Though there, they'd had a snoring Hippo in their bed. They'd assumed a college neighborhood would be better, up in Hillside. But this was just as bad as South. Silence prevailed, unbroken. The only hope for distraction was a stray pack of college students walking home from some house party. Perhaps a bus going by. A strong gust of wind that might make the bones of their old house creak.

With a final sigh as their heart stopped racing, Blanche reached for the tin on their nightstand and popped a gummy in their mouth. The "sleepytime" indica edibles still felt like a crime against nature. But as if the universe had wanted to put the final nail in the coffin for Blanche's time in Eastside, the Kum-and-Go where they used to buy their weed had closed the same day they'd moved out, destined to become yet another condo with some bougie boutique grocery store underneath it. The night manager who grew the best Northern Lights had found a job at a dispensary in Eastside, forcing Blanche to branch out.

The gummies calmed them down at least. Not enough to sleep, but enough to stop the screams in their head.

To distract themself until the edible kicked in, Blanche planned their day. Jazz had moved in a week ago, and her first morning, Blanche had stumbled downstairs to find her awake and making tea. She'd asked "what are your plans for the day?", a question Blanche had *never* considered before. They'd finally mumbled something about cleaning the kitchen, and Jazz had come up with a whole schedule before Blanche was even halfway through their tea.

So, what did Blanche want to do today? They'd done most of the cleanup yesterday, ending up putzing around with the record player in the den to give Jazz and her lovers privacy (after they'd overheard enough of an argument while doing dishes to know they shouldn't be hearing it). Only the nice one, Teddy, had stuck around by the time Blanche went to bed.

That was a conundrum. How much were they allowed to ask their much younger roommate about her relationships? Should they even get involved? Offer emotional support or a sympathetic ear? Something to ask their therapist, to help identify where the boundaries might be. With Lee, they'd listened to everything he was open to sharing; he'd set the boundaries. But Jazz wasn't her brother, their friendship was nothing alike.

Lee and Blanche had needed each other for years. Until they didn't. Jazz didn't need Blanche. And if they were honest with themself, they didn't need Jazz. At least, their therapist didn't think so, and so far Shayla had not steered Blanche wrong. Blanche had a mutually beneficial arrangement with Jazz—housing in exchange for company. But when Blanche had met Lee, they'd needed someone to take care of. And someone to take care of them.

Jazz was good company, and someone Blanche considered a friend, but they were still adjusting to living together. While Jazz was far too helpful and considerate, she also cheerfully chatted about her day when Blanche only wanted to listen, and always knew where to find things. So far, she was going above and beyond what Blanche had expected.

Having so much space left Blanche overwhelmed. When they were a kid, they'd lived in the barn loft, but that wasn't a house with cabinets and closets and doors that hid everything. That was hay and barn cats. After that, the closest thing they'd had to a home was Freddy's pullout couch that they'd shared with Daisy. Then the tiny studio apartment after Daisy's stepdad had finally died and she'd felt safe enough to take up a permanent residence somewhere. The one in the black and white brick building, where they'd rented three hundred square feet of mystery stains, with cockroaches painted into the wall.

Blanche had to breathe deeply again to keep from falling back into the nightmare. The three-bedroom apartment their patron—*former patron, good riddance*—had rented for them hadn't been large by any means, either. Blanche's bedroom had been a decent size, but the living space and kitchen were tiny, as were Lee and Tara's rooms.

To have a giant house with three stories, five bedrooms, and a yard and a shed and a garage and a basement... Blanche was overwhelmed. Things went missing so easily, disappearing into a cabinet or into a guest room that may never have guests. Luckily, Jazz had a knack for remembering where everything was. Blanche was waiting for the day when she finally snapped and told them to find their own damn shit.

They snorted to themself; the gummy must have been kicking in. Smoking would be so much faster, but Blanche didn't want their new house to have the pervasive skunky smell of their apartment. The den would be their smoking room, or outside.

If Daisy were alive, she'd probably make a plan for each room. A purpose, a theme, a vision for every space. When they used to sit on the bluff waiting for a john to come by, Daisy would dream out loud about how she'd decorate the big houses across the river. The den would be the lounge where they'd have a cigar and some scotch before bed. The tower rooms in the southeast corner would be where they kept all of their houseplants, until Blanche got around to fixing the atrium.

Daisy would probably set up the smallest guest room as an office for Tara and Lee to edit content for Blanche's channel. They should find some desks or a table for them to work at. Anything to fill the space. Because there was so much space!

But even the rooms they had filled with "stuff" felt unsettled. The den and dining room, despite the new furniture from their too-generous friends, still looked haphazard. The well-worn couch and chair looked depressingly out of place in the parlor, dilapidated and too small. This was their house, but nothing quite felt like the home they'd been hoping for.

Blanche had no idea what home was supposed to feel like.

Even when Daisy had been alive, *she'd* been Blanche's home, not whatever shitty bolt-hole they'd called theirs. Daisy had been Blanche's everything, just the way she'd liked it. Even seven years after her death, every decision Blanche made was based on what Daisy would tell them to do. Every goal they had, Daisy would have set for them.

But this was their fresh start, wasn't it? If this was to be Blanche's home—*and Jazz's, because Lord knows that girl needs some independence*—then Blanche should start figuring out what they wanted this sanctuary to be.

A bird sang sweetly outside, the chirps breaking their train of thought. The curtain over the window was lined with early morning light. With a sigh of relief, Blanche gave up on trying to plan their day. Instead, they turned off their lamp and let themself be lulled to sleep by the birdsong. Maybe they should get a birdfeeder. Or a dog.

JAZZ

"SHE'S GOING TO WANT to talk about Blanche more." Teddy pressed a kiss to Jazz's shoulder as she burrowed into the sheets. The quilt was in a pile around their feet; the sticky humidity never cooled off on the late summer nights. "You know that, right?"

Jazz sighed, blinking sleepily in the early morning light. Rainbows from the prisms she'd hung in the window danced across the lilac walls. Blanche—in their quintessential chaotic way—had called her without warning three weeks ago to ask what her favorite color was and promptly hung up. Jazz had moved in to find her new bedroom already painted in the same pinkish-purple of the hedges that bloomed along the front of her parent's house every May.

"What is there to talk about?" Jazz rolled over to pull Teddy closer, her hand tracing the soft skin of her waist as their bare legs tangled under the silky pink sheets. She'd splurged on bedding the second Blanche had told her that Gabe had an extra queen size bed if she wanted it. "There's nothing to be jealous of."

"I believe you, Jazz." Teddy kissed her sweetly and deeply, reminding Jazz how relieved she was to be out of her parent's house. Here, she could bring Teddy over and kiss her for hours. But Teddy pulled away too soon, leaving Jazz chasing her lips in an attempt to drown in them. "And yet, she's jealous. This might be a good opportunity to try out the preapproval process we came up with after the shitshow with Jules assuming she'd be Mimi's primary."

"Seriously?" Jazz huffed, burning with embarrassment. "You want a full rundown on my *roommate* because Mimi is convinced something is going to happen between us? They see me as Lee's kid sister. There's no point even considering that as an option."

Teddy's brown eyes softened. "Think about it like clearing the air. She's probably upset, like her feelings were dismissed last night. And you know Mimi is slow to adjust to change, and you moving in with Blanche is a big change." Teddy grinned and attacked Jazz's neck with kisses. "Plus you seriously undersold how hot they are. I might be a little jealous, too. How can I compete with someone like that?"

"There's no competition, Ted." Jazz's laugh turned into a soft gasp as Teddy's lips found that spot behind her ear. "Even if there was any remote possibility of *that* happening—which there isn't—there's no one like you."

"Keep talking," Teddy teased as she kissed her way down Jazz's chest.

"Who is in my bed right now?" Jazz asked, arching her back as Teddy swirled her tongue around Jazz's nipple piercing and sucked it into her mouth.

"Me."

Jazz bit her lip in anticipation as Teddy dragged open-mouthed kisses down Jazz's belly, her eager hands gripping her hips, her thighs. "And who is so irresistible that I couldn't help but kiss her the second she hinted her relationship was open?"

Hot air blew along the crease of her hip as Teddy laughed. "Me."

"And who do I love?" Jazz stroked Teddy's soft brown curls, caressing her face as she looked up at Jazz from between her thighs, the pastel sheets rumpling around her.

"Me." Teddy kissed Jazz's palm and nipped the inside of her thigh.

Jazz smirked. "And who is about to make me come so hard I forget my own name?"

A piercing alarm rang from Teddy's phone. They both groaned.

"Not me." Teddy planted one tantalizingly chaste kiss on Jazz's pussy, before crawling over her to turn the alarm off. "Fuck—is it ten already? I'm so late! I'm supposed to meet Ed, like, now!"

Jazz laughed into her parting kiss, before Teddy scrambled out of bed to find her clothes. Knowing Ed, he would also be late to meet Teddy. They'd been sweethearts since middle school, made for each other even then.

Rolling out of bed, Jazz pulled her house dress on as Teddy searched for her shirt. The soft periwinkle cotton stretched over her hips to swirl around her thighs. It was so freeing, being able to walk around the house with her legs bare and without a bra. At the risk of a lecture from her parents, Jazz would have never dared leave her bedroom without being covered from ankle to neck. Even leggings would get her a stern glare from her father, and a hint from her mother that perhaps her body was a little too voluptuous to pull those off without a dress over them.

But living with Blanche? She was free. Free to embrace her body and her sexuality and the power of her femininity. Free to love openly, including herself. Perhaps she should wear underwear, but Blanche only wore a bathrobe more often than not. Besides, Blanche had lived with Tara, and everyone knew that bitch always went commando, when she bothered to wear clothes at all. So Jazz forewent anything but the house dress as she walked Teddy to the front door and kissed her goodbye.

Jazz was about to walk back upstairs to finish the job Teddy started, when a loud clatter and an "ah shit!" came from the kitchen.

"You okay?" Jazz asked, swinging open the heavy walnut door. The wood grain dragged against her fingertips.

Blanche looked up from picking up the dozens of forks, spoons, and butter knives on the faded linoleum around them. "Sorry! Don't mind me!"

Jazz bent down to help them pick up the utensils, trying to ignore the tantalizing bronze skin of Blanche's chest peeking out from the gap of their silk bathrobe. "What happened?"

"Jazz, take a look and hazard a guess." Blanche snorted as they gestured around them. "I dropped them."

Jazz chuckled. "Yeah, I got that. But why were you carrying literally every single utensil you own?"

"I washed them all, but then I couldn't find a towel, so I went to look for one and lost my grip." Blanche crawled to retrieve the last knife from under the fridge, their back bowing as they bent over. "Any idea where the towels ended up?"

"They're in the drawer closest to the basement, so you can put them away as you come upstairs from the laundry room." Tearing her eyes away from Blanche's incredible ass and hips, Jazz dumped the silverware in the sink to wash again. "But also, you could leave the utensils in the sink while you go get a towel?"

"That is incredibly logical," Blanche laughed. "How do you come up with all of this stuff?"

"I dunno. It just makes sense?" Jazz retrieved a towel to dry the dishes, and a fresh sponge to start washing. "That's where my mom kept the towels in our house."

Blanche grabbed her wrist with a stronger grip than Jazz expected from their willowy figure. "Jazz, stop helping."

Ignoring the flutter in her belly, Jazz huffed, matching their stern glare with her own.

"I did not invite you to live with me to be a maid." Blanche adjusted their grip on Jazz's wrist to gently push her away from the sink. Jazz swallowed as their hand slid up her arm to grab the sponge. "I'm a lonely old biddy who wants a friend around. You don't need to do anything more than pick up after yourself and just *exist* around the house." Blanche gestured with the sponge, turning on the hot water tap with a squeak.

"First of all, you're not old." Jazz resisted the urge to touch her wrist, where she could still feel Blanche's firm grip. "Second of all, you're letting me live here rent-free. The least I can do is some dishes. And third of all, if you wanted someone to keep you company who wasn't helpful, you picked the wrong person. I *like* being helpful. Didn't you let Lee clean up when he lived with you?"

"Yeah, but he wanted to—"

"And I want to!" Jazz insisted. "Lee and I both have a Virgo moon. We like to be helpful. We like to be organized. I'm not in love with cleaning the way Lee is, but I can't stand mess." Jazz crossed her arms.

"The moon, huh?" Perhaps it was Jazz's imagination, but Blanche's gaze flickered to her chest for a brief second, before they raised a sardonic eyebrow. "And I'm sure your strict parents had nothing to do with that shared trait."

"Exactly. I chalk it up to astrology, so I don't have to acknowledge the trauma," Jazz laughed. "Seriously, let me help with washing dishes, or decorating, or whatever else strikes my interest. I will feel better knowing I'm contributing, instead of sitting around."

"Fine. You may help me dry," Blanche sighed dramatically and handed Jazz a clean fork.

"Thank you!" Jazz grinned and took the fork before they could change their mind. She opened the drawer next to the sink to find it filled with soy sauce packets and a few plastic jars of seasoning. "Why isn't this the silverware drawer? Spices should go by the stove."

"Just find an empty drawer. Lord knows there's enough of them."

A pang of annoyance flashed through her. "*That's* your process for unpacking? That explains so much!" Jazz rifled through the drawers until she found the utensil tray, and moved it to the drawer next to the sink. "Look I know this is your house, but silverware is going here from now on, okay? And your probably expired seasonings are going in the upper cabinet by the stove, where you can reach them while you're cooking."

"You gonna get a label maker for me, too?" Blanche teased. "Seriously, don't feel like you have to rearrange everything. I'll figure I'll find stuff when I need it."

Jazz turned, just in time to catch Blanche's gaze flick away from her ass, back to the sink. *Now you're being delusional.* "That explains why I keep finding stuff in nonsensical spots. Like the casserole dish on top of the fridge, when you have plenty of cabinet space."

Blanche shrugged. "I've never had this much space before. I didn't even know I had a casserole dish. Come to think of it, that might be Gabe's. He's always trying to get me and Tara—well, Tara mostly—to eat more veggies."

Jazz huffed. "Why are you like this?"

Handing her another fork, Blanche laughed. "Should I be honest and say that I've never really had a home before? Or that some parts of me grew up way too soon, so the rest of me never grew up at all? Or is there a chance we can chalk this up to some astrological sign?"

Jazz's irritation melted into eager curiosity. "Do you know where and when you were born? I could try and find some explanation in your chart."

"No. I was never legally adopted, so I don't have a birth certificate." Blanche shrugged. "The Family recorded my birthday as the day I was baptized, but I don't know how old I was when that happened."

"The Family?" Jazz held out her hand for the fork Blanche was rinsing.

Blanche handed it to her. Their fingers were already pruning. "Oh, that's the cult that kidnapped me. No relation to any well-known cult called the Family. Just a weird community of insular Swedes in the middle of nowhere Minnesota."

Jazz paused from drying the fork to stare at Blanche, who hummed to themself as they rinsed off a spoon. "The fuck? You were kidnapped by a cult?"

"Oh, did Lee not tell you that? Probably." Blanche snorted. "Strange, that's probably one of the least triggering subjects. Jokes on them for kidnapping a brown, intersex baby by accident. Grandma Rose said I was blond and blue-eyed until I was about three, though, so I can see why they might think I was white."

Jazz's throat tightened. "Have you ever tried to find your family? Like your biological parents?"

"Beautiful, I ran away at age thirteen for a good reason." Blanche shook their head with a gentle half smile. "The only ones who know who my biological family might be are the people who were going to cut my tits off. And considering I was raised as a boy, I wasn't *expecting* to grow tits, but I am rather attached to them." They winked. "Going back for answers isn't worth getting mutilated. Or killed, more likely."

As she blinked, Jazz was unsure how to react beyond a blank stare. Lee had warned her that Blanche had a tough past, and what to expect if they were having a hard day. But lighthearted stories of being kidnapped and threatened with mutilation by a cult had not been on the list of possibilities she'd considered.

Jazz realized Blanche was stacking up clean silverware next to the sink and remembered she was supposed to be drying them. She grabbed them all in the towel, wondering if she should say something sympathetic. But Blanche didn't seem to be asking for sympathy, despite telling the most heartbreaking story Jazz had ever heard. "What about a DNA test or something?"

Blanche's long nose wrinkled. "I don't want to end up a lab rat because my DNA is 'abnormal.' And besides, that shits the feds. I don't trust the government enough to give them my DNA." Blanche winced, waving a casual hand. "No, I've made my peace. I have a family, even if I'm not biologically related to Freddy or Chas. Or Tara or Lee or any of you ducklings, for that matter."

As she dried the serving bowl that Blanche handed her, Jazz wasn't sure if the twist in her gut was a sign that she was glad to be counted among Blanche's family, or disappointment because Blanche saw her as a "duckling." "Where does this go?" She raised the bowl, preemptively annoyed because she knew Blanche didn't have a place for it.

"Wherever." Blanche waved a hand. "I'll find it when I need it again."

"No." Jazz shook her head. "Sorry, I'm taking over your house. You can't live like this. I'm going to organize your damn kitchen. Hell, your damn house! You should know where it is when you need it and where to put it when you're done using it."

Blanche smiled, their green eyes thoughtful as they held Jazz's gaze. "You are very much Lee's sister. He was always rearranging my dishes and books and stuff and putting them in the most logical places."

Jazz opted to take that as a compliment, even if she was still annoyed at Lee for how rude he was to her partners yesterday. "So is the rest of your house like this too?"

Blanche grimaced. "Everything but the attic. Tara helped me arrange the film set, and I'm used to organizing the toys because we had less space at the old place. I just don't know what to do with all this room. I've never had more than a living area and a bedroom before."

Excitement unfurled in Jazz's chest. "Did you do any cleansing when you first moved in?"

"Is cleansing different from cleaning? Because Lee helped me clean."

"Like smudging, burning herbs, anything."

"Sounds like that nasty Satanism the Family always preached about," Blanche teased.

Jazz laughed. "It's not Satanic to clear out negative energy. It's more like...clearing the environment to get rid of lingering bad vibes from the previous residents. Adding your own energy and that sort of thing." Not that her parents ever would have bought that; her dad would have absolutely called it Satanic if she'd ever asked if she could do it at their house. Though if there was one place in Bellamy that needed a good cleansing, it was the Jones' residence. "I'd love to help make this space yours, if you don't mind. Give me something to do before classes start."

Blanche worried their bottom lip between their teeth. "Fine. Thank you, I am accepting your offer to help. But not the attic. Or my bedroom. And don't stress yourself out. You're allowed to relax, you know."

With a grin, Jazz hugged them. "I won't! This will be fun! Mom and Dad *never* let me do this shit, but I've always wanted to. And you deserve a home that enhances your life, not just a house where you sleep and waste time searching for a serving bowl. I want to help make your house something that fits you and what you need."

Blanche hugged her back, their arms tight around her waist with a firm strength that still surprised Jazz. "Just make it *your* home, too. We both live here, even if the deed is in my name. If there's anything you want or need, let me know. I'll make it happen."

Jazz swallowed heavily, her eyes burning. All of this was so different from her dad barking about his house, his rules. Or her mom's judgmental sniff, whenever Jazz dared mention something she didn't approve of. Life with Blanche was going to be better than she'd imagined. Blanche's only hesitation was out of concern for Jazz's well-being, and wasn't that a revelation? When was the last time anyone besides Lee or her partners worried about Jazz? The real Jazz, anyway, instead of the daughter her parents wanted her to be. "Trust me. This already feels more like home than my parents' house ever did."

CHAPTER FOUR

TARA

"Kitten, what the fuck is your hand doing?"

Tara looked down at her fingers tangled in her lap. Blood smeared across her finger, pearling up from where she must have yanked out a hangnail.

"Oh shit." She popped the finger in her mouth before she got blood on her nice clothes: khaki shorts and a mint green sweater vest. The tangy iron flooded her tongue. She shot a sheepish grin at Gabe, who was frowning while he switched lanes. His face softened when he glanced over at her. "I must be nervous."

"There are tissues in the console, you know." Gabe smiled affectionately when Tara defiantly sucked her finger harder. "And don't be. They're going to love you. And I think you'll love them too. Eventually." He blew out a sharp breath, tapping on the steering wheel.

"Eventually they'll love me, or eventually I'll love them?" Tara kept her tone teasing, for his sake. Gabe was just as anxious as her, even if he was pretending not to be. With Gabe's relationship history, she was prepared for a long slog of winning over his parents. Even if they had been nice at the wedding, before they'd found out Tara was dating their son.

And here she was, rolling into their lives as his live-in partner and pregnant with his kid. A mess of complicated feelings about parenthood, and clueless about how to win over a significant other's parents. While wearing *underwear*. Tara cringed. Only boxers and a bralette that was more there for protection than support, but still. The elastic itching her skin had become a necessity with her changing body. Parts of her now leaked and chaffed in ways she hadn't expected.

"Both. Try not to take any of my mom's initial reactions personally. She processes externally. Whatever the end result is, that's the one she truly means." Gabe tapped the steering wheel as he exited the freeway. "And my dad is hard to read, so don't worry if he just sits there and stares at you."

"Is this normal for families?" Tara asked with a laugh, rolling down her window to breathe in the sun-warmed country air. It was a rare occasion when she left the Bellamy metro, but the rolling hills past the outskirts of the suburbs, lined with apple orchards and cow pastures, were idyllic. If the Coopers didn't completely reject her today, she wouldn't mind visiting them out here more often.

"No." Gabe snorted. "Which is why you need to stop worrying if you're family-ing right. They just figured it out as they went, and we'll figure it out, too."

Tara grumbled, but he was right. They'd been figuring it out so far—or Gabe had, rather. More often than not, Tara felt like she was along for the ride, while he fussed over her. Gabe fed her, scheduled doctor appointments, and kept buying presents for her and their kid. He made her feel special and loved and shit. She'd lasted a full day after Blanche had left before she'd snapped at him to stop being so damn helpful, and let her figure some of it out. So far, all she'd done was take over dishwashing and sign them up for a queer birthing class. But that was better than sitting on her ass while he did literally everything. "What if they think I baby-trapped you? Like I'm a gold digger or whatever."

"They won't. Trust me." Gabe patted her thigh, letting his hand linger on her bare skin. His thumb traced her freckles without looking, as if he'd memorized them. "And we're middle class. Not really a good target for gold digging. Unless you're Richard's dad, who can't seem to grasp that Mom was disinherited."

"They own a *vineyard*." Tara rolled her eyes, fighting her grin. They'd had this argument so many times, it'd become comical. It was easier talking about this now that she lived with Gabe. She trusted that he wouldn't kick her out unexpectedly. And if he did, well, Blanche would welcome her and the kid without question. "I didn't have a bank account until I was twenty-two."

"Okay, fine—I *grew up* middle class. Now all of us are upper-middle class, including you. How's that for a compromise, broke ass?" Gabe patted her thigh. His warm palm lingered as he steered, one-handed, down the curved, sun-dappled road.

Swallowing, Tara stared at his large hand grasping the steering wheel. It was far more attractive than it should be, but her damn hormones made everything he did look hot. "I don't think my tiny emergency savings counts as upper-middle class."

Gabe grumbled. "You know what I meant, Kitten. What's mine is yours now."

Tracing the back of his fingers still on her thigh, Tara looked out the window, unsure of how to reply. Cows lay in the shade of oak tree strands dotting the fields to escape the sweltering August heat. Moments like this made her think too much about what she brought to his life. He was so doting and generous with her. Considerate to the point where she'd even started prepping the ingredients for whatever he planned on cooking before he got home from work, just so she felt like she was contributing.

His fingertips edged below the hem of her khaki shorts.

"Don't you dare finger me right now!" She pulled his hand away, but he brought hers to his mouth to kiss her knuckles.

"You seem anxious. Thought some stress relief might help," Gabe teased, spinning the wheel into a left turn one-handed. "You normally don't complain when I finger you in the car."

Tara swallowed to keep from drooling. "Normally I'm not about to meet your parents! Wait for the ride home."

He grinned, the anxiety in his own face melting away. "I don't think I'll ever get tired of hearing you call my house your home. Love you, Kitten."

"Back at you, Coop." Tara adjusted the hem of her shorts and wove her fingers between his.

With a grin, he kissed her hand again, seeing right through her prickly demeanor as always. He took another turn into a driveway flanked by a stone wall and a wrought iron gate, driving up the hill to a stunningly beautiful four-story modern building. The glass walls gleamed in the sunshine.

"That's not their house is it?" Tara's heart froze. *Middle class my ass. That's a mansion.*

"No, that's the main guest area of the property. They do some processing there for the sake of tours, but it's mostly the restaurant, tasting room, a couple of conference centers, and some accommodations for wedding guests, that sort of thing. The main winery and the wedding venue are further up the paved road. Their house is over there." Gabe nodded to the gravel road that branched off the parking lot.

"Oh. I see. Just the tasting room at your parents' vineyard. So much better." Tara chewed her lip. *You're not trapping him. Unexpected, but not unwanted. He chose this.* But his parents would think that. She wasn't exactly a catch. *You have to trust him to know what he wants. He'd want you to meet them, even without the kid.*

"Kitten, what are you overthinking now?" The gravel crunched beneath the tires as they drove.

"Just wondering how I'm going to convince your parents that I have your best interests at heart when I bring literally nothing to your life."

Gabe stopped when he got to a closed gate. He put the car in park and turned to her. "Tara, that is categorically untrue, and you know it."

"Do I?" Tara gripped his hand. "I thought I did when it was just us. But it's not just us. It's your parents, and your job that you hate that you're stuck at because of me, and your friendships—I don't know what was with Richard yesterday, but he seemed upset! And all the money you spend on me, and all the nice things you do, when I don't do anything nice for you in return."

Gabe waited patiently as she caught her breath. "You really can't think of anything nice you do for me?"

"I mean, the sex? And even that I kinda fucked up because I got knocked up right away because I told you to leave it in!" Tara groaned, trying to steady her breathing. "Sorry. I know I sound insecure, but I'm kind of freaking out."

"That's okay." Gabe kissed her hair. "Get it out."

"It's just...you could have been with anyone, but you chose me, and now you're kind of stuck with me. And your life is so different from what I grew up with. I was homeless most of my life, and you had all of this. I feel like an intruder, like security is going to knock on the window and tell me to go back to Eastside." Tara leaned into Gabe's shoulder, inhaling the sweet vanilla of his lotion and the comforting, woodsy musk of him. "I have a lot more sympathy for Sunny when she met Richard's parents now."

Gabe laughed. "Don't let my mom hear you compare her to Dick and Barbie." He rubbed her back. "Do you want validation, or did you need to vent?"

The idea of sitting here while Gabe showered praise on her—which he would, and he would mean every word—made her cringe. "Vent, I guess. Thanks for listening."

"Of course. And for the record, I'm not 'stuck' with you—I want all of you, and more." He caught her chin and drew her gaze up to look at him, his deep-set coffee-brown eyes searching hers. Biting his lip, he hesitated a moment, then added, "Let me worry about my job, and let Richard worry about Richard. His reaction has nothing to do with either of us, I knew it'd be a little triggering for him." He traced her lip with his thumb, softening into a smile. "Just be yourself when you meet my parents, and they'll grow to love you as much as I do. Okay?"

"Okay." Yup, the validation was making her cringe. Hearing her insecurities repeated back to her was awful, and she could tell Gabe was holding back the compliments and praise.

Gabe kissed her too briefly, drawing a sharp inhale from both of them when Tara's tongue traced his bottom lip. "Don't start that now, Kitten, or we're never going to make it to lunch." He pecked her lips once more. "Ready?"

"No, but we're here."

Gabe hit a button on one of the garage door openers clipped to his visor, and the gate swung open. They drove in silence through a copse of oak trees and up to a small blue rambler sitting prettily in the sunshine. The porch swing and shutters looked picturesque with the rusty pickup truck parked out front, filled with plastic buckets and tarps. After the picturesque glamor of the tasting room, the Cooper's home seemed almost quaint. Everything, other than the truck, looked new. Even the flower beds looked freshly planted, yet the small house was reassuringly unpretentious. The lawn was dotted with dande-lions, and the woods were edged by patches of wildflowers.

Hippo whined excitedly from the back as soon as Gabe turned off the car. The sun-warmed August humidity slammed into Tara as soon as she opened the door. Mere months ago, she would have embraced it. But pregnant? She hoped her deodorant was strong enough to last until she got back in the AC.

As soon as she unlatched Hippo's crate, Gabe's giant gray pittie mix hopped out, peed directly on a goldenrod, and waddled back to her side, snuffling her to make sure she was okay. He'd presumably figured out she was pregnant a few weeks ago and had turned into a Velcro dog.

She could barely hug Gabe without Hippo trying to wedge his way in between them.

Antonio and Lee had been voluntold to help with training, hugging Tara over and over, while Gabe rewarded Hippo for ignoring it.

"John! They're here!" came a shout from the house, the "r"s sounding more like "y"s.

Gabe sighed, grabbing a gift bag from the car so he could tuck it away somewhere when they walked in. The gift was for after lunch, not right away. "That's my mom. The accent gets stronger when she's excited."

Tara grinned. Miriam had seemed soft-spoken at the wedding, not even a trace of this East Coast accent.

The front door opened and out came Miriam on the front porch, beckoning them inside. Compared to the quiet wealth of the outfit she'd worn to Lee's wedding, her blue linen tank top and matching capris made Tara breathe a little easier. "I'm so glad you're here! Come in! Come in and out of the heat! Lunch is almost ready."

Gabe put his hand on Tara's back and led her inside, Hippo right beside her. *If nothing else, I can hang out with Hippo.* Miriam and John would be nice. Probably. But she was going from strangers at a wedding to Gabe's pregnant, live-in partner all in one day. It was a lot of bombshells for anyone, let alone the loving, supportive, and slightly overbearing parents of an only child with a history of horrible exes.

Her forced nervous smile soon turned genuine as Miriam greeted Tara with a tight hug before the door was all the way shut. "I'm sorry it's taken us so long to finally meet you properly, Tara!"

Tara hugged her back, relieved at the warm greeting. And the complete mess of their entry way. Shoes scattered everywhere, the lone framed photo of the vineyard was crooked on its nail. Gabe kicked more shoes out of the way to make room for theirs; his muttered "not one pair on the fucking shoe rack" made Tara grin.

Gabe's dad came out from the kitchen to join them. John's plaid shirt was stained and his jeans sported grass stains on both knees. Tara almost laughed at how overdressed she felt now, wearing shorts that buttoned. Though he didn't say a word in greeting, John's hug felt just as welcoming.

Forgetting his training, Hippo whined and nosed his way between them. Tara and Gabe exchanged a panicked look. But John simply laughed and bent down to pet him.

John's features were a near mirror of Gabe's: tall, dark, and handsome with a strong nose, olive skin, and kind, deep-set eyes. Yet, side by side, they were completely different. Gabe was muscles and curls and earnestness. John was lean and straight edges and reserve. Even John's quiet, dry laugh was nothing like his son's.

Tara couldn't help but feel relieved that his mom's genes and personality had influenced Gabe's appearance, along with her brown eyes, thicker frame, and curly hair. *Hopefully, something of me shines through with this kid too.*

"Lunch should be ready in about ten minutes." Miriam scratched Hippo's ears. "Can I get you anything? Wine? Sparkling water?"

"Sparkling water for both of us," Gabe said quickly, unobtrusively stashing the gift bag by the entry table. "It was a hot drive up here."

Tara raised an eyebrow at him for answering for her. He shot her a smug look in return, leaving her with a smile instead of a glare.

John disappeared to the kitchen as Miriam led them to the living room, where cardboard boxes acted as catchalls in the corners. The walls were bare, though a few framed photos were stacked haphazardly on the coffee table, including a family photo where John and Miriam held a pouting, chubby toddler. Gabe pinched her ass and muttered a quiet "don't you dare," in warning before Tara could say anything.

"Sorry about the mess. We moved in here a couple of years ago, but unpacking is really not a priority. Gabey was always the homemaker in the family. John and I could care less about decorating." Miriam perched on the edge of the sofa, beaming.

"Yeah, that happens when you're the only one who spends any time at home," Gabe muttered as he and Tara settled on the love seat.

Miriam's smile stayed bright, ignoring his dig. "So, how long have you two been seeing each other?"

"A few months," Gabe answered. "But we met through Lee and Tonio a couple of years ago."

Tara bit her lip to keep from laughing. Gabe wasn't technically wrong with that generous timeline. If Antonio hadn't been performing drag at the same bar where Lee worked, Tara never would have dragged Gabe into the Confessionals for the best sex of her life. Lee and Antonio hadn't formally introduced them until after they'd moved in together, six months later.

"That's lovely. I think friendships are the best basis for a good relationship, don't you, dearest?" Miriam asked John.

"Wouldn't know. I've never been your friend." John grinned at his wife, handing each of them a glass of fizzy ice water, decorated with lime wedges.

"Psh. You know what I meant." Miriam waved her hand, before explaining to Tara, "We mostly argued, until we didn't."

"Sounds familiar." Tara smiled. In the beginning, Gabe had been an attractive pain in the ass that Lee was forcing her to spend with. She hadn't exactly been nice to him either (outside of sex, anyway). Tara had stubbornly pretended he didn't exist, while Gabe did whatever it took to get her attention.

But she wasn't about to tell his parents that. She didn't want them to get the impression that their relationship was toxic. *We're in a good place. Now.*

"Oh, were your parents like that, too?" Miriam asked.

Gabe tensed as if he was about to speak for her again.

She squeezed his hand and answered honestly. *No point in hiding it from them. They'll find out eventually.* "Oh, no, that sounded like Gabe and I. To be honest, I don't remember what my parents were like together. My dad left when I was little, and I lost touch with my mom when I was a teenager. I'm not sure where they are now."

Miriam pressed her hand to her chest in sympathy. "Oh, I'm sorry to bring up a sore subject."

Tara shook her head, forcing a smile. Miriam's reaction was a little too practiced, but it was better than how most people responded. "No, it's okay. They weren't exactly good parents, so it was probably for the best. I ended up living with Lee's aunt when we were teenagers, and then we stayed with our friend Blanche—the one who officiated his and Tonio's wedding—after that." She turned to John. "Gabe said you were friends with Walter and Wanda. I stayed in their camp a few times over the years."

John looked at her thoughtfully for a long moment. "They were rare people."

"The best kind of people," Tara agreed, excited to find another person who knew the closest thing she'd had to grandparents. She'd looked up to Walter and Wanda her whole life, wishing they were really her family.

My kid is going to have grandparents. What the fuck. Tara still could not grasp the idea that any child of hers would have more people in their lives than their friends. Lee and Antonio's wedding party had been where her family began and ended. Gabe's life was so much...bigger.

"And where do you live now?" Miriam asked, seemingly glad to move to a lighter topic than Tara's unstable childhood. "I had thought you were living with Blanche, right? But Lee said his sister moved in with them."

Tara gaped, unsure how to break the news that she was living with Gabe. Especially since she hadn't realized that Lee and Blanche talked to Gabe's mom like that. But she was a co-owner of Confession now, and close with Antonio's family. How had Gabe's parents become a part of her whole life, before she'd had a chance to meet them? *This is like Gabe all over again.*

Gabe thankfully answered, "With me, actually. Since Blanche moved into their new house, we figured it was a good time since she had to move anyway."

Miriam's eyebrows disappeared into her curly hair. "So soon? Gabey, that seems quick, don't you think? You said it's only been a few months."

Tension radiated from Miriam and John's stiff postures. *Don't take it personally.* Gabe's parents were understandably protective of him, after what his ex had done to him.

Tara found her voice again when Gabe opened and closed his mouth wordlessly. "It is quick, but Blanche has a room for me at their house if it's too soon for us. I'd rather that we have a better relationship living apart than trying to force anything if we're not ready. So far, it's going great! Gabe's made me feel right at home." She smiled at Gabe, whose jaw worked back and forth. He squeezed her hand, though he still looked peeved.

The oven beeped, and Miriam hurried out of the room, muttering something about lunch being ready in a moment.

Tara's chest tightened. *Don't take it personally. Give them time to come around.*

John looked back and forth between them, his perceptive gaze lingering on her. Tara fidgeted. She read people like this, too, but this was a whole different level. This was Blanche-level of ocular interrogation.

Hippo rested his head on her lap, tail wagging. She was glad for the distraction, smiling and scratching Hippo's ears, looking at the family photos scattered on the table to distract her from John's examining stare. In every one, the younger version of Gabe looked like he wanted to be anywhere else.

After what felt like an eternity, John stood up and wordlessly gestured to the dining room.

"I'm sorry," Gabe murmured. He rose, holding out his hand to pull her up as Hippo ran ahead.

"Don't be. We knew this was going to be awkward." Tara leaned into him, glad for the reassurance as his hand found the small of her back to guide her to the equally haphazard dining room. *Don't take it personally. This is what Gabe wants.*

"Wine, Tara?" Miriam asked, pouring herself and John a glass. Despite the stacks of books and shopping bags on the side board, the table was set nicely, with a lace table runner and cloth napkins.

"Oh, no, thank you. Water is fine for me." Tara smiled politely, trying not to stare at the wine longingly. Just a sip would really help ease her anxiety. But one sip might turn into two, and so on. She missed the warm feeling she got when she drank the Cooper Winery house red. For someone who didn't drink wine much before she'd met Gabe, she sure as hell grew attached to it quickly. Or maybe it was just how Gabe made her feel.

"Are you sure?" Miriam taunted, waving the bottle with a teasing grin at the longing on Tara's face. Any trace of her apprehension from earlier seemed to be gone, as if Miriam was relieved to change the subject.

Tara's mouth watered as Gabe pulled out a chair for her. Hippo was under her feet before she could sit all the way down. Times like this were when she resented her parents' addiction issues. Her impulse control had never been great. Even with a very good reason to avoid alcohol, she was still tempted. How Antonio stayed sober was impressive.

"Water's fine!" She quietly asked Gabe, "Gift time?"

"I was just about to ask." Gabe jumped up to retrieve the gift bag from where he'd tucked it in the foyer. They had planned on waiting until after lunch, but Tara needed Miriam to stop offering her a taste of her favorite wine. She was scared she'd give in. Scared of becoming her mom, who prioritized vices over family. Gabe would step in before it got that far, but Tara needed the temptation removed completely.

Pregnancy had forced her to finally process her feelings, now that she couldn't save them up for getting drunk and high with Blanche and Lee on Saturdays. So far, the rational side that told her she needed to prove she was better than her parents was winning. But she had a long time before she could drink again.

"Here. This is for both of you. From both of us." Gabe handed Miriam a gift bag.

Miriam set down the bottle suspiciously and pulled out a stemless wineglass set from the Cooper Vineyard gift shop. "Our own wineglasses? Why are you giving these to us?" She looked at them closer, jaw dropping at the "Grandma" and "Grandpa" etched on each glass.

"Gabriel Fucking Cooper. Are you serious?!" Miriam's volume rose several decibels. The East Coast accent was back. Miriam burst out of her chair to hand the glasses to John, who took one look at them and, to Tara's relief, beamed. His smile was exactly like Gabe's, minus the dimples.

Those must be from Miriam. I hope our kid gets them too. She leaned close to Gabe, whispering, "Is that your real middle name?"

Gabe chuckled. "May as well be. But for the record, it's Zachariah. What's yours?"

Tara snorted; they should probably know each other's middle names by now. "Marie."

"When did this happen? How far along are you?" Miriam fired off questions as she circled around the dining table, not waiting for a response. Hippo followed Miriam, dogging her heels as she paced around the room. Gabe rubbed Tara's back as his mom shouted every thought she had. Tara was grateful; she hated shouting, even happy shouting. "Was this planned?"

Turning his head to follow her path around them, Gabe cleared his throat only when his mom took a breath. "There's a picture of the ultrasound in the bag."

Miriam snatched it up on her next lap around.

Gabe took advantage of the pause. "We just started the second trimester. Due date is February fifth. And no, not planned, obviously, as we've been together for three months. Tell them about your tea." He nudged Tara's leg with his own under the table with a grin.

Tara's cheeks burned as she muttered, "Apparently Saint John's wort can interfere with birth control pills."

John barked out a laugh. Saint John's wort was responsible for Gabe's own accidental conception. John had made a similar tea for Miriam after her mother died.

Miriam joined him, her laughter becoming tears as she held the ultrasound to her chest. "John, we're going to be fucking grandparents! Can you believe it? I knew it! As soon as you turned down that wine at the wedding, I knew. I didn't actually expect I was right! I thought I was reading too much into it! I'm gonna tear Richard a new one for telling us to give you space for so long! I'm so happy for you two!" She round-ed on Gabe and Tara excitedly. "So, when are you getting married? Do you want to do the ceremony here?"

Gabe coughed as the blood drained from Tara's face. Her head swam in alarm.

"Ma! We haven't talked about that yet!"

Miriam shot him a look, clutching the ultrasound to her chest. "What do you mean, you haven't talked about it? Gabey, you know the conditions of the trust!"

"Ma," Gabe said sternly. "We haven't talked about it yet, and we're not going to talk about it for the first time here. Phin is exploring the options, so please drop it. This is a conversation for Tara and I to have in private."

Miriam opened her mouth to protest, but John spoke first, putting his hand over hers. "Dearest, Gabe is setting a boundary."

Miriam huffed, throwing up her hands. "Fine. I'm proud of you for advocating for yourself."

Head swirling, Tara breathed deeply, trying to regain control as Hippo's head appeared in her lap. *Why would we need to get married? I didn't think his family would be that traditional.* She stroked Hippo's silky ears. She hadn't considered it as a possibility. *His parents really must think I'm a gold digger if the first thing they think about is protecting his inheritance.* She felt trapped, controlled and rejected by them all at once. *Oh my god, this is a literal nightmare.*

Tara let out an exhale, staring at her empty plate, zeroing in on a tiny chip in the ceramic as the rest of the room blurred. *Would Gabe even want to marry me? Do I want to marry him?* Anxiety rose with her train of thought. Unlike the usual fear that forced her to relive her past, this anxiety flashed to her future. Gabe glaring resentfully at her, because she was a horrible partner. Her future kid, unhappy and crying, while she tried everything to quiet them. Miriam and John, upset that Gabe had yet another shitty person who used and hurt him over and over.

The anxiety had been growing since she'd moved in with him. Really, since finding out they were expecting. But never had it been so sharp and clear. *How can I even consider that? Why would he want to marry me, of all people?*

Gabe nudged her leg again, drawing her attention to him. "Snap out of whatever overthinking spiral you're in right now, Kitten. You're not trapping me. You're not a gold digger." He put his hand in hers, squeezing her fingers. Leaning toward her, he spoke softly, "You're safe and loved and wanted. We're choosing this together, remember?"

Tara nodded, focusing on the feeling of his hand around hers, instead of the worried expressions from his parents on the other side of the table. They might as well know the mess their child had gotten himself into—*Nope. Breathe.* The smell of the lasagna with every inhale. The sound of the soft music playing in the kitchen. The look of concern in his lovely eyes. *He chose this. Me. Us.*

"Sorry." The panic threatening her lessened as she centered herself. The anxiety may be new, but her old methods worked. "Thanks for reading my mind."

Gabe chuckled. "No need to apologize, Kitten."

"And we'd never dare accuse anyone of being a gold digger in this family." The concern in Miriam's eyes matched Gabe's, despite her smile. "After all, John still married me after I was disinherited, because he loved me, not my money. A loving family is more important than money any day. And now you and your baby are part of this family, too."

Tara was struck with another surge; thankfully they were soft, happy emotions this time. Maybe she had read Miriam all wrong. "Thank you. I'm glad my kid will have more love than I did growing up." Tears welled up in her eyes at the thought that her kid would never experience the same loneliness, hunger, and insecurity that she had. She picked up her napkin to dab her eyes. "Sorry, just feeling a little overwhelmed. Blame the fucking hormones."

Miriam rounded the table to squeeze her tight, her hip catching on the table runner in her hurry to reach her. Tara's eyes welled up again as Miriam hugged her, her lilac perfume sweet against her nose. "You will never have to worry about running short of love ever again."

Gabe rubbed her hand with his thumb, where they were still joined between them. "Or money, Broke Ass. We'll talk more about the trust situation when you're ready."

She sobbed out a laugh as Hippo's head wiggled under their joined hand. "I still can't believe any kid of mine will have a fucking investment banker for a parent. Well, for now, anyway."

Miriam moved to sit next to her husband, admiring the glasses with John as she straightened the table runner. "For now? Are you changing jobs, Gabey?"

Gabe shot Tara a look.

She shrugged. "Sorry, is your undying hatred for your job a secret?"

"You hate your job?" Miriam asked.

Gabe grumbled, "It's complicated."

"It's not, Coop. Change jobs."

He gave Tara a sullen warning look. "I do want a change, but I need to make sure I can get parental leave and benefits lined up quickly, so this might not be the time. Also, I still don't know what I want to do instead."

"Don't stay in a job that makes you miserable for my sake. Or the kid's." Tara raised an eyebrow. "We'll work it out."

She hated how Gabe went to work in the mornings with a look of dread, the tension in his shoulders when he came home. He went to the gym every day after work with Richard to work off his frustration. Yet, he still came home with a storm cloud over his head that would only go away while they made dinner. But it would still reappear when he put his blazer on the next morning.

Leigh Anne better hope Tara never met her, because everything Gabe had shared about his awful boss made Tara want to put her in a choke hold. That Gabe felt obligated to stay there on her account made Tara feel like the shittiest partner on the planet. It was one thing when he doted on her because it made him happy, but when it made him miserable? Tara's fists tightened, but who could she blame but herself?

"Why don't you come work for the vineyard if you're unhappy there, Gabey? We can work out a parental leave for you, and our health insurance covers a lot more now that we've got so many employees." Miriam suggested, plating some lasagna for Tara. "Your dad has the touch for wine, and I can wrangle investors and events, but a lot of the day-to-day stuff of managing a business isn't either of our strong suits."

Gabe looked confused as he passed her his plate. "I thought you didn't need me."

Miriam's smile was uncomfortable. "Well, I mean, we get by. But we always could use your help, Gabey. We want this to be yours one day, if you want it. Your choice, of course. No pressure. I know it's not what you wanted in the past." Miriam handed Gabe his plate back, before grabbing John's.

Gabe stabbed his lasagna, clarifying in a harsher tone. "I thought *you* didn't want *me* to work at the vineyard." He looked angry, his face clouding. Tara rubbed his shoulder, and he leaned into her hand.

Miriam's voice took on a defensive edge. "Of course we want you to work here! We just don't want you to feel *forced* to work here. And it's not like we could pay you as much as where you work now. That's why we got our shit together—so you didn't feel obligated to help us out if it wasn't what you wanted. And then you went to work with Richard, so we thought that was it."

Gabe inhaled deeply and slowly.

"Do you need a pause?" Tara whispered. At his nod, she turned to John, asking the first "small talk" question she'd prepared in case things got awkward. "So... how do you get the wine to taste so good? I was never a big wine drinker before Gabe converted me. I'm looking forward to when I can drink it again!"

John gave her a thoughtful look, before nodding in approval. He cleared his throat. "It's the soil here in the Driftless region. The glaciers during the ice age never reached this area of the Midwest, so the soil here is nutrient-rich. We started with fruit wine from the orchard that used to be here, while I cultivated some cool-weather grapes. We've gotten more strains thanks to agricultural research from universities out of Minnesota and here in Bellamy. Lots of innovation in the past few decades."

This was the most Gabe's dad had spoken yet. She wondered if he was buying Gabe time, as well. "Where did you learn it all?" Tara asked.

John's face was unreadable, but his voice remained as even as ever. "The government placed me in a boarding school—Chilocco Indian Agricultural school—when I was young, that focused on job training. When I aged out, I went to San Francisco, like all the native kids in the '70s. I found work at a vineyard in Napa and fell in love with the wine business." John smiled in Miriam's direction. "I came out here as part of a sit-in to protect the Hopewell Mounds over Eastside, when there was going to be redevelopment in the park. That's where I met Miriam. She was the developer of the project I was protesting. Somehow I got her to stop arguing with me long enough for us to elope."

Tara liked the way John spoke. It was very deliberate and even, like whenever Gabe shared a story about his life. He wasn't giving a lot of details, but enough to answer the questions forming in Tara's mind.

"He corrupted me," Miriam joked, shooting a warm look back at her husband. "I was a New York heiress taken in by this handsome hippie and his radical rhetoric. My father could never have stopped me from running away with him, even if he had seen it coming."

Tara smiled, touched by how obviously in love John and Miriam were, almost forty years later. It was cute. She hoped she and Gabe could be like that when they were older too.

Finally finding his voice, Gabe spoke up, even though his face was still cloudy. "I got my MBA so I could help out with the vineyard. I *wanted* to work here. But I thought you didn't want me to, so I went to work with Richard instead. In hindsight, I think *she* convinced me that you didn't want me here."

Everyone at the table knew who "she" was. Tara put her hand on his thigh; comforting Gabe was all she could do, all he wanted and needed from her. Though she would love the opportunity to meet his abusive ex. Just to talk.

He covered her hand with his own. "I should have seen what she was doing. You said all of the same things as you said back then, but it doesn't feel like rejection like it did then. I'm sorry for holding onto that resentment for so long."

"I'm sorry for making you feel like we didn't want you here." Miriam had tears in her eyes. "You choose your path, Gabey Baby. We support you no matter what. You take time, talk about it with Tara, and let us know what you decide. We can get you set up to even do a lot of it remotely, so you don't have to drive out here most of the time."

Miriam paused, sipping her wine as she got herself under control, before adding, "I hope I've gotten better at showing support for your choices. Or at least found a better balance between being too involved, or not involved enough."

"I think we've all gotten better at communicating." John assessed Tara again as he spoke. "Do you know your parents' names and birth dates?"

Tara nodded. "Why do you ask?"

"I know some people. I can do some digging and see what I can find. If you want."

Tara smiled skeptically. She and Blanche had been searching for years for any trace of them. But ever since she'd found out she was pregnant, she'd been longing to know what her parents would be like. How they'd react to finding her again, and learning they would be grandparents. "Can't hurt to try, I guess. I'm not sure what you'll be able to find. I've never found them in any police reports. I figured at least one of them would be dead or in jail by now."

John nodded solemnly. "At least you have their names. That's more than I ever had. Hell, I never even found *my* name. I'll do what I can." He stood up to fetch a pen and paper.

Gabe leaned in close, his voice pouring quietly into her ear as he muttered, "That."

"That what?" Tara asked.

"Stepping in for me when I needed a minute. Supporting me when you saw me struggling. Calling me out on my bullshit." Gabe kissed her temple. "Being yourself, so my parents could see what I do, so they would trust me to know what I'm doing. That's what you bring to my life."

Saturday, September Fourth

Chapter Five

Lee

"So Lee," Sunny said, too cheerfully to be genuine. "What's this news that Antonio was talking about last weekend?"

"You're gonna have to try harder than that." Lee snorted as he tentatively sniffed a cute throw pillow. It *looked* clean, but it *smelled* like women's perfume had been sprayed over it to hide the wet dog smell. Wrinkling his nose, Lee put it back on the table, along with hundreds of other hoarded knickknacks cluttering up the driveway and front yard of someone's house. He and Sunny had tagged along with Blanche to an estate sale, in hopes of finding area rugs for their new house.

"What do you mean? I'm just curious!" Sunny batted her eyelashes, hand pressed to the neckline of her green sundress in mock offense. "You can tell me, I'm great at secrets!"

"Oh, so you're not doing this because Richard's a nosy little shit?" Lee teased.

"I don't know what you're talking about." Sunny's fake smile widened uncannily. She quickly turned to admire a painting of some boring landscape.

"What was it that Gabe's mom hired you for again?" Lee asked nonchalantly, finding a crate of vinyl to flip through. He'd overheard Miriam and Richard talking about it when they'd been at Confession for a meeting a few weeks ago.

"Oh, an immersive accessibility app for the art museum! They're installing sensory description checkpoints in all the exhibits next year," Sunny said, still staring at the painting. "This is really ugly. I kind of love it."

Lee turned to her with a smirk. "And is that app *public* knowledge yet?"

"Not yet!" Sunny groaned. "Seriously, that doesn't count—that was *my* secret to keep, I am great at keeping other people's secrets!"

Lee put his arm around her as they went to find Blanche, who had disappeared into the garage. "Sun, just forget there's any secret. Tell me more about this deal with Miriam."

"She's paying me out the wazoo for it!" Sunny beamed. "I've been saving up for my surgery, and the contract pays me by the milestone instead of the finished product, which is cool. Even though I'll still be working for her through next year, I should have enough saved up in like six months, if I keep on track."

"For real?" Lee squeezed her closer. All of his friends were overwhelming him lately with good news; his reactions felt disingenuous and lackluster. Bad news, he knew how to handle, because it'd been all he'd known until the past couple years. Good news still felt uncomfortable, unpracticed, like any "congratulations!" fell flat.

Between Blanche buying a mansion (a dilapidated mansion, but still, that house was massive!), Tara starting a family with the only person on the planet Lee felt might be halfway worthy of her, and this? Sunny had been dreaming about this for years, even when they were kids and didn't quite understand exactly why she was so averse to her own body. Even just a couple years ago, this had still been a "someday" goal for her, beyond a five, or even a ten-year plan.

"Yup! Wild, isn't it?" Sunny murmured as they found Blanche staring at a small cast-iron dog in a dated TV hutch. "Between that, and all the ass-kissing I've been doing at work to get this promotion, and helping Luna apply for scholarships, my life should be in order sooner than I expected."

"What do you mean?" Lee asked. "In order for what?"

"For being ready for the rest of my life," Sunny shrugged, as if that was something that would make sense to anyone but her.

"Meaning..." Blanche glanced over, picking up the dog from the shelf and turning it over to examine the worn and dusty metal from every angle.

"Meaning, I'm getting my life together, so Richard can propose sooner than I planned. Like, I was already pushing to get everything done, but I am gonna have to fast-track this."

Lee and Blanche exchanged a confused look. "Sun, you're gonna need to break this down for me. I'm not following."

Sunny huffed in annoyance. "I've been working on myself a lot lately, so I can grow into the wifey material Sunny I want to be before Richard and I get married. Get unstuck from my dead-end career track, help Luna finish school, pay for my surgery, all that sort of thing. And Richard says he's fine waiting, but the baby announcement last week messed him up more than he pretends, because he keeps trying to buy me expensive shit I don't want, giving me advice I didn't ask for, and he keeps asking me what I think about phoenixes." She screwed her face up. "That last one is kind of confusing, but the rest of them are usually signs he's spiraling. Because that's how he likes to show love when he needs to feel in control of something, but he knows I don't really vibe with receiving love that way." She rolled her eyes, tossing her hair over her shoulder. "Anyway, I'm trying to get my ass in gear so I can stop feeling like a charity case."

Lee blinked, unsure how the fuck to respond to that, while his phone buzzed in his pocket.

"Sounds like there's a lot to unpack there," Blanche cocked their head. "Do you want to talk about—"

"No. What did you find?" With her chin, Sunny pointed at the dog figurine in Blanche's hand.

"Oh, I think my grandma Rose had one just like this. She had a swinging door between her kitchen and the dining room, like I do, and she kept it propped open with this." Blanche smiled softly at the dog in their hand. "Getting nostalgic in my old age, I guess."

"You're not old," Lee teased, pulling his phone out of his pocket when it went off again. "You're barely middle-aged."

Blanche laughed. "Fuck off, I'm probably only thirty-five. That's not middle-aged yet!"

Lee huffed in annoyance, pocketing his phone without an answer.

"What's wrong?" Blanche asked, as they wandered the aisles of knick-knacks. Sunny had found a storage bin of old video games to dig through.

"My mom wants to know how Jazz is doing."

Blanche's face screwed up in confusion. "She's been great. Way too helpful, what with all of the furniture and decorations she keeps bringing home, and making me tea every morning, but I'm sure she'll learn she's allowed to relax eventually. Why is your mom asking you instead of her, though?"

"That's a great question." Lee pushed his glasses up as his chest tightened. "Apparently, Jazz told them that they can't come over without checking with her first, in case you're recording your uh...'influencer' content. And my parents aren't handling that well. My mom is basically asking me, without actually asking, to spy on Jazz for her. And I get they're worried about her, but also, why *don't* they ask her?"

"I never set that boundary, but I'm happy to be the bad guy. Good for her!" Blanche rubbed his arm sympathetically. "How do you feel about all of it?"

"Shitty, because I hate saying no. But Jazz deserves her privacy, and I don't want to turn into her helicopter brother." Lee groaned, because being Jazz's helicopter would mean seeing things he didn't want to, like his sister going down a path that would inevitably drive a wedge between her and their parents. It had taken them a decade to come around to the idea of him being gay, but for the daughter they'd smothered to be both a lesbian and polyamorous? Lee's life had been immeasurably hard; he wanted to protect Jazz's sensitive heart from that fate.

A man's most important role is to protect the women around him, especially those more vulnerable and impressionable than you. Your sister is your greatest responsibility.

Lee shuddered. A downside to reconnecting with his parents was his dad's sermons making an unwelcome reappearance. He pushed his glasses up his nose. "But if I can help keep our parents off her back, I will. That's my job as her brother, you know? That comes before being their son. I dunno, I might ask what she wants me to tell them."

"And what does Lee want?" Blanche asked, fiddling with some rusty tools.

"What do you mean?"

"Something my therapist keeps asking me," Blanche murmured. "I always make decisions in light of what other people want—what my clients want, or what my friends and family want, or what Daisy would want. I have all these roles that I play, but I never connect with myself. My therapist keeps harping on about figuring out what I want. And it sounds like you're doing that too. You're thinking in terms of what Jazz wants from you, or what your mom wants from you. What does Lee want?"

As Blanche left to inspect a table saw, Lee mulled it over. He wanted peace and quiet, to be loved, comfortable, and content. He wanted to be the best husband for Antonio, to make their shared dreams possible. He wanted his friends to be happy, to support them and be active in their lives. He wanted Jazz to flourish outside of their parents' control, to protect her from all the shit that came with real life, now that she wouldn't be forced into the strict, sheltered, smothering role their parents wanted for her.

And he wanted a relationship with his parents, but on his terms. An honest, genuine connection between the parents who were trying to meet him halfway, and the real Lee. And he couldn't do that by lying to them, or by spying on Jazz. Lee left his phone in his pocket; his mom could wait.

"Ooh, that's pretty!" Blanche exclaimed, making a beeline toward a round, burgundy Persian rug draped over a deep freezer. "Do you think that's big enough for the tower room?"

Lee looked at it skeptically. It was at least eight feet wide. "I think the bigger issue is that it won't fit in the car."

"Oh, psh!" Blanche handed the metal dog to Lee, who almost dropped it from the unexpected weight. They pulled up the sleeves of their blouse, and bent down to start rolling the rug up. "We can make it fit."

"That's what she said," Sunny quipped, arms full of old game cartridges.

Lee snorted, but helped Blanche carry the rug to the makeshift cashier's table and wedge it through the windows of his old ass Sonata. He glanced back in the rearview mirror to see Blanche, buried under the massive rug and clutching the cast-iron dog in the backseat, with a soft smile on their face. Their green eyes met his in the mirror, just for a moment, and Lee had to look away at the joy he saw there before he lost his composure. If even *Blanche* could find joy in putting themself first for once, maybe Lee should too.

Jazz

"You, uh…talk to Mimi yet, bro?"

Jazz blinked, snapping her head around so fast, she got a crick in her neck. In the driver's seat of his minivan, Ed looked resolutely at the road. His knuckles were white around the steering wheel, even though they were going about five miles an hour, watching the curbs for any gems among the free furniture left out from move-in day. Already a desk, a few side tables, and an armchair had made their way into Blanche's house, but Ed kept insisting they keep looking, even though it was close to sundown.

Now Jazz knew why he was so eager to help. "How long have you been working up the courage to ask me that?" she teased.

Ed huffed. "About four days. Give or take."

Jazz tsked. "Did Teddy put you up to this?"

"No, but I am asking on her behalf, because she wants to fix it, but doesn't know how, and she hasn't eaten in days because it's making her anxious." Ed cringed. "I even brought her pozole from the restaurant yesterday, and she barely touched it. And you *know* how much Teddy loves pozole."

Jazz huffed, a pang of guilt hitting her chest. Once again, she was removed from all of the fallout whenever she and Mimi fought. She might not live with her parents anymore, but she still didn't share an apartment with Mimi like Teddy did. "Look, Mimi is the one being weird."

"Because she thinks you're mad at her, duh!"

Jazz grumbled, "I'm not mad at her. *She's* mad at *me*."

Ed pulled over so they could look at a cluster of furniture with a "FREE!" sign taped to the couch. It had far too many stains on it for Jazz's taste. But there was a wicker shelf, spray-painted bright purple, that might add some much-needed storage to the downstairs powder room.

Ed opened the door for Jazz to load it in, his wispy mustache twisting in a wince. "Mimi *thinks* you're mad at her. You *think* she's mad at you."

Jazz checked her phone as it buzzed. Just another text from her mom. What good was a distraction from this conversation, when she was ignoring her mom too? She sighed, "And?"

With a pout, Ed groaned. "Neither of you are talking, because you're waiting for the other to stop being mad first and come back! But neither of you are mad, bro!" He hugged himself. "Last time you had a standoff like this, Mimi came to you. Maybe you might consider going to Mimi this time? Because all this not-fighting is making me itchy, man!"

Jazz scoffed. "Last time we had a standoff like this, Mimi's new girlfriend was so rude, I cried. This time, Mimi is accusing me of cheating with my roommate! Who isn't even interested in me!"

Ed raised an eyebrow at her.

"What?" Jazz crossed her arms, finger *tap tap tapping* her elbow. Ed looked back, his brown eyes digging into her. "Stop looking at me like that!"

"Is that what Mimi said?" Ed asked quietly, holding open the door for her.

Jazz frowned. Of course, that was what Mimi was upset about, what else would it be? They'd agreed to discuss potential new partners as a triad, but Blanche was *not* a potential new partner. Jazz slid into the passenger seat, foot *tap tap tapping* on the floor.

"Jazzy," Ed sighed, shutting the driver's side door gently. "I know you and Jules don't get along—"

"What, are you all buddy buddy with Julissa now?" Jazz scoffed. "She was way worse to you than me."

"But I'm not dating Mimi." Ed scratched the back of his neck, his thick ponytail bouncing. "I'm with Teddy, and Teddy wants to get along with Jules, so I'm letting Jules have whatever friendship with me she wants. She's not as bad as she was at first. We don't exactly talk, but I can breathe around her now. She's trying."

"Not with me." Jazz huffed as her mom texted again, asking how classes were going, if she had enough to eat. Jazz typed a snarky reply, deleted it, then typed another. Something reassuring, how she was doing fine, that wouldn't lead to more questions.

"Because you don't give her the opportunity to." Ed pulled off the curb as the sunlight faded fast. "Bro, you and I were friends before we all started this polycule stuff. Julissa's coming into this new, and yeah, she went about it all wrong, but we can cut her a little slack. For Mimi's sake. Because Mimi's feelings were hurt last weekend. You basically told her she was imagining your feelings for Blanche, and then made it about Julissa instead. Please don't hate me for saying that."

Deciding the text to her mom was as good as it was going to get, Jazz hit send and swallowed hard. How many times did she have to say that Blanche was not an option before it sank in? And why wouldn't it be about Julissa? She was the reason they had all of this approval nonsense. Before her, they were happy. Jazz's stomach tightened; she closed her eyes to fight the nausea. Foot *tap tap tapping* the floor again, her fist wrapped around the amethyst pendant. "I'm not replacing Mimi."

Ed sat quietly, the radio the only sound in the car. Another song began and ended before he finally sighed. "No one thinks you are, Jazz. But if you're feeling replaced by Julissa, maybe talk to Mimi about how you're feeling."

Jazz's eyes blurred as the sun disappeared behind the hills around campus. The lights from downtown brightened in the distant dark. The idea of bringing up a sore subject made her chest tight. But Ed was right; Mimi would absolutely be internalizing the silence. And it was Mimi's birthday coming up. This time, Jazz should be the one to reach out first. "I'll text her."

"Thank you." Ed patted her hand. "And uh... don't tell Teddy about this conversation. She told me to stay out of it. But I was about to break into hives from all the tension."

Jazz snorted as Ed turned back down the hill toward Blanche's house. Toward her new, beautiful, messy, comfortable haven, where Jazz was free to be her whole beautiful, messy, comfortable self. Toward home.

WAVING GOODBYE TO ED, Jazz hauled the wicker shelf up the front steps, watching out for the soft spot on the porch that made her feel like she was about to fall through every time she walked too quickly. Soon enough, this would be muscle memory. But after twenty-one years in her parent's house, even walking up the front steps took concentration.

She checked that the "On Air" sign above the entry table was off, Blanche's signal that they were recording (purchased after Jazz's shower world tour had unintentionally appeared in one of Blanche's solo livestreams), before swapping her sneakers for her house slides. Though the music playing from the den was reassurance enough that Blanche didn't have a client over.

Leaving the wicker shelf on the porch so she could disinfect it, Jazz went to the kitchen, only to find the tea kettle full, but lukewarm. A mug sat next to it, the tea ball already full. Jazz smiled, turned the kettle on again, and prepared another for herself. Two steaming mugs in hand, she followed the sound of music to the den.

"Oh! You're home!" Blanche paused mid-shimmy, joint hanging from their mouth, wearing a thin kaftan. Their hair was half-plaited, as if they'd given up partway through. "Oh, my tea!" Blanche took a tea cup from her. "Thank you! How was your day? You've really been in and out, haven't you? I found that side table you brought back earlier, I hope it's okay that I put it by the daybed. I needed a spot for my ashtray."

Jazz perched on the edge of the daybed. "You're welcome. It was fine. And yeah, drove all over Hillside, and of course, that's where I was planning on putting it."

Blanche laughed, loud and clear, until they snorted at the end. Jazz couldn't help but grin along. "Sorry, I was rambling a bit, wasn't I?"

"That's okay!" Jazz sipped her tea, just on the verge of scalding, the way she liked it. "What did you get up to today?"

"Went to an estate sale with your brother and Sunny, and I found a nice area rug for the tower room! It makes it feel super cozy in there now, and it leaves enough space around the edges of the room to wipe up any mess, in case any of the plants pee."

Jazz laughed, mentally adding rug cleaning to her list of chores to do tomorrow. "Good."

"And then I fussed around in the garden a bit. It's a bit overgrown, but I left the wildflowers so we don't have bare dirt all winter, until I can figure out what's actually growing there," Blanche tapped the joint in the ashtray. "Sorry, do you mind if I smoke in here? I was planning on making this my smoking lounge, but if you'd rather I smoke outside, I can."

Jazz shook her head. "No, go ahead. Your house, your rules."

"No!" Blanche waved a hand. "*Our* house, *our* rules! You get a say in how things go. Besides, you know more about what to do with all this space than I do." They kept talking before Jazz could respond. "It was just so nice to get my hands dirty a bit, you know? Feel the earth under my hands, the smell of it, the roots snapping, the sun on my neck, all of that. I hadn't realized how much I missed it. I should have left that apartment as soon as that damn condo went up across the street." They took a quick puff. "Today, during my vlogging, I decided that I'm a plant! I need sunlight, and that damn building blocked all of the natural light! That was my sign that it was time to leave."

"Vlogging?" Jazz asked, eyeing the joint in Blanche's hand.

"You want some?" Blanche offered hesitantly. "I don't want to corrupt you, but you're welcome to help yourself if you want."

"You won't corrupt me." Jazz snorted. "I don't smoke much, but I have a pack of gummies in my sock drawer. Don't tell Lee, he'll freak."

Blanche scoffed. "Please, Lee is in no position to judge a little puff."

"He might not judge *you*, but me?" Jazz took the joint Blanche offered. "What's this vlogging, though?"

"Oh! Shayla, my therapist, thinks I should journal, but I don't really like writing, and I can't read what I wrote, so I've been vlogging at least five minutes, twice a day." Blanche's hips swayed in time with the music as they talked, the thin cotton clinging to their hips. Jazz choked as she exhaled the smoke, coughing into her elbow. "Then before therapy, I watch it all back, and take notes on my phone about what I've noticed."

"What have you noticed?" Jazz passed the joint back, embarrassed at her cough. The smoke wasn't even that harsh.

"I don't know what I want," Blanche stopped dancing to take a deep drag on the joint, lighter flicking in their hand. "Everything I've been doing since I left the Family, I've done for other people. I've done what Daisy wanted, what would get me the most money from a john or a sub, what would keep Covey happy, what would help Freddy or Chas, what Lee or Tara or Sunny needed. But never what *I* wanted, other than what I've needed to stay alive."

"What have you figured out?" Jazz murmured. She wasn't sure if anyone had ever been this open with her. Her parents and Lee, certainly not. Maybe Teddy, to a degree, but Teddy was open with everyone. Jazz was touched that Blanche trusted her with all of this.

"I want to enjoy my life," Blanche sat on the daybed next to Jazz. "But other than that?" They shrugged, their brow furrowed and lips parted. "Fuck if I know." They fixed their face, giving Jazz a wink that made her heart thump in her chest. "But when I figure it out, you'll be the first to know!"

Sucking in a hesitant breath, Jazz tucked an ankle under her knee. "Can I ask you something?"

Blanche visibly perked up. "Yes!"

"So you and Daisy were together, but both sex workers, right?"

Blanche nodded, handing Jazz the joint. "It's a bit more complicated than that, but yes."

"How did that work? Jealousy-wise?" She flicked the lighter, the spark catching on the third try.

Blanche looked at Jazz softly. "I think I can better answer this question if we keep it about you. I expect our situations are apples and oranges, is all."

Jazz huffed with a billow of smoke, that nauseous feeling in her stomach from earlier coming back. Vulnerability, probably. It always made her slightly ill. She swallowed, passing the joint back to Blanche. A few puffs had probably been too much. "Mimi started dating Julissa a couple of months ago, and we got off to a rocky start. How do I get over my resentment? Because I don't want to let that situation with her come between Mimi and I, but also, that's exactly what I'm doing." Her thumb swiped across the handle of her mug, back and forth and back.

"Tell me more about this rocky start." Blanche tapped the joint out in the ashtray.

With a groan, Jazz muttered, "Our triad had been together, like six months, when Mimi met Jules. And we weren't like, closed or anything, but we never really discussed what to do when one of us wanted to start dating someone seriously. I didn't think it would happen, to be honest. I was so happy with what the three of us have together, that it was hard to accept that Mimi might want more. Teddy was still with Ed, so it wouldn't be fair if Mimi couldn't date anyone." Jazz gripped her mug, *tap tap tapping* on the rim. "But Julissa acted like we didn't exist, or said it was disrespectful for us to interact with Mimi like always if she was around, even though we're her girlfriends, too. And she didn't understand why Ed was around at all. I dunno, she just didn't seem to care about how our dynamic worked. She expected us to fit what she wanted."

Blanche hummed in sympathy. "Sounds like she could be more open-minded, but has she come around a bit?"

"Kinda," Jazz shrugged, *tap tap tapping* on the mug again, even though she hadn't collected all of the negative thoughts yet. "She still doesn't really acknowledge my presence when Mimi isn't around, but she doesn't insist Mimi only sit by her anymore, and she'll pout if we do anything romantic. I know I can only control my feelings, but I can't help but feel jealous, like I wasn't enough for Mimi. Because Jules is kinky, and I'm well..." Jazz's cheeks burned as she gripped the amethyst, fighting the urge to start the ritual over again. She'd messed it up, but it should still work. "Not. No offense."

"None taken. The lifestyle isn't for everyone." Blanche snorted. "It isn't even for me, sometimes."

Jazz smiled, reluctantly admitting, "I've always been jealous. Especially as a kid. And it's not like I don't want Mimi to explore that side of herself, but I'm jealous that I'm not part of it. But I don't know how to talk that out without it turning into an argument, and I hate arguing. Except with Lee, he's the only one I trust will come around eventually."

Blanche nodded. "Well, paying attention to and acknowledging your feelings seems like a good place to start. How have you worked through jealousy in the past?"

"I haven't?" Jazz laughed to hide her wince. "I just choose other emotions over it. Like, I was always jealous of Lee for being the favorite when we were kids, but I hero-worshipped him, even after he left. I was jealous that Auntie Alitrice chose him over me, but I missed her so hard that I would have given anything to talk to her again. I was jealous of Sunny for stealing so much of Lee's time, but she was so fun to have around, that I was always happy when she came over. I was *so* fucking jealous of Tara for becoming Lee's substitute sister after he got kicked out." Jazz's eyes burned. Should she restart the ritual now? Or was it too soon? It might backfire on her. Maybe she'd do it after she texted Mimi to apologize, to be safe. "But she's my sister now, too, so how can I still be jealous of her?"

Blanche tentatively wrapped an arm around her, squeezing her shoulders tight.

Jazz leaned into the half-hug, resting her head against Blanche's as a tear spilled down her cheek. "Sorry. I didn't mean to get this emotional."

"I'm glad you are. You carry a lot of stress with you, Beautiful. You can let it out." Blanche rubbed her shoulder, their strong hand warm against her bare skin. "Out of curiosity, and you don't have to answer this, but were you jealous of me too?"

"Oh, no!" Jazz sniffled, growing flustered at the memory of meeting the beautiful stranger who invited Jazz into their home, when she'd shown up on Lee's doorstep unannounced.

She'd been sixteen years old, venturing out into the world without her parents' knowledge or permission for the first time. Blanche had taken one look at her, and known exactly what to say to soothe her nerves. They'd made Jazz feel welcome and important and seen for the first time, while they waited for Lee to come home. For years after that, Jazz had carried a torch, one that had felt like real love to her teenage heart, for her brother's friend.

And now here she was, *living* with Blanche all on her own—without Lee, without their parents—feeling more welcome and important and seen than ever. Jazz smiled, tears rolling down her burning cheeks. "I was more jealous of Lee for having a Blanche."

Monday, September Sixth

Chapter Six

Blanche

THE PLANTS WERE HAPPY in their new home. Arranged in the tower room off the parlor downstairs, they were thriving in the sunny southeast corner of the pink house. As the soft dawn light broke through the trees outside, Blanche watered their prayer plant, murmuring praise to the beautiful survivor they'd found next to a dumpster years ago.

Their old apartment with the big window had seemed bright (at least before the condo next door went up). But their new home was filled with light. The new leaves on the pothos and philodendrons had streaks of variegation that Blanche never knew they possessed. The prayer plant was still a little crispy, but it sucked up water faster than it did in the old apartment, which Blanche took as a good sign. The snake plants... Well, the snake plant was the same as it always was.

Perhaps it was time to adopt more. They'd already hung a few pots, but the tower rooms were nothing but windows, and all of the plants in their old apartment could easily fit into the downstairs level alone. Though, Jazz had come home with some monstera cuttings; they should leave room for her plants, until Blanche could get around to fixing the glass in the atrium.

The wood floor creaked underfoot as Blanche moved around, admiring the view of the old basswood in their yard, and the hedge that shielded them from the view of the people waiting for the bus on the corner. Blanche hoped it was a lilac, but only time would tell.

Perhaps they could build a raised bed to grow veggies. Or herbs. *Could I grow weed? I wonder if my dealer would sell me seeds.*

Water trickled to the floor, splashing their bare feet with cold. Their parlor palm had spilled over onto the floor.

"Oh, shit! Stop peeing!" With a snort, Blanche went to get a towel from the very sensible location Jazz had picked for kitchen linens, only to find their tea steeping in the kitchen. "Why does everything disappear as soon as I close the door?" Blanche scoffed at themself; they'd only been up a few minutes, finally giving up on going back to sleep after another nightmare, and they'd already forgotten the tea?

Blanche took a tentative sip. At least it was still hot; they hadn't forgotten about it that long. They put a lid on the cup they'd made for Jazz, though she'd stumbled home well after Blanche went to bed at midnight, so she might not be up for a while.

Tea in hand, they returned to the parlor, wiping the wood floors before the dripping pot got their new rug wet. Leaving the towel, in case another plant had an accident, they settled into the window seat to watch the morning pass by. It reminded Blanche of when they were a kid, before they could conceive of a future where Chad might become Blanche, of summers when it was hot enough to sleep with the hayloft door open, waking to sweet, sun-warmed air and bright dawn light. Chad would sit in the open window after his morning chores were done, surrounded by the herbs and flowers he'd gathered to keep the mosquitoes away at night. The fresh air and herbs, a couple of dogs at his side, and warm hay poking his legs were some of Blanche's most peaceful memories.

"Good morning, Beautiful!" Jazz sang as she danced into the room, a mug of tea in hand. "Thanks for making tea!"

"Good morning to you!" Blanche grinned as Jazz spun around and collapsed into the wingback chair she'd found on the sidewalk on the other day. Any sign of stains in the yellow corduroy had been scrubbed out by Jazz's unending supply of elbow grease. The wood trim gleamed with polish. "You're cheerful this morning."

"I might still be a little drunk after Ed's party last night." Jazz crossed her legs, bare but for a pair of incredibly short shorts, and pressed her mug between her breasts. The barbells piercing her nipples were visible under her thin tank top. "I got home at like three."

"Why don't you go back to bed? Get some sleep!" Blanche dragged their eyes up to meet Jazz's brown ones, blinking sleepily at them. Her soft smile made their heart thump; the quiet intimacy of seeing Jazz with her guard down for once made Blanche's smile soften too.

With a cock of her head, Jazz shook her head stubbornly, her locs swinging around her ears. "I like our morning tea time."

That explained why Jazz was up by eight, like she had been every morning, even though it was the last day of her summer break. She'd kept herself busy around the house when she didn't have work or a get-together with her friends and partners. Every time Blanche saw her over the past week, she'd be bent over—always in the tiniest shorts—organizing some closet or bookshelf. The smoke of herbs and incense permeated the house, and the sound of singing bowls rang at the oddest times of the day. Secondhand furniture kept appearing, creating cozy seating areas throughout the house. Between Blanche and Jazz, dozens of paintings, wall hangings, and charming knick-knacks had found a new home there as well, including the cast-iron dog that reminded Blanche of Grandma Rose's house.

The big empty house, that had left Blanche spinning like a weather vane in a windstorm mere weeks ago, was slowly filling. Not cluttered, not crowded. Just, filled. With pleasant smells, and pretty sounds, and comfortable places for Blanche to simply exist peacefully. Or more often, fall into easy conversation with Jazz, whenever one of them found the other in some new, lovely corner. There was still so much to do, so many projects to complete. But their house was becoming liveable. Thanks to Jazz, it was becoming...homey.

"So, what's your plan for your last day before school starts?" Blanche asked, sipping the warm tea, the honey sweet on their tongue. When Jazz had given the loose leaf to them months ago, Blanche never would have imagined that they'd be drinking it together in their new home.

"Well..." Jazz pondered. "Sober up. Text my mom back with some lie that I'm getting a head start on the reading, so I can skip church."

Blanche chuckled into their mug.

"Then *actually* get a head start on the reading, because anxiety." Jazz wrinkled her nose. "Besides, I have enough to lie about. I should actually tell them the truth about some of my life."

"Have you seen them since you moved in?" Blanche asked, unsure if they should pry into Jazz's relationship with her parents. But if it'd keep Lee from feeling put in the middle...

When Jazz had moved in, Leland Senior had made a show of trying to intimidate Blanche when he'd brought Jazz's belongings (and completely ignored Antonio, strangely). After over two decades of sex work, it'd take a lot more than judgmental glowering. He'd snooped around a bit, but luckily Blanche had locked the attic beforehand, so Jazz's fib that Blanche was a "lifestyle influencer" had held up. Lee and Jazz had done their best to diffuse the tension, hurrying their parents out to dinner as soon as Jazz had unloaded her things.

She shook her head. "No. Dad's birthday is next weekend, though, so I'm going to have to go to church and pretend to be a nice girl again. At least Lee and Tonio will be at brunch after to take the heat off me."

Blanche raised an eyebrow; why was Jazz still going to church if she didn't want to? "You *are* a nice girl."

Jazz huffed, rolling her eyes. "You know what I mean. I've become everything I was taught was a ticket to hell."

Blanche blew a raspberry. "But you're also a straight-A student who wants to save the world, even if you spent the last week performing Satanic rituals all over our house."

"Oof. Saving the world is a bit ambitious. I just like plants." Jazz laughed. "But speaking of your new house, I wanted to introduce you to your home."

"Hi, house!" Blanche waved around the room. "I'm Blanche. Sorry in advance for all the sins I'll commit inside you."

Jazz slid to her knees onto the burgundy area rug that she'd spent half an hour the day before beating with a broomstick, and patted the floor in front of her three times. "Laugh all you want, but keep an open mind. I think this is a nice ritual."

Blanche left their mug on the window seat and sat cross-legged in front of her, thanking every deity that existed that Jazz was wearing shorts today, instead of going commando in her house dress like she was prone to do. Tara had often walked around the apartment barely clothed—frequently naked, for that matter—but for some reason, Jazz's comfort with casual nudity was impossible to look away from. *I did not invite her to live here to creep on her. I just need time to adjust to living with a new person in a new place.*

Jazz crawled over to the side table to light an incense, her full hips jiggling as she shuffled across the carpet. If she'd been a client, Blanche would have made her slow down and be more deliberate. But her awkward scurry was cute, in its own charming way. *Jazz isn't a client,* Shayla's voice murmured in their head. It was a reminder that Blanche didn't need, in a tone that implied an unasked question Blanche didn't care to consider.

"So!" Jazz returned to her seat in front of Blanche, crossing her legs. "How does your house feel today, compared to last week?"

Blanche considered it, grateful to ignore their therapist's voice among their thoughts. Their nightmares had been the same, but not even Jazz—magical as she was—could cure trauma with candles and crystals. Still, the "stuff" scattered around the house had found places it belonged. The new furniture shifted ever so slightly by the time Jazz was done arranging it, creating cozy spaces in every room. Everything was neatly tidied, instead of spread over every surface. Even the spare rolls of toilet tissue were neatly stacked within easy reach, with a scented candle decorating every bathroom. "Less scattered. Calming."

Jazz grinned triumphantly. "Good! That's the goal. You deserve a home that feels calming and sacred. Do you meditate?"

Blanche shrugged. "A little." They'd learned to meditate mostly for Tara's sake, but too much quiet time meant drowning in dark memories. Since starting therapy, Shayla's voice was popping up more and more, asking questions that Blanche struggled to answer.

"Close your eyes and place your hands flat on the floor. Let's just breathe for a while." Jazz spread her fingers across the rug, forming a triangle between her thumbs and pointer fingers.

Blanche mimicked her, closing their eyes and breathing with Jazz. "This reminds me of that time I worked at a tantric sex workshop with a cult leader," they joked, to distract themselves from feeling too exposed. The tantric sex workshop had been incredibly problematic on many levels, but Blanche had gotten paid. And learned about breath control and mindfulness—particularly during sex. One anonymous tip to the FBI an unsuspicious length of time later, and the cult leader had been arrested for human trafficking. Blanche and Daisy had been there by choice (well, Daisy's choice), but not everyone was.

"What's with you and cults?" Jazz teased. "Tell me the story later. We're focusing on your house now." She inhaled slowly. Then, in a rich, breathy voice, she murmured, "This is an opportunity to connect with your house, to thank it for providing you a home where you can feel safe, for creating space for peace and love. In your head and your heart, introduce yourself to your home, let it know you're going to take care of it as well as it will take care of you."

Lee would make a comment about how corny this was if he were here, but Jazz had managed to put into words exactly what Blanche wanted. They'd never had a home where they felt safe or peaceful or loved. Not as a child in their hayloft, not on Freddy's couch, not in the apartment where Daisy had— *No, not the time for that.* Blanche shook their head, taking a slow inhale in time with Jazz. Their fingertips bumped her blunt nails.

Even their apartment hadn't been Blanche's. It was their patron's playroom, where he came to get whipped and told what a miserable piece of shit he was for raising the price of NARCAN again. He'd invaded Blanche's bedroom like he was entitled to it.

In a way, he had been. They frowned. But not anymore. That was in the past. Yet another train of thought that would drown them if they let it. Blanche exhaled slowly, reminding themself that they were supposed to be greeting their house.

Covey wasn't safe or peaceful. He wasn't allowed in Blanche's new home.

The pink house would be sacred. This was where they'd heal, and...well, Blanche wasn't sure what they wanted to do. But this house would be full of potential that they could do anything they wanted, once they figured that out. Their mental Shayla reassured them that there was no timeline, no rush to start their future. They'd just started this new chapter; Blanche had nothing but time to figure it out.

Jazz's soothing alto continued, "Thank the energy lingering in this house, left behind the people who have called this home. The ones who built it and loved it and grew up in it. They've made a beautiful home for you to live in, and you'll be the steward for their lingering presence. Any harmful energy should be dispelled after the cleansing I did this week, so you're safe here. Feel it flow through you, the way it flows through your home."

Blanche breathed in with her, fingertips buried into the rug, interwoven with Jazz's. How many people had lived here since it was built over a century ago? How many children had slid down the banister, thrown their toys down the laundry chute? How many grandparents passed away peacefully here, surrounded by love and layers of floral wallpaper? How many lovers had kissed in these walls, stolen intimate moments in the butler's pantry? How many young people had shaped their future as they studied for finals, textbooks stacked on the built-in shelves in the parlor?

How many generations had called this place theirs, how many transient souls had found a home here?

Found a home the way Blanche hoped to do.

They exhaled slowly. That was why Blanche needed to keep their work in the attic. Before they'd moved in, Blanche had vowed never to sleep there themselves. That space was for Work Blanche, for their anger and bitterness. Not for love or family or home. Real Blanche wanted the love to stay on the downstairs levels, to make *that* their home.

Shayla hummed in their mind, a note of disapproval in her tone that Blanche didn't care to unpack.

"When you're ready, open your eyes."

Blanche opened their eyes to see Jazz's warm brown ones examining them. Blanche's hands searched for hers, still pressed to the floor. They kissed the backs of her hands in gratitude. "Thank you, Jazz."

Jazz bit her lip. "How do you feel?"

"Like I want you to cleanse my bedroom, too." Blanche laughed, the sound hoarser than they'd hoped. What was the point of lightening the mood, when the emotions were stuck in their throat? "It feels like a mess compared to the rest of the house now."

Jazz grinned. "Good. I'll do that today. Procrastinate on my first day of school anxiety a little longer. Still not the attic?"

"Still not the attic. I need the negative energy there." Blanche smiled tightly. "Where did you learn all of this stuff? I thought your parents were culty, too."

Jazz tangled their fingers together, her expression turning mischievous. "To be honest, I learned this from Marie Kondo's show on Netflix."

Tightening their fingers around hers, Blanche laughed loudly, a snort escaping them. "I was not expecting that!"

"I know." Jazz's smile faded. "In one of my last conversations with Auntie Alitrice, she told me about how my grandma—my dad's mom—was more spiritual than Christian. Apparently Dad got super religious when he joined the Marines and met my Mom at a church near base. I always wanted to ask her more, but Dad cut her off for taking in Lee before I could find out."

Sadness tightened Jazz's brow as she worried her bottom lip. "So I've been researching different traditions and rituals and stuff. Finding what works and makes sense for me. Like, I grew up learning this super religious controlling bullshit, where all this was Satanic. And now I'm pursuing a career in science, where anything remotely spiritual is completely discredited as pseudoscience, even if it's been practiced for thousands of years. There has to be a balance, you know? Like, the truth is in the liminal space, not the extremes." She huffed in a quiet laugh, her thumb *tap tap tapping* against Blanche's. "I never really had faith in anything my parents believed, but I've always wanted something to believe in. Just without so many rules that I'll feel guilty for not following." Jazz bit her lip with a bashful smile. "It's easier to make it up myself. So, I'm internet spiritual I guess. I know it's probably inauthentic, but it fits me."

Blanche nodded, feeling strangely vulnerable for so early in the morning. "I can't say I'm spiritual, but I've always been curious about where I came from. What practices and beliefs my birth parents or ancestors had, whoever they were. Because it had to be better than the Family's fuckshit." Blanche shook their head, as the voices in the past whispered to them. *Wicked. Bortbyting. Freak.* They forced a grin. "But that's never going to happen, so I've just been doing what works for me too. No wonder I became a dominatrix. Lots of practice being humiliated and beaten as a kid."

Jazz squeezed their hands in sympathy, brown eyes still searching Blanche's soul. "I find this fits me better than anything my parents taught me. Prayers don't help my anxiety. Debasing myself through servitude and penitence, or whatever the fuck my dad says, doesn't work for me. It doesn't make my anger and insecurity and jealousy any easier to manage." She shrugged, pointer finger *tap tap tapping* on the back of Blanche's hand. "Meditating and setting intentions and being patient and aware of myself does. I'm allowed to be angry and imperfect and worry without a solution. The 'pseudoscience' helps me. I can channel my emotion so it can flow away, instead of being bottled up until I snap."

Pulling one hand from Blanche's, Jazz fiddled with her necklace, eyes downcast. Blanche's jaw tightened. Jazz always seemed cheerful and at peace. To think of her suffering with anger and anxiety the way Blanche did felt wrong; Jazz didn't deserve that volatility.

"Anger's always been hard for me to control, too. I keep it bottled up until I have a scene to let it all out. I don't allow myself to think about it until then." Blanche snorted; they were the worst person to give Jazz advice on how to handle anger issues. "I focus on happy things—compassion and love and all the sappy corny feelings—until I can turn the anger into humiliation or pain for my clients."

They'd meant to sound lighthearted to break the tension, but Jazz frowned and scooted across the floor to pull Blanche in a hug. Her hand ran along their back, up and down. "That sounds like a lot to carry, Blanche. I worry about what that costs you."

"You sound like Shayla." Blanche scoffed, wondering how prying into her relationship with her parents had become a therapy session for them. *It costs a damn lot. It costs my future, my past. It cost me Daisy.* They wrapped their arms around her waist, pulling Jazz closer. The easy intimacy of their friendship was a balm on the raw edges, left exposed and vulnerable so early in the day. "It doesn't matter the cost. The benefit is survival."

"So, when do you get to live instead of just surviving?"

Blanche didn't have an answer. They'd always lived like their life had ended with Daisy's, like they'd be stuck in the past until the inevitable and imminent end. But now? They had nothing but time and endless projects to occupy them, while they figured out what they wanted their future to hold.

Friday, September Tenth

Chapter Seven

Sunny

With a wince, Sunny shifted in her desk chair, hissing as Dumpster's claws extended into her thigh. She looked down at the orange cat in her lap with an offended scoff. "Why do you treat me this way? I'm your mother!"

Dumpster blinked up at her, purring now that Sunny had stopped fidgeting.

"You want me to take her?" Richard asked from where he reclined on the guest bed. He was still naked from their scene earlier that evening, much to Sunny's delight. The summer heat was sticky even with the AC, and his newest tattoo—a phoenix on his thigh that he'd come home with the other day—was wrapped in Saniderm.

"No, it's just hard to sit in the chair after what you did to me with that flogger." Sunny pouted over her shoulder.

"Don't act like you weren't begging for it." Richard didn't look up from his book, but a smirk played at his lips.

Sunny laughed and turned back to her IM conversation with Gabe. She normally didn't go on her computer on Fridays—it was scene night, after all—but he had messaged her earlier that day, asking if she was free to talk. So far, though, Gabe had just been making his usual slightly sarcastic small talk; she didn't need to put her panties back on for *that*.

Sunnywith0meatballs: So what's so urgent that you need to talk?

Black_Hawk_Up88: It's not urgent. If you're busy, we can chat later.

Sunnywith0meatballs: No, you said you needed to talk, and you never talk about personal shit with me anymore, not since you stole my best friend from me.

Black_Hawk_Up88: She's my best friend, not yours. lol

Sunnywith0meatballs: Ass.

Black_Hawk_Up88: And I stopped talking to you about personal shit since I figured out I knew you in real life. It's not like you haven't done the same.

Sunnywith0meatballs: Whatever. What the fuck do you want?

Black_Hawk_Up88: You used to be nicer to me.

Sunnywith0meatballs: Sorry, treating you as an extension of Tara, but you're your own individual. I can be sweeter. What the fuck do you want, bestie?

Black_Hawk_Up88: lmao! So much better.

Black_Hawk_Up88: Don't tell Richard I'm asking, but how is he?

Sunny glanced over at the bed, where Richard was buried in his book as usual.

Sunnywith0meatballs: Uh... fine. Why?

Black_Hawk_Up88: Because having kids has been really important to him since before I met him, and he had to find out Tara and I are having one in front of a bunch of strangers. Every time I ask, he insists he's fine, but I know him and he's probably pretending he's fine while acting out in other ways.

Sunnywith0meatballs: Well, that explains the tattoo.

Black_Hawk_Up88: lmao seriously. Is he okay?

Sunnywith0meatballs: No, he seriously got a tattoo. It's on his thigh. Phoenix.

Black_Hawk_Up88: Does he often get new tattoos?

Sunnywith0meatballs: It's the first new one since I met him.

Black_Hawk_Up88: Fuck. Anything else going on?

Sunny shifted in her chair again as the welts on her ass started to throb. Gabe probably didn't want to hear that Richard had finally come close to her pain tolerance for the first time since they'd started their Friday night scenes. *But then again, he asked.* She'd assumed that Richard could tell she was extra stressed from work, taking on more leadership or whatever to make herself a better candidate for a promotion, part of her Future Wifey plan. But maybe Richard had been stressed too.

Sunnywith0meatballs: TMI warning.
Black_Hawk_Up88: Oh no
Sunnywith0meatballs: He normally is way too gentle with funishments, imo. Until last weekend. Seriously, I might ask him to get an ice pack for me to sit on.
Black_Hawk_Up88: Oh. Okay, that wasn't bad.
Sunnywith0meatballs: You want more details? Because I am ready to share!
Black_Hawk_Up88: Noooo

Sunny laughed.

"What's funny?" Richard asked.

"Just making Gabe uncomfortable. Nothing new." Sunny beamed at him. "Could you be a dear and get me an ice pack?"

Richard peered over his glasses. "I thought you said you were fine."

"I was fine in bed. Now I'm sitting up, and it burns." She wrinkled her nose, then quickly added, "In a good way!" in case Richard got any ideas that he'd gone too hard on her.

The corner of his mouth twitched, seeing right through her. "Need more aloe, too?"

"No, just an ice pack, please."

Richard tucked a receipt in his book and pressed a kiss to her head as he left the room.

Sunnywith0meatballs: Has he really been wanting kids that bad for so long?
Black_Hawk_Up88: I mean, I don't know how he feels about it now, but it took the better part of a year before he understood he could still have kids if he transitioned. And once he finally did, he was a completely different person overnight. Like having kids was more important than being himself, until he realized he didn't have to choose.

Sunny chewed the inside of her cheek. Was she taking too long to get ready for the rest of their lives, and delaying his? He had so many plans for his own future, beyond their life together, that were on hold until—

Black_Hawk_Up88: Sunny, stop overthinking. Don't let this freak you out if you're not ready for kids yet. Richard loves you, and if starting a family was urgent, he'd bring it up.
Sunnywith0meatballs: Fuck you. How did you know?
Black_Hawk_Up88: Because you and Tara are not that different.
Sunnywith0meatballs: wow double fuck you
Black_Hawk_Up88: lmao
Sunnywith0meatballs: You'll still have time for these conversations when you're a dad and shit, right?
Black_Hawk_Up88: Ugoihgohdtoiejoikfjsoihe

When Richard came back with an ice pack wrapped in a tea towel, Gabe's icon still showed "typing." Sunny made sure her moment of insecurity was buried in banter and off the screen, so Dicky couldn't eavesdrop. Carefully, she rose ever so slightly in her chair, so she wouldn't bother Dumpster. But the cat grumbled and jumped off anyway. Sunny sighed. "Dammit. She never sits on my lap."

"Because she likes me better," Richard teased dryly, sliding the ice pack underneath her.

"That's because you get to feed her. I just clean her litter box. No wonder." Sunny offered her cheek for Richard to kiss; he complied before burying his face in her hair.

Black_Hawk_Up88: Okay, so you might get this better than most people, but I'm just typing out loud because I need to process my thoughts. So don't take this too seriously but I think I've been feeling really... ughhigjdoirtjd idk...dysphoric?????? about being a "dad" and shit. Like, not physically dysphoric, but socially? I don't know how else to describe it. Like I've always felt a little nauseous anytime someone calls me a boyfriend or son or man or anything like that, but the "dad" thing is bringing it to a whole new level. I thought at first it was sympathy morning sickness, but it just keeps getting worse.
Black_Hawk_Up88: And Tara's been great about it because she's got her own feelings about being a "mom" but it's been so uncomfortable that I've been kind of questioning everything about

> myself. Like what if I'm not just queer, but like what if I'm not entirely a guy? But like I've questioned my gender before. Many times! And I'm fine with the he/him of my life and understand I am a big dude so everyone is always going to see me as a man, but I don't understand why this is making the heebie jeebies as bad as it is.
>
> **Black_Hawk_Up88**: Sorry to dump it on you like this lol I just don't know if this is normal fear about becoming a parent. But the part about having a kid and making a family with Tara is fucking amazing. It's the idea of being called dad by complete strangers for the rest of my life and all the social norms that go with that is freaking me out because it's going to be inescapable.

"Sunny," Richard breathed into her air, his raspy voice almost a growl. "Get dressed."

"What?" Sunny squeaked in surprise as Richard pulled her out of her chair. Her sore thighs screamed in protest.

With an unreadable expression, Richard handed her the ice pack. "Get dressed."

> **Black_Hawk_Up88**: Sunny?
> **Black_Hawk_Up88**: You there?

RICHARD

THE MOTION LIGHT OVER Gabe's front door flicked on, blinding as always, but Richard didn't bother with the key. Instead, he stormed through the backyard where the patio door was always left unlocked. It had been Gabe's habit ever since a fresh-out-of-rehab Antonio had once come over unexpectedly as a last-ditch effort to keep from calling his old dealer.

That night, Gabe hadn't been home, and Antonio couldn't figure out which key was Gabe's. Richard had reassured a panicked Gabe that he would go to Gabe's house instead, that he should finish dinner with Miriam and John at the vineyard, and that Antonio should sit in the backyard until Richard arrived. He then proceeded to tie the protesting Antonio to the kitchen chair with shibari ropes, and waited for Gabe to get home. Antonio's nonstop soliloquy had vacillated between desperation and shame, broken up by moments of delirious fits of laughter at Richard's methodology.

Richard had read a book.

"Dicky, should we be here?" Sunny asked, hurrying behind him in a pair of his sweatpants, still in her house slippers. "You didn't tell them you were coming, and Gabe seemed to be going through something."

"Exactly." The knot in his chest tightened. Richard yanked the back door open, trusting Sunny would shut it behind her.

Gabe wasn't in the dining room or the kitchen, but a mostly naked Tara was lying on the couch in the living room, wearing only a pair of Gabe's boxers. Hippo raised his head from the couch next to her, giving a soft woof in greeting.

Tara jumped up with a start, covering her chest. "What the fu—oh. It's you two." Her arms fell back on the couch. Her breasts—fuller now than when they'd gone skinny dipping a few months ago—jiggled as she lay back on the couch. "I was worried it was his parents or something."

"Hey Titties!" Sunny teased. "You really haven't changed, have you?"

"I have even fewer reasons to wear clothes now," Tara winked, then frowned, eyes narrowing at them. "What is happening here? Why are you both in sweatpants? This is weird."

Richard hadn't come here for social niceties. "Where's Gabe?"

Tara raised an eyebrow. "Basement. Everything okay?"

Richard didn't answer her, instead grabbing Sunny's elbow. "Don't follow me."

"I'll follow if I want," Sunny scoffed. "But sure, I'll hang out with Tara."

He turned on his heel toward Gabe's basement, where most of his gaming consoles and his PC were kept, along with the damn pinball machine that had taken up half of Gabe and Phin's dorm room.

As he descended the stairs, he found a sweatpants-clad Gabe nursing a glass of wine on the futon.

Gabe raised his glass in greeting. "I've been expecting you."

"What the fuck, Cooper."

"That one's yours." Gabe nodded to another glass next to the bottle. "Figured you were eavesdropping on that conversation. You're so predictable."

"First you're having a kid, now you're not cis? What else are you keeping from me, but telling everyone else?" Richard sat down in a huff and poured far more than the standard serving.

"Dicky, dude, you're such a lightweight!" Gabe took his almost-spilling-over glass and handed Richard his half-empty glass. "I wasn't intentionally keeping anything from you. I just...didn't know how to bring it up."

"I think 'Hey, I accidentally knocked Tara up' would be a start!" Richard downed the swallow of wine Gabe had handed him. "And 'I'm having complicated feelings, similar to what you experienced, and I want to talk about them' would be a great follow-up conversation."

Gabe groaned and snatched the bottle up to refill Richard's glass. "I'm sorry. But you've always wanted to start a family since before we met, and I never even thought about it. Like, having kids was so far in the future. Isa and I might have gotten there eventually, but things got offtrack with her so quick, and kept going further offtrack as my whole life derailed." Gabe shook his head. "Thank the Creator that Emily didn't want kids, otherwise I'd probably *still* be with her. But I'm glad it happened, especially with Tara. I love her *so* much."

Gabe smiled into his wine, before looking at Richard with far too much familiarity and vulnerability in his brown eyes. Richard's chest tightened.

"But *you've* had a damn cost-benefit analysis, planning how many kids you want to have and when you should have them, since you were sixteen. And you're thirty-two. That's half your life that you've planned Option A through Z so you can be a parent—a *dad*!" Gabe huffed. "And here Tara drank some tea that messed with her birth control, and I hate that I'm not as excited for this as I want to be. Instead, there's this cloud of gender fuckery hanging over my happiness."

Richard shook his head. Gabe was right. He wasn't handling Gabe's news well. He was making it about himself, when Gabe needed his support. Even if Richard was salty that half the office knew before he did. "So are you trans? Non-binary? Agender?" He paused. "Two-Spirit?"

Gabe winced. "I have no idea. Thinking of myself as a mom is just as weird as dad, so probably not trans fem. And I don't know if I should call myself Two-Spirit without knowing my dad's ancestry, because every tribe is different, and what if ours has some entirely different concept? I dunno. Nothing feels right. Maybe gender nonconforming?" He snorted. "I don't think it matters, really. I'm just Gabe, and that's all I want to be. Even if everyone else is putting their weird gender role shit on me."

"Why did you tell everyone but me?" Richard hated the way his voice trembled at the last two syllables. Here he was, making it about himself again, but Gabe was *his* friend. And yet he'd been hearing about everything in his friend's life from other people, namely Sunny. Sitting here with Gabe, the two of them in their fucking sweatpants and t-shirts with a glass of wine, like they were in college again... Richard resolved not to become the guy who relied on his girlfriend to maintain his friendships for him. He took a too-large swallow of wine to fortify his voice. "Why have this conversation with Sunny, instead of me?"

"Richard, you do so much for me." Gabe laid his head back on the futon. A heavy swallow made his throat bob. "I wouldn't be alive if it weren't for you. And I don't know the extent of how you've been protecting me since we moved back to Bellamy—and I don't want to!" He held up a hand as Richard opened his mouth. "I trust you to keep me ignorant of whatever fuckshit Emily might have tried. I just...I can't rely on one person, and I don't want to burden you."

Richard bristled. "You're not a burden."

Gabe laughed sardonically.

"You're not," Richard muttered. "You saved me first."

"I really didn't. I just gave you the support you needed to save yourself." With a sigh, Gabe ran his hand over his face. "All the same, your life has revolved around helping me for so long, and while I appreciate that, you can't do everything for me. If I told you that I needed to add Tara to my insurance, you would have been on hold with HR in seconds making it happen. I need to do that shit for myself, or let Tara help me. You have your own life."

"Not really," Richard muttered, his thigh itching under the bandage.

Gabe snorted into his wineglass. "Don't let Sunny hear that."

"I don't mean like that. Of course, I have a life, and Sunny is most of it." Richard shook his head. "But it's different with her. She doesn't let me help as much as you do."

Gabe snickered. "Bet that bothers the shit out of you, doesn't it? You're so controlling."

"I am not," Richard scoffed, grumbling as Gabe waited expectantly. He should have known Gabe would want him to be vulnerable too. He tapped his wineglass with a finger. "Fine, I might be a little controlling. But I have all this time and money and energy that I want to put into our future, and she's not ready yet. And I'm fine waiting however long it takes for her to be ready. We both want the same thing eventually." He huffed. "I need something to do, to focus on. Until then."

"So focus on *you*, not her or me." Gabe bumped his head against Richard's. "You'll have Confession to keep you busy soon enough."

Richard pushed him away. "Don't start with the cuddling. Why are you down here anyway?"

"Moping and waiting for you to come and yell at me." Gabe drew his feet up to curl around his knees instead. "It's easier for Tara if I keep the wine out of sight, so I've been having my sad bitch nights down here."

"How does she feel about that?" Richard asked hesitantly, unsure if he should be worried. Probably not, considering Gabe had just told him to mind his own business. In a kind and supportive way, but the message was the same. Besides, this was hardly "moping" by Gabe's standards.

"She likes it when I come upstairs wine-drunk and horny," Gabe laughed, leaning back to rub his belly under his shirt. "And I'm emo often enough that she doesn't mind me taking a night to myself down here sometimes. She wants me to keep living my life, even after the kid gets here. Gaming, and the gym, and my sad bitch nights. Let's see how it turns out though."

"Sounds healthy," Richard muttered, taking another swallow of wine he'd probably regret when he woke up with a headache later. Tara really was the polar opposite of Emily.

"It is. Strange that drinking by myself in the basement is healthy, but Joy supports me processing my emotions independently, instead of relying only on her or Tara." Gabe finished off his glass of wine. "We good?"

"Yeah." Richard finished his glass, too. "But just know you're never too much. Whatever you need. Seriously. You were there for me when I needed you. Let me return the favor."

"You have. A thousandfold, dude." Gabe tucked him under his arm and hugged Richard far too tightly. "And I'll keep you abreast of the gender situation. Still figuring it out."

"Get off!" Richard ducked out of his elbow, shaking off the crawling sensation along his skin. "You can do that with your naked baby mama upstairs."

Gabe sat up with a grin. "Tara's naked?"

Richard snorted. "Yes, other than your boxers, which is unsanitary."

"Isn't she great?" Gabe laughed, jumping off the couch and practically skipping to the stairs. "She says since she can't drink anymore, she needs a new hedonist outlet. We spend pretty much every weekend naked."

They found Sunny reclining on the couch, and Tara grumbling while she painted Sunny's toenails. Hippo had curled up behind Tara's bare back; his tail thumped the cushion when he saw them come up the basement stairs.

"How did we end up here?" Tara asked. A pillow was hugged to her chest as she bent over, squinting to carefully apply red polish to Sunny's toes. "I don't want to touch your nasty ass feet ever, and here you got me painting them?"

"Bitch, my feet are clean as hell!" Sunny smirked as Tara finished up her little toe. "Richard washed them during our scene."

"Whoa, TMI," Gabe coughed, giving Richard a confused look.

Richard shrugged, cheeks burning. "Sensory play." Gabe didn't want the details, but the scene—with Sunny blindfolded and tied up in the sex swing—had actually been quite sweet. At first. Lots of feathers and silk, a hot cloth and a scented oil massage. Followed by nipple clamps, a gag, and flogging, but still. Sweet.

Tara leaned back to greet Gabe with a sloppy kiss. Richard and Sunny exchanged a bemused look when Gabe's hand drifted places best left untouched in front of company. But then again, those parts should also be covered, and Tara still hadn't put on a shirt.

"Oh, were you drinking wine?" Tara asked, wiping her lip as Gabe pulled away. "Cooper house red?"

"You should become a sommelier," Gabe teased as he pet Hippo. "Sunny, you snitched? After I specifically told you not to?"

"I did not!" Sunny pressed a hand to her chest. "He eavesdropped!"

"You asked me to eavesdrop on you, anyway." Richard sprawled in an armchair, resigned to wait for Sunny's toes to dry, adjusting his itchy thigh and looking anywhere but Tara's chest. Gabe's home was certainly more lived-in, now that he shared it with Tara. Her camera and a laptop took up half the coffee table, along with several empty plates.

Gabe tsked. "Eavesdrop on Emily, not everyone else."

Richard grinned as he stacked the plates into a tidy pile, the knot in his chest a bit looser now that he and Gabe had finally talked. He'd been expecting Gabe to open up to him, but he did feel a bit better after opening up to Gabe in return. "Just be glad I don't read your texts with Tara."

ON THE WAY HOME, Sunny propped her feet on the dash of his Range Rover, admiring the red polish. The streetlights, enhanced by the steady drizzle, cast shadows throughout the car. "I think we should have kids."

Richard coughed. "Yeah. We will. I hope."

"No, I mean, like, soon."

"Oh." Heart racing, Richard forced his eyes to stay on the lanes as they approached downtown, the white stripes bright and glowing in the headlights. The wiper blades squeaked. A trickle of water ran down the side of the windshield. "I wish we weren't driving for this conversation."

"Why, you want to do things to me?" Sunny's smirk could be heard in her voice.

"You have no idea, Sunshine." He reached over to squeeze her thigh, pressing hard into a bite mark he'd left earlier. He would have left her covered in the bruises she loved, if he'd known they'd be having *this* conversation.

With a squeak, Sunny tangled her fingers with his. "I have almost enough saved for my surgery, thanks to you and your secret plotting with Miriam."

"It's called networking, not plotting."

Almost timidly, Sunny murmured, "I should have enough saved by the middle of next year to get my upgrade, even with Luna's tuition. And a team lead position is opening up soon at work, and my boss gave me an action plan to make me a good candidate for it. So maybe we start talking about what's next."

Richard's ears roared with his heartbeat. "Does your insurance cover your surgery?"

"That's my Dicky, starting off the sweet talk with insurance!" Sunny laughed. "But hell no! Are you kidding?"

"Mine does. We could add you," Richard mumbled, his mind already lost to his spreadsheets—which tabs needed updating, which lines could be moved up.

"This better not be you proposing!"

Richard shook his head, trying to focus on the here and now. "We don't need to be married for me to add you to my insurance. Gabe added Tara, and they're not married." *Yet.* "But it would ease the expense, and we're planning on that eventually anyway, so why not? Enrollment is in November."

"So, let's say I have my surgery. What's next on your plan, sir?" Sunny asked, her voice growing husky the way it did when she was trying to turn him on.

Richard bit back a grin, playing along in his dom voice. "If it's early enough in the year, we'll do a summer wedding. A long honeymoon wherever you want to go. Then we make an appointment at the fertility clinic."

Sunny laughed. "Let me guess, you already have a spreadsheet for this."

Richard snorted as he pulled into the parking garage of his condo—their condo, even if Sunny hadn't moved in officially. "I might have a few. I never expected that you'd beat me to the proposal."

"Dicky, if you think any of this counts as a proposal, you got the wrong idea." Sunny's hair brushed his arm as she flipped it over her shoulder. "You need to do it properly. Get down on one knee. Cry a little. I want a ring and romance."

Richard smirked. "But you usually like my spreadsheets."

"Dicky!"

"You'll get your ring, Sunshine. And your romance." She would get far more than that if Richard had anything to say about it. He'd been holding off on any ideas over the past year, beyond knowing he'd do it at home, in private (certainly not on *stage* like Antonio had). Finally, Sunny had given him permission to plan.

"And a strong, masculine tear or two?"

"I'll get down on one knee."

"Dicky!"

Richard bit his lip to hide his grin. After months of projecting all over Gabe, this conversation alone brought him so much relief, excitement, and no small amount of terror. He'd be surprised if he wasn't a blubbering mess by the time he actually got around to proposing. "Fine. I'll consider a tear or two."

Sunny flicked his ear affectionately. "Then I'll consider saying yes."

Sunday, September Twelfth

CHAPTER EIGHT

ANTONIO

LELAND SR. GLOWERED AT the veggie burger on Jazz's plate, brow furrowing further when Jazz poured an abundance of ketchup next to her fries. "Jasmine, there can't be much protein in that. And you should watch your sodium intake."

Jazz and Antonio exchanged a look; they'd ordered the same thing, yet Leland hadn't commented on Antonio's meal. His father-in-law had barely acknowledged Antonio's presence at all, let alone struck up a conversation with him about his dietary choices. Strange that they sat across the table from each other, and yet Antonio might as well be a stranger on the other end of the crowded diner.

But it was Leland Sr's birthday, so Antonio would sit quietly and eat his veggie burger and fries—the only vegan option at the restaurant in the outskirts of Eastside, where Leland had opted to celebrate—and get ignored by his father-in-law, like he had since the wedding. Antonio gave Jazz a sympathetic wince as he drowned a fry in his own ketchup lake. At least he and Lee hadn't had to go to church like Jazz.

"It has fourteen grams of protein, Dad." Jazz smiled tightly, scratching her hairline under the turban she'd worn to cover her hair for church. It still blew Antonio's mind how different Jazz was around her parents—the picture of modesty. No hint of crop top or nose piercing (or nipple piercings, but he was sworn to secrecy on that) in sight. "And a side of fries isn't going to kill me."

Leland opened his mouth to say more, but Althea put her hand on her husband's, cutting him off to force him to shut up. "So, Antonio, how's work going?"

Antonio looked up from his fries, pleasantly surprised that she'd asked at all. Althea usually only asked Lee questions, and fussed over Jazz. "Oh! Great! The middle schoolers seem somehow even smaller than they did last year, but it's a good group of kids." That was probably all Althea was asking about, but Antonio pressed on. "And Chas—who was the emcee at our reception—has been giving me more responsibilities at Confession since she's due in a couple of weeks but honestly, she looks like she could pop any day. And," he grinned at Lee, who tried to hide his excitement behind a warning look, but a giddy smile played at the corners of his mouth. "I have a feeling like our music career is about to take—"

"When are you doing your student teaching, Jasmine?" Leland asked, before taking a bite of his grilled chicken.

Lee and Jazz both frowned, their nostrils flaring in sync. Jazz met Antonio's gaze and gestured for him to go first. Antonio looked at Lee to step in, already low on patience.

"Yeah, we have some really exciting opportunities coming up for us," Lee said as if his father hadn't spoken, resting his hand on Antonio's thigh under the table. Antonio leaned against his shoulder in support and appreciation. "More so Antonio, but if things go the way we expect, I'll finally have a foot in the door for more production opportunities."

"That's great, sweetie!" Althea beamed. "Do you have new music coming out? Anything I can listen to this time?"

Lee and Antonio laughed. Antonio busied himself with a big bite of his burger, not trusting himself to keep anything inside. He hadn't even allowed himself to think about The News, just in case he blurted something out.

"No new music, but," Lee considered his words carefully, "you might want to listen to the radio in a few weeks."

"We don't listen to secular radio," Leland said sternly.

Antonio froze mid-chew as Lee stiffened, his hand growing clammy on Antonio's thigh. He quickly covered the flare of his jaw with the same tight smile Jazz always wore around their dad.

It was a good thing he'd taken such a big bite of his burger; if his mouth was free, he'd be cussing out his father-in-law. Antonio hummed quietly around the food in his mouth instead. Leland Senior may have deserved far more than a verbal barrage of insults, but his husband wanted to have a good relationship with his parents. And that meant Antonio would sit quietly by his side, while Lee managed that relationship the best way he could. Even if he was far more peaceable about it than Antonio thought was sensible.

"Well, I'm excited for it!" Jazz said brightly. "Even if you won't tell me anything."

"You'll be the first to know as soon as we're legally able to say anything." Lee gave her a grateful smile.

"A good job should have benefits and a pension plan. I can't imagine the music industry is consistent enough to make a living off of, let alone support a family." Leland spoke more to his plate than his son. "A business degree is the key to stability."

"Kicking me out is a funny way to show you care how stable my life is," Lee muttered.

"What was that?" Leland asked sharply.

For a half second, Antonio was sure that Lee was about to say it again. But to his disappointment, Lee offered only a tight smile. "We have stable jobs with benefits. Music takes a lot of hard work and luck, but Tonio and I are more than up to the task. Especially since we don't have any family to support besides each other."

"You might change your mind!" Althea piped up. "One day the clock starts ticking. Right, Antonio? I'm sure you've started to feel that longing."

I can't tell if she's calling me old, or assuming I'm the woman in this relationship. Antonio shook his head, tired of how often his mother-in-law brought up kids. Even *Gabe's* mom had a better respect for boundaries. "Not for us."

"But you love kids!"

"I love *teaching* kids! I love my niblings and cousins," Antonio conceded gently, yet firmly. He grinned. "And I love saying goodbye at the end of the day, and going home to peace and quiet."

Lee snorted as he took a bite of his shrimp scampi. "I might end up having to go back to school, though. One of the producers we've been collaborating with said I'd get farther with formal credentials, and BCC has a program in music production."

"Look at you, Lee, becoming a nerd like me,' Jazz teased.

"I have a long way to go before I'm anywhere as nerdy as you are," Lee teased. "You're literally trying to become a scientist. That's peak nerd. At least music production is cool."

"A scientist?" Leland frowned. "Jasmine, we talked about this. You're majoring in education."

Lee and Antonio exchanged a confused look. When had Jazz ever been considering a teaching degree?

Jazz sighed, tapping on the table. "No, Dad, *you* talked about it." Jazz straightened her shoulders, staring at her father with a neutral expression. She spoke slowly, "I told you two years ago that I wanted to major in ecology and botany. I have not changed my mind, no matter how many times you tell me I should be a teacher. In fact, I'm applying for a doctorate program at UB in ethnobotany, so I'm also minoring in anthropology now." Her finger rapped on the table again.

Leland's face darkened. Lee's hand gripped Antonio's leg painfully as he and Jazz stiffened. "You mean to tell me that the tuition that *I've* been paying has been going to a useless degree?"

Antonio's chest tightened with anxiety. But so far, Leland had been all bluster whenever he got like this, despite Lee and Jazz's reactions. He rubbed the back of Lee's hand, humming loud enough for just his husband to hear.

Jazz shook her head, finger tapping hard on the table. "I'll learn teaching skills as a grad student, and I plan to go into academia, so I'll still be teaching—" She froze, gripping her necklace. "No, you know what? I appreciate that you've been paying my tuition, but this is my life, and I don't want to be a teacher!"

If the tension had been a little less thick, Antonio would have cheered. Finally, someone was standing up to this bully of a man! Maybe this family dinner would take a turn for the funner. He gave Jazz an encouraging smile, though she seemed too upset to notice.

"Then you're wasting your potential, and I won't throw my money away on a mistake," Leland said, his voice dangerously low.

Althea's smile was plastered on as her eyes flicked nervously between them.

"I am not asking for your approval!" Jazz crossed her arms. "If you want to hold tuition payments over my head like this, I'll take out loans. I can do this on my own, without you. I'm making the best decisions for *my* life, even if you think it's a mistake."

Leland froze, his nostrils flaring the way his children's did when they were angry. His jaw worked back and forth for a few moments, before he finally spoke again. "It's more appropriate for woman to teach a younger age, not college students. You'd be more comfortable and adept at teaching children. If you were a man, of course, teach college." Leland sneered, "Men teaching children is—"

"I teach children," Antonio cut in, before he could stop himself.

Even Althea's ever-constant smile fell into an embarrassed wince.

"Yeah, well..." Leland waved his hand dismissively.

Lee sighed under his breath, as Antonio looked expectantly at him, humming his Intention Song to himself, because Lee was supposed to handle his parent's bullshit. A flurry of retorts to escalate all of Leland's bullshit ran just under the surface; it was better not to open his mouth. Antonio hummed harder.

"Well, what, Dad?" Jazz asked, before Lee could gather his courage to stand up for Antonio, like he'd promised he would. Antonio tried to ignore the pang of disappointment, but it grew bigger every time. Which thankfully, had only been a handful since the wedding. But Lee kept promising him he'd stand up to his father next time, and next time, and next time.

"I'm sure there are some exceptions for men who are, well..." Leland tried to stab a potato on his plate, but it rolled out from under the tines. The squeak of his fork on the worn ceramic made everyone cringe.

"Well, what?" Lee asked, a hint of a challenge in his baritone that made Antonio's heart beat faster in hope that Lee might finally, finally call his dad out. If this was Antonio's parents, they'd have already been hugging it out. Dragging it out like this was helping nobody!

"I'm just relieved one of my children is going to college." Leland stabbed the potato this time. "I always thought you'd be the one to go. You were so good at football."

"Yeah, well..." Lee muttered, tightening his grip on Antonio's thigh.

But Althea changed the subject before Lee could speak again. "Aren't these lovely centerpieces? Do you think these are real flowers?"

Antonio patted Lee's hand in sympathy, hating the bitter taste of disappointment. Yet another next time, and yet Antonio couldn't blame Lee. Antonio was new to this family dynamic. For Lee, this was a lifetime of ingrained patterns and trauma that he had to overcome. For how happy they were together, Lee's parents were a shadow over their newlywed bliss. One that Antonio did not expect to brighten anytime soon.

Lee

"At first I thought your parents assumed I was a bottom because I'm shorter than you, which was offensive enough." Antonio followed Lee inside Blanche's house, still ranting about all the slights they'd endured during dinner. The first crisp chill of fall evening air was replaced by the herbal haze of Blanche's house the moment Lee opened the door. He knew Antonio probably would prefer to go home, but Lee needed some time with his real family after that. Tara should be here, and Blanche, and Jazz...

Jazz had torn off to run inside the second Lee had put the car in park, refusing to look at anyone. But Lee had seen her glassy eyes in the rearview mirror as he drove. Yet another reason he was reluctant to simply drop her off.

He couldn't blame her for being upset. After two hours of trying to make nice while their dad didn't listen to a damn word anyone said (and jammed his unasked-for opinions down their throats), with their mom just smiling instead of disagreeing, Lee needed to debrief. And poor Jazz had gone to church all morning with them? No wonder she was on the verge of tears.

"But then I was pretty sure they thought I was a woman. Which, yeah, drag queen and pretty fem, but like, no. Definitely a man." Antonio ducked under Lee's arm as he held the front door open for him, kicking off his platforms next to Tara's ratty slides. "And now I'm pretty sure your dad thinks I'm a pedophile? I kind of want to punch him in the face."

With another pang of guilt, Lee wouldn't blame Antonio if he did. He'd forced his husband to grin and bear the insults, when he'd promised to protect him. Barely two months into their marriage, when he and Antonio were happier than ever, when everything was going better than he'd ever expected for everyone he loved, and yet Lee was utterly failing at the bare minimum. He leaned back against the door with a painful swallow as he toed off his shoes. Chest tight, Lee put them on the rack next to Antonio and Tara's. Despite Jazz's mood, hers were already neatly stacked at the top.

If it hadn't been his dad's birthday, Lee would have called his father out on his bullshit. But unfortunately (thankfully?), he only ever saw his parents on special occasions. They never reached out, unless it was to celebrate something. Or maybe that was Lee's convenient excuse to keep from having a real conversation. As much as he wanted them to be better, they were still the same parents they'd always been.

"So you don't regret getting marr—" Tara looked up as Lee and Antonio found her and Blanche in the dining room, drinking tea. Their laptops sat open on the table. "Oh hey! How was dinner?"

Lee shrugged.

"That bad, huh?" Tara winced.

"Take whatever you're thinking and it was worse." Antonio collapsed into an empty chair.

Tara snorted into her teacup. "I was imagining a lot of judgy comments and obtuse opinions, Lee sitting there and taking it, and you sitting next to him about to scream, wondering why he doesn't say just fucking say something."

"Well...yup, in a nutshell." Antonio laughed in exasperation. "But experiencing it was awful, so I'm saying it was worse."

"Sorry." Lee sat next to Antonio and took his hand. "I just—"

"I know, Angel." Antonio cut him off with a kiss. "I stayed silent, too. And I went with you, even though you told me I didn't have to."

Lee gripped his hand, guilt wracking him for letting his husband down. Why couldn't his parents be as easy as everything else? "I'm glad you did."

"Me, too!" Jazz sighed heavily as she came into the dining room from behind him.

"Jesus, Jazz—do you ever wear clothes anymore?" Lee covered his eyes as Jazz—the real Jazz, not the obedient daughter she'd pretended to be all morning—waltzed around the table to sit next to Blanche.

"No." Jazz's fingers tapped on the table impatiently. Her locs hung free without the turban hiding them, falling over her face. The septum piercing she always wore tucked into her nose had reappeared. And the long dress and leggings she'd worn to church were long gone, replaced by a thin house dress that barely covered anything. "Church was so awkward! Getting food after was better because at least I had you two there as a buffer. Mom is on my ass about never calling her. And you think *you* had the baby pressure? Mom doesn't even care if I finish college! She and the deacon's wife were in cahoots, so I got stuck next to the deacon's dusty-ass son. Who—by the way—kept breathing down my neck trying to look down my dress the whole damn time!"

"Well, at least you're going to college. I'm a failure because I didn't miraculously keep going to school and playing football after he kicked me out." Lee huffed, irritation bursting free after he'd swallowed it all evening. Not that Lee wanted to go to church, but he *would* to support Jazz. Even Antonio was curious, if only to see what it was actually like compared to his own not-Catholic upbringing. If only he and Antonio were even *invited*, which they had noticeably never been. "Yeah, completely my fault I've amounted to nothing and pursued a silly career that I'm passionate about."

"At least you're not a sissy pedo." Antonio rolled his eyes.

"He said that?!" Blanche and Tara asked, both of their fists slamming on the table.

Lee cringed, sinking into his chair. Why hadn't he reacted the same way? He'd been just as angry, and yet, he'd frozen. Barely able to form words, let alone fists.

Antonio waved them off. "Not in so many words, but pretty much."

"At least you can both be out," Jazz sighed. The *tap tap tap* of her fingers against the hardwood table helped Lee remember to breathe. "I wish I didn't have to hide. Do you know how long I've been trying to tell him I'm not getting a teaching degree? God, I really hope I don't have to take out loans!" She buried her face in her arms.

"Hey, you're safe from the worst of it. And Mom will talk him down about the loans, don't worry." Lee winced, hoping he wasn't lying. Though he and Antonio would hopefully have enough money coming in soon enough to help her with tuition. "If I hadn't been outed, I would probably never have come out, either. But I was, so let me take the heat for all the gay shit. You keep doing what you want in private. Hopefully, he's so distracted by how disappointing I am that he won't take it out on you."

"You're not a disappointment, Angel." Antonio squeezed his hand. "You're amazing, and if he had two brain cells to rub together, he'd see how wonderful you are. Both of you!"

"And how lucky he is to have you as a son-in-law." Lee pushed his glasses up his nose as his skin burned in shame. "I'm sorry I let him get away with saying that shit about you. Sometimes I don't know if he's worth the stress, but Mom..." He sighed as Jazz's anxious tapping reminded him he needed to stay calm. He wished there was an easy answer between wanting to keep the peace with his parents, without failing his husband. Most of the time, he could forget it. But during the couple days surrounding every dreadful meal with his family, Lee felt like the worst husband alive.

"I get it, Lee. It's complicated." Antonio's thumb traced his knuckles. "I still support you no matter what. I can ignore the shit your dad says about us, if that's what you think is best. We know you're not a failure or a disappointment, just like we know Jazz will be a great plant scientist, and that she would hate being a teacher."

Tugging on her necklace, Jazz laughed. "God, it's so true. He's such a sexist asshole!"

"He really is." Lee grinned. "I'm glad I somehow avoided that part of the indoctrination."

Blanche and Tara tittered.

"What?" Lee asked. "When have I ever been a sexist asshole?"

"You were never an asshole..." Tara trailed off.

"Okay? So I was sexist?" Lee looked between Blanche and Tara, who exchanged an amused look.

"Darling, you had a lot to unlearn when you first moved in with me." Blanche smiled kindly. "Remember the first night? You assumed that I'd have *expectations* since I wasn't charging you rent, and volunteered so Tara wouldn't have to sleep with me. Which of course was not even on the table, but you felt you had to protect her at the expense of your own sexual autonomy, and you were willing to pay that price so she'd have a roof over her head."

Lee burned with shame at the memory. Not so much his actions, because he had done that and would again. They'd been vulnerable, and Tara needed a safe place to sleep. He'd done worse to get Auntie Alitrice her meds. But the idea of Blanche ever taking advantage of either of them was so far from reality that he was ashamed he'd ever thought so poorly of them.

"And you completely freaked out when I fucked that dude in the supply closet at BCC," Tara grinned.

"You lost your virginity in a supply closet!" Lee waved his hands, wondering why he wouldn't be upset about that. "To a guy whose name you didn't even know!"

"First of all, I lost my 'virginity' a few months before that. It was still sex, even if a penis wasn't involved before then." She looked pointedly at him. "Second of all, the whole concept of virginity is stupid. I wanted to have sex with a guy. I had sex with a guy. Was it awful? Yeah, but I've had worse and better since. You were the one who had an existential crisis because I wasn't married yet."

"It wasn't the married thing! I just thought it should be special!" Lee cringed, hearing himself. Or hearing his father, rather. Damn, he had been a sexist asshole back then. "Or you know, in a bed?"

"Sex doesn't have to be special, Lee." Tara gestured as if he'd proven her point, which he had. "Sometimes, it's just fun. And I'm fortunate that now, the sex I have is both special and fun." Tara sighed dreamily. "Anyway, remember all the times that Blanche and I had to reassure you that you weren't a whore or a slut, or destined for Hell every time you sucked some dude off?"

Lee shifted uncomfortably, nodding to Jazz. "Do we need to be having this conversation in front of my little sister?"

Antonio groaned next to him, shaking their joined hands in exasperation.

"Why, you think I need to be protected from such a dirty topic?" Jazz teased. "Not that I want to swap stories, but you don't have to stop a conversation for my sake. I've been unlearning a lot myself. Partly thanks to living with Blanche."

"You have?" Blanche beamed. Lee had the same question, though he would have asked it in a much less cheerful tone. "How so?"

Jazz shrugged. "Just the casual conversations we have. They're so different from what I grew up with. You're nonjudgmental and share funny stories about former clients that reassure me that I'm normal. And you ask good questions that challenge my assumptions and set me off on a rabbit hole of research on a topic. Seriously, you should be a therapist or something."

Blanche laughed. "I think I have a few too many issues of my own to make a good therapist. But thank you."

Antonio snorted. "Don't let that stop you. Every therapist I've had has just as many issues as I have. Or more! If you ever meet Joy, you'll understand."

Lee politely smiled along with their laughter. Hearing that Blanche was sharing stories about their clients with Jazz made his gut clench. But then again—he forced himself to exhale slowly—Jazz was grown, capable of making grown choices and having grown conversations. If she didn't want to hear the stories, she would say so. Blanche would respect whatever boundary she set.

Still, he worried what their parents would do if they ever found out exactly what kind of "influencer" Blanche was. Or about Jazz's unconventional relationships with her partners. They'd assume Lee was leading her into sin (which Jazz was doing fine all on her own) and freak out. Who knows how harshly they'd come down, on both of them? While Lee was relatively secure, he wouldn't put it past his dad to sabotage Antonio's teaching career, or pressure Jazz into moving home. And Jazz seemed so much happier, even in just a few weeks of living here.

He gripped Antonio's hand tighter. Her happiness mattered more than any complicated, challenging relationship with his parents.

Tuesday, September Fourteenth

CHAPTER NINE

RICHARD

SINCE HE'D MET GABE fourteen years ago, there hadn't been many
times in Richard's life where he'd felt directionless. Once Gabe had taken
Richard under his wing, he'd been set free from the futile pursuit of
earning his father's approval. Instead, Gabe had put Richard on the path
toward the best revenge: a life well lived. And while Richard had shifted
course a few times along the way, mostly to make sure Gabe also lived a
full and happy life, he'd always had a purpose.

However, that purpose had somehow led him here: feeling incredibly useless and out of his element, hovering around Confession. As
luck would have it, it was a weeknight when Chas had gone into labor. Blanche was covering days, Richard weeknights, and, on behalf of
Miriam, Gabe, Richard, and Blanche would be splitting up the weekends. Chas had said he could consider himself on-call Monday through
Thursday, but what kind of business partner would he be if he didn't
pull his weight?

One who was less in the way, probably.

Richard stepped back to avoid the busboy hauling a tub of dishes
into the kitchen. He followed him in, dodging the chaos and heat to
find Darla, the back-of-house manager. "Anything I can help with back
here?"

"No offense, new bossman," Darla wiped her brow with her wrist as
she set a platter in the window, shouting "Order up!" loud enough to

make Richard flinch. "I don't like it when the usual boss is back here either, and Chas actually knows how to run a kitchen."

"So, stay out of your way." Richard nodded, relieved he didn't have to be in this sensory nightmare for a second longer than necessary. "Got it. I'll be up by the bar if you need me."

"I won't!"

Richard wandered through the dining hall, trying to smile and make eye contact with the customers; he was probably making himself look even more awkward. Why had he signed up for this? Oh yeah, because Blanche had needed a favor, and he could provide it. Because Gabe was right, he was a little controlling and nosy.

He nodded at Jackie, who didn't bother to conceal her eye roll when he sat on a barstool. Richard knew better than to dare to go behind the bar into her domain.

"What do you want?" she asked, hand on her hip.

"Just wondering if there's anything I can help with?"

Jackie huffed. "Look, gonna be honest. I'm not sure why you're here. Chas mostly comes here to socialize with her fans. And flirt with Freddy, without their kids and her mom as an audience. All the bills are paid up, and she already submitted payroll this morning, so you don't even have to start worrying about that until next payday."

"I want to get an idea of how things are supposed to go, so I know when and how I should step in when someone does need me," Richard said.

Jackie cocked her head at him, her long ponytail swinging behind her. "You've never worked in a restaurant before, have you?"

"How can you tell?" Richard tried not to squirm in his chair. Strange how he could argue with executives and present to boards no problem, but in a bar, he felt like he'd never worked a day in his life.

"You seem a little out of your element," Jackie laughed, the veins in her neck making her somehow even more intimidating. "My guy, we are a well-oiled machine. Unless you want to get yelled at by a drunk Karen, you're gonna be bored as hell. If you're gonna insist on hanging out here, enjoy the boredom, because it means we *don't* need you."

Richard nodded, wishing he'd brought his book. Or his laptop, to get ahead on his EOD reports for tomorrow. Or that Sunny wasn't busy working on the MIA app Miriam had commissioned, so he could text her.

He jumped when a tray full of silverware was set in front of him with a clatter.

"Here. Found something for you to do." Darla smirked, tossing down a stack of cloth napkins on top of the tray, before disappearing back into the kitchen. "Have fun!"

Jackie snickered as he looked at her helplessly, before she finally took pity on him. "Here, I'll show you once."

Richard watched as she rolled the napkin around the utensils. "Thank you. Sorry."

"We all start somewhere. Finish that, and I'll show you how the dishwasher works." She snorted. "We can always use another barback, especially one who doesn't get tips."

Richard got to work, wrapping the napkin the way Jackie showed him. After his third, he felt a bit more confident to ask, "Have you ever been married? Or engaged?"

"Oh god," Jackie muttered. "I'm aroace."

"Okay." Richard blinked. "And? You could still be married."

She huffed. "Still not interested, buddy."

"Oh, no! No!" Richard shook his head, his cheeks burning. "I'm planning how to propose to my girlfriend! And I don't know what to do about the ring."

"Oh!" Jackie scrunched her nose up. "Why the fuck would I know what your girlfriend wants? Ask her!"

Richard sputtered. "I have! All she says is that it needs to be ethically sourced, preferably vintage, and worthy of her. And I don't know what that means!"

Jackie blinked at him. "I think that means big."

Richard cocked his head. "Really? I figured it meant meaningful or something."

"It could be! You know her better than I do." Jackie shrugged. "But if she likes pretty shiny rocks, get her the biggest shiniest rock you can!"

Richard pursed his lips, concentrating on the napkin in front of him. He knew someone with quite a few pretty, shiny rocks that verged on garish. But that someone would definitely not be invited to the wedding. He huffed. Maybe he'd check out some vintage sites, before resorting to the dreadful route of acquiring family heirlooms.

BLANCHE

HOSPITALS WERE THE WORST. The smell of disinfectant clung to Blanche's nostrils, and the dry air leeched the moisture from their eyes. The constant beeping and hissing and whirring was unsettling. No matter where Blanche went in Sanctuary General of East Bellamy, a fluorescent light flickered like a horror movie.

The memories here were inescapable. Even the happy, cheerful infographics about babies and birthing on the walls of the birth center, were too similar to the ICU elsewhere in the same building. For six weeks, the sounds and smells and anxiety had permeated their subconscious while they lay in a coma. Even now, the sound of someone "paging doctor soandso" brought Blanche right back to being trapped in that hospital bed, waking up to the sound of Daisy's pleading tears. Then, as soon as Blanche got control of their eyes back, the blurry sight of her relieved smile.

Blanche paused at the receptionist's desk. "Sorry, can you tell me which room Chastity Gomez might be—Oh, it's you. Hi!"

Behind the desk, Mimi turned to them with a smile that fell as soon as they saw who it was. "Oh. Hi."

Blanche kept their polite mask on. "I didn't know you worked here!"

"I'm premed," Mimi said, gesturing to her nametag, which read *Miyako* and underneath *Volunteer*. "Looks good on the med school application to have volunteer experience in medical facilities." Blanche opened their mouth to say something polite yet encouraging back, but Mimi turned back to her computer. "Visiting hours are over. We're only admitting family right now."

Blanche glanced at the clock, which showed visiting hours had ended a mere five minutes ago at eight. They wondered if Mimi needed to work on her bedside manner for everyone, or if her chilly attitude was reserved exclusively for them. "I am family."

Mimi raised a skeptical eyebrow.

"I should be listed in her chart as an authorized visitor and emergency contact. If you'd look her up," Blanche added pointedly.

"Who did you say you were looking for?"

"Chastity Gomez."

Mimi eyed her computer screen. "There's no Blanche listed here."

"It's probably under Chad Hermanson." They took a deep breath to ease the tightening of their chest. Five kids, and this was the hardest time anyone had ever given Blanche at this damn hospital. Including when Daisy had practically lived here to chase away the med students from examining the freakshow intersex patient in a coma. Blanche had left against medical advice as soon as they could rip the IV out of their arm and walk with Daisy's help.

"You don't look like a Chad." Mimi frowned.

"Don't feel like one either." Blanche forced a smile, but the stern clip of Work Blanche had edged into their voice. Jazz's partner, who disliked them for some unknown reason, didn't need to hear about their endless struggle to establish an identity. There was a baby to meet. "Do you need ID?"

"No, I believe you." Mimi chewed her lip. "Room forty-two."

"Thanks. Enjoy the rest of your shift."

Mimi didn't reply. Blanche walked away with a slow exhale. Hospitals were the worst as it was. They didn't have the added patience for whatever imagined drama Mimi wanted to start.

Luckily, their irritation was washed away with a chorus of "Auntie Blanche!" as they knocked on the open door to room forty-two. Four small children, all mini variations of Chas and Freddy, ran to swarm them in a hug. Even Catalina, the youngest—second youngest, now—who could barely walk, toddled over.

"Hello, my chickies!" Blanche hugged them, showering everyone in kisses to the sound of squealing laughs. "And you're walking so well, my lovely! You're all grown up!"

"No, she's still my bebecita!" Chas's mother teased from the chair in the corner. "Venid aquí, cariños! Let Blanche into the room!"

"Lupe, looking good as always." Blanche greeted her with a hug.

Their relationship hadn't always been great; Guadalupe was very protective of Chas. Daisy, Blanche, and Freddy had never been the best influences on her only child. But for the sake of her grandkids, Lupe would do anything, including be nice to Blanche. Freddy had won her over long ago. Daisy had run out of time, but her death had meant all of her sins were forgiven; she'd been "that poor girl" ever since.

Lupe had even sworn to the police that the eight-month-pregnant Chas had been home on bed rest—doctor's orders!—the entire time Daisy's murderer had been out on bail. Blanche had still been in jail, unable to afford bail of their own before the charges were eventually dropped. Freddy had been running lights and sound for the show from the control room, after Chas insisted he go to work.

Karma had found a path through street justice, and they all had solid alibis when her murderer was found shot in an alley in Eastside, mere hours after he was released.

"Where are the parents of the hour?" Blanche asked quietly, leaning over the bassinet where the newest addition to the family lay, eyelashes fluttering and lips pursing in their sleep. *Her* sleep, based on the pink cap.

"Fred is helping Chas clean up." Lupe raised a stern eyebrow while the older kids—Marisol, Leo, and Sebastian—started to fidget and yell, playing with some action figures. They smiled innocently and returned to their toys more quietly.

As if on cue, the door to the bathroom opened, and Chas hobbled out, supported by Freddy's arm. "Oh, Blanchy! You made it!"

"How are you feeling?"

"Like I don't want another one!" Chas laughed as she eased into bed. "Give me two days, I'll get over it. This was the easiest one yet. Barely had to push."

"You say that every time," Blanche teased.

Lupe stood up. "Say goodnight, ninos! It's past your bedtime. Your mama is tired, and we'll come to see your sister again tomorrow."

Blanche joined in the bedtime hugs, before Lupe herded her grandchildren out.

"Mama *is* tired." Chas reclined her bed. Before she asked, Freddy was already adjusting her pillow.

"Do you need me to go?" Blanche asked. "Sorry, I couldn't get here earlier. I got your text right when Jazz and I were starting to make dinner, and it took us longer than we thought. We're not very good at cooking."

Chas waved them off. "No, stay! If you'd come any earlier, you would have been in the way while they were doing all those tests. I'm just resting my eyes."

"Well, we'll talk quietly," Blanche exchanged a bemused grin with Freddy. "Or at least I will. Freddy's the loudmouth here."

Chas's laugh turned into a groan. "Oh, don't make me laugh yet!"

Freddy nodded to the bassinet, pressing a hand to his throat. His raspy voice was barely louder than a whisper. "Want to hold your niece?"

"Bring me the baby." Blanche sat on the couch and held out their arms. They loved all of their niblings, but babies weren't really their comfort zone. They hadn't been the most present auntie until a few years ago. Picking up a sleeping baby would probably end in the baby screaming. But sitting down and holding the sleeping baby? That they could do.

Freddy deposited the sleeping bundle into their waiting arms, not bothering to press his hand to his throat again. He was close enough that Blanche would hear his whisper. "Meet Elena."

"Elena! Hello, my light!" Blanche tightened their arm around her to better support her head. They'd been a nervous wreck holding their eldest niece, but holding Elena's tiny, frail body was almost comfortable after so much practice. "You did good, Freddy."

"Don't give him the credit," Chas muttered from the bed, half-asleep.

"You did even better, Chas." Blanche exchanged a grin with Freddy.

"So do you and Jazz make dinner together every night?" Freddy asked, settling in close to Blanche on the couch. In the quiet of the room, it was less painful for him to be heard.

"Nosy," Blanche teased. "Not every night, but sometimes roommates eat together."

He grinned. "You never made dinner when you were squatting in my apartment."

"That's because you never had food. Seriously, you were a terrible host."

"You never paid rent." He traced the thick black hair peeking out from under Elena's tiny stocking cap. "I suspect you might want another tattoo soon. Music notes this time, maybe?"

Blanche shook their head with a scoff. "First of all, her name is Jasmine. That is also a flower. Second of all, what on Earth are you talking about?"

"Come on now, Blanchy. You know Freddy's got a sense about these things. Remember when Lee and Tonio met?" Chas coughed a laugh from the bed. Blanche blinked, dumbfounded. In their mind, Shayla and Daisy were laughing together. "He said they'd be head over heels within a week, and he was right. The only one he's been wrong about was hisself."

"Love, when we met, you were sixteen and wearing a Catholic school uniform," Freddy said, not bothering to speak up. Chas would hear him. "The only thing I sensed was that you'd ruin my life if I let you."

Chas tsked. "We're only four years apart."

"And by the time that wasn't wildly inappropriate, I had the sense to know I'd ruin yours."

"Good thing I never had sense, then," Chas chuckled, her eyes still closed. "Blanche, from how Jazz looked at you at yer party, and from how you're talkin' about her now, I'd say Freddy's on to somethin'."

Cheeks burning, Blanche opened their mouth to protest, but the words got stuck. Sure, Jazz had some lingering hero worship from that crush she'd had on Blanche when she was younger, but that wasn't romantic. She had partners! *Yes, multiple,* came their therapist's voice, unprompted, *which is kind of the point of polyamory, isn't it?*

Jazz and Blanche had always been affectionate; of course it would extend to their growing friendship as roommates. Besides, Tara and Lee were touchy too! *But to that degree?* Blanche grimaced. Sure, maybe Jazz's affection wasn't quite the same as— *And doesn't she trust you enough to be emotionally vulnerable with you, get flustered around you, ask you endless questions about yourself, light up when you come home, and check you out constantly?*

Blanche grumbled under their breath. They'd never mentioned any of this to Shayla; how could they possibly know what she'd say? *Blanche, really?* Okay, fine, maybe Jazz was into them. But *they* certainly weren't harboring any feelings for— Oh no. They sputtered helplessly.

"Yeah, that's what I thought," Chas laughed weakly.

They huffed. "Aren't you supposed to be sleeping?"

"I told you, I'm just restin' my eyes."

Blanche shook their head. Even if they thought about Jazz constantly, and looked forward to when she'd walk in the door every day, it wasn't an option. Doing anything about their—*it's a crush, admit it, you have feelings for her*, Daisy teased—could never happen. "She's my tenant for starters. She's Lee's little sister and in a happy relationship with two women her own age. Did I mention that she's almost fifteen years younger than me?" Blanche shook their head. "She's got a bright future ahead of her, and it doesn't include me."

Oh, and why did that make their stomach drop? That shouldn't ache!

"Sounds like you've found a lot of reasons to convince yourself you're not feeling anything." Freddy put an arm around them in a side hug.

Blanche leaned into it, bumping their head against his with a frustrated sigh, as they adjusted their hold on the sleeping baby. "I know you miss my sister, Blanche, but it's okay to move on. It's been seven years. You're always putting other people first. When do you get to look after yourself?"

Blanche shot him a look. Between Freddy and Shayla, Blanche was tempted to start carrying around a gag. "You talk too damn much, Fred."

Freddy's reedy laugh made his daughter's face flutter in her sleep. Blanche smiled; he had the same laugh as Daisy, with the little sigh at the end. He'd been a chatterbox when they were young. Now, speaking was too painful, even years after his and Daisy's stepdad had slashed his throat. Daisy and Blanche had just made it to the bottom of the fire escape from his apartment when the gunshot had sounded.

That had been Blanche's first venture back to this godforsaken hospital after their coma. Daisy had rushed to the hospital with him, and Blanche had stayed with a numb Chas until the cops arrived. When Blanche had finally been allowed to see Freddy—unconscious, with bandages around his throat—Daisy had given Blanche the good news that he'd pull through, but his vocal cords were permanently damaged. Blanche had given her the bad news that Chas had been arrested for murder, with the silver lining that her stepdad hadn't survived the bullet Chas put in his head.

Chas was eventually released on the grounds of self-defense, and Freddy learned to communicate his many thoughts and unasked for opinions in other ways—texting and exaggerated facial expressions. Blanche still teased him that he talked too much, and Freddy appreciated that Blanche didn't tiptoe around his injury. That was what family did for each other. And Freddy was the closest thing to family Blanche had.

They smiled down at the sleeping Elena as her tiny mouth opened. Daisy would have loved being an aunt, even more than Blanche did. She'd always wanted kids, and well, that was one thing Blanche knew they did *not* want. Strange, how it was easier to figure out what they didn't want than what they did. Stranger still that for Daisy, Blanche would have raised a thousand babies, even though they would have made terrible parents.

Elena made a noise that sounded like she was getting fussy, and Blanche handed her to her father, who appreciated small babies far more than Blanche did. "Here. She's about to cry."

Freddy laughed, taking Elena with ease. "Sure, we can change the subject."

Blanche's cheeks burned. Funny how thinking about the dark times, about Daisy, was easier than facing their growing feelings for Jazz. Shayla would be so proud, if they ever admitted any of this to her. "Dunno what you're talking about." What was the point in wanting things, if they couldn't have them?

Saturday, September Eighteenth

CHAPTER TEN

WITH THE KITCHEN FINALLY tidied from brunch, Gabe wiped his hands on the kitchen towel and pulled off his apron. The weekends when they had no other plans were dedicated to hedonism; other than boxers, clothes were discouraged. But Gabe had learned the hard way to wear an apron in the kitchen. No amount of chest hair would protect him from grease splatters while cooking hash browns and omelets.

A gentle autumn rain was starting to fall outside, the light gray skies still bright with the late-morning sun behind the clouds. Gabe patted Hippo, sprawled across his bed, on his way to find Tara. Normally, he'd cover the dog in a blanket, but it was far too hot for mid-September. The rain would hopefully cool the house off; the humidity was just as sticky as August.

Their weekends were everything he'd dreamt of when he'd imagined what it'd be like to live with Tara: just the two of them, enjoying each other's company. If they didn't volunteer at the museum, they'd sleep in—well, Tara slept in; his insomniac ass would hold her until she finally woke up—and meditate together. Quietly at first, and then eventually not quiet in the least, pulling breathy moans from each other.

Then Gabe would make them an obstetrician-approved breakfast, with healthy foods to help mitigate Tara's low body weight and history of poor nutrition. His weight was also going up, but Gabe was surprised to find he didn't mind as much as he expected. Their soft domesticity was a pattern he'd been thrilled to fall into.

Leaning against the doorframe, Gabe smiled as he found Tara curled up on the couch, wrapped tight in a blanket. Considering her hormones had turned her into a walking furnace, she must have been drenched with sweat under there. But Tara, despite her insistence on wearing as few clothes as possible, would always burrito herself into a blanket anytime she sat still.

With a sigh, Gabe steeled himself to interrupt her peace. They'd been avoiding a certain topic since she'd met his parents a couple of weeks ago. He'd been practicing what he would say with his therapist, so they could have a normal, healthy conversation. Putting his feelings on the line at the risk of their Saturdays—which were usually sweet, fun, and argument-free—was not how he wanted to start their afternoon.

But maybe he could manage to keep his emotions in check. And Tara might not have a panic attack at the very idea, like she nearly had during lunch at his parents' house.

"Coop, don't move a muscle." Tara's green eyes peered out of the blanket, her arm snaking out to grab her new camera. Fighting the urge to cover himself, Gabe stood still as the shutter clicked. "You could smile a little though. Come on, let me see those dimples!"

Gabe chuckled despite himself, as her shutter clicked again. "Really?"

Tara's unfiltered appreciation of his body had forced Gabe to finally confront the dysmorphia that had plagued him since he was a child. Joy, his therapist, had been thrilled he finally wanted to work on it. The treatment program had come with some...unexpected perks.

At Joy's encouragement, he'd asked Tara to take photos of him, so he could learn to see what she did. Candid photos of him around the house had quickly morphed into portraits of each other, often in very compromising positions. Joy didn't know about that, but Gabe suspected she'd approve. With their shared hobby of photography—and high libidos—Gabe was surprised it had taken them this long to curate a collection of nudes.

"This, by the way." Kissing her hair, Gabe sat next to her on the couch.

"This what?" Tara curled up against him, opening her blanket cocoon in a silent invitation to cuddle.

As she threw the blanket over them, a waft of her scent hit his nose. Just as he'd suspected, she was a little ripe. It was wonderful. Gabe put his arms around her to pull her onto his lap. Her back was slick with sweat, and he loved it, loved her. *It must be pheromones, because why isn't this disgusting?* He nuzzled against her neck, kissing her up and down.

"Focus, Coop. This what?" Tara teased, though she arched her neck to give him more room to scrape his teeth down her salty skin.

"You make me feel attractive." Gabe murmured in her ear, delighted by her responding shiver. "That is something you bring to my life."

Tara smiled, tracing his cheekbone with one finger. "You're beautiful."

He shook his head, opening his mouth to disagree. Tara raised an eyebrow. Gabe sighed, "I know."

"Good job." She kissed his cheek. "So what was the heavy sigh for when you came in?"

With a kiss to her collarbone, Gabe buried his face into her neck. He would prefer to keep going, kiss her everywhere, but there'd be time for tasting her after a conversation. As long as they managed to keep their feelings in check, anyway.

This was one of those moments where Gabe wished that he wasn't as fucked up as he was. It'd be nice to have an important conversation without having to mentally prepare and practice how to ask a simple question ahead of time. But he trusted he and Tara would get through it together and come out stronger for it. Just like every other hard conversation they'd had in the past three and a half months.

Gabe dragged himself away from her neck. "My mom isn't going to drop the marriage thing."

With a frown, Tara groaned.

Gabe's jaw tightened, but he exhaled slowly until the moment of frustration passed. It was difficult to not take her aversion to the idea personally, but this was a Tara Issue, not a slight against him. Even if it directly rubbed uncomfortably against several Gabe Issues. Tara had been unsettled after their dinner at his parents' house. So he'd given her space, even if he'd wanted to get on his knees and beg her to marry him as soon as they got home. But his insecure neediness was a Gabe Issue that he needed to manage, not something for Tara to placate.

That was why he'd practiced what to say with his therapist. Gabe and Tara couldn't have a normal proposal. If he piled his whole heart on her all at once, she would say no, and he would spiral. Tara was still building her confidence in having a relationship, and Gabe was still nervous about becoming codependent on his partner. Marriage was a lot to spring on her, even if they were both happy with their relationship, the pregnancy, and planned to stay together forever.

Tara put her hand on his chest, and Gabe realized she was breathing with him, the way they did in bed in the mornings. Heart melting, he smiled when she looked up at him. "I don't want to pressure you into doing anything you don't want. I only bring it up now because they are coming over tomorrow for lunch, and she's going to ask what Phineas found about the trust."

"What did he find?" Tara asked trepidatiously.

"Basically what I already knew. That if something happens to me, you can only access the money if we're legally married. The kid wouldn't be eligible to draw from it until they turn twenty-five." Gabe huffed, resentful of his mom's shitty parents. He shouldn't have been hopeful that Phineas might find a different answer this time; if they'd cut his mom off so thoroughly for simply falling in love with someone they didn't approve of, why would it be any easier for him? He kissed Tara's shoulder. "Again, only if something happens where I'm not around to manage it myself, but we should prepare for the possibilities."

Tara sat quietly, chewing on her fingernail.

"What are your thoughts on it?" he asked, pulling her hand from her mouth to lace their fingers together.

She scowled and kissed his thumb. "I already feel bad for getting you stuck with me. I don't want you to feel obligated to marry me too."

A pang of hurt and annoyance ran through him. This was another spot where a Tara Issue directly irritated a Gabe Issue. Thanks to many therapy sessions, he knew intellectually—and usually believed—that Tara wanted to be with him. But he hated feeling like he wasn't good enough for her. And hated even more how she felt she wasn't good enough for him.

Gabe took a breath to calm his temper before he spoke. "Kitten, can you please stop implying that we wouldn't be together if it weren't for the baby? I feel hurt when you say things like that. Like that's all we mean to each other. Like this is transactional. It's not true. Or at least I hope not."

Tara's lips parted softly and her brows furrowed. "I'm sorry. I didn't mean it that way. I just can't help but feel like I'm using you." Her hand moved over his heart. "And I know that's not what we are, but I still feel guilty for taking advantage of you."

The worry on her face erased his annoyance. Gabe covered her hand over his chest, stroking her fingers with his thumb. "I love you madly, and I want us to support each other the best we can for the rest of our lives. There's no way you can take advantage of me."

Tara smiled, bumping her forehead against his. "I love you too. I will try to be better about that. But I still don't want you to marry me out of some archaic sense of obligation. Down the road, what if we don't work out, and you're stuck with me? I don't want you to resent me."

Gabe's sigh sounded more like a growl. Luckily, Tara snorted in response. As much as Gabe adored her, he was equally as frustrated by her sometimes. She still didn't seem to understand that he'd been planning to spend the rest of his life with her, even before they found out about the baby. "How about this? If we weren't expecting, would you want to marry me? Not necessarily as soon as this, but at some point. Years, maybe, instead of months."

Tara Paused him then, gently tapping his nose as she considered his question. He had expected an outright refusal; the fact that she needed time to consider it gave him a tiny spark of hope.

Waiting patiently, Gabe kissed the inside of her wrist. She would hit Play when she'd said her piece. He slid his hands up her thighs, gripping her ass firmly.

"You're supposed to be Paused, not teasing me." Tara dragged his hands from her hips and laced her fingers through his. Her beautiful green eyes glancing up at him, she rested her forehead against his, her huffs of frustration blowing across his chest. "Marriage was never even a possibility for me growing up. And I worry about the future. Even if we love each other now, we might not always." She kissed his knuckles, even as she frowned. "I just don't want us stuck in a situation we can't get out of. And you actually have fucking assets and shit! I don't understand why you would even consider marrying me. I don't know how to be married, or a parent, or even this relationship shit."

His heart sank with resignation, wishing he wasn't Paused so he could remind her how much she brought to his life. From Tara's perspective, her arguments made sense. Marriage wasn't easy to end. She hadn't had the same experiences as he had. He'd grown up with loving, stable parents. Tara's parents had utterly failed her and each other.

Until they'd found out about the baby, he might have said a lot of the same things. He wanted to spend his life with her—however that worked out for them. A marriage certificate wouldn't change how he felt about her. But it would change how the executors of his grandfather's estate saw her.

"But…"

His heart rose a little. *There's a but?*

"You're the only person I can imagine spending the rest of my life with. I want us to stay together forever and see our kid grow up together. I want to have morning sex with you even when we're wrinkly and old. I want to kick your ass at Mario Kart when we're living in a nursing home in Miami."

"Miami will be underwater by the time we're old," Gabe laughed. "Oh, sorry. Still Paused."

Tara laughed with him, tapping his nose to hit Play.

"What if we had a safeword?" Gabe suggested, remembering the conversation they'd had about marriage, back when they were still friends pining after each other. A conversation he'd replayed in his head many, many times. "A prenup that lays out what happens if we need to end it? Like, I hope we never do, but we can hash out everything to protect our interests, figure out custody and child support for our future kids, all that shit."

He waited, giving her a chance to respond. As much as he hated even considering that she might leave, Tara would always be ready for the other shoe to drop. Her duffel bag, still fully packed, lived under their bed. It was a Tara Issue, not a reflection on him, even if it stung. That she'd also packed a suitcase for him helped. But still, she had an escape plan, always ready to go, the way life had taught her. Not even a baby would heal that.

The prenup could be a proverbial duffel bag for her, too.

"Future kids, huh?" Tara teased. "So presumptuous."

Gabe's cheeks burned, but he shrugged. "I mean, I hated being an only child. Your decision, of course."

Tara shook her head. "I hated it too. Not that I would have wanted another kid to go through what I did, but maybe things would have been different with someone else to look out for each other." Tara kissed his cheek before answering. "I like the idea of a prenup. It'd be nice to know that our kid is protected. Plus any future kids." She waggled her eyebrows.

"Is that a yes, Kitten?" Gabe swallowed, refusing to let his hopes up without a clear answer.

"I don't know!" Tara groaned in frustration as she rested her forehead against his again. "Do you want this? Or is this because your mom doesn't want a bastard grandbaby?"

Gabe huffed out a laugh. "She doesn't care about that, Kitten. She wants to make sure you won't be struggling if something happens to me. My grandfather made that trust fucking ironclad, so my mom couldn't touch it. Only me, my legally married spouse, and adult children. Not even a common-law marriage counts. *That's* why my mom is concerned about it."

He pulled his head away, stroking her cheek as he looked into her eyes, hoping she'd see how much he meant what he was about to say. "But yes, I abso-fucking-lutely want to marry you. You're everything to me. I want to spend the rest of my life with you. I've been all in on us since before there was even an us."

Tara looked doubtful. "Really? So this conversation isn't happening because you knocked me up?"

"I want to spend my life with you, married or not. And I've wanted that for an embarrassingly long time. The kid just accelerated things." Gabe shook his head with a frustrated laugh. He was gonna have to prove this, wasn't he? "Here, come on."

Gabe rose, carrying her with him as he headed to the bedroom, side-stepping Tara's backpack. Their clothes from last night were still scattered on the living room floor. Tara clung to his shoulders, wrapping the blanket around them tightly. Depositing her gently on the bed, he dug around in his sock drawer until he felt a hard lump of plastic.

He tossed her the toy capsule he'd won from a gumball machine months ago. "Here."

Tara caught it, the blanket falling off her shoulders as she popped it open. Out fell a fake gold ring with a plastic emerald. Just like the one she'd talked about when they were planning Lee and Antonio's wedding.

Looking between him and the ring in her hand, Tara's mouth fell open in surprise.

Gabe sat next to her on the bed. "I bought that the day after the flower arranging class. It took me like six tries to get a ring, instead of a dinosaur."

This was a lot for Gabe to admit; he'd bought that ring in a moment of vulnerability, while his feelings had been a confusing riot of hope and fear. He hadn't ever planned to give it to her, especially so soon into their relationship. But this was the right moment, if there ever was one.

Gabe tucked his hands under his thighs, staring at his bare knees. "I know you said you never wanted to get married. Hell, I didn't think *I'd* want to get married until we talked about it that one time. I bought that because, if you ever *did* want to get married, I wanted to be the one you married. To have the backyard wedding with the pizza and whiskey, like you talked about."

Gabe looked at her now, hoping she would see the truth in his face. "Me wanting to marry you has nothing to do with any obligation. I want to be with you forever, and I've wanted that since long before we were even together. Like I said, the baby only changes the timeline."

Lips still parted in shock, Tara stared silently, wrapping the blanket more tightly around her shoulders. Gabe's heart fell. *Too much, too soon.*

"Sorry. I know everything I just said is a lot," Gabe added in a hurry. "I can put it back in the drawer, and we can forget about it until you're ready. *If* you're ever ready. We're family now, and nothing will ever change that. I'll tell my mom to butt out." Why was the idea of putting it back in the drawer more dreadful than convincing his mom to drop this? The thought of losing Tara because he'd pushed her too far, too fast, was worse than going back to pretending that little plastic ball didn't exist.

He held out a hand for the ring, but Tara pulled it close possessively. "No, it's mine now."

Gabe tried to stop the hope that flickered in his heart. Tara was the most frustrating, wonderful, difficult, and captivating partner, and he adored her. "Is that a yes, Kitten?"

With a nod, Tara slid the ring on her finger, smiling as tears came to her eyes. "As long as there's that prenup, yes."

The smile that bloomed on his face couldn't compare to the joy exploding in his heart. "I'll sign as many fucking prenups as you want, Kitten." Gabe dove to kiss her hungrily, pushing her back against the pillows.

Tara responded with equal fervor, twining her fingers in his hair as she dragged her tongue against his, wrapping her legs around his hips. The blanket fell away from her completely. She broke away from their kiss with a grimace. "Holy shit, I stink. Why didn't you say anything?"

Gabe licked the sweat beading between her breasts, sniffing loudly. "I like the way you stink, Kitten."

"Fuck, you're so gross," Tara teased as he licked his way up her neck.

"Says the sweaty ass," Gabe shot back, relishing in her salty flavor. He sucked on a sensitive spot behind her jaw as she gasped in pleasure.

She wiggled a hand between them, cupping his hardening erection and pulling a groan from him. "Doesn't feel like you mind one bit."

"Never, Kitten. Get me sweaty too." Sitting back to pull off his boxers, Gabe ran his fingers along her thighs to push them further apart. Seeing her spread out beneath him—freckled chest already flushed with desire, the smallest bump swelling her belly, legs parted revealing damp auburn curls between her legs—sent a surge of lust through him, as always. "Fucking radiant," he breathed, bending down to lick a stripe up her pussy. She tasted wonderful. A bit more pungent than usual, but he loved her taste, her smell, the sounds she made. The dramatic motherfucker in him felt like Gabe had been made for Tara, to bring her pleasure, to love her.

He slid two fingers inside her as he lapped at her clit, grinning as Tara swore. Pulling his hair, her legs scrambled across his back. Within moments, she was pulsing and squirting over his hand, shuddering with a loud wail of his name. His cock throbbed with jealousy, desperate to be inside her.

"How are you getting even better at that?" Tara asked breathlessly.

"As much as my ego appreciates that, thank the pregnancy, not me, Kitten." He planted an affectionate kiss below her belly button, as he kissed and licked and sucked his way up her torso. Her pink nipples had darkened, and her breasts were heavy in his hands. Her hips were rounded, soft and grippable. The tattoos inked into her skin were as beautiful as always as her body had thickened. And, to his utter delight, Tara was so fucking sensitive now. Like hormones had lit up every erogenous zone on her body.

"Take the fucking compliment, Coop," Tara teased, whimpering as he gripped her thigh to pull it around his hip. His thumb pressed into the crease of her knee.

"Thank you—yes, I am a sex god." He teased back before kissing her, tentatively pushing his tongue against hers as his cock nestled between her thighs. She didn't always like when he used tongue—another Tara Issue they'd been working on together. Today seemed to be a good day for her though; she moaned into his mouth and slid her tongue against his.

Legs around his waist, Tara rutted against his erection. Gabe groaned back, rolling his hips in time to the rhythm of their kiss. He had been trying to take every opportunity to kiss her when he fucked her, before this position became too uncomfortable. Already she couldn't sleep on her back; he might only have weeks left.

"Please, Gabe," Tara whispered as her fingers found his hair again.

With a ragged groan, he slowly pushed into her. He didn't think he'd ever grow tired of the bliss he found between her legs. Of the sounds Tara made when she threw her head back, arching her back to take the last few inches of him.

Tara whimpered as he bottomed out inside her, tightening around him already. Sweat prickled his back as his muscles flexed. The filthy sounds of them echoed in their bedroom with each snap of his hips. Gabe gave into the love and lust, fucking her harder as she begged for more. Her moans and the taste of her on his tongue crumbled any reservation that remained after their vulnerable conversation.

Tara matched his need, crying out and bucking against him. Her nails dug furrows into his shoulders before she cried out, gushing again as she clamped around his cock.

"Fuck, Kitten!" Gabe couldn't hold back any longer. Her tits bounced on her chest as he chased his pleasure. He grabbed her curls with one hand, pulling her up to kiss her roughly. Her orgasm never ended, the hot pressure from her cunt squeezing him over and over again. He moaned her name into her mouth as his own overwhelmed him.

They were left panting heavily as they came down. He barely remembered to pull out to collapse next to her, instead of on top of her. Rough sex was one thing, his whole body collapsing on Tara might be a bit much; he should have some consideration for his future kid. And future wife. Excitement bloomed, flooding his body with delight that she'd said *yes*.

"Kitten, I fucking love you." He exhaled into her neck, running his hand through her curls to soothe where he'd pulled her hair. "And this isn't just the afterglow talking. I love you so much. You have no idea how happy you make me."

"And I'm going to love you forever." Tara's fingers traced the scratch marks she'd marked on his skin. "Though we should really get one of those waterproof blankets for the bed."

"I'll order a few. For the couches, too." Gabe smiled against her neck. Normally, they'd fall into silence and nap after. Instead, sheer giddiness made him blurt out, "So, when should we get married?"

Tara snorted, turning to him with a smirk. "How soon can we figure out the prenup?"

Chapter Eleven

I shouldn't have sat down.

Sprawled across the dining table, Blanche willed themselves to sit up. The stained glass light fixture overhead cast the room in a yellow glow that made their eyes ache, but they couldn't get up to turn it off. *Lift your head. Your hand even.*

The tea they'd poured was taunting them from a few inches away. *It will help. Sit up, you weak-ass bitch!* A plain white envelope lay next to it. It had been mailed to Confession, addressed to Blanche, with Covey's name on the return address. Blanche should have burned it without reading it. They should have known that any communication from Covey would be for him, not Blanche. But they'd been a fool, reading it mere minutes before a client's recorded session. Worse still, they'd decided to push through the session like nothing was wrong. Like they weren't feeling small and vulnerable and exposed, just imagining Covey's voice again. Like dominating their client wouldn't suck their already meager emotional reserves dry.

Blanche couldn't remember if they'd ever had a drop this bad. The sudden crash had caught them unprepared. The weed was upstairs, the whiskey in the living room, and no one was there to distract them, play with their hair, or indulge them with validation. Their phone was upstairs, so they had no chance to text Tara or Lee—or even Shayla—for help. Mimi's birthday party was tonight, so Jazz wouldn't be back until tomorrow. They didn't even know the time.

They were alone, stuck bent over the table and drowning in inexplicable guilt and shame. They should've had better control of themselves these days. Their clients were all good people, people they enjoyed working with, and the one who had just left was one of the easiest. He had simply wanted praise, along with ropes and suspension, and some sensory and impact play. Even his aftercare had been easy. *That's what I get for thinking I could handle Covey so soon.* Blanche scoffed, wishing Shayla's voice would make an appearance. Say something so obvious yet empowering that it would annoy Blanche to no end that they hadn't thought of it themself.

But Shayla's voice in Blanche's head was silent. Their own, depressing, hopeless thoughts were their only company.

The letter had reminded Blanche just how fragile their new life was. This bright, brilliant freedom they did not take for granted was a mere moment, a sliver of joy on the tail end of a lifetime of getting fucked over by everyone and everything. It was as if Covey had sensed that Blanche was happy, eager to ruin it with a reminder of the hell they'd clawed their way out of. The hell they refused to go back to, even if they'd carry reminders of it with them always.

Numbly, Blanche watched the steam from the mug dance, until their tea cooled to room temperature. *Why can't I move? I thought I was past this.*

Their back and neck screaming, Blanche wondered how long they'd been laying there. Their body was cold, achy from sitting in an awkward position for so long after a physically vigorous scene. Even their skin, which had been feverish after the session, was clammy. A draft from a vent as the old house breathed drew cold, basement air across their bare feet.

Perhaps it was from the effort of heaving the client into a suspended position, when he was much heavier than Blanche. Perhaps the Florentine flogging at the end had been enough to exhaust Blanche physically and emotionally. Keeping their sub positioned correctly as he swayed with the constant barrage of impacts had been draining.

I should upgrade to a pulley— Blanche scoffed, squeezing their eyes shut. *What good is it to plan for the future when I'm like this?*

The front door unlocked with a loud click, making Blanche's heart drop. *She can't see me like this.* Jazz finally gave Blanche the motivation to complete a herculean task: sit up. Seconds before Jazz waltzed into the kitchen, Blanche's back cracked as they straightened their spine.

Jazz stopped short when she passed the door to the dining room, propped open by the iron Scottie dog. "Beautiful, what are you doing awake? Don't tell me you waited up for me!"

"What time is it?" Blanche asked, rubbing one of the many cricks in their neck. At least they were too emotionally wrecked to over-think how to act around Jazz. Maybe this drop would have a silver lining of reminding Blanche how to be normal around their room-mate again. "I thought you weren't coming home until tomorrow."

Jazz looked at her phone, pulling it out of the pocket of her cutoff shorts. Her cropped pink hoodie rose with a flash of Jazz's midriff as she twisted. "It's a little after one."

I was lying there for three hours? Shame twisted Blanche's heart. *I can't even take care of myself. How am I supposed to be taking care of other people?* Blanche had to pull themselves together. They forced a smile, grimacing as they picked up their ice-cold mug.

Jazz danced around the kitchen to whatever music was in her head. Her eye makeup was smeared and her locs were falling out a scrunchie Blanche had never seen her wear before. "I dunno, just felt like coming home! Mimi's probably gonna be pissed, but whatever. She's got *Julissa* with her, so it's not like I'd spend much time with her anyway." She scoffed, rolling her eyes. Blanche raised an eyebrow; Jazz and Mimi must not have made up all the way yet. "Besides, sometimes I want to spend time at home. With you!" Jazz giggled, swaying as she spun enthusiastically.

"Jazzy, are you a little drunk?" Blanche found the will to stand up, back seizing painfully as they did. *I'm too old for this shit.* They crept to the pantry to get some crackers for Jazz, handing them to her as they shuffled to the sink to for a glass of water.

"Blanchy, I am a lot drunk." Jazz's smile fell, replaced with a look of concern as she waved her hand in Blanche's direction. "But you seem off. What's with your energy right now? Your vibes are really low."

Their heart melted, and Blanche struggled to get a smile back on their face, eyes burning. Blanche hadn't realized their drop was showing. Or that Jazz was sober enough to pick up on it. How were they supposed to ignore this absurd crush when she was so sweet? Why couldn't Jazz be inconsiderate? "Oh, sorry. My scene tonight took a lot out of me. I'll be okay." Forcing their usual mask of a half smile, they leaned against the counter.

"Beautiful, don't apologize!" Jazz cupped Blanche's face in her hands and kissed their forehead before they could react. She smelled like liquor and stale sweat, and Blanche had never smelled anything so lovely. Her lips seared a mark into Blanche's skin. "I'm just concerned. You seem down. What happened to the aftercare?"

Blanche allowed Jazz to pull them into a hug. They needed it, as ashamed as they were to admit it. Her warm touch and strong arms were so comforting, they couldn't help but melt into her. *This is not how you get over a crush, you fucking creep!* "Oh, I'll be okay. I did the aftercare for my client, but the drop hit me before I could get to my own. I didn't even see it coming today. But I'll be okay."

Jazz ran her hands up and down Blanche's back, swaying ever so slightly. "You keep saying you'll be okay, but right now you aren't." Jazz patted their shoulder, and Blanche sank a little further into her arms, like the pathetic piece of shit they were. "Tell me, what is your ideal aftercare? Like the perfect way you like to be taken care of?"

Blanche closed their eyes as they rested their head on her shoulder, rocking gently with Jazz's swaying. Danger had never felt so wonderful as Jazz's tight grip around their shoulders, the softness of her waist in the circle of their arms. "In a perfect world? I want to put on a record, drink whiskey, smoke weed, and have someone hold me and kiss me and tell me how wonderful I am." Blanche exhaled a chuckle, trying very hard not to imagine Jazz doing that, because that sounded like... Well, like something they wanted. But they couldn't want that, couldn't want Jazz. "But I'll make do with some music and an edible."

"Nonsense. Where do you keep your weed?"

Blanche pulled away from her embrace. Aftercare would be intimate, even if it wouldn't be sexual. Jazz taking care of them would absolutely drag this crush closer to feelings territory. *As if it's not there already*, came Freddy's annoying snark. Which was exactly why this could not go there. Fucking Freddy should never have opened his damn mouth. They shook their head. "Jazz, you're young enough to be my kid. And you're drunk. I can't ask that of you."

"Ask what? It's aftercare, not sex." Jazz stuck out her tongue. "And you are not old enough to be my parent. What, were you out having sex at fifteen?"

Blanche nodded with a shrug. "Thirteen, actually."

"The fuck? That was supposed to be rhetorical." A flash of concern crossed Jazz's face, before she put on a serious expression. "Look, you're not asking anything of me. I'm offering you support. Yeah, I may be a little drunk, and a little high, but I'm still in my right mind. And from the look of you, I'm in a better headspace than you seem to be right now. So where do you keep your fucking weed?"

What little of Blanche's willpower remained crumbled. They were a fucking mess and needed someone to take care of them. *Tara and Lee did this for me too. This is just platonic support from a friend.* Shayla finally appeared in their mind, laughing at how bad Blanche was at lying to themself. While they wanted this, *needed* this, they weren't supposed to want Jazz. But Shayla reminded Blanche that they were allowed to want things, to have things. *It's just aftercare.* A lump grew in their throat as they nodded. "My bedroom," their voice came out as a croak. "There's a pipe and lighter on top of my dresser."

"Go put on a record in the den and pour us some whiskey. I'll take care of the rest." Jazz ordered. "Okay?"

Blanche nodded.

By the time Blanche finished fiddling with the newfangled turntable Lee and Antonio had given them, and Edith Piaf's voice sang from the speakers (Blanche had always listened to grunge because that was what Daisy listened to, and it was time to see what else they might like), Jazz had transformed the den. Throw pillows and blankets made a nest on the daybed, illuminated by the fairy lights she'd strung up when she'd decorated the house. The room was bathed in a magical glow as the smell of patchouli and lavender filled the room from an incense burner on the table.

Jazz pulled the end table next to the daybed before hopping into it, patting three times between her legs for Blanche to join her. Blanche set the whiskey and two tumblers on the table, and fell into the nest, letting themselves be cradled against Jazz. Her strong arms squeezed Blanche tight, allowing Blanche to breathe deeply for the first time since Jackie had handed them the envelope at Confession that afternoon.

Jazz's lips on their neck made Blanche gasp quietly, igniting a burning sting behind their eyes. "Jazzy, you don't need to kiss me. I know I said that, but it's enough to be held." Blanche wasn't sure if they hated themselves for stopping her, or for wanting her to kiss them more.

"Blanche, let me do this." Jazz murmured against their skin, her lips warm.

The fairy lights blurred. Blanche couldn't answer, unsure of what to say and not trusting themself to tell her to stop.

Jazz's voice softened. "Look, I know you probably think this is weird because I'm Lee's little sister, and you're like a parent figure to him. And, like, it's probably obvious, so I won't deny I've been crushing on you for years. But it isn't some MILF fetish or Freudian shit or anything. I don't see you the same way Lee does. I just have a regular ol' crush on a total baddie. Who can blame me? Even Teddy wants you to step on her."

Blanche snorted, jealous of how easily Jazz talked about her feelings, while Blanche had been in panic mode all week. *Attraction is a common experience for most people, Blanche. Why would you be the exception? You're allowed to want things.* Maybe Shayla wouldn't judge Blanche too hard if they actually brought this up at therapy; they needed to hear what she'd actually say, instead of what their subconscious wanted her to say. Any reasonable person would tell Blanche to get over it, that crushing on their much-younger roommate was—

Jazz wrapped her arms around them and held them tight enough to silence any thoughts of how wrong this was. How could feeling this safe be anything but right? "And right now, me taking care of you is not in any way related to any non-friendship feelings I might have. As your roommate, as your friend, I genuinely want to make you feel better. Because you're a wonderful, giving person who deserves platonic smooches, because that's the bare minimum. Can I do that for you?"

Blanche's eyes stung again as Jazz's words washed over them. Tara and Lee helping with their aftercare had never ached so sweetly. They nodded.

"Say it," Jazz teased.

Blanche snorted. "Thank you, that would be lovely."

"Good. Drink your fucking whiskey, Beautiful," Jazz ordered, filling the tumblers with the golden brown liquor. "And we can talk and smoke and drink and listen to Edith Piaf. God, you're so gay."

With a quiet chuckle, Blanche took a glass. Relief and guilt warred in their heart, as Jazz pressed kisses into their hair and neck and shoulders. Jazz's arms tightened, and any last remnants of guilt were squeezed out of them. Blanche gave in, relaxing into her embrace, trusting their heart into Jazz's care. At least for tonight.

The numbness they'd been nursing for hours eased, washed away by all of the feelings Blanche didn't want to feel. They felt loved. They felt seen. They felt like someone's priority. Only two other people in Blanche's life had made them feel this way. Both of them were dead.

"This shit didn't used to take so much out of me. I must be getting old," Blanche sighed.

Jazz's rich alto voice spoke low in their ear, smooth and comforting. "You said you channel anger into your work. Do you think you have less anger than you used to?"

Blanche certainly still had plenty to be angry about, especially with that damn letter. But they'd had seven years since Daisy died, and over two decades since they'd left their adopted family. *Maybe time does heal all wounds. I thought I would be the exception to that.*

"I think I'm out of anger," Blanche murmured. "Or, I *was*. Covey sent me a letter."

"What?" Jazz gasped.

"Oh, it was delivered to Confession." Blanche patted her arm. "He doesn't know about this place. He's not going to show up."

"Blanche..." Jazz sighed, holding them tight. "That's not what I was worried about. Are you okay? What did he want?"

Blanche's heart clenched, struck that Jazz cared about them before her own safety. Getting over this crush was going to be impossible after tonight, but Blanche had already survived the impossible, over and over. "To apologize. To say goodbye."

It had been perfectly tame, as far as Covey went. Just a simple, genuine letter, asking for Blanche's forgiveness for how he'd wronged them, and wishing them the best, promising not to contact them again. Closure for Covey, pure and simple, with no concern that Blanche's own closure would be torn to shreds. The selfish asshole.

"But I'm okay. Or I will be." Blanche sighed. "I'm more sad than anything, and going back to all that anger after being free of it... I never realized how close I was to breaking for all those years." Their voice wavered, and they sipped their whiskey to clear the lump in their throat. "I never imagined I'd ever not feel angry. But the grief and pain are softer here. I'm even happy sometimes now. I suppose it's a good thing, but I don't know how to be happy." The words slipped from Blanche's mouth before they could stop them. The realization was sobering. *Have you ever been happy?* Shayla asked. Blanche hoped they'd remember that thought the next time they vlogged, because Shayla would love unpacking that.

"It just shows how far you've come, Beautiful." Jazz lit the pipe, taking a quick puff for herself, before holding it up for Blanche. "You deserve endless happiness."

As they inhaled, Blanche considered how much to tell her. As painful as it was, memories of Daisy were always close to the surface when Blanche was in a drop. She was going to come out of Blanche's mouth either way. "I don't know if Lee ever told you, but Daisy and I were married. We were happy, in a way. But even with her, I was always more angry than anything."

"Lee never said, just that she died."

Blanche took a slow drag on the pipe that Jazz held for them, breathing in the familiar comfort of Northern Lights.

"Will you tell me about her?" Jazz asked tentatively, as if sensing that Blanche didn't know how to answer that.

"I met her when I ran away from the Family. I was trying to hitchhike to New York, but I only made it as far as Bellamy. She saw me begging outside the bus station so I could afford a ticket, and told me how I could make money quicker." Blanche's heart swelled at the memory. This stunning girl, with jet black curls and a teasing bold red smirk. "She showed me the ropes when I was new to the trade."

"And you were thirteen?" Jazz asked, choking on her words.

They nodded. "I know how it sounds. She trafficked me when I was at my most vulnerable, but it didn't feel like that at the time. I was thirteen, yes, but she was only sixteen, and here she was teaching me how to suck dick for cash. That's how she knew to survive. She always said it was better to suck a stranger's dick for money than her stepdad's dick for free." Blanche shook their head as smoke billowed from Jazz's nose over their shoulder. "She was just so...charming that it took me a long time to accept the reality of our relationship. I fucking worshiped her from that first moment. I would have done anything for her, and I did."

"Sounds like her life was hard, too."

"Yeah, she was real fucked up. It just made her sweet side all the more addictive. Daisy saved my life over and over, even though she was the reason I was always in danger in the first place. She showed me softness, kindness, love—all of the things I'd never experienced growing up." Bringing the glass to their lips, Blanche inhaled the burn of the whiskey before rolling it over their tongue. Thinking about Daisy sober was hard enough, let alone talking about her. And yet, they'd talked about her so much with Shayla that all the memories, feelings, guilt could slip right out these days. Not easy, never easy, but possible, where it hadn't been before. "Looking back, we didn't have the healthiest relationship."

Jazz tittered. "Sorry. That is a massive understatement."

Blanche was surprised to find they were smiling along with her. "I know. But she was so encouraging of me. She was the one who got me connected into the kink scene, to get me off the street. But honestly, that was the least she could do after she asked me to jump a john who shorted her. She already had an assault charge on her record, and I didn't legally exist yet. I spent what we considered my eighteenth birthday in a coma."

Jazz froze, stiffening behind Blanche. "The fuck."

"I know! I know how it sounds. Anyway, I woke up in the hospital, and she came with a fucking dominatrix during visiting hours the next day." Blanche laughed at the memory. The nurses had been so curious, playing around with the floggers and making jokes about the weird objects they'd removed from people's butts over the years. Daisy could always make any situation fun. Even when Blanche had been immobile, watching this all unfold around them. "And she was right. It was perfect for me. I was an angry teenage kid, you know? Life had continually fucked me over, and she showed me a way to fuck it back. It was very therapeutic. Again, maybe not the healthiest, but it's what we knew. It worked."

They shook their head, sipping their whiskey as the bitter emotions raged inside of them at the memories they always tried to forget. Telling Jazz about her felt...good; they had told Lee and Tara what happened early on, but rarely spoke of her again, until they'd started therapy last year. Daisy had been murdered a week before they'd met Lee and Tara. Seven years was a long time to keep pain bottled up; talking about this with a friend was like releasing steam from a pressure cooker. They could hear Shayla laughing at them in their mind, as if she hadn't been telling them that for months.

"We were together for so long. Sixteen years, it was just her and I. Sometimes she'd date other people, and of course there were our regulars, but I didn't mind as long as I got to be with her. Once her stepdad died, she finally felt safe enough to love me back. We got married eight years ago on my birthday. And less than a year later, she..." Their throat clenched. Visions of blood and the echoes of screams and sirens took over. How many times had they repeated this story to strangers in the therapy clinics? Why was it so hard to talk about it with Jazz?

Sensing their struggle, Jazz pressed kisses down Blanche's neck, squeezing them tight. Hot tears that weren't Blanche's dripped onto their temple, and Jazz sniffled in their ear. They patted Jazz's arms, kissing her wrist. "Don't cry, Jazzy. It's in the past. No use crying about it."

"You miss her." Jazz's voice was low and raspy.

They nodded. "Every day. But it's different now. Before, I was getting vengeance on the world that exploited us, pissed at the world that took her from me, angry at her for using me the way she did." Blanche bumped their head against Jazz's gently. "Now, I'm more free and in control of my life than I've ever been, and it's like the pressure's off. The anger is escaping no matter how hard I try to bottle it up. I have people who love me, who look out for me, who help me when I need it. I have a fucking financial advisor, for Chrissakes!

"The anger doesn't matter anymore. How can I be angry at the world when someone named fucking *Alfie* does my taxes for me? When I have a home that's mine, and I'm safe every night when I go to sleep? When I can be picky about who my clients are?" They took another drag of the pipe as Jazz wiped her eyes. "Now, grief makes me sad, instead of angry. I don't know how to process it. But that's what Shayla is helping me with." Blanche ran their hand up and down Jazz's arm. "Maybe I should get in contact with the Family. See what the cult's gotten up to in the past couple of decades. Get more ammunition, you know?"

"You don't need more ammunition, Blanche. You've had a hard ass life." Jazz refilled both of their glasses, handing Blanche's back to them. She laced her fingers through Blanche's other hand. "But maybe going back would give you some closure."

Blanche snorted into their tumbler. "I've had enough closure for one night."

Jazz tsked. "I'm just saying, it sounds like your domme work served a purpose and helped you survive, and maybe it's no longer serving you. Maybe going back to where it all started—seeing how it's changed, how *you've* changed—will show you there's more possibilities now. Like how spending any time at my parents' house reminds me that I have outgrown it. And if I can't go back, that means I can go anywhere. And I know it's nowhere close to the same thing, but you're free, Blanche. You can do anything."

"What do you mean—retire from sex work? I'm not that old!" Blanche teased, hiding their skepticism at Jazz's naivete. The worst of the drop must have passed if they could make jokes. "I wasn't aware I had a pension plan with this gig."

"Not quit, unless that's what you want to do. Just *adapt*." Jazz tapped her glass. "Like, if you don't have that anger to vent, what is the work taking from you instead? What can you afford to emotionally invest into it, now that you have more stability? You have options, and time and money now that you didn't used to have." Jazz kissed Blanche's neck again. Blanche turned toward her reflexively, resting their forehead against hers to stop themself. "I hate seeing you like you're empty. It was scary seeing you like a zombie, you know? You deserve peace."

The turntable's auto-stop clicked into action as the album ended. Silence filled the room, leaving Blanche with only the soft crackle of the pipe as Jazz inhaled and blew out softly next to Blanche's ear. Once again, Blanche found themselves overwhelmed, this time by intimacy, by the profound sense of being seen, by how casually Jazz watered their soul. Shayla had been asking Blanche what they wanted, over and over to the point of frustration. But it'd never been so clear *why* they needed to know, until Jazz had put it that way.

They inhaled as Jazz held the pipe up to their lips.

Blanche exhaled, pressing a kiss into her wrist. "Thank you, Jazzy. I'm feeling so much better. And you've given me a lot to think about. I'm sorry for the roller coaster tonight. Me trauma dumping all over you probably wasn't what you had planned for your night in."

"Don't apologize, Beautiful. I'm glad I could be here for you the way you've been there for me." Jazz drew Blanche's face toward her with a soft hand on their jaw, her gentle brown eyes searching theirs in a silent question. Blanche froze, knowing what was about to happen. But they *refused* to pull away as Jazz's beautiful, full lips pressed against their own.

The soft, chaste kiss lasted an eternity, yet ended far too briefly in a mere moment.

Blanche's heart thudded in their chest as Jazz smiled breezily, as if they hadn't just kissed. Jazz had kissed them. *Jazz kissed me.* Blanche blinked, fighting the urge to kiss her again. To touch their lips so the feeling of her soft, fuller ones would linger. To keep that precious gift forever. *Jazz kissed me.*

Jazz laughed quietly, adding, "Trust me, I was just gonna go to bed and write an angsty poem about Mimi. This was a million times better."

Sunday, September Nineteenth

Chapter Twelve

ANTONIO

"MAYBE WE SHOULD WAIT and use the front door? Please?" Lee tightened his grip on Antonio's hand, dragging his feet along the cobblestone path.

The late afternoon air was cooling fast as the sunlight turned the clouds gold. Impatient and hungry (he was missing dinner at his mom's for this), Antonio swung the back gate open and tugged Lee along. "They didn't answer the front door, and Gabe never has his patio door locked." Lee and Antonio were a little early for the mysterious dinner invitation Gabe had sent via group chat last night. Maybe they hadn't heard Lee's knock.

"Knowing them, we're probably interrupting something I don't want to witness." Lee shut the gate behind them, reluctantly following Antonio along the stepstone path to the patio. "Tara isn't the type to leave doors unlocked—maybe she convinced Gabe to start locking it."

Antonio slid the patio door open, giving his husband a smug smile. "See? Wide open. If he didn't want us barging in, he'd lock it."

"If they're fooling around in there, please remove my eyes," Lee warned as he greeted a happy Hippo, whose body wagged vigorously along with his tail.

Gabe and Tara were nowhere to be seen. But soon enough, they could be heard. Antonio clapped his hands over Lee's ears as Tara's moans echoed from the other room.

The oven clock said they were only ten minutes early. Gabe's *mother* could be here any minute.

Lee grimaced. "Really?"

Antonio nodded, swallowing his annoyance at Lee's lingering purity culture bullshit. Sure, he and Gabe hadn't always been platonic like Tara and Lee had, so he was more comfortable with his friend's sexuality than Lee was with Tara's. However, Antonio would never let *anyone* stop him from fucking Lee as loudly and enthusiastically as he wanted, and neither would Lee, so he wouldn't hold their friends to a different standard. He didn't understand why Lee did, but at least his husband had started acknowledging that he *had* double standards.

Finally, after several painful—yet impressively long—moments, silence fell.

"Hello, anyone home?" Antonio called out, in case they weren't done yet. He tentatively removed his hands from Lee's ears. "I think they're done."

On cue, Gabe walked into the kitchen, tying his hair into a bun. He looked immaculate in a green sweater and black jeans. No stains or wrinkles or fluids in sight. "Sorry."

"You don't sound sorry in the least, Gabey Baby," Antonio teased.

Gabe grinned at him. "That's because I'm not. No one else is here, are they?"

Lee scowled. "No, we're the first. We let ourselves in, and I have serious regrets now."

Opening the fridge, Gabe tossed Antonio a can of sparkling water and wordlessly held up a bottle of wine in Lee's direction, who nodded.

"'Would you like some water, Antonio?'" Antonio teased, cracking open a can. He must be getting hangry, because normally this silent communication didn't get under his skin so much. "Why yes, I'd love some. 'And you Lee? Can I get you some wine?' 'Yes, thank you. That sounds delightful.'"

Gabe and Lee exchanged a shrug.

Antonio huffed. "Oh my god, can you please use your words instead of communicating through looks? I need sound to remember stuff!"

Gabe laughed as he handed Lee his glass of wine. "I didn't realize me offering you refreshments was a key memory."

"It's not, but you two are always annoyingly quiet together." Antonio tsked. "It drives me batty when I can't taste the conversation."

"Sometimes your brain amazes me, babe," Lee rubbed his back.

Antonio leaned against him, wishing every problem could go away so easily. "Sorry, I'm complaining to complain. I just wish I could tell my younger self to go to therapy, instead of getting high. It used to be so easy to remember shit. And eat! If past me knew that taking all those damn pills would leave us unable to eat junk food, I might have thought twice about my shitty coping mechanisms."

A loud knock on the door interrupted Antonio's rant, before Gabe's parents let themselves in. Antonio trotted over to hug them. Miriam was basically another mom to him, putting up with all of his antics as a teenager, with patience and a sassy streak that rivaled his own. She'd been the strictest parent in his life, and he loved her for it.

He hugged John tightly too, his flannel shirt and jeans a familiar comfort, which shouldn't be as needed as it was right now. But Antonio's chest was tight, and the nostalgia was easing it.

John had always been a font of wisdom for Antonio, who'd struggled being a mixed-race queer kid in a predominantly white suburb, hitting puberty just as his parents were getting divorced. Navigating blending families and bullying and his own identity was already a struggle, before intrusive thoughts and poor impulse control were added to the mix.

Compared to John, who had grown up in a boarding school with no idea if he had any family, teenage Emo Antonio had it easy. He'd only needed to accept his new stepparents and more siblings. John always had some story or asked the perfect question as a way to ground him. After spending time with the Coopers, Antonio had far fewer dramatic tantrums where he'd loudly burst into Yellowcard songs at the Flores dinner table.

Looking impressively immaculate considering the sounds he'd heard mere minutes ago, Tara emerged from the hallway to greet everyone with a hug and a suspiciously relaxed smile.

"I have a present for you two." John handed Tara and Antonio each a bottle of wine. "I've been experimenting with zero-proof wine. I was trying to get it ready for the wedding, but I couldn't get the taste quite right in time. Hope it's good."

"Oh, hell yeah!" Tara exclaimed. "You have no idea how much I've missed wine."

Antonio's gut tightened. He hadn't particularly missed wine—or rather he'd worked hard to not miss it. Risking all of that time, willpower and therapy for what? Pretending he wasn't in recovery? But he was touched nonetheless, so he forced a grin. "Ooh, I can sit at the big kids' table again!"

The small smile on John's face was practically a beam, as far as John went. It helped soothe Antonio's guilt for not particularly wanting his gift.

Richard opened the front door without knocking, letting himself in ahead of Sunny, Blanche, and Jazz, who trailed hesitantly behind them.

"Oh good, you're all here," Gabe said, filling more wineglasses. "We can get this over with then. Phin will be late, so no need to wait."

"Coop, relax," Tara chided. "Look, your dad made me wine that I can drink!" She held up the bottle excitedly. "Tonio, want some?"

"I'll try a little." Antonio ignored the dread curling in his gut. John had put in the effort for his sake.

Gabe passed Tara and Antonio stemless glasses—Antonio's just a splash of the burgundy-red liquid—and led the way to the living room. "Dinner should be ready in ten minutes. Think that's enough time?"

"Time for what?" Antonio asked. A shy whisper of temptation licked his throat at the sight of the drink in his hand. Taking a tentative sip, he nestled against Lee on the sectional. The wine was sweet, but without that burn he used to enjoy. And if it made him miss the burn, it was better not to drink it. He set the glass down.

Lee glanced at him in a silent question. Antonio shook his head ever so slightly. He'd "forget" his bottle here, leave it for Tara. Memory loss was a convenient excuse sometimes.

Lee squeezed his leg and moved the glass away from him.

"Yeah, what's this announcement?" Richard asked, perching on the arm of Sunny's chair.

"How do you know there's an announcement?" Gabe asked, sitting next to Tara on the love seat.

Richard crossed his arms. "You would never invite this many people over for dinner voluntarily unless you wanted to tell us something."

Antonio had also been puzzled why Gabe—renowned hater of having company, unless Tara happened to be included—suddenly invited all of their friends over for dinner with his parents. He had several theories: Gabe finally got a new job and they were moving to LA, so he could pursue a modeling career; Tara's baby was actually twins, but only one of them was his; they had somehow also been included on the same project that Lee and Antonio weren't allowed to talk about yet, but as—

"We're getting married. Welcome to our engagement party," Gabe said, without a trace of fanfare.

Ugh, rude. He didn't even let me finish.

"You're getting married?!" Sunny exclaimed, smacking Richard's arm. "How did you guess that?"

"Seemed logical, Sunshine." Richard elbowed her back.

Antonio glanced at Lee for his husband's reaction. Tara always told Lee everything before she told everyone else. But Lee hadn't told Antonio, and *all* tea was shared as soon as they were in private. Except for the time he and Tara had run into Jazz while getting their tattoos last year, because Lee did *not* need to know that Jazz had titty rings.

Lee's reserved smile told Antonio nothing. His husband was notorious for hiding his feelings, but at least his usual tells that he was upset—tight shoulders, sweaty palms and face—were absent.

Antonio put his hand on his shoulder anyway, squeezing in support. Lee patted his hand reassuringly, with a slight shake of his head. Antonio took that to mean "I'm happy, but this is news to me too." Again. It'd be nice if Lee *said* it.

"Wait—engagement party?" Sunny asked, the only one processing externally in the room. Everyone else seemed just as stunned. Even Miriam was speechless, though beaming. "We didn't bring a gift!"

Tara nodded. "That was kind of the point of not telling you that it was an engagement party. No gifts. Not a big thing, please."

Miriam clapped with joy, breaking the stunned silence. "I knew it! Tell me everything. How long have you been engaged? How did he ask? When are you thinking for the wedding date? Let me see your ring!"

"Fuck, Coop, we're engaged! This is weird." Tara bit her lip, cheeks pink as she and Gabe exchanged heart eyes.

God they're so fucking cute. Antonio glanced at Lee, wondering if everyone else thought they were that cute when they were dating. *They better have. We're still fucking cute. A literal power couple, who bring each other*—Antonio interrupted that train of thought with a quiet hum under his breath. He wasn't allowed to talk about that yet. His stomach clenched. With excitement. It had to be excitement. He should not be feeling *anything* other than excited for the thing he wasn't allowed to think about for another ten days.

Annoyingly, his chest tightened, too.

Tara smirked at Gabe. "He didn't so much ask, as suggest it on the couch yesterday morning. Then he calmed me down, and gave me enough rational reasons to say yes. So we've been engaged for a day and a half? And my ring is exactly what I wanted." She held up her hand, showing off a tiny plastic ring with a fake green stone. "Cost him a quarter."

Gabe raised a finger to clarify. "Technically, it cost a dollar fifty. It took me a few tries to get a ring instead of a dinosaur. And we're getting married as soon as we nail down the prenup."

"Gabriel Fucking Cooper!" Miriam flew out of her seat, burying her hands in her hair as she paced in circles around the living room. "I raised you better than this!" Antonio tensed at the emergence of her Queens accent, even if she wasn't yelling at him for once. "I have a fucking ring you could have given her. Several fucking rings, actually! And a prenup?! You're making the mother of your child sign a fucking prenup?!"

Lee stiffened, his hand around Antonio's shoulder tightening. Antonio leaned into him; like Gabe, Miriam felt everything more than most people. Lee couldn't know her anger would burn out as soon as the argument was over though.

Tara held out her hands placatingly, paling at Miriam's outburst. "I asked *him* to sign a prenup. It's the only way I would say yes." She smiled at Gabe. "And the ring is what I wanted, too. I made an offhand comment months ago about how if I ever got married, I'd only want a cheap toy ring and a backyard wedding with pizza. And he was very sweet to remember that."

Blanche raised their hand. "Can it be my backyard? One of my clients offered to put in a patio, and this would be the perfect excuse for me to call in that favor."

Gabe gave a nod to Tara, who grinned. "Sure! Want to officiate too?"

Blanche beamed, unphased by the daggers flying from Miriam's eyes. "As if I'd let anyone else officiate your wedding!"

Blanche had celebrated Lee and Antonio's wedding perfectly. At least Antonio thought so; the memory of the day was a blur for him. One second, he'd been nervously walking up the aisle, the next he was waking up next to his husband in bed at their hotel. The pictures looked fun, and the video had made him cry, but neither jogged any memories. A few moments stuck out, but he'd been so focused on being in the moment, that he barely remembered much.

"So what? Now you're not doing this at the temple? Or even the vineyard?" Miriam threw her hands up in the air.

"Vinyahd," whispered Sunny. "Amazing."

Gabe rubbed circles between Tara's shoulder blades, his jaw working back and forth. Historically, Gabe lost all arguments with his mother. His temper may rival his mom's, but he was still a people pleaser. He'd never mastered the quiet redirection of his dad, or the strategic questions of his mom. Now that Tara was in the picture, Antonio wondered who would win. If Tara's desire for a small backyard wedding could withstand Miriam's determination to give Gabe the very best, even if it wasn't what Gabe wanted.

Gabe rolled his eyes. "Ma, I didn't even have a bar mitzvah. Or a bris, for that matter! Why would I get married at a temple? And besides, it's going to be a small wedding. Literally, everyone here and maybe a few others will be invited, and that's it!"

"What's a bris?" Sunny whispered to Richard.

"Circumcision ceremony," he quietly explained.

Sunny narrowed her eyes. "But...he is circumcised!"

The room quieted as everyone turned to look at her.

"By a surgeon, not a mohel." Gabe scratched his head. "Do I want to know how you know that? Or why you cared to share that with the whole room?"

"What?" She shrugged. "We all went skinny dipping at the bachelor party! And I would hope your parents know! So pretty much everyone here already knew. Sorry Jazz, I guess?"

"It's not like I've never seen a cut dick before," Jazz said from behind him, her voice strangely bright.

Antonio practically jumped out of his seat; he'd forgotten she was there. He craned his neck to find her leaning against the mantle, back pressed to the wall so she practically disappeared into the built-ins. That was odd. Usually Blanche always made room for Jazz to sit by them.

"What dicks have *you* seen?" Lee asked, pushing his glasses up.

"None of your business!" Jazz rolled her eyes.

Antonio was strongly considering getting a squirt bottle to spray Lee anytime he went into Annoying Big Brother mode. But that would not be supportive husband behavior, and that had to be his priority now.

His chest tightened again.

Even a week later, Leland Senior's off-color comments still got his anger simmering. Antonio wasn't sure how much longer he could resist breaking it to him that (not that it was any of his business, or that it mattered), his son bottomed far more than Antonio did. Or keep from arguing that masculinity wasn't a virtue over femininity. Or that gays weren't inherently pedos! Antonio hummed a calming song to himself. That was Lee's battle. Antonio refused to cause conflict between his husband and his family. Even if the temptation to put makeup and glitter on Lee whenever they saw his parents was hard to resist.

Why wasn't being married as easy as every other stage of their relationship had been? Antonio missed when their biggest worry had been Lee's anxiety, when Antonio could soothe and distract him. Instead, it had become all these secrets and hard conversations, and needing to watch what he said. *Ten days, ten days and you can think normally again.* He hummed his new Surprise Announcement Song to himself; it contained a countdown to the finish line.

"Can we get back to the fact that my only child is not allowing me to throw him the wedding he deserves?" Miriam rubbed her forehead. "Gabriel. You mean to tell me that you're not inviting any other family, or friends, or connections to your wedding?"

"What family? The ones who disowned you? The ones who pretend we don't exist?" Gabe looked skeptically at her, a hint of accent leaking into his own voice. It only came out when he argued with his mom. "We don't want a big to-do. Only guests who are close to both of us." He folded his arms across his chest.

It's getting serious now. He's crossed his arms. Antonio caught Richard's smirk, who mimicked a perfect imitation of Gabe's stubborn posture. Antonio grinned and motioned as if he was eating popcorn. Richard turned away with a snort.

"I already had to talk him down from eloping, if it makes any difference." Tara leaned against Gabe. "He suggested Phin and his admin could walk down to the courthouse to be witnesses once the prenup was hashed out. But I couldn't imagine getting married without my family there." She grinned at Lee, who returned her smile.

Miriam looked ready to come out with a counterargument, when John interrupted. "Speaking of family, I have news." He handed Tara an envelope. "Got that from a friend of mine who works for the state of Illinois. Thought you should be the first to read it."

Antonio's jaw dropped. John changing the subject was a sign the debate was over. The argument might continue, but John had just wordlessly put his support with Gabe. Richard and Antonio exchanged another look. That rarely happened.

Tara stared at John, dumbfounded. "But it's only been a couple of weeks!"

John shrugged. "I know people who can find most anything."

"What is it, Buttercup?" Lee asked, leaning forward.

Tara set the envelope on the coffee table gingerly, not taking her eyes off it. "John offered to help track down my parents. I didn't expect you to find anything, especially so quickly. We've been looking for years." Lee whistled a long note as he exhaled heavily. Blanche sat up; both feet on the floor, they peered at the envelope with narrowed eyes. Tara stared at it like it might burst into flames, her face pale. "I think I need to open that after some food."

Gabe put his arm around her and pressed a kiss to her temple. "In that case, let's eat. Mom, you can yell at me more over the salad. Maybe at a lower decibel, please."

Chapter Thirteen

Blanche

To Blanche's relief, who'd been about to snap at Gabe's mom earlier for stressing Jazz—*everyone* out with her yelling—Miriam was calmer over dinner. Across the table from Blanche (who had taken the seat strategically, so Jazz and Lee could sit by each other, in case the arguing continued), Miriam politely ate her salad and casserole, offering gentle suggestions for the wedding. There was no further use of Gabe's unofficial middle name. She was holding back, but Miriam had seemed to quickly concede defeat.

Maybe she'd learned to take Gabe at his word, after all of these years of being "too supportive," in his words. Or maybe she wanted to get along with Tara. Or maybe she could tell Tara would win. Or maybe she was worried Gabe would pick Tara over her? Blanche couldn't imagine Tara putting Gabe in a position to choose between his mom and her, not when she was desperate to earn his parents' approval too.

"So, are you going to be Mrs. Cooper, then?" Sunny asked.

Tara looked at Gabe with a shrug. "We hadn't talked about it. I'm not particularly tied to Sanderson. Just the letters on my ID."

"We'd love it if you took the Cooper name," Miriam said proudly, adding hurriedly when Gabe shot his mom a look. "If that's what you want, of course. John and I picked it ourselves when we got married. It was very unheard of in the '70s, but it worked best for us. My family all disowned me in a heartbeat, so I couldn't wait to drop their last name."

"And I wanted to drop the commodity name the government gave me," John sneered, the first emotion Blanche had seen him display. "And since we were planning on going into winemaking, we decided on Cooper. Felt right."

"The government picked your name?" Blanche blurted out the question before they could stop themself. "And they let you change it when you got married? How did you swing that? You must have a birth certificate!"

John cocked his head, eyeing Blanche with curiosity. "Yes, but the one I have doesn't list my birth parents, or my original name. I've tried many times to unseal my adoption records, if they even exist, but no luck yet."

"Ah." Blanche nodded, jealousy churning their stomach. "They gave me a Letter of No Record, since all I had to go on was the church records where I grew up. I'm sure if I was determined enough, I could attempt to take on the bureaucracy, but I'm not sure if the headache is worth it."

John nodded knowingly. "I thought I had a chance after Chilocco closed, when I got my hands on my school records, but they just wrote 'unknown' under tribal affiliation."

Blanche chuckled, a little more bitter than they'd expected. "Another nobody. We're rare."

John didn't laugh. Instead, his eyes stayed on Blanche for longer than most could stand. "There's an online community who help each other out with research. I can connect you, if you want. That's how I found info on Tara's parents."

Blanche rubbed their neck, still sore from their drop last night, unwilling to be the first to look away. Awkward stares were their specialty. They could feel Jazz's eyes on them from down the table, and it was safer not to look. They'd already found themself mesmerized by her lips several times today, and that could *not* happen at the dinner table in front of all of their friends. "I'll keep it in mind, but I made peace with being a nobody a long time ago."

"This eye contact is intense," Antonio whispered, breaking the tension as everyone tittered. Blanche was grateful for the excuse to look away, shooting him a grin from his seat next to Lee. They hadn't realized they wanted to change their name as much as they did. Normally, explaining that they were legally Chad and socially Blanche, like with Mimi at the hospital, didn't bother them. Those were facts, irrefutable and unchangeable.

Yet another thing they wanted that was unattainable.

Their cheeks burned; they were staring at Jazz. Again. Namely Jazz's lips. The kiss—*the platonic, friendly kiss*—Jazz had given them last night was seared into their brain. Those perfect, plush lips formed an amused smile, and Blanche flushed hot when they noticed Jazz was staring back with a smirk. Blanche's sore neck pinched from how fast they looked to the other end of the table. Why couldn't they want things they could actually have?

Tara pressed her hand to her belly, looking at Gabe. "Is it cool with you if I'm a Cooper?"

Gabe nodded, smiling at her softy.

"Can we set up a chuppah in your backyard?" Miriam asked Blanche, turning away from Gabe and Tara's quiet moment with a smile of her own.

Blanche nodded, relieved for the distraction. "I have no idea what that is, but sure!"

Miriam beamed. "It's a wedding canopy. We have a freestanding one for our wedding venue, so we won't ruin your yard. Hopefully, we don't have it booked whenever they set their date, but the busy season is over at least."

"Is it okay if I smudge?" John asked.

"Have at it. You should coordinate with Jazz. She's the official spiritual cleanser of the house." Blanche smiled, nodding in Jazz's direction down the table.

Jazz must have overheard, because her expression grew flustered. Blanche's heart clenched as Jazz bit her lower lip and looked down at her plate, then raced when her eyes met theirs. Her soft lips formed a bashful smile.

LEE

AFTER DINNER, LEE FOLLOWED everyone into the living room, making sure Jazz had a seat this time before he sat down. He couldn't believe he'd left her lurking in the back before; he should have known she wouldn't feel as comfortable at Gabe's house as his or Blanche's. Blanche seemed to have a similar train of thought, gesturing for Jazz to sit on the sofa while they leaned on the arm. Jazz gestured back for Blanche to sit instead, so she could sit on the arm. Finally, after a silent battle of wills, Blanche conceded with a huff.

And thank god, because that meant Lee could finally sit, too. Before his thighs even touched the sectional, Antonio crawled into Lee's lap with a heavy sigh, burying his face in Lee's neck.

With a pang of guilt, Lee shifted him so Antonio was next to him instead. "Sorry," Lee murmured in his ear, kissing his cheek, making sure to keep his arm tight around his husband's shoulder. "The envelope. I might need to move quick."

"I'll try not to take it personally, Angel," Antonio pouted, breaking Lee's heart. Why was he always letting Antonio down?

But Tara's panic attacks could come quickly, especially when dredging up her past. Lee hadn't seen one from her in several months, but like him, her trauma would never disappear completely. Especially with the pregnancy, she was trying to stay as stress-free as possible. He had to support her. But also support Antonio, who had been in a strange mood all week.

"Kitten, you don't have to do this now," Gabe said as Tara picked up the envelope.

Tara shook her head. "No, I do. I just ate a delicious meal. I have some nonalcoholic wine to sip on. I'm with all of the people who love me. There is no better time." Tara gave him a teasing smile. "Besides, if you all find out *with* me, I don't have to talk about it ever again! Sounds like a win to me!"

"I could update everyone for you, you know," Gabe said softly. "If you want to do it privately. You've been waiting a long time for any information, a little longer won't hurt."

"I know you would, and I love you for it. But I'd rather do it this way," Tara insisted. "Remember, just be here for me."

"Always, Kitten." Gabe kissed her forehead.

"Can you play music, though?" Tara asked.

Gabe pulled out his phone. "The horny, toxic R&B playlist?"

"Yup!" Tara nodded and turned to Lee. "Can you get me—"

"On it!" Lee gave Antonio a squeeze and rose. He'd scoped out the pantry situation when she'd first moved in with Gabe. He knew exactly where to find the best sensory inputs for Tara.

"Blan—"

"Ready to guide you through your breathing exercises." Blanche knelt in front of her as he left the room, taking Tara's hands.

Lee found the cinnamon, grabbed a couple of ice cubes, and quickly sliced a lime. For good measure, he filled a spoon with peanut butter.

Hippo whined, licking his lips as soon as Lee closed the lid to the jar.

"This is not for you. You want peanut butter, ask someone who likes dogs." Lee shook his head before returning to the living room, Hippo on his heels.

Gabe took the lime and cinnamon, and Lee waited on her other side with the ice at the ready. Tara smiled apologetically at John and Miriam. "Please don't judge me for needing a whole emotional support team to open an envelope."

"We would never," Miriam insisted. "John has a whole routine for me, too."

With a deep breath, Tara tore it open and unfolded the papers within—two pages, each with a small photo clipped to the corner. Tara nodded once, her face grim. She handed the papers to Gabe.

Blanche must have seen something in her face, because they nodded to him and began the breathing exercise in their low, soothing voice. "Breathe, Tara. Stay with me. You're safe. Inhale. 2. 3. 4. 5."

Lee ran the ice cubes up and down along her spine. Tara shivered, but didn't say anything. Lee's chest tightened. The ice used to be enough to bring her back from dissociating.

"Tara, you're safe. You're at home. Breathe with me. Exhale, 4, 3, 2, 1."

Gabe held out the cinnamon under Tara's nose, whose shoulders and chest rose and fell at Blanche's count.

Tara's voice was breathy but firm. "I smell cinnamon."

Relieved, Lee sighed.

"Good. What's this?" Gabe switched out the cinnamon for the spoon.

Tara exhaled slowly and inhaled again. "Peanut butter."

"You got it. Open up." Tara obediently opened her mouth as Gabe stuck the lime in it.

Wrinkling her nose, Tara pulled her head away and smacked her lips. "Ugh. I thought it was gonna be peanut butter!"

Blanche laughed. "What are you feeling?"

"Your hands on my knees. The ice." Her normal pitch was returning to her voice. "And what I hope is Hippo licking my leg."

"Ah, damn he got the peanut butter." Lee snorted, pulling the ice away from her skin. "You with us, Buttercup?"

Tara nodded. "Can I have my not-wine? The lime was a lot."

Gabe passed her the glass. She sipped it, exhaling heavily, resting her head on his shoulder. "Thank you. How long was that?"

"Just a few moments, Babes. You did good pulling yourself out of that." Blanche patted her knees before returning to the couch, wincing as they stretched their back and neck.

Jazz muttered something under her breath as she pulled Blanche's hair over their shoulder to rub their neck. Blanche grimaced in pain, but didn't stop her.

"Thanks to you all. Seriously." Tara scratched Hippo's head as he licked her bare knee. "That was about to be a bad one."

Hippo looked at the ice cube in Lee's hand eagerly. Lee wasn't sure what else to do with it, so he gave it to him, before taking his place next to Antonio on the sectional. Antonio wound his fingers through Lee's with a tight smile. In reply, Lee pulled him into his lap, more confident now that Tara would be okay.

He really had to figure out what was up with Antonio. Between his weird reaction about the wine, his short temper all evening, and the sudden burst of affection, Lee was already wondering how soon they could leave, so Antonio could get whatever it was off his chest.

Cinnamon under her nose, Tara tapped the papers she'd handed to Gabe. "Okay, Coop. Share the update, please. I don't know if I can say it out loud."

Gabe nodded, then read the first report. "Carlos Anderson, deceased of drug overdose eleven years ago in Chicago." He shook his head at the report, eyes lingering on the photo before tucking it behind the other paper. Tara sipped her wine again, inhaling as she closed her eyes, rolling the sip over her tongue. When she reopened them, she nodded at Gabe to continue.

"Annamarie Sanderson, incarcerated for," he paused, "*several* felonies in Logan Correctional Center nine years ago. Sentenced to forty-seven years, eligible for parole in twenty."

Hippo put his head in Tara's lap with a whine.

She smiled down at the dog lovingly, still scratching him behind the ears. "'Several felonies,' that's how you make human trafficking, attempted murder, and drug conspiracy sound palatable. Oh, Anne. Walter was right. You always kept bad company."

Blanche crossed their arms, eyes narrowed. "How did we miss this? Those are police reports. We looked fucking everywhere and found jack shit, and somehow your friend found this in a matter of weeks?" They glared at John before reaching out to Gabe. "Lemme see."

Gabe handed them the papers.

"Fucking useless piece of shit," Blanche hissed. "They spelled their fucking names wrong! Carlos Anderson instead of Carl Sanderson. And Annamarie instead of Anne Marie. Useless fucking idiots. Why didn't we think to check that? We checked Carl with a K, Anderson, and Sanderson with an E, Anna instead of Anne. Where the fuck did the O in Carl even come from? His middle name was Phillip!" Blanche was pacing now, angrily tapping the papers with the back of their hand. "I'm so pissed at myself for not trying these!"

"Don't be, Blanche. You did everything you could. We just overestimated the justice system's data entry skills," Tara placated. "You've been nothing but helpful and amazing for me all these years. I appreciate you forever for that."

Blanche sat back down in a huff. Jazz put her arm around them to rub their neck again, murmuring something that made Blanche's cheeks go scarlet.

Fighting a frown, Lee leaned forward, resting his chin on Antonio's shoulder. "You doing okay still, Buttercup?"

"Yeah. I'm just pissed she told me to get lost right after my fucking dad died. I wonder if she knew? Is that why she didn't want me anymore? Because she didn't need to keep me around anymore if he wasn't coming back?" Tara's eyes filled with tears.

Gabe put his arms around her. His own eyes were red too. "Only she can answer those questions, Kitten. And now you know where she is, if you want to ask."

"I'm sorry to be the bearer of bad news," John murmured.

Tara shook her head. "It's not your fault. Thank you for bringing me the news at all. I'd given up on ever finding them. Sorry that I saddled your son with such a disaster of a partner."

Gabe swatted her thigh gently. "Kitten, we've talked about this. You're not saddling me or trapping me or any of that. We're both disasters, and we still chose each other, remember?"

John smiled. "I think my son chose an excellent person to be his partner. You two understand what each other needs. That's more important than anything."

Miriam stood up and sat next to Tara, tears in her eyes as she pulled Tara into a fierce hug. "Come here. I can't stand the thought of anyone fucking abandoning a sweetheart like you."

As Lee looked around the room, everyone looked a little misty-eyed. Even his own eyes burned a little. Richard was carefully hiding his face behind Sunny. Only Blanche kept their composure, as always. Despite the emotion, he almost laughed at Jazz's expression. As usual whenever anything remotely mushy happened, she was crying. But her confused frown at Miriam hugging Tara reminded him of the first dozen or so times Antonio's mom had hugged him. Althea had rarely been so affectionate, and never in front of company.

Tara clung to Miriam, sobbing against her shoulder. Lee envied her. There was nothing better in the world than a mom hug. Awkward and unaffectionate as his mom was, her rare hugs were so... healing. Like he was a little kid who was hurt and scared, and with one hug, everything would be okay. Part of the reason he was so reluctant to argue with his dad.

Tara hiccupped as she extracted herself from Miriam's embrace, looking utterly wrung out. "At least now I know I wasn't truly abandoned. He fucking died. She's been in jail the whole time. I just had shit parents." She swallowed, taking Gabe's hand. "Is it worth writing to her? I've had questions this whole time and now, maybe, she can give me answers."

The door swung open as Phineas let himself in. "Hey sorry I'm late!" He paused, looking around the room. "Damn, who died?"

Lee huffed as Antonio groaned, "Phin, I swear to god, you are the literal worst."

"What I'd do?" Phineas shimmied his blazer off. "I just walked in!"

"Tara received some bad news on what was otherwise a happy occasion," Richard glared at him. "So asking 'who died' was in really poor taste."

"Oh, what's the occasion?" Phineas rubbed his hands together with a grin.

Gabe ran his hand through his hair and shot an apologetic look to Tara. "Engagement party."

"Who's getting married?" Phineas beamed around the room. "Richard? You finally put a ring on it?"

"No," Gabe said carefully. "Tara and I."

"What?" Phineas's jaw dropped.

Gabe nodded, his jaw tightening as he avoided eye contact with Phineas. "We were gonna eventually get there anyway, but the timeline shrank with the baby."

"Baby?!" Phineas huffed, frowning at Tara, who still clung to Miriam. His brow was furrowed, eyes wide the way they got when he was in his feelings. "You're having a baby?"

Tara glanced up at Gabe, who ran a hand through his hair and grumbled, "Why did you think I was asking all those questions about the trust?"

"I assumed that was hypothetical!"

"Look, can we not do this right now? I'm going to need you, as my friend and lawyer, to help me and Tara figure all of this out." Gabe stood and reached for Phineas. "Come on, I made a plate for you in the kitchen. Let's talk in there."

Phineas backed up a step instead. "Of course! That's all I ever am. The lawyer. Phin's a flaky ass friend, let's never tell him anything until we need him for something!"

"Jesus Christ, Phin." Richard stood and grabbed Phineas by the elbows, pushing him out of the room. "Kitchen. Now."

Gabe cupped Tara's face. "Sorry. That has nothing to do with you."

Tara nodded, eyebrow raised. "I know. Go figure it out."

Gabe kissed her, before following Richard and Phineas into the kitchen.

"So..." Sunny looked around the room, her eyes wide. "Phin's in love with Gabe, then?"

Lee pressed his lips together as they all collectively agreed not to answer her. That hypothesis would explain a lot about Phineas Watkins, but Lee didn't want it to be true. For Tara's sake, Gabe's, and especially the Phineas who'd become one of his closest friends. "So, Buttercup, I'm going to be your best man, right?"

Tara winced apologetically. "If we were going to have attendants, of course! But I don't think we will?"

Lee frowned, but he didn't argue. Even if they didn't have attendants officially, Lee would still be her best man. The title was just a formality.

Tuesday, September Twenty-First

Chapter Fourteen

Tara

"I want to start by apologizing." Phineas steepled his fingers as he leaned back in his leather chair, looking uncharacteristically serious in a suit and tie. They were meeting during Gabe's lunch break, so her *fiancé* was also in a blazer and chinos.

Leaving Tara the only person dressed casually, in a hoodie and joggers. She tugged on the drawstring; the whole situation felt designed to make her feel like an imposter. A stack of paper was neatly clipped and fanned out on the massive wood desk between them. Out the window behind Phineas, skyscrapers gleamed in the afternoon sun. It was a far cry from Blanche's dining room table or the couch with Hippo, where Tara usually worked.

Phineas hesitated, then raised his eyes to meet Tara's earnestly. "For how I reacted at your engagement party, I mean."

Fidgeting in the club chair that sank a little too deep, Tara shot Gabe a confused look, who simply shrugged. Phineas might have had a little meltdown, but that didn't warrant an apology, as far as Tara was concerned. "Don't worry about it."

Phineas huffed. "All the same, I'm apologizing. Other than when we met briefly at Tonio and Lee's wedding, that was our first real interaction, and that's not the impression I want you to have of me."

"Dude, you're fine." Tara tried not to laugh at his earnestness. Sure, she *could* act jealous of the man Gabe shared so much history with. She *could* hold a grudge that Phineas seemed to be carrying a torch for her partner. But even if he was suffering from unrequited love with Gabe, despite Gabe's insistence otherwise, Tara only empathized; she'd been in the same boat a mere six months ago.

How that empathy might translate into a friendship with Phineas was still unclear, but she was determined to figure that out. Phineas was important to Gabe; that was all that mattered. She'd figure out how to get along with him, too. Maybe even see him as a friend one day, like Lee did.

"Well, if you're sure..." Phineas eyed her and Gabe warily, unclipping the first stack of papers. "Let's get down to business then. Here is our standard prenup agenda. I'll need your financial information—assets, property, income, etcetera—then we can discuss what you want to do with inheritance, estate planning, custody agreements, spousal support—"

"Spousal support?" Tara interrupted with a frown. "We don't need that."

"Don't we?" Gabe retorted, hand already reaching for his braid. "Because I'm not just going to abandon you without—"

"Abandon me?" Tara scoffed, pulling his hand away before he could start tugging on it. Strange how quickly she discounted the very idea, like it wasn't her driving fear the past few months—her whole life, really. "That's not what this is about! Inheritance is the main thing we need to cover, because your *trust* is what needs to be protected—"

"Kitten," Gabe groaned, sinking down into the club chair as he laced their fingers together. "The trust doesn't need protecting, I would give you all of it—"

"Hold up." Phineas raised a hand, his mouth open and eyes wide. "Can I get through my explanation first? Good Lord! You two went right at it. Am I in the wrong meeting? We're discussing a prenup, right? Not a divorce mediation?"

Gabe and Tara both huffed, then exchanged a small smile. Gabe touched his own nose. "Pause?"

"Good call." Tara touched hers too. "Pause. Go ahead, Phin."

"This is so weird," Phineas muttered. "Cute, but weird." He resumed his explanation without interruption (though her fight to stay quiet was a struggle), even getting through their list of assets—well, Gabe's list of assets. Tara had an LLC and a bank account that had barely started to grow since she'd moved in with Gabe.

The truce lasted until they started discussing the terms of the trust. Unexpectedly, Phineas turned to Tara conspiratorially. "Did he ever tell you about the night he secured that trust from his deadbeat granddad?"

Tara nodded, remembering the story Gabe had told her months ago; the undercurrent of pride in his honey dark voice was one she rarely heard. "Yep."

"Oh." Phineas's face fell.

"Oh, uh…" Tara floundered. "But if you want to tell it, I'm sure he left some stuff out. He doesn't talk about his college experience much."

"Well, I would love to overshare on his behalf!" Phineas grinned at Gabe, who groaned, as if anticipating the embarrassment he was about to endure. Tara sat up in her chair, eager to hear it. "So, the Gabe you know is very different than the Gabe I went to college with."

Tara nodded in agreement; Gabe had been through a lot, much of it when he was in grad school. She'd been curious what Gabe had been like before then. To hear Gabe describe it, he'd been miserable his whole life. But his stories from those times told Tara he'd also had fun.

"So we started rooming together halfway through fall semester our freshman year," Phineas explained, his voice deepening and slowing, the way Gabe's did whenever he told a story. With a smile, Tara settled in, hand on her bump as if it'd let the baby know to pay attention to the story their uncle Phineas was telling. Even though the kid wasn't developed enough to hear anything yet. "Our first roommates were friends, and they both smelled awful."

"So bad!" Gabe pretended to gag.

Tara grinned at their mutual snobbery.

"My roommate decided he didn't want to live with me anymore, so he accused me of stealing." Phineas rolled his eyes. "As if I wanted his nonexistent Xbox, and the RA knew that I didn't, so he gave us the option to switch. Gabe and I agreed so quick! It was a mutually beneficial arrangement." Phineas winked at Gabe, who pinkened.

"Oh?" Tara asked, delighted by the blush on Gabe's face.

"Nothing happened until after Richard and I secretly broke up," Gabe explained, as if defending himself. "Phin was still in the closet—"

"Still am, baby!" Phineas interjected.

"But I clocked him right away." Gabe's smile turned flirty. "We'd exchanged the subtle mutual queer eye contact when passing in the hallway a few times. And once Phinny here found out I was hooking up with people besides Richard, we started a regular thing."

"It made sense, more practical than anything," Phineas explained, as if placating Tara. "Just hooking up between friends!"

His explanation was unnecessary; Tara was enthralled with the whole conversation. She'd never seen Gabe this flirty with anyone but her before, let alone with someone as attractive as Phineas. She squirmed in her chair, crossing a leg. Gabe raised an eyebrow at her.

Cheeks burning, Tara turned her attention back to Phineas as he said, "We were young and horny. Gabe was officially dating Richard, who had finally accepted he was trans but then got hella uncomfortable with his body—remember how many sports bras he used to wear?" Phineas laughed, interrupting himself, and answered his own question before Gabe could speak, "Gabe bought him his first binder that Christmas, and he became a whole new person! That binder turned him into kind of an asshole, honestly. Anyway, I was excited to explore my sexuality halfway across the country from my parents, without commitment." Phineas's smile dimmed. "Like, I said, mutually beneficial. The three of us were tight."

Tara could easily picture the motley trio: Phineas was skinny, tall, and excitable. Gabe was even taller, heavier, and surly. Richard was short, blond hair buzzed short, and probably just as grouchy then. Amongst the cishet white majority she presumed made up Yale's student body, they would have stuck out. Even if they were all privileged rich kids in their own right.

"Anyway, I was tagging along to this alumni event Dick Carter dragged Gabe and Richard to, where he finally met Deadbeat Grand-dad." Phineas rested his hand on his chin, beaming up at Gabe. "I've never been so proud of him. He was always so smooth in social situations, but that night, it was like he gave into his spite. I've never seen him so confident, witty, sharp. He backed that man into a corner so fast!" Phineas laughed as Gabe muttered protests, demurring any compliments as always.

Tara's heart clenched at the affection and pride Phineas was broadcasting. It reminded her of the feelings in her heart whenever she looked at Gabe. If this was mere hero worship, then Phineas had put Gabe on a pedestal a hundred feet tall. Her heart went out to him; that was a lot of love to carry for a long time.

"Anyway, that facade completely crumbled as soon as we were back in our dorm." Phineas snorted. "He was a shaky, insecure mess. Completely freaked out, existential crisis about if he'd betrayed his mom by faking nice with Deadbeat Granddad. It was fun, getting to be the one who made *him* chill out for once." Phineas tapped his pen against the desk, a fond smile on his face. "I talked him down, made him email the accountant, then sucked him off as a reward."

"Nice," Tara nodded approvingly. Getting head always brought out a mood shift in Gabe, undoing him into a vulnerable mess that made her heart swell with the trust he had in her. Picturing Gabe falling apart, babbling praise for Phineas, the way he always did for Tara, made her mouth water. The warmth in her cheeks ignited her whole body.

"It's too bad you got pregnant so quick," Phineas said casually, dousing Tara in cold water. "You didn't get to have any fun together before jumping into marriage and monogamy."

"We can still have fun after the baby comes!" Tara protested, a pang of insecurity hitting her chest as she rubbed her bump protectively. "Hell, even *before* the baby comes!"

"Yeah, Phin, what the fuck?" Gabe grumbled, tightening his hand around hers. "Just because we're going to be parents doesn't mean we can't have fun."

"You're right! Sorry, sorry!" Phineas winced. "I'm probably projecting. My therapist suggested I might sabotage relationships because commitment freaks me out."

After a moment of awkward silence, Gabe burst into laughter. "That isn't news, Phin! You've been making that joke since we first hooked up."

Phineas's smile turned bashful. "Yeah, yeah, I know. But I'm trying to treat that a little less as a joke these days." To Tara, Phineas added, "Once again, I apologize. I'm sure your monogamous sex life will be very fulfilling for the rest of your lives." He winked. "Though if you ever want a—" Phineas cut himself off. "Nope, not finishing that. Not being a creep."

"No, no. Say it." Tara raised an eyebrow, crossing her arms. "If we ever want a what? A third?" Tara's grin spread with delight as Phineas blanched, wide eyes flashing to Gabe for help. "Phin, are you volunteering to be our unicorn?"

As Phineas stammered unintelligibly, Gabe snorted, giving her an amused look. "Oh, is this how these prenup meetings are going to go?"

"A little flirting will be a nice break from arguing." Nodding at the pile of papers that made her queasy just thinking about how many pauses they'd need, Tara traced her thumb along his palm. She liked seeing this side of Gabe; a fun, confident version of him who rarely emerged, except during quiet moments when it was just the two of them.

The Gabe Phin had loved back then (or perhaps merely admired, if Gabe could be believed) was not the Gabe that she loved now, but he was still the same person. Maybe Tara could help reconnect him with that fun, confident Gabe she wanted to know better, too. And she could do that by connecting with Phineas.

Slowly, Tara smirked at the panicked man across the table, thrilling at how Phineas's throat bobbed as he swallowed hard. "Besides, Phin doesn't mind. Do you, Phinny?"

Phineas paused, giving Gabe a panicked look. "Sorry, am I allowed to flirt with your future wife?"

Gabe shrugged, an amused smile on his lips. "Why are you asking me? That's between you and Tara."

"This is why I love you, man! Both of you! Everyone else tells me to stop being a horny creep." Phineas beamed, then snapped finger guns at Tara. "Flirt all you want! Just be forewarned, I'm not used to anyone flirting back, so I might panic."

"Love it." Tara's cheeks warmed, strangely touched by how quickly Phineas had included her in his love for Gabe. That was all it took to get Phineas on her side? If he made friends through charged flirting, well, Tara was about to be his new best friend.

Thursday, September
Twenty-Third

Chapter Fifteen

Jazz gasped, jolting awake when a scream cut through the dark. Sweat soaked her pajamas, and the sheets twisted around her legs. Her night-light cast a pink glow across the floor of her bedroom, but shadows danced in the moonlight from the tree branches outside.

A knock on the door made her jump.

"Jazz, you okay? Can I come in?"

"Yeah," Jazz replied, her voice hoarse.

Blanche peeked through the crack in the door. "What happened? I heard a scream."

Jazz shook her head with a sardonic laugh. "And here, I thought *you* screamed. Must have been a bad dream." *What else is new?* Strange how the closet that had been her childhood refuge in real life had become the setting where every nightmare started.

"You want to talk about it?" Blanche perched on the edge of the bed.

She scooted over to make room for them, wincing as her hand came away clammy when she patted the bed three times. "Sorry, I sweat the bed."

Blanche chuckled and leaned back against the headboard, pulling their robe tighter around them. "Trust me, I know how it is. I woke myself up too. Was just coming out of the shower when I heard you."

"I need to cleanse the house again," Jazz joked, but she fully planned to practically fumigate the damn place this weekend. Blanche's presence, their concern was enough comfort for now (especially since they'd been avoiding her all week). "Want to talk about yours? Distract me from mine?"

They shrugged. "It was the usual—one of the people who tried to kill me when I was younger either murdering me, or someone else I care about."

Jazz shook her head in exasperation. "I know I say this whenever you share anything about your past, but the fuck?"

Blanche snorted. "It's usually the night Daisy died." With a sigh, they added, "I wasn't in a good headspace last weekend to share this, but one of my clients murdered her." They grinned as they mouthed "the fuck?" in unison with her.

The nightmares about the father who hadn't raised a hand to her since Lee had left felt very silly now, when Blanche— *No, it's not a competition. Don't make this about you.* "What happened?"

"He was one of my long-term subs who had always been clingy, and it got out of hand. Daisy didn't think he was worth worrying about, so I ignored the stalking. He stabbed her. And fucking waited for me to come home, expecting I'd be proud of him and happy that he killed my wife." Blanche's swallow was heavy.

"Was he arrested?"

"Technically, yes. We both were. I tried to shoot him, but my aim has always been shit, and I was such a wreck." Blanche winced. "And of course, they bought his story that Daisy went crazy with jealousy, and attacked him first. He got bailed out within hours. I was there for a week before they let me go."

"That's fucked up." Jazz reached for their hand and wove their fingers together. "I'm sorry that happened to you. Did he get convicted?"

"No, karma worked its magic. He was found dead before I was released." Blanche squeezed her hand. "So I dream of that a lot. Finding her body. Him standing there waiting for me. But it's not always her who gets killed. Sometimes it's me, or Freddy, or Chas too. And it's not always my client doing the killing. Sometimes it's my Papa or Daisy's stepdad. Or the john that put me in a coma."

Another "the fuck," left Jazz lips. "Your dad tried to kill you?"

"You're asking a lot of questions about my trauma for someone who just had a nightmare," Blanche tittered. "You sure you don't want to talk about something lighter?"

Jazz bit her lip. "Takes my mind off my own. As much as the night-mares suck, I didn't have it so bad, compared to you."

Blanche huffed a laugh. "Don't minimize your own experience. You were a child who experienced trauma from a parent, and your abuser continues to be a part of your life. That's a lot to carry, especially for someone your age."

"My trauma wasn't that bad. He was harder on Lee."

"Because you hid your 'disobedience' better?"

Jazz shrugged. The reality was that Dad cared more about Lee than her. Lee had higher expectations to meet. Jazz just had to be quiet, obedient, and stay out of the way. Strange, to have the privilege of safety compared to what Lee went through, and still be jealous of her brother.

"You don't have to suffer directly to be traumatized. You witnessed traumatic events that shaped you. You lived in fear of someone who was supposed to protect you."

"That's true, I guess. Especially after Lee disappeared, I followed every damn rule to the letter. You couldn't catch me slipping at all!" Jazz snorted. "But yeah, you're right—if he did it to Lee, what was to stop him from doing it to me? I had to be perfect."

"You were home that day, weren't you?" Blanche asked quietly. "When Lee was kicked out?"

With a thick swallow, Jazz nodded. "That's what my nightmare always is. It never changes. Just me alone in the dark, hearing the yelling and screaming."

Anytime Dad got to yelling, she'd hide in her closet, like Lee had taught her. But her room was right next to her parents; she could hear every single word that was said when she was in there. Dad's never-end-ing sermon about sin and abomination. The cracks of the belt against bare skin. Lee's muffled screams. Mom praying in a weird voice, which Jazz only realized years later was her crying. Mom had always been so stoic and proper and obedient; Jazz had never heard her mom cry before that day, or after. Until she met Lee again.

And then silence. A silence that stretched on and on for hours, until her mom found her in the closet and scolded her for hiding. A silence that echoed through the house for weeks until Auntie Alitrice came for a visit, and asked where Lee was. Then Jazz hid in her closet again as her beloved aunt screamed at her dad, only to disappear like Lee, never to be seen again. Never to be spoken of again. A silence that lasted for years until a sixteen-year-old Jazz was finally allowed to have a cell phone and searched for her brother on every app, until she finally found his Instagram through Sunny's.

"I thought he died. He was just gone, and we weren't allowed to talk about him anymore. We were supposed to pretend he never existed." Jazz bit her lip to stop it from trembling. "I only found out he'd been kicked out when Dad told Aunt Alitrice what happened."

"How old were you?"

"Nine."

Blanche rolled to face her, tucking a stray loc back under her bonnet. "That alone is enough to fuck anyone up for life, Beautiful. You have every right to your nightmares and your trauma. Don't let comparison steal your pain."

"I thought the saying went 'comparison is the thief of joy.'" Jazz attempted a smile to show she was teasing. Her lips trembled, and Blanche's gaze flickered to her mouth. A resentful hope flickered to light. After the blow up fight she'd had with Mimi and Teddy for what she kept insisting was a "friendship kiss," Jazz should not be hoping Blanche was about to kiss her. Especially not when she was fighting tears. She had to stop deluding herself.

Still tracing her cheek, Blanche leaned forward and pressed a kiss to Jazz's forehead. "You want some tea?"

Tea would wash away the bitterness of disappointment and shame that burned in her throat, soothe the nerves still coursing through her after her bad dream. With a trembling smile, Jazz nodded.

GABE

"You didn't have to take work off for this, you know," Blanche raised an eyebrow at Gabe, nails tapping on the stainless steel bartop at Confession. "I appreciate the dedication, but this place isn't exactly going to fall apart without someone here on weeknights."

"I know," Gabe pulled his hair—still damp from the showers at the gym—over his shoulder to braid it. "But Richard can't let go of shit, and he is not meant to work at a bar, so I offered to cover for him this week."

Jackie snorted from behind the bar. The shaker in her hand rattled with crushed ice. "That's an understatement. I've never met someone so perfect for a desk job."

Fingers weaving through his curls, Gabe laughed. "Exactly! And I'm working through if I'd prefer to work in a different environment than the miserable job I have now, so this is my chance to see what it's like to do something like this instead."

"Well, more power to you! I hate the responsibility, but if you want it, have at it!" Blanche patted his arm. "Maybe you'll be more useful than I am, though. Jackie needs feedback on her cocktails for the winter menu, and my palate is nowhere close to refined. I just want my liquor strong and smooth. And preferably brown."

"Like your men?" Jackie teased, but backtracked as Blanche gave her a confused look. "Sorry, that sounded like a joke an allosexual would make. Forget I said that."

"Oh!" Blanche nodded. "That would be funny if I liked men more."

"Almost all of your clients are men," Gabe pointed out, dreading Blanche's reply. He'd always hoped for their sake that they remotely enjoyed their line of work.

Blanche shrugged. "I like *some* men, the ones I can connect with in some way. People who I respect or admire. I don't find most people very attractive, but I don't have any clients I don't *want* to sleep with." They paused. "Anymore. Women just tend to be easier to connect with. And prettier."

"Cheers to that!" Jackie said, pouring out the purple cocktail into a coupe glass. "What do you think?"

Blanche took the first sip, then passed it to Gabe. "It's sweet. Dangerous!"

Gabe rolled a taste over his tongue, the tart lemon bright against the sickly sweet lavender. Notes of juniper singed his nose as he swallowed. "It's good. Perhaps a little too much lavender, but I like the way it changes across the palate. The gin really hits at the end."

"See?" Blanche elbowed him. "This is way more up your alley than mine."

"You said sweet and dangerous," Gabe elbowed them back. "Basically the same thing."

"The lemon wasn't too strong?" Jackie asked, sipping it herself.

"No, that was good. Tart, but it fits the drink," Gabe said. "Though this feels more like a spring cocktail than a winter one."

Jackie glared at him, crossing her arms. "God dammit. You're right. I should do something with oranges for a winter citrus cocktail." Gabe practically preened; Leigh Anne never said he was right about anything. "We just have so much lavender. But it'll keep until spring." She turned away, opening cabinets and fridges. "Maybe pomegranate juice?"

"So do you want to go into the restaurant business?" Blanche asked Gabe, sipping the cocktail.

He winced. "Probably will have to, if I do change jobs. My mom said the vineyard would hire me as an admin, but they're getting older, so I would probably end up wearing all of their hats if I do. Learn from them while they're still working, you know?"

"Do you want to work for them?" Blanche murmured.

Gabe mulled his words, the indecision he'd struggled with his whole life weighing on him. He'd rarely known what he wanted in life, beyond someone to share it with. Tara, in particular. Especially since she encouraged him to pursue what he wanted, instead of what she wanted, the way all of his exes had. "I don't want to commute so far, but I'd much rather work for my parents than sit in a cubicle and report to my awful boss for the rest of my life. So, yes? I think so?"

"Jazz thinks I should consider a career change," Blanche slowly spun the coupe in their hand.

"Do you want to?" Gabe asked carefully. Privately, he'd worried about Blanche since finding out that their arrangement with Covey hadn't exactly been consensual. Nor had their start in the trade been, though they seemed content with it now.

"That's the question, isn't it?" Blanche chuckled sardonically. "What the fuck do I want? I want the patio and firepit one of my clients is putting in. I want a birdfeeder. I want the price of lumber to go down so I can afford to fix my porch. I want a cast-iron grate that is twelve-by-nine inches and patterned with roses. I want a dog, once all the holes in my house a dog might fall through are covered up." They shook their head. "But those are all little things, instead of big-picture! I want to be happy, but how does anyone get that?"

"Have you considered dating?" Gabe suggested, holding out a hand to stop Blanche's teasing. "Yes, I know how it sounds, coming from someone who went from single to engaged to Tara with a baby on the way in six months. But the point stands, loving and being loved has made me happy. And it might work for you too!"

"First of all." Jackie slammed down a knife and orange onto her cutting board. "*You're* Tara's baby daddy? Lee said she got knocked up, but I didn't know it was *you*!"

"Baby...parent, but yes." Gabe nodded.

"Damn." Jackie looked him up and down. "Good for her."

"Thank you," Gabe said hesitantly.

"Second of all, you're full of shit!" Jackie carefully slivered the zest from the pith, frowning at him while she carved the orange peel away. "Love doesn't lead to happiness."

"With the right person—"

"No." Jackie shook her head, juicing the orange into the shaker. "Love and happiness are both processes, not an attainable state of being. Contentment with your life choices, satisfaction in working toward your goals, celebrating your accomplishments—those things bring happiness, and you have to keep adjusting how you do those things to *stay* happy." She sliced the orange in half, juicing it into another shaker. "You may be finding those things in your relationship now, but not everyone does, and I'm not convinced Blanche would."

Gabe bristled. "'Now'? You think I'm going to be less happy as time goes on?"

Jackie shrugged, eyeballing the brandy she was pouring. "If you keep working at it, you'll be fine. Like I said, it's a process. I find my happiness working here, because I'm always learning and meeting new and interesting people who dump all their trauma on me. I'm getting stronger in my pole class, and celebrating the contests I win with my pole friends! Having one person, or several people, can be nice. But relying on other people for your own emotional needs isn't sustainable."

Gabe frowned; that was something Joy had been cautioning him on as well.

But Blanche leaned forward before he could argue back. "Jackie, you are the last person I'd expect to be a pole dancer!"

"What? Ace people can be sexy! You're demi, and you're a fucking dominatrix! It's not that big of a stretch." Jackie rolled her eyes, pouring the shaker into a glass. "Try this."

"Am I demi?" Blanche asked Gabe, sipping the rosy orange cocktail. "Ooh, that's delightful!"

"You might be. Do you want to be demi?" Gabe took the glass from them, catching some caramel notes in his nose as he sampled it. Once again, a hair too sweet, but otherwise balanced. "Maybe cranberry juice instead of grenadine? Perhaps some bitters?"

Jackie took the glass from him with another frown, sipping before she wrinkled her nose. "I don't like that you're better at this than me."

Gabe beamed; while he was competent (more competent than fucking Leigh Anne, anyway), the only thing he was truly good at when it came to his investment banker job was socializing.

"Don't let it go to your head," Jackie sneered, before turning to Blanche. "You said you're attracted to people you have an emotional connection with. Sounds demi to me."

Blanche hummed. "I've never been one for labels, but I suppose that sounds right. I dunno, I've always just been whoever I want, and done whatever I want at the moment." They paused, wrapping a blonde lock around their finger. "Now I need to remember who and what that is, for the long-term."

"You'll figure it out!" Gabe rubbed their back. "Just keep an open mind about it."

He wouldn't push, because Jackie was right: being with Tara had made him happy, but that might not work for Blanche. After all, if anyone knew how miserable love could be, it was him.

But that was in the past. Everything was looking up in his life, and being happy and in love was like breathing. Even the things that had been bothering him were all going to be fine.

Even if Phineas and Tara had gotten off on the wrong foot during their engagement party, their first meeting for the prenup the other day had gone well. They were already starting to gang up on him. Even if his awareness of his gender was uncomfortable and being called a Dad made his skin crawl, he and Tara were excited to be parents together. Even if he hated his job, he was taking steps to figure out his next move, with Tara's full support. After all, his mom trusted him to help with Confession, and he actually enjoyed this, unlike his dull office job. Even the notoriously rude Jackie was complimenting him. That had to count for something.

Everything would work out, because with Tara at his side, they could handle anything life threw at them.

Friday, September Twenty-Fourth

Chapter Sixteen

Blanche

Kneeling at Blanche's feet, their client batted her eyelashes at Blanche adoringly. "Did I do good today, Professor?"

With a fond smile, Blanche ran the brush through Sarah's soft brown hair. "You were wonderful, pet. Tell me all the reasons you should be proud of yourself."

Sarah bit her lip. "Well, I finished all my work before you got here, and I stopped doing my chores when the timer went off! And...I ate all of my dinner, and I didn't get angry when I was eating dessert today."

"That's right, pet." Blanche kissed the top of her head. If they'd known having a little could be this sweet—with the right client—they might have given age play a try long ago. "The meal you made was delicious, and I'm so proud of you for eating dessert. Was your ice cream good?"

Sarah nodded firmly. "Yeah."

"Are you going to have some more when I'm not here?"

"Do you want me to?" Sarah turned to Blanche again, searching for a sign of what she should do.

Blanche tweaked her nose. "Pet, our scene is over. You tell me what *you* want."

They adored Sarah, but damn, she was *such* a people pleaser. She had originally hired Blanche to help figure out why she couldn't orgasm, and why using toys was so painful. Her doctors had referred her to dilators that still hurt, and her therapists referred her to psychiatrists for medication.

But Blanche had known from the first rambling, backtracking message that Sarah had debilitating anxiety, decision fatigue, and a martyr complex—to name a few. Her hang-ups were a symptom of never being allowed—or allowing herself—to do what she wanted. She punished herself for wanting.

Her "formerly gifted child and eldest daughter syndrome," as Sarah called it, ran much deeper than orgasms. For the past few months, Blanche had been coming over on Fridays to help Sarah disconnect from work, to make her take care of the wants and needs that wracked her with guilt. They normally didn't take on littles, but Sarah didn't need sex, just affirmation and praise for being selfish.

And sure, Blanche would watch her touch herself, but that was to coach her through the panic that threatened to overwhelm her orgasms. To praise her for relaxing enough to work her way through the dilators. She was still a long way away from her "goal size"—a blue, tentacle dildo that was so big, even Blanche thought it was a little obscene—but they were proud of Sarah for setting her sights so high.

"I think...I think I want to make a boozy milkshake," Sarah whispered conspiratorially, eyes darting around the room as if her mother might appear around the corner and scold her. Even though Sarah was a grown adult who lived alone, with a graduate degree and a career at a company that matched her 401k.

But when Sarah was in pet mode, she leaned into her little persona. Even after Blanche left, Sarah preferred to stay in little mode and stay home alone on Friday nights. She'd already made her blanket fort and picked out the erotica novel that she wanted to read. She'd go to bed whenever she wanted, and she'd wake up again as Sarah the responsible adult after one guilt-free night a week to indulge in whatever she wanted. Blanche was working her up to do assignments outside of Friday nights, like eating dessert on weeknights, or reading her "dirty" books instead of self-help on Sundays.

"That sounds delicious, pet. Will you send me a selfie of you drinking it if you do?" Blanche separated her hair down the middle to start on her plaits.

Sarah nodded, resting her cheek on Blanche's thigh. "Yes, Professor."

"Remember, only if you *want* to. Okay?"

She nodded. "I want to."

"Good girl," Blanche said, making quick work on one braid and starting on the next. "What else are you proud of from today?"

"I came four times," Sarah grinned shyly. "And I didn't cry. That much."

"That's huge, pet. You've made so much progress." Blanche pressed a kiss to her head. "Remember your promise to me?"

Sarah pouted and clung to their leg, knowing what was coming. "To be honest with you about what I want at all times."

"That's right. And do you want more aftercare, or are you ready to go play in your fort?"

Sarah bit her lip. "Can you stay while I make my milkshake? I'm scared that if I rinse out the blender, I'm going to start cleaning again, and I don't want to clean tonight. I hate cleaning!"

With a nod, Blanche held out a hand to help her up. "I'm proud of you for remembering that cleaning time is over until tomorrow. Let's go make your boozy milkshake, pet."

"Thanks, Professor." Sarah slid her hand into Blanche's. "You should be a therapist. I've made so much more progress with you than I have with any of the therapists I've seen over the past decade."

Blanche chuckled politely, wishing they could— *You can,* came Shayla's voice. *If you want. Do you want to be a therapist, Blanche?* As Sarah beamed up at them, Blanche kept their domme mask on, cheeks burning at the respect and adoration in her pretty smile. Why couldn't they? Like Jazz had said, Blanche was free. Their heart bloomed with what Blanche imagined hope felt like. They could do anything they wanted.

Even become a therapist.

Blanche opened the front door of their house to the sound of Ed's raucous laughter. They winced; Jazz's board game night with her polycule had completely slipped their mind. Normally, after their sessions with Sarah, they barely needed aftercare. She was their easiest client; Blanche got to be soft and sweet and encouraging, no need for Viagra or anger.

But they still would have preferred to attend to their aftercare in quiet. That was the risk of living with a college student, though, and honestly, Blanche was feeling fine! The gummy and the long bus ride back was enough to return to their normal headspace without issue.

When Blanche kicked off their boots, they even remembered to tuck them into the closet, to keep the patent leather safe from the cluster of shoes scattered around the foyer. Lee would be so proud. After years of him nagging them to put their shoes away, it was finally Jazz's chaotic polycule that got Blanche to pick up after themself. They considered sneaking upstairs, but that might be rude. Mimi had been glaring at them extra hard since the kiss (which mortified Blanche that Jazz had presumably thought it important enough to share with her partners, when she and Blanche had never directly talked about it, but that was Jazz's business). Blanche decided to make some tea and make a short but polite appearance. An attempt at normalcy.

"Hey, Blanche!" Teddy waved from the dining room as Blanche filled the kettle in the kitchen sink, her eyes glued to her phone.

"Hi, Teddy." Blanche measured the tea leaves into the tea ball before leaning on the doorframe. The laptops, highlighters, and textbooks that usually graced the dining table had been pushed to the end to make room for a tornado of cardboard and dice. "What are you all up to?"

"Playing one of Ed's games," Jazz answered with a tight smile, fiddling with a small scrap of paper in her hand. "We're trying to conquer the galaxy."

"Fun. That looks like you're rolling a joint, though," Blanche teased, coming closer to inspect what Jazz was up to.

"Oh." Jazz laughed over her shoulder, her tongue darting out from between her lips to wet the paper. "Teddy's also teaching me how to roll a joint. Or at least she *was* before the latest Vamp trailer came out."

"I make no apologies," Teddy said, still glued to her phone. "This is so fucking hot!"

"Want one?" Jazz asked.

Blanche shrugged. "I won't say no to that."

"How was work?" Jazz frowned as she tapped the paper gently, biting her lower lip in concentration.

Blanche's cheeks burned when Jazz's lip slipped out from between her teeth.

"Work?" A young Black woman whom Blanche hadn't noticed—nor ever met before—spoke up. "Did you just come from a scene?!"

"Uh..." Blanche blinked at the eager, young femme, her hair in box braids and with a lip ring, beaming up at them excitedly. "That's confidential."

"Oh my god, you're so right. Sorry!" She pressed her lips together. "I'm just, like, your biggest fan. I love your YouTube channel! And your SubParty! I love you!"

"I have a YouTube channel?" Blanche asked Jazz quietly.

"You really need to pay Tara and Lee more," Jazz teased, licking the paper as she grinned over her shoulder. "They use your PG educational content to advertise the subscription-based platforms."

"Are Tara and Lee your editors? They're so funny!" The young woman gushed.

"Jules!" Mimi hissed, glowering at Blanche's hand on the back of Jazz's chair. "You said you were gonna be cool."

Jules as in Julissa? Blanche kept their mask in place, fighting the urge to react. Mimi's new girlfriend was the only member of Jazz's polycule that they hadn't yet met. Maybe Jazz hadn't told her partners about the kiss; maybe Mimi was upset because her other girlfriend was a fan of Blanche's? That had to be it.

"Yeah, but Blanche is so amazing, Mimi! Like, all the shit I know about kink came from their channel." Julissa turned to Blanche, hero worship in her eyes. "And honestly, you're even more magical in person."

"Aren't they gorgeous?" Teddy smacked the table, finally breaking free from her phone to wink at Blanche and blatantly check them out. "Seriously, Blanche, you look like you stepped off the cover of a fashion magazine, and you're not even wearing makeup!"

Blanche beamed, cheeks heating. "You're going to give me a praise kink, Teddy."

"Is this where you film your scenes now?" Julissa looked around the room in awe. "Can I see your set sometime?"

"Only clients are allowed there," Jazz said coldly, handing Blanche a slightly lumpy joint and a lighter.

"Thanks, Beautiful." Blanche took the joint and lit it. "And yeah, clients only, and I'm not taking any new clients right now." Better to nip that in the bud before Julissa got any ideas.

Julissa pouted. "Darn, I was hoping you'd be open to training me to domme. Like you did for that educational series you did over the summer."

"Well, if I ever decide to take on an apprentice, I'll post about it on my SubParty." Blanche exhaled the smoke from their lungs slowly, hoping the obvious sarcasm would get Julissa to drop it. Her attention was flattering, but Jazz's jaw was tight, and Mimi was frozen, staring hard at the table. And here Blanche had been trying to smooth things over.

"Oh my god, I'd love that!"

Julissa would need to learn to read a room before being anyone's domme.

Mimi glared at Blanche, faking a cough. "It's a little smoky in here."

Blanche raised an eyebrow at the half-full ashtray on the table, but took the hint and passed it back to Jazz. "Thanks, Jazzy. I'll bring my tea upstairs, let you get back to your game."

They were halfway up the staircase when Jazz called out behind them to wait up, holding out the tea they'd forgotten. Blanche descended a few steps to take it from her. "Thanks."

"Sorry." Jazz winced, her hands lingering on the mug and around Blanche's. "About that in there. I didn't know Julissa was a fan."

Blanche put on a tight half smile. "Never apologize for someone else's behavior, Beautiful."

"Will you come back? And play the game with us? Or just hang out?" Jazz asked shyly. "I can try and rein in Jules."

Blanche shook their head. "I think a few of you would like that, but not everyone would."

"Mimi. Sorry." Jazz sighed. "I can talk to her—"

"Jazz, go play your game." Blanche softened their smile when Jazz winced; their stomach soured at the thought of hurting her. "I don't want to impose on your polycule date night."

"You could, if you want though." Jazz's voice tugged into a hopeful question at the end.

Blanche sighed, their patience and willpower running equally thin. They had never talked about that kiss, and chaste as it was, Jazz shouldn't hope it might become something more.

They'd finally admitted what had happened with Shayla, who had listened to Blanche ramble for most of the session, before finally asking Blanche what they wanted to do about it. What choice did Blanche have? They had to set boundaries. Though she'd hid it well, Shayla had looked as disappointed as Blanche had felt as she helped them figure out what to say.

They cleared their throat, squeezing her shoulder. "I'm not part of your polycule, Jazz. And I am too drained for the energy in that room." Jazz flinched, and Blanche's chest tightened when her hands fell from theirs, leaving the mug with them. But they should have nipped this in the bud a week ago. While they might have some...feelings for Jazz, they did not want to navigate the murk of her extended relationships. "Look, I know we haven't talked about that kiss yet, but to be clear, we are friends and roommates. That's it."

Blanche wanted to take it back the second Jazz's face fell. To kiss the hope back into her eyes, and let them both live in delusion that they might have a chance of joy from whatever might blossom between them. Because Blanche could count on one hand the things they truly wanted, but wanting wasn't enough to overcome their rationality. Jazz was technically their tenant—their much *younger* tenant—and Lee's sister.

"I know." Jazz nodded, stepping back, her eyes downcast. Her lips, which should be smiling, trembled as she frowned.

"Good. Glad we could clarify that."

It was not good, and Blanche was not glad. Each step that Jazz shuffled in the opposite direction physically hurt. But reaffirming the boundary of their friendship was undoubtedly the right thing.

Normally, doing the right thing didn't suck so hard.

"Good night, Jazz." Blanche turned and walked upstairs.

Jazz didn't glance up as she walked past the staircase. "Night, Blanche."

Sunday, September
Twenty-Sixth

Chapter Seventeen

Sunny

"Where's Dumpster?" Luna asked, looking around as she sat at the dining table in Richard's condo. For once, it was decorated, with a lace tablecloth that Richard had dragged out from the depths of his linen closet, a bouquet of flowers, and a few candles lit for ambiance.

Richard had invited Sunny's mother and sister over for dinner to "lay the groundwork," as he called it, for their plans. Sunny wasn't sure what ground he was talking about, but she interpreted the gesture as an opportunity for him to ask for Birdie's approval to propose.

Since he *still* hadn't done that yet.

Sunny sucked her teeth. Instead of proposing, Richard had been *planning*. He'd created lists and spreadsheets and decision matrices galore, planning out the timeline for her surgery and their wedding and the honeymoon and the fertility clinic and how many kids they would have and how old Dumpster would be when their potential third child was born and—

"She's in the guest room. It's impossible to cook seafood with her around." Richard set a platter of seared salmon filets on the table. "She's been trying to get in the fridge since I brought this home."

As everyone helped themselves to the salmon, couscous, and lemony asparagus that Gabe had recommended as foolproof, Sunny decided not to mention that Dumpster had already succeeded. Neither teeth nor claws had punctured the butcher paper, but her precious demon cat had dragged the filets across into the living room before Sunny took them away. Neither Richard nor her mae needed to know that.

"So," Richard said, taking the first bite of his salmon. "We've been discussing marriage plans."

"Oh, finally!" Birdie pressed her hands together. "I thought you'd never get engaged! A few auspicious dates are coming up—it's a little fast, but I'm sure we could coordinate with your parents to find one that works before the holidays."

"Oh, no." Richard shook his head. "There are several milestones planned before then."

"Milestones?" Birdie raised an eyebrow.

Richard gave Sunny a questioning look. She nodded at him to continue as she took a big bite of salmon. To her surprise, the pepper-crusted skin was the perfect texture—maybe Gabe had been right; she and Richard hadn't managed to fuck it up. After all, this was Richard's plan. Sunny was happy to be along for the ride, as long as he eventually proposed, and she got everything she wanted. Namely, a better ring than Tara got, cute as her story was.

"Sunny's surgery, first and foremost. And even if she won't let me pay for it," Richard and Birdie shared an exasperated huff, "she is letting me add her to my health insurance to bring the out-of-pocket cost down. So, that won't be until next year."

Birdie tsked. "So I might be dead before I get grandchildren."

"Mae, you are so dramatic," Luna sighed. "How about congratulations?"

"Congratulations for what?" Sunny nudged Richard's foot under the table, mostly teasing but also not. Lee had bought Antonio's engagement ring weeks before he proposed, Gabe had Tara's hidden away for months. And while she'd spent months under the impression that he was waiting for her to give him the green light, Richard hadn't even made a proposal spreadsheet yet. At least, not one that he'd shown her, and her eyes had glazed over with how many of his spreadsheets she'd looked at the past few weeks. "*Talking* about marriage? I have no ring on my finger."

"Do you want a vintage ring or not?" Richard nudged her back. "I can buy you an overpriced diamond freshly released from the De Beer's stockpile if you'd prefer. Or perhaps one freshly mined by child labor?"

Sunny glared at him. "You wouldn't dare."

"Then you have to be patient. I'm still figuring out how to get the ring I want to give you out of my parent's safe."

Sunny growled under her breath; she wasn't thrilled about his idea to get one of his mother's rings. Sure, she'd insisted on something vintage (if he got her a new ring, she'd feel too guilty to enjoy it), but she hadn't meant for him to ask his *mom* for an heirloom!

"Are you planning a heist?" Luna asked eagerly.

"I wish." Richard shook his head. "I'll have to get lunch with my mother. Twice, probably."

"I'm coming with," Sunny and Birdie said simultaneously.

"What? No!" Richard looked between them. "*Neither* of you are going."

"So what, am I to meet your parents at your wedding?" Birdie shook her head. "Unacceptable. If we're going to be co-grandparents, I need to get on their good side so they don't try to steal the good holidays."

"You will never meet them because they will not be invited to the wedding. Nor will they ever meet their grandchildren." Richard's tone left no room for argument. "They are awful people who would traumatize any children we have."

"Which is exactly why you're not going to see her alone, Dicky. I'm coming with you," Sunny insisted, setting her fork down. The idea of playing nice with Barbie made her skin crawl, but the idea of Richard facing any verbal abuse alone was unacceptable. What kind of wife would she be if she didn't shoulder that with him?

Richard's blue eyes dug into hers, before he conceded with a minute nod. "Fine. But we're meeting her where she'll have friends. Hopefully, she'll be less...abhorrent with an audience. And without Dad."

"So when do grandchildren come into this plan of yours?" Birdie took a bite of asparagus.

"Mae, seriously?" Sunny and Luna asked.

"What? I have to wait for your surgery, the wedding—who knows how long that will take, and how long it could take to conceive?"

"Sorry our lives aren't moving fast enough for you." Sunny rolled her eyes. "I already have a surgery appointment for a consult in January, Mae. Hopefully, I'll be ready to walk down the aisle by summer."

Birdie pursed her lips with a nod. "I'll contact the temple and see if any of the good dates are still open for next summer."

"Actually, we were thinking of getting married at Gabe's family vineyard." Sunny tried to hide her grin. She didn't want to ruin the surprise.

"The Coopers have a nice wedding venue about an hour outside the city."

Birdie's jaw tightened. "You'd make the lama drive an hour for a wedding?"

Sunny bit her lip, trying to act casual as she shrugged. "Miriam can officiate, right, Dicky? Gabe's mom is super sweet. She's basically Richard's adopted mom."

"You don't want a Buddhist wedding?" Her mother's lower lip trembled, her eyes widened in hurt.

"Well, not for the legal wedding," Richard said, glancing in concern at Sunny. She nodded quickly; she'd expected her mother to get mad, not cry! "But the second one will be."

"Second wedding?" Birdie looked between them in confusion.

"I was going to make you sweat a little longer, but you looked so sad, Mae," Sunny laughed. "We're going to have a civil ceremony at the vineyard. And well, we should ask Yai for help booking whatever the best place to get married in Chiang Mai is."

"You're going to Thailand?!" Luna stood up with a shriek, couscous flying from her mouth.

Sunny's heart was close to bursting as she bounced in her chair. "No, *we* are. All four of us! But we might leave you home with table manners like that." Sunny wrinkled her nose, picking couscous out of her hair. "We were going to honeymoon there, but we figured why not have another ceremony? Courtesy of Richard, of course."

"If we schedule our PTO and Sunny's medical leave right, we can probably swing at least two weeks there." Richard studied his plate, likely envisioning his spreadsheets. "Longer if we can work remotely."

"Once we're back, and depending on the scheduling at the clinic," Taking Richard's hand under the table, Sunny exchanged a smile with him before turning to her mom, "We could be expecting your first grandchild within a year."

Tears streamed down her mom's cheeks.

"Mae, are you okay?"

"I haven't been home in thirty years." Birdie's voice trembled. "I never thought I'd see my parents again."

Luna and Sunny both leaned over to hug her.

Waving them off, Birdie wiped her eyes and collected herself. "Thank you, Richard. You're going to be a good son-in-law." Richard's cheeks pinkened. "Well, I guess we'll have to move in when the baby comes.

Might be crowded with Luna and I in the baby's room, but your condo is nice enough."

"No way in hell!" Richard barked, coughing in surprise at how sharply he'd spoken.

Sunny smacked his leg. "Dicky, that's my mother you're talking to."

"My apologies." Richard cleared his throat. "Respectfully, no way in hell."

Birdie raised an eyebrow. "You won't allow family to help when the baby comes?"

"Guess we're not going to ask if I *want* to move to help with the baby," Luna sighed, nibbling at her asparagus. "This is closer to school, though."

Richard narrowed his eyes. "The new house plan will have to accelerate, but if we've moved by then, you may stay for two weeks after the baby is born."

"New house?" Sunny asked. "There's a new house plan?"

Richard snorted. "I've shown it to you twice already, and you immediately glazed over both times."

"We will stay for six weeks," Birdie countered.

"A month," Richard returned.

"Done." Birdie extended her hand.

Richard shook it.

"I'm sorry, important question?" Sunny raised her hand, annoyed that she'd somehow accidentally chosen someone far too similar to her mother as a husband. *Capricorns, ugh.* "What's wrong with the condo? It's already paid off."

"I thought that would be obvious." Richard looked meaningfully at her. "Sure, we can convert the guest room into a nursery, but I assumed you'd want a separate *game* room."

Sunny scoffed. "I can just set up my computer in the living room or something—oh." There was a sex swing mounted in the ceiling of the guest room, as well as bolts in the wall to tie the cuffs to. And a rack full of floggers hanging in the closet that she definitely did not want her mom to find, let alone her future children. "Should we get something with a nice yard?"

"A fenced-in backyard is weighted highly on the decision matrix, yes." Richard nodded in way that told Sunny she should already know this. "I was thinking over South near Gabe and Tara, but I'm impressed with the neighborhood where Blanche and Jazz's house is. The schools there are excellent."

A tab popped up in her mind, demanding to know what exactly was wrong with Eastside. Three more tabs popped up after it, explaining exactly *why* Eastside wouldn't be the best place to raise a family. Sunny's stomach squirmed with guilt; would she really discount Eastside, the neighborhood she loved (despite its many problems), so quickly?

"Well, *Blanche's* house. It's not technically Jazz's, even if she lives there," Sunny corrected archly, instead of pressing on the new house location. She minimized the Eastside tabs, waiting to examine that until she'd had a chance to actually look at Richard's spreadsheet.

Richard shrugged. "We'll see."

"What's that supposed to mean?"

"Just that Blanche and Jazz seem very in sync, even for roommates." Richard got that glint in his blue eyes whenever he was sitting on gossip. The corner of his mouth lifted into the slightest smirk. "They're constantly watching each other and doing little things like neck rubs or refilling each other's glasses without asking. It's very...coupley."

"No. You think?" Sunny would have to pay more attention. She pointed at Luna. "You didn't hear a word of this conversation. Don't go gossiping about Jazz around campus."

"Oh, that's old news." Luna waved her fork. "Mimi's been pissy—well, pissier than usual—because Jazz kissed Blanche last weekend."

"They kissed?!" Sunny's mouth fell open. "Wait, how do you know this? I thought you and Jazz weren't buddy buddy."

"Ed's my lab partner in psych. He talks a lot." Luna took another bite of couscous. "And frankly, hearing about Teddy's polycule drama is way more exciting than watching rats go through a maze."

Richard chuckled, his wry smile smug. "That explains why Blanche kept blushing whenever they looked at Jazz last weekend."

"They were *blushing*?" Sunny groaned. "And I missed it?"

"You miss everything," Luna teased.

As her family laughed around her, Sunny took the teasing in stride, relieved that the conversation had shifted away from their future. It was a little annoying that she knew so little of the specifics, but Richard liked to handle those. She had told him what she wanted out of life, and he'd incorporated her desires along with his own into his decision matrices, to create a flexible yet incredibly detailed project plan of their future. She trusted Richard to make that happen, to let her know what he needed from her, and to adjust accordingly when she changed her mind.

Sunny smiled softly, watching his gossipy ass grill Luna for details on Jazz and Blanche in his too-serious way. Strange how their kink dynamic had leaked— No, not leaked. Strange how it had taken them so long to make their dynamic official. Because their relationship had always been one where Sunny gave him her desires, her limits, her trust, and Richard delivered, eager to give her everything and more. Even though he was the most awkward, snobby, uptight nerd she'd ever met, he loved so generously. And if this was what their future held? Sunny would happily be spoiled—

She frowned. Sunny didn't want to be spoiled and doted upon like a trophy wife. That wasn't wifey material. No, she would *help* him spoil their whole family, including herself. Yes, that was better. She wanted to love him as hard as he loved her, in all the ways he wanted to be loved. She nodded to herself, satisfied. Now she just had to get Richard to stop spoiling her so much.

Or at least find a way to spoil him back.

THURSDAY, SEPTEMBER THIRTIETH

Chapter Eighteen

Jazz

"Jazz, I love you, but if you mention Blanche one more time, I'm going to bed. Alone," Mimi threatened, waving her cup in Jazz's direction. Curling further into the corner of the couch, Mimi chewed on her cheek the way she did when she was in one of her moods. With only the purple Christmas lights strung around Mimi and Teddy's apartment for illumination, she looked positively dejected in the dark corner as she pouted. Her knees were even tucked under her hoodie as she hugged them.

Jazz's stir of annoyance might have been ignored any other time. But she had just poured herself her fourth vodka lemonade, and she had been cramming all week for the bio test that had kicked her ass earlier that morning. Her patience was slower than her temper today, and Mimi could be *so* melodramatic. In the privacy of her apartment, Mimi's Virgo pettiness always came to a head. "Damn, I'm not allowed to talk about my roommate now?"

"Oh, here we go." Teddy sighed heavily from where she sat on the floor between them, legs tucked under the coffee table. She closed her textbook with a snap and pulled out her laptop.

"Of course, you can talk about your roommate. I just don't have to hear it." Mimi swung her legs over Teddy's head and stood up, swaying slightly.

"Mimi, sit your ass down." Teddy pushed her back down onto the couch, pinning her there with a strong arm across Mimi's hips, still focusing on her laptop. Mimi crossed her arms but didn't fight her. "I can't take it anymore. It's been constant bickering for weeks. You two gotta figure this shit out."

Jazz sipped her drink. "What's there to figure out? Nothing has changed except where I live."

"And who you live with!" Mimi snapped. "Living with your parents is a lot different than living with someone you have feelings for, Jazz, and you know it!"

"It doesn't matter!" Jazz protested with a frustrated sigh, finger *tap tap tapping* on her drink. "It doesn't change anything! Nothing is going to happen with them!"

"Except for a *kiss* apparently," Mimi muttered. "On my *birthday*."

It took all of Jazz's willpower to keep her anger down. Forcing herself to keep her voice low and calm, she replied, "Mimi, I've told you. It wasn't a romantic kiss. They needed aftercare, and I helped them. As a friend."

"And that is exactly why we're preclearing Blanche tonight," Teddy announced, turning around on her knees and waving her hands in the air as if to clear the negative energy between them.

Jazz huffed. "Teddy, I don't want to. There's no poi—"

Teddy pressed her finger to Jazz's lips. "The point of preclearing someone is not to give you our blessing to go bang someone else." Teddy's brown eyes looked earnestly into Jazz's. Freckles dusted her cheekbones and nose. "It's so we all know what it means for us if and when something *does* happen. And right now, Mimi and I don't know where we stand with you since you've been growing closer with Blanche."

Mimi curled into the couch again. "It feels like they're all you think about. Like you're putting more into your relationship with them than you are with us. And if that's the way you want it, fine! But be honest about it."

Jazz's chest tightened, her stomach roiling in guilt and vodka lemonades. Her finger *tap tap tapped* again. "I know I've been spending a lot of time with someone I've been crushing on since I was sixteen, but I'm not trying to put them before you. Blanche and I are friends, and that's it."

Mimi bit her lip. "I didn't say you were doing anything. I said that's how it feels."

"Okay, sorry," Jazz groaned. "I don't understand why my living with Blanche makes things different with us!"

"So let's talk about it so we can clear the air!" Teddy nodded encouragingly. "Mimi and I are both feeling a little unheard, and as much as you keep insisting everything is fine, it's not. Otherwise, this wouldn't keep triggering hurt feelings and arguments." She sat back down to find a file on her laptop. "I knew you'd never make this yourself, so I took the liberty of preparing a PowerPoint with all of the information I could find about Blanche."

"Teddy, that's fucking weird." Jazz laughed in exasperation, finger *tap tap tapping. What part of "Blanche doesn't like me" don't they understand?* But of course, it was Libra season now; the peacemaker Teddy's time to shine. "When did you even do this?"

Teddy shrugged. "It was this or my International Relations paper. Looking up Blanche was way more fun than researching European energy politics after the fall of the USSR. I told my prof I was sick and got an extension." She pushed her laptop back on the coffee table. "Ta-da! Aren't they gorgeous?"

On the screen was a photo of Blanche reclining in a lawn chair with Gabe's dog, taken from their Instagram. Jazz sighed, wrapping her hand around her pendant as Teddy dove into the information she'd found on Blanche. It was a surprising and strangely invasive amount, including shoe size (twelve in women's) and zodiac sign (Cancer Sun).

"Blanche is on wikiFeet?" Jazz asked.

Teddy nodded. "They have four and a half stars."

For someone as private as Blanche, it was odd that it had ended up readily available online. At least Teddy hadn't delved into their Sub-Party content. Everything in Teddy's PowerPoint was fairly vanilla.

Eventually, Teddy ran out of information. "Okay, now time for the hard shit!" She tapped the space bar again and a series of questions popped up on her screen:

What would you like out of a partnership with this person?

Are any needs not being met with us that you hope they can fulfill?

How would they fit into our triad/polycule? (ex: parallel, kitchen table, etc)

No matter how much she tried to keep an open mind for the sake of her partners, Jazz's eyes burned. "This is humiliating. You know that, right?"

"Tell us more," Teddy murmured, resting her head on her elbow as she looked up at Jazz. "Why do you feel humiliated?"

Jazz scoffed. "Because Blanche doesn't want to be with me! Why are you making me pretend they could? Why am I the one who has to get interrogated, when Blanche has repeatedly made it clear that they don't see me that way!"

"But *you* see them that way, Jazz!" Mimi finally snapped. "That's the point! I don't care what Blanche wants. I care about what *you* want! Yeah, I'm jealous because you're always talking about them, and you kissed them on my *birthday*!" She scoffed. "But the point is that you never open up about *your* feelings! Are you upset because we're asking questions about what you want, or because you have to admit that your crush is one-sided?"

Resentment burning in her tight chest, Jazz tried to fight the words, but they slipped out anyway. "Why do I have to do this when *Julissa* is the reason we needed to preclear partners in the first place?"

"Oh, god." Teddy rubbed her forehead.

Mimi's jaw tightened. "You said you were fine with Julissa."

"I am! She just—" Jazz caught herself. "I *feel* like she would prefer it if I wasn't in the picture. I feel shut out when she's around. Like I'm not allowed to talk to you, let alone be affectionate with you." She sniffled, hating the hot trail of a tear that rolled down her cheek.

"Baby..." Mimi softened, crawling across the couch. Her small fingers brushed Jazz's cheek. "I know it hasn't been easy, but Jules is trying. She's coming to game nights. She's making an effort to get used to seeing me with you guys, because she wants to be more involved with everyone. She wants to be friends with you. But this is all new to her—to us—and she's figuring it out."

Jazz swallowed, willing the tears to stop, for her lungs to take a deep enough breath to work through the ache in her chest. "I know not everyone is going to be my bestie like Ed is, and I don't expect her to be. I just hate feeling like I'm being replaced."

"She could never replace you, baby." Mimi cupped her cheeks, curling up in Jazz's lap. "You are both so special to me, and I love you both! You're so sweet and understanding and loving. And Jules, well...you know I can get a little more needy than you're comfortable with, and

Jules satisfies a lot of those needs. But that doesn't mean I don't love you too."

"I do like my independence," Jazz conceded. "Aquarius rising and Sag venus. Or maybe it's my attachment issues."

Mimi snorted. "Exactly. And I want to be possessed like a Victorian doll. But that's not you. You're so levelheaded and chill and generous and caring, and I love that about you. You just put everyone first, and it drives me nuts. Even with Blanche, I see you wanting something, but refusing to admit that you want it, let alone do anything to make it happen." She stroked Jazz's cheek. "Be *selfish* for once, Jazz. Be open about what you want, instead of accepting what you think you can get."

"I am selfish!" Jazz countered.

"Are you selfish, or are you finally making decisions for yourself, and you feel guilty about it?" Teddy teased, resting her head on her arm as she leaned on the couch to face them. "Because if you're selfish, you are the most considerate, generous selfish person I've ever met."

"Okay, fine!" With an exasperated laugh, Jazz squeezed Mimi's thigh. "I admit my feelings for Blanche might run a little deeper than a crush."

"You're in love with them," Mimi corrected.

Jazz huffed, her eyes burning again. "Okay, yes. Fine. I'm in love with them. That doesn't change the fact that they do not return my feelings. I don't understand why this is necessary." She gestured to the PowerPoint.

"Jazz, this is hypothetical." Teddy thought for a moment, then amended, "But, if anything changes, and something does happen—because I'm not entirely certain your crush is one-sided—Mimi and I would both be fine with that, if you're honest and open with us about it.

"For now, this conversation is just what you *would* want *if* something were to happen with you and Blanche. Okay?" Teddy gestured to the laptop. "*This* way we all are on the same page, and we know where we stand and what we can expect if anything ever does happen. We're doing this so we don't end up with another Jules situation, right? Think about this as practice for us, if any of us do want to add any new partners."

"Fine." Resigned that there was no delaying this any longer, Jazz breathed as much as she could through the knot in her chest. Identifying exactly why she wanted Blanche was difficult to articulate. "I don't think I have any needs that aren't being met. I've just had a crush on Blanche since I met them, and we're close friends now. Living with them has been maddening because I feel like the more I know about them, the stronger my feelings get. Like we already have the emotional intimacy, but not the physical intimacy. A relationship would be a natural progression of our friendship is probably the simplest way I can describe it."

"A new opportunity for love, and more love is good?" Teddy summarized with a questioning eyebrow raised toward Jazz.

"Yes. More love is good. Way simpler," Jazz laughed.

Still in Jazz's lap, Mimi snorted, genuinely smiling for the first time since their argument had started. The knot in Jazz's chest unwound enough for her to let out a relieved sigh. Finally, the conflict she'd expected to be resolved a month ago seemed like it finally might be ending.

And yet, Jazz dreaded the last question. Even considering these hypotheticals felt incredibly humiliating, but her partners would feel better discussing it, so she'd do it for their sake. "I cannot imagine Blanche even wanting to be with one college kid, let alone metamours with three or more. No offense. So I think parallel would be the best. Not to say there can't be kitchen table moments. I live with them, so it'd be hard to avoid. But I doubt they'd want to come to Ed's frat parties and shit. Or let Julissa play around in the attic."

"Fair," Mimi and Teddy said together. "Any more questions before I flip to the last slide?" Teddy asked Mimi.

Mimi chewed on her cheek for a few moments, before asking quietly. "When are you going to bring this up to Blanche?"

"I'm not." Keeping her voice level took every ounce of willpower Jazz had. "There isn't a point." She groaned, dropping her head on Mimi's shoulder. "Do I need to repeat that doing this felt really shitty? Nothing is going to happen between me and Blanche, and I don't appreciate the reminders that this is hopeless."

Mimi side-eyed her. "They're attracted to you. They kissed you back."

Admittedly, Jazz had caught Blanche checking her out. She'd noticed it more and more since the kiss. And they *had* kissed her back, as chaste as it'd been. "That's just physical attraction, Mimi. They've been very clear that they don't have feelings for me. How many more times are you going to make me say that out loud?"

"Ugh, I have so much more empathy for Ed now! Watching you talk yourself out of this is torture! How did he watch all three of us do this for a fucking year without snapping?!" Teddy slapped the table. "I'm fucking sick of you pining over them and not making a move! You're a bad bitch, Jazzy! Blanche is probably pining over you, too, telling themselves they're not good enough for you! So just fucking kiss them already!"

Jazz couldn't help but laugh, grateful for her supportive partners. "I will consider thinking about asking if they're up for more kissing. If they give me a sign they want that."

"That's all we ask. On that note," Teddy flipped to the last slide. On it was the SubParty content Jazz had been expecting: a picture of Blanche stepping on a client's neck, a flogger strategically placed to hide their...Jazz realized she'd never asked Blanche what language they used to talk about their body. Teddy smirked up at Jazz. "Are you sure you're vanilla, Jazz? Have you been holding out on us?" Teddy's phone buzzed in rapid succession and fell off the coffee table. She bent to pick it up. "Shit."

"Holy shit. Julissa was right. Blanche is stupid hot," Mimi muttered. "Have you considered getting into BDSM, Jazz? Because me and Julissa cou—"

"No! I'm very much vanilla, thank you," Jazz interrupted. "Besides, that's Blanche's job. They try very hard to separate work from the rest of their life."

Teddy grinned. "Ed will be so disappointed to hear you like dick, just not his dick."

Jazz groaned. "Seriously? Just because they're AMAB doesn't mean I like men. Even Ed. I love him, but no...!" She shuddered at the memory of her and Ed making out; neither of them had been particularly into it, both taking things so slowly to delay the part they never got to. They'd taken one look at each other's awkward expressions and started laughing, finally confessing they'd both only agreed to try dating for Teddy's sake. "Trust me, as much as I enjoyed our date night, trying to have sex with him definitely affirmed that I'm a lesbian."

"I'm teasing, Jazz," Teddy laughed and grabbed her hand, speaking quickly. "But speaking of, if anything does happen, can you please use a condom? It's one thing for Ed and I to go without since I'm his only partner, but Blanche and you wouldn't be exclusive on either side."

"Of course," Jazz nodded. "I can't imagine Blanche would have sex without protection."

"Good." Teddy nodded, her grin giddy. "Because the Vamp soundtrack just dropped about three seconds ago, and since we couldn't get tickets until tomorrow, we need to wrap this up. Mimi, anything else?"

Mimi finally tore her eyes from Blanche's picture. "Yeah, but it's something I can talk to Jazz about, while you listen to your gay vampire music."

"Just talk quietly," Teddy teased before hooking her phone up to the Bluetooth speaker with a squeal as the music started.

Jazz wrapped her arms around Mimi's hips and held her tight, finding comfort in the weight of the tiny woman in her lap. "Are we okay, Mimi?"

Mimi nodded with a shy smile. "I'm sorry for pushing you, but it felt like you were pulling away from us. And you might be an avoidant attachment rising, but I'm an anxious attachment moon." Jazz snorted, and Mimi rested her head on her shoulder. "I didn't know what would happen to us if something did happen with Blanche. And you kept refusing to acknowledge it. I felt like you were denying my feelings, but I didn't realize you were trying to reconcile your own. Communicate with us when you're struggling like this, okay?"

Jazz squeezed her girlfriend closer, struck by the simple ask to solve what had felt like an insurmountable conflict for weeks. As if it'd be that easy, after a lifetime hiding everything from everyone. After living with a father who would punish her for a hint of selfishness, and a mother who had trained her from infancy to ignore her instincts and emotions. But what was the point of moving out, if she didn't start leaving all that behind? Especially when it was Mimi and Teddy asking it of Jazz. They were her first two friends, these two women who loved her fiercely. Loved her, the real Jazz, not who they wanted her to be. With a thick swallow, Jazz nodded. "I will. I just don't want to feel this way, you know?"

"I know. It's a shitty position to be in. And not to push you more, but you should tell Blanche how you feel. I know you said there isn't anything you're missing with us, but if there's anything from being with Blanche that you're not getting now, you deserve the chance to get it." Mimi stroked Jazz's cheek, dragging her thumb across Jazz's lower lip. "And if there's anything Blanche could get from being with you, they deserve the chance to make that choice. You're doing both of you a disservice by keeping your feelings to yourself. More love is good, after all." Mimi's eyes crinkled with amusement.

There was no way to respond to that aside from kissing Mimi, who melted in Jazz's arms. That was what she loved about Mimi; she gave herself over so completely and enthusiastically and passionately. She showed Jazz how good it felt to be needed, appreciated.

Swallowing the shuddering gasp from Mimi's lips, Jazz threw herself into Mimi's kiss. Mimi's small hands roamed under Jazz's tank top, thumbs pressing against the barbells piercing her nipples.

Arching her back, Jazz squeezed Mimi's thighs before sliding higher, hand disappearing under her skirt to pull aside her panties.

Mimi whined as Jazz's fingers circled her clit. That delicious wordless beg for more, more, again, again, that Jazz would always be thrilled to give her. Jazz kissed down her jaw, murmuring praise and encouragement into Mimi's ear, as Mimi clung helpless to Jazz's arm.

"Oh, shit. Some talk," Teddy teased, finally tearing her eyes away from her laptop to climb onto the couch. "Room for me?"

"Always," Jazz broke away from Mimi to kiss Teddy. A moan escaped her as Mimi's mouth latched onto Jazz's neck. Jazz kept her hand between her legs, but kissed whatever, whoever she could reach.

Clothes were soon discarded as the three enjoyed each other, sharing touches and kisses in a familiar entanglement of legs and tongues and fingers after so long together. Music thumped along with their moans, the rhythmic beats and powerful guitar setting the pace for Jazz's fingers deep inside both of her partners.

Mimi ground on Jazz's palm, soft exhales panting against Jazz's neck as she came with a soft cry. Jazz pinned her hips down and brought her to climax again, while Teddy devoured Mimi's small breasts one after the other.

Pushing both of them away, Mimi climbed off Jazz's lap. "Your turn, baby."

As the song changed to a house track, Jazz devoured Teddy's kiss. Mimi parted her thighs to kneel in front of her, the rhythm slow and sensual.

The music built to a crescendo as Mimi licked everywhere but her clit. Just as the beat dropped into a rapid bounce track, Mimi finally pressed her tongue where Jazz wanted her most, and a familiar voice was added to the mix.

"Tonio?" Jazz sat up, inadvertently pushing Teddy away.

"Excuse me?" Mimi sounded offended. "You did not just call me by your brother-in-law's name!"

"No!" Jazz pointed to the speaker. "That's Tonio. He's on the fucking song!"

What was undeniably Carlita's voice sang over the speaker.

Teddy jumped away to her laptop. "Holy shit! Your brother-in-law has a feature on the Vamp soundtrack?!" She passed the computer to Mimi. Listed among the many names in the credits were Carlita Asada, along with Antonio and Leland Flores-Jones. Teddy shrieked, "Your brother produced a song on the Vamp soundtrack?!"

"Where's my phone?!" Jazz swung her leg carefully over Mimi to grab it from the coffee table. Her brother-in-law's voice had already killed the moment; Teddy jumping around and screaming left it dead.

She sent a rapid succession of nonsensical button-mash texts, before finally managing to send Lee and Tonio a relatively coherent "Omg wtf congrats I can't believe it!"

In response, she got an incoming video call. Jazz groaned. "Seriously? Of all the times, you have to do video when I'm naked?" She declined it and called him on the phone instead.

Antonio answered with an echoey shriek. He must be on speaker. "You heard it already?!"

"Hell yes! Teddy bought us tickets for the midnight showing tomorrow, too. Oh my god, that's so exciting!"

Antonio rambled, his excitement tangible in how fast he spoke. "We were going to use the song on our next album, but Lee sent it to the creepy producer we worked with on the first album, who happened to be working on the Vamp soundtrack, and he made it happen! Can you believe? They picked a lot of unknown queer artists of color for the soundtrack, but even so, we got so lucky."

"Why'd you decline my Facetime?" Lee asked. "We're all dressed up."

Jazz snorted. "Lee, don't ask questions you don't want to know the answer to. Let's just say hearing Tonio's voice ruined a moment." Jazz winked at Mimi and Teddy, who both grinned back at her.

"Jazz!"

She tsked. "What, like you've never listened to music during sex before?"

Lee's groan was drowned out by Antonio's cackle.

Saturday, October Second

CHAPTER NINETEEN

LEE

"Everyone, today is a very special day!" Carlita Asada announced to the buzzing venue. Lee's husband looked gorgeous as always in a red glittery cocktail dress, with layers and layers of purple tulle underneath. A blonde wig was piled high into a beehive. "Twenty-seven years ago on this very day, a very special little snowflake sashayed his way out of his momma's pussy. I want everyone to shout a Happy Motherfucking Birthday to my fine-ass husband!"

Wincing at the comments about his mother's vagina, Lee raised his glass to the audience's roar of "Happy Motherfucking Birthday!" from the VIP table next to the stage. His ears rang as his friends shouted with them.

The ice in his vodka tonic smacked him in the face. The cup was empty. Again.

With the spotlight following her, Carlita pranced across the stage, picking up dollar bills that had been thrown during her number. "And on top of that, Lee and I just had a new single drop two days ago, from the Vamp soundtrack!"

Lee grinned as the crowd exploded. It was such a relief that the restraints in the NDA were finally over. He hated not being able to tell anyone for so long. Antonio's complete inability to keep a secret had threatened to give him an ulcer. Finally, they could talk about the biggest accomplishment of their fucking lives.

Their single had been all he and Antonio could think about, talk about, dream about, for weeks. And for the song to come out so close to his birthday? *I can die happy. Or at least we can finally buy a new car.*

Someone handed Carlita a shot on stage. "Thank you, sweetie, that's very kind of you. I also take cash." The crowd laughed. She sidestepped over to hand it to Lee, holding it at arm's length. "I'm sober as a judge, so Lee is my designated shot boy tonight."

Lee tossed it back, wincing as the rail vodka burned down his throat. The things he did for love. Though no one else would see it through Carlita's makeup and stage presence, that shadow was lurking in her eyes again when she'd passed the shot to Lee. A shadow that Antonio had refused to acknowledge for weeks. Lee had been hoping that it had merely stemmed from keeping such a huge secret. That once the song was released, Antonio would be back to his usual, effervescent self. Maybe it was just from handling alcohol; Antonio had worn a similar look when he'd tried the Coopers zero-proof wine.

"Don't get him too drunk now. It's his birthday! He can't have a whiskey dick tonight!" Carlita teased as someone handed her another shot, the shadow nonexistent as she winked at Lee.

The crowd laughed again. Lee laughed with them, raising the shot glass before shooting it back. Even if Antonio might be nursing some complicated feelings, tonight was a celebration. Not just for Lee's birthday or the song, but for everything good in his life, and he deserved a fun night to enjoy it.

He was married to a wonderful, charismatic, sexy, confident man who adored him. His friends were all happy and thriving. His sister was independent, doing well in college, and in a happy relationship. *Or would it be relationships, plural?* His parents were kind of trying (and failing) to build a relationship with him again. Lee winced. But he had a production credit on one of the most anticipated movies of the year—a guaranteed hit with plenty of royalties coming their way, if the streaming numbers were anything to go by—so his dad could choke!

Before he'd met Antonio a mere two and a half years ago, Lee never would have imagined his life could transform so completely.

"Y'all know I'm not going to stop talking about this song for the rest of my fucking life! If I can be sappy for a moment, all of our dreams when we set out to make music together came true this week." Carlita blew Lee a kiss, who grinned with a dopey smile at his husband as Tara and Gabe pulled their cameras out. Tara propped her elbows on the monitor to stabilize her video, giving a thumbs-up. Carlita beamed. "With no further ado, enjoy the first ever live performance of 'Vice'!"

The lights flashed right as the music started. Lee frowned, confused. And the song was playing at the right timestamp? Freddy had agreed to come in from his parental leave to give Lee his birthday off, but that transition was too clean for Freddy. Lee sat up, craning his neck into the window of the control room. From next to the stage, Lee could see the mop of black hair belonging to the oldest Coleman kid, sitting next to Freddy in front of the soundboard.

Somehow, that made Lee feel both better and worse about sitting in the VIP booth, getting shit-faced when he should be working. Everyone else was pulling their weight with Chas and Freddy's parental leave, except Lee. Stomach churning from guilt and cheap liquor, Lee reminded himself that literally everyone, including Chas, had forbidden him from working tonight.

Tara dutifully recorded Carlita's performance, as Gabe took pictures to use in their promo on social media—one of the conditions they'd agreed to as part of the contract. *Not that we wouldn't post the hell out of it already.* Lee had already scheduled dozens of posts and stories across Carlita's social media accounts.

A crowd of girls, including that Teddy character Jazz was dating, waved dollar bills along the stage, waiting to tip Carlita as she did a handstand split. Glittery red panties peeked out from between the layers of tulle. Blanche and Gabe waited with them. As part of their choreography, Blanche held up a money gun to make it rain on Carlita, while Gabe recorded. The two of them stuck out like a sore thumb; Gabe towered over everyone, and Blanche danced in a black leather bodysuit among the sea of flannel, broken up by only a few white dresses and veils from bachelorette parties.

On cue, Carlita slid on her knees in front of Blanche to belt the chorus into Gabe's camera. Dollar bills shot into the stage, landing on Carlita's chest and face as she sang into the camera. She pushed into a backflip to collect the many tips from her waiting fans.

Lee loved how acrobatic his husband was. And flexible. He sighed happily, appreciating that he was married to such an athletic, sexy, fun, talented man.

"You okay, Lee? You look like you're about to cry," Sunny handed him another vodka tonic as the bridge started.

Lee's throat tightened. "I just love him so much."

"Oh, no. You're drunk." Sunny frowned at the drink she'd handed him. "I should have brought you water."

The song ended before Lee could get too emotional about his husband's flexibility. Carlita gratefully accepted more tips, sending a couple more shots his way. Lee took them cheerfully, even though taking tequila and whiskey right after one another was a terrible idea.

Blanche set the money gun down on the table, took one look at Lee, and disappeared into the crowd.

"So how much have you had to drink?" Sunny asked, sipping on her vodka cran.

"Who cares?" Lee cried, lifting the last shot of tequila as a toast to Sunny and Richard. His vodka tonic was already empty. "I'm drunk on glory and joy!"

"Drunk on too many shots is more like it," Tara teased, reclaiming her seat next to him. Gabe slid into the booth next to her. "Though it is nice to see you let loose for once. I didn't get to witness you this drunk at your bachelor party."

"Where did Blanche go?" Sunny asked. "Do you think they went to dance with Jazz—Ouch, Dicky! Stop pinching me!"

Lee screwed his face up in confusion. "Why would they go to dance with Jazz?"

"I'm just saying, they kind of coordinated their outfits today. They look cute together!" Sunny said, before turning to Richard. "I swear to god, Dicky if you don't stop pinching me, I'm going to smack you."

Jazz had been wearing... Lee couldn't remember. It was at least more modest than the last few times she'd been to Confession. It was opaque; that was all he cared about. She had worn a mesh shirt to the show a few weeks ago that exposed *far* too much. Hopefully, she wasn't dressing so— Lee huffed, annoyed. There was that judgmental asshole mentality again.

As if summoned, Blanche, in a leather bodysuit and lace maxi skirt, set a plate of fries and a pitcher of water in front of him. "Here, shot boy. Eat some carbs and grease."

"Blanche, I love you!" Lee crammed a handful of fries into his mouth. "Where is Jazz, anyway?"

"She went downstairs to dance with her partners." Tara was eyeing the fries too, so Lee nudged the basket in her direction. She beamed at him, popping a few in her mouth, shoulders dancing as she ate.

Lee stared at her. "You're going to be a mom! Like with a baby! And married!" Something else the Lee of two and a half years ago would have found impossible to believe.

"Yup, that's happening all right." Tara grinned. "But 'parent,' please. Still feeling weird about someone calling me 'mom.'"

Lee nodded. "Moms can suck, can't they?"

Tara laughed. "They can. I don't want to suck."

"You won't suck, Buttercup. You're fucking fantastic!" He hugged her, squeezing Tara tight. "And so smart! And cool!"

"Drink your water, Lee."

"Ooh, fries!" Jazz said as she appeared, reaching a hand to grab them. Lee squinted to focus on what she was wearing. Faux leather pants and a lace blouse. She and Blanche *were* coordinating. *Huh. Sunny was right.*

"Wait, no!" Lee smacked at her hand as she reached the basket, but Jazz was too quick. *It wasn't like this when we were kids. She was always the slow one.*

His sister grinned at him as she ate her prize.

"Blanche! Jazz stole a fry!" Lee whined.

Blanche smiled kindly at him. "Sorry, Lee. I don't care. I'm not your parent."

Lee stuck his tongue out at Jazz. "Obviously. You took me in instead of kicking me out. Not all of us had the privilege of staying in the closet until it was safe."

Jazz's face fell.

Lee groaned out an apology immediately; he'd fucked up. This was why he never drank this much. He couldn't keep the inside thoughts from escaping. He was still so angry at his parents, but that wasn't Jazz's fault. They were fucking up her life, too.

Blanche patted his hand from across the table. "Don't blame her for that, Lee. She saw the other side of what happened when you were outed. Can you blame her for not telling them?"

"I'm going to tell them." Jazz didn't meet his eyes. "I just needed to move out first, make sure I could take care of myself, in case they did it to me too. And now I have, and I want to tell them. I just...it's hard."

"I'm sorry. I should have been there for you." His eyes burned.

Jazz grabbed his hands from across the table. "It's not your fault. Blame Dad."

"Eat all the damn French fries you want, Jazz." He wiped the tears rolling down his cheeks away on his sleeve. *Damn, I must be drunk if I'm crying in public.*

Tara put her arm around him, rubbing his back.

When Jazz finally looked at him, her eyes were wet, too.

Blanche pulled her into a hug. "You two are both so drunk."

"Welcome back— Excuse me, why the fuck is my husband crying on his birthday?" Carlita had returned to the stage to emcee the second half. She put her hand on her hip, now wearing a blue bodysuit and thigh-high fishnets. The lights fell, spotlighting her as the crowd hushed.

"Sorry, it's my fault," Blanche teased. "I bought French fries. Accidentally set off drunk sibling feelings."

Carlita laughed, sitting on the stage so she could kiss Lee's cheek. "You're crying over French fries, Angel?"

Lee nodded, wiping his eyes. "Jazz stole one." He'd probably be embarrassed by this tomorrow, when he remembered the literal spotlight had been on him when he was crying in public—at *work*. But considering they'd gotten engaged and married on this stage, this was at least the third time this had happened. Lee didn't need to care.

Besides, the spotlight was technically on Antonio; Lee just happened to be at his side.

"Oh god, I love you, but I'm cutting you off." Her hand covered the headset mic as she murmured in Lee's ear. "Let the tears out for once, my love. You're going to feel so much better." Carlita smoothed her bodysuit as she rose. "Okay, time for a new shot boy! Gabey Baby, stand up, wave to the crowd."

Glaring at Antonio, Gabe waved once, before crossing his arms and slumping in his chair.

"My best friend Gabe here is about to get married and has a baby on the way. And this motherfucker won't let me plan a bachelor party for him, so help him celebrate tonight! Don't get him too drunk though, he's gotta be able to walk in the door. He's tall and big—if you know what I mean. I don't think his fiancée could carry him."

"Challenge accepted, Tonio!" Tara called.

Carlita laughed. "She said challenge accepted. Bitch, worry about carrying your baby, not your man."

The crowd laughed, and Carlita introduced the next performer. Lee poured himself some water. It may be his birthday, and it may be a celebration, and no one would judge him if he let loose and had some fun. But Lee was still himself, and he didn't like feeling so out of control. Especially not at work, or when Antonio was still secretly upset, or when Lee was making Jazz cry by not watching what he said. He needed to sober up if he couldn't act right.

CHAPTER TWENTY

BLANCHE

AFTER THE SHOW, BLANCHE helped Lee downstairs to the dance floor. A task that should have been far easier than it was. By this point, he and Gabe were both fucked up after downing shot after shot, despite Antonio's constant reminders that he was sober.

Tara was faring slightly better with helping Gabe down the stairs. He was holding his liquor better and—in his usual doting manner—he was attempting to help her, too. Which meant he kept stopping to feel her ass every few steps with a foolish grin on his face.

Lee, on the other hand, was a fucking anchor around Blanche's neck.

At least he'd recovered from his earlier emotional spell, so Lee was back to his easygoing self. Just deeply uncoordinated. Eventually, Blanche got him down to the dance floor and deposited him on a barstool next to Mimi. Jazz's partner merely nodded in greeting as she sipped a White Claw.

"Taking a break from dancing?" Blanche asked her as they caught their breath. They were regretting the leather bodysuit; sweat coated their skin.

Gabe must have caught a second wind from the thumping music, because he dragged a grinning Tara to the dance floor with a mischievous grin.

"Yeah, got too hot. Looks like he's having a fun night," Mimi said dryly, smiling at Blanche before nodding toward Lee.

Blanche blinked in surprise at Mimi *smiling*. At *them*? "Too much fun, I think. The crowd was a little too generous tonight." Carlita had eventually started calling Venus out to start taking shots after Gabe tapped out, and Blanche had had their fair share of any brown liquor. This level of raucousness was more typical of Pride weekends, not a random Saturday in October. But the Vamp movie already had a feral sapphic fanbase, and word had spread quickly that a local drag queen had been featured on the album. Most likely thanks to Teddy, Blanche imagined.

Swaying on his barstool, Lee danced with his eyes closed. His hand stayed on Blanche's shoulder, pulling on them as he moved. Probably for the best. He'd fall off otherwise.

"You know Jazz talks about you all the time," Mimi said, too casually.

"Does she?" Blanche tried to ignore the pleased glow in their heart. They thought about Jazz too much as it was, especially since that kiss. Hopefully Mimi wouldn't notice their blush in the pink and blue lighting of the bar. With how much whiskey they'd had, Blanche had no hope of controlling it.

While the first week or so had been awkward, in the past few days, there'd been a shift between them, despite Blanche's best efforts to create space. Jazz had always been affectionate and sweet, but it was now apparent that Jazz had been showing restraint this whole time.

Jazz didn't have just one love language; she used all of them. She gave Blanche compliments and touches and gifts and favors and movie nights every day from sunup to sundown. Blanche felt powerless to stop their crush from deepening. She was so...sweet. They couldn't find it in themselves to talk about boundaries or ask her to stop. It was easier to be generous and affectionate in return.

Even when they'd been getting ready to come here tonight, Jazz's energy had been infectious. Blanche had found her trying on clothes in front of the full-length mirror in the bathroom, wearing only the lace blouse and a thong. Once their brain had regained any function, they'd offhandedly suggested they both wear lace, since they had a skirt in the same pattern as her blouse. Which had led to Jazz helping Blanche pick out what to wear. Which led to Blanche lending her their pants (which hugged Jazz's round hips *far* better than they'd ever graced Blanche's), which led to Jazz doing their makeup. Which led to Blanche sitting at her desk, while she straddled their lap, their jaw firmly grasped in her hand, while they were mere inches from her full, soft lips. Nearly irresistible, they'd been parted in concentration as she winged Blanche's eyeliner.

"We had to have a talk about jealousy." Mimi pursed her lips, snapping Blanche out of their fevered memory. "I was under the impression that she was hiding feelings for you. But after our talk, I'm good."

Mimi's words drenched Blanche in cold water. If Mimi had been jealous, it was no wonder she'd been so standoffish before. Blanche's heart hurt at the thought that Mimi no longer had anything to be jealous of. That the kiss had just been platonic for Jazz, while Blanche was completely melting down, unable to drive it from their mind. That the increased affection between them was simply Jazz being more comfortable as friends and roommates. That Jazz's crush had faded, as Blanche's grew.

They took a breath, trying to play it off, fully aware of overprotective Lee behind them. Even if he might not remember the conversation. "Oh, there's nothing to be jealous of here. Just dear friends and roommates."

Mimi shook her head, her black hair glinting blue and pink in the lights of the dance floor. "You've been preapproved by the polycule in any case, whatever happens."

Blanche didn't know what Mimi meant. With Lee in earshot, they were reluctant to ask.

Before they could find a way to phrase it subtly, Carlita joined them. Freddy and three of his kids were right behind her, like ducklings waddling after their mama. Freddy held a sleeping Catalina to his chest; the noise-canceling headphones over her ears matched her siblings.

"You brought all the kids to the bar?" Blanche teased. "Dad of the year!"

The three who were still awake hugged them to a chorus of "Auntie Blanche!" Blanche scooped up Sebastian, the third eldest, before he could toddle into the dance floor. "Are you having fun tonight, my lovelies?"

Marisol nodded. "Grandma had bingo night, so we came to work with Daddy, so Mama could sleep when Elena did."

Leo wrinkled his nose. "Elena's boring. All she does is sleep."

Blanche snorted. "Were you good helpers?"

They all nodded. "I got to hit play on the music!" Marisol beamed.

"Freddy, can you be a dear and help me get Lee to my car?" Carlita asked.

Lee opened his eyes with a grin that lit up his face at the sound of his husband's voice. "Babe, I can walk! I'm so good at walking!"

"I'm sure you can, Angel, but not in a straight line. Sorry for getting you so drunk." Carlita kissed his cheek.

"S'ok." Lee bashed his head against Antonio's. "I'm having the best fucking birthday."

"Then let's go home and make it even better, okay?" Carlita patted his chest as Tara and Gabe emerged from the crowd.

Lee nodded and stood, wavering as he blinked slowly. Blanche was not jealous of the hangover he'd have tomorrow morning. Freddy quickly handed the still-sleeping Catalina to Tara to help steady him. He signed to his kids, telling them to stay with Blanche.

"Can we have cherries?" Leo asked.

Freddy flagged Jackie down, who gave them a cup full of cherries. She showed Marisol and Leo how to tie the stem into a knot with their tongues to keep them busy.

Teddy emerged from the dance floor with Jazz, only to drag Mimi back instead. Jazz took her vacant barstool instead, putting her arms around Blanche's waist from behind and pulling them against her. "You found a kid!"

"My nephew, Bash!" Blanche explained, leaning into her arms. Sebastian buried his head into Blanche's chest, suddenly shy.

Sunny was flushed pink when she found them again, and Richard was smirking. Blanche knew they should probably pull away from Jazz before Sunny said anything, but they couldn't find it within them to care. *Let Sunny talk shit.* After all, this was just affection between friends, apparently. Blanche fussed with their nephew's shoe, unsure why they were so bothered by Jazz respecting the boundary they'd set.

Gabe sat down on the barstool Lee had left unoccupied. He grinned stupidly at Tara holding the sleeping toddler, wedging his hands into the pockets of her jeans to pull her closer. Tara smiled patiently as she let herself be pulled between his legs, awkwardly readjusting Catalina in her arms, checking how Blanche held Sebastian to make sure she was doing it right.

"Babes, you're going to be a good parent. The look suits you." Blanche offered with a nod. Tara huffed at the compliment, lifting the toddler a bit more comfortably against her chest.

Gabe apparently agreed; his hands rested on her belly under her shirt. The bump was barely noticeable under her baggy sweater, until Gabe's giant hands highlighted it.

Lips brushed Blanche's neck as Jazz whispered in their ear, "What a cute family they'll—" Jazz huffed. "One sec. Teddy's waving me down. Be right back." Her absence chilled Blanche's back as Jazz returned to the dance floor.

Sunny stole Jazz's chair. "You two look cozy. What's going on there?"

Blanche shook their head. "Nothing like what you're asking about, Babygirl. Just two affectionate roommates."

"Sure, okay. I believe you," Sunny teased.

Blanche simply shook their head. "Was there a line for the Confessionals?" they teased to avoid the question.

Sunny flushed red. "I have no shame in my mild exhibition game. Just saying, if that changes, I'm happy for you. You deserve someone sweet like her to have your back. She might be able to handle you better than anyone."

Blanche shook their head. Jazz was surprisingly levelheaded, a good communicator, assertive, and compassionate. But handling difficult conversations between partners who were all college students was very different from the difficulties and dangers of being with Blanche. And Jazz should have light, fun, relationships. She shouldn't need to be emotionally mature; she'd experienced enough heaviness in her life. Blanche refused to add to it.

Not that Jazz wanted them to, *apparently*.

"Keep an open mind," Sunny said in a singsong. "We've all taken risks and grown from them. Even if they didn't work out the way we wanted right away, it's all been for the best. You've been so good about taking risks with your career, maybe it's time to do the same with your heart too."

Blanche laughed as Sebastian yawned against their chest and slumped over with a snore. "Babygirl, here I thought you were about to talk shit. Instead, you're sitting here giving me a therapy session."

Sunny laughed, pulling them into a hug and ruffling the sleeping toddler's hair. "You've given me enough of them over the years. But speaking of talking shit, was that a kiss on the neck I saw? That certainly is very affectionate for a roommate."

Blanche scoffed. "She was talking, and her lips happened to touch my neck!"

Richard must have overheard, because he narrowed his eyes. "Sunshine, are you meddling?"

Sunny rolled her eyes. "I might be. What are you going to do about it?"

Richard gripped her elbow. "You have been getting on my last nerve tonight, Doll. One offhand observation, and you start causing trouble. We're going home."

Sunny winked at Blanche as they left. Blanche shook their head, fighting a proud smile. The shy Sunny who had asked for their help discovering her sexual side had blossomed into a vibrant woman. Richard had grown into a quiet confidence himself, right alongside her. While they couldn't take all the credit, Blanche considered them a personal success.

Freddy returned to take Catalina back from Tara, who shook out her arms. "Let's go, Coop. You know how I feel about driving at night. Better to leave now before the bar closes."

"Gladly, Kitten. Unless you need to use the bathroom first? I can come with you." Gabe kissed her neck once more. Tara laughed and walked away. He dutifully followed her to the Confessionals, stumbling after her. His hands stayed firmly in her back pockets to keep himself upright.

Blanche rose to follow Freddy to his minivan in the parking garage, stroking Sebastian's cheek. Freddy's child slept peacefully in their arms, blissfully unaware of the sadness rolling through Blanche. The tuft of dark hair that he and all of his siblings got from their father always reminded Blanche of Daisy.

Daisy would have loved Bash. All of her brother's kids. She'd been so excited when Chas got pregnant, only to have her life cut short weeks before Marisol was due.

Marisol and Leo laughed as they ran ahead to reach the car first, letting out the same sigh that their dad did—that Daisy had—as they caught their breath.

Daisy and Blanche had discussed kids a couple of times, but with Blanche's conundrum of a body, who knew if that ever would have happened? Besides, kids were something Daisy had wanted. Blanche...well, Blanche didn't. Even if they loved Freddy and Chas's kids, Blanche was perfectly happy being an auntie, a friend to their ducklings, and a domme to their clients. They wanted to live life for themself. For the first time, they didn't feel guilty for wanting something different from Daisy.

"THE THING I MISS most about my old apartment was how close it was to everything." Blanche's thigh muscles burned as they climbed the bluff that earned the Hillside neighborhood its name. A brisk October breeze, scented with the promise of rain, blew against them, encouraging them to hurry home. "And how flat it was. I'm too old for this shit."

Jazz laughed, equally breathless from the walk. She held out her arm, a silent offer of support. "I said we could call an Uber."

Blanche looped their arm through hers, even if it wouldn't necessarily make it easier for either of them to walk so close together. But her body was warm as they huddled together. "I said I'm old, not dead. I can walk two miles." A car slowed as its headlights passed over them. The blaring music cut through the silence of the early morning hours. Blanche and Jazz both stiffened, their hands finding each other with a squeeze. They both waited silently until it sped away. "Still, it'd be a good idea to catch the last bus home in the future."

Jazz hummed in agreement as they paused to catch their breath once the street leveled out. Neither let go of each other's hand. Instead, their fingers laced together tight.

"Jazzy, can I ask you something?" Perhaps they were looking for trouble by asking a question they could probably guess the answer to, but it was going to come up at some point. Or at least that's how the Shayla in Blanche's mind rationalized it. With how much Blanche had to drink, mixed emotions roiled under their skin. The walk and chill night air had helped sober them up, but not enough to keep them from running their mouth.

"Of course, Beautiful!"

Just as the rain started to fall in a cold spritz across their face, Blanche flicked open the gate latch at their front sidewalk. The house looked gray in the rainy evening, the only pink visible on the porch, where the light was on to guide them home. "Mimi told me I was preapproved by the polycule. What does that mean?"

Jazz tripped over the step as they held the gate open for her. Without letting go of her hand, Blanche caught her around the waist to steady her. The gate swung out against their hip. Oh, that was a terrible idea. Jazz's body pressed against theirs was the best torture.

"Of course she did." Stepping away, Jazz rubbed her forehead with the hand that wasn't holding Blanche's, leaving them cold as they hurried along the sidewalk to get out of the rain. "So obviously, we can have partners outside of our triad. But after Mimi started dating Julissa, it triggered some jealousy issues in all of us. So we agreed we needed to get any potential partners preapproved before we pursue another relationship."

Blanche waited expectantly as they unlocked the door. They weren't a new partner.

"And Mimi was jealous because I... Well, because I moved in with you, when I've been crushing on you for literal years. Not that I'm letting that impact our living situation or friendship or anything," Jazz added in a rush. "Anyway, Teddy insisted that we test out our preapproval conversation to give Mimi a chance to voice her worries. Even though I told them you didn't want anything like that." She grimaced, groaning, "Sorry she mentioned it—I've been trying very hard to not make it weird, and that's exactly the kind of shit that'd make it weird. She's very encouraging, but sometimes it crosses over into meddling."

Blanche pursed their lips, confused. Maybe they'd had more to drink than they expected, because this wasn't clicking. Jazz *did* have feelings for them? Then why was Mimi's jealousy no longer an issue? "Don't be sorry. I was just curious what she meant." While they'd also been trying to keep their own crush away from this friendship, they were a hot mess about it. Some things were best left unacknowledged. Wanting was bitter when it was hopeless.

Tossing their keys on the entry table (missing the dish Jazz had put there to hold the things that went missing easily for Blanche, like keys), Blanche kicked their shoes off. Before Jazz could say anything, they stacked them neatly on the shoe rack and put the keys where they were supposed to go, preening at Jazz's silent nod of approval. "Sorry for causing relationship drama. You can do way better than someone like me."

The house groaned with a strong gust of wind, and the sprinkle outside turned to heavy drops, beating against the windows.

Jazz frowned. "Don't sell yourself short. You're gorgeous and funny and confident and sweet and so resilient and wonderful. I want you. I'm not ashamed or embarrassed to say it. I've accepted that my feelings are one-sided, so I try not to bring it up because I don't want to make you uncomfortable. But that doesn't make it any less true."

Blanche snorted. *If only things were that easy.* "I was talking more about how it'd look for someone like me to take advantage of the sheltered young college student living with me."

"You can corrupt me anytime." Jazz winked over her shoulder, tucking her shoes next to theirs on the rack.

"You know what I mean, Jazzy. We both know I'm not a creep preying on you. But as far as the world sees it, you can do better than a trans femme sex worker who is fifteen years older than you." Blanche huffed. "It has nothing to do with how we feel about each other."

Jazz whirled around, her eyes narrowing. She stepped closer to Blanche, eyes bright. "'How *we* feel about each other?'"

"Shit." With a heavy swallow of regret, Blanche backed away as Jazz's warm brown eyes examined them, bumping into the front door behind them. The oak creaked, and the oval window cutout made Blanche shiver when their bare skin grazed against it. "Forget I said that. Blame the whiskey."

"Uh no. Not forgetting that." Jazz shook her head, stalking slowly toward them with a pleased glint in her eye. "Frankly, I've seen you much drunker than you are right now, and you've never said anything like that before."

"It doesn't matter what I feel, Jazzy." The door handle prodded Blanche's hip, and the cold glass sealed against the exposed skin between their shoulder blades. Goosebumps erupted over their whole body, their breath growing shallow as their heart pounded.

"Hard disagree, Blanche. What *you* feel? That changes everything." Jazz pressed them against the door, her hips and breasts brushing Blanche's as she cupped their jaw, an echo of how she'd done their make-up earlier. Their faces mere inches apart, Jazz's thumb stroked Blanche's lower lip, eyes searching for permission.

The only answer Blanche could muster was a shuddering inhale, before they raised their mouth to meet hers.

Vulnerability tasted like gin and vanilla Chapstick. Desire burned like Jazz's tongue delving between their lips. Honesty ached like their shared sigh of relief as Blanche gripped the back of Jazz's neck to pull her closer.

Jazz's mouth devoured them, first in breathless kisses, then in harder bites down Blanche's neck. Hands roamed down Blanche's torso, fingertips tracing the exposed skin of their back. Blanche's thigh instinctively hitched around her hip when she squeezed their ass and rolled her hips against theirs.

The lips sucking the hollow of their throat smiled against their skin when a moan escaped them. "Fuck, Blanche, you sound gorgeous."

She wanted a performance then. Moans and vocal approval, sensuality. Maybe she'd pay more if Blanche— "Stop."

Jazz froze and immediately stepped away. She looked as wrecked as Blanche felt, panting with swollen lips. Her pierced nipples were taut against the thin fabric of her bralette under the lace blouse. "What's wrong?"

"I can't..." Blanche shook their head. Around them, the house creaked in the wind.

"Blanche, don't tell me you didn't want that. That you don't want me." Jazz shook her head, her voice breaking as she pleaded. "Please. I know you did!"

"No, I did. I do! I just..." Rubbing their forehead, Blanche searched for the right words. For once, Shayla's voice had fallen completely silent. "I don't know how to...we're both drunk, and it's late, and..."

Jazz pressed her lips together and nodded. "You want space to think."

"Yes." Space to think about what had just happened, and overthink if Blanche could ever want anyone without losing themself, and hate themself for wanting someone who they shouldn't. Someone who had shown Blanche what it meant to feel safe and whole and to live again. Someone who it would kill them to lose.

"Okay." Jazz stepped closer again, taking Blanche's hands. Her thumbs pressed Blanche's palms as she kissed the inside of their wrists. "But we *are* going to talk about this tomorrow. So think long and hard about what you want. Not what anyone else would think, or what you're supposed to say. Not what *I* want, not what *Lee* would want, not even what Daisy would want. Okay?"

Blanche nodded. Before they could overthink it, Blanche leaned forward to press a single kiss against Jazz's lips.

Jazz's smile was impossible to read, but her eyes were wide and vulnerable as she stepped back. "Good night, Blanche."

"Night," Blanche whispered. They stayed pressed against the door, hip aching where the handle still pressed into their bones as their pulse

raced. Rain pattered against the windows as Blanche sighed, and the back
of their head hit the glass with a *thunk*.

Sunday, October Third

Chapter Twenty-One

Jazz

JUST AS DAWN BROKE, and rosy light filled the tower room, Blanche stormed in, tightening the belt of their velvet dressing gown as they paced around the parlor. Their hair was tangled and frizzy, as if they'd been rolling around in bed all night. "I have too much baggage for a relationship."

Still half asleep, Jazz blinked and inhaled the warm turmeric scent of her golden milk, before taking a slow sip. "Good morning."

"Sorry! Good morning," Blanche huffed, not slowing their steps.

"Didn't sleep much?" With an amused smile, Jazz tucked her legs up on the love seat to keep her toes safe from Blanche's frantic pacing. She hadn't either, but seeing what a mess Blanche was this morning was a little validating that Jazz wasn't alone in her apprehensive yet thrilled insomnia last night. Though Blanche probably hadn't written any awful poems about their feelings, the way Jazz had.

Blache scoffed, then groaned, rubbing their eyes. As if the makeup they hadn't removed last night needed more smearing. "I'm sorry—I got caught up in the moment last night, and I should never have—"

"Blanche." Jazz shook her head, disappointed yet unsurprised at the frantic excuses flying from Blanche. "Sit down."

With a sigh, Blanche sat on the other end of the love seat, back and shoulders rigid.

"Drink your tea."

"What tea?" they snapped.

With an affectionate smile and a heavy heart, Jazz nodded to the still-steaming mug of calming tea on the side table. "We're going to drink our tea and start our morning with our usual sleep-deprived comfortable silence. Then we'll talk, okay?"

With a nod, Blanche softened into the couch as they picked it up. "Thank you." The smudged mascara circles under their eyes made them look drained, instead of their usual glorious chaotic self.

If everything was going to change between them, Jazz wanted this moment of normalcy. The peace and calm of watching the morning pass by together, even if neither Blanche nor Jazz was peaceful or calm. Despite the overwhelming hope that had kept her awake, Jazz was a little irritated, a little hungover, and a lot anxious, dreading the awkwardness of this conversation.

And Blanche? Well, their vibes were all over the place.

Their foot bounced the entire time they inhaled their tea. Jazz was barely halfway through her golden milk, when Blanche set their mug down with a loud *thunk*. By the time Jazz drained the grainy dregs at the bottom of her cup, the sash of Blanche's robe was twisted and wrinkled from where they kept twisting and yanking the ends of it.

Jazz took a breath and set her mug down on the table. "What do you want, Blanche?"

"Last night was a mis—"

Gripping her amethyst, Jazz shook her head. There weren't any concrete negative thoughts to *tap tap tap* away, but she wanted the comfort of the cool crystal in her palm. "What do you *want*, Blanche?"

Blanche huffed. "It doesn't matt—"

"What. Do. You. Want."

Their jaw tensed as they glared at the floor. "What do *you* want?"

Jazz's laugh sounded as bitter as it tasted. "Beautiful, I laid my cards on the table last night. My answer hasn't changed."

"Tell me."

"I want you." Her head fell back on the couch, letting the words spill from her heart. "As a roommate, as a friend, but also as a lover, as a partner. I don't care if it lasts one night or a decade. Let me adore you in whatever way we're comfortable with, for as long as we want, and I'll let you do the same." She swallowed, her throat thick. "As long as we don't lose each other when it's over, and as long as you don't pretend it's casual or meaningless, or feel guilty because of how you think others will see it. I know what I'm about."

"I don't."

"Don't what?" Jazz rolled to her side to look at Blanche.

They bit their lip. "Know what I'm about."

"Tell me more."

"She always made the plans for us." Blanche fussed with their hair, smoothing it over one shoulder, tugging their fingers through the snarls. "She decided what we wanted and made it happen. I was just along for the ride on her grand adventure."

"Daisy, you mean?" Jazz asked softly, taking Blanche's hand in hers.

Blanche nodded. "And she's gone, and I've been living for everyone else since. Freddy, Chas, Tara, Lee, Sunny—everything I've done is to keep them safe and alive and healthy and happy. Even my online stuff—that was for Tara and Lee. Yes, I benefited too, but they needed a safety net, when my former patron started caring more about his fiancée than himself." They squeezed Jazz's hand. "And now they don't need me anymore, and I'm not sure what to do with myself. I forgot how to be selfish. The only time I put myself first is when my survival is threatened."

Jazz laced their fingers together. "You deserve to be whole, instead of splitting yourself into pieces for people. You deserve to love yourself and dream and get everything you want. You deserve better than surviving, Blanche."

Blanche squeezed her hand. "You always say something that made me wish I could cry."

"And you always say shit that blows my fucking mind, because I didn't know someone could experience everything you have without crying." Jazz huffed. "When's the last time you did?"

"I don't remember." Blanche's brow furrowed. "Before Grandma Rose died, because I kept waiting for the tears when I found her body, but they never came."

"The fuck?" Jazz sighed, fighting the urge to curl up alongside them, like she did every time Blanche said something heartbreaking. This conversation needed to be had at a distance. "You haven't cried in over twenty years?"

"I know. I'm a terrible Cancer," Blanche laughed. "You keep asking what I want, and everything I can think of is so...simple yet impossible. I want someone to care about me. I want someone to put me first, the way I put everyone I care about first. I want someone who loves me and cares about me, like Daisy—no, *better* than Daisy did. I adored her, but she never listened. I want to be heard."

"That's not simple, but it's not impossible either," Jazz murmured. "Do you get any of those needs met now?"

They shrugged. "In some ways. Shayla hears me, but I pay her to. My ducklings care about me, but they have to put themselves and their relationships first. I would never ask Lee to put me before Tonio, or Freddy to prioritize me over his family. I like the relationships I have with the clients I have left, but that's not me. That's who they need me to be."

"You can be loved, safely and wholly, not just for whatever services you're providing." Jazz gave in. Leaning against their side, she rested her head on their shoulder. "Even if you don't want me, you can find someone to experience that with. It's not a betrayal to move on with your life, Blanche."

"That's what Shayla said, too," they scoffed. "It would be nice to have a partner," Blanche admitted into Jazz's hair. "At least one who doesn't use me, or make me paranoid that they're going to be the next stalker like some of my old clients did."

"Anyone who uses you or makes you paranoid is not a real partner, Blanche." Jazz scoffed. "If *you* want, *I* want to be that person for you. Someone who cares about you and listens to you and—well, I can't put you first because I'm twenty-one, and I need to put me first—but we can put *ourselves* first, together."

"Jazz," Blanche sighed. "We shouldn't—"

Jazz interrupted their rehearsed excuses with a finger to their lips. "Let me finish before you tell me what we 'should' or 'shouldn't' do, just because of what other people will say. I'm not asking for expectations or exclusivity or commitment. Even if you want that, I can't give that to you. I haven't even told my parents about my fucking nose ring yet, let alone being queer or polyamorous. At this rate, it'll probably be years before anyone who isn't in my polycule knows who I'm dating.

"What I can give you is someone to look out for you, the way you look out for me. I can love on you, and have fun with you, and remind you to prioritize yourself. I want to add kissing and dancing and romance to our friendship. I want us to adore each other when we're alone, without holding back for the sake of other people's comfort who aren't even here. I want you in whatever way we decide that we want. Do you want that, too?"

Blanche opened their mouth, and closed it repeatedly, as if unsure how they wanted to respond.

Jazz's heart clenched; their indecision made her already floundering hope sink. "And I don't want a yes if it's because you're too nice to tell me no. I'd rather gracefully get rejected than fuck up our friendship with something you don't mean. Do you, Blanche, the inner selfish 'living and not just surviving' version of Blanche, want a relationship like that with me?"

Blanche's "Yes" was immediate and sure.

Jazz tittered in surprise. "What?"

"Yes," Blanche repeated.

Jazz blinked, her stomach in knots that hadn't been there before. She'd spent all night figuring out what she wanted to say, because she finally had the chance to say it, all while fully expecting to be gently rejected. "Shit, I didn't think you'd say yes!"

Blanche huffed. "Really, you give me a speech like that and then act surprised? Don't make me question it. I'll overthink it. I'm already overthinking it!"

Jazz laughed, still in shock that this was real, that this was happening. That the speech she'd drunkenly composed last night had been enough to convince Blanche, who had hundreds of fans begging for their attention, to take a chance on Jazz. "Can I kiss you?"

Blanche nodded again, holding up a hand against her chest as Jazz leaned in. Jazz froze, wondering if she'd fucked this up already. "Just...can we take it slow? I...I don't know how to be present. Last night, I stopped us because Work Blanche took over. And I don't know how to have intimacy where I'm not performing for someone else. Even with Daisy, I've never...I've never really had that."

Jazz nodded, fighting the "what the fuck" simmering on her tongue. "We'll take it as slow as you want. You tell me what you want and need, and I'll tell you what I want and need, and where that aligns, that's what we do. Okay?"

"Okay." Blanche hesitated. "I want...I want you to kiss me like you did last night."

With a smirk, Jazz cupped their jaw, her thumb tracing their plush lower lip. "How did I kiss you last night?"

Blanche's lips captured the tip of her thumb in the tiniest kiss. "Like you needed me."

"God, Blanche, you're so fucking precious." Jazz surged forward to devour the shy smile that bloomed on Blanche's face.

Blanche gasped that adorable shuddering sound into her mouth again, giving Jazz more access to kiss them senseless. They felt just as perfect under her as they had the night before: muscles firm under curves that she couldn't wait to explore. Their blunt nails dug into her shoulder. Soft whines fell from their lips, so much more delicate than Jazz expected from someone so collected and confident. The reality of Blanche was better than Jazz had ever imagined.

When Blanche tensed under her, she pulled away, sitting back on her heels. Jazz traced down Blanche's arm to take their hand. "You okay?"

"Yeah." Blanche bit their lip and crossed their legs as they sat up. "Just don't want to escalate before I'm ready."

This might be new, but Jazz could see something was worrying them through the way they bit their lip. "And?"

Blanche threw a look at her. "You uh...know I'm intersex, right? And non-binary, or whatever. Genderqueer? Fem-ish?" They scoffed. "Maybe I should use labels."

Jazz raised an eyebrow. "Are you asking if I know that you have a dick? Or whatever word you prefer? Because I love all women, trans women included."

"For the record, any word is fine. It's my body, and it's perfect, regardless of what anyone calls it." Blanche hugged themself. "But yes, that's just it. Specifically, my gender, more than my body. You are a lesbian, and I'm not sure if I fit into what you want. Even though I present quite feminine, I am not a *woman...*" Blanche huffed. "Why is this so hard to explain?"

Jazz took their other hand. "Beautiful, I want you exactly as you are, assuming you're cool with me being exactly who I am. Me being a lesbian is not a reflection on you." She laughed. "Do I know you're intersex? Really? Have you ever Googled yourself with the safe search off? Yes, fully aware of what you look like naked."

Their light bronze skin darkened into a rosy blush. Blanche pressed their fingers to their lips. "You Googled me?"

Jazz snorted. "Blanche, I hate to break it to you, but you are internet famous. You have four and a half stars on wikiFeet! Not only have *I* Googled you, but Teddy has a PowerPoint of your nudes, Julissa subscribes to your channel, and even Mimi has been sending me screenshots as encouragement to make a move on you." Maybe she shouldn't be spilling all of her polycule's secrets like this, but it felt one-sided; the world had full access to Blanche, and they seemed to be under the impression that they were known only to a few strangers on the Internet. Jazz counted herself fortunate that she was one of the few who got to see the real Blanche.

Blanche covered their laugh with a hand. "God, they're so cute. But no offense to anyone, I don't want to do game nights."

Jazz chuckled, just imagining the chaos Blanche would bring to their already chaotic game nights. Mimi would be relieved; Teddy's disregard for the rules already drove her up the wall. Blanche would be ten times worse. "No offense, I don't want you to. I already told them you'd be a parallel partner, if it came to this."

They sagged in her arms with a sigh of relief. "I'm far too old for that drama. Obviously, they're still welcome whenever you want them to, but I don't..."

"We'll figure it out, Beautiful." Jazz stroked their hair, still in awe that this conversation had turned out so much differently than she'd expected. "You tell me what you want when it comes to my other partners, and I'll handle it. Okay?"

Blanche nodded and kissed her again.

Sunday, October Tenth

Chapter Twenty-Two

RICHARD

His mother was a pitiable creature.

Though Richard might have had more sympathy for Barbie, if she hadn't brought his *father* to lunch.

He and Sunny waited silently at the heavy oak table in the back of the Yacht Club, the members-only restaurant and social club for the wannabe elite of Bellamy. There were boats in the small marina outside, and some of them could conceivably be called a yacht without stretching the definition too far. But from the toile de Jouy wallpaper and the coastal decor so ostentatious it verged on camp, the Yacht Club was for people who conflated money with class, and thought the high membership fees and semiotics of wealth meant they were important.

Which is why it was taking his parents so damn long to reach their table. In what Richard imagined was his attempt at a power play, Dick Carter was greeting every single person in the restaurant as if they were old friends. Even the ones who were obviously not thrilled by the disruption to their meal or conversation, which was most of them. Dick was embarrassing himself for the sake of humiliating Richard.

Barbie kept pressing her lips together in an apologetic smile at them every few minutes, trying and failing to hurry her husband along. Richard gave her a tight smile back, leaning back in his chair to wait, fussing with the stiff white cuffs of his button-down. His father would not be happy if Barbie left his side to greet Richard and Sunny without him; Dick would see it as losing face if his wife didn't play her role.

Hopefully, the audience of what his father considered his peers would keep him in line when it came to losing face himself.

"Who would name their boat 'Bittersea'?" Sunny asked, looking out the window at the boats docked in the marina. She'd quickly lost interest in watching his parents' glacial approach, and was fiddling with the pearl necklace Richard had given her long ago. Her light blue cashmere sweater (that she'd borrowed from her "prep of a sister") was Sunny's attempt to "roleplay the upper crust." Fittingly enough, she matched the wallpaper. "That's a weird name for a riverboat."

"Who indeed?" Richard held back a snort. It was a happy coincidence that the cruiser his father had purchased long ago was docked outside the window. Though perhaps it wasn't a coincidence; seating their members with a view of their boats seemed like something the staff of the Bellamy Yacht Club would try to do.

"Lizzie!" Barbie finally broke away from her husband's arm to greet them, when the rudeness of ignoring them a few feet away outweighed the rudeness of excusing herself from Dick's latest victim. "So lovely to see you."

"It's Richard, Mom," Richard corrected as he rose to hug her. "And if you can't manage that, please don't call me anything."

It was a strange feeling, trying to enforce boundaries face-to-face. He'd given up before he'd ever tried, knowing he'd end up enduring the deadnaming and misgendering either way. He'd instead opted to simply cut off contact, outside of the rare occasion when he had no choice but to see them. But that was when it was just Richard in the picture. If Barbie wanted any chance of being a part of his life with Sunny and their future family, she'd have to respect them.

Barbie chose not to say anything, smoothing down her bubblegum pink dress.

"You remember Sunny, of course."

"Of course!" Barbie hugged her before Sunny had a chance to stand up. "Hey, you!"

Sunny's pleading look for help as his mom squeezed her around the neck made Richard grin as he sat back down. At least Barbie was being nice. Depending on how much she drank with lunch, that might change. Sober, his mother wanted to be everyone's best friend. Drunk, Barbie could turn nasty and bitter. And as a bored, lonely housewife whose husband treated her like an ornament, whose only "daughter" refused to cooperate with her dreams of being codependent gal pals, and whose younger son treated her like the help, Barbie was often drunk. Part of the reason he'd intentionally not extended the invitation to his father, who was also often drunk, but didn't let that stop him from driving.

"While we wait for Dad, can I ask for a favor?" Richard poured a glass of wine for everyone—a standard pour, in hopes it would slow his parents down—from the carafe he'd ordered for the table. "Do you still have Grandma Betty's ring?"

"Which one?" Barbie beamed. "The emerald, that gaudy silver thing, or the baguette diamond?"

Richard glanced at Sunny, who gave him a confused shrug back. She would probably like the gaudy silver thing—which was a glorious display of art nouveau filigree, though not blingy enough for his mother's taste—but Grandma Betty's third marriage had been a short-lived scandal. "The baguette."

Her fourth marriage had been the happiest. And longest, lasting until her husband passed before Richard was born.

"So is that the occasion?" Barbie whispered conspiratorially. "Am I finally going to get to be the mother of the bride?"

Richard huffed. "Well, yes and no."

Sunny snorted into her wineglass.

"We are planning on getting married, but Sunny's the bride." Richard opted not to break it to his mom that she would likely not be invited to the wedding. Even if he explicitly told her not to, she'd bring his father, who would ruin it. That would have to be a conversation in private.

"You're not getting married." Dick finally joined them without greeting or apology. "Unless it's to the Cooper boy."

Richard felt Sunny's muffled sigh in his soul. "This may come as a surprise to you, but I don't care what you want. I am going to marry Sunny."

Sunny scoffed. "Besides, Gabe's getting married and has a kid on the—Dicky, you gotta stop pinching me! You know it doesn't stop me!"

"Do not tell *anyone* outside of our friends about Gabe's life." Richard tried to keep his voice calm, low enough that his parents wouldn't hear. "Especially my parents."

Sunny must have heard his panic, because she stilled. "Sorry."

Richard shook his head, dread sinking his stomach; Miriam was going to kill him. "Don't be. I should have said something earlier."

"Who is he marrying?" Barbie asked. "And he's having a baby? That's so exciting!"

Dick was silent. Not a good sign. If he'd known his father was coming along, Richard would have gotten a table closer to the front. Faster escape route, closer to the other patrons that Dick would want to impress. As it was, their table in the back was isolated, out of earshot.

"With another friend of ours," Richard admitted, trying to be as vague as possible. "And yes, they're very happy together."

"You stay close," Dick finally said, refilling his wineglass. "It probably won't last and then—"

"And then what, Dad?" Richard scoffed. "Do you want me to swoop in if his relationship falls apart? Give up the life Sunny and I have together, for the chance that you might get some social clout out of it?" Richard scoffed, wondering where this audacity had come from. But he wasn't about to stop. "How did that work out for you? Miriam and John are still happily married, and you dragged Mom all the way to Bellamy to drink herself to death on the off chance you could set her aside the second Miriam was single? Give it up already!"

"Lizzie!" His mother scolded, her face scarlet as she forced a smile at the other tables looking their way.

"Oh, sorry. I forgot we're not supposed to acknowledge that." Richard rolled his eyes. Any hope of getting Grandma Betty's ring was wasted, but he refused to cower again. Maybe the shock of speaking to his parents this way would make them forget they'd found out about Gabe's engagement. Either way, Richard had never felt so alive.

"How dare you!" Dick growled. "Elizabeth, everything I do is for the betterment of our family—"

"You do it for your ego," Richard snapped. This was going very poorly. He'd lost his temper, and his skin burned so hot, his face was probably bright red. His hands were shaking so hard, it was a miracle he managed to catch the wineglass his father threw at him a second later, though not before it spilled on Sunny.

"Oh, you are *so* not invited to the wedding." Sunny wiped her cheek, grimacing at the wet splotch darkening her pastel sweater and eggshell slacks. He'd have to get Luna's top dry-cleaned, but at least he'd ordered a white wine for the table. "I don't think we picked a safeword for today, Dicky, but safeword. Whatever it is."

"No." He gripped Sunny's thigh to keep her in her seat, and to keep his hands from trembling. Another miracle: his voice was steady. "*They'll* be leaving."

"You can't tell me to leave!" Dick's face was as red as Richard's felt. "I'm a platinum member here!"

"Not for much longer." Richard nodded gratefully at the manager who approached with extra napkins. "Could you please escort the Carters from the premises?"

"We will do no such thing! I'm a shareholder!"

"You *were* a shareholder." Richard's voice went low, resonant in his chest. "Other than your precious platinum membership, you signed your investment here over to me years ago." Richard looked to the manager, who nodded in confirmation. Richard leveled a look at his dad. "So you can leave, or be escorted and trespassed."

"I did no such thing!" His dad sputtered, face perhaps redder than Richard's now. "I would *never* have signed anything over to *you*."

Richard had heard that transphobic *you* from many people over the years, but his father's was especially cruel. His resolve hardened as Richard smiled coldly. "I assure you, you did. Considering you often conveniently forget that my name has legally been Richard Carter for over a decade, I can see why you might be confused. Call your lawyers if you don't believe me." Richard turned to Sunny. "Sunshine, what should we rename our boat? You're right, *Bittersea* is such an odd choice for a river cruiser. Especially considering 'Miriam' means Sea of Bitterness. What an odd coincidence."

"You stole my yacht?!" Dick snarled and reached for the empty wine carafe.

Barbie caught his wrist first. "Dick!" she hissed. "You're making a scene. We will call your lawyers and get this all straightened out." As she stood, Barbie spoke in a chipper voice, loud enough to be heard by everyone watching. "Is it so late already? We'll miss our tee time, Darling! We must be going, but it was so lovely to see you both!" She dragged the still fuming Dick behind her.

Richard exhaled.

"Um, I assume we won't be ordering lunch?" The manager asked with a sympathetic smile.

The idea of food, when his anxiety was running the highest it had been in years, made his stomach turn. And Sunny deserved far more than the bland cuisine at the yacht club. "Perhaps some sparkling water?" He needed a few moments before his legs would work again. His whole body was shaking so badly that he didn't trust himself to stand.

As soon as the manager walked away, Sunny whispered, "Dicky, that was so hot. You used your dom voice and everything."

Oh. He had? Richard let out a trembling laugh and found her hand under the table, grateful beyond measure that Sunny had insisted on coming with him. That conversation would have unfolded much differently without her. "I'm going to have to find another ring for you."

"Fuck a ring, you bought me a yacht!" As if sensing he needed more than her hand, she pressed her arm against his, steadying his shaking.

"I didn't buy it. I stole it—legally—along with many of my dad's assets over the past five years. Some petty revenge scheme I don't fully understand anymore." After a few deep breaths, Richard finally trusted himself to look at her without bursting into tears. "It must have made sense five years ago, because I don't want to be a minority shareholder of the Yacht Club. I don't want a boat. I just wanted to piss him off! And I already did that by being myself!"

"Dicky, slowly undermining everything your dad cares about is one-hundred-percent being yourself." Sunny's smile was brilliant. "You sadistic motherfucker, I love you."

Richard laughed. The hot burn of adrenaline started to cool with Sunny's encouragement, her teasing, her smile. Something shifted in his chest as his breath steadied. Even if he would have to find a different ring for her now, she was by his side, supporting him the way she always did. "Love you, too."

"Can we have sex on it? This yacht of yours."

Richard snorted. "In theory, yes."

"No, I mean like right now." Sunny bit her lip as she eyed him. "I want to blow you on the yacht that you stole from your dad."

He coughed, hoping the waiter approaching with their waters didn't hear her. "I think it's already been winterized."

"Pity. I'll just have to do it in the car then." Sunny winked, thanking the waiter, whose red cheeks revealed that he'd definitely overheard. "So, what else do you have that I don't know about, besides a boat and a stake in a bougie restaurant?"

"Oh," Richard paused, mentally running through the list of things he'd taken: his dad's old bachelor pad in New York that'd been sitting empty since Richard had moved back to Bellamy, some modern art currently on loan to the MIA that Dick had purchased to impress Miriam,

Richard's own Range Rover, a collection of vintage watches and cuff links that Grandma Betty had given Dick as a wedding gift, and so on. In short, any assets Richard had some sentimental attachment to, that would strike a blow to his father's ego.

Other than the condo on the Upper East Side, nothing worth a tremendous amount of money, nor anything his dad would miss until long after Richard had disappeared from his life. He'd left any lucrative investments, the real estate and hedge funds, in his dad's name. Other than some apartment complexes in Eastside, which Dick had invested in early on when they'd first moved to Bellamy; Richard had assumed Dick was a horrible landlord.

Disappointing but unsurprisingly, "horrible landlord" hadn't begun to cover it, once he'd started digging into the financials. Richard had switched management companies to a more reputable firm and lowered rent to market-rate, but he'd left them alone for the past few years. Come to think of it, Sunny might have a lot to say about those assets in particular.

He sucked in a breath. "We should discuss finances."

Tuesday, October Twelfth

CHAPTER TWENTY-THREE

GABE

PHINEAS TAPPED A REAM of papers covered in pen marks into a tidy pile, before clipping it together. "Knock on wood, but I think we're done."

Tara leaned across the desk to rap on his forehead.

"Seriously?" Phineas sighed before laughing.

Gabe grinned. After Phineas's meltdown a few weeks ago (that had not helped the "Phin is in love with Gabe" rumors which had floated around their friendship for over a decade), he seemed to be doing better. Phineas was not, and had never been, in love with him; he was just...clingy. Being incredibly clingy himself, Gabe was simply more patient than most people. Their friends with benefits arrangement in college hadn't helped the perception.

Not all of Gabe's partners had understood his history with his three best friends, all of whom he'd had relationships with, even if none of them were particularly romantic. Any physical intimacy between them had only been fun with friends, like playing a video game, daring each other to do stupid shit, or getting high and listening to Kid Cudi.

Luckily, Tara understood and trusted him, the way she always did. Even if she thought Phineas might be harboring some feelings for him that ran deeper than friendship. She'd done her best to smooth over the lingering tension the past few times they'd met with Phineas to discuss, draft, discuss, argue, redraft, argue, and finally agree upon the prenup.

"Smoothing over" for Tara meant talking shit about Phineas, who took it in self-deprecating stride. It was Tara's *flirting* Phineas couldn't handle. Bi panic erupted on his face whenever Tara so much as smirked at him. Gabe found it highly entertaining; Phineas had finally been out-hornied by his future spouse.

"I'll have this updated for signatures next week." Phineas tossed the file in the wire bin on the filing cabinet behind him. He leaned back in his chair, adjusting his glasses. "You know, I don't think I've ever had anyone argue as much as you two over a prenup, especially since you were trying to give the other one everything."

Gabe huffed, "I'm still keeping too much."

"No, you're not, Coop—"

"Nope!" Phineas covered his ears. "No, I don't want to hear anymore. It's over, it's done. I'm going to start charging for mediation if we have to revisit any of this."

"We'll save it for later when we're alone," Tara winked at Gabe.

"See, now that sounds hot!" Phineas teased. "Why couldn't you have the sexy arguments in my office, instead of squabbling over custody agreements?"

"What, spousal support doesn't do it for you, Phinny?" Tara shot back with a smirk.

Phineas grinned. "Fun fact, when we were roommates, we used to settle arguments with bets. Whoever came first had to take out the trash, or vacuum, or whatever. Once, we took turns with this baddie I was seeing to see who could make her come the most times, and the winner got out of hall duty." Phineas smiled appreciatively at Gabe. Gabe chuckled; those had been fun times. Weird how many good memories Phineas always managed to stir up. "It set me up with very unrealistic expectations for how to handle conflict."

Tara smacked Gabe's arm. "Why don't *we* do that?"

"We make bets!" he protested.

"Not to solve arguments!"

Gabe snorted. "I think our lifelong financial decisions require a little more conversation than garbage duty did."

Tara shook her head. "Coop, we settled on a paint color for the nursery over a game of Smash when I could have *edged* you?"

Gabe smirked at her, eyeing her slowly until her cheeks tinged pink. "Did you want to win or not, Kitten?"

Tara scoffed. "You think I would lose? At edging?"

"In the middle of your second trimester?" Gabe teased, his hand drifting to his stomach. "Kitten, I barely have to touch you. My ego is huge."

Phineas coughed politely. "Still here, and trying really hard not to be a creep."

Gabe's cheeks burned; their flirting had gotten a little out of hand. "Sorry, that was TMI."

"Nah, you're good. You two are cute. Even if you argue a lot." Phineas untied the ribbon that kept his locs out of his way, shaking out his waist-length hair. "So, when's the big day? I'm still invited, right?"

"Of course, dude." Tara rolled her eyes.

Yet another thing Gabe appreciated about Tara. She liked everyone in his life, even Phineas. He was a good guy, but he came across as an anxious, insecure fuckboy—an acquired taste for most people.

"We still have to get the license, so probably sometime in November?" Gabe said. "We'll let you know."

"You should!" Phineas wrapped the ribbon around his wrist, using his teeth to tie it. "I want to be more involved. With you, with Richard, Lee, and Antonio. Everyone! My therapist says I use work as an excuse to preemptively reject myself before anyone else does. Which is a rude thing to point out, but he's not wrong." Phineas waved his vulnerable moment off like it was nothing. "So can I plan your bachelor party or something?"

Gabe sucked in a breath through his teeth. Even if he and Tara had a joint bachelor party like Lee and Antonio, any night of partying where he was the center of attention sounded like hell. That night as Carlita's shot boy had been *humiliating*. God, and Halloween was coming up? If he wasn't careful, Antonio would absolutely find a way to get him on stage. "Oh, we're not doing all that."

"What?" Phineas exclaimed. "Gabey, you have to! It's one last hurrah! Tara, you're having one right?"

Tara shook her head. "I told you, dude, our 'hurrahing' isn't going to end just because we're getting married and having a kid. We'll have a low-key wedding, and keep being us. Anyway, I'd rather hurrah when I can drink and smoke again. The only hurrahing I can do right now is fucking, which I don't really want to do with our friends." Tara smirked. "Well, *most* of our friends."

Phineas's eyes went wide. He cleared his throat, whipping to look at Gabe. "So I'll come early! Help set up or something."

"You're gonna come *early* to help *set up*?" Gabe asked, trying to hide his skepticism. At Phineas's eager nod, Gabe shrugged; he'd believe it when he saw it. "Okay, cool. I'm sure Blanche and my parents could use the help."

"Speaking of Blanche..." Phineas winked. "I don't suppose you're inviting any baddies who want to date a workaholic lawyer?"

Gabe laughed as he and Tara stood to leave. "You're relentless, Phin. Blanche is still off-limits." Safer that way, especially if Tara's suspicions about Blanche and Jazz growing closer were true. She'd interrupted a few moments where they'd jumped apart suspiciously, and immediately told Gabe to make sure she wasn't imagining things.

As soon as the elevator doors closed behind them, Gabe twisted his fingers in Tara's hair and roughly pulled her back against him. He sucked her earlobe, biting kisses along her neck. "How hard was it to keep yourself from propositioning Phin right in the office?"

Tara reached behind him to squeeze his ass. "Busted. Dude, the idea of him sucking you off? And the two of you working together to get someone off? If I could lay on my stomach, I would have volunteered to be spit-roasted over that desk so fast."

Gabe did his best to muffle his groan as his heart pounded through his veins. Tara was the best partner he could have imagined. "I mean, I'm down if you are."

Tara shook her head. "Maybe not Phin. At least, not yet. Flirting with him is fun, but I still think he's hung up on you. Let's give him time to move on if he needs it."

Gabe grumbled, "He's not hung up on me."

"Speaking as someone who pined over you the better part of a year, you're not the most aware of when people like you, Coop," Tara said pointedly.

"With you, I thought I was delusional." Gabe kissed her cheek, his hand sliding around to cup her growing bump. The prenup, which had been a proverbial duffle bag for Tara, had become Gabe's way of ensuring that no matter what, he could still support their family. It had been their biggest obstacle to overcome together, figuring out how to align their shared values to their mutual satisfaction. The marriage license, decorating the nursery, planning the ceremony—all of that would be easy after weeks of negotiating the hard shit. Everything was starting to become real. In a month or so, they'd be married. A few months after that, raising a child together.

He'd never imagined any of this happiness, let alone with someone who had turned his world upside down with her passion and confidence and patience. Someone who saw him for all that he was. Who understood him because she was so similar—pridefully queer, and argumentative, and impulsive, and stubbornly determined to keep going despite everything. Who trusted him, *loved* him through it all. Who wanted a future with him, because she wanted the same peace, happiness, and security for him that he wanted for her.

"This," he murmured, kissing her jaw.

"This what?"

"We got through a lot of conversations that brought out difficult parts of both of us, and we still can't get enough of each other." He held her tight, inhaling the warmth of her skin. "For trying to make this work with me, even though we're both learning how this all works. For being patient with me while I adjust to everything."

"Yeah, same."

Gabe snorted; Tara was the master of understatement. "And for reminding me that sex can just be fun. It doesn't have to be so intense and passionate every time. I love that our sex life can also be playful."

"Me, too." Tara paused. "But how about Angie, though?"

"Oh!" Gabe's mind jumped tracks as the elevator doors regretfully opened, erasing their illusion of privacy right when his dick had started to harden again. "Yeah! I'm down for that if you are, and if she is."

"Good. Because I'm still offended that you think I would lose any sex competition," Tara winked. "What do you want to wager that I'm better at eating pussy than you?"

"You can pick whatever stakes you want, Kitten, because there's no way you're better than me." Gabe was certain he would lose, but he was more than willing to try. How lucky was he that he'd found a partner like Tara?

"I'll text her." Tara typed furiously as they headed to the parking ramp, so he could drop her off at Blanche's before returning to work himself. As they reached the car, she burst into a loud laugh. "Oh, she sent me a link to a survey." She snorted, smiling up at him. "The form says congratulations on being one of the few couples she'd consider unicorning for, and asks a bunch of questions about why we're doing this and what we want out of it."

"I expected nothing less from her," Gabe chuckled, already looking forward to filling out this survey on the way. Hopefully, with his hand down Tara's joggers. Considering she was squirming with that sparkle in her eye merely getting into the car, he would be late getting back to work.

For Tara, he'd call off the whole afternoon.

JAZZ

JAZZ STUCK HER TONGUE through her teeth, flinching as the knife in her hand slipped around the avocado, almost slicing her palm open. She jumped again when Blanche spoke up; she had no idea they were home.

"Watching you cook is scarier than that one time Tara tried to make a salad." With a laugh, Blanche ducked behind the fridge as Jazz chucked an avocado peel at them.

"I can cook!" Jazz pouted. Her stomach was rumbling after a long day of classes. She'd only had a bag of chips, some licorice that Teddy gave her, and a can of soda for lunch. "But I grew up cooking dry-ass chicken and unsalted veggies because my dad hates when anyone enjoys life. This," she held up the avocado that had almost caused her to need stitches, "would never be allowed in my dad's house."

"What are you making?" Blanche asked, dropping the avocado peel into the compost bin and wrapping their robe around them.

"Ed gave me a recipe for black bean and sweet potato tacos from the restaurant he works at." Jazz scraped the last of the avocado into a bowl, wishing the counters were four inches taller so she didn't have to stoop so much to prepare food. Or at least that they had some task lighting in the tiny kitchen, so she could see what she was doing. "I figured I should learn to make guac to go with it."

Blanche hovered nearby, their hand tentatively raised, as if they were thinking about touching her.

Jazz bit her lip to keep from grinning; Blanche was so much more hesitant about affection than she'd expected. They'd made out a handful of times in the ten days since they'd agreed to be together, but Jazz was doing her best to let Blanche lead. However, Blanche's idea of initiating was to stand awkwardly close to Jazz, blushing and not actually touching her. Until Jazz finally took pity on them and touched them first.

She stepped closer, so Blanche's hand landed on her hip, and pulled the cutting board along with her.

When Jazz peeked over her shoulder, Blanche had turned pink, but their hand still slid to her lower back. *God, they're so cute.* When she'd imagined what a relationship with Blanche would be like, Jazz never once considered they'd be so shy. They were night and day from their dominatrix persona. Hopefully, they would get more comfortable with the idea as time went on. *It's only been ten days. Lord knows I was a wreck for a good two months after Mimi, Teddy, and I got together.*

"I think it's great you're trying new things, Beautiful."

"Yeah? Does that mean you're going to cook with me?" Jazz teased. "Finally make something besides leftover takeout and frozen shit?"

"Oh, no!" Blanche grinned. "I wouldn't know the first thing about cooking."

"What, the cult didn't make you cook for a crowd?" Jazz did her best to mash the avocado in the bowl, but chunks kept sliding away from her fork. When Ed had shown her how to make it, this step had seemed much easier.

Blanche laughed. "No. That was women's work, and my adopted parents couldn't have children, so they only had me to feed. Mama would bring my food out to the barn, so I never watched how she did it."

Jazz froze. "You never ate inside?"

"I'm sure I did when I was a baby." Blanche's thumb stroked her hip. "But I only remember living in the barn. I only went inside the house for a bath before church on Sundays."

With a flare of that annoyed heartbreak whenever Blanche said something messed up, Jazz threw the fork down with a clatter. "The fuck? You lived in the *barn*? Did you at least have a bed and, you know, heat?!"

"The dogs kept me pretty warm," Blanche shrugged. "And honestly, it was safer there. Out of sight, out of mind, you know?"

"No!" Jazz scoffed. "Why did they make you sleep in the barn?!"

"I was the bortbyting," Blanche said as if that explained anything.

"The what?"

"The bortbyting. The...changeling, I guess it would be in English?" Blanche waved a hand. "The Family had adopted—or maybe kidnapped—what they thought was a white baby, because I was blond and pale and had blue eyes when I was very young." Blanche rolled their eyes. "And after a year or so, I...changed. Happens to a lot of white children—their hair and eyes change as they get older—but normally their skin doesn't turn brown like mine did."

"So they thought what—the fairies got you?" Jazz picked her fork back up to resume mashing the avocado, channeling her rage on Blanche's behalf. The chunks still slipped past her fork, but it was starting to look mushier.

Blanche nodded, absentmindedly running their thumb along Jazz's spine. "There was an old folktale that if you mistreat the changeling, the Trolls will trade their baby back. Since they couldn't kill me—because the Trolls would kill the real Chad—they treated me like an outcast."

Jazz blinked. "Trolls."

"I know how it sounds." Blanche laughed. "But it was an insular cult of Swedes who prided themselves on how unassimilated they were. And I didn't mind the barn. I learned a lot when I was left to my own devices. Carpentry. Sewing. Treating the livestock when they got sick or injured. Eavesdropping without anyone noticing you." They frowned. "That's how I figured out when they finally noticed my body wasn't entirely male. Papa and the Fadern were talking about cutting the sin out of me, so I ran to Grandma Rose. She lived nearby, but she wasn't in the Family. She threatened to report the child abuse if they did anything."

"She protected you," Jazz murmured. Like Lee had for her, always lying to take the blame for whatever she did wrong. Even after they'd kicked him out, his absence had changed everything.

"As best she could." They shrugged. "I was still a source of shame. Papa almost took it into his own hands one day, but he missed."

Jazz gave up the rubbery avocado, dropping the fork completely to put her arms around Blanche's waist. "And when you say he missed you mean..."

Blanche hugged her. "He said he was aiming at the wolf behind me. Missed me by inches, though." Blanche snorted in Jazz's shoulder. "Then I found Grandma Rose dead in front of the TV, I knew it was time to go. Stole her car and drove it as far as I could get, then hitchhiked until I got here."

"How can you be so nonchalant about it?" Jazz asked, resting her cheek against their hair and pulling them in tight. And here she'd thought *Lee* was bad whenever he brushed off what happened to him. "You've been through so much."

"It was a lifetime ago. Two lifetimes ago." Blanche's swallow bobbed across her collarbone. "That happened to Chad Hermanson."

"But that was still *you*," Jazz insisted.

When Blanche pulled away, their smile looked sad. "It's easier to disconnect, Jazz. Chad was scared and ashamed and alone, and Blanche is not. Don't you do the same thing when you brush off bad memories? Try to move on, pretend it never happened? With your tapping?"

Jazz froze. "You've noticed the tapping?"

Blanche nodded.

She cringed; no one was supposed to notice it. She thought her childhood habit of doing everything in threes had found a new, more subtle home that her mom wouldn't yell at her for. "Everything just builds, up and up and up, and then I explode." Jazz bit her lip. "The tapping is how I make myself sit with it, so I can understand myself better." Jazz sighed. "Three sets of taps to catch the negativity, and I release it through the amethyst." Her cheeks burned. "I know how it sounds, there's no way it actually does anything measurable. I shouldn't rely on it."

"But it helps?" Blanche asked.

Jazz nodded. Now that she was using it as a way to process her emotions, instead of hiding them, like she had when she was young.

"Then it works." Blanche stroked her cheek. "And maybe you're right not to disconnect. Daisy was the one who taught me I could be a new person. She said we were in the 'happily ever after' part of our fairytale, and we could just pretend the old us were characters we'd played for a while. Anything bad that happened, it happened to someone who didn't exist anymore. She was Cinderella, free from her evil stepfather. And I was the ugly duckling who finally found out I was beautiful all along."

"That's sweet. A little fucked up, but sweet." Jazz snorted; Blanche in a nutshell.

"Was everything sweet? No, but I loved her all the same." Blanche huffed. "Sorry, you probably don't want to hear me wax poetic about my dead wife more than you already have."

"Of course I do, Beautiful." Jazz leaned back to tilt Blanche's chin up to her. There was a hint of trepidation in those dark green eyes that Jazz needed to ease. She never wanted Blanche to hold back with her, not when she knew how important Daisy was to them. "I wanted to before we started this. I still want to hear about her now. Our friendship stays the same no matter what, remember?"

The adorable blush tinged Blanche's cheeks again, as Jazz brushed her lips against theirs.

A cough by the door made them both spring apart. Tara glanced between them, eyebrows raised. "Sorry to interrupt."

"You're not interrupting!" Blanche said, too cheerfully, as Jazz turned back to her avocado, mashing it with more vigor to get out the heat of her embarrassment. She'd forgotten Tara was there. "We were just talking about my traumatic childhood. Lovely topic, right?"

"Right. Okay. That's all I interrupted. Sure." With a shrug, Tara set her backpack down, digging through it. "I finished the edits on your video for this weekend, and I scheduled the posts on your socials for this week. I was about to head out, but on the topic of traumatic childhoods, would you mind reading the letter I wrote to my mom?" Tara held out a single leaf of paper. "I've rewritten it like eight times. Gabe just says as long as I write from the heart or some shit, it'll be fine. So, like, can you tell me if it's *actually* okay before I send it?"

"Of course, Babes." Blanche took the paper, squinting with their mouth open as they scanned it. Jazz frowned as she smashed the avocado; Blanche had probably never gotten their eyes checked.

"It's so weird. I never thought I'd have the chance to talk to her. Especially sober." Tara shook her head. "Assuming she hasn't found a way to get heroin into prison—though if anyone could, it'd be Anne. I don't know if I want her to write back, you know?" Tara picked at a hangnail, looking at the floor. "Part of me wants to be all, 'See? Turned out fine!' and never hear back from her. And another part wants to know how she's doing? And I'd probably be pissed if I do write to her, and she doesn't fucking write me back! But also, I got a life to protect now, and what if she tries to use me like she used to?" Tara sighed. "Maybe closure will actually suck, and I shouldn't send this letter."

"Send the letter, Babes." Blanche handed it back to her. "I think it's perfect. It's a good first communication if you both decide to keep communicating, and if she doesn't write to you, you said everything you need to."

"Would you write a letter if you could?" Jazz asked, adding lime juice to her avocado now that it finally resembled something like guacamole. "To the Family, I mean?"

"Write a letter to a cult?" Blanche teased.

Jazz tsked. "To the people who adopted you. Get your questions answered. Get your own closure?"

Blanche shrugged as Tara shoved the paper back in her bag. "I don't so much want closure as I want them to know I survived out of spite. And to see how a cult lives in the new millennium! I do wonder how the Fadern keeps everyone brainwashed in the Internet age."

Jazz winced, choosing not to comment that she'd been born in the new millennium.

"That's closure, too," Tara said, swinging her backpack over her shoulder.

"Maybe," Blanche sighed.

"Well, let's see how mine goes. If it's a disaster, you'll know not to," Tara teased, then looked between them again with a smirk.

For a moment, Jazz was worried she was about to call them out on their kiss. That she might tell Lee, and he would lose his shit and try to Dad her. This was all so new for them. Jazz wasn't sure if her and Blanche's budding relationship would survive her brother's pissy fit.

But Tara simply eyed the bowl in her hands. "Is that guac? Can I have some?"

Saturday, October Sixteenth

CHAPTER TWENTY-FOUR

TARA

WATER SPLASHED IN THE sink as Tara scrubbed the coffee stain out of a mug. Through the kitchen window, Hippo stretched out on his back in the grass, sunning himself. Excitement and anticipation had been coursing under her skin all afternoon; Angie had been more than happy to judge their skills and cleared her Saturday evening.

Now that their ongoing half-teasing, half-serious joke was about to become reality in a few short hours, her nerves were going haywire. What if she'd lost her skills in the last two years of only sleeping with Gabe? What if Angie felt weird about having a threesome with a pregnant woman? Tara looked at her rounded belly, her bare skin wet from when she'd rinsed the spoons. What if Tara got jealous? What if *Gabe* got jealous? Would this make Antonio's family cookouts awkward? Her throat tightened as she rinsed the mug; she really liked going to those. The food was amazing. Lee's in-laws were so wonderful. Would this be worth it? What if she lost the bet?

"Kitten, breathe." Gabe's hands on her hips brought her back to awareness. "Stop overthinking."

"I'm not overthinking."

"You've washed that glass three times for fun, then? You do know that could just go in the dishwasher, right?"

Tara rinsed the glass and set it to dry on the rack. "I have two hands that are perfectly capable of washing dishes."

"Clearly." Gabe's lips brushed her neck. "What's on your mind, Kitten?"

They'd discussed the whys and what-ifs that could come out of adding Angie to the mix for an evening. But still, Tara was unsettled. "We kinda rushed into this, didn't we?"

"Our plans with Angie, you mean?"

Tara nodded. "What else would I mean?"

"Having a kid, getting married, literally anything else going on in our lives," Gabe teased, his mouth trailing up and down her neck. His hands wrapped around her hips to pull her back against him. The hair of his chest and belly tickled the bare skin of her back. "Want me to text her to reschedule or cancel?"

Shaking her head, Tara rinsed soap off a plate. "No, I want to do it. As long as you do too. Like, I've only ever had one threesome, and I was the unicorn. It feels weird from this side. What if this makes things awkward, you know? Will this change how we interact with Angie?"

Gabe hummed. "I could see how it'd get awkward, being friends with a woman who thinks you give trash head compared to me."

Tara laughed and flicked the water on her hands over her shoulder at Gabe. "You wish. I mean like, what if this changes things between you and me? Or what if something happens to make it weird with her from now on? Or us? Like, I can't imagine it would, so like, I'm not going to let it stop me, but I'm just...worried I guess."

Her brow furrowed and her throat tightened, but Tara forced herself to keep talking; she'd promised Gabe he could emotionally support her or whatever. "Like, I don't know if a good mom or loving wife is supposed to be out here proposing threesomes." She groaned. "But also, maybe that's the kind of wife and mom I'm going to be, and I have to accept that, and that doesn't make me a *bad* mom or wife." Tara leaned back against Gabe as she tried to slow her breathing. "I think I just talked myself out of my spiral. I was thinking like Lee, that being a hedonist would make me a bad person. But it's who I am, and just because I have shitty impulse control doesn't mean I can't be a loving and supportive parent and spouse. Thanks for listening."

Gabe chuckled, kissing the crown of her head. "Well, we're going to debrief after, and of course we will check in during, but is there anything else you want to discuss now, before she gets here?"

"No, that rant just about covered it." Tara dried her hands on the towel hanging next to the sink, taking a few slow breaths to make sure there were no stray hard feelings floating around. "At least for now. I'm sure I'll spiral more tomorrow. Are you feeling anything we should talk about?"

Gabe's thumbs traced her hips, warm hands sliding across her skin to embrace her as he rested his head on hers. "I thought I'd be more worried about jealousy, given my own history of insecurity and shit. But then again, you two had your hands all over each other at the wedding, I wasn't jealous then." He shrugged. "I couldn't blame her, it was hard to keep my hands off you myself. I think I'm more confident now, in myself and us. I trust that you're still going to want me, even if we argue or I have a flashback, so the idea that you'll like Angie more than me seems silly at this point."

"Good, because it is." Tara put her hands over his, luxuriating in the skin-to-skin contact like she did every weekend. "I've never seen you with anyone else. I'm not sure how I'll react."

"We objectify strangers all the time, Kitten. Does that make you jealous?"

Tara smiled. They often mutually admired eye candy of all genders. "No, that's just fun. Why do you want to do this anyway? Like what are you getting out of it?"

Gabe laughed. "Well, you've been practically drooling all week every time we talk about it. And why wouldn't I want to? I'm already incredibly lucky to be with you, but then you also want to have the occasional threesome? You're literally the partner of my dreams. Kitten. Even if things today get weird, or we have confusing feelings, we'll figure them out. I can't imagine anyone or anything coming between us."

"You and your damn sweet-talking." Tara ran her hands up his bare chest and looked up into his lovely brown eyes. His hands drifted to cup her ass through her boxers as she turned. He always knew what to say to soothe whatever new worries and anxiety she had. "You're incredibly charming sometimes, did you know that?"

He pulled her against him, kissing her forehead. "So I should add in how you're a walking wet dream into the wedding vows somehow?"

Tara nodded earnestly. "Yes, great idea. Let's tell all of our friends and your parents all about our sex life."

Gabe beamed. His dimples still made her heart flutter whenever she saw them. "Maybe we get a slide show going of all of the photos we've taken? Let them see the filthy side of us."

Tara laughed. "Poor Lee would probably pass out."

Gabe kissed her in reply, his tongue tentatively swiping her lip. With a quiet gasp, she kissed him back so enthusiastically that she practically sucked his tongue into her mouth, ignoring the more-manageable flare of fear that often erupted when they kissed like this. "Wait."

"Too much?" Gabe immediately pulled away.

She shook her head. "No, but what if Angie kisses me, and I get panicky?"

"Then we will take a break, and I'll be here to help you work through it, and Angie will understand and not take it personally." He kissed her forehead. "Are you comfortable trying? Or we can just skip kissing completely."

Tara considered it before she nodded. "Guess it'd be nice to know if I actually like kissing, or if it's a you-only thing."

"As long as you don't like kissing her more than me," Gabe teased, hesitant enough that insecurity leaked into his voice.

Tara frowned. "I'm not dignifying that with a response, Coop."

He pecked her lips once more. "I wouldn't expect you to, and I don't need you to, Kitten."

"I don't know what I was so worried about." Tara lay her head back on Gabe's chest, as they cuddled in bed while Angie showered. "Seriously, look how hot you are."

She zoomed in on the picture she'd taken during their competition. Toes strained against the duvet left the pale soles of Gabe's feet exposed to the camera, creating motion in his ankles and calves. The tension in his ass formed dimples above it as he rutted into the mattress. The expanse of his back was framed by dainty feet with painted toes and pillowy brown thighs. Angie's clenched fist around his long hair she pulled Gabe where she needed him. His fingertips created divots in the skin of her breast, brown nipple rolling between his thumb and finger. The flare of her nostrils, teeth sinking into her lower lip, and the gleam in her hazel eyes as she smirked directly into the viewfinder, all showed Angie on the verge of her first orgasm.

"Damn, that is good framing. Good eye, Kitten."

Tara scoffed. "I wasn't showing you the framing. I *know* that's good. I'm showing you how hot you are."

Gabe laughed. "Okay, fine. I'm hot."

Tara snorted at his sarcastic tone; one day he'd believe it. He'd recognize what she saw in him if she had to take thousands of pictures of him at his hottest and most confident moments. She would keep showing him that, even when his depression had him at his lowest, or when the nightmares woke him in the night, or when he was frustrated and angry, that he was still the same Gabe she knew and loved.

"How are you feeling?" Gabe asked. "Anything you want to talk about before Ang comes back out?"

Tara shook her head, relieved that this moment of fun indulgence hadn't changed the love between them. No hard feelings had erupted from her, and Gabe had the same lovesick smile on his face that he always did. "Not yet. Still pussy-drunk and sleepy. You?"

Gabe chuckled. "No. I just...love you a lot."

With a grin, Tara turned around to kiss him. "Love you, too."

"You two already going at it again?" Angie teased from the bathroom door, her curls piled high in a messy bun. She shook out her dress from where she'd tossed it on the floor earlier. "I want whatever you two have. Seriously, you are so open with each other. It's beautiful to see so much passion."

"We got lucky," Tara murmured.

"And then we worked for it," Gabe added.

With a soft smile, Tara pecked him on the lips once more. "Be right back, need to pee."

"Again?" Angie teased.

"Always these days," Tara huffed as she padded to the bathroom.

By the time she returned, Gabe and Angie were both unfortunately clothed, talking about the wedding plans, and standing an awkward distance apart, considering they'd all been naked in bed less than half an hour ago. Tara frowned. Gabe was only in boxers and a t-shirt, but still, it was Saturday. They didn't wear clothes on Saturday. He must have started feeling insecure being exposed without Tara there. What would it take to convince him that he had nothing to be insecure about? That he was hot, not despite his belly and chest hair, but because of it?

"No, no flowers, please," Gabe waved his hand. "We're doing the bare minimum. My mom is already bringing a whole truck of wedding shit from the vineyard that we don't want."

"Fine, if you insist," Angie sighed, holding out her arms for a hug. "Anyway, back to the shop tonight to finish the last few bouquets for a wedding tomorrow!"

"I thought we were giving you a night off," Tara teased, hugging Angie goodbye.

Angie grinned and gave her a lingering kiss. "Nope! You were a temporary distraction. But if you know any single hotties who fuck as hard as you two, let me know. I'd love distracting on the regular."

"Did you meet Phin at Antonio's wedding?" Gabe asked, wrapping his hand gently around Tara's neck.

Tara grinned and let herself be pulled close to him, dreaming of the day when they could add choking back to the menu after the kid was born. "Phin? Now there's an idea."

"Oh! Who is this Phin?" Angie asked, flashing a bright smile at Gabe.

"He's single, a successful lawyer, a workaholic like you. Hot, very enthusiastic in bed." Gabe paused, then added, "A little on the submissive side. And after sleeping with you, I can confidently say you might be into that."

Tara snorted. While she had proposed a threesome where Angie could "just lay back while we take turns eating you out," it'd quickly become more about taking direction from Angie. A pleasant surprise for both her and Gabe, who usually took turns being more dominant with each other. It had been fun, teasing each other while Angie bossed them around.

"Oh Gabe, you know me so well now," Angie laughed, fanning herself. "You said he was at Tonio's wedding?"

Gabe nodded. "Tall, glasses, long locs."

"Oh." Angie's face fell. "*Him.*"

"Oh no," Tara sighed. "What did he do?"

"Ghosted me!" Angie scoffed. "Me! Can you believe it? He was so sweet and charming. There was no small talk shit. We just dove right in like we'd known each other forever. I felt like we really connected, you know?" She huffed. "We spent a phenomenal night together, and then the fucker never texted me back! Like who does that?"

"Phin," Gabe grumbled. "If it helps, he's been going to therapy? It's kind of working! He's acknowledging his issues now, and *intends* to work on them."

Angie rolled her eyes. "Actually, that *doesn't* help, Gabriel. What would make me feel better is an apology and some groveling. I'm not saying he has *no* chance. Just maybe a nice dinner, a little begging, and some follow through this time, you know?"

"I'll let him know." Gabe nodded before asking, "So, have you decided who won?"

Angie's frown bloomed into a smile. "Oh yeah, the whole reason I'm here! Come with me!" She led the way to the dining room to find her purse. From it, she pulled two flower crowns, protected by clear, plastic boxes. "I made these to crown the winner. So I made two in case it was a tie."

Tara laughed. "We would've gone into overtime if it was a tie."

"Unfortunately for me, it wasn't. There was a clear winner." Angie turned to Gabe. "Gabe, you made me come harder and faster than I think anyone's ever made me come before."

With an offended gasp, Tara's heart fell. Though, she could believe it; Gabe was the best in her experience. No one else even came close.

"However," Angie continued, "half of the pleasure was from Tara talking me through it. So, congratulations, you're in second place."

Tara whooped as Angie settled a flower crown over his hair, laughing at Gabe's sullen look. The yellow dahlias in his long hair undermined his surly attitude.

"And Tara, you know what you're doing." Angie fanned herself. "You can multitask like no other. Like, that tongue is magic. Can you stick it out for me?"

Tara complied, sticking her tongue out as far as she could.

"Gabe, your fiancée is hung. Look at that thing. Appreciate her." Angie was pointing at her emphatically, while Tara wiggled her tongue at him.

"She's *very* talented with it," Gabe agreed.

"So Tara Sanderson, I crown you the winner." Angie settled the other flower crown over her hair. "Congratulations."

Tara wiped a fake tear, putting her hand dramatically over her heart. "This has been my dream since Gabe first ate me out."

"Okay, Kitten. Good job. Glad you're happy," Gabe muttered. He planted a kiss on her cheek before leaving to let Hippo out of his crate, where he'd been since he'd tried to push Angie away from Tara when they'd first kissed in the dining room.

"Well, this was fun, but I should go finish up for that wedding tomorrow," Angie said, snapping her purse shut again. "You let me know if you two ever want a rematch."

Tara nodded eagerly as Angie cupped her face, leaning in to kiss her goodbye. Pride overcame the fear as Angie's tongue parted hers once again, pleased that she could let herself enjoy the feel of it sliding against hers as their mouths moved together. Not as intense as kissing Gabe, who could turn her into a weak-kneed puddle with just a glance at her lips, but Tara enjoyed it all the same.

"Angelica Maria Garcia Flores!"

They broke apart to find Antonio standing in the open patio door, rage darkening his face.

"What the fuck is this?" Antonio gesticulated in their direction.

"Tonio—" Tara began. Hippo bumped her out of the way to stand in front of her protectively. "Hippo, calm." Hippo sat as trained, but stayed alert at her feet.

Antonio sputtered, "Don't 'Tonio' me! How could you do this to Gabe?"

"What is Tara doing to me?" Gabe leaned against the doorframe, wearing his flower crown over his loose flowing curls and boxers, and nothing else. He tossed Tara his t-shirt, which she reluctantly pulled over her head to cover her nakedness. "Heard we had company."

Antonio looked at him, mouth gaping open, looking for words as he took in the scene.

"Yeah, what *are* we doing to Gabe?" Angie crossed her arms.

Antonio rounded on Gabe. "My cousin, dude? What the hell?!"

"Relax, Tonito. We're all adults here. Just some casual fun. They asked and I came." Angie shrugged. "Four times, if you're curious."

Antonio covered his face with his hands. "I was not!"

"Good. Forget I was ever here, and we'll never talk about it again." Angie turned to Tara and Gabe, giving them each a quick peck on the cheek, before she headed out the front.

There stood Lee, frowning in confusion when Antonio's cousin opened their door instead. Angie gave him a warm greeting as she stepped around him and left.

Lee walked in. "So, I'm confused."

"Me, too, babe." Antonio still looked flustered, but more out of embarrassment than anger.

Hippo must have sensed the danger was past. He let himself out the patio door Antonio had left open.

Tara rounded on Antonio then, crossing her arms the way Angie had just done. "Dude, *you're* confused? You're the one who let yourself into our house, and then accused me of cheating on Gabe. I think we get to be the confused party here."

Antonio looked chagrined. "I'm sorry! I just get very protective of him. I don't want to see him hurt again."

"And I do?" Tara asked, anger rising. "You think that poorly of me? That I would cheat on him?"

"You're right. I'm sorry for jumping to conclusions! I don't think you would ever do anything to hurt him." Antonio raised his hands to plead for mercy. "However, I was not expecting to see my cousin with her tongue down your throat when I walked in!"

Lee made a pained sound. "Babe, this is why I said we should wait at the front. We learned our lesson last time. I don't want to get involved with their sex life."

"Maybe you should text us that you're coming over?" Tara huffed. "Or you know, knock? Shit's going to change, Tonio. It's not just our sex life, but we're gonna have a kid soon. Coming over after the show on Saturday nights might not be the ideal time anymore!"

Antonio winced. "I know. I'm sorry."

Gabe put his hand on her lower back, rubbing circles with this thumb. Tara knew it was meant to calm her, and she was annoyed that it was working. She didn't want to be calm, but his warm hand was very soothing.

"Tonio, what the fuck are you doing here?" Gabe asked, the irritation plain in his voice. Tara admired his restraint; he probably wanted to tear Antonio a new one, too. She put her arm around him in return. If she had to be calm, so did he.

Antonio's mood turned on a dime. His apologetic expression bloomed a smile so big, it seemed fake. "Oh yeah! We got invited to go to do an interview and photo shoot for some big magazine whose name I cannot remember right now!"

"Comette," Lee supplied. Tara raised her eyebrows; "some big magazine" was an understatement. Comette was as big as Billboard or the Rolling Stone.

"Which is great and wonderful and we're very excited about the opportunity. But! It's in New York…" Antonio's voice trailed off, heavy with meaning.

Gabe sighed. "You want me to be your emotional support friend."

"Exactly," Antonio winced. "Lots of demons everywhere. I was never able to get sober when I was living there, and I'm worried I'll relapse. Lee won't be able to be by my side every minute. I need backup. We were hoping you two might want to come with us?"

Tara's anger deflated with concern. Gabe always left his door open in case Antonio needed support. That wasn't something Tara wanted to change, even if it meant fucking up their kid's sleep schedule. They were part of Antonio's support system, a responsibility she didn't take lightly. If only her mother had had anyone besides Tara to lean on, she might have stood a better chance at getting sober too.

Tara had never mentioned it to Gabe, but the bottle of zero-proof wine John had given Antonio had been left behind. Antonio might have forgotten, but Lee wouldn't have. They must have left it on purpose. If that little sip was enough to make Antonio anxious about his sobriety, what would going to New York do?

"When is it?" Gabe asked.

"First weekend in November." Antonio wrung his hands, humming as he waited.

After a moment of intense eye contact, Gabe shrugged and turned to her. "Want to go to New York?"

Tara frowned. That shrug was quite nonchalant, considering all of his nightmares were presumably still living in that city. "You told me to avoid New York."

"Yeah, but it's been years, you know? And the city is huge, there's no way we'd run into…" Gabe paused, glancing at Lee, who—unless Antonio had told him—did not know about Gabe's history of abusive exes. "…trouble."

Tara wasn't so sure, but they could argue about it later. "Fine. Honestly, a trip to New York is a pretty good apology after accusing me of cheating." Tara shot Antonio a glare, who winced guiltily.

"I might regret asking this, but what's with the flower crowns?" Lee asked, staring at Gabe, though he wasn't looking at the crown. "I feel like I missed a lot by waiting outside."

For once, Gabe wasn't shying away or hiding behind her. He was letting Lee look, standing confidently beside her. Tara grinned. "Angie made flower crowns for the winner of our pussy eating competition. Gabe's is more of a participation trophy."

Gabe scowled in mock anger, pinching her ass. "I'm not sure how objective Angie was. I think she likes you more than me."

"Don't be a sore loser, Coop," she teased.

"I regret asking," Lee muttered, still blatantly checking Gabe out. As he should. He looked fantastic; he should show off like this more. In fact, there was a great opportunity coming up to ease him out of his comfort zone.

She grinned up at Gabe, who took one look at the mischief brewing in her mind, and muttered, "Oh no."

"I figured out what I want my prize to be," Tara announced. Gabe rarely showed skin in front of anyone but her. If she had to be by his side to bring that confident Gabe out, she would happily do so. Maybe Gabe telling her all the things she brought to their relationship was working; she might be better at being Tara Cooper than she'd given herself credit for. Even if her version of Gabe's wife would be one who flirted with his friends, proposed threesomes while pregnant, and made bets that put Gabe in revealing Halloween costumes. "You're gonna hate it."

"Gabey, can you put a shirt on or something?" Antonio covered Lee's eyes with a pout.

"You're looking too," Lee teased. "Heart and hole, still all yours, babe."

With a trepidacious look that turned into a smirk the longer Tara beamed up at him, Gabe shook his head. "No, we have a rule against clothes on weekends."

Saturday, October
Twenty-Third

Chapter Twenty-Five

FOLLOWING TARA AND GABE, Lee stepped into the classroom at the Modern Art Institute with an eerie sense of déjà vu that made him feel like he was sixteen again. He hadn't been in this room since he was a kid. Back then, making music was the only way the timid, indecisive Lee could express himself, without requiring an actual audience. Through music, Lee could be his proud, Black, gay self, while still staying safe from the world. "Damn, it's weird to be back."

It was even weirder to be teaching the damn class, with the credentials to back up his "expertise." A record he'd poured his heart and soul into was topping the charts, his idols in the industry were DMing *him* to work on projects, and he was getting flown out to New York alongside Antonio, as if he was the artist, too. He would have been happy to work in Antonio's shadow, but the spotlight found Lee right alongside his husband. It was...well, good, mostly. Uncomfortable, and a little frazzling with how quickly his schedule was filling up, and how many messages he had yet to respond to, but good.

"Tell me about it." Tara smiled over her shoulder at him. "Check the ceiling."

Lee looked up and laughed. "The paint! It's still there!"

"Good times, right?" Tara threw a poncho over her already-baggy sweater and yoga pants. "I still can't believe you did that!"

"*I* did that?" Lee shook his head. "No, Buttercup, *you* did that! When you tried to steal *my* paintbrush."

"You weren't supposed to let go!" Tara protested.

Lee set his laptop on the podium to hook it up to the smartboard. They had made technology upgrades, at least. He'd been worried about burning himself on the touchy projector that used to be there. "In my defense, I never thought I could get it up that high."

Gabe chuckled as he sat on the front table. "From what we heard at the bachelor party, I didn't think getting it up would be a problem for you."

Tara snorted.

"Buttercup, don't laugh at that. That was so bad." Lee sent a strategic kick underneath the table, hitting the lever that kept the tabletop horizontal. He had never considered himself a class clown, only remembering how uptight and anxious he'd been. But he may have had more fun than he gave himself credit for, because this thrill felt familiar.

Gabe landed on the ground with a curse and a bang, as the table flipped to a vertical position. Lee and Tara laughed as they bumped fists. Maybe they had caused trouble back then.

"I didn't know they could do that!" came a voice from the doorway. Syl, the funny kid that Tara had picked up during the vigil last spring, grinned like he had just won the lottery.

Gabe glared at Lee as Tara helped him up. "I didn't either. Not sure I wanted *Syl* of all people to find out."

Lee grinned sheepishly, and warned Syl, "Use that knowledge responsibly. So, don't do it when there's stuff on the table. And make sure the table is facing the right way."

Syl simply grinned, ducking to examine the underside.

"Lee, I'm going to send you an invoice for any and all cleaning fees. Or tablets that need replacing," Gabe threatened, as more kids trickled into the classroom.

"Gabey, lighten up," Lee teased. He'd been nervous about teaching this class, but he was strangely confident now that he was here. There was a lightness in his chest he hadn't often experienced. The dopamine rush was akin to when their first single had gone viral, or when he'd first woken up to a dozen DMs from industry legends and thought "We did it." Was this how Antonio felt all the time? He grinned, elbowing Gabe. "A little mess won't kill you. It'll be good practice when your own kid gets here."

"Coop, you're having a baby?!" Syl asked, the whole class going silent to listen.

Tara and Gabe both shot him a reproachful look. "Lee!"

Lee refused to feel guilty when they should have told everyone by now. "Sorry. Was that supposed to be a secret? Your bump is bumpin'!"

Tara gestured to the poncho she wore. "You think I'm wearing this because it's cute?"

"Honestly, with your fashion sense? I didn't even question it." Lee side-eyed the garish lump of fabric as Tara flipped him off, her finger hidden from the class by her bump. "Hopefully, your wedding outfit is more flattering than that."

"You're getting married?!" A tall girl asked.

"Can we come?" A short girl squealed.

Gabe ran his hand through his hair. "We're never having Lee come teach again," he muttered to Tara, before turning to the classroom full of teenagers. "Yes, Tara and I are having a baby and yes, we're getting married. No, you cannot come. We're having a very small wedding. Honestly, Lee might get uninvited after this."

"You're not getting uninvited," Tara reassured him.

"I hope not, you asked me to take pictures!" Lee pressed a hand to his chest in mock offense. Honestly, this might be his best opportunity to get out of photographer duty during the ceremony. "Who else could possibly step into that role, if not me?"

When he said he'd do anything for their wedding, he meant he'd be Tara's best man and walk her down the aisle. If he couldn't do that, he preferred to get caught up in his feelings and hold hands with Antonio instead. For Tara, he would suck it up and take photos, but he'd rather watch his Buttercup get married. Maybe even shed a tear or two.

"You need a photographer?" The small blonde girl raised her hand eagerly. "I'll do it! You don't even have to pay me!"

Lee grinned, leaning into his plan. "No, they'll pay you. Never work for free."

Tara shot him another look. "As much as I don't want to admit it, that's not the worst idea. We are doing a photography class next."

Every student in his class immediately raised their hands to volunteer.

Gabe waved them down. "Tara and I will talk about it privately and let you know next class. For now, get a tablet from the cart and find your seats. We're going to get on with today's class if you—and Mr. Flores-Jones—can get yourselves under control."

Lee grinned and waved to the class. "Call me, Lee. None of this Mr. stuff."

"Lee is another alum from the Eastside Community Center youth program like me," Tara introduced him, as everyone made their way back to their seats. "And despite his big mouth today, he is my bestie. So be nice to him. He's going to teach you about music production. He got his start selling tracks after we learned how in this class, and he's been growing his business since. Most recently, he produced one of the songs on the new Vamp soundtrack."

"Thanks for the lovely introduction, Buttercup!" Still riding this strange high of what he could only describe as confidence, Lee turned to the class without a touch of the nerves he'd expected. Perhaps being married to a drag queen and middle school teacher had rubbed off on him, because he felt just as comfortable standing in front of a dozen teenagers as he did giving directions backstage at Confession to the tech crew. But before Lee could start on his slide deck, a bang sounded from the tables.

Syl was curled up in a ball on the floor, wincing in pain and his tabletop vertical. "Ugh, I just got sacked by my tablet."

Lee laughed with the kids and Tara, while Gabe muttered something about a lawsuit waiting to happen.

"I warned you, man." Lee set the table back to rights. "This is your first lesson of the day: Don't hit the lever when anything's on the table. And it tilts the opposite way of the brakes, for future reference."

Lee met Hippo's brown eyes stubbornly. *I'm not going to lose to a dog.* Hippo had been standing in front of him, staring, since Lee had sat next to Tara on the couch. But Lee was on fire today, having led a fun, if a bit raucous, class and securing two production projects over lunch. He refused to let a dog bully him out of sitting next to his best friend.

"You're in his spot," Tara teased.

"I'm sitting here. It's my spot." He crossed his arms, sitting back further into the sectional. The staredown had been going strong for a good fifteen minutes.

Hippo woofed in response, practically stamping a foot.

"It's usually my spot," Gabe pouted from the love seat, curled up next to Antonio. His laptop sat on their legs.

"Am I making your life hard for you today, Gabey?" Lee teased. He should probably go easier on Gabe, considering how out of control the kids had gotten under Lee's lax teaching style (honestly, had Gabe expected anything but a dance party with Lee in charge? There was a reason he and Antonio worked so well together). But Gabe was so fun to tease.

Gabe scoffed. "A little, yeah."

Lee put his arm around Tara. "Once you and Tonio figure out the hotel situation, you can have your Kitten and your spot back."

Tara smiled fondly at Gabe. "We're trusting you to make all the good decisions for us. It's not like we can help you decide where we're staying. I've never even been on a plane, let alone know where to stay in New York."

"This is so hard," Antonio sighed, leaning into Gabe's shoulder, squeezing his eyes shut. "I can't remember any of these places, but as soon as I look at what street they're on or a photo of the lobby, I get hella anxious, and I have no idea why."

And just like that, the bubble popped. Lee's chest tightened in shame. While Lee'd had a fun, easy morning, his husband had been home alone, dreading the afternoon of planning their trip. He should have insisted Antonio come to class, but Antonio hadn't wanted to risk Carlita being recognized by a student as Mr. F.

Pulling him into a hug, Gabe rubbed the back of Antonio's neck. "There's probably not many places in Manhattan you're going to feel good about. We can always stay in another borough, if it helps."

Antonio shook his head, sitting up. He didn't look directly at Lee, but Lee didn't need to make eye contact to see that shadow was back. "No, I can handle it. The closest we can get to the studio and the tourist shit, the better."

"How do people take vacation days?" Tara asked Lee quietly, looking at her own laptop perched on her knees. "Like, do you email your clients and let them know and stuff? Or do you just get everything done before you go?"

Lee chuckled. "Buttercup, fuck if I know. I'm planning on working from the hotel." The blessing and curse of freelance work was that he and Tara could work from everywhere.

"Do not work from the hotel!" Gabe huffed. "Why are both of you like this?"

"We freelance!" Lee protested, hot under his sweater; working on music was the only part of his life that he still felt in control of. "We don't work, we don't get paid!"

"Angel, your job is to get interviewed, look hot, and emotionally support me," Antonio teased, still not quite meeting Lee's eyes. "Take the time off. Same goes for you, Tara. Unplug, enjoy yourself."

"I'd set an out-of-office saying you won't respond until we're back that Monday, and block the days off on your calendar," Gabe suggested. "And if you have newer projects, maybe give longer time windows?"

"Wait, so I'm not supposed to respond at all while we're gone?" Tara looked confused. "What if they need something?"

"Then they'll wait until you're back," Gabe shrugged.

Tara grumbling under her breath made Lee laugh. "What are you planning to do once the baby is here? Keep working?" he asked.

"I was going to take fewer clients, but I wasn't going to stop." Tara pursed her lips at Gabe and Antonio's collective dismayed groans.

"Kitten, please take time off after the baby is here. I get four months of leave." Gabe rubbed his forehead. "Take it off with me, and then ramp back up when you feel ready. You'll have enough to worry about without thinking about work."

"And lose all my income?" Tara teased with a scoff. Lee could tell she was trying to hide her fear. Not working had never been an option for them before. "I suppose you're right. But I should probably still hire an assistant, so I don't lose some of my bigger clients while I'm out."

Lee was impressed she was doing well enough to afford an assistant. Maybe he should do the same with his and Antonio's social media, because it was getting out of hand, even for him. He was spending more time responding to messages than making music, but Antonio had been even busier than Lee with teaching; this was Lee's responsibility. His chest tightened, as his phone vibrated in his pocket again; he wouldn't have time to check it until after the show that night. "Does Syl need a job? He seems creative."

"I think Syl has some growing up to do before I trust him with my clients." Tara snorted. "But that is a good idea. Coop, maybe we should help the older ones find part-time jobs and internship opportunities. Or contests they can apply to?"

"I'm full of good ideas today," Lee teased, grinning at Gabe's glare. Even if life was making him feel like he was splitting at the seams from stress, at least his bromance with Tara's lover boy was still easy. He may not know shit about tummy time or maternity leave, but he could tease Gabe. And help his Buttercup fold all the tiny baby clothes Miriam had started bringing over by the bagful.

"What about this one?" Antonio interrupted, pointing to the laptop. "I'm not getting any bad feelings about this one."

Gabe nodded. "Works for me." He took the laptop from Antonio, clicking away to book the rooms. "By the way, Phin says he'll be *early* to our wedding to help set up and shit. I guess he was feeling out of the loop, and this is his way of being more involved and supportive. Hope that doesn't cause any issues for either of you. Since he was at your wedding, I figured it'd be fine, but I can tell him to back off if you need."

Lee exchanged a confused look with Antonio. Lee and Phineas were friends, and even Antonio had begun to ease up on minimizing time with him (though he didn't often hang out with Lee and Phineas's other friends). Why would Gabe think *Lee* might have issues with Phineas?

Antonio raised his eyebrows. "Yeah, that's fine. I appreciate the warning, though."

"Sorry, is there an issue I didn't know about?" Tara fiddled with a hangnail. "I should have checked with you before I told him it was fine. Is it because he ghosted Angie?"

Antonio let out a frustrated groan. "Why are all of my friends sleeping with my cousin?!"

"No, Tonio just needs a buffer around Phin," Gabe explained, then winked at Lee. "Although at least you don't have to worry about him doing a line off anyone now that he's California sober."

Lee was seriously confused now. How did Gabe know about *that*? "Did he... Did he do that with you, too?"

Gabe winced, as if realizing he should have kept his mouth shut. "Snow jobs were his go-to party trick."

"Am I the only one who hasn't slept with him? How was it?" Tara asked, turning to Lee.

Lee shrugged, more concerned with the closed-off, distant shadow that had darkened Antonio's face. It was no longer just a hint. He'd been acting weird lately, saying he was fine anytime Lee asked. Since it hadn't been the secret causing it, Lee had assumed it was the awkwardness with his parents.

But reliving all of his feelings about New York had probably been stressful without adding Phineas—who tended to trigger Antonio's demons—into the conversation. Lee swallowed, skin hot; when he'd told Antonio that they'd hooked up before, he'd never mentioned the details. Hopefully, Antonio wasn't upset about the omission.

Oh no, he was probably mad. Lee should have said something.

Gabe looked cautiously between them. "Sorry if I wasn't supposed to know that. Phin told me when he was drunk."

Antonio forced a smile that didn't reach his eyes. "Don't worry about it."

The mail slot rattled. Hippo's ears perked up, but he kept his eyes on Lee, waiting for him to get up.

With one last guilty wince at Lee, Gabe got up to grab the envelopes that had fallen through. He handed Tara a letter. "I think you got a reply from your mom."

Relieved for the distraction, stress-inducing as this one was, Lee looked over her shoulder. The return address on the envelope was a correctional facility in Illinois. "Are you going to read it now?"

Tara sighed. "Might as well rip the Band-Aid off."

"Give me two seconds, Buttercup. I'll get you some food."

The toxic and horny R&B playlist came on over the sound system, while Lee grabbed some ice and a mandarin orange (the nearest food he could find that would give her something to feel, smell and taste). He returned to find Hippo curled up next to Tara. Gabe had found a way underneath her on her other side, so she was in his lap.

"I see my spot's been taken." Lee shook his head in dismay.

Tara grinned apologetically, as Lee handed her the orange and the ice to Gabe.

As annoyed as he was that the dog had won, his place should be next to Antonio anyway, who—despite pretending to be otherwise—was on edge. And he had to trust that Gabe could help Tara on his own. Lee pulled Antonio into his lap, squeezing his arms around him. "You okay, Babe?" he murmured as Tara opened the envelope.

"Of course," Antonio replied tightly. "Why wouldn't I be?"

"Tonio," Lee coaxed, drawing Antonio's face toward him to look at his hazel eyes.

Antonio took a shuddery breath, before replying in a whisper, "Lee, please. I'm barely keeping it together. Worry about Tara now. I don't want to lose my shit when she's about to lose hers. I'm holding it together. Worry about me once we're home."

Lee frowned, chest tightening, but gave his husband a nod. Antonio was trying so hard to be strong, especially with the constant attention now that the soundtrack was out. Between invites to music podcasts, their contracted movie promo on social media, and meetings with other artists in the industry, they'd had no off days in weeks. And Antonio was teaching on top of it all. "Okay, but if you need anything, tell me."

"I'm fine, Angel." Antonio gave him a tense smile.

Lee kissed his cheek as Tara handed Gabe the letter. Dabbing her eyes, she peeled the orange and shot Lee a smile. That was encouraging. She might be crying, but she didn't seem to be dissociating.

Tara took a deep breath, inhaling the citrus as she peeled it. "She says she's glad to hear I'm alive and doing well. She is sad to hear about my dad. Guess she didn't know that he died either. She apologized for kicking me out like she did, and that she never expected me to reach out to her after all this time."

"Did she explain why she kicked you out?" Lee asked.

Tara nodded. "She saw I was getting older, and she didn't want me to get caught up in her shit. I didn't even know she was involved in fuckshit like sex trafficking, but apparently she'd been involved with a worse crowd than I thought. She thought I had a better chance of a good future without her. I guess she was right." She huffed, wiping her eyes. "And here I thought it was because of me. But she never kicked me out because I wasn't good enough, or because I was queer, or any of the million ways I'd told myself I'd messed up. It's because she was trying to protect me. I can't imagine being in her position to make that decision."

Lee's gut twisted at how easily Tara empathized with the mother who'd abandoned her; Anne had Tara's best interests at heart, in her own twisted way. He fought to quell a rush of anger in comparison; his dad had been selfish in his unwillingness to change. From what Tara had said over the years, Anne had fought her addiction constantly, getting sober dozens of times so she could be the mom Tara deserved, only to give in soon after every time. Even now, Leland was barely trying.

Antonio hummed in his ear, a soothing song that Lee could tell was meant for him. Lee relaxed his grip on Antonio's thigh, murmuring an apology.

Gabe held Tara close. "We're going to give this kid the best chance for a good future. They won't have to go through what you did. You've learned from her mistakes, and you'll be a better parent because of it."

Tara smiled tearfully at Gabe. "You and your mind reading."

"Hurts, doesn't it?" Lee asked softly, rubbing the spot where he'd been gripping Antonio, who settled deeper into his arms. "Feeling all of the emotions right now?"

Tara nodded. "Very confusing. Very achy. You were right. This sucks."

His heart went out to her. She'd have a lot of feelings to sort through as time went on. He'd been on a roller coaster of pain and relief, gratitude and resentment, since reuniting with his parents. "Just give yourself time to process. I put so much pressure on myself to get along with mine for the wedding that I swallowed all of my feelings, and now I'm on the verge of cussing my dad out every time I'm around him."

Cussing him out was an understatement. Lee was ready to cut him out again completely. Except his mom was trying, even if his dad wasn't. He couldn't give up the chance to repair his relationship with her.

Still humming, Antonio stroked Lee's hand with his thumb, still there for him even when he was on the verge of spiraling himself. Lee kissed his shoulder.

"At least I don't have to try and figure it all out before the wedding like you did." Tara shook her head. "I can't imagine adding the stress of meeting her right now to the fucking wedding shit and the baby shit."

Lee hummed in agreement, feeling a hint of that cocky confidence from earlier coming back, now that Tara seemed to be through the worst of it. "Yeah, it's not like she's going anywhere anytime soon."

"Dick!" Tara laughed and threw the orange peel at him.

THE SECOND LEE CLOSED the door to their apartment, Antonio shoved him against it, pulling Lee down to kiss him.

Lee kissed him back, confused but matching his heated urgency. He hadn't known what to expect from Antonio. Apparently, he was getting a needy, desperate husband. He wasn't sure if that was reassuring or not.

Antonio tore his own jacket and t-shirt off first, while Lee's phone vibrated loudly in his back pocket. Fumbling with the buttons of Lee's shirt, Antonio let out a frustrated moan when Lee slowly kissed down his neck, ignoring the string of notifications buzzing against his thigh. The fabric of his shirt tightened until the buttons popped off, pinging on the floor of the entryway.

"Impatient today?" Lee teased against his husband's ear. He hadn't seen Antonio this desperate since they'd first started dating. Heat bloomed under his skin, but Lee wasn't sure if lust or anxiety was fueling Antonio's fire.

"I need you," Antonio's voice shook, pushing Lee's jeans and boxers down around his thighs.

Fighting a pang of doubt, Lee trusted Antonio to know that for himself. Hopefully, this neediness stemmed from Antonio's desire, not his demons. Lee kissed him, working with Antonio to strip him naked of his joggers, groaning as Antonio fisted his growing erection and sucked on his neck.

Before Lee could take control and slow things down, Antonio climbed up his body, wrapping his legs around Lee's waist. Lee grabbed him and turned them around, pressing Antonio roughly against the door. He spat in his hand to wrap around Antonio's dick, pressed between them. "What do you need, Tonio? Tell me."

Antonio's whines were desperate. "Lee, please." Antonio let out a breathy moan as Lee rubbed a thumb over the precum, beading on the head of his dick. His phone buzzed again, somehow louder than Antonio's gasp of pleasure. "Fuck me."

Doubt grew teeth to gnaw, churning in Lee's gut; Antonio did not bottom at the spur of the moment. And he wasn't going to fuck Antonio against the door like this, without lube, no matter how desperately Antonio begged. Instead he reached around to press hard against his perineum, hoping that'd be enough to satisfy Antonio.

"More. Make me feel something," Antonio panted into Lee's mouth. Squirming down Lee's body, he reached behind him to line himself up with Lee's dick.

Lee set him down to pin him against the door, searching Antonio's face. His damn phone buzzed again as he pulled his jeans back up. "Let's go to the bedroom, so I can make you feel good."

Hazel eyes shining, Antonio pressed his lips together, before saying in a strained voice, "No, I need to hurt."

"Nope." Worry shot through Lee, tightening his chest until it hurt to breathe. This wasn't the Antonio he knew. This wasn't his husband, even on his darkest days. "Tonio, I can be rough if you need that right now, but I'm not going to hurt you."

Tears streamed from his husband's eyes. "Please."

"No. You deserve to feel good." Lee pulled him close and brushed away the tears dripping slowly down his husband's cheeks. Steering him to the couch, Lee gathered his husband into his lap. "Talk to me, Tonio."

With a loud sniffle, Antonio swallowed before he answered, "I just... I want to feel alive. I don't want to be alone."

Lee's heart broke as he ran his hands up and down Antonio's spine, holding him close and humming the song he didn't know the words to, but it always calmed Antonio down. "I'm here with you. Whatever your demons are telling you, they're wrong."

Lee's damn phone went off again, shaking the whole couch. With a frustrated growl, Lee fished it out, checked to make sure it was only social media and not from anyone he cared about. Turning the phone off, Lee chucked it onto the chair across the room.

As if he'd been waiting for Lee's undivided attention, Antonio let out a sob into Lee's shoulder that left his husband shaking in Lee's arms. "I'm scared."

Humming quietly, Lee kissed his neck, not needing to ask what. The New York trip. As excited as they both were for their big break, Antonio had been increasingly anxious since they'd gotten the invitation. Like their quiet life together was coming to an end, and the new successful chapter of their lives would leave him exposed and vulnerable.

Lee had been trying to make sure his husband knew he'd always have his back, to protect him from the endless notifications. No success was worth losing each other. Lee would become a recluse, never make music again, if it made Antonio happy. "We don't have to go. We don't *need* to go. If you want to go, you'll be okay. You're safe and loved and so strong, and I love and support you no matter—"

"We're going." Antonio's voice was stronger, more determined. "We're fucking going, and I'm going to be okay. I'm not going to ruin anyone else's life again, especially not yours."

Lee paused. That was an intrusive thought he'd never heard before. "Tonio, what do you mean? Whose life do you think you ruined?"

Antonio sat back with a frown. "Gabe. I left him when he needed me, and now I'm dragging him back to New York. And all that shit with Phin? I got him into that shit." His hazel eyes flicked up to Lee's, distraught. "You never said that about the snow job before. He picked that up from *me*. Told me it was the coolest thing he'd ever seen, and I just let my ego get inflated. I fucked up his whole life and never thought twice about it."

Lee exhaled slowly. That explained his shift in mood earlier. "You didn't fuck up his life, Tonio. Phin's or Gabe's. Their choices were always theirs to make. And both of their lives are going well. Phin is successful, he sobered up, and he's going to therapy." After a pause, he added in a lighter tone, "And it sounds like he's hit it off your cousin. As did Gabe and Tara."

Antonio's huff crackled with frustration. "I don't need to be reminded of *that*."

Lee nuzzled his neck; apparently, Antonio needed more validation before Lee lightened the mood. "The point is, you didn't ruin his life. You didn't ruin Gabe's. You didn't ruin yours. All three of you are happy and thriving." Lee kissed his neck. "And I'm so happy because that means I get to have you in my life. And I love and appreciate you so much. No matter what happens, you can't ruin my life, so long as you're in it, okay?"

"I love you, too, Angel." Antonio kissed him. "Thank you."

Lee kissed him back, relieved and reassured that the desperation now was because Antonio wanted it, not because his demons were telling him he deserved to be used and abused. Even if Antonio's eyes were still wide and teary.

As he pulled Lee on top of him, Antonio pressed the small bottle of lube they kept tucked under the couch cushion into Lee's hand. "Make me feel good, Angel."

"You sure?" Lee teased, sensing Antonio was ready for laughter. For their easy, lighthearted love again. "Because this feels very spontaneous for someone with IBS."

With a snort, Antonio rolled his eyes. "I've been too anxious to eat today, we should be okay."

"Oh, so all of this could be because you're *hangry*?" Lee smirked, pumping lube onto his fingers and coating his dick. "You know how you get when you don't eat."

"Fuck you!" Antonio burst into laughter, his easy, wide smile brightening the shadows that had been lingering over him all afternoon, all week, all month. He bit his lip as Lee slowly worked a finger inside him, trying to show Antonio the love and care he deserved. To reassure him that Lee would always take care of him. "I'll eat *you* if you don't hurry up and fuck me already."

"That's not the threat you think it is, babe." Lee relished in Antonio's gasp as he pressed into him slowly. Since he was apparently too impatient to let Lee do this properly, Lee made damn sure to give his husband plenty of time to adjust. He huffed, fighting the surge of pleasure at Antonio, tight and hot around him. If Antonio wasn't ready for loving reassurance, Lee could shut the demons up a different way.

In reply, Antonio bit his neck.

Lee moaned as Antonio's teeth scraped his skin, "Oh, it's gonna be like that, huh? You want me to be rough with you?" Antonio whimpered under him as Lee pulled out, thrusting slowly to make sure he was ready. "To fuck you so hard, you feel it for days?"

Antonio bucked against him in reply. His legs wrapped around Lee's hips to take him deeper.

With a grin, Lee pinned his hands to the cushion. "This not enough for you, sweetheart?" He snapped his hips harder. "How rough can you take it, Tonio?"

"More, please. Faster." Antonio bit his lip, cheeks puffing out as he panted. Tears formed in his hazel eyes as he and Lee's bodies moved together. The slap of skin echoed in the living room. "Fuck me so hard, I forget my own name."

With a strained laugh, Lee shook his head, tightening his grip on Antonio's wrists. "No, I'm gonna fuck you so hard that you remember who the fuck you married." He leaned down, sucking Antonio's neck. The change in angle sent sparks up his spine. "You'll feel this for days, and remember who made you feel this good."

Antonio let out a shuddering whine. "Lee."

"That's right, Antonio." Lee released his wrists, cupping the back of Antonio's head to kiss him. His other hand worked between them to stroke Antonio's erection. "Me. I love you so fucking much, you're never going to forget it." Lee kissed him again, gasping as Antonio's nails gouged his back. He managed to get a few words in between each sharp thrust. "No matter what happens, no matter where we go, I'll still be here, making you feel good. Making you feel loved. Making you happy."

"Lee, please," Antonio whimpered against his lips. "I'm so close, don't stop."

"Never, my love," Lee murmured, pressing his thumb under the head of Antonio's dick, the way he'd learned long ago drove him wild. As if on command, Antonio cried out, cum dripping over Lee's hand, coating their stomachs. With a relieved groan at how tight Antonio clenched around him, Lee slowed his strokes. The gentler pace did far more for his building orgasm than the desperate fucking Antonio had needed. "I'm not going anywhere."

Antonio laughed under him, tear streaks staining his cheeks. "You better not." He kissed Lee firmly, sucking his lower lip between his teeth. Shuddering as he lost control, Lee groaned, burying his face in Antonio's neck as he came.

"I love you, Tonio." Lee kissed his collarbone as his heart rate slowed. Pulling out, he sat up on his elbows to smile at his husband. "Never forget that."

"As if I could," Antonio murmured, straightening Lee's glasses. "I appreciate you, Angel." His soft smile became a smirk. "Dirty talk included. 'I'm gonna fuck you so hard you remember who the fuck you married.' Cocky ass!" Antonio teased. "Was that my Lee, my sweet Angel, talking like that? Normally you're the one begging me to fuck you harder."

Lee snorted, returning his husband's grin. How far he'd come, if the person who knew him better than anyone could describe him as cocky unironically. "You needed to hear it." He kissed Antonio's chest, the golden brown skin damp with sweat. Lee had needed to say it, too. If only to remind Antonio of exactly what they'd promised with those vows.

Friday, October Twenty-Ninth

CHAPTER TWENTY-SIX

SUNNY

AGAINST ME! BLASTED OVER the speakers in Richard's condo as Sunny jumped around in the bathroom. In between careful pauses to get her eyeliner perfect, she yelled off-key along with the music while she got ready for their Friday evening scene. The outfit he'd laid out for her before he'd left for work was surprisingly comfortable, compared to the lingerie he usually had her strap herself into for their scenes. Today's teddy was silky and sweet, a soft lavender with lace trim that swished around her hips as she danced. Other than the fox tail butt plug, she'd barely had to prepare at all.

She froze. "Wait, why am I so comfortable?" Trepidation warred with excitement; this soft, sweet outfit hinted that Richard was going to go hard on her tonight. Ever since that lunch with his parents—where she'd accidentally let it slip that Gabe was getting married—he'd been stressed. While she was happy to be the beneficiary of his stress, she was starting to worry. "I should really start reading the scene notes when I get here."

Richard—in his typical neurotic fashion—had printed their scene plans from his spreadsheets and stuck it to the fridge, so she could review before he came home from work, when the scene started.

Sunny never actually read them; she liked the surprise, and she'd agreed to it all last weekend. It wasn't like Richard would add anything that she didn't want. The list was already carefully mapped over for their remaining scenes.

The thought made Sunny groan. Nine Fridays left between now and the end of the year, and then they would wait until her consult to schedule more. Sure, their sex life outside of their roleplay time was fab, but she'd miss their Fridays. Work had been on her ass (Why had she told her boss she wanted to be promoted again?); she missed when she could just do her job and go home without being in anyone else's business. It was nice to take a break, one where only Richard was on her ass, in a fun way.

On top of her work stress, analyzing Richard's new home spreadsheet had shown that yes, she really was going to buy a home and raise a family anywhere but Eastside. Sunny pouted, huffing as she applied her lip gloss. She was proud of where she'd grown up. But the schools were awful, the property tax rates were far higher than the public services warranted, and the Eastside of today was not the Eastside that had raised her. Nostalgia only factored in so high in a decision matrix. Hopefully today's scene would be an outlet for the weird mix of emotions sitting heavy in her chest.

Adding the finishing touch of fluffing her hair around her fox ears, Sunny put her makeup kit away. Bopping down the hallway to the music, she headed to the kitchen to make sure the cutesy outfit meant she could be bratty today.

Only to find Barbie in her living room, hands covering her ears as she bent over the sound system.

Sunny screamed.

Jumping back, Barbie screamed too. "What are you doing here?"

"What are *you* doing here?!" Sunny hurried over to turn the music off.

The silence echoed louder than Laura Jane Grace singing moments ago.

Wrapping her camel trench around her as if *she* was the mostly naked one, Barbie looked her up and down. Her eyes widened comically, yet her brows remained stiff from Botox under her perfectly styled bangs.

Sunny crossed her arms in an attempt to hide her tits. Her teddy was far from opaque; Barbie had already gotten an eyeful. "How did you get in here?"

"Lizz—" Barbie caught herself as Sunny raised an eyebrow. "*Richard* gave me a key when...*he* first moved back to Bellamy."

"Why?" Richard had never mentioned that his mom had a key to his place before.

"Because I'm her—*his* mother." Barbie sniffed haughtily. "What are *you* doing here? I wasn't aware you lived here."

Sunny gestured to her outfit. "It's date night."

"It's four in the afternoon." Barbie leaned over, blinking. "And you're wearing a tail?"

"And?" Sunny shrugged. "Did you come over to judge us? Because I can lecture you about sex positivity for hours, if you want to keep this conversation going."

"Well, I suppose it's better if you're here." Barbie dug through her purse. "I know neither of you is likely to feel very forgiving after what happened a couple of weeks ago. Dick has been..." Barbie shook her head. A far-off look in her eye lingered, before she could plaster on a fake smile. "Well! We're just so very hurt that things have fallen so offtrack with...*Richard*. I may not understand everything about his life, but I want my children to be happy."

Sunny nodded, waiting for anything other than the bare minimum that was supposed to make her feel sympathetic.

"And even though our financial situation seems to have taken a turn thanks to *Richard's* actions—not that Dick will ever admit it or tell me anything, even though it's my money..." Barbie's smile tightened. "I come with a peace offering in hopes that my...*child* and I could rebuild our friendship someday."

She handed Sunny a padded envelope. "I kept the boxes in the safe, so Dick doesn't know they're missing, but the certificate and appraisal value are there. You can get new boxes when you get them resized." A sneer creased her nose as Barbie eyed Sunny. "My mother had the daintiest hands."

"These big hands can still slap a bitch," Sunny muttered as she took the thick envelope, feeling a lump that could only be the ring that Richard had asked his mother for.

The uniformity of Barbie's fake smile was unnerving. "And it's best that Dick doesn't find out about this. They're legally mine as they belonged to my mother, but he can be so sensitive about these things. Especially after the lawyer told him the extent of everything that..." She shook her head. "Well, I suppose you know better than I do what Richard did."

"I'm not sure what you're talking about," Sunny said carefully, in case Barbie was fishing for some evidence that Richard had intentionally misled them. Richard—during the damn presentation he'd prepared to discuss their financial assets—had said it was all above the books. He was very clear that he'd only taken assets that would hurt his father's ego, not his financial health. As if a swanky condo in Manhattan wasn't worth millions! From the sound of it, Dick had hurt their financial health on his own, though Sunny had already tuned out by then, too hung up on just how rich her Dicky was. "But thank you—this will mean a lot to Richard."

He'd been incredibly grumpy at the prospect of finding a new ring for her. As much as Sunny teased him about how he had to propose properly, she didn't *actually* need a meaningful, vintage ring. Something affordable and lab-created would be perfectly sensible. But Richard—the incredibly stubborn man he was—would not be redirected.

"I only hope it's enough to warrant an invitation to the wedding after the scene Dick pulled." Barbie's smile turned simpering. "Can I trust you'll put in a good word with Richard?"

Sunny snorted before she could catch it. "Oh. You're serious. Uh... That is for Richard and I to discuss. Later."

Barbie's mouth twisted, but she nodded. "I'll keep the insurance up until the wedding regardless."

"Insurance?" Sunny asked without thinking.

"Yes, insurance!" Barbie huffed. "All jewelry—heirlooms especially—need to be insured. I don't know where Richard found you, but you're marrying into a legacy. The Carter name carries weight in society, now that it's tied to my parents. Best to brush up on what's expected of you."

Sunny didn't reply as Barbie let herself out.

As RICHARD FUSSED AROUND in the bathroom to get himself ready, Sunny knelt in the living room, waiting for their scene to begin. She gnawed on her cheek, eager for Richard to tell her what to do. She'd stashed the envelope in their bedside table, unsure if she should tell Richard right away that his mother had been there. Or if it could wait until after their aftercare. The bedroom was safer than the guest room where they ended their scenes; she might be tempted to bring it up before the right moment—

"Doll, when I told you to kneel, I didn't mean sit on the floor." Dressed in a black suit, Richard strode into the living room, circling her. "You know better than that. Kneel properly."

Sunny straightened up, putting her hands behind her back like she was supposed to. "Sorry, sir."

She should wait until after she was safely out of subspace. If she got to subspace, anyway. One, to buy more time to figure out what to say, and two, because it would probably be hard for both of them to get in the right headspace—

"Sunshine, come here."

Sunny snapped to attention, trying to close the tabs in her head about the ring and Barbie, to maximize the Scene tab. The rug fiber dug across her knees, the pain grounding her enough to focus on her crawling. Her hips swayed as she slunk slowly across the floor. With a sweet smile, she approached Richard, still fully dressed and sprawled across the couch. Her eyes stayed downcast as she resumed her kneeling position at his feet.

He held out a hand to cup her jaw, and she leaned into his touch, trying to focus on him as he tilted her head back. Richard sighed. "You didn't read the scene plan."

"I did!" Sunny insisted, even though she hadn't. Barbie had interrupted before she could get that far. "I'm being sweet and obedient—like you wanted!"

Richard's eyes narrowed. "Strange, because the scene plan says to be as bratty as you want."

Sunny winced; normally bratty was her default. "Oh."

"What's wrong, Sunshine?" He leaned forward, stroking her hair.

"Nothing! I can be bratty!" Sunny bit his arm. His black sleeve was silky under her teeth. *Oh, that's what the fox outfit is for!* "See?"

Richard's mouth twitched. "You're very cute. But what's wrong?"

"Nothing! I promise, sir!" Sunny whined. She just wanted to do the scene; they only had nine left. "I'll be better!"

"Come here." Richard patted his knee. Sunny jumped up and sat on it, fluffing her tail out behind her. Finally, he was going to play with her, and she could put these thoughts to rest. He wrapped his arms around her and cuddled her close, strangely affectionate. Richard was normally not this soft during scenes. "What's wrong?"

Sunny groaned. "*Nothing*...sir."

"Sunny, I'm just Richard right now, asking my girlfriend what's wrong. I can tell something is bothering you, and it's taking you out of the scene."

She pouted. "Can I tell you during aftercare?"

"No. Because we won't make it to aftercare if it's bothering you this much." Richard nuzzled her neck. "Tell me."

Sunny huffed. "I'll tell you if you promise we can reschedule this one."

"Oh," Richard sat back. "We're stopping if you tell me?"

Sunny reluctantly nodded. "Probably."

"Okay, we can try the scene again tomorrow."

Sunny tsked. "Good try. It's Confession's Halloween party tomorrow, and you can't get out of it because our costumes are fucking amazing. How about Sunday?"

"Worth a shot." Richard huffed. "Sunday is acceptable. Tell me."

Sunny bit her lip. "Your mother came by today."

Richard sat up straight. "What."

"Your mother. She was here. Let herself in with the key that I didn't know she had and saw me looking like this." Sunny waved her hand over her torso, still on display in the translucent lavender teddy. "The tail and the ears and everything!"

"Is she okay?" Richard's voice took on a darker edge.

"I mean, once we both stopped screaming, yeah, she seemed fine." Sunny shrugged. She hadn't expected Richard's reaction at finding out that his mom broke into his condo to be concern for Barbie's well-being. Sunny had been more worried about changing the locks. "Bitchy as usual. Why?"

Richard sighed. "Just—I gave her the key as an escape plan from Dad. I never thought she'd use it unless it was an emergency."

Sunny bit her lip, unsure if she should feel bad that she didn't care about Barbie's safety as much as he did. "I don't think she intended to pay a social call. She was surprised I was here."

Richard pulled her lip from between her teeth with his thumb. "What did she want?"

"She left something for you. A peace offering, she called it, in hopes that you might rebuild your friendship." Sunny stood and held out her hand. She led him to the bedroom and handed him the envelope.

He turned it over in his hands. "Our *friendship*." Richard scoffed. "I assume she wants an invite to the wedding?"

Sunny nodded. "I told her that was our decision. She also said it's best if your dad doesn't find out about this, but all the paperwork you need should be in there."

Sitting on the bed, Richard pulled out the neatly folded documents as Dumpster jumped up to investigate. Dumpster promptly laid on them the moment he set the papers aside, as Richard poured a ring into his hand. Out fell a silver band, with engraved geometric swirls encircling tiny diamonds.

"Ooh, that's pretty."

"It is. Art nouveau. From my grandmother's third marriage." Richard set it safely out of Dumpster's reach on the nightstand. "But it isn't the one I asked for." He reached back into the envelope to pull out—

"Mother fuck!" Sunny's jaw dropped at the sight of a massive, gleaming, rectangular diamond, flanked by two smaller rectangles. Even the "smaller" diamonds were bigger than any diamond Sunny had ever witnessed in real life. "Is that real?"

Richard nodded, holding out the ring to her. Sunny took it, eyes bulging out of her head as she inspected it. They'd had a diamond the size of her thumbnail, just sitting away in a safe? She glanced at the other ring, sitting next to a flickering candle on the nightstand. The silver filigree looked positively drab in comparison.

Dimming the lights, Richard took the ring back from her, sitting beside her on the bed. "Can I do this now?"

"Do what? Buy an island? Or a small country?"

Richard cackled. "Propose."

"What? Now?" Sunny looked around their bedroom. While she'd been busy losing her mind over the ring, Richard had lit candles. They flickered gently in the dim, romantic lighting of the room. Soft classical music was playing on his phone. "I'm wearing a fox tail butt plug."

"And?"

"And ears!"

Richard guided her to sit on the bed next to him, taking her hand. "You look stunning, but if you prefer to change, I can wait. Unless you'd prefer to do this tomorrow when we go out for Halloween?"

"Oh, no, not in public! Please, no!" Sunny's heart pounded, and she couldn't seem to close her mouth. "This is just very spontaneous for you. Are you feeling okay?"

"Better than ever. I wanted to do this months ago." With that ghost of a smile that always made her heart beat faster, Richard calmly waited for her permission.

With a heavy swallow, Sunny nodded.

Richard kissed her knuckles with a deep breath:

"You and I

Have so much love

That it

Burns like a fire,

In which we bake a lump of clay

Molded into a figure of you

And a figure of me.

Then we take both of them,

And break them into pieces,

And mix the pieces with water,

And mold again a figure of you,

And a figure of me.

I am in your clay.

You are in my clay.

In life we share a single quilt.

In death we will share one bed."

He paused to take a deep, shuddering breath. But before he could continue, Sunny asked with a wet laugh, "Did you write me a poem?"

"No, I recited one by Kuan Tao-Sheng. Yet another attempt to convince you that Taoist poetry is not boring." Richard's smile was apologetic as he shifted nervously on the bed next to her. "You know anything *I* wrote would be awful. And I wanted it to be beautiful for you."

Sunny huffed. "You're such a nerd, Dicky."

"I know."

"I love that about you."

"I know." Richard kissed her fingertips; his lips trembled under her touch. "Sunny, you mean so much to me. You've brought me more j-J-" He frowned, blinking rapidly. "Damn it, I practiced this dozens of times."

"Stop trying to give a speech, Dicky. Just talk."

Richard huffed and gave her a look, but continued, "You've brought so much to my life, that I can't remember who I was before I met you, or imagine who I would be without you. And I never want to find out, because I want us to spend the rest of our lives together, and support each other's dreams, and give your mom more grandbabies than she knows what to do with."

Sunny laughed, her eyes burning.

"Sunny Boonmee, would you—"

"Wait." Sunny looked archly at him, namely at how he was sitting on the bed. Richard looked at her in panicked confusion. His blue eyes were practically teal from the tears reddening his eyes. She tsked. "You know better than that. Kneel properly."

Richard let out a wet laugh and slid off the bed to get on one knee, holding the ring over her finger. "Sunny Boonmee, would you do me the honor of being my wife?"

Sunny nodded wordlessly, vision blurring as the cool band of gold slid up her finger. Before she could wipe her eyes, Richard's lips crashed into hers, pushing her back into the bed. Dumpster yowled and ran out of the room as Sunny landed on her tail.

Ignoring the cat, Richard's mouth trailed down Sunny's neck, sucking hard enough to embed the most pleasurable bruises into her sensitive skin. Sunny gasped as he yanked the satin ribbon holding her teddy together out in one smooth motion. Cool air pebbled her nipples seconds before his hot mouth and fingers found them.

She arched into his touch, wedging a knee between his thighs. The stiff fabric of his slacks scratched her leg, giving him something to grind on, while his fingers pressed her plug into the spots he knew better than she did.

Normally, their Friday nights involved vibrators and straps, the smack of a leather flogger against her ass, and both of them naked and shining in sweat and lube. Tonight, they were both too worked up, too needy for self-control. Sunny needed him fully dressed, with her clothes half torn off. His raspy voice saying her name around her tit in a shuddering exhale. Fingers and mouths and body parts working in tandem. Just them, raw and desperate and sweet.

As her pleasure mounted from his skilled fingers and mouth, he shuddered around her knee with a moan. Teeth sank into her neck with a sharp ache. She held him there with her nails digging into his scalp, and wrapped her other leg around his hips to trap him in place.

"Fuck, Sunny, you play dirty," he laughed, grinding on her knee to bring himself off again.

With a pleased grin, she let him up. "I know. Making you come twice—how rude of me."

He climbed over her further to kiss her, pressing her into the bed as he hitched her leg around his shoulder. Sunny groaned as his hand massaged her muff against the plug. Within moments, she was shuddering under him as pleasure tore through her body. He swallowed her cries, bringing her to her peak over and over again until she finally pushed him off, begging him to stop.

He rolled off of her with a smug look, his suit rumpled and his hair askew.

Struggling to catch her breath, Sunny let him kiss his way down her arm and up her neck. As she shifted into a more comfortable position, she picked up the papers squished under her shoulder to set them on the table with the other ring, when a dollar sign caught her eye. "Dicky, what the fuck?"

"What's wrong?" He pulled away from her neck. "What is it?"

"You just put forty thousand dollars on my finger?!" Her heart pounded, no longer from arousal.

"Well, we should get it reappraised for insurance purposes, but I imagine it's closer to fifty." Richard silenced her with a kiss. "Don't worry about the price."

She scoffed. "Easy for you to say, I'm gonna get jumped!"

"Good luck to them," Richard said dryly. "But we can get you another ring for everyday wear, if you prefer to save that one for special occasions. Okay?"

Nodding, Sunny bit her lip as she grinned. "After I'm done showing it off to everyone."

Richard snorted. "Want to have some fun before we tell our friends?"

She sat up on her elbows, her curiosity piqued. "Always. What do you have in mind?"

"Want to see how long it takes for anyone to notice?" He smirked, a glint in his eye.

Sunny laughed, delighted that even after putting forty fucking stacks on her finger, Richard was still his quietly mischievous self. That he wanted her to be his conspirator in his schemes, instead of a demure, obedient trophy like his mother. That her chaotic, kinky, bratty self was exactly the wifey material he wanted. "Sure, but with this ring, it won't take them long—" She gasped. "Wait, tomorrow is the Halloween thing at Confession! They'll think it's part of the costume! Yes, this will be so fun!"

Saturday, October Thirtieth

CHAPTER TWENTY-SEVEN

Jazz

STRAIGHT MEN SMELLED AWFUL. Jazz loved Ed, but the stale odor of unhygienic college-aged boys permeated every room of his frat house. Music thumped around her as she sat quietly in a chair—sitting on a couch by herself would just be asking for some dude to hit on her—and smoked the joint Teddy had handed her.

Tugging on the hem of her dress as the crusty upholstery scratched the back of her thighs, Jazz almost regretted dressing up as Poison Ivy for the frat's Halloween party. Or at least she could have worn a longer green dress under the faux vines wrapping her body.

Maybe one day she'd look back at her college years with embarrassed regret for acting so wild the second she was free to dress without suffering her parent's judgment. But not yet. Jazz was still thrilled by every second. Crusty frat house chairs aside.

"Care to share?" Julissa asked, perching on the arm of Jazz's chair.

Blinking in surprise, Jazz passed the joint to her along with the lighter. "Having fun?" Julissa had never acknowledged her presence before, not without Mimi there, anyway.

Julissa leaned back, crossing her arm under the leather bustier that made up the top half of her Cat Woman outfit. "Greek life—especially frats? Not my scene. And considering you've been sitting here by yourself ignoring everyone, I'd guess it's not yours either."

"It can be fun. Sometimes." Jazz normally found some stoned philosophy major who wanted to talk about the universe, or a quiet engineering student to infodump about their special interest, so she wouldn't have to make small talk with creeps. She usually had a good time.

Julissa snorted. "Not tonight. This is a shitshow."

Admittedly, this was a little more crowded, the partygoers drunker, and the house significantly more smelly. It was hard to hear the nerds talk about roller coasters over the music; the goth girl she'd been talking with about the weight of a soul had decided to take molly and lock herself in the bathroom to dance with glow sticks. Jazz might have joined her, but she didn't want to lose track of time. She had two more hours before she could feasibly leave without hurting anyone's feelings, but she didn't want to risk taking an Uber to Confession dressed in so little *and* high out of her mind.

Mimi and Teddy—dressed as Bat Girl and Batman—cheered from across the room at the pong table as they finally got a ball in the cup, just before Ed (dressed as Robin) easily sank the ball in their last one.

"Oh good, maybe she can hang out with me again," Julissa muttered under her breath.

Jazz rolled her eyes. "She's allowed to hang out with other people, you know."

"I know." Julissa's voice was reproachful. "I just...I'm not good at this."

"At what? Polyamory?" Jazz kept the "obviously" to herself.

"Well, that too. But I've been reading some of the books Teddy lent me, trying to understand it all."

Jazz shifted uncomfortably in her chair; she hadn't even read any of the books Teddy had recommended. Maybe she should do that, if even *Julissa* was doing her research.

"No, I meant this..." Julissa waved the joint around the room. "Socializing. Talking to people I don't know. I get anxious, not knowing the people I'm with, or what's safe to talk about."

"I think everyone does," Jazz huffed. "At least I do."

"And yet we're not all social butterflies like you." Julissa teased, passing the joint back. "I feel like such a poser. You know, I'm not even from Chicago? I just tell people that so they think I'm cooler than I am. I'm actually from Lake Forest. I never even went to a party before I met Mimi. My dad would flip out if he knew I was here."

"That doesn't make you a poser. That just makes you a nerd." Jazz snorted, resisting the urge to talk shit about the Lake Forest lie. She wasn't sure if she and Julissa were there yet. "Besides, I've literally been sitting by myself for twenty minutes, while there's a whole-ass party happening around me. Some social butterfly."

"And? I was too anxious to do that. Mimi went to play beer pong with Ed and Teddy, and I immediately got sweaty because I didn't know what to do besides find someone to latch onto." Julissa laughed, looping her arm through Jazz's. "You're my victim until Mimi's back. I'm so glad she likes how clingy I am."

Jazz chuckled with her, confused at what felt like sympathy. "Why did you come then, if you knew you weren't going to have a good time?"

Julissa raised an eyebrow. "Why did you?"

Jazz didn't answer. She came for the same reason Julissa did. Mimi. Because Mimi—and Teddy...and Ed, though he'd never admit it—would have been upset if she outright ditched them for Blanche. Even if it was more accurate to say she was ditching a frat party for Confession. But she could suck it up for a few hours to keep the peace.

Besides, her dad would throw a fit if he ever found out she was dressed like she was, drinking and getting high at a frat party. That in and of itself made the night worth it.

Jazz sighed. Maybe she and Julissa had more in common than she wanted to admit. Being proven wrong, when she was just starting to trust her instincts, was the worst. But Ed, Teddy, and Mimi had been right; Julissa was trying, and Jazz could cut her some slack. She flicked the lighter, taking a deep drag of the joint. Maybe she should embrace her Pisces side more, instead of clinging to the detachment of her Aquarius rising. To keep an open mind, and recognize others in her life could change as much as she did. To allow bad situations to improve.

Mimi collapsed into Jazz's lap with a grin. "Hello, my lovelies!"

After she returned Mimi's kiss, Jazz smoothed her latex miniskirt down, so her girlfriend wouldn't inadvertently give the guys lurking across the room an eyeful of her ass. Mostly to distract herself, as Mimi and Julissa swapped spit inches from her face.

"How do you feel about getting out of here?" Julissa traced Mimi's neck with her thumb.

"We can't leave this early! It's not even ten!" Mimi pouted.

"Baby, your two introverted girlfriends—"

"I'm not an introvert," Jazz corrected.

Julissa huffed. "Your two socially anxious girlfriends?" She looked to Jazz, who nodded. "Are not having the time of our lives. It's very loud, and crowded, and drunk, and very cishet—"

"Don't forget smelly!" Jazz chimed in.

"And smelly!" Julissa nodded.

"But what about Teddy?"

Jazz spotted Teddy's legs wrapped around Ed's waist, as they made out on the kitchen counter. "She's fine."

"Besides," Julissa leaned down to whisper into Mimi's ear. But Jazz caught enough, involving "latex," "begging," and "screaming," to have a clear understanding of exactly what Julissa and Mimi would be doing, when they got back to Mimi and Teddy's apartment.

Mimi's cheeks turned pink, biting her lip as she nodded eagerly. "But what about Jazz?"

Jazz patted her thigh. "Don't worry about me. I have another party calling my name."

Mimi winced, before she kissed Jazz's cheek. "Sorry."

"Don't be. You want us to have a good time, and I appreciate that." Jazz patted her thigh only twice; for once, she didn't have many negative thoughts to capture. She was more excited about finding Blanche. Which was a nice change, being excited about seeing her new partner, instead of feeling guilty for ditching her partners to hang out with her roommate. "I'm just not vibing with frat boys tonight. And I can probably make it to Confession in time to watch the show!"

JAZZ THANKED HER UBER driver, taking care not to flash anyone as she exited the car. She adjusted the hem as she stood, pulling down the back where it was riding up. Her forced modesty days might be behind her, but she didn't want to show the world her whole ass. Not when it was this cold outside.

With a shiver, Jazz shut the car door. The joint she'd shared with Julissa began to hit as she walked down the sidewalk, her head spinning with the strangeness of being both unbothered and paranoid. She tugged gently on the faux vines that wrapped around her legs and torso to a more flattering position to accentuate her curves. Patting her phone tucked into her bra three times to make sure it was there, Jazz then triple-checked the scrunchie around her wrist to make sure her house key and belongings were still zipped securely inside.

She always did this sober, too. But the weed made it seem even *more* important to make sure she had everything right now, that she was clear of any negative energy from the frat party. Satisfied she was all put together, she took three deep breaths, tugged her amethyst gently, and walked into Confession.

"Poison Ivy—nice! I love the hair, Jazz!" Jackie, the front-of-house manager checking IDs, greeted her as she entered.

"Thank you!" Jazz spun in a circle, showing off her outfit for her brother's friend. Blanche had helped her dye her locs burgundy to fit her costume. "You look scary as hell!"

Jackie was dressed as a nun, a little blood running from her mouth. "Thanks! I got these cool fangs. I'm the vampire nun from that gay ass movie!" Jackie showed off the retractable fangs in her mouth, tongue flickering. "Should have thought this through, though. I keep getting hit on," Jackie scoffed. "Anyway, Lee is up in the control room for the show, but his friends are around downstairs somewhere."

Jazz thanked her for letting her bypass the line without paying the cover. Jackie's assumption that she was here to hang out with her brother was not entirely accurate; Jazz was on a mission to find Blanche.

It didn't take long. Their blond pigtails were easily found in the crowd on the first floor. Weaving her way through the glamorous, glitter-coated crowd (which smelled like perfume, liquor, and clean sweat—delightful after the stale sock smell of the frat house), she greeted them with a hug from behind and a kiss on the cheek. "Hi, Beautiful!"

Blanche turned to face her, their face breaking into a grin. Blue and purple Harley Quinn makeup crinkled as their eyes lit up. "What are you doing here, Jazzy? I thought you'd be with your partners!"

"You look so good!" Jazz gushed. "Your thighs are amazing in those shorts!"

Harley was a great costume on them. Temporary hair dye brightened the tips of their hair. Their curves were luscious in red shorts and a crop top, paired with a jacket over their shoulders.

"Jazzy, you helped me get ready," Blanche teased. "Did Teddy and Mimi come with you? Or is there drama you want to vent about?"

Jazz waved her hand. "Nah, no drama or anything. Jules and I weren't really feeling the frat house vibes, so she took Mimi home and I came here."

Blanche's hands slid around her waist. Jazz half leaned in for a kiss, before remembering they were in public. "Let me buy you a drink before we go up for the show. Bombay and tonic?"

Jazz nodded. "You know it!" Jazz didn't particularly like drinking, but at least gin tasted more alive and less like poison than most liquor. The botanicals saved it. After the joint and the couple of seltzers at the party, she didn't *need* a drink, just something to do with her hands.

Gin and tonic in one hand, Blanche led her upstairs by the other, their fingers lacing together. Every time Blanche held her hand or kissed her or—a recent development—squeezed her ass, Jazz felt like she was in a dream. She was still anxious that one day Blanche would come to their senses and realize they were dating their friend's kid sister, when they could have literally anyone else.

No self-doubting, Jazz. That's your dad talking. She still had so much bullshit to unlearn. *You have a lot to offer in a relationship.* The mantras and affirmations were going to be her new attitude, her new outlook on the world. Eventually. As soon as she could get his deeply-rooted opinions out of her head. *You have intrinsic value beyond being an obedient housewife.* It wasn't always him, either. Her mom's voice could be just as biting.

But, she was free now. Aside from the occasional dinner with her parents, Lee, and Antonio. And the frequent texts and calls from her mom that she ignored, because Jazz had *told* her mom that she would only respond twice a week unless there was an emergency.

Now she simply had to retrain her brain; it still hadn't gotten the memo that she was free.

When they joined the rest of their friends upstairs, Lee and Antonio were with them, hanging out before the show started. Jazz admired their costumes, laughing when she saw Gabe's. He was dressed as Lara Croft, in tiny shorts and a tank top, strapped into various holsters. "Gabe, you look hot."

Gabe scowled, crossing his arms around his wide chest. Even as he tried to hide it, it only emphasized his muscular frame and massive pecs. "Thank you, but I would much rather have dressed on theme if I had been given a choice."

Tara patted his arm, dressed in a glittery blazer and black maternity pants: Beyonce's pregnancy reveal outfit. *Teddy would be so proud of me for recognizing that.* "I keep telling you, there was no planned theme. This is a complete coincidence that Lee, Tonio, and I all dressed as Beyonce. I just wanted an iconic pregnancy look."

"And I do this number every year." Antonio wore the black one-sleeved leotard and heels from the "Single Ladies" music video. He huffed, "Sorry I didn't check to see if you wanted to be matchy matchy this year."

"He didn't ask me either, but I wanted to coordinate with him." Lee twirled, wearing the long, yellow dress from the "Hold Up" music video. One of Antonio's wigs gave him the iconic waist-length honey-blond hair.

"Does Dad know you're in drag?" Jazz teased.

"Does Dad know your ass is hanging out like that?" Lee shot back.

"Not my concern if he did." Jazz scoffed. "But where's your bat?"

Lee scowled. "I had a dick joke ready for that question, but I wasn't expecting *you* to ask it."

Jazz wrinkled her nose, luckily interrupted by the arrival of Sunny and Richard, dressed like a sexy Morticia and Gomez Addams. Sunny wore a plunging long-sleeved black dress and costume jewelry, while Richard's pinstripe suit had nothing underneath it, showing off the deer head and flowers tattooed on his chest.

"Hello, Titties!" Tara reached for Sunny's chest, who laughed and smacked her hand away. Instead, Tara grabbed Sunny's hand. Her jaw dropped as she examined the diamond ring on her finger. "Got something to announce there, Sunny?"

"Seriously?" Sunny sighed. "I was hoping we could at least make it to intermission."

Richard shook his head, frowning at Tara. "Spoiled our fun."

"Wait, you two got engaged?" Blanche asked with a squeal. "Baby-girl, that's amazing! Congratulations! When did this happen?"

"Last night. We thought it'd be fun to see how long we could go before anyone found out." Sunny shrugged at Richard as everyone congratulated them. "Lasted five seconds."

With a low whistle, Lee admired the ring. "Damn, I'd be sweating if this was on my hand."

"I am," Sunny admitted. "Especially since we haven't resized it yet. But I think it fits okay? Or at least it didn't come off around the house, so fingers crossed! Literally!"

"Angel, we gotta go." Strangely quiet up until then, Antonio tugged on Lee's billowing yellow sleeve. Even in drag, Antonio seemed subdued. "Any of you up for the costume contest? I can bring you up."

Richard shook his head. "I'm already wearing a costume for the first time since I was a child. I am not getting on stage, too."

Sunny shook her head emphatically in agreement. "I'm not really an onstage person."

"We should, Blanchy!" Jazz grabbed Blanche's hand. "Ivy and Harley are canon, you know."

"Oh, are they?" Blanche smiled as if they hadn't coordinated their costumes for that reason, putting their arm around her waist. Jazz leaned into their touch. "Let's do it."

"Anyone else?" Antonio pointed around, searching for more volunteers. "Gabey, you're looking positively edible tonight. You'd have a chance."

Gabe shook his head resolutely, awkwardly hiding his body behind Tara. "I'm already out of my comfort zone. I'm only wearing this because I lost the bet."

Tara grinned. "I asked you who your celebrity crush was as a kid. Not my fault you were a pervy nerd, Coop. You could have said literally anyone else."

"You look good tonight, Jazzy," Blanche murmured in her ear as they sat down at the VIP table Chas had booked for them. Their hand trailed from her waist to where her dress rode up her ass, their fingers teasing the hem.

Jazz realized belatedly that there were only four chairs at the table for the six of them. Before she could look for another, Blanche pulled her into their lap.

She hoped no one else could tell how high she was, even if her cheeks hurt from smiling like an idiot at the onslaught of affection from the normally hesitant Blanche. "Let me know if I'm crushing you."

"I would never complain about being crushed by you, Jazzy," Blanche muttered. "Best way to go, I think."

Jazz laughed too loudly, then whispered. "Are you high, too?"

Blanche shrugged. "A little. Tara brought Gabe over to smoke with me to help him be less self-conscious, but I think it backfired."

Gabe pulled Tara onto his lap, hiding behind Tara's body as best he could. "Am I paranoid, or is everyone judging me?"

Sunny sat next to him. "Everyone is staring, but they're drooling, not judging. Seriously Gabe, I knew you were in good shape, but I had no idea you were hiding all of that. Do you ever take a day off from the gym?"

Tara shook her head. "No, he works out in the basement on his 'rest' days. Hopefully, our hotel in New York doesn't have a gym. We'll never leave the hotel."

Richard frowned. "You're going to New York?"

Jazz smiled, not following any of the conversation anymore. She loved how Blanche's hands rasped across her skin, with the thump of the music in her bones.

"What did you take, Jazzy? You're grinning like a fool." Blanche murmured, smirking as they leaned into her. "And did you bring enough to share with the class?"

"Teddy gave me a joint earlier," Jazz laughed. "I have a gummy, though. You want it?"

Blanche nodded. "Sure, if you don't mind. I feel like I need to catch up with you."

"It's not like I'm going to take it. I'm high as shit!" Jazz fiddled with the scrunchie on her wrist, unzipping it and retrieving the tangerine-flavored gummy from within. "Here." Blanche opened their mouth, sucking on Jazz's fingertips subtly as she fed it to them. Their lovely dark green eyes smiled up at her as Blanche kissed her fingers.

Sunny cleared her throat. "You two look cozy." She raised her eyebrows as she looked between Jazz and Blanche. She turned to Richard. "Really? Not going to pinch me?"

Richard didn't reply. His jaw was working back and forth as he glared at Gabe.

Still grinning, Jazz zipped up the scrunchie again so her house key and cash wouldn't fall out. Her phone, with her ID and debit card tucked into the case, was still wedged into the top of her dress. She touched the scrunchie three times to reassure herself that everything she needed was still there, and tapped three times on the phone. Then with a grin, she tapped Blanche's head three times, too. Everything was in order. Her fingers touched the pendant.

The lights went down as Jazz settled against them. Tracing up and down her thighs, Blanche's fingertips dipped along the hem, nails scraping her skin. She tried not to squirm; Blanche was probably not trying to tease her. They were barely comfortable making out for too long, let alone driving Jazz mad with want on purpose.

Jazz cheered as Carlita took the stage with two other queens, flawlessly recreating all of the Single Ladies choreography. Blanche sang along to the music with Jazz, and to the number after that and the one after that.

"And to think, you only listened to grunge before I moved in," Jazz teased.

Blanche stuck their tongue out. "I'm not *that* old, Jazz. You listen to this pop stuff often enough that I can't help but learn it."

From when she'd met them, Blanche had always been fun to be around, always coming up with some scheme or game to play together as they observed everyone. But since moving in, Jazz had found the side of Blanche that let loose. That danced while they did the dishes, that giggled until they snorted, and then giggled more because they snorted.

There were dark sides, too, like the night she had come home to find a zombified Blanche barely able to move. Or who woke her up at night with a scream because they were having a nightmare. But Jazz loved seeing all of the new sides she'd found, not just the in-control survivor mask they always wore.

Carlita took the stage after Chas finished a rousing performance of "The Devil Went Down to Georgia" to announce the costume contest. The individuals went first, the crowd cheering for their favorites. A person wearing full body paint as Mystique won easily, with second place going to a shirtless fireman who strategically tore away his pants to reveal a glittery jockstrap to the crowd's delight.

"Coop, I think you could have come in third at least," Tara teased Gabe.

"What, only third?" Gabe scoffed. "This skimpy ass costume isn't good enough for first?"

"Maybe we should have made some tearaway shorts. Next year." Tara winked.

Gabe shook his head vehemently. "Kitten, I am never agreeing to another wager without naming the stakes first again."

"You could have backed out," she taunted.

"You'd never let me live it down." Gabe kissed her shoulder with a grin.

Blanche and Jazz got up excitedly as Antonio called up couples or groups for the costume contest. Jazz handed her phone and scrunchie to Tara. "Promise me that you'll keep this safe."

Tara nodded solemnly. "I promise."

"I'm trusting you, Tara."

"I got you, Jazz." Tara laughed and put the scrunchie around her wrist, holding it up so Jazz could see.

"Are we about to make fools of ourselves?" Jazz asked, ascending the stairs with Blanche right behind her.

"Beautiful, if you're feeling anything like me right now, we should not watch any videos of this in the morning." With a giggle, Blanche gripped her hand as they waited on stage.

Jazz giggled with them, unable to focus on anything Carlita was doing with the other contestants.

However, as soon as Carlita got to them, Jazz's muscle memory of dancing with Blanche in the kitchen took over. Jazz strutted around Blanche and brought them into a spin. She caught them around the waist and dipped them, as Blanche hooked a leg over her hip. The crowd cheered.

She looked into Blanche's eyes, who grinned up at her. Their tongue poked out between their teeth like always, when Blanche was happiest. This was normally when Jazz kissed them. She *really* wanted to kiss them.

But they were on stage and in public. Even as high and slightly tipsy as she was, Jazz made herself settle for pressing a kiss into Blanche's hand instead.

"Everyone give it up for Poison Ivy and Harley Quinn!" Carlita shouted as the crowd cheered. In a quieter tone, Antonio added in her ear, "Sorry Jazz, but Lee is asking me to do this." Carlita gently tugged on the back of her dress as Jazz set Blanche upright, pulling the hem down over her ass again.

Jazz flipped the bird to the control room, rolling her eyes while the crowd and Blanche booed.

Carlita covered her face. "Yeah yeah yeah, boo me. I deserve it. You know I would never want anyone to hide their bodies—especially such a prodigious ass like Miss Ivy has—but in my earpiece, my husband is complaining that he can see his little sister's tuchus on stage, and I live to make him happy." Carlita explained, waving a hand in the direction of the control room, before putting it on her hip. "Are you happy, Lee? You got me booed! The things I do for you!"

He moved on to the next couple, dressed as Korra and Asami. Jazz stopped paying attention, closing her eyes as Blanche wrapped their arms around her waist. Carlita came back and announced them as the second place winners, giving first place to a group of four dressed as Sexy Golden Girls.

"Chas is calling me, babe. I'll meet you back at the table in a minute," Blanche murmured in her ear.

Jazz nodded, going to reclaim the chair next to Tara. Gabe and Richard must have stepped away, because only Sunny and Tara were at the table. Tara handed her back her belongings.

As usual, Jazz checked everything. Not that she didn't trust Tara; it was just her habit, especially when she was not the soberest. Phone with ID and debit card went back in the reliable storage space in her left bra cup, wedged against her titty. Jazz patted it three times. The scrunchie, stiff where the metal key and her cash was rolled inside of it, slipped back over her wrist. She patted it three times once it was in place.

Jazz looked up to see Tara and Sunny grinning at her with twin smiles; she forgot to complete the triplet.

"What?" she asked. "Did I make a fool of myself? How much of my ass could you see?"

Tara shook her head. "No, you guys were great. It was barely peeking out; Lee is just a drama queen."

"Then what's with the looks?" Jazz waved between them, unnerved at how wide their grins were.

"I'm just happy," Sunny beamed. "Happy that you're happy. Happy that Blanche is happy."

Tara nodded, practically smirking. "I've never seen them this silly."

Jazz snorted. "I think we're both just high."

Tara raised an eyebrow at her. "I have seen Blanche high many times, and never have I seen them *that* geeked."

"It's sativa. They usually go for an indica," Jazz muttered in a weak protest. But her grin felt comically huge.

"I know you probably can't confirm or deny anything, but if something happened to be going on between you, we're supportive," Sunny said, patting her hand. "Blanche needs someone like you in their life."

"And we'll keep it quiet. This isn't something I'll tell Lee, but you should. Soon." Tara raised her eyebrow again. "Because that little show up there? The chemistry was sizzling."

Blanche rejoined them before she could answer, perching themself in Jazz's lap without a word. Gabe and Richard returned soon after, passing out drinks for the table.

Gabe sniffed a glass and took a sip, before putting it in front of Tara. "That should just be sparkling water with lime. But I got confused with the two gin and tonics I was carrying. Someone was distracting me."

Richard frowned at him. "Someone needs to use his fucking brain!"

"Are you arguing with him now, too?" Tara teased.

"I told you, I'm not arguing with anyone." Gabe huffed. "Phin and I are cool now, you know that."

"Yeah, but Antonio's been acting pissy as hell."

"If *he's* mad at me, he hasn't told me why. And there's nothing I can fix if he doesn't tell me." Shaking his head, Gabe gestured to the drink in her hand. "Does that taste like booze to you or not? I'm not sober, so you should double-check."

Tara huffed, but she sipped it with an approving nod. "Unless you asked for the smoothest gin ever, this is water."

Blanche turned to Jazz suddenly. "Do you want to go dance?"

Jazz nodded, worried. Their vibes were off. *Everyone's* vibes were off. "Sure!"

Following Blanche downstairs to the dance floor, she put her arms around their waist, pulling them close. "Is everything all right?"

Their hands settled on her hips as Blanche pressed a kiss to her neck. "Chas let me know that Freddy told her that Lee is a little pissy about our bit onstage."

Jazz rolled her eyes. "Seriously? Well, Sunny and Tara are glad you're happy, at least. I didn't confirm or deny anything of course, but they could tell."

Blanche smiled. The tip of their tongue peeked out again. "That's very sweet of them. I wish Lee wasn't so opposed to the idea. I don't like hiding this from him."

Jazz nodded, her chest buzzing with two warring ideals; being open and being safe shouldn't have to be mutually exclusive, not when it came to Lee. "Me either." She looked around for signs of anyone they knew in the crowd. Seeing no one, she risked a quick kiss as they danced among dozens of strangers.

As if they'd been waiting for her, Blanche pulled her in deeper. Their hand cradled the back of her head as she tentatively licked the seam of Blanche's lips. Blanche wasn't super comfortable with being affectionate in public; Jazz needed to take this slow, even though she wanted anything but.

Fortunately, Blanche seemed to have the same idea as they slid their tongue over Jazz's. A happy whine escaped her as she kissed them enthusiastically, bringing her hands down to their ass to pull them close against her.

Blanche eventually pulled away, sighing with regret as they did.

"Sorry, too much?" Jazz asked.

Blanche shook their head as they murmured in her ear, "No, I feel someone staring. We should probably stop."

Jazz looked around at whatever creep was making her partner feel uncomfortable, ready to fight. Or at least glare.

Instead, she locked eyes with Lee. Arms crossed, he stood glaring at them from the edge of the dance floor. He might have looked more intimidating without the honey blond wig and yellow dress, but Jazz still breathed out an "oh shit."

Blanche sighed. "Time to face the music, Jazzy? Or do you want to hide it from him longer? We can chalk it up to being intoxicated, if you want. I can take the heat."

Jazz laced her fingers through theirs. She was already pissed off that Lee was acting like Dad, and he hadn't even said a word yet. "No, I'm tired of hiding shit. Is that okay with you?"

As much as she wanted to go cuss out Lee, there was no way she'd spill Blanche's private life without their permission, even to her own brother. Their secret went both ways; Blanche had a stake in this too.

With a bite of their lip, Blanche nodded. "It can't hurt if just close friends know, I suppose."

Jazz nodded. "If you're sure."

Relief washed over her. The same relief when she had first confessed to Teddy that she didn't want to just be friends. That same relief when she'd turned around and kissed Mimi moments after Teddy. The same relief she'd had when Antonio had tapped on her shoulder with a message of love and support from Lee on her birthday, when she'd been drunkenly making out with Teddy, having totally forgotten her brother might see. The same relief when she'd put her heart on the line for Blanche, and they'd said they wanted to be with her too.

Honesty was so freeing. Exhilarating. Terrifying. Like the time freshman year, when Ed and Teddy had dared her and Mimi to climb up the old bell tower on campus with them. She knew she shouldn't do it, but she was going to anyway. And it was going to be fun—or at least worth the experience in the end.

Hopefully, being open with her brother about her relationship with his friend would be worth it too. Even if he looked constipated with anger at the moment.

Blanche smiled, tracing her cheek with their thumb. "To be honest, I'm not sure, but neither are you. So let's talk to him before we change our minds."

Jazz snorted and led them over to Lee, hand in hand.

"Lee," Jazz said coolly, trying to keep afloat of her emotions. Anger was battling anxiety. Resentment fought her rational brain, telling her that Lee wasn't their dad. Blanche's fingers lacing through hers helped keep her in control.

"Jazz. Blanche." Lee pushed his glasses up with one finger. "Please tell me I didn't just see what I think I did."

"Do you want us to lie?" Jazz snapped. "Because I'm pretty sure you just saw me making out with Blanche."

He always reminded her of Dad when he got like this. Like he had some right, some authority to tell her what to do. Like she was someone to be protected from the world, hidden away from reality. Kept safe on a shelf, waiting for a future that would keep her there.

"What the fuck, Blanche?" Lee huffed. "That's my sister! What the fuck were you thinking?"

Blanche pursed their lips in annoyance. "That I wanted to kiss her? I don't know how else to answer that, Lee."

"You're fifteen years older than her! She's a fucking kid!"

Jazz's blood boiled. "I'm not a fucking kid, Lee! If I want to be with someone older than me, that's my choice."

"Is it? You're their tenant, Jazz! You just turned twenty-one. How long have you known them? Six years?" Lee frowned at Blanche. "You gotta admit, it's—"

"Don't you dare finish that sentence!" Blanche put their free hand on their hip, green eyes flashing in anger. "Leland Jones, how fucking dare you? The whole time you've known me, I've always talked about consent and boundaries. The first night you moved in, I told you that I would never ask for a damn thing from you in exchange for a safe place to stay. And you dare to accuse me of grooming your sister?!"

Lee's eyes widened as his glasses slipped down his nose. "I didn't mean it like that."

"Bullshit, Lee. That's exactly how you meant it." Jazz fired back, poking Lee in the chest. "You know what's funny? Dad would be saying the exact same fucking thing. He'd be telling me I look classless, and that I should cover my body. That I'm not capable of making decisions for myself, that he needs to make them for me. You know what? I'm finally free of our fucking dad. I don't need you to turn into him. No one can make me do anything I don't want to do. Not Blanche. Not Dad. Not you."

Lee stared at the floor.

Jazz knew her brother well enough to know he wouldn't say anything back anytime soon. Lee didn't fight. He didn't argue. He just shut down, taking his punishment without complaint. He'd always been more obedient than Jazz. Lee was the golden child…until he wasn't. That he'd even lasted as long as he had just now was a surprise.

Unfortunately for him, Jazz wasn't done.

"And Dad would absolutely be accusing Blanche—your *friend*—of all sorts of 'perversions and sins,' like you just fucking did. And for what? For daring to live their life? Or god forbid, for kissing me while we're dancing? How dare someone like Blanche be happy for once?" Jazz let the sarcasm drip, like their mom would, knowing it would go straight to Lee's heart. He'd always taken her lectures like a knife to the chest. After years of putting up with his bullshit protectiveness, Jazz was happy to twist it. "When's the last time you saw Blanche this carefree, Lee? When's the last time you saw them smile like they did tonight? How's it feel to fuck with their happiness, Lee? With *my* happiness?"

Lee straightened his shoulders. "I'm sorry. I do sound like Dad, and I hate that." He took off his glasses, rubbing his forehead before looking up at her with the same eyes Jazz saw in the mirror, the same eyes as their mom. "Just, why didn't you tell me? Why do I always gotta find out shit about your life from other people? We're family, Jazz. We're the only blood relation either of us can count on. So why'd I have to find out from Freddy of all people, instead of you?" He put his glasses back on to look at her with hurt twisting his face.

Jazz opened her mouth, unsure how to answer. He'd never been so vulnerable with her. The Lee she'd grown up with would have taken days before he dared to look at anyone again, let alone speak.

"It's new, Lee," Blanche spoke up softly. They must be feeling more forgiving than she did right now. Jazz wanted to make him stew in it longer. She was still angry with him, despite his pitiful expression and heartfelt words. "Don't blame Jazz for keeping it a secret. It's only been a few weeks. We were going to tell you eventually, once we figured out where this is going." Blanche tentatively touched Lee's shoulder. "And for the record, Freddy doesn't know shit. He just saw my feelings coming before I did. He really needs to stop running his mouth." They tittered in nervous laughter before biting their lip, looking hesitantly at Lee.

Jazz softened, squeezing their hand.

Lee made a frustrated sound and played with his dress, looking like a little girl making her skirt flutter around her. "I'm sorry. I will respect whatever you two consenting adults want to do, and I'll do my best to not be a dick about it. Just, if either of you get hurt, I'm kicking both of your asses. Okay?" He pointed to both of them in turn.

Jazz snorted, relieved that he'd seen sense. Or at least hated being yelled at enough to get them off his back. "You'd probably look a lot scarier if you had brought a bat, Lee. The blonde wig and the dress really take away the threat."

Lee huffed out a laugh, pulling her and Blanche into a hug. "I told you, you're my sister, so it's weird to make that joke." He squeezed both of them tightly. "Are we okay? What can I do to apologize?"

"I'm okay, Lee. I know you didn't mean it, not truly," Blanche said. "Jazzy?"

Jazz's jaw tightened, less forgiving than Blanche, but just as conflict avoidant as her brother. Their dad's voice was hard to uproot. "Just figure yourself out, Lee. I'm unlearning all sorts of shit that Mom and Dad put in my head. You should too."

Lee nodded. "I will. I promise. I'm sorry."

Jazz hugged him tighter, wanting to believe him. But Dad said sorry a lot too after he started therapy; he still never fucking changed. And Mom just kept making excuses for him and apologizing on his behalf.

Jazz refused to have another person like Dad in her life. Lee had to prove it.

CHAPTER TWENTY-EIGHT

RICHARD

RICHARD CHECKED HIS WATCH for the eighth time in as many minutes, tapping on the steering wheel as he waited in the parking ramp. Music still emanated from Confession, despite being past bar close.

"Why are we still here, Dicky?" Sunny asked. "Are we gonna fool around or something?"

He shook his head, jaw tight. "Don't worry about it."

"Damn, what's got you so grumpy?"

Richard shook his head again, keeping his eyes trained on Antonio's shitty ass car. Squeezing her thigh, he added a hint of dom edge. "Sunshine, don't worry about it."

"Oh, because that's reassuring. Seriously, you're freaking me out."

"I'll explain later." Richard hoped he sounded calmer than he felt. He was fuming inside. But Sunny didn't need to know that. It wasn't her business, and it wasn't about her. He had to get answers before he could explain. Gabe's insistence that he'd be fine hadn't been reassuring in the least.

Lee and Antonio emerged into the parking ramp, still in drag. *Finally.* Unfortunate that this had to happen on Halloween. Confronting Antonio-as-Carlita-as-Beyonce, while he was dressed as Sexy Gomez Addams, added several layers of discomfort. But it had to be done.

"Wait here." Richard got out of the Range Rover without looking at Sunny, stalking toward Antonio, who had his back turned to unlock his old Civic. He did his best to keep from stomping, trying to keep his cool.

He lost it as soon as Antonio saw him coming. "Lee, save me!"

Richard pushed him against the car, forearm pinning him against the door. "We need to talk."

Lee looked between them as he loaded the suitcase into the trunk. "Uh, are we good?"

Antonio looked up at Richard with a resentful glare, as he struggled against Richard's arm pinning him. Richard glared back.

Antonio sighed, resignation dimming his eyes. "I'm fine, Lee. This is all bark. Richard only bites when he's fucking."

Sunny laughed. "It's so true."

Richard took a breath to keep the anger out of his voice; Sunny would hear it, and he wasn't mad at her. "I told you to wait in the car."

"And miss this drama? I don't think so." Sunny crossed her arms and leaned against the passenger door of his Range Rover.

"Sunny, this isn't my drama. Wait in the car," he begged.

"You too, Lee," Antonio said. "Please."

"No." Lee shook his head. "Y'all are freaking me out. I'm staying."

"If he's staying, I'm staying."

Antonio huffed. "This isn't about me. I'll explain later."

Lee sighed. "I'll wait over there with Sunny, but I'm right here if you need me."

Richard's temper was a little mollified that Antonio was taking this seriously, for once in his damn life. He always treated everything like a joke. The second anything got too serious or heavy, he would flutter away for easier distractions. Part of the reason Richard didn't include him in Gabe's shit; Antonio never handled stress well, and neither he nor Gabe wanted to push him toward anything potentially self-destructive.

"Can you let me up now? My outfit is gonna get dirty." Antonio struggled against his arm as soon as Lee and Sunny were out of earshot. "Damn, when did you get so strong?"

"What's this I hear about a trip to New York?" Richard pressed harder.

"Ugh, God. Why is this so hot?" Antonio laughed. "The fake mustache is really doing things for me, Dicky."

"Answer the fucking question." He kept Antonio pinned.

Antonio sighed heavily. "Lee and I got invited to interview for a Comette feature about all the 'up and coming' queer artists featured on the Vamp soundtrack. We're going next week. Four days."

"So why does Gabe need to go?"

"You fucking *know* why, Dicky!" Antonio huffed. "Do you need me to say it out loud? Admit just how shitty a friend I am?" He looked balefully at Richard; his eyes narrowed uncannily in the exaggerated stage makeup. "So what, Gabe isn't allowed to leave Bellamy for the rest of his life? He's stronger now. It's not like he's going back to that bitch."

Anger flared through Richard. "It's not *him* going back to *her* that I'm worried about. It's only an hour and a half between Newtown and Manhattan, Tonio. You're putting him at risk."

"How the fuck do you even know she's in Connecticut?" Antonio rolled his eyes again. "She's not gonna know he's in Manhattan. He's excited to show Tara around New York. It's her first vacation. Let him move on, Dicky!"

Richard growled, "You think Emily gave up that easily? Especially now that he's getting married and has a kid on the way? Of all the fucking places to bring him to, you're bringing him to New York?"

Antonio scoffed. "How would she know he's getting married, or the baby? Besides, he's got a protection order against her, hasn't he?"

Richard's jaw ached. "He's gotten six calls from unknown East Coast numbers in the past three weeks. Which is how long it's been since my mom found out he's getting married." Sunny knew not to post pictures of Gabe on social media, but she couldn't have known not to tell his parents anything about Gabe. He should have warned her. He'd caused this mess, and Antonio was making it worse. "Normally, he gets one a month, if that."

"What, you screen his calls? Are you his personal security or something?" Antonio asked sarcastically, before noticing the look on Richard's face. "Oh shit, you have been his personal security this whole time! Does Gabe know?"

Richard shrugged, his forearm still pressed against Antonio's chest. He really wished he was wearing more than the pinstripe suit without a shirt underneath. The cheap costume jewelry that Sunny made him wear was especially humiliating; the chain was clinking and cold against his chest. At least the parking garage was practically empty. "He knows enough. I send her contact attempts to Phin, who manages the rest. Gabe is blissfully unaware of the specifics, by choice." He shook his head with a sigh. "You can't bring him to New York, Tonio. She's still trying to get him back."

"But I need him." Antono's voice was strangled as tears sprang up in his hazel eyes. "Richard, I can't *not* go. This is the break Lee's been working for, since before I met him. I can't hold him back, and I can't rely on Lee alone to keep me straight. I need Gabe, Tara too! You've been keeping him safe from her, but Gabe keeps me safe from myself. I won't come back in one piece without him and Tara and Lee there to help me."

"Fuck." Richard hated that he was right. "Can't I come instead?"

Antonio's laugh was wet enough to be worrisome. "What are you going to do? Tie me to a chair again? Dicky, I love you, but your kind of support is not what I need. I need a friend, not a wannabe mafia boss." He exhaled. "What do I need to do? How do I keep him safe?"

Richard growled out a sigh, resigned. He couldn't keep Gabe safe in Bellamy forever. If Emily did find him, it may be enough to finally prove to the court that she was attempting to violate the protection order. If she did find him, hopefully he'd come back whole. Alive. They'd been so close to losing him. "Don't post him on your social media. Even in the background. Block him out with emojis or however if you need to do it. Hopefully she'll never even know he's there. But if she does—"

"She won't!" Antonio emphatically shook his head. "I promise."

Richard sighed, wishing he was half as optimistic. "*If* she finds him, don't touch her. Make sure Tara knows that, too. She can't lay a damn finger on her, or it'll all go to shit. Just record what you can. Take pictures or recordings as evidence to prove she's violated the protection order. And make sure there are always witnesses. Don't let her talk to him alone. Send everything to Phin." Richard shook his head, hating that it'd come to this. "And if she does show up, mention Phin and I somehow. It should be enough to scare her off."

Richard had enough dirt on that bitch that she should be scared of him. Her last victim had been covered up well as a suicide, but Richard had found the truth: He'd killed himself on her orders.

Phineas had helped him confront her when they'd rescued Gabe, before it was too late. Hopefully, the memory of that barely legal interaction had stayed with her. They'd recorded the whole conversation. Phineas had assured him repeatedly that they'd stayed above the board, but Richard was worried she'd try to file a countersuit for intimidation and blackmail. Because as far as Richard was concerned, he *had* intimidated and blackmailed her into letting Gabe leave, not-so-subtly threatening to take the letters she'd hidden from her last victim to the press.

"Do you want me to text that to you?" Richard asked. Antonio's face was screwed up in concentration, like it did anytime he was trying to memorize something. Antonio made his annoying bubbly personality seem so effortless; sometimes Richard forgot how hard Antonio had to work to function.

Antonio snorted. "Please. I've got it in a song, but I might not remember if I'm stressed."

With a nod, Richard let Antonio up from the car and drew him into a hug instead. "I'm trusting you to keep him safe. And yourself. Don't put yourself in a situation where you're going to relapse for Lee's sake. He loves you more than he needs a break in his career."

"I know. He doesn't want me to go, either." Antonio hugged him back. "But it's not just for him. I'm doing this for me, too, even if I don't understand it fully."

"Everyone wants you healthy and whole, Tonio."

"I promise to bring us all back in one piece." Antonio sniffled against his shoulder.

Richard scoffed. "Don't get snot on my suit."

"Love you, too. Dicky."

Richard groaned as Lee joined, but he didn't pull away, especially when Sunny hugged them all too. His fiancé kissed his cheek with a teasing, "You're hating this, aren't you?"

He didn't answer. For once, a group hug with Antonio wasn't the worst experience of Richard's life.

Sunday, October Thirty-First

CHAPTER TWENTY-NINE

BLANCHE

BLANCHE SQUINTED AT THEIR laptop in the dim light of the dining room, struggling to make sense of the admissions requirements for the counseling program at the University of Iowa Bellamy. They wrapped their blanket tighter around them, tucking their ice-cold feet up onto the dining chair. Where had their slippers gone? With the shift to autumn, the downstairs floor had become freezing. They'd have to get house boots for winter.

Jazz held up a spoon in front of them. "Try this, tell me what you think of it."

Blanche jumped, minimizing the form. It only managed to expose another window with instructions for a name change. With a squeak, they minimized that one too, revealing a forum about BDSM apprenticeship advice, followed by a DNA test kit order form, the GED program at Bellamy Community College, the map of the country roads surrounding Marshall, Minnesota, and the sex therapy certificate from the U. Cheeks burning, Blanche finally reached a window that they didn't mind Jazz asking questions about: their SubParty.

"You know, most people would be trying to hide their porn, not their college search," Jazz teased, still holding out the steaming spoon. "Should I pretend I didn't see any of that?"

"Please, if you don't mind." Cheeks still on fire that Jazz had basically seen the list of everything Blanche was tentatively considering wanting, they blew on the steam from the spoon. "Not quite ready to talk about any of it."

"Any day now," Jazz teased. Unlike Blanche, who was freezing in their witch costume (a gauzy black robe embroidered with spider webs), Jazz seemed perfectly comfortable in her short, sleeveless purple dress and thigh-high socks.

"It looks hot." Blanche tentatively took a bite of what Jazz claimed was chili. It looked more like bean mush to Blanche. Tasted like bean mush, too. Scalding hot bean mush. They puffed around the bite burning their mouth.

"Too spicy?" Jazz asked.

Blanche shook their head. It was far too bland for anyone to consider it spicy. But Jazz probably didn't need to hear that. "No, temperature hot. It um…it needs salt. Or seasoning, perhaps? Meat?"

Jazz hummed. "I can do everything but the meat."

Blanche grinned. "Sorry, I don't know what it needs other than more flavor."

"I'm trying to make it healthy but good, so 'needs seasoning' is still helpful." Jazz went back to the kitchen. "What are you working on over there? If there's anything you're comfortable telling me about, anyway."

"Oh, just browsing estate auction sites for a replacement grate for that hole in the foyer." Blanche found that window, keeping the rest minimized. They were still simply dreaming, unsure how to tell if they really wanted these things, or if they were simply whims. Shayla had said that if Blanche kept coming back to something, there was a good chance it was a want worth pursuing. "It's giving me a headache trying to read my screen."

"Have you considered that you might need glasses?"

Blanche laughed. "Many times. I have done nothing about it though. I can get by."

The doorbell rang.

"Ah! Showtime!" With a burst of giddy energy, Blanche threw the blanket from their shoulders and pulled on a witch's hat on their way to answer it. Jazz had never been able to decorate for Halloween, and Blanche had never had trick-or-treaters at their old apartment. Admittedly, they might have gone a little hard on the decor: crystals and dried herbs hung in the windows, fake crows and cats were tucked around the house, midnight blue tablecloths glittering with stars covered all of the side tables, and candles were everywhere. Blanche suspected most of it would become year-round decor, considering the house now matched Jazz's bedroom.

"Trick or treat!" A group of college students in costume held out pillowcases.

Yet another group of trick-or-treaters, who were much older than Blanche had anticipated when they'd envisioned their first-ever Halloween as a homeowner. But they hadn't had anyone younger than fifteen come by since sundown, so Blanche still complimented their costumes and gave them candy bars.

"More college kids?" Jazz asked when they returned.

"Yup." They leaned on the counter. "When does trick-or-treating end? Like, how do I know when it's over?"

"I don't know. We didn't do that Satanic shit at my house," Jazz laughed. "Maybe turn the porch light off, and pretend you're not home?"

"So you and Lee never wore costumes and went trick-or-treating?" Blanche asked. They'd been giving Jazz space to process her feelings after the argument with Lee last night. Jazz had to be upset still, even if she was pretending everything was normal.

"Of course not!" Jazz rolled her eyes. "Now it's all well and good for him to do what he wants, dress in drag and shit. But not for me, apparently!" She huffed as she stirred the chili. "Sorry."

"Get it off your chest—" The doorbell rang. Blanche huffed and apologized as they went to give more candy to a trio of teenagers who hadn't even bothered with a costume. But Blanche still had four bags of candy, so they gave them some anyway.

"College students?" Jazz asked, turning off the heat.

Blanche shook their head, wrapping their thin robes tighter around themself. "Seemed younger. They didn't even have costumes."

"And yet you rewarded them."

"I gave them the candy I don't like."

Jazz laughed, then sighed. "I think I'm so angry at Lee because, well, frankly, it hurt. Hearing him say the shit he did, the assumptions he made, the conclusions he jumped to. He doesn't think I'm capable of making my own decisions. He's always had this older brother mind-set—Dad never let him forget it—but he's never thought less of me for it before." She tapped the wooden spoon against the pot with more vigor than usual. "Like, he would do all this shit when we were younger to cheer me up, keep me safe from our parents, but I...I guess I just didn't expect him to be such an ass about me making decisions for myself."

Lee had reacted exactly the way Blanche had expected him to, including accusing them of grooming Jazz. While it hurt to hear, that was how Lee'd been raised, not his true feelings about Blanche or their friendship. He seemed to have forgotten how much baggage he carried, hiding it so he wouldn't have to address it. They swallowed. "Over the years, I've noticed that when Lee's upset, his first reaction is always what he learned from your parents. Not that it excuses anything he said, but with some space and distance to mull things over, he always comes around to see sense."

Jazz grumbled, "I can't forgive him as easily as that. He knows what it's like, to constantly hear that shit—I dunno. I know we'll figure it out. We are the only blood relation we can count on, like he said. I just..." She shrugged.

Blanche pulled her into their arms. "You need time?"

Arms slipping around Blanche's waist, Jazz nodded into their neck. "And he needs to prove he meant it. That he wasn't just saying what I wanted to hear because I was yelling at him."

A knock sounded at the door as Blanche's phone buzzed from...somewhere in the dining room. Jazz stole Blanche's witch hat with a grin and a peck on the lips. "I'll give out the candy. You answer that."

Blanche found their phone on the chair they'd been sitting in, just as Sunny's call went to voicemail. Knowing Sunny as they did, they waited, and the phone buzzed again seconds later.

"Hello?"

"Hey, do you and Jazz want to go on vacation?"

Blanche blinked. "Uh...this is a little out of the blue."

Sunny huffed through the speaker. "I know, but Richard is looking up tattoo ideas again, and I don't know what else to do."

"Let him get a tattoo?" Blanche suggested. "Is a tattoo mutually exclusive from a vacation?

"No, but he only wants a tattoo because he's having an existential crisis about being unable to control every aspect of existence. Namely, Gabe and Antonio going to New York. So I was thinking *we* should go somewhere, like a road trip or something, so he can drive, make all the plans, and feel useful. It'd just be for the weekend while they're out of town."

Blanche covered the phone when Jazz returned. "Sunny wants to know if we want to go on a road trip the weekend after next, when Lee and them are in New York."

"We? As in 'us'?" Jazz grinned. "Like a *couple*?"

Blanche ignored the burning of their cheeks; after last night, they'd been worried Jazz would want to pull back from them around others. "Is that okay?"

"Of course! It's nice to be included by the rest of your friends, even though Lee is being a little bitch about it." Jazz gave a tiny skip as she went to stir the chili. "Where are we going?"

Her easy giddiness made them smile, as Blanche squinted at the phone for the speakerphone button. "You're on speaker. Jazz is in, but she wants to know where we're going."

Sunny hummed. "I haven't thought that far yet. Where do you want to go?"

Jazz shrugged and gestured to Blanche to answer.

Blanche bit their lip, mulling over the idea that had been forming over many conversations with Jazz, Freddy, Tara, and Lee. One of those quickly minimized tabs on their laptop had been searched at least a dozen times; if that wasn't a sign that they wanted it, then what was? "How do you feel about Nowhere, Minnesota?"

Jazz turned from the stove, a slow smile spreading across her face. "Blanche, you wanna go back home?"

Blanche winced, inhaling a sharp breath before saying, "Yes? For you know, closure and shit."

"Oh, Dicky would *love* to bring you to your cult! That's exactly what he needs!" Sunny squealed. "Are there corny roadside attractions?"

"Oh, uh…" Blanche fiddled with their hair. "I've only driven through there once when I was thirteen, but I vaguely remember seeing signs for a SPAM Museum on the way here."

"Hell yes!" Sunny cheered. "This is going to be so much better than New York!"

Friday, November Fifth

CHAPTER THIRTY

GABE

SHRUGGING OFF HIS TOO-TIGHT blazer, Gabe draped it over the break room chair, greeting Richard with a nod as he sat next to him. The bright room was practically empty; most people worked from home on Fridays. Despite not even living in the same time zone, Leigh Anne insisted Gabe work from the office five days a week. As a manager, Richard felt obligated to be in the office as much as he could.

Richard responded to Gabe's greeting with a grunt, barely deigning him a glance.

Still pissed, then. Raising his eyebrows, Gabe opened his sack lunch of apples, cheddar, and some crackers he'd scrounged from the pantry that morning (he was still getting used to Tara's portion sizes; leftovers were not as reliable as when he'd been cooking for one). "You know, we're the only ones here. If you want to air it out."

"Dunno what you're talking about." Richard stabbed his pasta salad with more force than necessary.

Gabe popped a cheese cube into his mouth. "Don't you wanna yell at me more?"

"Why would I yell? I'm not mad." Richard's jaw flared as he stared hard at the table.

Gabe fought to keep from laughing at his surly expression. "You look mad."

"I'm not!" Richard snapped. "Am I worried? Yes. Am I stressed? Yes. But you want to go for Antonio's sake, and Antonio is determined to go. So I am not going to get involved, and I'm going to cope by taking Sunny to the fucking *SPAM* museum, apparently."

Gabe blinked, confused by the turn his rant had taken. "What?"

"Don't ask. I don't understand it." Richard waved a hand as he continued venting. "She got this idea to go on a road trip. Something about closure for Blanche and corny roadside attractions. So I have mapped out every corny roadside attraction between here and wherever the fuck Marshall is."

"Well, that sounds like a productive use of your nosy, micromanaging-ass energy," Gabe teased, crunching on his apple. His phone buzzed in his left pocket, which he ignored, because the phone in his left pocket was his work phone. And he was on break.

"My nosy micromanaging is my greatest strength," Richard snarked. "One that has directly benefited you greatly over the years." He finally looked up at Gabe, his too-serious expression causing a pinch of dread in Gabe's gut. "Gabe, you should know—"

"Nope! I should not!" Gabe waved the apple in warning. "Everything is going to be fine! No one will know or care that I'm in New York except Antonio, Lee, and Tara. It's going to be okay, because it has to be."

Richard frowned, narrowing his eyes at Gabe for a moment, before returning to his pasta salad. "Fine."

They ate in tense silence, the only sound Gabe munching on the crisp apple. For as pessimistic as Gabe could be, he had to be optimistic about this. What was the point of worrying about what would probably never happen? This was exactly why Gabe hadn't been burdening Richard with anything; he always invented these practical solutions to abstract problems. Like his gender weirdness, or his anxious excitement about his and Tara's kid, this New York trip was not something that had practical solutions.

His left pocket buzzed again; probably fucking Leigh Anne calling again. Gabe ignored it, half wishing Freddy had taken more time away from Confession, so he'd have an excuse to take more time off and work there instead.

Either something bad would happen, or it wouldn't. Richard would worry his way into endless what-ifs, account for every imagined problem, and stress himself into a nervous wreck before the trip even happened.

Gabe had to hope for the best, and do what he could to make the best happen.

Like how Antonio had been weird lately, quiet and distant. Sure, it was probably partially Gabe's fault for asking his cousin to have a three-some with him and Tara, but he never would have expected Antonio to react so strongly! There was no way this was about Angie; it had to be about the trip. But Antonio kept saying everything was fine! Despite his worry, all Gabe could do was keep showing up, keep communication open, and hope for the best. And when Antonio was ready to confide in him about whatever it was that had him upset, Gabe would—

He paused, mid-bite. *Oh*. Maybe that was what Richard had been doing. Waiting for Gabe to share what had been going on, and getting increasingly annoyed that he hadn't. It was probably how Phineas always felt, unsure of his place in their lives, unless he was invited in to help clean up their mess. Maybe he'd been putting all of his emotional support eggs in Tara's basket, or relying on his therapist, when he could have turned to his friends.

As his left pocket buzzed again, Gabe turned it off. He still had fifteen minutes of his break, and Leigh Anne and this whole job could fucking wait.

Gabe looked at Richard, who was still slowly eating his pasta salad. He had one egg, so to speak, that he could give Richard. One that didn't have any easy solutions that he could think of; none of the worries that kept Gabe awake at night had easy answers.

"I wish I could unsubscribe from gender completely," Gabe murmured. He fought a grin as Richard perked up, sitting up in his chair to turn to Gabe. The faintest ghost of a smirk on his face was a sure sign that Richard was about to give Gabe a perfectly reasonable solution, except it wouldn't quite fit Gabe's problem. "Like if there could be a mod to my stats that everyone could see, so they know I am just *me*—not a man, or a dad, or a boyfriend, or any of that. And just like, accept that, so I wouldn't have to explain the vague wrongness every time I feel weird about gendered shit."

"You could get an agender or non-binary pin," Richard suggested. "Or whichever flag suits you best, I mean. I guess that wouldn't solve the problem of everyone understanding and accepting it without question, but it would be a start."

Gabe lost the fight against his laughter. "You're so fucking pre-dictable, Dicky." Maybe Richard would never have all the answers.

Maybe Phineas would never quite believe they all loved and wanted him in their lives. Maybe Antonio would always wriggle his way out of being vulnerable about the hardest parts of his life with humor and deflection.

And maybe Gabe had flipped a full one-eighty from his trademark pessimism to delusional optimism, to keep himself from worrying himself sick now that he was happy, yet scared of losing the life he loved. But his friends all wanted to be there for him, he just had to let them, the way they let Gabe be there for them. He hid a sigh behind his fading smile, worry nagging him. His growing pains with Richard and Phineas were more straightforward to manage; Antonio was the one friend who never had an easy answer.

TARA

TARA LOOKED AT HERSELF in the mirror, adjusting the sleeves of the suit she had been planning to wear to her wedding.

Annoyingly, her eyes welled up, but in a bad way. She didn't look like herself. She looked okay, just not...herself. She didn't *feel* like herself.

Her shoulders were so tight, she couldn't move properly. The waistline cut into a weird spot on her stomach, pushing on her bladder, which was already a constant worry considering how much pressure the kid was putting on it. The stiff fabric of the dress shirt scratched her nipples and belly and made her look like she was trying to hide her kid. It only succeeded in making her look like a balloon.

And her skin—her face was different. Tara was always pale despite the freckles, but now she was puffy and pink and *glowing* or whatever.

She looked like a sick penguin. She *felt* like a sick penguin.

And now she looked like a sick penguin who was ugly crying in the mirror.

"Ugh fuck this shit!" Tara freed herself from the jacket and waistband cutting into her bladder. "I'm not a balloon. I'm not a penguin. And I'm not trying to hide the damn kid!"

She left the expensive custom-made suit Gabe had paid for scattered on the floor across the closet and the bedroom, before she peed for the thousandth time that day. Burying herself in bed sounded amazing, but too pitiful, so she went to the basement and buried herself in the weighted blanket on the futon, still fully naked. Hippo curled up behind her calves. His comforting presence added to the weight of the blanket and the scent of Gabe.

That was where Gabe went on his sad bitch nights, when there was nothing Tara could do to help him besides give him space to mope alone. Maybe it would work for her, too.

And that was where Gabe found her when he came home from the gym after work. Wordlessly, he stripped and unwrapped the blankets to join her in her cocoon.

Tara played with his chest hair as he wiggled underneath her, wrapping his arms around her. Hippo grumbled, but flopped down on Gabe's legs, resting his head on Tara's hip. With deep breaths, she breathed in the faint sweat clinging to Gabe's hair and neck, the artificial manly-scented soap from the gym locker rooms, the vanilla from his lotion. Breathed in his comforting, familiar oaky smell that was all Gabe. "Do you ever feel like someone cut your head off and put it on someone else's body?"

Gabe's loud laugh moved her whole body. "Constantly!"

Tara groaned. "This is still me, but it's not me. My body is just so...wrong right now. I've never looked like this before. I don't recognize myself."

"Your body is glorious, Tara. Then, and now, and forever." Gabe pressed a kiss to her hair.

"I know." Tara grinned against his collarbone. "Tell yourself that more often."

"Yeah, yeah," Gabe grumbled. "What brought this existential crisis on?"

"The suit came." She huffed. "I feel awful in it. It's stiff and scratchy and tight in awful places, and it looks like I'm trying to hide the fact that I'm pregnant. I don't want to be stiff and scratchy. I don't want to hide the kid. I just want to look like me, but a nice, put-together version of me. And I thought the suit would do that, but I hate it. But you already spent a shit ton of money on it, and now I feel like shit because I wasted your money."

Gabe's hand ran up and down her back. "You don't have to wear the suit if you hate it."

"I kind of do. We're getting married in three weeks."

"We can find something else."

"Can we?" Tara's eyes burned again. "Because I'm trying to pack for our trip, and nothing fits. I don't have many clothes to begin with. Most of it is lazy, comfortable shit, and the stuff that's not doesn't fit anymore, and I don't want to embarrass anyone by walking around New York wearing leggings and one of your sweaters when everyone else looks nice."

His touch was warm as he slowly stroked up and down her back. "Don't worry about what other people think. I would never be embarrassed by anything you wear. Walk around naked for all I care."

"You might not, but we're literally going to a fashion shoot," Tara grumbled. "I don't want to give Antonio and Lee any reason to feel like they don't belong there."

"Want to raid Antonio's closet?" Gabe offered. "Or maybe ask Blanche if you can borrow something? I don't think Sunny or Richard share your style."

"Even Blanche is way too fem for me." Tara snorted. "And they dress like a grandma. Seriously, I don't know if you know this, but their collection of bedazzled jackets is obscene." She paused. Antonio had been acting strange lately. Every time she or Gabe tried to clear the air, he'd take one look at Lee and force a mask of "I'm fine" on. But right now, Lee was working the burlesque show at Confession. And Antonio was home alone. "Antonio can sew, right?"

Gabe hummed in assent. "He makes all of Carlita's dresses, and he made the outfit he wore for the wedding."

"Do you..." Tara swallowed her pride. "Do you think he could make one for me?"

"Are you feeling okay?" Gabe pressed a hand to her forehead. "You're considering asking someone besides Lee and Blanche for help?"

"Shut up, Coop." Tara bit his shoulder. "Desperate times, okay? I want to look hot for our wedding. And I want to look cool enough in New York to make Lee proud."

"You're going to look hot no matter what—"

Tara laughed. "Gabe, I love and appreciate you, but I don't need validation. I need help figuring out what to wear. Being told I look good no matter what isn't very helpful, because what I have now doesn't make me *feel* good."

"Fine. I will call Antonio, but I don't want to stress him out. Or you!" Gabe pinched her ass. Hippo grumbled as his head was knocked off her hip.

"Me either, but he's probably sick of people worrying about him." Tara wrinkled her nose. "And besides, you two need to hash whatever weird shit is going on between you about the Angie thing."

Gabe groaned. "I don't know if anything but time will fix that. He refuses to admit he's pissed about it, but why else would he be such a crabby ass lately?"

Tara kissed his chest. "At least you can say your piece so you stop moping about it."

"I'm not moping."

"You've been moping hard." Tara pushed up on his chest to sit back. Hippo clambered off the couch, ready to follow her anywhere. "Okay, let's go."

"What? Now?" Gabe gripped her hips with a pout. "But we're already naked, so..."

Tara smirked. "Okay, after a quickie."

ANTONIO LOOKED OVER THE outfits Tara had put together for their trip, strewn across his coffee table, with a skeptical twist to his mouth. "Tara-Bear, this is sad."

Tara huffed. "I know. That's why I'm here. I have no idea how to look cool."

"But you always look cool." Antonio paused, then amended, "When you're not swimming in athleisure."

"Yeah, but I'm normally not six months pregnant. None of my cool clothes fit anymore, and there's not a lot of masc maternity wear, so I've been wearing Gabe's sweaters whenever I have to look nice." Tara glared at the suit in the garment bag she'd brought. "And I can't wear that to get fucking married in."

"I mean, you can," Gabe chimed in. "Small backyard wedding, remember?"

"Yeah, but your tux looks amazing, and I don't want to look schlubby next to you." Tara huffed. "I don't want to wear a dress, but the suit makes me look bloated instead of pregnant."

"Jumpsuit?" Antonio suggested.

Tara shook her head. "I don't trust my bladder enough right now to wear a jumpsuit."

"Stand up and turn around?" Antonio raked his eyes over her. "You want to emphasize the bump?"

"No? I just...don't want to hide it." Tara touched her belly. "The kid is in there, you know? I don't want to minimize or maximize it."

"Normalize the bump," Antonio suggested. At Tara's nod, he grinned. "How do you feel about tearaway pants?"

"Oh, yes!" Tara laughed. "I feel great about tearaway pants!"

"Perfect. I have a couple of patterns I could probably Frankenstein together into a backless flowy jumpsuit thingy, so you could pee with one quick yoink of fabric. Or would that be too fem?"

"Dude, fem or masc isn't the issue. The closer I feel to naked, while also looking like I'm not complete trash, the better." Tara shrugged. "As long as it's not white, and I can pee in a hurry, a backless flowy jumpsuit thingy sounds better than a dress."

"Cool. Stand on the coffee table. I'll get my measuring tape." Antonio disappeared into the guest room, while Tara climbed onto the table. He reappeared with a bolt of forest green velvet in his arms. "I knew this would come in handy one day, even if it's not Carlita's aesthetic. This will look amazing with your autumn coloring."

He took far more measurements on Tara than they'd needed for the suit, calling out numbers for Gabe to write down.

Tara held her arms up so he could measure her bust for the third time. "Sorry to add this to your plate on top of everything else. I wasn't expecting you to custom-sew me a whole outfit. I was just thinking you would send me shopping somewhere."

Antonio glared at her, his hazel eyes narrowing. "Tara-Bear, this is one of the few things I'm good at that doesn't make me the center of attention. I kind of need that right now, so don't get weird about me making you a damn backless flowy jumpsuit thingy with tearaway pants."

Tara exchanged a loaded glance with Gabe. "You want to talk about it?"

"Not really." Antonio sucked his teeth. "But if I *did*...I would say I'm feeling a little in over my head these days. There's just been so much attention, even at school where no one knows that I'm Carlita. Like, my students are singing our song around me constantly, and thank God they don't know it's me, because that'd be even weirder! Lee had to completely take over my social media because the flood of messages from blogs and labels and other artists was overwhelming. We might need to hire an assistant, because it's starting to wear on him, too, even if he won't admit it." He huffed.

Gabe shook his head in warning when Tara opened her mouth to offer her help. She was already adding to Lee's burden by taking time off Blanche's channel when the kid was born. Gabe was right; she couldn't add to her plate.

"And like, it's so strange, you know?" Antonio draped her in velvet, working effortlessly as he spoke. "Fame, and attention, and *all* of this is what Old Antonio wanted, and I reconciled years ago that I would never have it. That I couldn't want this anymore, and that maybe I'd been self-sabotaging all this time because I never wanted it in the first place, I just thought I should!" He hummed to himself, waving a pin before spearing it through the fabric. "Like, I knew it'd be a lot, but I didn't think I'd hate it." He sighed. "But I just want to go back to making raunchy house music that barely anyone listens to. So I keep reminding myself this will be good for Lee. He wants the opportunities to work with bigger names and labels and shit. I just gotta tough it out until he can establish a good reputation as a producer, and then I can step back."

"So *that's* why we're going to New York." Gabe sat behind Antonio on the couch and pulled him into a hug.

"Partially." Antonio rested his head on Gabe's chest. "And partially because I need to prove I can handle it. Because if Lee *does* make a name for himself, it's not like we're going to hide in Bellamy forever. Networking is a huge part of the industry, and if that means being his arm candy at parties and shit, I want to support him."

"You should tell him all of this." Tara sat on the coffee table and took Antonio's hands. "Let Lee have a say in this, too."

"This may come as a shock, Tara-Bear, but I do talk to my husband," Antonio laughed. "Lee knows. He trusts me to advocate what's best for me, but he would absolutely put me before his career. I can't be the reason he holds himself back, so we're going to New York as a compromise of sorts. He gets the opportunity to put his name and face out there, and I get to see if I'm strong enough to handle it.

"And that's why I'm dragging you along with me." Antonio winced at Gabe. "Sorry. I know going back will be hard for you, too. You're just the only one besides Lee I trust to support me the way I need."

Gabe shrugged with a resigned sigh. "Don't be sorry. I need to stop hiding eventually. It's been close to four years, she's probably gotten over shit."

Antonio winced. "Richard says she—"

Gabe put his hand over Antonio's mouth. "I don't want to know what Richard says about it. I live in blissful ignorance about everything unless Richard, Phin, and my parents decide that I need to know. I just assume she moved on, unless I need to testify otherwise." He smiled at Tara. "Everything will be fine."

Tara's stomach sank in dread. The anxiety in Antonio's eyes told Tara that Emily had, in fact, not moved on. But Gabe didn't want to know that, so the understanding that passed between her and Antonio stayed between them.

"Okay," Antonio said, behind Gabe's hand muffling his mouth. "I won't say anything."

"Thank you." Gabe removed his hand from Antonio's mouth. "Anything else we need to clear the air on? The Angie thing, or anything else?"

Antonio cried out in laughter. "God, no! Please stop bringing her up. I'm sorry I made a big deal of that! It's nothing!"

"Are you sure? Because you were pissed, dude," Tara said, still skeptical. Something about Antonio had been off since that night, but maybe it'd been a coincidence; Antonio seemed more concerned about New York than his cousin.

"I was," Antonio admitted. "But only because it felt like one more thing that was out of control, and because in hindsight, I was more than a little jealous of Gabe's crush on her when we were kids. But I don't control what you do—or what she does for that matter. So I am choosing to focus on the things I can control. Like not being a dick about things that are none of my business."

"You want to tell that to Lee, please?" Tara teased.

"Look, Lee's reactions to his sister's love life are out of my control. When he's ready to accept that he's being a dick, he'll figure it out." Antonio scoffed, waving a finger at Tara. "Can we get back to things that are in my control? Namely, the sorry state of your wardrobe."

Tara groaned. But a fashion emergency was her excuse for getting Gabe and Antonio to talk shit out. And they'd talked shit out. Now it was her turn to suffer. Playing dress up was already torture; trying on endless clothes when her body was so unfamiliar would be worse. She shot a pleading look at Gabe.

He shook his head with an affectionate smile. "You asked for this, Kitten. I'm just here to tell you you're hot no matter what."

Thursday, November Eleventh

Chapter Thirty-One

BLANCHE

FINGERS STIFF WITH COLD, Blanche clenched the knife in their hand tighter, scraping against the sandstone to deepen the "y" as they squatted precariously in front of a rock face. Freddy worked next to them, carefully chipping away at the dates below Daisy's name where the river had eroded them to nothing. Despite the midday sun, a sharp breeze made Blanche shiver beneath their denim jacket.

"Be careful down there," Chas called from the ledge, wrapping his coat tighter around the sleeping baby strapped to his chest. "I can't exactly jump in after you."

"You can barely swim anyway," Freddy exhaled in his raspy whisper, so quiet that Blanche barely heard him over the water rushing below.

"I heard that!" Chas retorted as Blanche laughed.

The sandstone rock face on the southern tip of the island had crumbled over the years. When they'd first scattered Daisy's ashes here, all three of them could comfortably stretch out on the outcropping. Now, Blanche hoped the root they were gripping with one hand was sturdy enough to keep from falling into the icy Mississippi.

Blanche brushed the dust away from Daisy's name, more legible now that they'd carved deeper into the sandstone. Graffiti in a public park was the only headstone Daisy had, the river her final resting place. Daisy wouldn't have wanted anyone to spend money on a grave site or a headstone—not when Freddy and Chas were new parents, struggling to keep

Confession afloat. Even if Blanche finally had money these days, they could only imagine what Daisy would say about contributing money to the "death industrial complex" or whatever Daisy would have called it.

No, being slowly absorbed into nature was what Daisy would have approved of. Even if Blanche was getting too old to climb crumbling cliffs with Freddy every few months, to make sure her name and dates stayed entrenched in the sandstone: Daisy Coleman, April 13th, 1982-2014. They'd been married on the birthday she'd chosen for Blanche, and Daisy was murdered on her own less than a year later.

Freddy sighed, digging his screwdriver into the straight lines once more for good measure, before he stood up carefully and passed the screwdriver up to Chas. Blanche closed their knife and pocketed it, helping Freddy climb to safety before taking his hand, so he could pull them up.

"This used to be easier." Blanche winced. Their back protested as they strained to haul themself up by a sturdy root.

"We used to be younger," Freddy whispered, grunting as he held Blanche's weight steady, while they scrambled for balance at the top.

"From the looks of it, you might not be able to get down there next year." Chas peered over the edge. "We should find a more permanent way to memorialize her than riskin' our necks."

"*Our* necks," Freddy teased via sign, sitting on a bench nearby to stretch his knees.

"Fine, *your* neck. Which I happen to value very highly." Chas glared at his husband. "Can we plant a tree or get a plaque made instead? I was sweatin' up a storm just watchin' y'all down there."

"A statue perhaps?" Blanche grinned. "Or a park bench in her honor by the mounds?"

They all laughed at that. Daisy would have adored a memorial park bench—an ironic ode to the countless hours spent there, talking about life with Blanche, while they waited for a john to approach them, or Chas to get out of school, or Freddy to get off of work.

When the laughter had died away—complete with that heart-wrenching sigh from Freddie that was exactly like Daisy's—Blanche gathered their courage. "I'm going home tomorrow."

They could feel the look between Freddy and Chas, before both of them turned to Blanche. "What do you mean, goin' home?"

"Sunny wanted to go on a road trip this weekend, and well... Jazz and I have been talking a lot about closure lately."

"Closure?" came Freddy's raspy voice.

Blanche nodded, their eyes trained on the gray water swirling past the island. Foam caught in the eddies where logs and rocks lay under the surface. "I think it might be time for me to have some. At least see if anyone in the Family is still around. And if they are, hopefully get some answers about where I'm from. So we're driving up to where I grew up and…I guess, see what it's like now?"

"You and Jazz?"

Blanche chuckled, not needing to look at Freddy to know he was raising an eyebrow at them. "Yes, me and Jazz. And Sunny, and Richard—he's driving us. Jazz's last class ends around lunchtime, so we're leaving Friday afternoon."

"No, *you and Jazz*?" Freddy pressed a hand to his throat to speak louder.

"Like your gossipy ass didn't already know that." Blanche leveled a look at him. "How else would Lee have been under the impression that I was taking advantage of his little sister?"

Freddy raised his hands in innocence, signing quickly, "I didn't tell him anything. He jumped to conclusions. He always does."

"I'm not taking advantage of her." Blanche scowled.

"But you are sleepin' with her, then?" Chas sat on Freddy's other side. "Not judgin', just clarifyin' the facts. Even if Lee was up his butt about it."

Blanche shook their head, admiring the fall colors lining the river. Blurs of oranges and reds, pops of yellow fading to bare brown. "We're…together. I'll spare you the details, but I need to take it slow, and she's been so sweet and patient with me. I don't know how to do all this. I haven't been with anyone—let alone had a relationship—since Daisy."

"Weren't you and Sunny…" Chas trailed off.

"That wasn't…" Blanche sighed. "This feels real. Since I moved into my house, I've been questioning everything about my life. And Jazz somehow gets what I'm going through, even though I don't. I have never been in control of my life, and neither has she, and now we can, and she's so much better at this shit than I am. I can barely admit I want her without having an existential crisis. She's the easiest part of all of this."

"I'm happy for you. You've been alone too long," Freddy whispered as he put his arm around them and rubbed their shoulder. "What are you questioning?"

Blanche leaned into his side as a gust of wind scattered dry leaves into the river. "What I want from life, mostly. I have all these ideas floating around, and I don't know what to do. And Jazz just listens as I think out loud, go back and forth, and she encourages me to do what I want." Blanche fiddled with their hair. "I loved her, but Daisy always told me what was best for me, and I never figured out how to do that on my own. Not to speak ill of the dead, but I've been living based on what she'd tell me to do for seven years, because that's how I lived when she was alive. I don't know how to live for me."

Freddy rested his head on Blanche's head. "You don't have to tiptoe around the fact that my sister had issues. Daisy could be controlling, temperamental, and opportunistic."

Blanche snorted. "Don't forget entitled. Remember that time she rolled up with a dead guy in the trunk, and expected us to thank her?" Just because he'd been stalking Chas didn't mean Daisy should have *murdered* him. But of course Blanche and Freddy had helped her dump the body at the island, because what was the alternative? Turn her in? Let her get caught?

"Way to prove my point," Freddy's raspy laugh made Blanche smile. "I'm just saying, you bore the brunt of that more than anyone. Speaking the truth is not speaking ill of her."

"Her favors, especially that one, always left stains on my soul, and you always were her favorite." Chas sighed. "You think goin' home will help you find your closure?"

"It can't hurt at this point. I doubt anyone would recognize me, and if they do, then I can ask all the questions I've been saving up for two decades." Blanche shrugged. "Something's got to give. Domming isn't serving me anymore. At least not the harder stuff. But do I give it up? Or switch to soft domming? What do I do with my channel? What can I do instead? Other than buying my house, the last decision I made that was right for me was running away from home." Blanche bit their lip. "So maybe going back will help me reconnect with that version of myself. At least, that's the hope."

"Just come back safely," Freddy said. "All this talk about going home, but remember your real home is here. With us."

Blanche's throat was thick when they swallowed, nodding against his shoulder. "You can't get rid of me that easily."

Chapter Thirty-Two

Antonio

AMIDST THE SWIRL OF clothes racks squeaking as interns wheeled them by, lights flashing from a nearby room, and calls for "quiet on set!", Antonio had found a quiet moment cradled in Lee's arms, leaning on a stack of equipment storage cases in a back hallway. He'd forgotten how frenzied New York was.

When he was young, he'd found the whirlwind exciting. The unstoppable bustle had matched his brain. But after being back in the slower pace of Bellamy for three years (almost to the day since his third and final overdose), this city was hell.

Sinking deeper into Lee's embrace, Antonio sighed and tried to ignore the demons. One pointed out that one of his favorite dealers would be mere blocks away. Another reminisced about a party he'd attended with some minor celebrity, at the hotel just across the street. The loudest one unhelpfully kept pointing out that they were on the same street as the hospital where he'd spent weeks in detox. After a sleepless night in the hotel, even his reliable Intentions Song couldn't shut them up. Maybe he should have brought Richard, if only to tie him to the bed so everyone else could go to dinner without worrying.

"Remember your boundary phrases, babe?" Lee asked, cutting through the hubbub.

Antonio leaned his head back onto Lee's shoulder, careful not to get makeup on Lee's borrowed head-to-toe designer outfit. The artistic team had dressed Lee like a wet dream in a pink jacket over leather pants covered in buckles. He'd been pampered by the makeup team too; his subtle pink eyeshadow brought out the golden flecks of his brown eyes. Carlita's dramatic pink and black midi-dress by the same designer coordinated with Lee's. They gave power couple vibes, even if her makeup was significantly less subtle than Lee's.

"Tonio? You with me?" The nutmeg in Lee's voice was extra strong, as his sweet baritone murmured in Antonio's ear.

"Yup. You're just...really great." His gratitude for his husband was endless. The shadows on the edges of his mind hadn't been this dark since he'd moved back home. Antonio barely remembered his time here, but somehow his demons did. He'd forgotten how loud they could get, but their screams were constant. Even last night at dinner, he'd tried to put on a brave face, take Lee and Tara to a restaurant he and Gabe had gone to often that year they'd lived together here. But midway through, the dread had sunk in, and he'd slowly fallen silent. It left him shaking with nausea; Lee had brought him back to the hotel before dessert. The echoes of lost memories that whispered in his head threatened to surface, simply because he was closer to where he'd lost them.

Swallowing the whisper of dread in his throat, Antonio did his best to quell the fear that bubbled in his gut. At least he wasn't alone, like before.

"You're really great, too." The corner of Lee's mouth twitched into a smile. "Can you give me your boundary phrases, though?"

Antonio nodded, humming the memory song with the scripts he and his therapist had put together in anticipation of their trip. "That sounds lovely, but we have to decline. I'm in recovery, so please respect my decision. I'm not obligated to explain my choices," he recited.

The more he practiced, the easier it should be for them to leave his mouth without having to think about it. Hopefully. He'd already used them when another singer they'd met here had invited them for drinks after the photoshoot. It'd been awkward, but manageable. More awkward had been responding to a few DMs of old friends, who had seen the poorly thought-out selfie he'd posted from the restaurant yesterday; he should have waited until he was home before posting anything. Even if Gabe had been blocked out with an emoji, Antonio realized too late that he didn't want anyone to know *he* was here either. He'd been pretending to be fine too hard.

"You doing okay?" Lee pressed his hand flat against Antonio's stomach to draw him closer.

Antonio leaned into the embrace. His husband's familiar rosemary and shea butter scent soothed the panic in his throat. He nodded. "Yes, but I'm glad that you're here. And Gabe and Tara."

Gabe and Tara were nearby in the studio, staying out of the way until he needed them. There was enough chaos without making a giant and a pregnant woman follow him around. Lee was enough to keep the demons at bay for now.

"Carlita Asada, as I live and breathe!"

His whole body tensed; that silky voice, an echo from his darkest memories, was real. Antonio's heart sank as a screaming shadow dug its claws in and dragged it, still beating wildly, down to his stomach. That voice belonged to one of his former friends. Enabler more than friend, he'd discovered over time. He should have guessed Monique would be here; she was featured on the soundtrack too. Maybe if he hadn't blocked her three years ago, he would have remembered.

He plastered on a fake smile as he left the circle of Lee's arms. As much as he wanted to run screaming, Antonio could play nice for the sake of professionalism. "Monique! Bitch, you're still alive?" He awkwardly hugged and air-kissed the cheek of his drag stepmother—as Monique had called herself—who had taken Carlita under her wing. In doing so, she'd introduced Antonio to every dealer, party, and prescription in New York.

"What are you doing here?" Monique was in full face, dressed in a neon green faux feather outfit. Hopefully, her interview and photo shoot were over, and she would leave soon. "I thought you swore off New York."

Antonio nodded. "We're only here for the interview. I wish we could have done it from home, but you know I'd never turn down a chance for self-promotion!" His laugh sounded empty even to his own ears. Lee's steady hand anchored itself on Antonio's hip. "Oh, Lee, this is Monique Unique, another featured artist on the album. Monique, this is my husband, Lee."

Monique had glued down her eyebrows, but the makeup caked on her forehead broke into cracks. "*Husband*? Carlita Asada—the biggest slut of us all—got married? It has to be open, right?" She checked out Lee blatantly. "Oh hunny, *please* tell me it's open!"

Antonio bit back the jealousy that rose in his gut. Not that Lee would ever entertain Monique, but the principle irked him. "Nope, he's all mine." He blinked slowly at Lee, desperately hoping Lee could see he was begging for an exit.

Lee's subtle nod in return flooded him with reassurance that he'd get out of this in one piece.

Monique laughed. "Well, let's see how long *your* monogamy lasts. You free tonight? There's a new underground place to test out those vows. Or test other things, if you're up for extra fun."

"Oh no, that sounds...lovely. But we have to decline." Antonio put his fake smile back on. It didn't sound lovely. It sounded like a terrible idea. Luckily the boundary phrase had come out, instead of the other words he wanted to say.

"Oh, come on! I'm sure Lee's seen your wild side before."

Jaw clenching, Antonio fought a sigh of annoyance, exhaling it out carefully instead to cool the anger licking his heart. "No, and he never will. I'm straight edge now. Been sober for a few years."

Monique laughed again, until she saw his face. "Oh, you're serious? Bitch, please! One night of fun won't hurt you. I know you. You can never say no."

Antonio struggled to find the words for another boundary phrase, but the demons had found a foothold. *She's right. You never can say no. Not to Monique. You owe her. What's the harm in one night for old time's sake?*

Lee tightened his arm around Antonio. "He's already given you an answer. Please respect his choice. Excuse us."

Antonio looked at his husband gratefully as Lee pulled him away toward the set, back to the bustle and away from Monique. "Thank you. She was starting to make sense."

Lee kissed his hand. "That's why I'm here. We'll get you through this. We can leave now if you want. Fuck the article."

"No, we're already here. I can handle it. We only have a few days, and today is the hardest—"

"Lee Flores-Jones?" An aide with a clipboard in her hands was making a beeline for them. "We're ready for your interview, if you'll follow me."

Lee nodded. "Be right there." He turned to Antonio. "Will you be okay without me?"

Antonio was doubtful, but he nodded anyway. "I'll find Tara and Gabe. Go ahead. I can survive on my own for a few minutes."

Lee nodded, kissing his hand before following the aide deeper into the studio. Taking a few breaths while Lee walked out of sight, Antonio lasted all of thirty seconds before his anxiety kicked into full gear. Nausea rose in his throat.

Antonio pressed his lips together, fighting the urge to retch. Monique or someone else he couldn't say no to would find him. Alone. Vulnerable. His last deep breath shuddered, fear clawing at his throat as he ducked back into the hallway. Thankfully, Monique was nowhere to be seen.

> Lee just got called into the interview. I'm going to hide in the single-stall bathroom in the hallway.

> SOS to Gabe or Tara. :|

> Please. Urgent.

> Thx! Love u.

With that, he ran to lock himself in the bathroom. Thankfully it was empty. And clean. Because he fell to his knees, retching bile into the toilet until his stomach had turned itself inside out. Praying his makeup wasn't ruined, Antonio panted, wadding toilet tissue to dab his teary eyes and wipe the spit on his lips, before he sank back against the wall.

The spacious bathroom was swankier than he'd expected. A diffuser on a little table filled the room with a sickly sweet floral scent, and there was a gold laundry basket for the terry cloth hand towels next to the matching garbage can. He'd broken down in far worse places than this. Pressing back against the cold tile, Antonio willed himself to breathe.

He'd fucked up. The demons whispered to him, darkness creeping into his brain as they spoke. He was already here in New York, where he knew he'd make bad decisions. At a place where he knew Mo would be. He'd put himself in this situation. He knew it would happen.

Might as well go find Monique now. She always had Xanax on her. That euphoric detachment was exactly what he needed.

We should have stayed home.

Tears welled up in his eyes. All of his hard work—building up practices to fight temptation and figuring out his triggers—was all going to shit. He'd set himself up to fail. Antonio couldn't even last twenty-four hours in this goddamn city without being reminded of all of his sins, his weaknesses. How easy it would be to drown out his demons. How comfortable he'd be if he gave in.

It would feel *so* good too. To slip into that quiet nothingness again. He would fuck up his head. Could erase his few remaining memories, all the little songs he'd written over the past few years to keep track of things.

Maybe that was why he'd insisted on coming here, despite Lee, Joy, their friends, his whole family telling him that he had nothing to prove. Maybe he'd *wanted* this to happen.

Antonio squeezed his eyes shut as a pitiful whimper escaped him. The demons were so fucking *loud!* He needed to forget them, forget everything. And he'd be glad to, because remembering a time when Antonio was happy would hurt like hell. The memories of how he'd failed Lee, Gabe, and his family would mock him as soon as he was alone in the darkness again.

A soft knock on the door made him jump, pulling him out of his spiral.

He panicked, thinking Monique had found him, like she always used to when he was having a breakdown. She'd give him a few somethings to take to make him fun again.

Antonio shook his head, humming his Intentions Song. He'd come here to prove he could handle it. He had to handle it. He didn't want to lose himself again. Not yet. Not ever.

The knock sounded again.

"Occupied!" Antonio called, his voice hoarse.

"Tonio, that you? It's Tara."

Antonio scrambled, crawling to the door, and fumbled the handle with shaking hands. When it finally clicked open, he threw his arms around her hips. The hard floor was painful against his bare knees, but he was too relieved to care.

The shadows receded as Tara's arms circled his shoulders, her prominent belly and breasts cradling his head. Antonio swallowed hard, resting his forehead against her sternum. The olive sweater vest he'd dug out of his closet for her was soft against his skin. Squeezing her hips so he wouldn't crush the kid, Antonio inhaled deeply; the smell of home, of Lee, of happiness centered him enough to hum his Intentions Song.

"That's good, deep breaths. You're okay, Tonio. You're safe. Let's sit down." Tara closed the bathroom door behind her, locking it again. "Did something happen?"

Antonio slid back down the wall, tugging his skirt over his knees so it wouldn't wrinkle any worse. "No. Kinda? Not really. It's inside, more than anything. Someone who knew me then is here. She wants to take us out tonight. Lee told her no." He paused. Words failed him.

Tara tilted her head, her green eyes searching his face. "Because you couldn't?"

Antonio nodded. "I thought I was stronger than this." He tilted his head back as the tears threatened to fall. "Fuck! My makeup looks too good to cry."

"Breathe with me." Inhaling slowly, Tara knelt in front of him, pulling toilet paper off the roll to dab at his eyes. She smiled at him encouragingly when Antonio took one breath with her, then another, and a third. Somehow it was easier to catch his breath when he was following her lead. "Right now, you're doubting yourself, but you are strong enough, Tonio. You've gone this long without giving in, and you're gonna keep going." She knelt back and grabbed his hands, kissing his wrists before she turned them to face himself. "What's this say?"

Antonio looked at the tattoos on the inside of his wrists. "Not Today. Not Tomorrow."

"You put those words where you could see them, because you knew there'd be hard days. This is one of them." Tara took another deep breath with him. "But today isn't the day you give in, is it?"

Antonio nodded, exhaling with her. "Not today. Not tomorrow."

"You already got through the hardest part of getting sober. And you gave yourself all the support and reminders you need to keep going. Not just the tattoos, or what you practiced with your therapist. You brought us with you, too. We're here to support you, okay?" Tara held his hands, still kneeling between his legs. "You have so much to be proud of."

Out of all of his friends, only Tara really understood how bad temptation could get. She'd witnessed her mom at her lowest, unable to resist the desperation, even when she had a kid to take care of. If Tara still believed in him, maybe Antonio would get through this.

"Thank you, Tara-Bear." He leaned forward to hug her, eyes burning. No one had been there for him like this when he'd relapsed before. No one had seen how weak he was, how powerless he was against himself, against his demons. Maybe if he'd allowed anyone worthwhile to get close to him before, he might have tried harder to stay clean.

Antonio needed his people with him. Lee and Gabe and Tara. His phone background was a photo of his mom and sisters. He needed the reminder that he wasn't alone. Other people cared if he slipped up. Other people were impacted if he gave in. People he loved.

Tara stroked his back. "So I don't need to handcuff you to the sink, I take it?"

"Did I accidentally bring Richard with me?" Antonio laughed into her neck. "Sounds hot, but no."

Tara gave one last dab at his eyes with the tissue as they broke their hug. She leaned back, awkwardly standing up from where she'd been kneeling on the floor. "You don't mind if I pee in front of you, do you? Gabe was talking to some guy who knows his mom when we got your text, and the kid has been pressing on my bladder all morning. I came instead, since you were in the bathroom anyway."

He averted his eyes as Tara pulled down her leggings. More out of politeness; he'd seen her naked enough times to know she wasn't shy about her body.

For Tara's outfit, Antonio had picked one of Lee's button-downs for her to wear as a dress, with a cropped olive green sweater of Antonio's over it. It wasn't Fashion, and certainly didn't hide her bump, but she was comfortable and looked dressier than the assortment of hoodies and sweatpants she normally wore in winter.

"Do you want to push our flights up?" Tara offered as she washed her hands. "We can try to get out of here tomorrow instead of Sunday."

Antonio wanted that very much, but he shook his head. "No, it's your first vacation. I don't want to ruin it."

Tara shot him a look. "Yeah, because we're having so much fun in the bathroom!" Her face softened as she eased her body down to the floor, sitting against the wall next to him. "You're more important than a vacation. It's not like Gabe enjoys being back here either. He's trying to stay positive, but he's anxious." Her jaw tightened as she glared at the floor. "He slept horribly last night—more than usual I mean. He needed two rounds before I could get him to sleep, and he *still* woke up crying from a nightmare."

Antonio laughed, his heart bubbling with love. Tara was so good for Gabe. "I'm glad we're friends, Tara."

"Even though I fucked your cousin?" Tara teased.

Antonio groaned. "What you and Gabe do with Angie or anyone else is your business, not mine. It only becomes my business if anyone gets hurt."

"I know. Want me to check with you next time we sleep with someone in your family?"

Antonio made a face. "No! Please don't involve me in any way. But also, stop sleeping with my relatives! Go find someone else to be your unicorn."

Tara leaned her head on his shoulder as she grabbed his hand. "I'm teasing, Tonio."

They sat in comfortable silence for a while, hands clasped tightly together. Antonio appreciated the moment to think without the demons clawing at his brain. *Maybe we should go home early.* Guilt tightened his chest, but objectively, he wasn't handling the trip as well as he hoped. Making everyone walk on eggshells around him might be worse than cutting their vacation short.

Another knock sounded on the door. "Babe, you in there? It's Lee."

Antonio got up to let him in, greeting him with a kiss. "Welcome to the grand deluxe bathroom suite. We're having a party in here."

"I see that. They'll be ready for us in thirty for photos, they said." Lee kissed him again. "Oh, and Gabe said to tell you that she's here? He didn't really explain, just told me to tell you guys."

"Fucking shit." Antonio's heart froze, stomach plummeting. "Dicky's gonna kill me."

Tara scrambled to her feet and lurched for the door.

"Wait." Antonio grabbed her sleeve, stopping her in her tracks, hating that he was too much of a mess to do anything for Gabe. "You can't lay a finger on her."

Tara whirled around, her green eyes wide. "She's not getting a finger, she's getting a whole ass fist down her throat!"

Antonio shook his head. "You can't! Do not touch her. It'd fuck with whatever legal shit Phin has going on."

Tara growled, "Can I be a cunt to her at least?"

"You can try." Antonio pulled out his phone to check the text from Richard, ignoring the flush of shame that he'd minimized his warning. "She'll be a catty bitch to you, and she's good at it too. Just don't get physical. Keep it short, get Gabe away from her. And Richard said to find a way to mention Phin and him in the conversation. Dicky says she'll get the message, but I have no idea what the message is." He pulled up the camera on his phone and started a video. Slipping it into the pocket of Tara's leggings, he aimed the camera poking out. "Try to get her on video if you can, but this should capture the audio at least."

Tara nodded before she slipped out.

Antonio took a deep breath. His demons were powerless now; Gabe's were more important.

He turned to Lee, whose eyebrows were furrowed in confusion and concern. "We need to bump our flights up."

Chapter Thirty-Three

Gabe

Missing Tara already, even though she'd just left, Gabe made small talk with yet another older man—a label executive this time—who knew his mom when they were young. For someone who'd been happily married for forty years, his mom had retained a cult following of men who viewed her as "the one who got away"—Richard's dad included. Gabe was in the middle of halfhearted assurances that he'd pass the hello along, when a hand clapped his shoulder from behind.

"Gabe Cooper! Now there's someone I never thought I'd see again."

Gabe turned to see who was greeting him, and an icy trickle of fear sent shivers down his spine. He forced a polite smile at a man he hoped never to see again. "Mr. Stone!"

If he's here, that means...fuck. Hopefully, his daughter wasn't with him. The thought of *her* made his heart ice over in fear. *Fuck fuck fuck.*

"Please, son, you can call me Rob. No need to stand on formalities with me." Rob Stone's dark hair was flecked with salt and pepper. It had only been a handful of years since Gabe had seen him last, but he looked older now.

In the part of his head that wasn't screaming at his frozen feet to run, Gabe considered using one of Antonio's boundary phrases. He strongly preferred to stand on formalities with the entire Stone family. He should have gone with Tara to find Antonio.

"So what brings you to New York?" Rob Stone asked with a friendly grin. His light blue eyes were kind enough, but Gabe knew he didn't care. He never had. Everything was business to Rob Stone. Impersonal. Gabe was merely a bystander, a side character, a potential pawn.

Why I'm here is none of your business. But every rational response was iced under his familiar mask of a polite smile. "Plus one for a featured artist," he bit out, hating that he cared if he didn't seem friendly enough. His mom would already be cussing Mr. Stone out. Gabe should already be gone, not making small talk. But his feet were stuck, and his mind was trapped, and the ingrained politeness went unchecked.

"That Antonio character, right? I remember you mentioning him a few times."

To his utter disgust, the survivor in Gabe, the part that had kept him going all those years, preened that Rob Stone had remembered something about him. He recognized the fawn taking over, yet Gabe was powerless to stop it. His stomach clenched as he beamed. "Yeah, that's right." *How did he know Tonio was here? There's no way he actually remembers that.*

"How's your mom doing? She still trying to get that old vineyard off the ground?" A tempered sneer crossed Mr. Stone's face.

Gabe half-suspected Mr. Stone was one of the assholes in his mom's fan club of entitled men. "She's good, as is my dad." Good, something had gotten that past the fawn instinct that told him not to piss this man off. People like Mr. Stone intentionally forgot that his dad existed; they only ever asked about his mom. He fought the urge to gush about the family business, to boast about its financials and his mom's booming wedding empire; he didn't want to give the Stone family any information. "The vineyard is doing wonderful these days."

"Good, good. You still working at that investment firm with Dick Carter's kid? How's that going? You been there a while, right?"

Mr. Stone had never given two shits about Gabe before. The fact that he kept tabs on his work history— The thought sent another chill down his spine. Someone must have refreshed him on what to talk about with Gabe Cooper, what questions to ask.

There was only one person in Mr. Stone's life who would know all of this about him.

He scrambled for an excuse to leave, but adrenaline flooded his brain, freezing Gabe in place with a polite mask. Memories of shivering on wood floors whenever he'd "misbehaved" flashed into his mind. Repressing a shiver, he swallowed. "I'm still there, for now."

Mr. Stone nodded. "For now, huh? I get it. Can't be in finance forever. Eventually you gotta play with big money. You ever want a job in the music business, you let me know. I know things didn't work out with Emmy and you, but you're still part of the family."

"Thanks." Gabe wanted to vomit at the ingratiating smile he felt on his face. He wanted no part of the Stone family, or their connections.

"Ah, here she is now. Emmy, darling, come say hi. Don't be rude. It's been years now, I'm sure you can get past whatever happened between you."

Fuck. Gabe's heart froze, his mind sluggish as another set of icy blue eyes joined them. Until last night, it'd been so long since he'd had a nightmare about them. The reality was worse than any of his worst terrors.

Smiling the same cold smile as if no time had passed, his ex appeared at her father's elbow. "Gabe. It's been a while."

"Emily," he bit out. *How did she find me?*

He had to get away, but his feet refused to unfreeze. *Tara, Tonio, Lee, please come.* He willed Tara to somehow sense his need, even knowing she would be in the bathroom with Antonio until Lee was done with his interview.

He was on his own.

He willed his feet to move.

He didn't. He couldn't. He was stuck.

"You look *good*, Gabe."

Good. He wanted to vomit at the word. In an act of bravery, he didn't return the compliment, even though Emily wanted him to. She looked beautiful, as always. Long black hair, ice-blue eyes, and that cold, calculating smile. When they'd first met, that smile had charmed him into seeing confidence, wit, self-assurance. Looking at her now, he never understood what he'd found attractive in her. Emily had no life in her, no heart. That smile never reached her eyes.

A hand on his forearm made him jump. Fear flashed through him with a memory of restraints, but it was merely Lee at his elbow. Gabe practically collapsed in relief. He'd never been so grateful to see him.

"Hey, Gabey, you seen Tonio?" Lee pushed his glasses up his nose. "He has my phone, so I don't know where he ended up."

A spark of hope ignited. "Yeah, I can show you where they are. Tara's with him."

"Leaving so soon? Surely you're not running away again already," Emily asked coldly.

Anger flashed through him, cracking the ice. He hadn't *run*. He *should* have run. Gabe had been stupid not to. Instead, he'd been left with a note instructing him to leave. Emily had probably given her father a different story to save face. Something that made her look *good*.

"Oh, I don't want to take you from your conversation. I can find him," Lee said, always too polite for his own good.

Gabe couldn't blame him; he hadn't told anyone the truth about his ex besides Tara and his therapist. His parents, Antonio, Phineas, and Richard knew some of the story, but he doubted even they would have any idea what he was experiencing right now.

I can't pull myself out of this. The tiny flicker of hope fading, Gabe nodded. "They're in the single-stall bathroom in the back hallway."

Lee nodded, his hand falling from Gabe's arm as he turned to go.

Desperation won out before Lee could get far. Gabe grabbed his shoulder, muttering into Lee's ear, "Can you tell them that she's here?"

Lee nodded once, looking at him with concern.

And then Gabe was alone with his nightmare again. He clung to the hope that he'd wake up soon, that Tara or Antonio would find him before it was too late.

Emily still wore that cold smile. Her blue eyes narrowed at Lee's disappearing silhouette. "Friend of yours?"

Gabe nodded. "Antonio's husband."

"I thought I recognized him," Emily said. "From his Instagram."

Is that how she found me? Antonio had posted a selfie at dinner yesterday. Gabe's face had been blocked out, but she must have recognized the rest of him, or hoped it would be him. *Did she fucking plan this? What happened to the protection order?* He swallowed heavily. The court would see him coming to New York, to an event Emily's father would reasonably be at, as evidence that he didn't need it anymore. *Fuck. Richard was right.*

Her smirk deepened as she read his thoughts. "So Gabe, have you been *good*?"

That nauseating word again. Her emphasis on it brought up memories of his training—brainwashing would be more accurate—to be obedient and docile and supplicant, past the point of self-destruction.

Before he could answer, a familiar touch landed on the small of his back. He exhaled in relief as he leaned into the warm hand. Smiling down at the mop of red curls that appeared next to him, Gabe put his arm around Tara.

"Another friend of yours?" Emily's cold eyes narrowed, flickering as she took in Tara's appearance. The baby bump was obvious under her cropped sweater.

Gabe fought the urge to push Tara behind him, out of sight from her chilling gaze.

"Fiancée, actually." Tara wore a cold smile of her own directed at Emily. "I'm Tara. And you are?"

"Rob Stone." Mr. Stone stuck his hand out. "And my daughter Emily."

Emily didn't extend her hand.

Neither did Tara. Instead she eyed the offered hand haughtily, pressing her right hand firmly on Gabe's lower back, until Mr. Stone eventually lowered it.

The matching glowers from both Emily and Rob Stone sent cold fear flooding through Gabe again, but Tara's hand anchored him through the storm.

Mr. Stone spoke first, "I heard some rumors about your engagement. Congratulations!"

Gabe should have guessed Barbie wouldn't be able to keep her mouth shut. "Thank you," Gabe said, hating the polite mask he couldn't fight.

"So when's the big day?" Mr. Stone asked.

"In a few weeks." Even through gritted teeth that passed for a grimace, Tara had more heart, more life in her than Emily ever had. "We were planning on a longer engagement, but you know, things happened to *bump* along the timeline."

She put her hand over her belly and looked up at Gabe with an encouraging smile; it was more genuine than the one she'd worn seconds before. He couldn't help but smile back, even if his instincts screamed at him to stop giving Emily ammunition. Assuming he got out of this in one piece, he'd have to ask Phineas if it was possible to extend the protection order to Tara and their baby too.

"Is that the ring he bought you?" Emily sneered.

Tara admired the plastic adorning her finger. "It is! It's really very sweet. I made an offhand comment long before we started dating, how I would just want a cheap toy ring. And well, he was so sure he wanted to marry me that he went and bought one for me the next day."

"Still, at least he had the decency to buy me a real one." Emily's gaze dropped to Tara's hand resting on her belly. As Tara blanched, Emily's sneer became a triumphant leer. "You mean he didn't tell you we were engaged?"

Rage ran through him that Emily dared think herself better than Tara in *any* regard, breaking through the fear freezing him in place. "You mean the ring you bought for yourself with my credit card without ever talking to me about it? Didn't think that sham of an engagement was important enough to mention." The anger and resentment in his voice surprised him. He'd never dared speak to Emily that way.

"Now, Gabe," Mr. Stone said. "That's water under the bridge."

Gabe worked his jaw back and forth, unable to form words.

Tara rubbed her thumb against his back soothingly. "So true, Mr. Stone. All of that is *ancient* history at this point." Tara gave another fake smile. "Besides, Miriam is giving us family rings for our wedding bands. She's so excited to have me join the Coopers!"

Emily frowned.

Gabe could have laughed. He wasn't sure how Tara guessed had it, but he was proud of her for finding a weak spot. His mom had hated Emily, and treated her accordingly, from the moment he'd introduced them.

"Although, I'm sure nothing will compare with the ring Richard proposed to Sunny with, right, sweetheart?" Tara turned toward him. "My friend just got engaged to Richard Carter. Absolutely gorgeous ring. It belonged to his grandmother, if I'm not mistaken."

"Oh, that's Dick Carter's eldest, right?" Mr. Stone asked. "I wasn't aware he was engaged." He said the pronoun with a question mark. Dick refused to acknowledge Richard's transition, but Richard had transitioned so long ago that it was uncomfortable for anyone else to follow Dick's lead in misgendering him.

"It's still pretty new. I'm happy for them though, Richard is a really good friend to Gabe, and he and my friend are such a perfect match." She sneered at Emily, whose already pale face had drained of any color. "They're planning a big wedding, unlike us. We're practically eloping. Just close friends and family."

Gabe didn't know where Tara was going with this. She'd given them too much information already. They needed to get away, not talk.

"You know, we should invite Phineas to the wedding, too! He's been so cooperative and helpful, always at our beck and call for the past few months." Tara looked up at Gabe, hand on his chest, green eyes hypnotizing him with softness and concern.

He nodded, playing along. His brain was too sluggish to understand why Tara was talking about this; Phineas was already invited.

"Daddy, we have to go." Emily's tense face paled.

Gabe pulled Tara tighter against him at the anger in her cold eyes.

"Emmy dear, didn't you want to meet some of the talent?" Mr. Stone asked.

"We're leaving." Emily turned on her heel and walked away.

"Well, good to see you're doing well, Gabe. Congratulations again." Mr. Stone waved as he followed his daughter.

With a tentative flutter, Gabe's heart began to beat again. Light-headed, he finally took a breath.

That warm hand on his back pressed him more firmly, guiding him away. "Come on, Coop. Let's go somewhere to decompress. Antonio had his breakdown in the bathroom, you can join the party."

Still frozen, he followed Tara to the hallway, where she knocked on the bathroom door. Antonio let her in, taking his phone from her. "Oh thank god. I was getting worried."

"It took a while to figure out how to work Phin and Richard into the conversation, when all I wanted to do was punch her in the throat." Tara locked the door behind them again. She touched Gabe's chest, looking up at him. "Coop?"

Still numb, Gabe could only stare at the green eyes that swam with worry for him. He was struck with just how grateful he was for her. How ashamed he was that he was so weak. That he froze up, that she'd needed to rescue him.

But Tara had been there. She'd come for him.

He collapsed to his knees on the hard tile, ready to fulfill whatever Tara wanted. She was everything, the only person that mattered.

She kissed his forehead. "Coop, talk to me," she whispered against his hair. "You're kinda freaking me out."

Gabe fought a smile, trying to be good as he waited for instruction. Her concern meant so much to him. He didn't even care about himself; it was a miracle someone as wonderful as Tara did. Guilt flared through him again. He was a burden to her, when she was his light.

"Is he okay?" Gabe was vaguely aware that Lee and Antonio were still in the room. That they still existed. It didn't matter. Only Tara mattered.

"He's fine. He just needs a moment to pause." Slim fingers wound their way through his hair. "Coop. Look at me. Play when you're ready."

Blinking, Gabe focused on Tara's face. Horror dawned over him as he took in the tears brimming in her green eyes, looking at him with fear. He needed to be good for her, not make her cry. What had he done wrong?

"Gabe? Play?" Tara's voice trembled, her finger tapping his nose. "Please, say something, Coop. I'm calling red on whatever this is. Hear that? Red!"

With a crash, Gabe remembered where he was, what he was doing. It'd been so easy to fall into that horrific headspace again. That dark place that haunted him. His legs giving out, he recoiled from her, disgusted with himself.

But Tara stepped forward to hug him, not giving him the chance to pull away.

"I'm sorry." he whispered, burying his face in her hip. He couldn't get a breath, too overwhelmed by shame to breathe. "I'm sorry."

"Gabe, you're safe." Her hands cradled his head, pulling him to her to hold him against her belly. Her arms circled his head and shoulders, rocking him gently. "You're here with me, and you're safe. She can't hurt you again. Just breathe with me."

Hot tears poured down his face as he cried against her, against their baby, as he breathed with her. The familiar breathing pattern brought him to soft, warm mornings in bed with her in his arms, instead of the cold place he had been. *Fuck, I love her.* Tara was too good for him. He could spend the rest of his life fulfilling her every desire, and it still wouldn't be enough. Letting him love her was more than he deserved.

"I'm sorry." The more Gabe thawed, the more shame filled him. He wanted to take a hot shower and scrub his brain until the nausea went away, to wrap himself and Tara in a blanket and hold her until the shame burned to nothing. Gabe couldn't believe he'd reverted right back into the machine she'd tried to turn him into, with just one cold smile at him and that damn *"good"* worming into his psyche. Resting his forehead on her bump, Gabe wrapped his arms around her hips. "I thought we were gonna be okay."

"We will be, I promise," Tara murmured. "She really did a number on you, didn't she?" Her fingers ran through his hair as he gripped her tightly, breathing deep in time with her. "I'm sorry I couldn't get you out of there sooner. I hope I did enough to keep her away until we're home safe."

Fresh tears welled up in his eyes. "I should have gotten myself out. I froze. Even when it was just her fucking dad there, even the idea she might be nearby, watching to make sure I was nice enough to him, was enough to fuck me up. I should have left when Lee was there."

"You did everything you could in the moment. You kept yourself safe, and you sent Lee for help when you needed support. You're not in this alone. That's what we agreed on, remember? You help me with my shit, I help you with your shit." Tara stroked the tears from his face. "And you would have found a way out, even if you were alone. You are strong. You stood up to her for me when she was talking shit about my ring." She pressed a kiss into his hair. "I was very proud of you for that."

"How did she find you?" Antonio asked, sitting on the floor next to Lee.

Gabe pulled away from Tara, finally remembering Antonio and Lee were there. He leaned against the door and guided Tara down into his lap. As she wiped away his tears with a gentle touch of her thumb, he pulled her close in his arms. Burying his face in her neck drowned out everything else as he breathed in her familiar scent. He didn't want to think about Emily again—especially so soon—but it was easier when he was holding Tara. "She saw your post on Instagram, and guessed that the person you blocked out was me. Her dad has connections here, so she probably made him get her in somehow."

Antonio blanched. "Oh, fuck. I'm so sorry, Gabey. Richard's gonna kill me."

Gabe shook his head, grateful for Richard and Phineas now more than ever. They'd been keeping him safe from her for years, and he'd never realized the extent of their help. "Don't blame yourself, Tonio. I didn't even think about the protection order until I remembered it was useless here. The judge in New York put limitations on it a couple of years ago."

"In good news, our flight is now tonight at seven," Lee announced, looking up from his phone. "We finish this up, pack up our shit, and we can go back to the airport."

A surge of appreciation for Lee flooded Gabe. With it came a renewed surge of shame for breaking down like this in front of him, for cutting his vacation short. "I'm sorry you had to witness me like this, Lee. I didn't think I'd ever experience that headspace again, or I would have warned you."

Lee shook his head, a soft look he usually reserved for Tara or Antonio on his face. "Tara trusted you to snap yourself out of it. You did. I'm sorry I didn't realize how bad off you were out there. Like, you were a little out of it, but damn, I should *not* have left you alone with that creepy-eyed bitch."

Gabe huffed a laugh. Tara ran her fingers soothingly through his hair. "You couldn't have known. My abusive ex is not exactly something I like talking about. And apparently she's keeping tabs on me."

Lee shook his head. "Fuck New York, man. This place sucks."

Gabe laughed out loud this time. He buried his face in Tara's shoulder. "God, I hope Joy can get me in tomorrow."

Antonio held up his phone. "I already texted her. If we don't mind having a joint session while she eats breakfast, we can come first thing in the morning." He laughed, his head falling back against the wall. "God, we're still such emo kids. One bad day of vacation and we need emergency therapy."

Gabe couldn't stop giggling. "Maybe you should go back to flat ironing your hair, Tonio. Dye it black with box dye again."

Antonio shook his head, snorting at the memory. "I thought I looked like a Black Mikey Way. And those glasses I wore? They didn't even have lenses!"

They both sounded insane. Gabe and his oldest friend, giggling uncontrollably, while their partners looked on with confusion and affection. Tara and Lee eventually joined in the laughter as Antonio's infectious giggles spread to them. Gabe buried his face in Tara as he shook, warmth and relief spreading through his body.

Eventually, an alarm went off on Lee's phone. Lee took a tissue and dabbed at his eyes with a sigh. "Okay babe, just a quick photo shoot together, and then we can get the fuck out of here." Lee pulled Antonio up off the ground before helping Tara and Gabe up.

With more tissues from the roll, Lee dabbed at Antonio's eye makeup, cleaning up the tears of laughter and despair that threatened to fall, without smudging his husband's lashes. "Ready to look hot and get our pictures taken?"

Antonio nodded, looking worn out and delirious. "I'm always ready for a photo shoot, Angel. And even more ready to go home when it's done."

Lightheaded from the ebbing adrenaline and laughter, Gabe gripped Tara's hand as they followed Lee and Antonio out of the safety of the bathroom, tugging her closer. "This," he murmured in her ear.

"Yeah, yeah, Coop. I get it." Tara's voice was gruff, but she kissed his knuckles with so much tenderness, his heart ached. "Let's just get home safe and sound."

Gabe grinned. While he couldn't wait, guilt still stirred in his chest for cutting short her first real vacation. "What do you think about Hawaii?"

"What about it?"

He shrugged. "I won a vacation package for a trip there at a silent auction a while ago. We're getting married soon. So, honeymoon?"

Tara smirked over her shoulder. "Sounds way more romantic than this shitshow."

Friday, November Twelfth

Chapter Thirty-Four

LEE

"You sure you want me to come in with you?" Lee asked, staring with trepidation at the clinic as he parked the car.

"For the last time, yes, Angel," Antonio grabbed his tea and the vanilla latte he'd brought for Joy, as a thank you for the early morning emergency session. "Joy said it would be helpful to have both you and Tara there, so our primary support partners could debrief, too. You don't have to, but both Joy and I would like it if you did."

Despite his discomfort, Lee grabbed his own cold brew and followed Antonio inside. While he fully supported everyone else seeing a therapist, this felt a little too much like *Lee* was going to therapy. His dad's voice in his head had a *lot* to say about that.

He wasn't sure what he was expecting, but to his pleasant surprise, Joy was a middle-aged Black woman. A little shorter than Antonio, she greeted him with an "Oh my god, I love you!" when he handed her the latte. Her outfit reminded Lee of an art teacher, long and flowy layers in bright colors, with salt and pepper streaks braided into plaits that hung down her shoulders.

"So, you must be Lee?" With a warm smile, Joy extended a hand, which Lee shook politely. "Pleasure to finally meet the hot-ass beefcake Antonio hasn't shut up about in two and a half years."

Antonio laughed. "You did not just say that!"

"Thank you," Lee grinned, feeling more at ease than he'd expected.

"Anything you want to discuss before Gabe gets here?" Joy asked, wordlessly inviting them to sit on the couch. "Last time we were talking about self-advocating. This might be a good opport—"

"No," Antonio cut her off, flashing a glance at Lee. A glance that told Lee nothing, and yet everything: they'd been talking about Antonio advocating for himself, because Lee wasn't standing up to his parents on his own. His chest tightened. Antonio rested a hand on Lee's knee. "We can wait for Gabe to get into anything juicy. I just want to focus on this weekend."

"Okay." Joy sipped her coffee. "Small talk it is. I saw your movie last weekend."

"It's not our movie," Antonio scoffed. "We have a song playing in the background of one scene." As Joy raised an eyebrow, Antonio hurriedly added, "Don't read into that. I'm not minimizing my accomplishments, I'm just on edge. What'd you think of the movie?"

Lee focused on capturing the pitches of Joy's voice as she spoke, to distract himself from the guilt burning under his skin. He'd known reconnecting with his family hadn't been easy on Antonio, but to know that it'd been a focus of his therapy sessions? Lee felt like the shittiest husband on the planet. By trying so hard to be perfect for everyone, he'd fallen short on everything. He was a shitty husband, son, friend, and brother. It was one thing to be an imperfect friend for Tara and Sunny, because he trusted them to tell him when he was fucking up. But he'd been awful to Blanche, to Jazz. An apology wouldn't be enough. He had to prove it.

Gabe knocked on the door, another coffee in his hand. "Sorry we're late! We stopped to get you a latte— Oh, you already have one!"

Joy reached for it with a grin. "Gimme! I got a long day ahead of me— Oh!"

Tara froze as she followed Gabe into the room. "Oh." She looked at Gabe and back to Joy. "Oh!"

Gabe looked at them both, realization dawning on his face. "Oh."

Lee sighed. That could only mean one thing. "Oh."

"What?" Antonio asked, his brow furrowed. "Why are we all Oh-ing?"

"Hello Stargirl," Joy smirked. "Fancy meeting you again, under these circumstances."

"Stargirl?" Gabe murmured. "There's a story."

"Oh!" Antonio huffed. "Really, Tara? You slept with my therapist?"

Tara shrugged, sitting next to Lee. "I didn't know she was your therapist! Wait, is that gonna cause a problem for Gabe?" She jolted up. "Should I leave and pretend I was never here?"

Joy waved a hand. "I think given the circumstances under which we were previously acquainted, enough time and life has passed that I don't expect any conflict of interest. Unless either of you are uncomfortable?" she asked Gabe and Tara, who both shook their heads.

"What about me?" Antonio pouted. Lee was wondering the same thing, but he didn't want to be called a sexist, controlling asshole. And it was none of his business, so he kept quiet. "First you sleep with my ex, then my cousin, now my therapist? What's next, my husband?"

"No!" Tara and Lee protested in horror.

Gabe frowned in confusion. "Which ex did she sleep with— Oh, me. I get it now." He laughed. "So really, she slept with your therapist, your ex, and then your cousin."

"Well, the ex, then the therapist among a bunch of other people, then the ex again, then the cousin." Tara paused, then leaned forward to ask Antonio, "Are you related to the guy who runs the taco truck that's always parked by the museum?"

"*Him*?" Antonio gasped. "No, but he's so old!"

"No, it was his nephew," Tara shrugged. "But old people can be hot, too."

"Wait, was it *in* the taco truck?" Gabe asked.

Tara's cheeks turned pink. "I will neither confirm nor deny that."

"Nice." Gabe held out a fist, which Tara bumped.

"Aren't we here to talk about the weekend, not this road trip down memory lane?" Lee rubbed Antonio's shoulder, uncomfortable with hearing so much about Tara's sex life. Sure, he'd known there was someone Tara had slept with at the museum who'd called her Stargirl. And sure, he'd been aware of Tara's rendezvous in the taco truck. But he liked that she was happily partnered with Gabe now, instead of putting herself in all these risky situations for a meaningless—

Lee sighed. This was what Jazz had been talking about. This judgment, this discomfort, this was his dad talking again. Maybe not the echo of his voice or a direct quote, but that was still Leland Senior in his head.

And Lee had been the controlling asswipe to his sister, because that was how he'd been taught a big brother should be, the kind of son his dad wanted. He couldn't be both a good brother, or a good husband, *and* be a good son. Not to his parents. Given the choice, Lee would rather be a shitty son than lose Jazz's trust, get disowned by his parents again than fail Antonio.

Gabe's laugh made him jump. "Yeah, I admit I was a little over-confident about going back there. Everything has been going so well, so easily, that I thought this anxiety was me being a dramatic pessimist again, but I should have trusted my instincts better." Gabe squeezed Tara's hand. "But even if it's not as easy as I expected, I'm still confident that we will work through whatever we face together. This was a shitty reminder that love doesn't fix shit. Not on its own. Instead, *we* have to fix shit, and we will, because we love each other."

"Damn straight!" Tara snorted. "I just wish I could have permanently fixed her, but we'll have to trust Phin can use that recording."

"You did the right thing, Kitten. Fighting her wouldn't have helped anyone."

"I know," Tara huffed. "That's why I didn't! I guess..." She smiled up at Lee. "It's like when we were young. You didn't need me to fight for you, like my mom did. You were safer with me at your side, just being there for you. That's the kind of parent and partner I need to be, a wall to protect and lean on, instead of a fist," Tara pouted. "Even though I would much rather snap her fucking—" She paused. "Not gonna finish that sentence."

"Just remember to lean on me too, Kitten," Gabe murmured.

Joy smiled, eyes drifting to their end of the couch. "Antonio, you've been quiet. Anything you want to add? Anything to advocate for yourself, perhaps?"

Antonio huffed, then turned to Lee. "I can't be famous."

"Okay!" Lee nodded, swallowing his pang of disappointment. "We won't be famous, then."

"No, Lee, *I* can't be famous. Not *we*." Antonio's hazel eyes turned shiny as his lower lip trembled.

Ears rushing, Lee's chest ached. Had he been that bad of a husband? "Are you...are you leaving me?" Scooting down the couch closer to him, Tara silently took his hand.

"Oh wow, he does have abandonment issues," Joy murmured. "Lee, what did Antonio say that led you to the conclusion that he was leaving you?"

"He doesn't want us to be a 'we' anymore." Lee frowned, skin burning. How else was he supposed to interpret that? He swallowed, listening for anything to focus on, finally finding a quiet *tick-tick-tick* from Joy's clock as he squeezed Tara's hand.

"Lee, of course, I'm not leaving you!" Antonio groaned, clutching Lee's arm. "I love being your husband. I *want* to be your husband for the rest of our lives. I just can't be in the spotlight. You have so much talent and passion, and I love that you want to use it to make me shine, but I can't be the face of your career." Antonio looked up then, his hazel eyes earnest. "If it weren't for you, I would have sabotaged this months ago, and that tells me I'm doing all of this for you, not me. I'm burning out, and we've barely started. *You* need to shine, and you're in a great place to take off. But *I* need to step back to keep myself grounded."

"Okay," Lee nodded, the knot in his chest loosening ever so slightly. "I'm sorry—"

"No, don't apologize, Angel!" Antonio huffed. "You're sorry! Sorry for *what*? Being supportive? For being sweet? No! We can still be perfect for each other, we can still be the baddest power couple in Bellamy, but our lives can be a little less wrapped up in each other's. You can do anything and everything you set your mind to, and I am happy being an underpaid public school teacher and a never-was drag queen. There are other artists who want the spotlight more, who need you to light them up."

The waver in Antonio's voice told Lee that his husband needed a distraction from the demons. He smirked. "You kind of lost me on the metaphor. I'm the sound guy, Freddy runs lights."

"I can't with you!" Antonio laughed. "Oh, and I can't be your parent's son-in-law, unless they seriously fix their shit. And before you jump to conclusions again, no, I'm not suggesting divorce. I simply do not want to see them unless they start treating us better."

"Oh okay! We'll just tack that on to the conversation," Lee teased, his stomach plummeting despite his light tone. His ears found the *tick-tick-tick* of the clock again, as his mind raced for what to say. "I promise to say something next time." He paused, skin burning as his chest tightened again. "Wait, that's Thanksgiving, so maybe not—" Tara pinched his side; Lee groaned. "No, yeah. If we're gonna ruin some relationships, Thanksgiving is the time to do it. I promise, I will call them out on their bullshit. Set some boundaries, clear expectations for what's acceptable or not. Is that okay?"

Antonio's relieved smile and nod melted Lee's anxiety away. This was what his husband needed, and being a good husband was what Lee had to—no, what Lee *wanted* to prioritize. Himself, being Antonio's husband, and a better brother.

Once the conversation moved away from him, Lee discretely pulled out his phone to text Jazz.

> **Lunch today?**

> I'm literally leaving for a road trip in a couple hours. Why aren't you in New York?

> **Some shit went down.**

> …that's not concerning at all.

> **We're good, promise. Just came home early. Lunch when you're back then? Does Monday work?**

> What's going on?

> **We haven't had lunch together in a while, so I thought we could catch up. Just the two of us, like we used to.**

> …Yeah, okay. Monday works.

Lee tucked his phone away, before anyone could call him out for being rude. Part of him wished he could talk to Jazz now, clear the air after everything, apologize for how he'd been acting the past few weeks, months—her whole life, honestly.

But he had no idea what he wanted to say yet. The weekend would give him time to think on how the fuck he could fix things with Jazz.

RICHARD

RICHARD AND SUNNY MIGHT have overpacked for a weekend away. Their suitcase alone took up half of the trunk; their food would take up the other half. Sunny trotted up the sidewalk to Blanche's front porch, lugging the massive cooler inside to pack with road trip snacks. Richard huffed, his breath frosting. The bite of winter was already sharp in the air, and the hedges surrounding Blanche's house were bare. Everyone's sleeping bags and coats would have to go in the third row. As Richard shut the trunk to follow her, his phone vibrated in his coat pocket.

Gabe: Hey, so good news and bad news.

Phin: Ooh, good news first.

Gabe: All four of us made it back safe and sound from New York.

Richard frowned, closing the front gate behind him. They were supposed to come back on Sunday.

What happened?

Antonio: More of who than a what.

Richard froze at the top step of the porch, fighting to keep his heart rate down. *They're safe. He's home safe.*

"You okay?" Sunny asked, looking over her shoulder. Her twin braids framed her face under her purple knit beanie.

"Go ahead without me. I'll be there in a second." He waved his phone. "Gabe stuff."

Sunny rolled her eyes. "At least it's not work. Make it quick—Jazz will be back from class any minute. I want to get going!"

Hitting the "call" button on the group chat, Richard pressed the phone to his ear before the front door swung shut, waiting impatiently for the first person to pick up. "What happened," he demanded as soon as the line connected.

"Oh, you know, you were right," Antonio groaned. "Just her stalker ass creeping on my Instagram."

Richard's jaw tightened as two more beeps joined the call. "Tonio, I told you to blur him out."

"I did!" Antonio protested. "He and Tara were both barely visible, and I emoji-ed him out."

"I told him it was fine before he posted it," Gabe said. "I wouldn't have recognized myself."

"You do cut a rather distinctive figure," Phineas added. "You should crop him out next time."

"There won't be a next time," Gabe reported.

"Read my mind." Richard paced a circle around the porch, minding the spots that felt dangerously soft. "Did you record it at least?"

"Tara did," Antonio said.

"Ooh, *Tara* talked to her? Catfight! Rawr!"

Antonio groaned. "Oh my god, Phin!"

With a heavy sigh, Richard rubbed his forehead. "Seriously, do you think before you speak?"

"Not if I don't have to."

Gabe groaned. "Yeah, Tara talked to her and recorded the whole thing. Tonio emailed it to you this morning, Phin."

"I didn't fight her, though!" Tara called from the background.

"Surprised you hadn't already slept with her, honestly," Antonio muttered.

Tara laughed. "Sorry that I unintentionally slept with your therapist like two years ago. It won't happen again!"

"She called you Stargirl! I'm going to think about that every time I have therapy!"

"To be honest, I think Joy understands my two years of pining a lot more now." Gabe snorted. "Do you remember which exhibit it was?"

"Can we focus?" Richard asked, doing another lap of the front porch, nodding at Jazz who waved as she climbed up the front steps. "So we have evidence that she violated the protection order. That's useful."

"Sure is!" Phin said. "You got a nice camera angle at the end there. We can definitely use this."

"Watch out for the soft spot. We haven't fixed the rotten bits out here yet." Jazz pointed to the edge of the porch where the wood was worn.

"Thanks."

"You're welcome!" Antonio chimed in.

"I was thanking *Jazz*, Tonio, not you." Richard rolled his eyes as Jazz grinned before she went in. "What are you taking credit for?"

"I put the phone in Tara's leggings pocket so she could—Wait, why are you with *Jazz?*"

"Oh. Uh...we're going on a road trip?" Richard shoved a hand in his pocket; his fingers were starting to go numb. "Sunny wanted to do something fun while you were out of town." Richard was half-tempted to cancel it now that Gabe and Antonio were back, but Tara would be who Gabe needed more than Richard. And he did need to invest more energy into friendships other than Gabe's; Blanche and Jazz were pleasant enough to be around.

"Where was my invite?"

Unlike Phineas, whose friendship was a lesson in patience. Richard was unsure if he should share that they were bringing Blanche back to their hometown. His only option left was to make the trip sound as unappealing for Phineas as possible. "We're going to the SPAM museum."

"I still wanna come! I love road trips!"

"Don't you have to do...whatever it is you need to do with Gabe's case, with the video?" Richard hoped the others wouldn't hate him; he could already feel himself caving to the hurt in Phineas's voice.

"I've got a new junior associate who wants to move into criminal defense. She can work on it, and I'll review it on Monday before we submit anything," Phineas said. "I've been trying to have more work-life balance or whatever, and I've been out of the loop with y'all. This sounds like that social bonding shit my therapist has been after me to do."

If Phineas ever did it on purpose, Richard would consider him one of the most skilled emotional manipulators he knew. Because Richard had been after him for years to work fewer hours, to spend time with his friends, to go to therapy. It was rare that Richard spent any significant time with Phineas, let alone with Sunny too. They barely knew each other. And Antonio wouldn't be there, so he wouldn't have to buffer between them... Richard sighed. "I'll ask, but no promises."

"Yessss!"

"I kind of want to go now, too!" Antonio chimed in.

"Hell no," Richard said.

"Fuck you, I wasn't inviting myself along, Dicky. I also had an emotional roller coaster in the past forty-eight hours. My normal routine sounds like heaven right now."

The bitterness in Antonio's voice made him pause; Antonio must be a little too raw for their usual banter. "I'm glad you're back home then. Both of you."

"Love you too, Dicky!"

For once, Richard didn't snark in response. The four of them said their goodbyes as Richard slipped into the house, blinking in surprise. He hadn't been inside since the housewarming party, when it'd been empty and stuffy and reeking of furniture polish. He'd expected it to be as cluttered, cramped, and chaotic as Blanche's apartment had been. But the house was...homey. Lived-in. The cozy warmth was scented with incense. Candles and crystals surrounded a catchall bowl of keys on the entry table. Blankets were tossed casually over the sofa, and plants overflowed their pots in the windows.

"Blanche—are you blushing?" Sunny's voice teased from the kitchen. "This is so fucking cute!"

"Babygirl, stop pointing it out!" Blanche pressed their hands against their cheeks as Jazz grinned into her fist. "I can't control it!"

"And miss the opportunity to tease you? Hell no! You remember how much shit you gave me when I started seeing Richard?" Sunny pealed with laughter, clapping in delight as Blanche hid their face in their bedazzled jean jacket.

Richard cleared his throat. "I was emotionally blackmailed into this, but is anyone strongly opposed to Phin coming with us?"

Sunny cocked her head, her frown suspicious. "I don't mind, but do *you?* He talks a lot."

Richard wrinkled his nose. "Less than Antonio, and we survived driving him to the cabin. I'm fine with it if you all are."

"Aren't we renting a two-bedroom?" Blanche asked, biting their lip. "Where will he sleep?"

"There's a pullout couch," Sunny suggested. "It sleeps six."

Blanche and Jazz exchanged a look. Jazz shrugged. "As long as he doesn't flirt with me, I don't mind."

How soon can you get here? I want to leave.

FUCK YES!!!!

I'm already on my way home to pack. I had a good feeling about this.

You're not allowed to flirt with anyone in the car.

Who would I flirt with? You?

Sunny, Jazz, and Blanche are coming. No flirting with any of them.

Boo, no fun. But fine. I'm sure I'll find some hot nerds at the SPAM museum.

Richard snorted. Of course. Maybe it was a good thing he'd be coming along. Much like Antonio, Phineas made everything an adventure. Without a push, Richard would probably spend the whole trip fretting about the Emily situation. There was nothing Phineas's team couldn't handle, and nothing that needed Richard micromanaging everyone. Gabe and Antonio would need a quiet weekend with their partners to recover from their short-lived trip; Richard was free to have fun with Sunny, and their other friends.

CHAPTER THIRTY-FIVE

JAZZ

JAZZ HAD HAD LOW expectations walking into the thinly veiled commercial for mystery meat, a mere hour before it closed. Driving through a small town (where the only sign of a Black community was a Sudanese grocery store), when she'd only ever taken weekend trips to Chicago with her parents, had Jazz out of her comfort zone. Their motley crew stood out like a sore thumb—from Blanche's bedazzled jacket to Phineas's white wool trench—amongst the Carharrts and flannels.

Despite her trepidation, she, Blanche, and Phineas had stayed entertained enough, especially in the gift shop. Meanwhile Sunny and Richard had read every sign, inspected every display, and played all of the interactive games in record time. Of all the new experiences Jazz had expected from living with Blanche, this had not been one of them. Still, Blanche looked adorable in their new SPAM hat.

"So what was Lee like as a kid?" Phineas asked Jazz, holding the door open for everyone as they trooped out of the strange museum that Sunny had been looking forward to. They still had three hours to go before they reached their rental (Blanche admitted that they had perhaps underestimated how close the SPAM museum was to their hometown), but the break in driving had been nice.

Shivering from the sharp wind, Jazz wrapped her cream puffer jacket tighter on the walk through the parking lot. "Honestly, not much different. Overprotective doormat."

Sunny laughed. "I mean, he's lightened up a little. He's less uptight now."

"Yeah, now he's just controlling." Jazz scoffed.

"Controlling? Uptight? Are we talking about the same Lee? He's so chill." Phineas clambered into the third row of Richard's SUV, where he'd been unexpectedly respectful and quiet so far. Especially compared to the Phineas she'd met at Lee's wedding. Jazz had to endure weeks of "Councilman Watkins's son was so nice! And he seemed to like you!" from her mom afterward, always followed by disapproving grunts from her dad.

"Oh, that's all an act so you don't find out he's an anxious mess," Blanche said as they buckled into the bucket seat across from Jazz, far enough away that Jazz wished they had taken the third row instead, so they could sit closer. "Though he has gotten better over the years."

"Has he?" Jazz teased. "Because he called you a groomer mere weeks ago when he found out about us."

Blanche groaned. "Because he was spiraling. He didn't mean it!"

"You're too nice, Beautiful."

"Why do all the anti-abortion billboards have toddlers on them?" Sunny asked. She'd been either reading billboards aloud, or commenting on them, or yelling "cow!" out the window as they drove.

"To emotionally manipulate people with how cute babies are," Phineas responded. He'd been the main person engaging with Sunny. Jazz didn't mind; she always felt a little bad for ignoring Sunny's off-topic commentary, but everyone else did, too. "So," Phineas grinned between Jazz and Blanche, leaning between the seats. "Are you two like, a couple then?"

Her heart tightening, Jazz exchanged a look with Blanche; they shrugged hesitantly, cheeks flushed. "We're...together?" At Blanche's approving nod, Jazz continued, "We're—well, I'm polyamorous, and you're...you. So...we're open?"

"Really?" Phineas hummed.

"That doesn't mean they're open to you, Phin." Richard pulled out of the parking lot, heading back through the quaint town toward the highway. "You promised no flirting."

Jazz snorted. That explained why he'd been so polite.

"I wasn't going to hit on anyone, bro!" Phineas protested, reminding Jazz of Teddy at her thirstiest. "I was just curious how it all worked. That polyamory shit sounds cool. Like, low-key but honest."

"Or you could just come out to your parents, so you can date who you want instead of trying to meet their expectations." Richard accelerated, merging back onto the freeway.

"Woof," Jazz and Phineas said together.

"Why have we seen, like, eight million billboards of this real estate guy with his arms stretched out?" Sunny asked.

Phineas must not have had an answer for Sunny, because instead he asked Jazz, "You not out either?"

"After what they did to Lee? Hell no!" Jazz shook her head. It was a nice change to not be the only person with one foot still in the closet; Mimi and Teddy had been out to their families before Jazz had even met them. "What's your excuse?"

"The real me doesn't fit into Councilman Watkins's political ambitions," Phineas scoffed, sitting back. "He wants me to run for his city council seat after he becomes mayor or state rep or whatever. Which is why I live in Bellamy instead of Chicago." Phineas's smile looked more like a sneer, a pleasant change from the smarmy smirk when they'd met at the wedding. "Close enough to show up and smile and wave when he needs me to, but with a residential address in Iowa, so he can't pressure me into anything."

"At least he's got goals for you. My dad thinks that if I must work, instead of churning out babies, I should be a teacher. Instead, I'm applying to grad school." Jazz was surprised she was relating to him as much as she was; she and Phineas had seemed like opposites.

But the past few hours of respectful small talk, and an easygoing hour in the SPAM museum (where Phineas had been surprisingly friendly with a herd of white kids who kept staring at their group, and charmed a tour guide into letting them tag along for free), Jazz was starting to warm up to him.

First Julissa on Halloween, and now Phineas? Jazz was becoming strangely comfortable with people who had once rubbed her the wrong way. It was weird, like breaking in a new pair of shoes. Her parents had taught her to distrust people, to hide her feelings. But what was the point of living for herself, if she kept all but a few select people at arm's length? She had to trust her Pisces intuition, instead of reacting to her mom's voice in her head. Now that she'd given Phineas a chance to be himself, he wasn't so bad.

"Yeah, but they're not the goals I want for myself. Honestly, I just want..." Phineas sighed. "Gotta be honest, who knows what I want?

To escape the constant demands of my parents? To work a reasonable amount of hours? To find someone who... No, even if I found someone who loves me for me, I'd fuck it up."

Blanche and Jazz exchanged a concerned look at the strangled crack in Phineas's voice.

"I don't really know what I want either," Blanche offered, twisting around to face him. Jazz was relieved; she hadn't known the first thing to say that wouldn't sound disingenuous. "But if you want something enough, you'll find a way to make it happen."

"Yeah, maybe," Phineas sighed. "So what'd your parents do to Lee when he came out?"

Sunny audibly groaned from the front seat as Jazz grimaced. She preferred not to talk about it; remembering that day always made her feel weak and helpless, and she'd done so much work to become stronger, more independent. She was capable now. She didn't hide anymore. *Other than from my parents, but that's why I moved out.*

Breaking the awkward silence, Jazz said, "Honestly, I hid in the closet once I heard Dad start yelling, so you might want to tell this story, Sun."

"You sure?" Sunny asked. "We can tell him to mind his own business."

Jazz laughed. "If you're up for it, go for it."

Sunny turned around in her seat, a mischievous glint in her eye. "Okay, so. Picture it. Eastside. 2009. I was fourteen, egg uncracked, and Lee was fifteen and so closeted that it didn't register to him that he might be gay, even though we were fooling around after school almost every day."

Sunny's emphatic storytelling made Jazz smile, despite the awfulness of that day. She'd never heard Sunny's side before. Her only memories were of a dark closet and hearing her father shout, her mother cry, and her brother scream.

"We'd been arguing for weeks because he was *my* secret boyfriend, and he not only let this bitch Chrissy kiss him during the homecoming dance, but he kissed her back!" Sunny tossed her hair over her shoulder. "So he was giving me a handy to make up for being a lying, cheating dirtbag."

"Ooh, TMI." Jazz shook her head.

"You wanted me to tell it, Jazz. This is what happened." Sunny waved her off. "Anyway, the door opens with a bang, and Mr. Jones takes one look at us and says, 'Oh, hell no.' Before I know it, I'm being dragged out of the house by my hair, pants undone and junk still out. Not a word, he just pushed me off the stoop and locked the door behind me. And that was the last time I saw Lee for five years. For all I knew, he was dead."

"Same," Jazz muttered. For three weeks, she'd been forbidden from asking about her brother. Her parents had refused to admit that Lee ever existed.

It wasn't until Auntie Alitrice had shown up and asked after him that Jazz had found out the truth. A month after that fight, her aunt had returned to let her parents know that Lee'd been living in the homeless encampment, but Dad had refused to let her in. Alitrice had shouted and yelled outside their house for almost an hour, until she gave up and went home. She'd even addressed Jazz directly when she spotted her looking out the window. Her mom had quickly sent her to her room.

"Wait, but what happened?" Phineas asked.

Sunny, Jazz, and Blanche all looked between each other.

"Have you ever asked Lee?" Blanche asked.

Phineas shrugged. "I mean, we're cool, but not like heart-to-heart cool. From his side at least—I can't shut up. Which I get. I can be a lot, and it's a little weird to be besties with a married couple when you slept with both of them before they got together."

"Whoa." Sunny raised her eyebrows. "That's news to me."

"To all of us, I think," Blanche said.

"Sorry. I panicked when I found out he and Antonio were together and asked him not to tell anyone." Phineas laughed. "But I'm the one running my mouth. As always!"

Jazz sighed, suddenly understanding Lee's prudishness on a whole new level. "Please don't give me any details."

Richard cackled loudly.

Jazz jumped; Richard was normally quiet and serious. The screaming laugh that tore from him was wholly unexpected.

"Your dad was at their family reunion! Oh, that conversation makes so much more sense now!" He cackled again. "You thought you were related!"

"Bro, don't remind me! I was fucking panicking!" Phineas groaned. "I thought I'd unintentionally fucked my cousin or something!"

"Wait, so if you and Lee..." Jazz made a face, "Why did you hit on *me* at the wedding? That's even weirder!"

Phineas winced. "I don't even know. That's why I'm in therapy. I see someone who I want to step on my neck—I swear I'm not hitting on you again—and make a fool of myself. Even when it works out, I panic afterward and ghost people."

An awkward silence fell over the car. Jazz was not the type to step on anyone—much to Mimi's disappointment—especially not Phineas. But also that was none of his business. It was safer not to say anything. Jazz *tap tap tapped* the arm of her seat. Just like it was safer to never talk about the day Lee was kicked out.

Everything was easier to deal with when she could pretend it didn't affect her. Even if she should know better by now. Her relationships with Teddy and Mimi would be far simpler if she let herself admit when she was upset, or when she wanted something, or when she didn't want something. She and Blanche might have gotten together far sooner, if Jazz had ever advocated for her wants. She could have saved herself months of heartache. *Tap tap tap.*

For all her talk about being free since moving out, her passive acceptance of silently suffering was insidious. And she couldn't keep blaming it on her parents. Lee blaming his assholery on Dad infuriated her to no end; he'd been free for years, and her brother was *still* stuck in the same cycle she was trying to get out of. Even hearing Phineas blame his parents for his issues, when he was a decade older than her, was a future she wanted to avoid. She *tap tap tapped* on the armrest once more. Something had to give.

"Oh, look. Cows," Sunny said as if they hadn't passed a dozen cattle farms already.

Jazz snorted, touching her pendant, exhaling all of her whirling thoughts and uncomfortable feelings through it.

"That's very...insightful of you, you know," Blanche eventually said to Phineas as the silence stretched on. "The first step to changing a habit is admitting it exists."

"You don't have to do that." Phineas patted their shoulder. "We can change the subject. Or just not talk. I made it awkward. It happens."

"What's a land trust?" Sunny asked.

"Oh, I know this one! What's the context?" Phineas asked, eager to change the subject.

"The sign said the river we just crossed was conserved by the Minnesota Land Trust."

"Oh! That is probably a nonprofit designed to protect natural lands through voluntary land conservation agreements, but there are also community land trusts, too." Phineas's voice deepened and slowed as he spoke; he sounded like a different person entirely. "The goal of most land trusts is to protect property for future generations, like preserving family farms, conserving natural lands, or ensuring affordable housing."

"That's sick!" Sunny whipped out her phone. "Going into a rabbit hole. Dicky, smack me if you need me to navigate."

Richard snorted. "We have a hundred miles until we get off this highway, so have fun, Sunshine."

They rode in silence the rest of the way to Marshall, where they'd be staying the weekend in a two-bedroom cabin nearby. Blanche didn't remember exactly where the Family had lived, but on trips into "town," they'd gone to Marshall.

"This looks different," Blanche murmured as they rolled through the main street just as the streetlights flickered on.

"Do you remember any restaurants that might be good?" Sunny asked. "I'm getting hungry."

"I don't remember any of these stores, but the buildings look familiar." Blanche shrugged. "We only went to town for groceries and animal feed, but it looks like there's a diner up ahead."

"Well, let's go. I'm starving, and old people love diners," Sunny said.

"What do old people have to do with anything?" Blanche asked.

"If the cult isn't around anymore, someone might remember them," she explained as Richard parked the car. "That way we're not driving around a bunch of dirt roads, while you look for something that looks familiar."

Phineas ran ahead to open the door for everyone.

"You know, we can open doors by ourselves," Sunny said as she passed him.

"He's not doing it to be chivalrous," Richard said. "He does it so he doesn't have to be the first one to walk in."

"Dicky, stop spilling my secrets. Also, if the hostess is cute, it makes me look gentlemanly."

All eyes in the diner turned to them as they filed into the dimly lit restaurant. Jazz straightened her shoulders and raised her chin, irritation flaring as the dozen or so gray-haired white people looked at them like they'd never seen so many people of color at once before. She'd have to get used to this reaction if she wanted to pursue a career in botany. Fieldwork wouldn't be in cities, but in small towns in the middle of nowhere.

"Table for two?" The hostess—an older white woman with a deep smoker's rasp to her voice—asked Richard. Her eyes darted between him and Sunny as if the other three didn't exist.

He blinked, frowning at her before answering, "No, five."

The hostess pressed her lips together in that awkward way white people pretended was a polite smile. "Right this way."

She sat them at a table in the back as their waitress—the only other person in the diner under the age of forty, though she looked exhausted enough to have lived for a century—took their drink orders.

"Forgive my nosiness, but have you ladies lived here long?" Phineas asked both the hostess and their waitress, a skeezy smile on his face. His hands gracefully interlaced as he leaned forward in interest.

Predictably, they both ate it up. The awkward half smile the hostess had given them before broke into a crooked grin. A blush crossed the waitress's face.

"We're both locals, born and raised," the hostess said. "Are you passing through or visiting?"

"We're here for the weekend while we do research for uh..." Phineas smiled conspiratorially, lowering his voice, "a documentary we're making."

"Ooh, a documentary? About our town?" The waitress asked, adjusting her apron self-consciously.

"That's right..." He made a show of reading her name tag. "Katie. We're making a documentary about insular faith communities, and we got a lead about a Swedish community that used to be in the area. Would either of you ladies have any suggestions for where we might begin our search?"

"Swedish community?" The hostess pursed her lips. "That's ringing a bell, but my memory isn't what it used to be."

"They called themselves the Family?" Blanche asked. "Their commune was called Vitt Hem?"

"Oh, you looking for that cult?" another diner, an elderly man with suspenders over his t-shirt, asked. "The one that got busted back in...when was that, Earl?"

"Oh, yeah, yeah," said another older man, rubbing his belly through his overalls. "That was back...let's see. At least twenty years ago, wasn't it, Neil? Oh-two? Oh-three?"

"What happened to them?" Blanche asked, their voice shaking slightly. Not enough that most people would catch it, but Jazz noticed. She took their hand under the table.

"A couple of their leaders got arrested, for child abuse I think. They're still locked up, as far as I know, up in Lino." The man in suspenders,

Neil, shrugged. "The rest fell apart. Most of them with kids went out west—Montana or Idaho or somewhere. A few of the fellas went up to North Dakota to work in the oil fields. None of them stuck around long after their farm went into foreclosure."

"Where was the farm?" Phineas asked. "We'd love to get some footage, if the current owners don't mind."

Earl scoffed. "Most of the buildings were torn down. Some corporation owns it now, along with half the county. Just don't get caught by an employee who drinks the Kool-Aid, but I'm sure no one would care if you're poking around there."

"Where can we find it?" Richard asked.

"Oh, go up Fifty-Nine til you get to Normania, then hang a right past the church for a couple of miles, until you see the burned-out oak tree." Earl waved his hands, as if that would help them navigate. "Take the left after that, and it's just past the cow pond."

"The burned-out oak tree," Richard repeated, his expression dead-pan. "Are there any other landmarks? Like a sign? Or an address?"

"You can't miss it!" Neil insisted.

"Found it." Sunny had her nose buried in her phone. "Or at least I found what looks like a cow pond."

"Thanks for your help! We'll be sure to credit you in our documentary." Phineas winked at Earl, who cleared his throat and looked away. The tips of the older man's ears were bright pink.

"So, we're making a documentary?" Jazz muttered, once everyone stopped paying attention to them and returned to their conversations. Had there been a plan she'd missed, or was this just Phineas freestyling?

"It's a good cover in case anyone wonders why we're poking around." Phineas shrugged. Freestyling then. "I'm sure even the Kool-Aid drinking employees know Katie at the diner and Earl the bachelor farmer. Both of whom can vouch for us now."

"How do you know he's a bachelor?" Sunny asked.

Phineas raised an eyebrow, fiddling with one of his many necklaces. "Earl was admiring the view a bit too hard. Took a risk, but I clocked him right."

"That's impressive actually," Jazz said, jealous that he'd picked up on it so quickly. She, Mimi, and Teddy had all pined for the better part of a year, before Ed finally lost his patience and forced the conversation.

Phineas waved off the compliment. "I'm an extroverted lawyer with social anxiety, if there's something I'm good at, it's getting people talking. I may be a walking disaster, but I am useful sometimes. Right Dicky?"

"You contain multitudes, Phin," Richard muttered dryly.

"You okay, Beautiful?" Jazz murmured to Blanche. "You've been quiet."

Blanche nodded. "Just processing."

"You want to talk about it?"

They shook their head, forcing a smile as Katie brought their plates to the table. "Later."

JAZZ WAS SECURING HER bonnet over her locs, when she realized Blanche had been staring at the bed for longer than necessary, their shoulders hunched tight around their chest. The sash of their bathrobe was twisted around their hands.

"You okay, Beautiful?" Jazz asked, sliding her arms around their waist with a kiss on their cheek. The rose-colored silk warmed quickly under her palms. Blanche was always so classy; Jazz's boxers and ancient youth group t-shirt made her feel very underdressed.

Blanche leaned into her. "Just overthinking. As usual."

"What about?"

"Everything. But in particular..." They gestured to the double bed with a patchwork quilt spread smoothly over it. "I haven't slept with anyone—as in actual sleeping—in years."

"Do you want me to take the floor?" Jazz offered, ignoring the twinge in her heart.

"Of course not!" Blanche swatted her hand. "I'm not going to kick Phin off the couch either. I just...what if I snore? What if I kick you? What if I have a nightmare and wake you?"

Jazz smiled into their hair, relieved that their worries weren't *about* her, but *for* her. "I probably won't get much sleep anyway. New places are hard to relax in. It took me like a week after I moved in with you to actually sleep through the night."

"What? Why didn't you say anything?" Blanche asked.

"Because I'm too proud to admit any weakness," Jazz teased. "But also, what would you have done if I had told you?"

"I don't know," Blanche huffed. "But I would have tried to help."

"Of course you would have, Beautiful." Jazz kissed their cheek again. "Now, what side of the bed do you sleep on? Please say the left, because I like the right."

Blanche laughed. "I don't really have a side, so left is fine."

"How do you not have a side of the bed? You sleep in the middle?" Jazz untucked the top of the quilt and wiggled her way under it. The bedding pulled tight over her bare legs, just the way she liked it.

Blanche disrobed, revealing a matching silk nightie under their bathrobe. "For the most part, yes. Daisy didn't want us to get complacent, so we would switch it up. Left one night, right the next, perhaps we'd sleep stacked in the middle or upside down."

"With all due respect, was Daisy a psychopath?"

Blanche snorted as they climbed into bed, fanning their long blond hair out over the pillow as they got comfortable. "I have many theories about what was going on in her head, but it's all speculation. All I know for certain is that she had a tough life."

Trying to get comfortable on the stiff mattress and dusty linens, Jazz hesitated, wondering if Blanche would be a cuddler. Before she could ask, Blanche rolled onto their side. Away from her.

Her heart fell. *Guess not.* Jazz breathed through the lump in her throat. *They're not rejecting you, they just don't want to be...close to you.* Jazz scolded herself for taking it so personally, but she couldn't even rationalize her hurt away.

"Do you want to keep the light on?" Blanche asked.

"Yeah, if you don't mind," Jazz replied, her voice husky.

Blanche stiffened and rolled back over, their knees bumping against Jazz's. "What's wrong?"

"Nothing." Jazz forced a smile, grasping her amethyst. "You'd think I'd have outgrown my fear of the dark by now. I appreciate you thinking of me."

"Jazz." Their eyes narrowed.

She huffed. She'd just been telling herself she needed to be better about speaking up for herself, so she wouldn't end up like her brother who accepted the bare minimum from everyone. Or like Phineas, who had a whole second persona ready to go when he needed it. "Your emotional well-being is the priority this weekend, not my immature needy ass."

"And what does your wonderful ass want to be immature and needy about?"

Jazz sucked her teeth before whispering, "Can we snuggle?"

Blanche's cheeks burned bright pink. "Did you think I don't want to snuggle with you?"

"It's silly, I know—"

"No, it's not."

"I just...this is our first time sharing a bed, and I dunno." Jazz groaned. "I guess I thought we'd make out a little, spoon or some shit. But then you wanted to go right to sleep, and it felt like rejection, but you're totally entitled to go right to sleep, because you had an emotionally draining day, and tomorrow is probably going to be worse, so of course you should focus on yourself. Because I am here to support you—not the other way around—and now you're listening to me verbally vomit everything instead of processing your own shit and—"

Blanche silenced her with a kiss, their soft lips warm against hers.

Jazz sighed with relief, then with pleasure as Blanche rolled her onto her back, wedging a leg between her thighs and bracketing her with their arms. The mint of their toothpaste was sharp on her tongue, a delightful contrast to the floral aroma of their hair between her fingers.

"Beautiful," Blanche kissed down her jaw and neck, "anything you want, you only have to ask." Their hand traced down her body to grip her thigh and pull it around their hip.

Jazz groaned, fingers tightening around their hair, as their thigh pressed between her legs. Her hips bucked involuntarily.

"That's it, Sweetheart," Blanche cooed, pressing their thigh against her harder. "Take what you need."

"Are you—" A whine escaped her and her hips rocked again as they cupped her breast, thumbing a nipple through her shirt. To think that after all these years of crushing on Blanche, the months of pining as their roommate, the weeks of hesitant kisses that make her heart clench, she was here, dry humping their leg, at Blanche's encouragement. "Is this okay?"

"Give me some credit, I will slow us down if I need to." Blanche dipped to devour her mouth again, until Jazz was dizzy and panting. "But I can't let you worry yourself sick thinking I don't want you, when that is the farthest thing from the truth. I thought I should give you space here, since this is new for us, and our friends are on the other side of the wall."

Jazz huffed. "It's almost like we should talk about things."

Blanche snorted in laughter, pulling her tighter against them and kissing her neck. "Exactly. Why are we like this?"

Jazz wrapped her arms around them, tightening her thigh around their hip to pull them closer. Their erection was pressing into her belly. She nipped their earlobe. "Can we keep going?"

"How far do you want to go?" Blanche rolled their hips, thigh pressing firmly against Jazz's pussy again. Pleasure shot up her spine in a shiver.

Jazz heard the hesitation in their question. Even though they were present and encouraging now, they were nervous. And they were right—Phineas was in the next room on the couch, and the walls were thin. Her original plan of making out and spooning was still the right call. "More of this. Clothes on. If you want."

"I can do that. You're a glorious diversion from the storm cloud in my head." Blanche smirked, before capturing her mouth again in one of their dizzying, soul-devouring kisses.

Thrilled to be their distraction, Jazz kissed them back eagerly, tongue massaging theirs. Her hand dragged down their spine to cup their ass, preening at Blanche's resonant groan.

Blanche's lips and teeth found a spot on her neck that made Jazz clap a hand over her mouth to muffle her cry as pleasure coursed through her, sending her toes curling.

"You have to be quiet, Beautiful," Blanche murmured in her ear. "Can you do that for me?"

"Can you?" Jazz rolled her hips again, smirking at the whimper against her neck. She always enjoyed kissing with Blanche, but this was the first time they'd indulged this much. Blanche normally pulled back when things got this hot and heavy. But if they were taking things this far, perhaps they needed the escape from their head. Jazz was honored that Blanche trusted her enough to be that safe person they could turn to.

Bucking her hips, Jazz twisted them over so she straddled them, pinning their hands above their head.

Blanche's cheeks darkened again, their green eyes glassy. Their tongue swiped across their lower lip as they panted, chest heaving in their silk nightie.

"Is this okay?" Jazz circled her hips, relishing in the way Blanche bit their lip as she did. Her boxers were soaked and slick against her, pussy clenching as she found a spot against Blanche's hip that sent sparks through her belly.

Blanche nodded, still feverish. "Do what makes you feel good, Beautiful."

"Tell me if it gets to be too much." Jazz waited for their nod before rocking against them slowly, examining their face as their brow knotted and their breath quickened. She sighed as tension climbed up her spine and trembled through her legs. The firm pressure against her clit rolled through her again and again.

Jazz bit her lip to muffle her groan as Blanche surged up to capture her nipple between their teeth, through the cotton of her sleep shirt. If she'd known this would be the first time Blanche made her come, she would have dressed sexier. "I'm close."

"Keep going. I want to see." The rasp humming against her nipple sent her over the edge, spasms tearing through her body as she collapsed over Blanche; they wriggled their hands from her grasp to wrap around her waist. "You are so gorgeous, Jazz."

Jazz buried her face into their neck. "What do you need?"

"Oh." Blanche blushed scarlet again. "I uhh...I'm good."

Blinking in confusion, Jazz pursed her lips. "You came already? Or you don't want to?"

"Both? I had a couple of small ones. And honestly, that's more than I can usually manage. My window for a big one has passed."

"What?"

Blanche huffed with an embarrassed smile. "I have a dick, but I don't come the way most people with penises do. Since I don't have testicles, it's more like a large clit in functionality? But kind of a lackluster one. And without Viagra, my erections don't last long. I had a couple of small orgasms after you rolled us over—because that was incredibly hot—but I think that's all I'm going to get."

"Sad. I didn't even get to enjoy it." Jazz grinned into their neck, relieved that even if she couldn't make Blanche fall apart completely, she'd done enough to make them feel good.

"I would argue that you did enjoy it." Blanche smirked as they rolled them over, pressing one last kiss against her lips. "Can you..." They blushed again. "Can you be the big spoon?"

Jazz chuckled, her heart melting at how sweet Blanche was in private, when only Jazz got to see. "I would be honored to be your big spoon." As they climbed back under the covers, she shifted so Blanche could curl up in her arms. With a kiss to their spine, she murmured, "Good night, Beautiful."

"Good night Jazzy." They sighed contentedly. "I'm glad you're here."

"I'm glad we're both here." Jazz stiffened as Blanche's feet pressed against her shins. "Even if your feet are freezing. What the fuck, get those away from me!"

Blanche giggled and trapped her calf between two blocks of ice. Jazz laughed and let them, relishing in Blanche's joy. It only served to make them both laugh harder, shushing each other for being too loud. Teddy always teased Jazz for being a furnace; they'd warm up eventually.

Saturday, November Thirteenth

CHAPTER THIRTY-SIX

BLANCHE

It was gone.

Not all of it. The barn was still standing, and the wooden fence surrounding the commune still ringed the property. But all of the houses and huts the Family had built were gone. Not even a pile of bricks from the chimney, or the limestone from the foundations remained. Just evenly mowed grass and gravel that had been dumped for a makeshift parking lot. A half dozen pickups, loaded with water tanks and marked with some corporate logo on the side, were parked in the late morning sunshine.

"Is this the right place?" Sunny asked, looking around as she pulled her beanie over her ears. "Or is there another burned-out tree around here that we're looking for?"

"This is it." Blanche couldn't tear their eyes away from the barn. They swallowed the tangle of conflicting emotions choking them. "The main house was there," they pointed to a clearing amid the oak trees nearby, "And the meeting hall was there." What was now a gravel parking pad was where Blanche had been prayed over for hours. Dozens of hands had forced them to lay prone, while the Family wished for their human baby back, instead of the changeling the Trolls had left.

"Where did you live?" Phineas asked, buttoning his coat up to his chin, The white faux-fur ruff of his trench hid his beard. "The main house, or somewhere else?"

The laugh that left Blanche was heavy, sardonic. They pointed to the barn. "The hay loft."

"Oh, damn. Did all the kids stay there?"

Blanche shook their head, barely bothered by the cold seeping in through their thin jacket. "The other kids weren't allowed to talk to me. Some of them did at school, but not when we were at home."

"What? Why?"

"I was cursed." To avoid more of Phineas's questions, they took off toward the barn, ignoring the nerves roiling in their stomach with each step closer to their past. The doors were locked, but Blanche peered through the windows. It looked much the same, as all old barns do. Gray-brown dust covered everything. Old cars and machinery cluttered up the empty space, where stalls had existed long before Blanche's lifetime. Not the same cars and machinery as when they were a child, but it felt the same.

The Family had farmed, but never had livestock to necessitate clearing the junk out of the barn. Instead, there'd been goat and pig pens, chicken coops, and a smokehouse to cure the side of beef they'd get from the cattle farmer down the road. Blanche's home had been used to store hay and animal feed, the downstairs a garage for tractors and machinery.

"You okay?" Sunny asked, peering into the window next to them.

With a shrug, Blanche walked around to try the side door under the lean-to, but a heavy padlock cut that short. They looked around for a stepladder or something to climb—wondering if it was worth risking arrest to break in through the window, when they weren't even sure if they *wanted* to go in—when a deer path through the woods caught their eye.

It was still there. A shiver trembled through them; Blanche pulled their jacket around them tighter. They'd walked this path hundreds of times. This one had brought them to the only good memories of their childhood. But it was also the path Blanche had been on when they'd resolved to leave forever.

They were a few feet into the woods when Jazz caught up to them; a stick snapping under her foot made Blanche flinch. "I know you probably want quiet, but is it okay if I come with you? This place is giving me bad vibes."

Blanche's nerves soothed somewhat. Jazz was so understanding, so supportive, yet still so endearingly her. They smiled. "Let's go. I'm not going far."

Zipping up her puffer jacket, Jazz wordlessly followed Blanche down the narrow path, climbing over fallen logs. Dormant underbrush snagged their jeans with each step. Eventually, they came to a clearing, with a fork in the path that split around a boulder. Blanche looked around, until they spotted a tree with bark scarring over an old wound.

"This is where my Papa shot at me." The burl was rough under their hand. "He said he was aiming at the wolf, but then why did the bullet hit the tree right above my head?"

He was trying to scare the wolf off, Blanche had told themself at the time. Only to realize that maybe he was trying to scare off the changeling. He'd succeeded. Blanche frowned, wondering where Papa had gone, how long ago he'd left, if he regretted that day at all. Strange how the tree was still living, growing as if the trunk hadn't exploded from the impact. Strange how Blanche was still living, growing older and wiser and happier, and the Family had been the one to fall apart.

They kept down the path, their anxiety growing about what they would see, or not see, once they were through the stand of trees. And what that would feel like. Maybe they should have taken an edible with breakfast. Already today, they'd remembered more unpleasant memories from their childhood than they'd had in two decades. Each one churned their stomach and squeezed their lungs.

But as the tree cover broke into a meadow, the little blue house still stood in the dale between two rolling hills. The squat, run down rambler, with the paint mostly peeled away from the graying wood siding, looked one bad storm away from caving in. The porch sagged under the weight of the roof and time.

Grandma Rose's car was there. The one Chad had stolen after he'd found her body in front of the blaring TV, her coffee long since cold. The car he'd ditched when it ran out of gas in Marshall. He'd left it on the side of the road and hitchhiked. But someone—Papa most likely, since Mama wasn't allowed to drive—had brought it back to the house and parked it where Grandma Rose always kept it.

Which meant they likely knew Blanche had taken it, that Blanche had run away. Perhaps that meant they'd come after them. But no one had ever come looking, so perhaps not. Perhaps they'd just gone after the car. Blanche wasn't sure which they wanted to be true.

Blanche walked through the front door, before they could stop to question if they should. Someone else could have moved in, or it might be unsafe after being abandoned for so long. The porch creaked under their feet, but the half-rotted wood held under Blanche's steps and Jazz's, who followed at their heels.

Just like when they were a kid, Blanche barged right in without knocking, trusting the door was unlocked.

Based on the smell, some critters had made it home, but Grandma Rose's perfume still permeated the bones of the house. Like a time capsule, everything was the same as the day she'd died. The April 1998 calendar was still on the wall, with a hair appointment she never went to circled in red. Her coffee cup with red lipstick staining the rim was still on the folding table next to her recliner, the footstool still up. The ashes from her Marlboros in the ashtray, sculpted to resemble a rose, sat next to the engraved Zippo lighter her first ex-husband had bought her as a wedding present.

It was as if the coroner had simply moved the table aside before removing her body from her chair, and then no one had ever returned. Only nature had visited, the rodents and spiders, dried seedheads from weeds peeking through the windows.

Strange that the Family had never claimed her home, or that whatever company owned the property hadn't utilized it in some way. But it was in an odd location, a small valley flanked by hills that were too steep to be convenient. And knowing the Family, they probably thought it was cursed by Blanche.

Bitterness churned in their stomach on behalf of Grandma Rose, who had lost her daughter to their influence. Who had prayed every day that she would come back to this side of the woods, if only for a visit. Who taught her daughter's strange, outcast, adopted child about the real world outside of their insular community via reruns of sitcoms. How different would Rose's life have been, how much less lonely if she wasn't stuck in stasis? How much different would Blanche's life have been, if the two of them had just left?

"There's no changing it." The rasp in Blanche's voice sounded like a stranger's. They turned to smile at Jazz, who was waiting patiently by the kitchen table. Her arms were wrapped around herself as she smiled back. "The past I mean. And there's no going back."

Instead of telling Blanche that their obvious revelations were common sense—because of course Blanche knew those things—Jazz stepped closer to take their hand. Standing in the time capsule of Grandma Rose's house made Blanche hyperaware of how much they'd changed after twenty-some years. The house that had been Chad's refuge seemed tiny now, just four small rooms and a low ceiling. With the same too-short countertops as in Blanche's pink house, which had seemed perfectly sized when Chad was a child.

Blanche rested their head on Jazz's shoulder. "I should have taken an edible this morning."

Jazz's booming laugh filled the small house as she reached into her tote bag. "I brought a preroll in case you needed it."

"God, you're a lifesaver!" Blanche bit her shoulder affectionately as Jazz opened the tube and passed them the joint. They hesitated only a moment, before picking up Grandma Rose's old Zippo to see if it worked. The tiny flame flicked to life on the third strike.

Smoke filled Blanche's lungs, comforting and settling their stomach. They passed it to Jazz, holding the lighter for her.

"You gonna keep that?" she asked, nodding to the lighter.

"I suppose I could. Heirloom." Blanche laughed. "Grandma Rose didn't like hippies, though. She'd probably think I was a degenerate with how much grass I smoke. She was a classy lady who only smoked Marlboros. She wore nylons every day, even in the summer." Blanche kissed her cheek, appreciation for her consideration surging through them. "I'm glad you're here."

"Any other souvenirs you want to bring with?" Jazz asked, tucking the lighter in her bag.

"The ashtray?" Blanche suggested, carrying the ceramic rose, the same magenta as Blanche's shutters, to the ash-bucket next to the fireplace to dump it out, the way Grandma Rose had them do as a child. *Careful not to chip it. My boyfriend made that for me for art class in high school.*

It was there, while Blanche was bent over in the corner of the room, that a wrought iron grate in the wall caught their eye. Decorated in roses, the heating vent was about the right size. "Jazzy, I don't want to stereotype here, but do you have a tape measure and a screwdriver in that tote bag of yours?"

Jazz's laugh boomed again, overwhelming the quiet of the tiny house. "What, because I'm a les, I must carry around tools? You know I'm a femme, right?" She pressed her keys into Blanche's hand, where a small tape measurer and Swiss Army knife dangled from the key chain. "I just happen to be prepared. I learned my lesson when I dragged a bookshelf all the way home, only to find it was three inches too big for the alcove."

With a smile (because that bookshelf had found a home in the attic, holding all of the stuffies and blankets Blanche had on hand for aftercare), Blanche knelt down. Sure enough, the grate was the right size. The screw holes even lined up perfectly with the measurements that Blanche had saved in their phone.

"We're taking this, too." They popped open the Phillips head on the knife to unscrew the grate from the wall.

Jazz poked around the kitchen while they worked, returning with a few sack flour towels and an apron draped over her shoulder. "Here. We can use these to keep the rust out of my bag. The apron is just cute, though."

Together, they wrapped up the grate in the towels, carefully tucking it into Jazz's bag along with the other souvenirs. Blanche closed the door behind them, leaving it unlocked; Grandma Rose had always left it open for Blanche, or in case Mama came back.

By the time they'd rejoined the others by the barn, Sunny and Phin were deep in conversation with a couple of farm employees. They made an odd group: Phineas in his bright white trench coat and Sunny in her ripped black jeans, peacoat, and combat boots, talking to farmhands in their dirt-stained canvas coveralls and flannels.

"Sorry, we took longer than I thought," Blanche said to Richard, who hung back next to the barn, leaning against the building with his arms crossed.

"Phin and Sunny are staying entertained," he shrugged. "They're 'interviewing' the workers about the cult that was here for the documentary. So far it sounds mostly like ghost stories. The former employees found a lot of references about the Forbidden, or something along those lines, in the journals that were left behind when they first took the property over. It's become kind of an urban legend among the employees now."

"Forbannad?" Blanche asked, their heart seizing in their chest.

Richard nodded. "Something like that."

"It means 'cursed' in Swedish." Their swallow was thick. Even after twenty-some years, hearing their title hurt more than they'd expected.

Richard tilted his head as his bright blue eyes examined them. "The guy on the left said they blamed the Forbidden for losing the farm, but in reality, they never paid the property taxes."

Blanche grinned. Their legacy was evicting the Family? "Good."

With a smirk, Richard turned the handle of the barn door with a squeak. "And he let us in, if you want to check it out."

The smell billowed out of the open door—the earthy dust, the sharp tang of rust transported them right back to their childhood. Being woken up to little dream barks from the dogs piled around them, a tail whacking them in the shins. The fresh sun-warmed air cutting through the must when they opened the loft door. The ice-cold shock of water from the pump waking them up faster than any coffee or tea had since.

Throat thick, Blanche swallowed as they took their first steps inside. As the dust swirled around their boots, they could practically feel the cool stone and grit under their bare feet again. The pools of oil and spare bolts and washers they always had to avoid, from where Papa was constantly repairing the ancient tractor.

The stairs up to the loft still creaked as they climbed them, so similar to when they were young that they turned, half expecting to see a half dozen dogs rushing up the stairs behind them. Instead, Jazz looked up at them. Concern creased a line between her eyebrows.

"Careful, Lovely." Blanche's heart melted at the sight of her, still following quietly in support, toting all of Blanche's good memories in her bag. "These stairs have never been up to any code."

With a nod, Jazz hiked her tote up to her shoulder and pressed her hands to the narrow walls to steady herself.

Their footsteps echoed through the hayloft, ringing against the ancient wood beams soaring above them. Blanche's heart sank at the unfamiliar ring to the sound, before they flicked the light on.

Everything was gone.

It'd been twenty-some years. Of course, everything was gone. The hay bales, the straw-tick mattress that had been Chad's bed, the table and chairs by the giant door where they had done their homework, the metal shelf that had functioned as a closet—everything had been swept clean. As if Chad had never existed.

"This is where you lived?" Jazz murmured.

Blanche nodded, their jaw clenched too tightly to speak. They shivered, the brisk, November chill finally penetrating their thin jacket.

"Do you want to leave?"

Another nod, this time because Blanche didn't trust themself to speak.

Jazz's arm wrapped around their shoulders, guiding them back toward the stairs. Blanche took one last look around the expansive loft, a narrow beam of light shining around the drafty gates. The vast emptiness held no trace of home, of the tiny corners of nostalgia that Blanche had eked into existence. As Blanche stepped through the door, they flicked the light switch off.

Chapter Thirty-Seven

BLANCHE

"So, how does closure feel?" Phineas asked as they all settled into the living room. The cabin was quaint, if rustic. The hunter green leather couches sagged, the deer antlers on the walls were rimed with dust, but it was cozy. Knit blankets lay across the back of every chair, dry wood was stacked next to the fireplace, and framed photos of dogs hung on the walls.

Blanche draped themself over Jazz's lap in the recliner, curling up on her thick thighs and tucking their head on her shoulder. "Kinda shitty, to be honest. But I'm hoping it feels less shitty as time goes on. That's the point of it, right?"

At least, that's what Shayla had told them to expect. So far, she was right.

Jazz wrapped her arms around them, cradling them in a tight hug. Blanche didn't bother to analyze why being held like a child felt so perfect; they were too emotionally numb to put up any walls between them.

From his spot alone on the couch, Phineas watched them for a moment, his gaze wistful, before he pulled out his phone and buried himself in it. "You should be proud of yourself for doing this. Reclaiming your past and shit."

"More of an attempt to let it go, so I can finally focus on my future." Blanche sighed. "Richard, can we smoke in here?"

Richard looked up from where he was arranging wood in the fireplace. "Technically no, but I'm sure greater sins have been committed here."

"Sunny, can you very carefully pass me my tote bag?" Jazz asked.

Sunny made a face. "If you two weren't so fucking cute, I'd say no." She got up and hefted Jazz's tote from next to the couch. "What do you have in here? Bricks?"

"Blanche stole a bunch of shit from their grandma."

"No one but raccoons has been in that house in twenty years," Blanche shrugged. "I'm not sure if it counts as stealing."

"Your Grandma's house was still there?" Sunny asked. "I wonder why they left that one up, but tore down the rest."

"They might not own it," Phineas suggested. "You two were gone a while. How far was her house from the barn?"

"Maybe a mile, at most?" Blanche guessed. When they were a kid, they could run there in ten minutes.

"Want me to dig around and see if I can find out who owns it?" Phineas looked up from his phone, his mouth twisting into a forced smile. "Who knows? Maybe she left it to you."

Blanche blinked. They'd never considered that anyone but Mama, and therefore the Family, would inherit what little Grandma Rose had owned. What would it mean to own the property where they'd spent their worst years? This sounded like they'd need to go to court as Chad, and they weren't sure it'd be worth it. But if she'd left anything to Chad, Blanche couldn't pass up the chance. There might be answers for them, too.

Jazz gave them an odd look as she fished another joint, lighter, and the rose-shaped ashtray out of the bag. She offered a second joint to Sunny, who took it with a grin and sat next to Phineas, who dug in his pocket for his own lighter.

"Could you?" Blanche finally decided, as Jazz lit the joint and held it out for Blanche. Their curiosity, their want to know anything, had won out. "If it's not too much trouble."

"Of course! I like to be helpful." Phineas grinned a bit more genuinely than before.

"You don't have to be helpful," Richard grumbled as the fire crackled to life. "You can just be you."

"Yeah, yeah, yeah. I am enough!" Phineas scoffed as he took the joint from Sunny. "Do you ever take your own advice, Dicky?"

"You okay?" Jazz asked quietly, while Blanche pursed their lips around the joint, rubbing out a knot in Blanche's neck.

Blanche exhaled, before burying their face in her shoulder "Yes, but the more you ask, the more I doubt it. Why? Do I not seem okay? Are my vibes off?" they teased.

Jazz snorted, taking a quick puff of the joint. "Make fun of me and my vibes all you want, but honestly, yes. Your energy is all over the place."

She wasn't wrong. Blanche felt scattered, like they'd been beamed through time and space on the Star Trek reruns they watched with their Grandma, and their particles had coalesced slightly differently than they'd been arranged before. Blanche merely shrugged and burrowed closer to Jazz, while Phineas and Sunny carried the conversation toward inheritance law and blissfully away from Blanche's feelings. Being held by Jazz, with a belly full of more diner food, staring into a crackling fire, and an effervescent buzz easing through their body... Blanche could exist like this for hours.

"Beautiful, we should go to bed."

Blanche blinked. The fireplace glowed merely from the coals of a few barely-lit logs. A knit blanket was tucked up to their chin. "Did I fall asleep?"

"Yeah, you've been snoring," Sunny said, brushing her hair across the room. She was already dressed in black silk pajamas. "I wanted to draw a Sharpie mustache on you, but Jazz wouldn't let me."

"Thank you," Blanche kissed Jazz's shoulder before standing up, bringing the knit blanket with them.

Jazz winced as she stood, the recliner creaking. "I think my legs fell asleep."

Blanche huffed as they gathered her in their arms. "Why didn't you say anything?"

"Because you were sleeping!" Jazz shrugged, leaning on them while they walked slowly to their room. "It was cute! Like having a cat on your lap. You can't just stand up when a cat is sleeping on you."

"God, I'm so fucking single!" With a groan, Phineas dove into the pullout couch that had reappeared while Blanche was sleeping.

"And what are you going to do about it?" Richard asked, poking the coals in the fireplace. He set the poker in the rack and brushed his hands clear of soot.

Phineas sighed. "Give myself a chance to be happy, and trust other people to give me a chance, too."

"Good boy, Phin." Richard smacked his ass as he passed by.

Phineas yelped out a laugh. "Bro, do that again. The praise and everything."

"No." Sunny caught Richard's wrist. "Don't take advantage of him when he's high, Phin. You know he gets handsy, and these are *my* hands."

Blanche snorted, pulling Jazz behind them into the bedroom as they called their good nights to the others. To shut the door on everyone but the two of them filled Blanche with relief. Not that they felt on edge around the others—though having Phineas along was certainly an interesting crash course in being his friend—but Jazz was...home. After years of friendship, months of living together, and weeks of being partners, she was ingrained in Blanche's life in ways that no one else was.

Jazz sighed in relief as she unsnapped her bra, her full breasts bouncing heavily on her chest. She stripped quickly, efficiently, shedding layer after layer until her smooth brown skin was prickling from cold. With a shiver, Jazz reached for her sleep shirt.

Blanche stopped her with a kiss to her nape, their hands sliding down her arms to pull Jazz close. "Thank you for today."

Jazz leaned into them, resting her head against Blanche's. "I didn't do much, but I know you would do the same for me."

"You were with me all day. Just...there. Not prying. Giving me space." Blanche kissed the warm skin of her neck again, breathing in the fruity aroma of her hair as they nuzzled behind her ear. "I appreciate that. I appreciate *you*."

A sigh escaped Jazz as Blanche's hands roamed up the soft skin of her waist to cup her breasts; thumbing the nipple rings turned her sigh into a gasp. Blanche guided her to the bed, climbing over her when she fell into the pillows. "Is this okay?"

"I don't know what you mean by 'this,' but yes." Jazz arched her back as Blanche kissed down her neck. "Literally anything and everything you want to do, the answer is yes."

"So if I wanted to fist your asshole?" Blanche teased.

"Really? *That's* what you want to do?" Jazz shot them a look. "You underestimate how freaky Mimi is, and how open-minded I am. Wouldn't be the first time. Though I will say, Mimi has the tiniest hands, so it might be more of a challenge with you."

"I was teasing, but good to know." Blanche laved her nipple, tongue teasing the barbell. Jazz's brown eyes rolling back as her back arched sent a thrill of power through them. "I want to go down on you."

Jazz eyed them thoughtfully, stroking Blanche's cheek. "I want that, but only if you're in a good place mentally. You had a hard day, and I want you to stay present."

Blanche ran their hand down her hip. "Again, I appreciate you. I want to do this. And I will stop if I can't stay present." The idea of being intimate with Jazz like she was a client made Blanche a little queasy; they doubted stopping would be a problem if they went into their work headspace.

"Then get to work, Beautiful." Jazz's tongue peeked out to wet her lips before she grinned. "Appreciate me."

Blanche grinned back before surging up to kiss her, devouring her mouth like Jazz was oxygen, catching Jazz's squeak as Blanche gripped the waistband of her leggings and pulled them down her hips.

Blanche only pulled back to yank them down her feet, tugging her thick wool socks off for good measure. They paused to kiss her ankle as the clothes landed somewhere on the floor. "You are so..." they kissed the hollow of her knee, "everything."

Jazz smirked. "Show me."

At the command in her voice, Blanche shivered. They were so used to everyone they fucked begging and pleading, submitting. Jazz... They weren't fucking Jazz; they wanted to worship her.

Blanche sank to their knees on the cold floor next to the bed, dragging her to the edge. Running their hands along her thighs, they pushed back to spread her open. They took their time, admiring the sweet pink peeking past the smooth brown skin and short coils of black hair.

Normally, they would tease and build anticipation, make sure the client got their money's worth. But this wasn't a client. This was Jazz. Their...partner? Lover? Girlfriend?

The label didn't matter. Her pleasure was tantamount.

Still Blanche indulged, inhaling the earthy musk of her and scraping their teeth along her innermost thigh. Swiping their tongue up her slit, they swirled around her clit for the barest second.

Jazz's groan resonated through the room.

"You have to be quiet, Lovely," Blanche murmured, their lips brushing against Jazz's curls. "Don't want Phin to hear us. Can you do that?"

She nodded, biting her lip.

Blanche rewarded her with another slow lick of her clit, preening at how it throbbed under her tongue. They were surprised to find, just like last night, that Work Blanche never tried to rear their head. There were no tips from Daisy telling them how to perform better, how to earn more. Instead, Blanche did what felt right for themself and Jazz. The steady, unhurried pace of their tongue and fingertips worked in tandem to get Jazz whimpering into her fist as she fluttered around Blanche's hand.

Blanche brought her over the edge twice more, before their knees ached so much they had to stand.

"Come here, Beautiful." Jazz cupped their jaw to pull them onto the bed, kissing them as she pushed them back against the pillows. "What can I do to make you feel good?"

Anxiety twinged through Blanche. They felt good going down on her. They felt good kissing her. They felt good making her fight to stay quiet. But Jazz was asking how to make them come. And wasn't that the million-dollar question? With most clients, they faked it. But they didn't want to do that with Jazz.

"I don't..." Blanche sighed, gripping Jazz's hips as she straddled them, grinding her pussy against Blanche's erection, soaking through Blanche's denim. "Can we do what we did last night? I didn't bring any Viagra or anything, so I probably won't be able to fuck you for long, if at all. And I don't have condoms with me."

"That's fine, but can we be naked this time?" Jazz winked.

Blanche laughed, wiggling their jeans off. Pleasure shot through them as their bare erection came into contact with Jazz's wet heat.

Jazz bent down to kiss them, grinding against them. "Look at me, Beautiful."

Blanche forced their eyes open, meeting the brown eyes smirking down at them.

"What can I do to make this phenomenal for you?" Jazz asked.

Blanche huffed, taking her hand, guiding it between their legs. They pressed her hand into their muff, biting their lip at the pressure against their prostate.

"How does this feel?" Jazz pressed her fingers in time with her rocking hips.

Blanche took a shuddering breath to keep their voice from cracking, as Jazz's swollen clit dragged along their cock. "Like everything."

"Good."

They kissed and touched and sucked and loved on one another for what felt like hours, Blanche's erection came and went as small orgasms overtook them, the way they had the night before.

If Blanche had never experienced a true, toe-curling orgasm that made them black out and fight for consciousness, they might have thought their "small orgasms" were the real thing. But their body was perfect like Daisy always said, with so much untapped potential for pleasure waiting to be discovered.

They would get there with Jazz eventually, perhaps with support from medication and vibrator, but this ongoing...lovemaking, for lack of a better word, was exactly what Blanche needed tonight. The nails scraping down their chest, the tug of Jazz's lips against their nipples, the bruises they left on each other—that was what Blanche craved. A sign of their future with Jazz, after a long day of their past. A sign that they were with someone who cared for them, who saw them and made them feel special; not exploitable like Daisy had, but cherished like no one else but Daisy had. The way Blanche had been craving for longer than they could remember.

Exchanging soft kisses, until gentle snores overtook Jazz, Blanche tucked her into the bed. They found the bonnet she'd discarded on the nightstand and pulled it over her hair, tucking every last loc into it. They plugged in her phone and set Jazz's water bottle next to it. Jazz always got so thirsty when she smoked, and she'd had most of the joint.

They paused before climbing back into bed with her, wondering if Jazz was wearing makeup that needed to be removed, and where her makeup remover might be. But there was a line between fussing and caretaking, and Jazz loved her independence.

So they climbed into bed with her, pressing a kiss to each vertebra in her neck. Chewing their lip while they waited for sleep to overtake them, Blanche sighed. A strange sense of freedom and optimism was mixing with the more familiar apathy and listlessness. As if they were cast adrift from their anchors, seeing where the current would take them and powerless to change it.

But they did. They could steer and row and anchor themself.

"How would you feel about me hiring Julissa?" Blanche murmured.

Jazz groaned in her sleep. "Hmm?"

"I think..." Blanche paused, trusting Jazz was too out of it to pay them any real mind. They'd have this conversation again when they were home. "With Tara going to be out, and Julissa having filmmaking experience, I think I will need help. And I think I want...to go back to school, eventually. And taking on an apprentice or two to help run the channel wouldn't be the worst idea. The editing gig would be a good trial run, to see how I well I can work with someone besides Tara and Lee."

"That'd be hella cool," Jazz groaned.

Blanche grinned. "Are you sure?"

"Yeah."

"She'd be over all the time. I thought you didn't like her."

"She's cool," Jazz shrugged. "I wouldn't have said anything if we weren't getting along better. I'm not that tired."

Blanche snorted and kissed her behind the ear. "Okay, Lovely, I believe you."

"I'm not! You should ask Jules," Jazz murmured sleepily. "She'd shit herself. But Mimi says she's a good dominant. Sadistic, but sweet."

That was exactly what Blanche was looking for. They could keep the soft clients, and mentor the harder doms. But Jazz had been snoring minutes ago; she might not want the reality of that. "Go to sleep, Jazzy. You weren't supposed to actually hear this, you know," Blanche murmured. "This was me thinking out loud."

Jazz grumbled, burrowing deeper into Blanche's arms. "I'm a light sleeper. What are you going to school for?"

"Go back to sleep. We'll talk about this when we're home."

"Blanche?"

"Yeah, Jazz?"

"Can we do this when we're home? Sleep together sometimes? I slept great last night."

With a smile against her neck, Blanche melted. They'd slept great the night before, too. Even if they'd woken up with a sweaty back from Jazz's inhuman body temperature. "Yeah, Jazzy, we can sleep together sometimes."

Monday, November Fifteenth

Chapter Thirty-Eight

JAZZ

JAZZ LAUGHED TO HERSELF when she walked into the café. The bustle of conversation and the warm smell of coffee was a familiar comfort after so many years of coming here. And there, at their normal spot in the corner—with the order number card on the table and a mug of tea already next to his cold brew—sat her brother. She should have known Lee would be early.

"If I'd known Antonio wasn't coming with you, I would have left sooner," Jazz teased, dropping her bag into an empty chair. She steeled herself for his annoying reaction as she pulled off her coat, revealing a pink crocheted sweater that probably showed more cleavage than he wanted. "Didn't mean to make you wait, even though I'm ten minutes early."

Surprisingly, Lee merely laughed, swirling the iced coffee in his hand, despite the freezing temperatures outside. "Yeah, no, I just got here."

"And yet, you ordered our food already," Jazz sat, pulling the steaming mug of hibiscus tea closer. Her favorite, had been since she was a kid, because she liked the color. "Thank you."

Jazz had walked in a little trepidacious (Lee was being so weird about meeting with her), but now that she was here, the nostalgic familiarity made her hopeful. They'd met up like this for years, once a month since she was sixteen.

And yet, when was the last time they hung out, just the two of them, like this? Not since he'd started bringing Antonio along. She'd never realized how much she missed him. Lee might look different, with the long hair and beard, in a Coogi sweater, instead of the usual thrifted crewnecks he used to wear. But he was still her brother, still the only family she could count on.

Lee merely shrugged off her thanks. "How was the road trip?"

"Is that really what you wanted to talk about?" Jazz raised her eyebrows as she sipped her tea. "It was fun. Interesting. Glad to be back in Bellamy, though. I don't think I really vibe with small towns like that." She snorted. "It was giving sundown town, until Phin started chatting with the locals. They were friendlier after he started sweet-talking them."

"Phin was there?" Lee frowned. "I didn't know he actually went. Tonio and I figured he was kidding when he asked to go."

"Yeah, he tagged along last minute." Jazz bristled preemptively at Lee's attitude. If he didn't trust his friends to be respectful around her, why was he friends with them? "Honestly, Blanche probably wouldn't have learned anything if it weren't for him." Her chest twisted; the closure she'd been hoping for Blanche wasn't very *closed*, but that was as much as Blanche would get. Blanche seemed to be at peace with how few answers they'd gotten, but Jazz wanted more for them.

"And how is Blanche?" Lee asked, stirring his cold brew absentmindedly. The ice cubes clinked in the glass.

"They're good," Jazz bit her lip, *tap tap tapping* her finger on the mug. Had her rapport with her brother always been this awkward? It couldn't have been; she'd always left their sibling lunch dates lighter than when she'd arrived, like talking with him was an outlet for the anxiety that always built in her chest. *Tap tap tap* went her finger. Her monthly get-togethers with Lee had been a relief, every time. Maybe now that she wasn't living with their parents, she didn't need the outlet. *Tap tap tap.*

But she still needed *Lee*. She missed who Lee had been to her for all those years, the sympathetic ear, the understanding support, the hope that maybe she'd be free too, one day. She wanted to get to a point where they had that same openness, that implicit understanding between them again. Jazz wrapped her hand around her amethyst, exhaling the wish into the world.

"You don't do that as often." Lee nodded to her hand around her necklace. "The tapping, I mean."

Jazz flushed hot. "Was it always that obvious?" Here, she thought she'd hidden it so well that only the ever-perceptive Blanche had spotted it.

"I don't think Mom and Dad ever noticed, but you've done it, ever since you were little." Lee smiled softly. "I listen for it, when I'm anxious. It was quiet, but it was always there, anytime Dad was in a mood. Even now, I get stressed, and I just listen for a pattern, a rhythm, anything to remind myself to stay calm. Even if you're not the one I'm staying calm for. Luckily, Antonio never stops humming."

Her smile twisted in sympathy as Jazz sat silently, her chest aching.

"I'm sorry," Lee murmured, eyes on his half-empty coffee. "For not supporting you like you needed to be. Not just with Blanche, but your partners, how you dress, all of it. I wanted to protect you, keep you safe, because I'm your older brother, and that's what's been drilled into my head since you were born. But I never questioned that Dad's idea of protection and safety was a way to control you, even when it was him I was keeping you safe from."

"Thank you," Jazz muttered, shifting in her chair. Lee had never been one to discuss problems so openly. They would complain about their parents together, but never talk about any issues between them. "That means a lot to hear."

"I went to therapy—" Lee raised a hand preemptively as Jazz's eyebrows shot up. "No, don't get that idea! I am not *going* to therapy. I *tagged along with* Tonio to one of *his* therapy sessions."

"Okay, but have you considered that you might—"

"Shh..." Lee grinned as he gestured for her to stop talking. "Very aware that I would probably benefit from therapy. But it's not like *you're* going anytime soon either."

"Oh, absolutely not!" Jazz laughed with him. "God, we're so fucked up."

"Honestly," Lee huffed. "Anyway, Tonio's therapy session made me realize how hard I've been backsliding, because I thought Dad and I were trying to meet each other halfway this whole time. But no, I went halfway, and Dad keeps moving the goalposts farther and farther back, and now I'm deep in the end zone on his side of the field."

"I know you're the one who actually played it, but I don't think that's how football works," Jazz teased. "Don't you want to be in the other team's end zone?"

Lee snorted. "Let's just say it was a good thing I played defense. I was trying so hard to pretend to be straight, I had no idea what I was doing on that field."

Jazz's smile faded, ever so slightly. Sometimes Lee would say things that reminded her of how Blanche would drop horrifying tidbits about their past; hearing her brother, the only guy she'd always looked up to, allude to his own trauma so casually was heartbreaking. "Moving in with Blanche helped, with the tapping I mean," she admitted. "It was getting bad. Near the end there, I couldn't stop because I was always anxious and overwhelmed." Jazz bit her lip, resisting the urge to tap again. "But now, I don't need it as much. There's less to cope with."

"Good." Lee nodded. "I'm glad. It's all I want, for you to be happy, and safe, and like you're getting everything you need."

Jazz sipped her tea, gathering her courage. "I'm sorry, too."

"For what?" Lee frowned.

"For coming down so hard on you." Jazz groaned; doing this with Mimi and Teddy had been hard enough, and they were the ones who had taught her conflict could be healthy. Doing this with Lee—who had always been on the same page as her, that they'd get over everything and keep moving, no discussion needed—was so uncomfortable. "Like, you were being an ass, don't get me wrong. But I know you, what you've been through, where you're coming from, and I know you didn't mean to make me feel so...*incapable* of making my own decisions. You were working through your own shit. And Blanche understood that before I did." She traced the rim of her mug, uncomfortably warm against the pad of her thumb. "I guess I forget that you're not ahead of me, just because you're older or because you've been on your own longer. We're not even on the same track! Yeah, we come from the same family, but we got different lessons that we need to unlearn, and we aren't coming from the same starting place."

Lee nodded, his jaw tight. But instead of anger, like she would expect to see in their father's face, Lee's eyes only held understanding.

"I lost faith in our parents, in everything they stood for, the day they kicked you out." Jazz shook her head, bitterness tight in her throat. "I've been knowing they're wrong about everything since I was nine. I've had Mimi and Teddy forcing me to have these intentional, vulnerable conversations since we became friends, helping me see a new way of thinking and seeing the world." Jazz laughed, because she had initially hated those challenging discussions, all wrapped in therapy-speak; they'd made her feel so small and sheltered and ignorant. But Mimi and Teddy had been growing right along with her, fucking up with her, forgiving each other for every misstep. "And you've had that, too, with Blanche, and Tara, and Antonio. But Mom and Dad put so much more pressure on you, for so much longer, and now they're expecting you to be the same obedient kid, even after they abandoned you for a decade."

"It's not fair, is it?" Lee asked, his deep voice gentle.

Jazz shook her head. Her brother and father may have looked eerily similar, but Lee was nothing like their dad. She had to remember that, and she could remind him too, when he needed it. "For either of us."

"So we're our own people now, right?" Lee smiled as he waited for her nod. "Good, then let's be ourselves with each other. I'm not the controlling older brother. You're not the sheltered little sister. From now on, we're the adult versions of Lee and Jazz. Whatever that means for us. And I'll remember to keep an open mind about whoever you are now, and whoever you become, and not who I expect you to be. Is that okay?"

With a nod, Jazz smiled. Lee made it sound so simple, but she supposed it would have to be a start. "I'll do my best to remember that you're a new person too. Shouldn't be too hard, you're barely sweating right now, and we're actually talking about real shit for once."

"Damn, you did not need to call out the anxiety sweat like that," Lee laughed, pushing up his glasses. "So what do you want to share about your life? How's everything? School, life with Blanche, your relationship with Mimi and Teddy, all of it."

Jazz snorted to hide the glow in her chest that Lee had finally acknowledged her partners by name. "Honestly? Great. I'm a little scared where all of this is going to go with Mimi and Teddy, because we're so young, and we all have such different plans about what happens after next year, but I'm happy right now. Even with Blanche, who knows what our future holds? But we're so happy together, honestly."

"What *are* your plans for next year?" Lee settled back into his chair, slurping his iced coffee. "And your partners?"

"I plan on staying in Bellamy for grad school. My advisor says with my grades and the anthro minor I'm adding, I'll be a shoo-in for the ethnobotany program, and Blanche says I can stay as long as I want, so I'll still be here." Jazz bit her lip, still anxious about how everything would pan out. But she was so relieved by everyone's confidence that she could pull it off. "Mimi is ready to move to whatever med school accepts her, but she's hoping for SoCal, because Jules plans on moving to LA to get her foot in the door in the film industry." Jazz considered telling Lee that Blanche was thinking about adding Jules to their SubParty team while Tara was out, but decided against it. Blanche could manage their business however they wanted. "Teddy and Ed plan on moving to Chicago, assuming Ed gets into grad school for social work. So yeah, most likely going to end up long distance, or breaking up." She winced, dreading the day they came to that bridge. "But honestly, we'll figure it out. Right now, we're happy, and that's all I need out of a relationship right now."

"Good. I'm glad you're happy." Lee smiled, his expression soft.

Jazz could still see the inner judginess in the twitch of his eyebrow, but thankfully, Lee kept it to himself. And that was what Jazz needed to see, what she'd been needing from Lee for years. She didn't want to control his thoughts, just not feel so persecuted for being herself.

"One question though..." Lee hesitated, nodding to the server who finally brought them their food. Lee looked increasingly nervous about the delay, as he thanked the guy setting their sandwiches in front of them. Just as Jazz prepared to take it all back and cuss him out for being a judgy little bitch, he leaned forward. "What the fuck is ethnobotany?"

Jazz burst into laughter. "I don't know what I was expecting, but it wasn't that."

Lee popped a chip in his mouth. "Gotta be honest, I still don't get what botany is in the first place, let alone adding ethno to it. You got all the book smarts in this family."

"I want to study the relationship between plants and people. How people and cultures shape and are shaped by the flora around them, how they use those plants for food, medicine, spirituality, clothing, etcetera." Jazz fussed with the sandwich on her plate, pulling out the skewers holding it together. "I like the science of botany and ecology, but what really interests me are the applications for real people, especially how plants that are native, easily grown, and readily available can improve normal lives. Like, imagine cities growing plants in parks and boulevards that are not only beautiful, but ecologically advantageous for soil health and local ecosystems, and can also be used medicinally by the general public." Jazz's cheeks heated as she caught herself from the rave she'd been about to go on about goldenseal and echinacea.

Lee ate another chip as he processed. "I still don't really understand what all of that means, but I can tell your nerdy ass is gonna be good at it."

"Thanks, Lee." Jazz snorted. Even as she and her brother matured into the dynamic individuals they were in the process of becoming, some things would never change.

FRIDAY, NOVEMBER NINETEENTH

Chapter Thirty-Nine

Sunny

Squirming against her restraints, Sunny longed to adjust her bra. Mostly for the excuse to touch herself. The restraints bound her hands and feet to Richard's desk chair, a vibe filled her ass, and a leather cleave gag was wedged between her teeth. Straddling her thighs, Richard was using her as a chair; Sunny melted into a puddle of goo at the thought. And since he had just joined his final meeting of the day (an unexpected escalation to his calendar, scheduled after he was already on his way home), she would be there for at least another thirty minutes.

She really hadn't thought this through. Not the idea of being naked and used as human furniture, while he was fully clothed and held the remote for the plug in her ass—because she'd been *really* looking forward to this scene. Moreso, the whole "being quiet" part. Because chairs didn't move, and chairs didn't orgasm. At most, a chair might only squeak.

So far, it was a pleasurable experience. Except the whole not being allowed to move, talk, or come aspect. Sunny pouted to herself, even if Richard wouldn't see it. She was supposed to be good while he was on his call, but he couldn't stop her from making a face.

Fully clothed in the suit he'd worn to work that day, Richard straddled her lap. He passed the remote casually back and forth between his hands while participating in his work call, as if she wasn't there at all. She narrowed her eyes at the back of his neck resentfully, even as she admired his strong shoulders, muscular thighs, his weight in her lap. Her skin was slick with sweat. Anticipation, need, and the hazy glow of subspace slowly taking her over made heat burn under her skin.

The remote clicked only once. But Sunny still had to close her eyes to fight the moan that shuddered through her, as the vibrator buzzed to life deep within her. Forbidden from coming, she ran through a project at work, replaying the code in her head to try and find where the damn defect was. Because that was her responsibility now, the responsibility she'd asked for in hopes of making team lead: fixing other people's shit. She found a couple of extra keystrokes that she mentally flagged to fix after the scene, but she couldn't find the extra bracket that was in there somewhere. Probably wherever Greg had made his edits.

Richard clicked the button again, and Sunny bit the leather gag to keep silent. Richard had chosen a moment where he was casually adding his opinion about risk assessment to take her up to level two. Once he'd muted himself, he murmured, "Good girl."

Sunny preened, but tried to keep her mind focused, so she could stay good. Fucking Greg. Her annoying coworker was a safe train of thought to stave off an orgasm. He was useless. And somehow condescending and arrogant, despite his ineptitude. If Sunny fucked up as often as he did, she'd have been fired years ago. He probably got paid more than her, too.

"Sorry, I'm not able to turn my camera on right now for privacy reasons. My girlfriend is working in the same room," Richard said calmly.

"Fiancée," she corrected with a smirk, the sound muffled by the leather.

Richard clicked the remote again as a reprimand. She bit back a squeal as pleasure coursed through her. She might be feeling brattier than they'd planned, but Sunny knew better than to moan while he was on a call.

"Yes, that was her. And yes, I haven't shared it at work yet, but we did recently get engaged." Richard scowled over his shoulder. She grinned unapologetically. "Thank you, we are very excited."

He doesn't sound excited at all. Richard's coworkers saw a different side of him than she did. They didn't see the softness and sweatpants, the snores when he fell asleep on the couch with his glasses on; the delighted laugh that rang out when he was playing with Dumpster; the tender way he brushed Sunny's hair before bed. They only saw the cold, hard-ass persona he hid behind around anyone but her.

With a quiet giggle, Sunny squirmed again as Richard leaned back against her, crossing his ankle over his knee. The plug pressed harder against her prostate. The leather creaked under her teeth as she tried to get back to the code.

"My chair is moving a lot," Richard quietly reprimanded, pressing the remote again.

Sunny whimpered. *Where is the bracket? What was fucking Greg working on again?* The replay of the code running through her brain kept getting jumbled, whiting out as Richard cruelly adjusted his hips, his ass pressing against her clit.

She glared at the back of his head as she barely held back a cry. Sweat prickled Sunny's chest and back as pleasure threatened to overwhelm her.

"Quiet, Doll," Richard reminded her. "I might be muted, but good chairs should be silent. You've already earned a couple punishments."

Sunny grinned in anticipation, as Richard unmuted himself to say some corporate bullshit she couldn't follow when she was like this. The fact that he could effortlessly talk, while still grinding against her, was so irritating. She wanted to come so bad, and he was fucking talking about compliance reports? *Honestly at this point I don't even care about the punishments. I just want him to stop ignoring me.*

As Richard muted himself and pressed the button to the highest level, Sunny stopped holding back. She set the coil of tension building within her free, flying over the edge, shuddering under him as the orgasm tore through her. By some miracle, she remained silent.

Richard's head whipped around as he glared over his shoulder, a hard edge in his voice as he simply said, "Doll."

The disappointment and warning in his voice flooded Sunny with guilt. "Whoops."

"We agreed that you could be a little bratty later in the scene, but this is a whole other level. That was deliberate."

"You can't prove anything, sir." Sunny rolled her eyes, playing up the smart-ass attitude more than she felt. *Why did I do that?* Doubt crept in. Guilt ate at her. *The whole point of the scenes is to fucking listen to him, to do what he tells me, to be good.*

"Fine. You'll stay there then. I'm not done with you yet." Richard turned back to his meeting, turning the remote off completely.

Sunny twitched, emptiness gnawing at her as shame set in.

He still had fifteen minutes on his call. Fifteen more minutes of this torture.

And I deserve every minute. She waited patiently, without a squirm or squeak, for her punishment.

The second his call was over, Richard slammed his laptop shut and stood to face her. His jaw tightened as he crossed his arms.

"Doll, what the fuck was that?" Richard asked. His blue eyes flashed in anger.

"Sorry, sir," Sunny tried to hide how sheepish she felt behind a bratty smirk around the gag, desperate to be good, to keep the scene going. He'd probably get mad at her for not using the safeword, for not asking him to slow down, but she'd wanted this.

"No, you're not. But you will be." His quiet tone was a warning that brought tears to Sunny's eyes, and a wobble to her lip. "Oh, Doll..." Richard breathed instead, his frown softening. He pulled the gag from between her lips. "What's wrong?"

"I'm sorry," she whispered, biting her lip to fight from crying.

"This was too much for you." Richard knelt to untie her feet. "I should have been paying more attention, I'm sorry. Let me take care of you, okay?"

Sunny thought about protesting, considered arguing that she could keep going. But then Richard kissed the bare sole of her foot, massaging where the ropes had dug into her ankle, and the soft haze of subspace returned. He was the dominant right now; she would have to trust him to know what she needed.

He's so good to me. Sunny was in heaven, her body floating as the last remnants of subspace faded away. The weird mid-scene drop was a forgotten memory in the safe cradle of Richard's wiry and delightfully naked body. The sunset cast an orange glow through the gauzy curtains of their bedroom as she leaned her head back on his shoulder. Dumpster had joined them, happily purring in Sunny's lap, while Richard cradled her from behind. Sunny's happy place.

"Sorry for coming," she whispered. "I shouldn't have been that bad."

"Did you forget you've already apologized for it eight times?" Richard kissed her neck. "Sorry I was too hard on you. I'm still stressed from the shit with Gabe, and I shouldn't have been working. My focus was split. We should have rescheduled."

She arched her neck to give him more room to kiss her. "We already rescheduled this twice, and now we know I don't like being ignored," Sunny teased softly, regretting that the scene hadn't been the outlet he needed.

"I know I worry about him more than I should. My therapist thinks I feel guilty that I let him get into that situation to begin with." Richard buried his face in her hair. "But Gabe can handle himself without me. He has Tara to look out for him now, and I need to get used to that."

It was a little disappointing that the road trip hadn't been enough to distract him. But soon enough they'd have their own family to occupy his worrywart tendencies.

She wished he would tell her more, so she could at least listen and support him, but it was Gabe's business. Gabe's ex had never been her favorite person; E had rarely let Gabe game when they were together. Apparently, she'd been much more controlling than that, but that was all Richard would tell her.

Sunny scratched Dumpster's chin. "So when do we meet with Phin to figure out *our* prenup?"

Richard's laugh shook her body. "Why would we do that?"

"Because you have actual assets, and I barely have an LLC." Sunny rolled her eyes. "You probably already have the meeting scheduled in a spreadsheet somewhere, right?"

"I wasn't planning on us having one. What's mine is yours, Sunshine. If you want one to cover your assets, I'm happy to agree to whatever you want." Richard snorted. "There's a plan for the recovery time needed from your surgery, insurance deductibles between that and potential fertility clinic fees later in the year. Where the wedding and honeymoon fit in. No meeting with Phin on there, but we can always add one."

"You're so romantic. Talking about deductibles and our major life events like it's a project to plan." Sunny laughed. "But you know I'm not a project, right?"

"Of course you're not!" Richard scoffed. "Look, I know..." he huffed. "I know I've been a little uptight lately, but I just...itch."

"Uh oh," Sunny teased.

"You're ridiculous," Richard retorted. "I mean, I want to do...*any-thing*. Everything. It's ambition, or drive, and I've always had Gabe as an outlet for that. Or my Dad to piss off. And now I can't put all of my energy into them. I have to trust Gabe to figure his own shit out with Tara, other than the stuff he asks me for help for, and I want nothing to do with my dad anymore, and I have all this mental energy, and time, and money, but it feels like you don't want it."

She huffed. "I don't want to be your charity case, Dicky."

"You're not. And you're not a project. You're my...inspiration." Richard kissed her neck.

"Oh, Dicky, keep going." Sunny liked the sound of that better. That Richard saw her as a guiding light, not a puzzle to be solved, was actually quite validating. Maybe she should have taken his money for the surgery. Maybe she didn't need to push herself to get this damn team lead promotion that she didn't want.

He huffed a quiet laugh against her skin. "You're my ally."

Sunny tsked. "That's slightly less romantic."

"Conspirator?" Richard tried.

Sunny wrinkled her nose. "We'll stick with inspiration."

"If you want, I can go back to the insurance jargon. Whisper about deductibles in your ear," he teased, kissing her neck again. "Show you what a good spreadsheet really does for me."

"You're such a nerd." Their laughter shook her weary body. "How did I end up with someone who makes cost-benefit matrices for fun?"

"Oh, I'm a nerd?" Richard bit her neck. "And how many code errors did you find during the scene today?"

Sunny growled at the reminder of Greg's incompetence. "Three."

With a quiet chuckle, Richard held her tight. "And that's why we work. We get each other."

"I don't wanna be a team lead," Sunny confessed, relieved to finally say it out loud. Someone else could fix Greg's many mistakes. "I hate being responsible for grown adults who can't pull their own weight. I feel like I should want to climb the career ladder, but it's awful."

"Then don't." Richard shrugged. "You're allowed to change your mind. You're allowed to be an individual contributor. You're allowed to quit and do your apps full-time if you want." He tutted, cutting off her protests before she could voice them. "I know you don't want to quit completely. My point is that whatever you want, I support you."

Sunny smirked. "So you'd wear a thrifted tux for the wedding?"

Richard cackled, the sound exploding in her ear. "You wouldn't dare! Bespoke only, or the wedding is off." He tickled her sides as he planted kisses on her neck.

Sunny giggled, pushing him away unsuccessfully. She wasn't trying too hard; it was nice that she could make Richard this playful, after the weird turn the scene had taken. "I take it back. I was kidding!" She squirmed, trying to get away from his tickling hands.

Dumpster ran away with a hiss.

"Look at what you did—you scared her away."

"No, that was all you." Richard smiled against her neck. "She was scared off by your talk about a used tux."

Sunny laughed, shaking her head as Richard's tickles and quick kisses became a tender embrace. Until an idea had her bolting upright, tabs popping open one after the other. If she was no longer going to waste her brain power on that promotion, she should lean into being Richard's inspiration, or conspirator, or whatever. If he was going to insist that they didn't need a prenup, she should warn him what that level of trust in her would look like. "Hey, Dicky? Can I *inspire* you to invest your obscene fortune in affordable housing in Eastside?"

"Sunshine, you can use whatever money you want, however you want. As long as we have enough to live on and send our kids to college, if they want, what I have is yours." Richard bumped his head against hers. "Tell me what you're thinking."

"I was feeling weird about the idea that we wouldn't buy our new house in Eastside, but I get why we aren't looking there." Sunny bit her lip, excitement replacing the guilt that had been nagging her since the new house plan had come up. She turned around to straddle him, placing his hands on her hips. "Remember that rabbit hole about land trusts from the road trip? The way for communities to buy land to protect residential homes from development, keeping it affordable in perpetuity? Well, there's a community land trust in Eastside, but it's underfunded and their website looks like it's from thirty years ago. And I'm almost done with the app Miriam commissioned." She paused, wishing she could simply show Richard the tabs in her mind. "Maybe we can become this super hot, radical philanthropy power couple? Not just with money, but with your micromanaging, and that apartment complex you stole, and my tech skills. Maybe we can find out if they want our support?"

Richard grinned up at her, thumbs stroking her hips. "Oh, Sunshine, keep talking."

Sunny beamed. It was clear; she was not meant to be a chair, silent as she was used. That had sounded fun, but it didn't fit her, and it didn't fit Richard. She was meant to infodump about all of her brilliant ideas, her dreams and desires, all over this man. Her Dicky was there, waiting for inspiration, for her direction, to help bring them to life.

Saturday, November Twentieth

CHAPTER FORTY

"ANY CHANCE I CAN make a last-minute request for a menu change?" Miriam asked, folding her hands on the dining table. "I know this caterer who—"

"Ma," Gabe sighed, his elbows thunking against the polished wood. "We're doing pizza. I already placed the order with the place around the corner."

Jazz wasn't sure if she was *supposed* to be sitting in on Tara's wedding stuff—she'd been studying when everyone came over to set up for the wedding tomorrow—but no one had asked her to leave. Sitting off by herself at the other end of the long table, far from Blanche, Tara, Gabe and his parents, gave Jazz a sudden sympathy for how Blanche must feel on game nights. Allowed in the space, yet not part of the group. Pretending she wasn't eavesdropping, Jazz kept her head buried in her ecology textbook, while everyone (mostly Gabe's mom) chatted.

"Not to make light of the actual traditions in our ceremony, but pizza is the only part of all this I'm contributing." Tara winced. "Lee, Blanche, and I always order pizza for special occasions."

Jazz looked up from her notebook to exchange an amused look with Blanche. She would probably have more luck studying in her room, but being a fly on the wall was more entertaining. As long as Miriam didn't start yelling, of course.

"Did your mom have any ideas?" Blanche asked Tara.

Tara shook her head. "We talked on the phone last weekend. I asked, but she and my dad got married in Vegas, and she doesn't remember any of it."

Blanche leaned forward, chin on their hands. "How was that?"

Tara sighed, grabbing one of the snickerdoodles Miriam had brought. "Weird, but not what I expected. She's not the same person I remember. She was funny. Sarcastic. Sober." Tara snorted, a half smile on her face. "Either way, not super helpful in terms of wedding traditions. So pizza it is."

"Then pizza you will have!" Despite her smile, Miriam's eyebrows knit together. "How does a layer cake sound?"

"Dearest, you already made far too many cheesecakes, which is what the bride and groom asked for." John rubbed his wife's shoulders.

Tara and Gabe winced. "I appreciate the cheesecakes, but can we keep the bride and groom stuff to a minimum?" Gabe asked. "Along with any gendered words related to weddings and families?"

Jazz tensed; Tara had mentioned that gender and family roles had been complicated for them both several times, but Gabe was bringing it up to his parents? Just like that?

A wordless conversation passed between John and Miriam in a quick glance. "Of course," Miriam said brightly. "Anything you want to share with us?"

Jazz blinked, confused. She'd expected Miriam to have a larger reaction than that.

Gabe shrugged. "Not exactly. Gender is weird right now, and getting weirder the more people assume we're a cishet couple. I've been leaning agender, but we'll see how that develops." Frowning, he fussed with his hair. "It was easier to ignore when I wasn't constantly bombarded with how everyone else talks about weddings and babies. I'll let you know if I decide anything like with labels or pronouns and shit. Just, less gendered language is appreciated."

"And I've been in a state of existential crisis about adding 'mom' and 'wife' to my identity for six months," Tara added, shuddering. "Being called a bride makes my skin crawl."

"Okay. Gender-neutral terms until further notice." Miriam smiled kindly, patting Tara's hand. "And if there's anything you want to talk through, I'm here to listen. Marriage and a baby is a huge change, for both of you."

John leaned forward in his chair. Everyone at the table turned to hear what he had to say, Jazz included. "If you want someone to talk to, Gabe, I can connect you with some Two-Spirit Elders I know."

Gabe winced. "I don't know if that's the right label for me?"

Jazz's chest tightened; her own dad would not take that subtle refusal well.

John looked at Gabe for a long moment, which did not help her anxiety. "Even if you may not connect to that identity fully, it's not always simple for you and I to understand where we fit, and you have a community to lean on when the answers aren't easy." John gestured to Tara as well, his voice soft. "Both of you. We certainly needed support when Gabe was little, and the Native folks in Bellamy became our village. Everything we learned about raising a kid came from our community. It's been a while, but I still know of some Native-run parenting groups you might like."

Jazz blinked, bewildered at the kindness in his tone.

"Yes, please," Tara sighed in relief. "We're doing a queer parenting class, but I want more friends who have small kids, besides Chas and Freddy. Especially since our kid will be Native, too, and I don't know enough about that beyond what Gabe has told me."

Expression soft, Gabe nodded, gently playing with his hair. "I'll take you up on that too, I think. You're right, the gender stuff has been...complicated. Not hard, but not easy. And I probably do need to talk to someone who gets what I'm feeling better than Joy can." He snorted. "Or Richard, for that matter."

"Just remember to—"

"Yeah, bring a gift. I remember," Gabe chuckled. "I'll pick up some tobacco or something. Thanks, Dad."

"Anytime." John smiled, settling back in his chair. "Your mother isn't the only one who knows everyone after all. Whatever you need, we support you. Both of you."

"What the fuck?" Jazz muttered under her breath, wondering if everyone's parents were like this. If so, her childhood had been worse than she'd thought. For once, she wished her mother and father were here, so they could witness how "supportive" parents were supposed to act. She would probably answer her mom's texts and calls more often, if Althea was even a fraction this understanding.

Even if Miriam was a little pushy, she listened and accepted what Gabe wanted, instead of insisting on her way and actively working against her wishes, the way her dad did. Miriam and John didn't take it personally whenever Gabe expressed an opinion that didn't match their own, like her mom.

"Do you want to read the wedding script?" Blanche asked Gabe and Tara. "I took out all of the gendered language, but there might be some things you want to review before tomorrow?"

Tara shook her head. "Nah, we trust you."

"Yeah, you made me cry at Tonio and Lee's wedding, so I'm sure it's great." Gabe waved them off.

Jazz exchanged another amused look with Blanche, biting her lip to keep from grinning. Blanche pressed a subtle finger to their mouth to shush her. Blanche had complained multiple times that Lee and Antonio kept vetoing the funny bits from their speech. If Gabe and Tara weren't even going to look at it... Jazz turned back to her textbook to hide her grin. Tomorrow would be entertaining.

Her phone lit up with an incoming text from Teddy to the polycule, minus Blanche (who understandably did not want to be in a text thread with a bunch of college students). Julissa, on the other hand, had finally asked to be added.

Teddy: Hello lovers! (Jules—you're included in that even if you're not literally my lover) My mom wants to know how many of you are coming to Thanksgiving.

Ed: Me! And my brother and his boyfriend if that's cool. They had fun last year. Actually, my parents might come, too. Is that okay?

Teddy: Duh.

Mimi: I'll be in Chicago for the weekend, but Julissa might stop by.

Julissa: If that's okay, of course. I don't want to impose, but I'd appreciate an excuse to get away from the extended family asking if I have a boyfriend. Doesn't matter how many times I come out, they keep insisting it's a phase.

Teddy: Ofc! Our house is open to whoever wants to show up whenever they feel like between the hours of the Macy's parade and midnight.

Teddy: Jazzy babe, hbu? Does Blanche want to come?

Jazz fiddled with her phone, unsure of how to respond. Going to Teddy's sounded a million times more fun than her own parents. But not going to her parents for Thanksgiving would put the last nail in the coffin of their already fragile relationship. And Lee and Antonio would be there this year, at least for a little while. They would count on Jazz's presence for support, just like she counted on theirs. But unlike her, Lee and Antonio had an excuse to escape back to the Flores family.

She wished Teddy's family could be her excuse. Or Mimi's. Or Blanche. Or that she could be open about who she spent time with, instead of keeping her parents in the dark. Because as awful as they could be, she understood why Lee was giving them so many second chances. Why he wanted them back in his life in the first place.

They were trying.

The progress was slow, but there was progress. The dad she'd grown up with wouldn't have let her move out, unless it was to get married to a man. But he'd helped her move into Blanche's with minimal fuss. The Leland who raised her would have cut off her tuition unless she majored in what he wanted, instead of merely grumbling about what he thought was most appropriate.

Maybe one day she wouldn't have to hide from them. One day she could talk about her partners, Blanche included, without fear of how her parents would react.

Don't count on me, but I'll try.

"I think we've covered everything, right?" Tara asked.

"Who did you pick for your photographers?" Miriam asked. "The photo contest was a hit with the museum guests."

"Good. We'll do it again next cohort," Gabe grinned. "And Syl and Lily tied for first. Syl's aunt will bring them by around ten-thirty tomorrow to get some photos ahead of time."

"I think that's it then." Miriam closed her notebook. "Though compared to most of the weddings I plan, you don't have much to cover."

"Sorry." Tara smiled apologetically.

"Don't be." Miriam waved her off. "Richard asked if he and Sunny could get married at the vineyard, so I get to organize a big wedding for someone at least, even if it's not my own son—sorry, child."

Gabe grinned. "He can have the stress then. Even a small backyard wedding is stressful, and we've had enough of that this week."

"How are you after...you know?" Miriam asked. "And don't do that thing where you say you're fine and don't mean it. You gave us a scare."

Gabe chuckled. "I'm fine."

"Is he fine?" John asked Tara.

Tara held her hands up, palms out. "He says he's fine."

"What happened?" Jazz asked, regretting it as everyone turned to her at the far end of the table. "Sorry. Not my business. I'm just nosy."

"I mean, everyone else knows, you may as well, too." Gabe gave a warning look to Blanche. "Do not do the armchair psychoanalysis thing on me. I have a therapist, and I don't need my friend to be one, okay?"

Blanche blinked innocently. "I would never dream of it."

"Sure." Gabe snorted. "Long story short, my ex was abusive. Turns out she's also been keeping tabs on me and, when she found out I was in New York, got access to the photoshoot that Lee and Antonio were at. Tara scared her off, we all made it back in one piece, I've met with my therapist, and I'm managing."

Tara hugged his arm, pressing a kiss to his shoulder.

Blanche fiddled with the pen in their hand as they eyed him.

"What did I say about psychoanalyzing me?" Gabe teased.

"I'm not! Just wondering if she's still in the hospital after Tara 'scared her off,'" Blanche teased.

Tara scowled. "I didn't even touch her. I channeled my inner Sunny, but without the right hook. I hated every second. Self-control is over-rated."

"You were wonderful." Gabe smiled softly at her. "Even if you were way too nice to her. And at least now we have evidence of her violating the protection order in New York. Hopefully Phin can get that shit handled."

Miriam stood up to wrap her arms around Tara and Gabe, who both leaned into the Mom hug far more naturally than Jazz ever could. "You're going to get the best fucking cheesecake in your life for this wedding."

Jazz smiled, struck once again with how much she wished her parents could see how parents were supposed to act. They were supposed to stand up for their kids. Protect them without restricting them. Not make them feel like they had to hide a secret life.

BLANCHE

"BEAUTIFUL, DO YOU HAVE soy sauce somewhere? I'm out." Jazz called from the kitchen, barely loud enough to be heard over her pop music as she made herself, and hopefully Blanche, dinner.

Cradled amongst the hodgepodge of pillows and throw blankets on the daybed, Blanche looked up from their laptop. "Maybe?"

Grandma Rose's apron tied around her waist, Jazz poked her head into the den. "What do you mean by maybe?"

"It means that I might, but I might not," Blanche teased.

Jazz rolled her eyes with a laugh. "Seriously. Do you mean like you think there's a chance that there's a bottle somewhere in this house, or you don't know if you've ever bought soy sauce?"

"Jazzy, you know what's in this house better than I do," Blanche shrugged, doubting they'd ever bought soy sauce. "But 'maybe' as in there are probably some packets from takeout in a drawer somewhere?"

Jazz walked over to the daybed, an affectionate smile on her oval face as she kissed their cheek. "Oh, Blanche. I hope for your sake that you never have to live alone."

Blanche wrapped an arm around her hips, turning their head at the last second to give her a quick peck on the lips. "I hope so too. Who would feed me...whatever it is you're making with the soy sauce?"

"Oh, you think you're getting any?" Jazz put her arms around Blanche. "I have two exams next week, so that's supposed to be my dinner until break starts."

Blanche pouted. "Not even a bite?"

"It's tofu and broccoli over brown rice."

They wrinkled their nose. "I'll order takeout."

Jazz laughed. "Thought so. I'll convert you to my healthy food eventually. You'll wonder how you ever ate fast food."

"Jazzy?" Blanche asked, enjoying the lingering hug. "Is it supposed to smell smoky?"

"Oh, fuck!" Jazz ran back to the kitchen. "My broccoli!"

Blanche turned back to their laptop with a grin, busying themself with revising some details in the ceremony, in light of the new information they'd learned about Gabe's past today. Unintentionally referencing trauma at their wedding would be cruel. The ceremony should be about the good parts of their life, the happy memories they'd made together.

Besides, the changes added to the theme of celebrating their mutual support. Tara and Gabe may be polar opposites, but they balanced each other well. Tara had never been so serene in all the years Blanche had known her, and the moody Gabe had mellowed out.

I want more details on some of these stories. When was the moment that Gabe fell in love with Tara? When and how did he know? And why was Gabe so adamant about pushing Tara away when they first met? What was going through his head when they'd broken things off for a month? Maybe they *should* have gone over this with them. *No, that'd mean I'd have to cut half the stories. Fuck it. I'll just ask him during the goddamn ceremony.*

Blanche conceded they may have tried a little too hard to armchair diagnose Gabe back when they'd first met. But he and Tara had been on a collision course, and Blanche had been worried. They wrinkled their nose. Strange how things had reversed. Their ducklings might have needed Blanche's help when they were younger, but everyone had a better handle on themselves now. Better than Blanche did, anyway, but they were working on it. *Yet another reason to do this therapy shit for real.*

Jazz came back into the den, bowl in hand, somehow comfortable wearing only slippers and her house dress, despite how freezing it was downstairs. She stood next to the daybed, a silent request to sit next to them. Lifting the blankets, Blanche scooted over, leaning into her once she'd made herself comfortable in their cozy nest.

"That smells good. How'd the broccoli turn out?" Blanche asked, peering into the bowl. It didn't look bad, just burnt.

"You mean my *seared* broccoli?" Jazz laughed. "Delicious."

"Looks more like blackened broccoli, Jazzy." Blanche teased, opening their mouth expectantly.

Jazz rolled her eyes and scooped a little broccoli, rice, and tofu on the fork for them. "Here. A perfect bite because it's going to be your only one. I have everything already portioned out for my meals this week."

Blanche ate it slowly, savoring the salt and spice. "It's not bad. For tofu," they teased.

Jazz rolled her eyes and ate, cuddled against them in silence. With a satisfied glow at how comfortably their affectionate friendship had deepened, Blanche turned back to their laptop, pulling up the application they'd been opening and closing over the past few weeks. Like the directions back to Marshall, the dozens of times they'd come back to this window should be a sign.

"Is that what I think it is?" Jazz's smile was smug.

Blanche nodded. "It's an adult learner program at the community college. They combine GED prep with prerequisites for the U."

Jazz hummed, almost hesitant. "I know I wasn't supposed to see this, but you had a window up before, about changing your name. Do you want to do that, before you start getting degrees? I don't know how easy it is to change that after you graduate."

"You're sweet," Blanche smiled, then sighed. "I don't think I can, even if I wanted to. Phin offered to help, but I'm not sure what I'd change it to?"

"Not Blanche?" Jazz cocked her head as she ate a bite of tofu.

Blanche shook their head. "Blanche is the name Daisy picked for me. While it fits now, I'm not sure it'll fit forever. But I'm not sure what my next chapter holds, let alone what name will fit me best for it." Outgrowing the life Daisy had intended for them was all sorts of uncomfortable, but Shayla's voice in their head reminded them that Blanche wanted that discomfort. Blanche snorted, hardly believing they were saying all this out loud. They'd loved becoming Blanche, loved that Daisy had so easily reinvented them. But now, they wanted to reinvent themself. "Blanche already gets the fame and fortune from being the LLC. Chad can have a few degrees."

"Okay. Well, let me know if you want me to test out any names on you." Jazz nodded at the computer casually, as if Blanche hadn't confessed something that they'd barely admitted to themself yet. "What do you need to do to apply?"

"I have everything but the letters of recommendation." Blanche grimaced. "The downfalls of being a sex worker. Who do I have to recommend me? A client? A subscriber? Covey?" They laughed sardonically.

"You have two independent contractors named Tara and Lee." Jazz leaned against them. "And you own part of Confession, right? I'm sure your co-owner Chas would write one for you. Besides, they won't actually look into who wrote it."

Jazz always made everything sound so easy. As much as they wanted to chalk it up to naivete, or perhaps optimism, Shayla's voice reminded them that Jazz simply believed in Blanche. Perhaps they could do with a bit of believing in themself, too. Curling around her warmth, Blanche fought a smile, reviewing the answers they'd written and rewritten dozens of times. "You think I can do it?"

"Beautiful, you're one of the smartest, most driven people I know. Of course, you can do it!" Jazz tsked. "You make six figures a year, own your own home, and you're doing the hard work of healing from your past. All because you want to. You're not trying to impress anyone, or worry what people might think. When you set a goal for yourself, you achieve it, and you don't let anyone hold you back. That's..." Jazz paused, her voice catching. "That's admirable."

Heart quickening, Blanche leaned in to kiss her. To press the ache in their chest into her lips, so Jazz could taste the gratitude, the peace, the happiness that Blanche felt for her. "I love you," they whispered against her lips.

Jazz's lips parted and for a moment, Blanche worried they'd misstepped. But her smile grew, splitting her shocked face into a grin. "Really?"

Blanche nodded. "You're wonderful, Jazzy. And you don't have to say it back. I know we're in very different places in our lives, but I never thought I would feel this...whole again. And I have you to thank for pushing me to get here."

"I love you, too." Jazz pressed a kiss to their lips. "I wouldn't have risked our friendship in the first place if I didn't. And it doesn't matter that we're in different places in our lives. We love and support each other now."

With a grin, Blanche passed the laptop to her. "Since you support me, would you mind looking over my responses to the essay questions?"

Jazz snorted, setting her food down. "Can I finish eating?"

"Multitask, Lovely." Blanche slid down the daybed, burrowing under the blankets as they went, and pressed a kiss to Jazz's knee. They smirked when her legs parted to reveal the short curls between her thighs.

"Blanche!" Jazz laughed. "Do you want me to read these or not?"

"*Multitask.*" Blanche kissed their way down her thighs, hands tracing her curves under her short house dress, pressing her thighs apart.

Jazz shot them an amused look, before perching the computer on her knee. "I'm not gonna be able to read any of this."

The laptop whirred above their head as their thumbs spread her open. Blanche's heart pounded, desire coursing through them, a shuddered groan escaping both of them at the first taste of her earthy musk. They adored how Jazz let them be so sweet to her. How she let them shower her with affection, the way she did for them.

"Fuck, Blanche. Right there." Jazz arched her back, her knees falling open wider as she thrust against their mouth. The laptop slid into a pillow.

Blanche pulled away. "Are you multitasking?"

Jazz groaned. "Oh, you were serious?"

"Focus, Beautiful. Eat or read, your choice, but I'll stop when you do." Blanche flattened their tongue against her clit, as Jazz picked the computer back up, delighted when she moaned.

"Don't stop."

"Keep reading, then." Blanche slipped two fingers into the gorgeous pussy spread open for them, curling them the way Jazz liked. Her thighs clamped around their ears. With a grin, they worked her until their jaw ached, until their cock throbbed against the daybed from going untouched for so long. Until they'd gotten her off at least four times.

Jazz threw the laptop down as she shuddered with another orgasm. Her fingers gripped Blanche's hair as she rode their face, while her thighs squeezed their neck. Her back arching, Jazz writhed on the daybed while her final orgasm tore through her.

She laughed. "Okay, I corrected a few typos, but I want to read it again when you're not blowing my fucking mind with that damn tongue of yours."

"Was it okay?"

Jazz melted against the pillows. "Fucking phenomenal."

"I meant the essays. I know I give good head." Blanche winked.

"Sure, the essays seemed fine. I was distracted." Pulling them close enough to kiss, her tongue delved into their mouth. "Fuck, I love when you taste like me."

Blanche smiled against her mouth, their cheeks burning. They'd been a sex worker for decades, and yet Jazz made them blush like a schoolgirl so easily. They ground against her, pressing their still-clothed erection against her hip.

"Will you fuck me?" Jazz asked.

The excited squeak that left Blanche's mouth was so humiliating they had to clap a hand over their mouth. They'd been following her lead. While she'd gone down on them occasionally over the last couple of weeks, Jazz had never asked for Blanche to fuck her. Blanche had already found more pleasure simply being present with her, as they discovered all the new ways their bodies worked together. Penetrative sex hadn't even crossed their mind. Their erection twitched at the thought. Cheeks burning, they asked, "Are you sure?"

Fighting back a teasing smile, Jazz nodded. "I might have optimistically stashed some condoms in the side table."

Blanche laughed. "Oh, really?"

She nodded with a smug grin. "But only if you want to."

Opening the drawer, Blanche pulled one out. "I might not last long, but I can get one of the straps from upstairs if you want more. I normally take Viagra when I—"

"Blanche, you just made me come five times," Jazz shook her head with an exasperated groan. "Yes, I want you to, but this is for you, for as long as you want or need. I'm honestly not sure I can move after all of that, so I'm just going to lay back, while you fuck me and kiss me and tell me you love me." Her smile turned bashful. "If that sounds good to you, of course."

Blanche threw their head back in laughter that ended in a snort. "I love your honesty." They pulled off their camisole, preening when Jazz's eyes dropped to their chest with a bite of her lip. "I love how needy you are." They sucked her nipple ring through her house dress as they pulled down their silk loungers. The fabric kissed their skin as it slid from their long legs. "I love the sounds you make when you come." Settling between Jazz's bountiful thighs, they rolled the condom over themself, trailing kisses up her neck. "And I love how you like to taste yourself after I eat you out."

Jazz captured their mouth in a kiss as Blanche pushed slowly into her, savoring each quiver of her pussy around them as her heat sucked them in. They thrust shallowly at first, checking for her reaction. Until her calves wrapped around their hips and pushed them in all the way, sending pleasure shooting up their spine and a gasp from their throat.

"Stop being gentle with me." Jazz's foot slid down around their thigh, pressing her heel hard against Blanche's muff. "Fuck me like you mean it. Like you need me."

Spreading their thighs under hers with a moan, Blanche rolled their hips, exalting in Jazz's satisfied grin before they kissed her. Each pump of their hips pushed them between the euphoria of her pussy, and the blissful pleasure of her heel. They wouldn't last long if they kept this pace up, but Jazz didn't seem to care, especially not when Blanche stroked her clit. She wanted them to feel good, prioritized their pleasure as much as they did hers. And that care, that selflessness, was everything Blanche had never expected to experience. "I love you."

"Love you so much, Blanche," Jazz murmured in reply. Her back arched, trembling in their arms as her muscles clamped around them. As her pleasure sent shock waves down their spine, Blanche rocked their hips. Each movement sent a deep wave through their belly, flooding their whole awareness.

Blanche kissed her again as their own orgasm overtook them. Collapsing against her, Blanche panted into her neck to catch their breath.

"What do you usually do for Thanksgiving?"

Blanche blinked. That sentence did not belong in the post-orgasm haze. "What?"

Jazz shrugged casually. "What do you usually do for Thanksgiving? Like, do you go to Freddy and Chas's house? Stay home and pretend it's another day?"

Blanche sat up on their elbows, unsure why Jazz was curious about this *now* of all times. "I used to spend it with Freddy and Daisy, but Freddy goes to Texas with Chas these days. Tara, Lee, and I used to do movie marathons, but since Antonio came in the picture, it's just been Tara and I. Not sure what I'll do this year since Tara will be with Gabe's family." They paused, heart twinging. They hated being alone. "I'll probably stay home, I guess."

"Do you want to come to my parents with us?"

They froze, sitting back on their knees. "Jazz—"

She sat up with them, taking their hands, her alto voice low and reassuring. "I don't mean as my partner. Just as my friend and roommate, because you *are* my friend and roommate. They don't need to know that you're also my partner." Jazz looked away, her brow furrowing. "I would like having you there. I know Lee and Antonio would, too."

Unsure if this was a good idea, Blanche kissed her. "If you want me there, and if your parents want me there, then I'll be there. As your friend and roommate." They'd seen the wide vulnerability in her eyes before she'd glanced away; Jazz wanted them there, and Blanche didn't want to be alone. No need for their mental Shayla to make an appearance; that alone was enough for them to know they wanted to go. Assuming they would be invited by the Joneses.

With a shy smile, Jazz nodded. "I'll ask."

Sunday, November Twenty-First

Chapter Forty-One

GABE

THE SMELL OF WOODSMOKE and herbs emanated in full force as Gabe opened Blanche's front door for Tara and Hippo. He couldn't resist patting Tara's ass as she walked past, shapely under the velvet jumpsuit draped around her, courtesy of Antonio's creativity.

"Really?" Tara smiled over her shoulder. She looked radiant, like a forest nymph or a renaissance painting. The green fabric made her eyes luminous. Her red curls tumbled over her heart-shaped face like a crown. The billowing velvet created a vee, exposing her spine down to the small of her back. "Are you going to be looking at me like that all day, Coop?"

I hope Lily and Syl get good photos of her today. He itched to take some himself in the midmorning light streaming into Blanche's foyer. To capture how her green eyes seemed to stare into his heart. Instead, he simply closed the door behind him, unhooking Hippo's leash to adjust the flower wreath around his neck. His buddy deserved to look pretty today, too.

Not that the leash mattered. Hippo clung happily in Tara's shadow wherever she went, more Tara's dog than his these days. Hopefully after the baby came, his firstborn son would be back to climbing in his lap for pets, instead of constantly laying at Tara's feet. After all, Hippo was supposed to be *his* emotional support dog, a calming presence to distract Gabe from bad memories and sleepless nights. Not Tara's security detail. Although after the run-in with Emily a few weeks ago, maybe he wouldn't mind the lazy goofball acting like he would protect his family. Even if Hippo was a big softie.

Scratching Hippo's ears, Gabe smiled up at her. "How am I looking at you, Kitten?"

"Like you want to worship me," Tara explained as she hung up the leash. "Or eat me. I can't tell."

Gabe nodded, wrapping his arms around her. "Then yes, I am going to look at you like that all day. All the time, really."

She kissed him, pulling on the lapels of his white tuxedo jacket. Grinning against her mouth, he bent down so she wouldn't have to stand on her toes.

"I thought you were supposed to do that after the wedding," Blanche teased from the parlor, dressed in the same navy jumpsuit they'd made for Lee and Antonio's wedding. Hippo's nails clicked against the wood as he scurried to greet his soulmate.

Gabe ignored them until Tara pulled away with a sigh, smiling up at him. "Sorry, he's too irresistible. I'll try and save it for later."

He pouted before turning to Blanche. "Can we help with anything?"

Blanche shook their head. "Everything is pretty much ready. Although, your photographers seem nervous. The little one thinks Jazzy and I are witches. She asked if the house was haunted."

"Can you blame them?" Gabe teased, gesturing at the dried herbs and half-melted candles everywhere, as they followed Blanche to the backyard. He had expected Lily would be nervous, but he was a little amused that Syl was. He always acted tough as nails in class, even if Gabe could see right through it.

Blanche's yard had transformed over the past few weeks. The old trees and hedges lining the yard now framed a lovely curved patio. A stone walking path led to a firepit, emanating the same scented smoke that had soaked into Blanche's house. The chuppah from the vineyard was set up in front of the firepit. Sunbeams danced through the white lace canopy.

"It's perfect," Tara murmured.

"I told you, man!" Phineas called out, hauling a folding table into the backyard. His sleeves were rolled to the elbows. "Here early! Helping set up! Mr. Involved! Mr. Best Friend!"

Gabe laughed, pleasantly surprised that Phineas had followed through. Maybe their days of keeping Phineas at arm's length from Antonio were finally over. "Thanks for coming, Phin."

"Oh, great! You're here!" Miriam came around the corner, dressed in a light blue pantsuit. Her usual set of pearls she wore to fancy events were roped around her neck. "We scoped out some good spots in the yard for photos. Beautiful day, isn't it? We got lucky with the weather."

Syl, Lily, and Syl's aunt followed, both with DSLR cameras in hand, as dressed up as Gabe had ever seen them. Syl had even found a suit coat that was too big for him.

"Damn, Coop. You look sharp!" Syl said.

Syl's aunt and Miriam shot Syl twin looks. For someone who cussed as much as his mom, she always held children to a high standard.

"I mean, darn," Syl amended.

"Thank you, Sylvester." Miriam smiled at him. "Do you two want to take photos of our happy couple, until the rest of the guests arrive?"

"Or maybe just Tara?" Gabe offered, ignoring Tara's elbow in his side. "I don't need to be in them."

Miriam shot Gabe a look this time. "Gabriel Fucking Cooper, if you try and dodge any pictures today, I will post your baby pictures all over my social media."

"Talk about language," Syl muttered.

Gabe's jaw dropped. That threat was low, even by his mother's standards. He'd only been half-joking, anyway. "Fine," he said sullenly. "Lead the way."

Lily smiled at them shyly, and took Tara by the hand around the corner, where the old atrium sat in the sunlight. Most of the glass from the greenhouse was still missing, but the light was perfect. The run-down look of the stone walls and metal frame would create an interesting aesthetic. With the gray and black background, and his white tux, he'd blend in while Tara popped. *Perfect.*

To everyone's surprise, Lily—Gabe's quiet, timid, "no-favorites-but-she's-his-favorite" student—became a director when given a little power, bossing them both around for where to stand and how to pose. Tara and Gabe obeyed, exchanging looks of surprise at this new side of the shy Lily. A few minutes in, Hippo got tired of standing, and laid at their feet. But even his lazy ass got back up with a groan to sit pretty when Lily scolded him. Ordering Syl to hold the reflector higher, she climbed up the iron frame to get a better angle.

"Careful, Lily. We can get a ladder or a chair or something," Tara cautioned.

Lily looked at her like she was stupid, in the way that only eighth graders can. "I'm not going up that high. You worry too much."

"Did I just get bullied by a kid?" Tara muttered.

Fighting a laugh, Gabe stood still behind her, hands curled around her bump as Lily had instructed. Tara grinned over her shoulder at him, heart-achingly beautiful in the soft light filtering through the oak trees.

"Coop, keep that look but kiss her cheek," Lily called from her perch, adjusting her settings as she zoomed in.

Tara laughed as Gabe eagerly followed Lily's instructions. He planted kisses over her face and head, hearing the clicks from Lily's camera and her scolding Syl to hold the light higher. Gabe cupped her jaw to kiss her tenderly, before scooping a hand under her knees to pick her up in his arms.

Tara squealed in surprise, throwing her arms around his neck. Hippo barked, jumping at them playfully.

"Okay, Coop. That's cute and everything, but I'm about to be sick. It's getting a little disgusting." Lily's newfound teenage attitude cut through his reverie.

Gabe put Tara down gently. "Yes, ma'am. Do you want help down from there?"

Lily shook her head with a dirty look, easily climbing down without a scratch. "I swear to god, that kid is going to be so safe with you guys."

Tara snorted at Gabe's confused face.

"Why does that feel like an insult?" he muttered, wondering if his and Tara's kid would be half as sassy, and already knowing they would be worse. He squeezed Tara's hand as they followed their photographers to another spot; he couldn't wait to find out.

Lily took the reflector from Syl as he popped the lens cover off his camera. Syl walked them over to an oak tree with red leaves still clinging to the branches. Box hedges lined the back fence in green in the background. The two created a color scheme that was a muted version of Tara. It would make him stand out, which he wasn't particularly excited by. But Gabe remembered his mom's threat and obeyed Syl's every command.

Syl was a lot nicer than Lily had been, giving them more free rein over their poses and expressions. Gabe was actually having fun, proud that his students were doing so well at directing their subjects and each other. Not counting their collection of nudes, Gabe had never had fun getting photographed before. Soon his parents were joining them, and then all of their guests. Gabe had Syl snap a candid picture of Phineas speaking quietly to Angie on the edge of the lawn, a charming smile on his face and a smirk on hers.

"Okay, let's get this ceremony started," Miriam announced, directing everyone where they should stand. "It's almost noon."

With fewer than twenty people in attendance for a ceremony only ten minutes long, it didn't make sense to set up chairs. Instead, everyone circled the chuppah. While Tara and Gabe waited by the house, Miriam and John distributed various items. To Richard, John handed a folded wool blanket, then passed Sunny a drinking vessel with two spouts. "Please don't spill," he warned quietly, wrapping her hands around it securely and patting her arm.

Eyes widening, Sunny blushed and nodded seriously. Gabe snorted; Sunny seemed to be just as affected by his dad as Richard did. Not that Richard would ever admit he'd been crushing on John since Gabe first introduced them.

Tara took Gabe's hand in a vice grip. He squeezed her hand gently in return, rubbing his thumb over her fingers to soothe her nerves. Outside, she was calm, smiling. But her jaw was clenched, her breathing too steady to be natural.

Miriam handed Antonio and Lee a ring box each. "Don't you dare fucking lose this, Tonio."

Antonio put a hand to his chest in mock offense. "I can't believe you don't trust me after all of these years. *Me.* I'm basically your son."

Miriam shook her head. "I still haven't forgotten about my sapphire necklace you dropped in the lake."

"In my defense, I was twelve and obsessed with Leo."

Gabe smiled at the memory of him and Antonio diving over and over again into the muck and weeds under the dock, trying to find the necklace his mom didn't even know they'd borrowed to recreate *Titanic*. For as panicked as they'd been, and as many leeches as they'd gotten, it was one of Gabe's fondest memories from middle school. And they had found the necklace. Eventually.

"Anything I can help with?" Phineas asked eagerly.

"Hold the tissue box for me, and keep 'em coming." With an already watery smile, Miriam patted his arm before taking her spot outside of the chuppah. She nodded to Gabe and Tara. "I think we're ready."

Blanche hit play on their phone, and an instrumental version of "If I Ain't Got You" played softly from a nearby speaker. Gabe's throat tightened, his eyes already burning at the first notes. They had carefully selected every element included in this ceremony, every song on the playlist. This whole wedding had been planned for weeks. But hearing those chords made it real.

They were actually doing this. A year ago, he'd been resigned to a life alone, told himself a hundred times that he'd never get the chance to love Tara. That he couldn't treat her the way she deserved, that she'd never want him back. And now they were starting a family together.

Throat tight, Gabe risked a glance at Tara, who glared up at him.

"Get it together, Coop," she hissed. "I need to get at least halfway through this before I let myself cry. Don't ruin it for me already. I'm on the verge of fucking tears just looking at you."

He nodded. Smiling tearfully at her, he took in a shuddering breath.

"God, I can't even look at you right now," she muttered, bringing his hand to her mouth to kiss the back of it.

"Love you, too, Kitten." Gabe took another breath to calm himself as they walked through the circle of their loved ones and under the chuppah. Traditionally, both sets of parents would stand under it with them, but they had all agreed that it should just be Tara, Gabe and Blanche under the chuppah today. And apparently Hippo, too, who lay at Blanche's feet, snoring softly. The flowers around his neck pushed his wrinkles up around his ears.

Tara smiled at him shyly as they finally faced each other in front of Blanche.

Blanche cleared their throat. "We are gathered here today to celebrate the union between Tara and Gabe. I don't believe in much anymore, but I do believe in love. And I've seen the love these two have for each other longer than Tara would probably care to admit."

Tara nodded in agreement as everyone chuckled.

"I've seen softness overtake their hard walls, the defensiveness between them turn into protectiveness, pain to comfort, and mutual attraction grow into love for each other. You'd think that love for each other is the heart of their story, but their love for themselves is just as vital.

"These two have both been through shit I wouldn't wish on anyone. But they healed from it. Not for the others' sake, but for their own. Because despite the pain and rejection and hurt they've been through, they wanted love. And they had to overcome everything to love themselves, so they could love each other."

Asking Blanche to officiate had been the best decision. Gabe couldn't imagine anyone else would do their relationship justice like they could. They'd seen their relationship more than anyone, except maybe Sunny. And Sunny would spend the whole time telling embarrassing stories. He trusted Blanche not to do that, especially after their beautiful ceremony at Antonio and Lee's wedding.

Blanche smiled at Tara. "In April, I opened my door to find Tara wearing nothing but Gabe's shirt and having stolen his car."

"What the fuck?" Gabe sighed.

Shaking her head with a sigh, Tara wore the same *really?* expression he guessed was also on his face. "Not sure I wanted *this* story told at our wedding."

"Hey, I offered to let you read the ceremony in advance, you said you trusted me. That's on you." Blanche shrugged, waving their protests away as their guests tittered. "Anyway. For a whole month, Tara was a mopey ass bitch, sighing around the house, always going on about 'why is he so good to me?' and 'I don't deserve him.' I can only imagine Gabe here was in a similar state, but Hippo refuses to snitch."

Gabe's cheeks burned as Blanche looked at him expectantly, painfully aware that everyone he cared about was standing around them, listening intently. But this was important to Tara (and him as well, if he was being honest), so he would play along with being emotionally vulnerable in front of his whole world. "I can confirm I was also a mopey ass bitch who didn't deserve her. I still feel like she's too good for me."

Tara smiled ruefully at him with a shake of her head.

Blanche continued, "Over the course of that month, Tara got on a massive self-help kick. She was trying new things with her business, drinking tea instead of coffee, and cooking with actual vegetables with, like, a knife and cutting board and shit. And if you know Tara, you know she's been a Cup Noodle and Easy Mac girl since long before I met her. And suddenly, she's making salad and stir-fry? She even started doing her own laundry, and folding it—"

"They get the point, Blanche! Loud and clear." Tara cut in, cheeks red. "I am a disaster of a human being."

Blanche waved a hand. "That isn't the point, babes. You *were* a disaster. And you decided one day you couldn't be such a disaster anymore. And I know it wasn't to prove to yourself that you deserved him, because you were *so* determined he had to move on from you. You did it because he showed you what life could be like if you allowed yourself some love and care. And so you showed *yourself* some fucking love and care!"

Blanche met Tara's smile, before they turned to Gabe. "The first time I met Gabe, he was a sad wreck. Just a big, sad, insecure giant, who tried not to make heart eyes at Tara every time she was in the room. He followed her around like a traumatized puppy dog who wanted her to pet him, but growled when she got too close. It was really cringe to watch."

"Are you going somewhere with this?" Face burning, Gabe cocked his head, resisting the urge to tug on his hair; he didn't want to crush the flowers plaited into his curls. Tara was trying not to laugh, green eyes lit up in amusement. "We should have read this first."

"He was always talking about what his therapist told him, and how he was working on himself and shit. But he still looked like that sad kicked puppy dog, and I never understood what his deal was. He and Tara were crushing hard on each other. Like, a crush should be fun and exciting, so why was he so fucking sad all of the time? It finally clicked for me one day, when he forgot I was there and called her Kitten. He'd been hiding his feelings from everyone but her. And Tara was too bullheaded to see it for what it was. But I finally understood."

"Oh great. At least it wasn't the chair situation," Gabe muttered.

"Or bowling," Tara added.

"But this was no mere crush. He was madly in love. He didn't just like Tara, he *needed* her. This whole time, he was holding himself back because he wasn't ready for her. *That's* why he was working on himself, why he was so obsessed with therapy. He didn't want to need her."

"I wanted to choose her. I couldn't choose her if I needed her," Gabe said softly, looking into Tara's eyes, before shooting a teasing look at Blanche. "You got all this from one nickname? You need a new hobby."

"Can you tell the class why you needed her, Gabe?" Blanche ignored him. "What was it about Tara that made you love her so desperately? I completely understand of course, Tara's very loveable. I just don't know the story because you guys didn't want to go over the damn ceremony with me!" Blanche scoffed. "And please remember to keep it PG. There are children and your parents present."

Gabe rolled his eyes before looking back to Tara, remembering the night they met. She blushed, an apprehensive look on her face, probably wondering if he was about to tell the story of their anonymous bar hookup. "She was so self-assured and decisive, she just went for what she wanted. She was everything I wanted to be. And she treated me with respect. Like I was a decent person. Like I was someone worth wanting. She didn't play games or bullshit anything."

He shook his head, remembering the deep depression he'd fallen in after she ran from him the first time. "And I was in such a low place that someone treating me with basic decency was enough to make me fall hard. But I never thought I'd see you again, so you became my wake-up call that I had a lot of healing to do. You became the person I aspired to be, to love, and be loved by. And now that I know you—the real you, not the you I built up in my head—everything about you makes me love you more and more."

Blanche whistled. "Wow, Gabe. That's lovely. Who knew a bathroom quickie with a stranger could feel so romantic?"

Gabe scowled as everyone laughed, feeling his mom's eyes burn into the back of his head and hearing his dad's quiet chuckle. When they'd asked Blanche to officiate, this public flaying was not what he'd had in mind. Tara's hand slipping into his still made him smile; they were in this together, and always would be.

"Okay, I'm done telling stories! Unless I think of another one," Blanche teased. "Anyway, you did that healing for your sake. Not because you thought you'd ever find Tara again, but because she showed you what respect could feel like. She held a mirror up to your heart, and you didn't like what you saw in it. You healed because you wanted to love yourself, to be strong enough to fall in love. You both wanted it, and you both did the work. You both grew into confident people who love and support both yourselves and each other." Now this was what Gabe had expected: the heartfelt, genuine support from a close friend, who had been rooting for their relationship from the rocky start. "And now you're getting married and having a fucking family together. That's some beautiful shit." Blanche smiled at both of them proudly. "Before your vows, you both wanted a chance to read a message for each other. Gabe?"

Gabe took a breath, feeling more vulnerable than he'd expected already, and now he was about to expose his heart even further. "Tara, thank you for being patient and compassionate with me. I know at times, many many times, I have been a tactless asshat who said the wrong things and pushed you away." With a huff, Tara shook her head. But Gabe pushed on, "Despite my flaws, you're always there for me. You listen to my silence until my emotions can be put into words. You show me resilience when everything feels hopeless. You love the painful parts as freely and easily as you love the rest of me, even when I struggle to love those parts of myself.

"Most importantly, I'm so grateful that you want to be my family, and that our baby is with us. They can hear our vows to each other, how madly in love their parents are. I can't believe I get to call myself yours every day for the rest of our lives and I'm so happy that we chose us, Kitten."

Tara's eyes were glassy as she stepped forward to kiss him. The tears dampening their cheeks came from them both.

"Hey, we're not to that part yet." Blanche swatted them with their script.

"I slipped," Tara joked as they broke apart. Behind him, his dad asked Phineas for a tissue; his mom whispered to hand her one, too.

"Yeah, yeah, do your bit, Babes."

Tara pulled a paper out of her pocket. "I didn't even try to memorize this. And fair warning, I'm going to cry." Those green eyes smiled up at him, before she looked down at the paper trembling in her hands.

"Gabe, when I met you, I was convinced I was destined to be alone. I had spent my whole life telling myself that I wasn't good enough for anyone to care about. I had built up walls that no one, not even myself, could get close enough to prove me wrong. But then you came along, with your pretty eyes and dimples and respect for my boundaries. You showed me your heart, your honesty, your patience, and I was so scared by how much I wanted that. Because why on earth would a gorgeous, sensitive, funny man who likes to cook want someone like me? You were perfect, and I was broken."

His heart ached at the strain in her voice. Gabe opened his mouth to protest that of course he wasn't perfect, that she had never been broken.

But Tara stopped him with a finger to his nose. "I didn't think I needed to pause you, but you're paused!" She huffed, finding her place on the paper again. "Interrupting me right now? Really?"

She cleared her throat, rubbing her eyes with the back of her hand. "But the more you stuck around, you showed me you wanted me, and you weren't scared off by my issues. You showed me you weren't perfect, and how we could be imperfect together. The more I got to know you, the harder and harder it was to isolate myself. You were undeniable, and you were always going to be there for me. All I had to do was let you in."

Tears ran down her freckled cheeks, dripping from her quivering chin. "And you've given me more joy than I could ever have imagined. You've given me you, you've given me a family, a home. Hell, I even was able to reconnect with my mom because I met you. So you not only gave me you, you gave me a life I never dared to hope for. I hope I can live up to your example as we build our future together, to be compassionate and kind and loving, even though I'm still learning what it means to be a family. I can't bring you anything but myself, but I trust I'm enough for you to keep choosing me for the rest of our lives."

Gabe pulled her to him, gently kissing the top of her head, his heart in his throat. He knew how hard all of this was for her to say. Even just to him, let alone in front of everyone. She tilted her head back, tears welling in her green eyes again when he sniffled.

"You're more than enough, Kitten. You're everything." He kissed her to keep from crying again. It didn't work.

"I need a fucking spray bottle for these two," Blanche said, voice choked with emotion.

Gabe and Tara broke away with a wet laugh.

Blanche cleared their throat and exhaled before continuing the ceremony, leading them through their vows and explaining the seven circles they walked around each other, and calling for Antonio and Lee to bring the rings. Since his parents had opened their wedding venue, Gabe had seen countless ceremonies—some similar to this one, most bigger and more involved—all through the lens of his camera. He'd never expected to be standing under the chuppah himself, a blubbering mess overwhelmed by love. As surreal as it was to be here, Tara had been right; he couldn't imagine marrying her without their friends and families to witness this moment.

Gabe slid a simple gold ring with three small opals dotting the top onto Tara's finger. Miriam had tried to insist on a nicer diamond ring, but Tara had held firm that this was the ring she wanted. In turn, she adorned his own finger with a turquoise and silver band. The weight of the ceremony sank in, as they looked at each other with a strange serenity.

Gabe turned with Tara to face Blanche. His right hand rested on her lower back, tracing the freckles under the velvet. John brought them the drinking vessel Miriam had given to Sunny to hold earlier. The glaze created a blue and green gradient, reminiscent of a hilly landscape. Gabe and Tara's fingers touched as their hands wrapped around cool rasp of clay.

"Do you, Tara, take Gabriel Fucking Cooper to be your lawfully wedded spouse?"

"I do," Tara said with a smile. "And, in case it matters legally, I also take Gabriel Zachariah Cooper."

Gabe supported the drinking vessel as she took a sip from the opening closest to her. Her eyebrows went up in surprise, but she didn't spill anything. Gabe chalked her reaction up to the awkwardness of drinking out of the odd-shaped vessel that two people were already holding.

"Do you, Gabriel, take Tara Marie Sanderson to be your lawfully wedded spouse?"

"I do," Gabe said simply. He crouched, guiding the other opening of the drinking vessel to his lips as Tara tipped it slowly into his mouth, a grin on her face.

He'd been expecting water. This was not water.

Gabe fought a cough as he forced himself to swallow, before turning to his dad. "You could've warned us you used wine instead of water!"

Pretending to adjust the collar of his nice flannel, John shrugged, a ghost of a smile on his face. "It's nonalcoholic!"

He waited until Tara's muffled laughter died down, before he crouched down so they could drink from the vessel together, draining the rest of the wine without spilling.

"For a giant nearly a foot taller than his wife, I'm impressed you didn't get a single drop of wine on that white tux," Blanche teased as Miriam approached.

She placed a small bundle on the flagstone in front of them. "As is Jewish tradition, we remember that even our happiest moments are fragile. You both have a painful past that can never be forgotten, and Gabe, you carry the weight of two cultures full of tragic history that needs to be honored, even in moments of celebration. As you enter into marriage today, you commit an irrevocable act—permanent and final. As you break this glass, you also commit an irrevocable act. Your love can no more be undone than this glass could be made whole again."

Gabe nodded solemnly. Growing up, there had been even fewer opportunities to engage with his Jewish culture than his Native side, but this ritual—the whole ceremony—felt right. He wouldn't erase his or Tara's scars, even if it was an option; their past had made them who they were. He put his heart behind his leg, the glass crunching under his foot as he stomped on the cloth bundle.

"Mazel tov!" cried Miriam along with their other guests.

"With no further ado," Blanche beamed. "By the power vested in me by the State of Iowa, I now pronounce you married! You may kiss!"

Gabe eagerly captured Tara's lips as his parents spread the heavy wool blanket over their shoulders. The patterns and stripes of blues and greens, red and orange were bright in the sunshine. He grasped the corners of the blanket tightly to hold it around them, her arms wrapping around his waist as they kissed.

When they parted, Miriam and John enveloped both of them, still wrapped in the blanket, in a hug. "Welcome to the family, Tara." Miriam patted Tara's cheek. "Now, go take some time for yichud, and we'll get the pizza."

As she helped Gabe fold the blanket, Tara murmured, "Can we uh...yichud in a bathroom? Our kid was quiet until the drinking vessel, and now they're jumping on my bladder again."

"The bathroom?" Antonio teased, overhearing her. "Get your earplugs, everyone."

Miriam smacked his arm. "Tonio, head out of the gutter."

Antonio rubbed his shoulder. "Says you! I haven't been able to look at our en suite the same way since they defiled it."

With a wink back at Antonio, Tara led the way to the small powder room downstairs, untying the waistband of the jumpsuit in record time. The velvet crumpled to the floor as she pushed it out of the way.

"No underwear, huh, Kitten?" Gabe teased. She never wore underwear if she could help it. Why would her wedding day be any different?

Tara grinned at him. "Spoilers, but no bra either." She rubbed her bump, lifting it slightly to adjust as she peed. "God, I hope we didn't traumatize Lily and Syl. Blanche said some things I was not expecting. We really should have read their ceremony first."

Gabe smiled. "After the initial shock, I'm happy with how it turned out."

"It was very us."

He stood behind her as she washed her hands, tying her jumpsuit back in place and resting his hands on her hips. Tara leaned back against him, meeting his smile in the mirror. His heart clenched, reminded of how they'd met looking into a mirror at Confession, years ago. That first jolt of overwhelming yearning for the stranger in his arms was nothing compared to the riot of love he held for Tara now. They'd looked good together then, mussed hair and a postcoital glow. But today, dressed up, and happily married? They looked perfect.

"This reminds me of the night we met." Tara spoke his thoughts out loud. "I thought of those pretty brown eyes of yours in the mirror for months."

"Me too, Kitten." Her green eyes had haunted his dreams in the best way. They still did. Only now when he woke up, she was there with him in real life, too. He rested his cheek on her head as his hands laced together under her bump, taking some of the weight off her back. "Who knew we'd end up here?"

With a contented groan, Tara leaned against him. "I know we just barely hit the third trimester, but you need to do this until the baby comes. Quit your job so you can follow me around like this constantly."

"Happily, Kitten." Gabe might, even if she didn't genuinely mean it. "I think I am going to quit though. Take my parents up on their offer to work at the vineyard. It'll be less money—"

"Do it," Tara cut him off. "You're more important than money. That place sucks the soul out of you."

Gabe swayed with her. "I'll stick around long enough after leave so we don't have to pay back the insurance, and then that's it."

"You can go sooner than that," Tara murmured. "But it's your choice."

A knock on the door interrupted their peace before Gabe could explain his decision. Through the door, Antonio called, "Your mom sent me to tell you to come eat. No one else wanted to risk being traumatized."

Gabe smiled, still holding Tara. "I still can't believe she actually let us have the pizza."

Tara chuckled. "I think she backed off after the whole 'pizza is the only family tradition I'm contributing' thing yesterday. I hope I didn't insult her, because I know she was trying to be nice, but I wanted to be in our wedding too, even if it's just the food."

"Trust me, you are far more than just the food." Gabe kissed the top of her head. His mom had only ever wanted what was best for him, what made him happy. By now, it was apparent to everyone that what made him happiest was Tara. "But I can't wait to have you for dessert."

"God, you're so corny, dude!" Tara laughed.

"You love it."

Tara leaned back to kiss his cheek, her green eyes full of the love Gabe held in his heart, too. "I do."

Chapter Forty-Two

Tara

"Coop, you look fucking hot here." Tara smiled at Gabe over her shoulder, reclining on her side with his naked body as her pillow. She zoomed in on one of the photos Syl and Lily had taken earlier that day. *Our wedding day.* It was still a surreal thought.

The photo on her phone was from the greenhouse, where he'd looked at her with so much love she'd felt faint. Lily had captured it beautifully, just like Tara and Gabe had taught during class. The lens focus was on her face, but the motion of the composition drew the eye to his profile and down his body. It made him look like the cover model of an old romance novel.

"What do you know, I *do* look hot in that one," Gabe chuckled in her ear. His deep voice tingled against her skin.

With a smug grin, Tara ran her hands along the thick arms that surrounded her. She appreciated that they'd gone with a noon wedding; she'd been emotionally exhausted by the time they'd left at four, and both of them eager to be alone together. Despite her exhaustion, they'd found the energy for a quick photo shoot of their own, in various states of undress, the moment they were home again. The camera had been quickly forgotten as their need for each other took over, but she couldn't wait to develop one shot she'd taken of Gabe on his knees, looking up at her with hunger in his eyes as he kissed her inner thigh. The green velvet had been crumpled in his fists as he'd pushed it out of the way.

Their first time as a married couple had been surprisingly rough, with Gabe fucking her from behind vigorously against the headboard, one hand gripping her hair tightly. If she hadn't been pregnant, he probably would have been choking her.

Or maybe it wasn't so surprising; vulnerable emotions always brought out their needy, impulsive sides. After a day like today, Tara had been as desperate for him as he was for her. They hadn't bothered getting dressed since.

"We should send this one to Ang and Phin." Gabe showed her a photo of Angie and Phineas talking. In the background, Antonio scowled in their direction.

Tara laughed. "They would make a cute couple. If they can get their shit together."

"I hope they do. Maybe Ang would stop hitting on you so much."

With a snort, Tara rolled over in his arms to kiss his collarbone. "And maybe Phin can catch feelings for someone besides you."

"He doesn't have feelings for me." Gabe groaned. "We're friends."

"And Angie's not truly hitting on me," Tara returned. Gabe could be so obtuse about people's feelings for him; she knew from experience. "I'm not saying he's in love with you, but he pedestalizes you. And flirts with you relentlessly."

"Don't pretend you don't like it," Gabe teased. "You got so turned on when I told you about all the times I sucked him off in public."

Tara's cunt throbbed at the thought. "I don't mind the flirting. But we're a package deal, and I don't think he's come around to that quite yet. Just like how I don't see Angie's crush on me, but I still agree with you that she's more into *me* than *us*." She shrugged. "Let's give them time to figure their shit out, and adjust to us being an us. Who knows, if they work out, maybe we can invite them over for an evening. Just some friends having fun together, on a night when your parents are spoiling their grandkid with a sleepover."

Gabe laughed, nipping her earlobe. "This conversation was hot until you mentioned my parents."

Tara giggled, remembering how high Miriam's eyebrows had risen when Blanche told the story of how they'd fucked in the bathroom at Confession, before they even knew each other's names. Or the far-off look in her eyes, when Sunny had loudly shared during dessert that Gabe had caught feelings mid-nut that same night. Or how her new mother-in-law had smiled politely, nodding like she wasn't even listening, when Antonio made a joke during the toast (that neither of them had asked him to give) about learning to knock at their house since he'd walked in on them too many times. Even the normally quiet, discreet Richard had made more than a few comments about the number of hickeys Gabe had sported over the past couple of years.

"Your mom doesn't hate me, does she?" Tara asked, tentatively. Immediately, she hated that she'd asked, because she knew that wasn't true.

Gabe scoffed. "No, of course not. Why would you ask that?"

"Because I showed up pregnant with your baby, she knows far too much about our sex life, and I made her eat cheap pizza at her only child's wedding day." She looked over her shoulder, matching his skeptical look with one of her own. Gabe and his mother were so similar, but it was easier to trust his moments of frustration were temporary, now that they'd learned to work through them together. Tara had spent her entire adult life believing that her mother had abandoned her in a moment of anger; learning how to handle her mother-in-law's mercurial emotions would take time.

"Kitten, my mom loves you. Trust me, she wouldn't hide it if she didn't." Gabe laughed. "And Richard is basically letting her act as his mom for their wedding, and he has even less of a backbone with her than I do." He kissed her neck. "Besides, she knows I'm on the uh... libidinous side."

"'Libidinous?' I didn't realize I married a thesaurus," Tara teased.

"Literally nothing we do would shock her after how many times she walked in on Tonio and I in high school. Plus, it's not like her and Dad are any better. I'm still surprised I was an only child. There's a certain point where walking in on them all over the house, and sometimes in public, isn't traumatizing anymore."

Her thumb brushed his jaw. "I wish I could have known you back then. I mean, not in real life because you're like six years older than me, and that'd be weird. But it sounds like you and Tonio had a good time."

Gabe shook his head against her neck. "Oh, I'm so glad you didn't know me back then. I would have been a raging asshole. You think I have issues *now*? I hated myself then. Obviously." He took her hand and put it on the scars on his thighs.

She tenderly traced the lines marked in his skin, determined to love all parts of him (even the parts Gabe didn't yet love himself), scars included. She squeezed his thigh more firmly before teasing the soft skin of his hips, fingers playing with the trail of hair on his belly.

"But did we have a good time?" Gabe chuckled as her hand trailed lower. "I suppose we did. I had trouble letting myself enjoy things, and Tonio always made me let go and have fun."

Tara wrapped her fingers around his stiffening cock. "I'm glad we learned to enjoy each other."

"Me too, Kitten." Gabe ducked his head to nuzzle against hers, his husky voice warm honey in her ear. Teeth scraped the shell of her ear as his hand traced a line down her body. "Are you happy you married me? I know marriage wasn't in your plans. Or having a kid. Or a relationship at all, let alone with me."

"You didn't listen to a damn word I said today, did you?" Tara teased, propping herself up on her elbow to look at him better and drape her legs over his. Stroking his cock slowly, she rolled him onto his back and smiled gently at the vulnerability in those deep set brown eyes. She'd happily reassure him of everything she loved about him, as many times as it took, even at his lowest moments. "I meant everything I said, Gabriel Fucking Cooper. I'm really fucking happy that you're going to be mine forever."

He smiled fondly at her before she bent down to kiss him, luxuriating in the feeling of his lovely full lips on hers, his warm hand cradling her cheek, the wet heat of his mouth as she slid her tongue against his. Though climbing into his lap was a much more awkward process at six months pregnant.

Gabe helped, adjusting her thighs around his hips. His hands massaged her ass, gripping her cheeks firmly to pull her against him. "I've been thinking about this all day, Kitten. I couldn't stop staring at your ass anytime we had a moment alone, thinking how easy it'd be to bend you over, eat you out, and put you back together without anyone noticing," he whispered against her lips. "Fuck Tonio for giving you tearaway pants, when I wasn't allowed to tear them off of you."

"Want me to put it back on?" Tara teased, kissing her way down his neck and grinding against his hard cock. The veins in his neck tensed under her tongue when she sucked on a sensitive spot. A honeyed groan sounded loudly in her ear. She loved how he gave himself to her so wholly. "Your hand was on my ass often enough, I was fantasizing about it too."

"Maybe later, Kitten." Gabe's fingernails dug into the globes of her ass as she dragged her clit along his erection. "Wanna fuck you first. *Need* to fuck you first. Need you, this ass, your tits, constantly. And your fucking tattoos. And your eyes. And your freckles. And your cunt? Always on my mind." He craned his head to suck on her earlobe. "It's amazing I don't have a constant hard-on."

"You don't?" Tara teased, running her hands into his hair. "Uh oh. Dealbreaker."

Gabe chuckled into her ear. Her brain turned to liquid as the sound poured over it. Everything about him made her melt. She pulled his hair roughly, yanking his head back. His dick twitched underneath her as he moaned her name.

Tara's heart melted. The fire in his pleading brown eyes matched the desire she always felt for him. She reached a hand behind her and lined him up, before working herself slowly down his cock.

Her cunt wasn't as prepared as she thought from their earlier round. The stretch of him burned as she took him inch by inch. Gabe's hands firm against her back kept her balanced. He groaned under her, biting his bottom lip, his head thrown back against the pillows. Tara loved making him come apart. She clamped down around him, teasing him as she ground against him.

"I like seeing you like this." She sounded breathy even to her ears.

"You like seeing me try really hard not to come?" He huffed out a laugh.

Tara rose up to the tip before slamming back down, gloating at how Gabe's brown eyes flew open, searching hers desperately. She loved how he stretched and filled her, how he looked at her like she was everything. "I like making you feel good."

Gabe moved a hand up her body to draw her face to his. "Kitten, I love you."

"And I love you, Coop." Tara kissed him again as she set a slow pace, her fingers tangling in his lovely brown curls. His hand worked between her legs until he could press against her clit. White heat flashed through her at his touch, sending tremors through her body.

"Fuck, Kitten. You feel amazing." Gabe groaned as she slowly dragged herself up and down around his cock. The ache in her hips from the effort only added to her pleasure.

She wasn't sure how long she would last; already the tension had built in her legs and back. Gabe was barely hanging on. If she came, he would too. Tara wanted him to feel good for as long as possible. She slowed her pace even more, torturing herself too.

"Kitten, stop holding back," Gabe scolded, sucking on her neck. "I can feel you're close. If you want to come, come."

Tara chuckled, gasping, "I want to make you feel good. I want to make this last for you."

"Kitten, I'm yours. We're going to make it last a lifetime." Gabe bit her collarbone as he bucked into her roughly, sending jolts of pleasure that pushed her over the edge.

Her muscles rolled with pleasure as she cried out his name. With a strangled moan, his hips stuttered against her, his own orgasm following her own. She loved feeling his cock flexing inside her when she bore down on him. The sound of his deep voice around her collarbone reverberated through her neck and chest as he bit her hard enough to bruise.

She collapsed against him as the last tremors stilled, wrapping her arms around his shoulders as she lay her head against his chest. After a few moments of quiet breathing together, the baby stretched again, pushing against her ribs and lower back.

"I think we woke them up," Gabe grimaced. "I gotta pull out, sorry. That's a weird feeling."

"Tell me about it. Wish I could pull out," Tara laughed, lifting her hips so he could slip out of her. "At least they waited until we were done. They're probably wondering why they're not being rocked anymore."

She settled back down against him, letting him feel the movement of their baby with his hand instead. "We should probably figure out a name, huh?"

"Eventually, yeah. Can we veto dead relatives as a rule? And living ones, for that matter."

The baby settled under his touch. Right on her fucking bladder. Again.

She nodded, climbing off of him to go to the bathroom. "Can you imagine how fucked up it'd be if we named them Carl? 'You're named after your deadbeat grandfather who died of a heroin overdose.' They'd need therapy for sure."

"So Carl is off the table. Noted." Gabe laughed, a little uncomfortably. "I'm glad you can joke about it, Kitten."

Tara smiled at him as she rushed to the en suite. "Me too. I wasn't expecting that to come out of my mouth." She felt surprisingly light about the heavy topic; she'd already meditated and cried out as much of her feelings about her mom's letter as she could.

She was still blown away that she could simply write a letter, or call her mom. After over a decade of not knowing where she was, or if she was even alive, to suddenly have regular contact with her again was hard to wrap her head around. Her mom actually wanted to hear from her. And her mom was sober, albeit not by choice, but she hadn't come close to any of the boundaries Tara and Gabe had discussed.

Anne seemed glad that Tara was doing well for herself. She wanted Tara to come visit with Gabe, before the baby came. Tara was still thinking about it. The correctional facility was a three-hour drive away. Between the drive, the prison and seeing her mom again, all of it would be stressful for her pregnant body. It'd be stressful with an infant, too. But like Lee said, Anne wasn't going anywhere. Tara had time, and a damn good excuse, to figure out what she wanted.

When she came back from the bathroom, Gabe wordlessly lifted the corner of the duvet. She eagerly crawled under the covers, tucking herself under his arm.

"Do you know why your parents named you Tara?" he asked.

She shook her head. "Not a fucking clue. Anne probably doesn't remember either, but I can ask I suppose. Why did your parents name you Gabriel?"

"It means Strength of God. Zachariah means God Remembers. Apparently they each picked a trait they wanted me to have, and my mom found the Hebrew names to match it," Gabe explained. "Which I find hilarious because she was raised secular, but a Hebrew name seemed important to her at the time. Her mom had just died, I suppose grief influenced her decision."

Tara liked the idea of picking a characteristic first. Like a wish or intention for the baby. "Do you want to give our kid a Hebrew name, too?" Tara asked.

Gabe shrugged. "I'm ambivalent about it. If there's a name that fits the baby, we should go with it. Regardless of origin. I don't want anything particularly religious is all."

"Will your mom be upset if we name them something hella Gentile?"

Gabe laughed. "I doubt it. Besides, if she does, I'll just tell her you picked the name, and she'll give up without an argument."

Tara smacked his shoulder. "Fuck off, Coop. You better not be using me to avoid conflict with your mom."

Gabe kissed her head. "Never, Kitten. Arguing is my mother's love language."

She ran her fingers through his chest hair. "Naming a person is a lot of responsibility. And there are so many damn options."

Gabe chuckled. "And yet somehow every name I like, there's someone in Tonio's family who already has that name."

Tara smiled. "What trait do you want them to have?"

Gabe considered it, stroking her hip with his thumb. "Peace. Or Happiness. Something calming and uplifting."

"So, Hunter is off the table," Tara teased.

"Kitten, if Hunter was ever on the table, I got tricked into marrying a redneck." Gabe pinched her ass.

"You're such a snob," Tara teased. "You married down, Coop. You might end up with a white trash name for your kid."

Gabe shook his head. "What trait do you want them to have?"

"Common sense," Tara said without hesitation. "Auntie Alitrice always said I never had a lick of it. Usually after I did something like accidentally light the bed on fire."

Gabe kissed her head. "Kitten, you might not have learned many basic life skills when you were younger, but you are incredibly intelligent, confident, and resourceful. I consider that common sense. More than most people have. Myself included."

"You just say that because I haven't accidentally set anything on fire yet." Tara looked up into his soft brown eyes. "But thank you for being sweet."

Gabe kissed her hair again. "Why don't we try and find a few names we both like to put on a short list that mean intelligence or happiness or something similar? Then we can see which one fits best after we meet them." He smiled at her before adding, "Even if it is 'hella Gentile.'"

She smiled back. He could be so overwhelming, yet so fucking easy to be with. Like he shook her world upside down, but then made it so manageable to handle the aftermath. He was everything she needed. Tara hoped she would be what they needed too.

"I hope I'm a good parent," she sighed.

"I hope I am, too. We'll figure it out together." Gabe ducked his head down to gently kiss her lips. "Just like we do with everything else."

Thursday, November Twenty-Fifth

Chapter Forty-Three

Jazz

Jazz woke up with a start. Her pounding heart shook her whole body with each *thump thump thump* against the mattress. As the old house creaked—*just the wind*, she tried to reassure the adrenaline rush—Jazz checked the time on her phone, wincing at the bright screen.

Just past two. Too late to go to Blanche now. Jazz slept better with a partner nearby, but Blanche was a light sleeper. Jazz always felt bad when she woke them with how much she tossed around, usually opting to sleep in her own room unless Blanche invited her, or they happened to fall asleep together.

But tonight? She could have used Blanche's help getting to sleep, their comforting presence to help calm her down again. Her vibrator did the trick the first time, finally getting her to sleep around midnight. But she had woken up in a cold sweat just before one.

Her first nightmare had been her most common: the day Lee was kicked out. As usual, she'd been curled up in a ball in the closet, listening to Lee's cries of pain and screams with her hands pressed over her ears, like she had been in real life.

Only in the nightmare, it was never her mom who opened the closet door, like she had that day. It was always Dad. The sight of him looming over her, angry and disappointed—already terrifying in real life—had left her shaking and crying when she woke up.

No vibrator would have helped her sleep after that. She didn't even try. Clutching the selenite under her pillow in one hand and her amethyst pendant in the other, Jazz had meditated instead. Breathing on a seven count, she imagined herself floating in space, light flowing through her like waves to pull the bad energy out, over and over again.

Jazz wasn't sure exactly when she'd managed to fall asleep, but she barely remembered the dream that had woken her up just now. Something about a walk with Teddy and Mimi along the river, and there'd been a boat, but it was also a bus? Mimi and Teddy were on board, but she couldn't get to it. Then the water had risen, and it was murky. It kept rising, and she couldn't reach the busboat. And was there a little dog swimming in the river next to her? The water was crystal clear once she slipped underneath the surface, and the sky looked murky instead. With a shudder, Jazz groaned into her pillow. Her heart rate was increasing again just thinking about it.

Maybe I should just lay here and not think.

The bones of the house clacked in the night, as if tutting her for the idea. Jazz scoffed out a laugh. She didn't know how to not think. If she didn't direct her mind, the intrusive thoughts would take over. And at this time of night, they'd be fucking dark. She picked up her phone again, going to her meditation app, scrolling through the options with one eye closed against the bright light.

She finally settled on a bedtime mantra, nice and long to calm her down. A man's deep voice welcomed her to the guided meditation.

Jazz groaned, picking up her phone again. She didn't want a *man* to put her to sleep. Or at least not one with such a deep voice. She found another one that was only about twelve minutes, but at least the guy on this one didn't sound like her dad.

As she breathed to the soft music playing on the recording, the soothing voice told her that she was free, powerful, and in control of her life.

Jazz wished she believed that.

In the daytime, she might, but not at two in the morning. Even the simplest mantras were hard to believe at this hour. The voice could tell her she existed, and right now, she would doubt it. But Jazz listened politely, not arguing with the voice calmly telling her how easy it was to sleep...

Jazz sat up, chest heaving. The sheen of sweat over her skin cooled quickly, making her shiver in the chilly night air.

"I'm so fucking tired of this," Jazz growled, snatching up her phone to check the time.

Three-thirty.

She fell back with a groan. The sheets were soaked with sweat, too. Throwing off her blankets with an angry huff, Jazz rolled out of bed. Chucking her sweat-soaked nightie into the hamper, she traded it for an oversized t-shirt. At least her bonnet had stayed dry through the nightmare.

Leaving the safety of her night-light, Jazz stalked down the pitch-black hallway, wishing she could stamp her feet or flick on the too-bright hallway light. But she didn't want to wake Blanche by sounding like an intruder. If she must wake them, Blanche should be woken up gently and sweetly. And considering they were about to spend the day with her parents, they needed as much sleep as they could get.

She eased the door to Blanche's room open, wincing at the squeak that always woke them. "Sorry, Beautiful. I can't sleep," she whispered.

Bathed in moonlight, Blanche responded with a whimper, tossing in bed. Jazz hurried over to their side. *Guess I'm not the only one with nightmares tonight.*

"Blanche?" she called gently. Shaking them awake would probably make their nightmare worse—or at least, it always made hers worse—but she would if it came to that. "Wake up, Beautiful."

Blanche slept on, a sob tearing from their throat.

"You need to wake up, Blanche," Jazz said a little louder.

Blanche woke with a scream.

Startled by the echo of her own nightmare, Jazz flinched, fighting the urge to hide. She took a breath to recover her nerves; Blanche needed her right now. She eased onto the bed next to them, taking them in her arms. "Hey, Blanche. I'm here. You're safe."

Blanche desperately clung to Jazz as she stroked their back, breathing steadily for them to match her. Eventually, Blanche's breathing slowed, and they leaned back against the pillows. Jazz climbed into bed, tucking herself under Blanche's arm so they could hold each other.

"I'm sorry. Did I wake you up?" Blanche asked.

Jazz kissed their chest. "No. I was having a bad dream too and came to find you. Do you want to talk about it?"

Blanche took a deep shuddering breath. "Can you just hold me?"

"Always, Blanche. I'm here for you."

Blanche sniffled. They trembled and shook as Jazz held them. After a long moment of silence, they asked, "What was yours?"

She hated replaying it, but if it would help distract Blanche... "The closet again, the day Lee got kicked out. Only this time, you opened the closet instead of my dad. You were there to help me run away, and your house was in a field of wildflowers. It had a tail and paws and floppy ears, and it licked us when we got home. But then Lee screamed again, and then my dad's belt wrapped around my ankle and dragged me back." Jazz snorted. "We don't need to dig too deep into that one. My dreams are not subtle."

"My house was a Baba Dogga?" Blanche snickered. "I love that."

"It was cute." Jazz buried her face into their chest. "What about you? Ready to talk about it, or not at all?"

Blanche's sigh was heavy. "You know the deer path we took to get to my grandma's house? I was Chad again, but dressed as Little Red Riding Hood, cloak and everything, going down the path, when I ran into a wolf, just like I did the day she died. Big thing, beautiful. Yellow eyes and thick gray fur. We simply looked at each other, and I was somehow both the wolf and Chad at the same time. But then Papa showed up and shot at me—both of me—and we ran, howling and screaming to Grandma Rose's house.

"But when we ran up the steps, it turned into the apartment building Daisy and I used to live in." Blanche's arms tightened around Jazz. "And when I opened it, I found myself split again, this time I was both Daisy's murderer and the real me, still screaming." They took a breath, body pulsing in Jazz's arms. "But when I picked up her body like I had in real life, she was you. And you were dead, and I hated myself for letting it happen again."

Jazz swallowed, her heart wrenching not in fear for herself, but compassion for Blanche. "I'm here, Beautiful. I'm okay. I'm safe. So are you."

"I know. You came back to life and told me I had to wake up." Blanche exhaled a chuckle, sniffling. "And then I did and you were here. Safe and alive and lovely."

Tears splashed against Jazz's neck, but she didn't say anything. Most likely, that was her imagination; Blanche didn't cry. Never had. Jazz simply held them tighter to show them she was alive and whole, that they both were.

Eventually, soft snores filled the room.

Jazz didn't dare go back to sleep. Even with the bright moonlight, it was still too dark. With Blanche holding her, it was safe to think, even during the witching hour. Blanche's snores scared the intrusive thoughts away.

Once she was sure Blanche was safely asleep, Jazz whispered, "I think I'm going to tell my parents I'm gay tomorrow." Blanche would support her, but she felt safer admitting it here in the quiet dark when they slept. "I hate lying. But I also hate fighting. But if I do it tomorrow, I'll have you, and Lee, and Antonio there to support me. And I live with you now, and I can take out loans to finish undergrad, and my advisor says I'd be eligible for grants and scholarships if I get into the grad program I want. Why not come out to them? This is the last thing holding me back from being truly free."

"Would your dad try to beat me up?" Blanche asked sleepily. "Keyword try, because I *would* win."

Jazz laughed. "Sorry, I thought you were asleep."

"I can multitask," they murmured against her neck. "You sure you don't want to start by telling him you're vegan, or that you have a nose ring? Do they know you dyed your hair? Maybe test the waters first?"

"I'm sure." Jazz snorted. "I won't tell them about us, if that's what you're worried about. Or Mimi and Teddy for that matter. Like you said, I have a lot of secrets from them. Our relationship will stay between us—and our friends—for as long as we want. I just don't want to end up like Phin."

"Fair," Blanche yawned as they laughed. "I support whatever you decide, as long as you stay safe."

"We will." Jazz smiled. The darkness lifted from the room as early dawn light spilled into the window, filtering through the bare branches of the basswood outside. The birds were quieter now than they had been in summer, but a few chirps greeted the sun. As Blanche snored next to her, Jazz finally drifted off again.

Chapter Forty-Four

BLANCHE

BLANCHE POKED AT THE dry turkey on their plate, still unsettled from their dream the night before, and the conflicting emotions it had dredged up. But they were determined to keep their "vibes" up, as Jazz would put it. Jazz needed them today, so they'd put on a relatively tame outfit (wide-legged slacks and a green sweater that brought out their eyes, nary a sparkle in sight) and their Work headspace to stay polite and composed for Thanksgiving dinner.

The Joneses home was exactly what Blanche had pictured. A little too quiet, formal, a little too sterile—even the sofas were covered in plastic. The sparse decor was either religious, or highlighted Leland Senior's time in the Marines. Thankfully, the heavy curtains were wide open to allow in the overcast November skies, presumably for the plants.

The whole house was decorated with thriving houseplants that put Blanche's collection to shame. *Althea must have a green thumb.* African violets were arranged on the table as a centerpiece. A purple velvet vine hung in front of the dining room window, and calatheas dotted the room. Blanche wondered if Althea would notice if one of her orchids disappeared.

When the houseplants were the highlight of the meal, it really spoke to how unappetizing the spread was. All the best parts of this holiday—the stuffing and mashed potatoes—were notably absent. The green beans weren't bad, but all of the nostalgic carbs that were Blanche's favorites were nowhere to be seen on the Joneses table. It was so...*healthy.*

Blanche looked around for hot sauce—*any* sauce, gravy, or anything remotely flavorful—but only black pepper sat on the table. Not even a salt shaker. *Leland must have a heart condition. There's no reason anyone would choose to be this miserable.*

Looking as wretched as the food, Antonio caught their eyes across from them on the table, blinking deadpan at them as he took a bite of the turkey. Blanche bit the inside of their cheek to keep from laughing.

The four of them were planning on leaving right after the Jones's early dinner, stopping by Teddy's for dessert, then loading up to-go plates at Tonio's rotation of parents and aunties, who would keep food on the table long into the evening. They would regroup at Blanche and Jazz's house to eat leftovers with Tara, Gabe, Sunny, and Richard. Blanche was relieved to strike a nice balance between their past Thanksgivings, and the new reality that everyone had more families to celebrate with. Only a few minutes into this meal, and Blanche was already looking forward to retreating to the comfort of home.

Besides the sounds of eating and forks scraping the plates, it was eerily quiet. Leland had insisted on a prayer before they ate. Blanche had politely held hands with Jazz and Althea as he'd said grace, swallowing their discomfort. Overt displays of religion always brought up bad memories of their cult-like upbringing, especially after that dream about Papa and the wolf last night. Once grace was said, the conversation had stayed polite, stilted, and short.

"So," Althea started, too cheerily, over the silence, "What are we all thankful for? I am thankful to finally have a Thanksgiving dinner with both of my children! Blanche, what about you?"

Blanche froze, unprepared. Most things they were thankful for were inappropriate to mention in front of Leland and Althea. "I'm thankful for the support of all of my friends to help make my new house a home."

Best not to mention that their daughter was a big part of the reason their house felt like a home now. Blanche couldn't imagine what their house would be like without Jazz's touch all over it. It'd be mishmashed, found items and stressful clutter, instead of the cohesive decor, witchy touches, and feng shui intentionality she'd brought into every square inch.

"Antonio, what about you?" Althea asked.

Antonio coughed around the piece of turkey he'd been chewing for a while, trying to swallow it so he could talk. He sipped water, clearing his throat with a smile. "I'm thankful for the opportunities we had this year. I never imagined we'd blow up like we have. I already bought like six copies of the cover issue we're in."

He and Lee grinned at each other.

"Oh, I bought a copy too!" Althea said excitedly. "I was telling everyone at church about it. I never imagined my son would be famous enough for a spread in Comette!"

"Althea," Leland said sternly. "Fame isn't a virtue."

Althea's face fell.

Blanche was trying to be polite for Lee and Jazz's sake, but they detested Leland. Even if they hadn't known about how he treated Lee or Jazz, just the way he talked to his wife made Blanche want to cuss him out. Althea was awkward and timid, and a little judgy, but she seemed to have a loving heart and a sharp mind. Jazz and Lee had to get their dry humor from somewhere; it certainly was not from Leland.

"I don't think the good brothers and sisters at church want to read about men wearing makeup and parading as women." Leland shot Antonio a glare.

Blanche's hackles rose.

"It was a fashion shoot. Makeup is part of the deal," Lee said, too calmly. His measured tone sounded rehearsed. "And the article was about queer artists of color. Drag is more than just men impersonating women. It's community and art, and inherently a part of Black culture."

"My son should not be dressing like a woman in a nationwide publication!" Leland snapped. "Nor should my wife boast about it to our community!"

"So I've been eating vegan lately," Jazz said to nobody in particular. "I think I'm going to give up meat and dairy completely after today."

Blanche's heart went out to her; Jazz hated when her dad got like this.

Lee ignored her attempt to change the topic. "A little eyeshadow, and suddenly I'm a woman? So much for being supportive. You're still ashamed of me, aren't you, Dad?" He shook his head. "Why is being feminine so shameful to you? Are you ashamed of Mom or Jazz, too? Or just me?"

Leland slammed his fist on the table. "We raised you to respect God's design. We were created differently for a reason."

Blanche flinched along with everyone else, squeezing Jazz's thigh under the table. Her hand squeezed theirs. Pulse thudding in their ears, Blanche forgot that they'd been roleplaying someone *quietly* supportive. "I think self-determination outweighs what a doctor sees between someone's legs when they're born."

Jazz squeezed their hand again, and Blanche couldn't tell if it was in support or reprimand. But that shit always pissed them off.

As a child, Chad had fully believed he was an imposter, desperate to keep people from finding out his secret. He just hadn't understood what the secret was until puberty. A part of them must have always known they were intersex, even if everyone had told them they were a boy. It wasn't until their body changed to how it was supposed to look that they felt truly themself, free of the constrictions placed on their behavior.

Leland glared, uncannily resembling Lee when he was upset. Lee rarely got upset, but when he did, the same vein twitched in his left temple as Leland Senior's did now. "You're a guest in my home, so I won't say what I want to say to you." The *you* at the end of his sentence was venomous.

Trying to regain control of themself, Blanche seethed, keeping a lot of choice words for Leland Senior in their head.

"I got my nose pierced," Jazz announced, too cheerful. She couldn't quite pull it off; her anxious tone sounded more manic than chipper. She fiddled with her septum piercing, revealing the jewelry she always hid around her parents. "A couple years ago actually."

"Admit it, Dad. All your words about being supportive don't mean shit unless I act man enough." Lee scowled. "You'd think a huge break in my career would be important, but I wear pink eyeshadow one time, and your empty words about supporting me fall apart."

Antonio squirmed in his seat, humming to himself as he exchanged a nervous glance with Blanche. Despite the tension in the room (Jazz and Althea wore the same wide-eyed expression as they looked between the two Leland Joneses), pride bloomed in Blanche's chest. Finally, Lee was standing up for himself against his dad.

Leland matched his son's scowl. "I can tolerate you being the man in your marriage. Am I happy about it? No, but for the world to associate our name with queerness and perversion? We raised you better than that."

"You didn't raise me! You left me on a goddamn park bench to fend for myself!" Lee threw his napkin down, laughing sardonically and shaking his head in disbelief. "And 'the man'? Antonio and I are both men in our marriage! Just because he is more feminine and does drag doesn't mean I don't have *his* dick up *my* ass most of the time. I'm not ashamed about it, either. Queerness isn't a perversion. Your control issues are more perverse than anything we do in our bedroom."

Antonio's shoulders shook as he pressed his lips together, eyes wide and brows raised. Blanche covered their grin. Lee was never going to live this down. This conversation was long overdue, and they were not going to ruin it by bursting into laughter.

With a growl, Leland stood up. The table clattered, killing any trace of humor.

As everyone seated jumped, Lee rose to meet him, his chair falling over. "What are you going to do, Dad? What? Try and beat my ass like you used to? Think you still can?"

Leland's hand formed a fist, but it stayed by his side.

Jazz clawed Blanche's wrist. They rubbed her thigh, unable to tear their eyes from Leland, in case they needed to step in. Lee would forgive Blanche for kicking the shit out of his dad faster than he would himself.

Mirrors of each other, father and son stared the other down, as the table sat in silent anticipation. Shoulders back, they stood tall with their fists at their sides, jaws clenched in anger. The physical similarities were uncanny. The two Lelands were echoes, separated by a deep chasm of values and understanding.

"So I'm gay."

Blanche eased their grip on Jazz's thigh, as she finally got everyone's attention away from the conflict at the table. Every head snapped in her direction.

Picking up his chair, Lee fell onto it with a laugh. "Jazz, your timing needs work."

"I think it's perfect timing," Jazz shrugged. "When better to come out than during an argument about heteronormativity, gender essentialism, and anal during Thanksgiving dinner?"

"Did you know about this?" Still standing, Leland pointed at Jazz but glared at Lee.

Lee glared back. "Did I know Jazz is an adult capable of making her own choices? Yes. Do you?"

A surge of pride rose up in Blanche. Their confrontation last month had really changed his tune.

"This is your fault." Leland jabbed an angry finger in the air toward Lee.

"Dad!" Jazz interrupted, irritation plain in her voice. "This has nothing to do with Lee. I've been a lesbian as long as I can remember. I just never told you because I didn't want you to treat me the same way you did him."

Leland opened his mouth to retort—

"Leland, I won't let you do this again." Althea's voice was sharp, the timidness gone. She gave Jazz a gentle smile. "We love and support you no matter what. Like how we love and support Lee no matter what. We would never dream of *repeating our mistakes* again." She glowered at Leland, until he finally sat down. The smile reappeared on her face, as she turned back to her daughter. "Thank you for trusting us to be more understanding with you than we were with your brother. And your nose ring is beautiful!"

Leland opened his mouth again, but closed it as Althea glared at him. Blanche barely knew Althea, but they were incredibly proud of her right now.

Jazz smiled at her mom. "I thought I'd have to lie to you both for the rest of my life. But then you wanted to meet Lee again, and you were so happy to have him back. I want you guys to know everything that's going on in my life, not just what I feel safe telling you."

Althea beamed back, full of love. "Do you have a girlfriend?"

"No one I'm ready to tell you about right now. But once I know something is serious, I'll be sure to bring them by." Jazz squeezed Blanche's hand under the table. Blanche fought a blush. They were happy to stay her secret for as long as Jazz wanted. It was safer, even if Blanche wanted nothing more than to put their arm around her right now.

"When you're ready. But I want you to be happy. And settle down with someone who treats you right." Althea winked. "And maybe eventually have kids of your own."

Catching Blanche's eye, Antonio gave them a shit-eating grin.

Composing any reaction *that* might have brought to their face, Blanche squeezed Jazz's hand. They did not want to listen to a one-sided conversation about this. The already awkward dinner had taken a deeply uncomfortable turn, without the reminder that they were in very different places in their lives. That the comfort and support they gave each other would, in all likelihood, be impermanent. So much had happened in Blanche's life since they were Jazz's age, and Jazz's life held far more promise than Blanche's had. Who knew where their relationship would be by the time Jazz was ready to consider having a family of her own?

Luckily, Jazz made a face and gave a vague answer. "Oh, I don't think that's happening for a long time, if it ever does. I'm only twenty-one, Mom."

"And I was twenty-two when I had Lee!" Althea beamed innocently. "You know, I joined a PFLAG group. A lot of the other parents there have grandkids."

They were all ignoring Leland at this point, still glowering but thankfully silent. Althea was the head of the table now.

"My point is that *if* I have kids, it'll be when I choose to, and only because *I* want them." Jazz shook her head. "Lee's older. Make him have babies."

Lee shook his head right back at her. "Nah. We're good."

Blanche rubbed Jazz's thigh with their thumb. What mattered was they were happy together now. They wanted each other, no promises of undying commitment or unrealistic fidelity needed. The joy, serenity, and love that Jazz brought to Blanche's life outweighed her parents' dry ass turkey, tense conversations, and discomforting thoughts about the future any day.

Chapter Forty-Five

The crackle of the fireplace filled the room with a warm glow, as Lee settled into the floral couch in Blanche's parlor. They'd arrived just after sunset, exhausted from the half dozen stops they'd made, yet he and Antonio had been unwilling to go home yet; there was one more family to celebrate with.

He moaned around a bite of sweet potato pie, nostalgia hitting just as hard as the flavor. The texture, crust, and spices were all perfectly balanced. "Who made this, and are they single?"

Antonio elbowed him, looking cozy in the gray sweatpants and a cropped hoodie he'd changed into when they got to Blanche's. "My auntie, but I'm not telling you which one because it doesn't matter if she's single or not. You're mine, Angel. You have to get that pie through me."

They'd been the first two to declare defeat against the leftovers. Everyone else was still eating to-go plates in the dining room. They had both grabbed dessert on their way to the couch, though; there was always room for dessert.

Unbuttoning his fly, because none of their friends would care if he wasn't entirely put-together, Lee grinned at the jealous pout on his husband's face. "It's the one who called dibs on me, isn't it?"

Antonio didn't reply, instead hitting him with a pouty side-eye, while he ate a dairy-free cheesecake tart that Gabe had brought.

Lee balanced his plate carefully as he leaned against his husband. "You know I love you, right? You and only you," Lee murmured in his ear, before he kissed Antonio's cheek. "And not just because I have to get this pie from you. I'm crazy about you."

Antonio gave him a small smile as he bit his lip. "I'll see if I can get the recipe," Antonio conceded, before kissing Lee on the mouth. Lee let the kiss linger, tasting the cheesecake on his husband's lips.

"You better not be about to stick any dicks up anyone's ass," Blanche teased as they entered the room, carrying a plate of dessert. With a snort, Jazz followed them with two glasses of wine.

Lee groaned, flushing with embarrassment, pride, and relief. "God, that was such a fucking disaster." He'd lost his temper, but somehow still managed to say everything he'd wanted. And then some things he *didn't*. "Honestly, I might start acting more fem just to piss him off at this point."

Jazz settled into one of the armchairs, setting the glasses of wine on the side table before Blanche draped themselves across her lap. They were seamlessly comfortable together, wordlessly offering a bite of dessert, or taking the plate so the other could sip their wine. As uncomfortable as he still was with his friend and his little sister shacking up, Lee had to admit they were cute together. They worked. They seemed to get each other. *And it's none of my business. They're adults, making choices. And I can deal with it.*

He had never seen Blanche smile as much, or as brightly, as they did when they were with Jazz. In all the years he'd known them, their mask had never slipped. Now that it had, the difference was palpable. They were happy, present, excited.

And he had tried to ruin that. Shame burned through him that he'd never realized how toxic his behavior had been. The prejudices he didn't even know he'd internalized from his dad had come between him, and two of the people he trusted most in the world.

"I'm proud of you, Lee," Blanche said as they washed down the crust of the apple pie with their wine. "I never expected you stand up to anyone like that, let alone your dad."

Lee huffed, ignoring the burst of confidence that made him want to puff out his chest. The whole confrontation had been too long overdue for him to be proud of himself. "Honestly, I've been complaining about his attitude enough that it just came out. He's so frustrating. If it weren't for Mom, I probably wouldn't bother."

"I'm glad you were there." Jazz hugged Blanche tightly. "I don't know if I could have gotten through that without y'all."

Same. Lee snorted. Just like always, Jazz had played the peacekeeper in the family again today. The one who caused just enough of a scene to defuse their dad's temper, to distract him enough that whatever he was mad about took a backseat.

Blanche kissed her with a proud smile. "You would have gotten through it just fine, but I'm glad I could be there for you. Even if I almost choked to death on that dry ass turkey."

She'd gone to dinner with the intention of coming out? Lee raised his eyebrows, pushing his glasses up his nose. Even now, he was terrified of his dad, despite actually standing up to him for once. He would never understand where Jazz had got her boldness from.

As if reading his thoughts, Antonio exclaimed, "You *planned* that announcement? That took guts."

Jazz shrugged, but a quiet smile teased her face. "Living a lie isn't free enough."

Gabe and Richard wandered in from the dining room, Richard filling him in on his Thanksgiving with the Boonmees, namely how much quieter it was than the Floreses. Which left Tara and Sunny still at the dining table. Tara was a bottomless pit, even with the baby encroaching on her stomach. And Sunny was probably egging Tara on.

Lee missed his chosen family these days; they were all so busy with their own lives. Not that they were growing apart, but he had to make time for them now. It was different than when he'd lived with Tara and Blanche, when Sunny would come over to their apartment all of the time to escape from her mom.

After stoking the fire, Richard sat in another armchair with a glass of wine, while Gabe made himself comfortable on Antonio's other side. His plate was full of cheesecake tarts, lemon cookies, and two kinds of pie.

Antonio leaned over, looking at it. "Gabey Baby, look at you, eating carbs!"

Gabe nodded, taking a bite of the lemon cookie. "Tara's determined to make me eat the food I make. But even if she didn't, I should've been eating this stuff the whole time. I've been missing out." He smacked Antonio's hand creeping toward the tart. "Get your own. This is mine."

Shaking his hand, Antonio hissed, but then sighed dramatically, leaning into Gabe's side. "You're so mean to me, Gabey."

Lee privately preferred when Antonio snuggled with him instead, but he would never begrudge his affectionate husband the opportunity to cuddle with his best friend. Gabe was even more touchy-feely than Antonio.

Gabe put his arm around Antonio. "Tonio, I literally retraumatized myself for your ass mere weeks ago, and I'd do it again if you asked, and you think I'm *mean*?"

Lee couldn't let a perfect opportunity to stir the pot pass by. "Yeah, but you also had a threesome with his cousin."

Antonio shot him a look. Lee hid his grin.

"Consenting adults," Gabe shrugged. "Besides, get used to it. Her and Phin seemed to hit it off again last weekend."

"Surprisingly, those two might work out," Tara said, as she and Sunny finally joined them. At the sight of Antonio hogging all of Gabe's personal space, Tara pouted and went to sit by Lee instead.

Lee beamed, patting his thighs as he took her plate of desserts so she could sit. Tara grinned back as she settled on his lap. Lee briefly considered faking a groan of pain to shit-talk how large her bump was now, but Tara was barely heavier than she'd always been.

"Getting the party started, Lee?" Tara teased, tugging on his waistband where he'd undone his fly. "You should have worn maternity pants like me. I might wear them every Thanksgiving."

"Don't be jealous just because I can wear pants that zip, Buttercup," he teased back.

He was glad that despite their new directions in life, they were still besties. It was like nothing had changed between them. Even if they'd become completely different people since Antonio's hazel eyes had turned his life upside down.

Now, they'd both made families for themselves, instead of relying only on each other. Instead of hoping for a break, he was being choosy about which calls he returned, which projects wouldn't disrupt the peaceful life he'd built with Antonio. Instead of stressing about her student loans, Tara was complaining about needing an assistant while she took parental leave. Their days of clinging to each other because they were all they had were gone. Their days of avoiding being vulnerable with the world were in the past. Hard to avoid it when his picture, makeup and all, accompanied a heartfelt interview in an international magazine. Or when he'd openly shared with his dad that he was a bottom vers.

Lee wrapped his arms around Tara as she balanced the overloaded dessert plate on her bump. "Buttercup, I'm impressed you can eat all of that with a baby in there."

Tara smiled proudly. "Me too. My OB keeps telling me I still need to gain weight though. Although she'd probably prefer if I ate shit like brown rice and steamed broccoli, instead of cheesecake thingies."

"Kitten, you *do* eat shit like brown rice and steamed broccoli. You just don't realize it because you eat whatever I put in front of you," Gabe teased, adjusting his long legs over Antonio's lap. His feet nudged Tara and Lee's thighs.

"Yeah, but you make it taste good. It can't be *that* healthy if it tastes good."

"Can you send me some recipes so we can meal prep healthy shit, when we get there?" Sunny asked. "Obviously it won't be until after the wedding, but we're going to go to the fertility clinic basically as soon as we get back from the honeymoon."

Gabe nodded. "Of course. I went down a rabbit hole on gestational nutrition. I have a whole doc full of recipes. I'll send you the link on Discord. There are even some that are supposed to boost folic acid for helping with conception."

"Planning the next one already, Gabe?" Blanche teased.

Gabe blushed. "Not right away, but neither of us liked being only children. Obviously we gotta get through this one first before we decide anything."

"I dunno. I kind of miss being an only child," Lee joked.

Jazz flipped him off. "This fucker literally asked if the hospital would take me back every year on my birthday, like it was the funniest joke in the world." Jazz softened into a smile. "Having you as a brother wasn't always a joy, but it got a lot harder after you weren't there anymore. Mom got so mad when I joked about going back to the hospital on my tenth birthday."

Lee's chest ached. "I wish I could have been there."

"You're here now, that's what matters." Jazz smirked. "And you told Dad off today, so I think this is officially my favorite Thanksgiving."

"Did you?" Tara asked him. "Lee, that's amazing! Good for you."

"He stood up and proudly told Dad he takes it up the ass." Jazz sighed. "My hero!"

Lee grinned in embarrassment as everyone laughed. Even the fire snapped, the house wheezing along with them as the furnace kicked on.

"I had one moment of glory, before Jazz stole my thunder and told him she was gay."

"Wow, this sounds way more exciting than our Thanksgiving." Tara nudged her feet against Gabe's. "Don't get me wrong, I enjoyed helping with landscaping around the mounds, but maybe we should have gone with them."

Antonio shook his head as he reclined against Gabe's chest. "No, you would have hated it. Leland must have hypertension because that food had *no* salt."

"Or heat. Or fat. Or really any flavor," added Blanche. "Let's just say we absolutely needed all of your leftovers after that sad dinner. No offense to your mom's cooking, but wow."

Jazz shook her head. "None taken. She *can* make good food, she just *doesn't* because Dad thinks it's indulgent." She made a face. "Although I do like one Thanksgiving tradition of hers: What are we all thankful for?"

Lee snorted; he hadn't even gotten to say his after their had argument broken out. He opened his mouth to say he was thankful for Antonio, when Jazz added "And you can't say you're thankful for your partner. It's too easy."

Lee closed his mouth.

Blanche spoke up. "I'll go first. I'm thankful for Gabriel Fucking Cooper." They raised their wineglass in his direction. "You asked me what was holding me back from getting my GED, and I still haven't been able to come up with a good answer. And...I'm starting a GED program in January! So thank you. You might make a real therapist out of me yet."

Gabe beamed. "You'll make a great therapist. Just as long as you remember I'm not your patient." He turned his gaze to Sunny. "I'm thankful to you, Sunny, for always listening to my emo ass when I'm going through it. Even if you didn't always know you were listening to my emo ass in particular, you always gave me great advice. You still do."

Sunny grinned. "So did you. I'm thankful for Tara." She grinned at Tara, who narrowed her eyes in suspicion. "For always being my friend, and especially for getting knocked up and married. It got Richard jealous enough to get his shit together and propose."

Richard merely shrugged, his cheeks pink.

Tara laughed. "Glad I could help, I guess. I'm happy with how it turned out. Even if we only were together like a week before I got pregnant." She smiled fondly at Gabe, patting his feet where they rested against her thigh.

Gabe winked. "You're the one who said to leave it in, Kitten."

"As if you hesitated."

Lee shook his head, patting Tara's thigh. "I don't need to hear this while you're sitting in my lap."

With a snort, Tara turned to Antonio instead. "I'm grateful to you, Tonio. Because I got to see how happy being with you made Lee, and it made me want that for myself. And now I have a whole-ass family, and I'm fucking married and shit."

Antonio grinned. "Does this mean Lee and I get full credit for your whole relationship?"

"No, because I get partial credit!" Sunny piped up. "I have it in writing and everything."

"Honestly, you get some credit," Gabe conceded. "I only went to Confession in the first place to see you perform that night. Not that I saw much of your set."

Antonio clapped happily. "I'm going to tell your kid that they exist because of us." He grinned up at Gabe. "And all of your embarrassing stories from when we were kids."

Gabe shook his head. "Maybe not all of them, Tonio."

"All of them. It's going to happen, Gabey Baby," Antonio grinned. "I am thankful for Dicky, because the mere mention of your name was still enough to make that bitch shit herself in fear. I don't know what you did, but I am grateful you're a scary motherfucker."

Richard nodded grimly. "Glad to know I haven't lost my touch." He looked up at Blanche. "I'm thankful for you, Blanche. You've been a big influence on us. In many ways."

Blanche beamed. "I'm glad I could help."

Lee met Jazz's eyes as they both realized no one had said they were thankful for them. "Wow, fuck all y'all. No love for the Joneses?" Lee asked, clutching his chest to lay the guilt on thick. "I'm hurt. I thought we were friends."

"That's homophobic, honestly," Jazz scoffed.

Lee grinned. "And racist!"

"So racist!" Jazz laughed.

Tara threw her arms around him, spilling a lemon cookie in between them as she hugged him tightly. "I am so thankful for you!"

"Too late, Buttercup. You love my husband more than me. I get it."
Antonio joined her, and soon even Gabe's arms were around him too.
Lee laughed as he hugged them back. As always, Lee was grateful for his
chosen family, practically doubled in size over the past few years and still
growing. Not just in number, but in direction. All of them supported
and successful, happy and loved in ways Lee would never have dreamed
possible before he'd met Antonio.

"This is way too much affection," Richard muttered to Sunny, who
snorted and ruffled his hair.

As Blanche pressed kisses all over Jazz's face, squeezing her in a tight
hug, Jazz raised her wineglass. "I'm thankful for you, Lee. Fuck these
guys."

Smiling at his sister over Tara's shoulder, Lee retrieved the lemon
cookie stuck between them to toast her with. Out of everyone he loved,
he'd always worried about her and Blanche the most. But their futures
were brighter than ever, bursting with possibilities. "Cheers to you,
Jazz!"

CHAPTER FORTY-SIX

Jazz

WATER THUNDERED FROM THE tap, a light scent of lavender floating in the steam. Putting a CBD joint to her lips, Jazz took a deep drag as Blanche wrapped her locs up in a shower cap, their hands massaging the back of her head. Candles flickered against the marble walls in the luxurious upstairs bathroom, as Jazz curled up in a bathrobe on the chaise.

Blanche had taken one look at her after their friends had left and guided her upstairs to draw her a bath in the jacuzzi tub. Jazz had never been in the attic before; this was Work space, not Home space. And here she was, too exhausted to take in the surroundings. Too weary to comprehend what it meant that Blanche had brought her into this space, beyond the numb awareness that Blanche's upstairs bathroom was so big that it had a fucking chaise.

As Blanche stirred Epsom salts into the tub, the lavender aroma soothed Jazz's soul. Gratitude washed over her that Blanche was taking care of her after they'd both had an exhausting day. Neither had slept well the night before. Though her brain was still too full to sleep now, perhaps Blanche's was too. If she'd gone to bed right away, she would have stared at the ceiling for hours.

Dinner at her parents had left Jazz drained, vulnerable, and unsatisfied. But she was glad she had finally let them into more of her life. While she wanted to tell them more, it was better to give them that little piece of her to digest first. Her parents' house had been an emotional roller-coaster, jolting into so many unexpected directions and intense dives, that Jazz still felt slightly nauseous.

Afterward, she'd been thrown into the zoo of Teddy's family, and then four different stops with Antonio's extended relations—all of which were the complete opposite of the tense silence of her parents. Everyone was amazing and welcoming and lovely, but they were so much. She didn't know how Lee handled so many people and smells and kids and noise. Leland and Althea were ghosts compared to the explosion of life that Antonio had grown up with.

Ending the evening with Blanche's chosen family had been lovely, but by the time Lee and Antonio finally left, Jazz needed alone time to decompress. Well, alone time with Blanche anyway. She was out of steam, but Blanche didn't drain her the way most people did. She could recharge if it was just the two of them.

Blanche filling the bath with Epsom salts and essential oils, undressing her and rolling her a joint, made Jazz's heart clench with love and appreciation. Blanche somehow always saw exactly what she needed. Jazz hoped she made them feel at least a fraction as cared for.

When Blanche held out their hand to lead her to the enormous bath, she followed, hoping Blanche wouldn't comment on the tears in her eyes as she left the fluffy robe behind. Jazz sighed as she sank into the perfect scalding heat, seeping through her skin to warm her soul. Leaning back against Blanche, Jazz ran her hands along the long legs that surrounded her own under the water. "This is exactly what I needed."

Blanche kissed her neck, murmuring softly, "Do you want to talk about any of it?"

Jazz shook her head. Talking took energy, as did replaying the day. She would need a decent night's sleep before she was ready to process anything.

Blanche wrapped their arms around her, running their thumbs along her hips. "I'm here whenever you're ready."

Jazz smiled. "You're always there for me, Blanche. No one supports me like you do."

"Your mom seemed supportive today." Blanche rested their head against hers.

"My mom's support is the support she wants to give; not the support I need. I have her support as long as I meet her expectations. It's still conditional." Jazz sighed as Blanche kissed her neck again. Closing her eyes, Jazz basked in their affection. "No one gets me like you do. Not even Mimi and Teddy. I love them, but what I have with them is very different from what we have."

Teddy was fun and goofy and sweet. Mimi was intense and assertive and encouraging. But Jazz had finally realized what had been missing from her relationship with them. Ed was dorky and goofy like Teddy was, the fun partner for Teddy the way she was for Jazz and Mimi. Julissa bossed Mimi around and obsessed over her the way Mimi needed, because Jazz and Teddy couldn't do that for her. Jazz had been pouring herself into Teddy and Mimi, and not getting watered enough in return. Because they couldn't nurture her the way she needed.

The way Blanche loved her was most similar to how Jazz loved—giving and passionate and quietly supportive. And Jazz couldn't imagine losing any of them. All three of her partners balanced her in different ways.

"I cried last night," Blanche murmured. "You woke me up from my nightmare, and I was just so fucking relieved to see that you were safe."

"Blanche," Jazz whispered, looking over her shoulder at Blanche in the tub behind her. She hadn't known. Never even considered that the tears she'd imagined were real. She had felt them shaking, but Blanche never cried. That had simply been an irrefutable fact about Blanche. Jazz had assumed the trembling was from fear.

Blanche's green eyes were soft and sad when they met hers. "I didn't even know I still could. I've been emotional, choked up before, but tears? Even after Daisy died, I sobbed and screamed, but no tears came out. So thank you for holding me and being there for me, while I rediscovered I'm still a weak ass bitch."

Jazz laughed, settling back against their chest with a shake of her head. "You're not a weak ass bitch. You're a human with emotions. A very strong human who has been through too much shit. If *you* don't cry sometimes, what right does anyone else have?"

Blanche's lips pressed against her neck again. "I never expected I'd feel love again, Jazzy, or if I ever knew what love felt like in the first place. But I'm glad I found it with you."

Jazz looked over her shoulder, a smile growing on her face at the nervous vulnerability in their green eyes. "Love feels like this, Blanche. It feels like us."

Her lips melted into Blanche's as their tongues danced; a contented sigh escaped them both. Jazz settled herself into their lap, grateful for the giant tub that was wide enough to stretch her thighs comfortably over Blanche's hips. The heat between them made the steaming water bubbling around them feel cool in comparison.

Blanche's hands danced along her body, expertly gripping and pinching all of Jazz's favorite places Blanche had discovered over the past couple of months. Jazz's pussy clenched in anticipation. Despite her exhaustion, she needed this. She needed Blanche, to be close with them.

"Please," Jazz whispered, as Blanche's skilled fingers roamed between her thighs, skirting the places she needed to be touched the most. She thrust her hips toward their hands as she panted against Blanche's mouth, grasping Blanche's shoulders and neck.

Blanche took pity on her begging, massaging her clit gently between two fingers and their thumb. Jazz cried out, her stomach tightening at each roll of their fingers. Blanche's other hand pressed two long fingers inside her. Pleasure coiled up her back. Toes curling, calves cramping, her eyes rolled back in her head. Her nails dug into Blanche's shoulders and their name flew from her mouth as Blanche brought her over the edge.

Jazz kissed them again, desperate for more. She reached down and massaged Blanche's muff, her lips sucking softly on their neck. She needed them to feel good too.

"I came up here to take care of you, not me," Blanche moaned, not stopping her.

"So take care of me then, Beautiful." Jazz teased before she kissed them again, still pressing gently against their muff. Her other hand teased their breast. She loved the gasps Blanche made under her. "And I'll take care of you, too."

Blanche shot her a look, any sternness softened by the temptation in their eyes. "We'll get to me." They smiled against her mouth, biting her lower lip before sucking on it gently. "But this bath is getting cold."

Jazz nodded, pouting again.

Kissing her pout away, Blanche guided her carefully out of the bath and toward the walk-in shower to rinse them both free of Epsom salts and soapy bathwater.

"You should open a spa," Jazz teased once Blanche finished toweling her off and brought out a bottle of lotion. "I feel so pampered."

"Should I call it Aftercare?" With a wink, Blanche rubbed the moisturizer in their hands and massaged Jazz's skin, taking extra time with her tits and ass. Their calloused hands ran along her body as they kissed her neck and lips.

"Sit up here, Lovely." Blanche patted the countertop. "I need to get your feet." Blanche knelt as Jazz scooted onto the cold marble top. Want coursed through Jazz from Blanche's touch. Her heart went into overdrive as she looked down at her lover's green eyes, looking at her with adoration from between her thighs.

Blanche kissed her feet and ankles and calves and knees as they massaged the moisturizer into her skin. Jazz bit her lip with anticipation, breath catching as Blanche's talented mouth kissed her inner thighs. Desperation coursed through her.

Jazz's breath was shaky as she gasped as Blanche planted a soft kiss over her pussy. Their tongue darted between her lips in tiny licks, flickering on her clit. Jazz moaned, leaning back on her hands. She spread her legs wide as Blanche buried their face deeper against her, pushing into her with two fingers.

Her hips bucked as those fingers curled oh so perfectly. "Fuck, you're so good at this."

"I know," Blanche murmured, sucking messily on her clit and twisting their hand expertly to tease all of her pleasure points. Bliss simmered up her spine as they devoured her. She gasped as Blanche worked her steadily toward her climax, begging them not to stop.

Blanche kissed her clit gently but relentlessly, increasing pressure with their fingers. Whimpering, Jazz looked into those green eyes staring hungrily up at her again, before her orgasm crashed over her like a tidal wave. Her brain melted as the simmer of pleasure climbing up her back boiled over.

Steady and sweet as always, Blanche worked her through it, licking gently as Jazz shuddered around their fingers, blissed out on love and affection and touch.

Blanche always made her feel so desperate and needy, so alive. Making love with Blanche was like when lilacs bloomed in spring and took over the world with their scent. Like how fresh rosemary lingered on Jazz's fingertips after she burned it. Like letting the water for her tea slightly cool before she poured it over the leaves, so she could have the perfect first sip. The fleeting, intimate moments overwhelmed her senses, and made a home in her psyche forever.

"Your turn?" she asked, eagerly.

"Be patient." Blanche held up a fluffy towel for her.

Jazz whined, "Ugh, you're such a tease."

Blanche laughed. "I just made you come twice, Jazzy. That's literally the opposite of a tease."

"Fine." She hopped off the bathroom counter and wrapped their arms around Blanche, gripping their ass as she kissed them, while they tucked her bathrobe around her.

They stepped out of the bathroom and into the main recording room. Jazz admired the rest of the attic in the dim glow of the room, more awake now than when she'd entered it. Tastefully arranged shelves and hooks lined one wall, holding various tools such as ropes, dildos, riding crops, leather restraints, and gags. Mats and furniture lined along another wall: a St. Andrews cross, suspension frame, a couple benches, and a large cage, with some stockades tucked behind it along the wall. Cleaning spray clung to the air.

She'd expected to feel uneasy up here, around all of this stuff that had made her anxious when she'd experimented with Mimi's interest in kink. But Jazz merely felt as relaxed and safe as she always did with Blanche. Even if she wasn't remotely interested in trying most of it out. "It looks like a gym up here."

"In a way, I suppose it is," Blanche laughed. "Want a tour?"

"Can I?" Jazz asked, trying not to show her eagerness. This was a part of Blanche's life she had never been invited to, and while she didn't particularly want to get tied up or flogged, she wanted to know more about Blanche.

They showed her the different areas of the attic: the storage area, the set with a Murphy bed tucked away, leaving the camera rigs pointing at bare hardwood floors. Blanche snorted. "Surprisingly, I put everything away when we're done."

"I respect that." Jazz grinned. "But would it kill you to put some flowers or an area rug in here, though?"

"Are you going to decorate my set, too?" Blanche teased. "That might help with the mic echo that Lee keeps complaining about, though."

The aftercare zone looked cozier. A wide chaise was strewn with blankets and pillows. A cushioned mat on the floor, under the dormer window, looked perfect to recline and cuddle on.

Jazz lingered; she wasn't particularly interested in being dominated or recorded. Blanche wanted to keep their relationship sweet and vanilla; Jazz was happy with that. But aftercare? Moments like this, where Blanche took care of her and spoiled her? That hit all of her love languages.

Blanche wrapped their arms around her, nuzzling her neck. One hand was creeping under the bathrobe to cup her breast; their thumb grazed her nipple ring. "Seeing you up here is giving me ideas for new ways to love on you."

Jazz grinned. "Wanna show me those ideas?"

They exhaled into her neck, sounding a little sad. "I never thought I'd want you in my work space. I've compartmentalized Work Blanche from the rest of me for so long, that I thought I needed to keep it physically separate too."

Jazz put her hands over theirs, rubbing the backs of their hands with her thumb.

"But you are a flood, Jazzy. You're leaking into all parts of me." Blanche kissed her neck. "I think I like it. You make me feel whole."

"You deserve to feel whole, Beautiful." She kissed them again as she wrapped her arms around their waist, holding them close. Jazz closed her eyes as Blanche ran a tentative tongue across her lips. Their tits and erection pressed into her as Jazz lost herself in their kiss.

Jazz needed more; the couple orgasms in the bathroom were appetizers. She gestured to the cushions arranged in the nook of the aftercare area. "You know, you never finished telling me that story about the tantric workshop."

Blanche grinned at her, the tip of their tongue poking between their teeth. Jazz's heart pounded as she grinned back. They took one step and another with a bright glint in their eyes, backing Jazz toward the cushions. "I didn't finish that story? Well, let me show you everything I learned."

"I take it we're not going downstairs, are we?" Jazz teased.

Blanche shook their head. "Not yet, Jazzy. Be patient."

"Does this tantric workshop include you coming, too?" she asked eagerly, biting her lip.

Blanche's eyes fell to her mouth, before their green eyes flicked back up to hers. "Several times, hopefully."

Jazz squealed as Blanche lowered her gently onto the cushions, peppering her with kisses until Jazz was shrieking with laughter. Loving Blanche was so freeing, so boundless, so filled with delight, that Jazz never wanted it to end, only for their love to grow with them, in whatever directions they went. Her heart warmed at Blanche's lovely face and those shining green eyes, looking back at her with so much happiness and hope.

Thursday, May Twelfth

Epilogue

Blanche

Repairing their vintage home was exhausting, expensive, and never-ending. Forearm cramping from squeezing the caulk gun, Blanche squinted as they dragged a line of silicone along the glass, their fourteenth windowpane of the day. Only three windows to go after this, just as they were finally getting the hang of how to squeeze consistently. The silicone sealing the panes on the roof of the atrium would probably cure thick and uneven, but no one would ever see it.

With a wince, Blanche shook their arm out once the glass was fully sealed into the steel frame. After repairing and painting the front porch earlier in the spring, and flogging people professionally for almost two decades, their muscles should be used to this. A caulk gun must have used some neglected muscle. But, they only had so long before Jazz got back, before they had to leave, and they wanted to finish this project.

Renovating the atrium would have been easier, faster, cheaper if they'd gone with polycarbonate instead of real glass. Or just hired someone to do it. But this was their home, and Blanche wanted to learn to do it right. "Like therapy," Blanche quipped to themself, clipping the pane of glass into the frame. The thick work gloves were clumsy around the sharp edges.

From beyond the fully bloomed lilacs perfuming the air, Jazz sang to herself as she walked up to the house. Blanche smiled, waiting for her to come in. To tease them after Blanche had promised she'd come home from her exam to a finished atrium. They didn't have long to wait; Jazz walked around to the backyard without going inside.

"This looks amazing!" Jazz practically skipped through the door, chest bouncing in her cropped lavender sweater. She didn't need to open it; Blanche was saving the largest pane of glass for last, so Jazz merely stepped through the frame. She dropped her backpack inside the door to the kitchen, pulling her own gloves on as she came over to help, just as she had last weekend when Blanche was carefully cutting all of this glass. "A little draftier than I expected, after all your talk of finishing this project before I finished finals, but it looks *so* good!"

"Yeah, yeah!" Blanche took the teasing in stride, greeting her with a quick peck when Jazz carried the next pane of glass over. "How was your final?"

"Not as bad as I thought, but more importantly, it's over!" Jazz beamed, shimmying a little as she held the glass, while Blanche ran a bead of silicone along the edge. "I am free until my internship at the urban farm starts in June." She slid the glass into place, holding it steady until it was secure. "You're getting good at that, by the way. Way better than yesterday!"

"I am," Blanche agreed archly. Then added, "Just in time for our last pane of glass." They exchanged a wary smile; Blanche had had to recut the door glass three times last weekend, either due to it breaking or somehow getting the measurements wrong twice. Funny how their basic math course hadn't taught Blanche to read the tape measure better.

"Well, let's do it!" Jazz clapped her hands. "Lee and Antonio will be here any minute."

"Wait, I thought we said four! What time is it?" Blanche looked at their wrist, as if they had a watch below their leather gloves.

"Just after three. But you know Lee!" Jazz held the tall pane of glass so Blanche could run the caulk gun along the edge. Together, they worked it carefully into the clips, letting out a shared sigh of relief when it fit perfectly. The birdsong and traffic that had been Blanche's soundtrack muffled as the atrium was, at long last, finished.

"Are we...done?" Blanche hesitantly opened the door, wincing at the squeak of the hinges, to make sure the glass hadn't shifted the swing.

Jazz checked the equally squeaky vents to make sure the hinges held up with the added weight. "Other than cleanup and a little lube on the hinges, I think so."

Blanche glanced around at the discarded bottles of silicone, the towels all over the brick floor, the packaging the glass had been stored in. "Can we clean up tomorrow?"

"Honestly, I don't really want to clean up right after finals. So sure!" Jazz laughed, pulling her gloves off. "Besides I have a present for you, as a belated congratulations for passing your GED tests last week! I wanted the atrium to be done before I gave it to you."

"For me?" Cheeks warming, Blanche removed their gloves too, dropping them on the sawhorse. "No, I should have a present for *you*!" they sputtered. "You just finished finals! Why didn't I think of getting you a present?"

"You finished the atrium!" Jazz cocked her head, looking at them like they'd grown a second head. "I'm about to propagate all of my mom's herbs. They have to fit somewhere. I'm going to take up at least half of this room." With a bashful smile, she fished a small bottle out of her backpack. "This is for you, for the other half that I'm not using."

Blanche held up the bottle. A dozen or so round, brown seeds rolled around the glass. "Are these cannabis seeds?"

Jazz beamed. "Yup! Gabe got them from his dad for me, along with some growing tips. Now you can grow your own Northern Lights! In here!" She gestured to the atrium around them. The sunlight gleaming through the glass was as bright as her smile.

Their heart glowing, Blanche pulled Jazz into a hug, kissing her plush lips in profound appreciation.

Jazz smiled against their mouth. "Does that mean you like it?"

"I love it." Blanche kissed her again. "I love you."

"Love you too." Just as Jazz deepened the kiss, a series of honks blared from the front walk. Jazz groaned. "Sounds like Lee is here to pick us up."

They washed up quickly in the kitchen—Jazz pulling some silicone string off of Blanche's fuzzy, pink cardigan that they'd been trying *so* hard to keep clean—and went to climb into the leather backseat of Lee's shiny black Escalade.

"Are you ever going to park and text us like a normal person again?" Blanche teased as they buckled in.

"Nope!" Lee grinned from the driver's seat. "The horn on my old car didn't work. The novelty isn't going to wear off anytime soon."

Jazz muttered something about a "grandpa ass car," but Lee ignored her, turning up the house music playing on the top-of-the-line sound system. The addition was completely impractical, especially for the practical Lee. But then again, Antonio was still driving his death trap of a Civic, despite the steady royalty income from the Vamp soundtrack, and Lee's increasingly large paychecks from the record labels hiring him. One of them should indulge. "Are we ready?" he asked.

"Yup!" Blanche's chest tightened, especially when Antonio turned around to examine them thoughtfully. "And before you ask, yes, I'm sure. This has been a long time coming."

Blanche's hand found Jazz's in the backseat, as Lee took the streets on their way over Eastside. Students from the university celebrated the last day of finals, with parties underway on the front lawns of the frat houses. Downtown, commuters waited at their bus stops, carrying briefcases and produce from the farmer's market along the riverwalk. A busker strumming her guitar outside of Confession made Blanche's heart clench with the reminder of how Walter used to sit there with his harmonica, too.

As they crossed the river into Eastside, the spray from the splash pool on the island created a small rainbow next to the bridge. Blanche caught a flash of their old apartment building between the new high-rises when Lee turned to head up the bluff. Surprisingly, the ache in their chest felt more like nostalgia than anger.

"You all right, Lovely?" Jazz murmured.

"Yes, why?" Blanche startled at how raspy their voice was. They touched their cheeks to find them damp. "Dammit, am I crying again?"

Jazz smiled softly, and nodded. "Maybe you really are a Cancer."

Blanche snorted, wiping their eyes. "Just feeling unexpectedly nostalgic. I thought the waterworks would wait until we got there. I should never have started crying again. I can't stop it."

Lee parked the car next to John Cooper's rusty pickup truck. "Damn, it's weird being back here."

"You can say that again," Blanche murmured, stepping out of the car. The mounds park hadn't changed much from when they were still working the street fifteen years ago. Fresh paint on the benches and new signs shared the history of the park—the Nations who had buried their dead at the sacred site for thousands of years, and the story of how it was protected and preserved into a living memorial—were the only new additions. The trees had grown taller, the flowers a little wilder.

But the neighborhood surrounding it had transformed. The boarded up rowhouses had been renovated, with new windows and beautiful gardens, as if the graffiti covering the brown brick had never existed.

The people had changed. Children were running around the daycare playground across the street. Old men were playing chess and talking shit at a picnic table. A few women (not anyone Blanche used to know, but who they could clock from yards away) loitered on a bench in the distance, a mere fraction of the sex workers and dealers who used to frequent the park.

Blanche jumped as Jazz's hand slid into theirs; Lee and Antonio were already halfway down the path, where Miriam and John waited for them next to a bench with a tool bag. Blanche let Jazz guide them along, almost numb from the warring emotions stirring in their chest.

"Wait up!" That was Blanche's only warning, before Phineas's arm wrapped around their shoulders. His dress shirt was rolled up to the elbow, rings and bracelets on display. "Look who's actually on time today!"

"You made it!" Blanche beamed, hugging him around the waist with the arm that wasn't intertwined with Jazz's. "I wasn't sure if you were coming."

"Gonna be honest, Richard and Sunny drove me, since we were all coming from downtown," Phineas admitted. "Otherwise, I probably would have missed it."

"As always, I admire your honesty." Blanche looked over their shoulder, nodding a greeting to Richard. He was busy helping Sunny, as she gingerly slid from the passenger seat of his Range Rover. Blanche's thighs tightened in sympathy; almost three weeks after her surgery, Sunny struggled to sit down, and struggled more to get back up. She was healing though, and Richard was always at her side, doting on her as much she allowed.

"Also, got a notice about your probate court date for your grandma's estate!" Phineas blurted out. "I will email you the deets tomorrow morning, because I am officially off the clock for the day! Work life balance, baby!"

"No Angie today, Phin?" Jazz teased, her hand tightening around Blanche's. Blanche snorted, relieved for the distraction from the probate court mess. Grandma Rose's property had been in care of the state, waiting to be claimed by anyone. Claiming it had sounded much easier than the reality, but Phineas was doing the complicated stuff on their behalf.

Phineas groaned. "Look, man, I get enough of that from your brother. Just because she's technically my date to Dicky's wedding doesn't mean we're a couple."

Jazz hummed skeptically. "The last time we went to one of the Flores parties, Antonio's mom told us that Angie's mom said that you also invited her to your cousin's wedding this summer."

"And you're going to be her plus one to Antonio's stepsister's wedding this fall, right?" Blanche added. "At least, that's what Richard said Antonio's stepdad said."

"Can't keep anything private around here," Phineas muttered, pulling away from Blanche. "Look, we might be attending some weddings together, but that doesn't mean it means anything. And I'm not just saying that because I'm scared of commitment."

"Sure, Phinny." Blanche patted his shoulder as they caught up to Lee, Antonio, Miriam, and John, who greeted Blanche with a hug, passing them a screwdriver without a word of explanation.

Miriam gestured to the bench, where a plaque was loosely attached with two half-sunken screws. "We thought you might want to do the honors, or perhaps say a few words to make it official."

Blanche nodded, wondering what the fuck they were supposed to say. But they had time; Chas and Freddy hadn't arrived yet, and Gabe and Tara were understandably running late.

As if summoned, shrieks of "Aunty Blanche!" and footsteps slapping on the pavement made Blanche turn around. Marisol, Leo, Sebastian, and Catalina all streamed out of Freddy's van, dashing around Sunny and Richard, who still slowly walked toward the bench. Blanche greeted them all with hugs and kisses, exchanging heartfelt greetings with Freddy and Chas, who held a wide-eyed Elena.

Sunny and Richard eventually joined them. "I hate being so slow!" Sunny huffed. "Sorry, we're technically late. We would have been on time if I could walk faster than a turtle!"

"I'm just glad you made it." Blanche greeted her with a kiss on the cheek and Richard with a nod. "Would you prefer to sit?"

"Fuck no!" Sunny snorted. "I just stood up!"

"Sorry, we're late!" Gabe called from the parking lot, slowly extracting a car seat from his Outback. "We're coming!"

"My Fi-fi is here!" Antonio lit up, making grabby hands. Miriam got an equally feverish gleam in her eye.

Dressed in her usual athleisure—hoodie decorated with a spit up stain on the shoulder—Tara hurried in front of Gabe down the path. "Here's the thing!" she announced, pointing in warning to Antonio. "Fia just got to sleep. If we stop moving the car seat for even a second, she will wake up. And her sleep has been regressing lately—of course, as soon as I decide to start working again—and she's been crying whenever she wakes up, and getting her to calm down out here will be—" Her face crumpled as Miriam drew her into a hug.

"You're doing great, sweetheart," Miriam murmured, rubbing Tara's back soothingly. "None of us want to wake her up."

"May I take over car seat rocking duty?" Antonio asked, eyeing the car seat Gabe was slowly swaying. "You better believe I will give her back the second she starts crying."

"Go for it." Gabe held out his swaying arm. His olive green sweater was cleaner than Tara's, but the burp rag was still over his shoulder, as if he'd forgotten it was there.

Antonio carefully mimicked the same pace and motion as Gabe, even while peering under the blanket to coo at the sleeping Sofia.

Blanche put their hand on Gabe's arm; he was still rocking in time with Antonio's swaying. "You can stop moving now."

Gabe frowned at his hand. "I don't think I can, honestly. My body is on autopilot. I'm so tired."

With a snort, Tara grabbed his wrist and wrapped his arm around her shoulders. Gabe kissed the top of her head.

"Yeah, I don't think I want kids," Jazz whispered in Blanche's ear, her hand slipping around their waist.

Blanche bit their lip to keep from laughing, but Tara and Gabe had never looked so frazzled. "Me either."

"Are we waiting for anyone else?" Miriam looked between Blanche and Freddy, who shook their heads. "Wonderful! Let's get started then. Welcome everyone. On behalf of the Friends of the Hopewell Mounds, I'd like to thank you for your donation for this dedicated bench." She gestured to the park bench, the plaque hanging loose on the top plank. "Normally, dedicating these benches don't involve much pomp and circumstance, but for memorials such as this one, we like to give the families an opportunity to say a few words." Miriam smiled expectantly between Chas, Freddy, and Blanche.

Freddy and Chas both muttered "not it" before Blanche could think. They sputtered, still at a loss for what to say, but they cleared their throat.

"Daisy always said she wanted to have her funeral before she died, so she could give her own eulogy and party with her friends one last time." Blanche's voice caught, and Jazz's arm tightened around them. "But that chance was stolen from her, before she ever considered that she might not grow old enough to get sick."

As if summoned, Daisy's voice in their head resurfaced. She'd been quiet these past months, aside from quietly praising them whenever Blanche made a breakthrough. But she was loud and clear now: *Get on with it, Blanchy. We ain't got all day!*

Blanche laughed, the sound wet, and they knew without touching their face that they were already crying again. "If Daisy were here now, I don't think she'd bother with her own eulogy. She'd take one look at this screwdriver in my hand, and ask me what I was waiting for."

"Let's get this shitshow on the road," Chas said, in an uncanny impression of Daisy's dramatic affect. Blanche and Freddy laughed, his with the little sigh on the end that still made Blanche's heart clench.

Saying goodbye to Daisy in this way, giving her a permanent spot to rest in the park where she'd irrevocably changed Blanche's life—Chas's and Freddy's, too—was strange after living with her in their heart for so long. She'd been a blessing and a curse in all of their lives; the ripples of her choices still impacted every person standing beside them. Some in small ways, like Sunny, who had unknowingly lived in Daisy's shadow for years.

Others in larger ways, like how Chas and Freddy would never have met without Daisy. Or how Blanche would never have stumbled across Tara and Lee in that alley years ago, if they hadn't been wandering Eastside aimlessly after that first session with Covey. The one they'd gone to a mere week after Daisy's death, because she had scheduled it. They would never have heard Tara's sobs, or been struck by the sight of her peacoat. All black, except faded white paint on the buttons, chipped off until the daisies that had been painted on were no longer recognizable. A coat Blanche hadn't seen in years, because Daisy had put her favorite coat around the shoulders of a shivering and panicked young Black boy. One who she'd found on a bench in this very park one cold November night, and sent him to St. Mary's for a bed.

Without Daisy's influence, Jazz might never have found the brother she'd lost on the worst night of their lives. And without Daisy's death, Jazz and Lee might never have reconnected, rebuilt the trust and love, or the sibling rivalry, back stronger than ever. None of Blanche's ducklings might be here now, their lives blossoming together. Blanche would never have found the happiness, the stability, the love they had found with all of them, with Jazz.

Their throat tightened again, chest aching as they sniffled. Shayla's voice spoke up in their head, with a reminder of what they'd been working through for the weeks leading up to today: the consequences of Daisy's choices, the guilt of her death, that sorrow that her life had been cut short. None of it had ever been Blanche's burden to bear. It was time to let her go, and finally be free to move on.

Eyes still swimming with tears, Blanche smiled at their nieces and nephews, all huddled around their parents' legs. They all looked so much like Freddy, like Chas, like their aunt Daisy. Blanche held out the screwdriver to them. "Who wants to help me?"

Acknowledgements

Where do I begin the acknowledgements for Carte Blanche?

I will start, as always, with my editor, Mikko, who is supportive and amazing and encouraging, even as they tear my manuscript apart. May your queer hostel always keep the lights on, no matter what happens next. And to my cover designer, Marta, who created my favorite cover of the series for this book (don't tell Sunny).

To my besties, beta/sensitivity readers, and author friends who keep me going and let me talk through all of my questions, get me back on track, and let me rave about the the little things that no one is gonna notice (like, the pockets, did you catch the callback to Tara's first POV chapter in *Loving Lee* about the pockets?!): thank you! Your support is invaluable, and I cannot imagine where this series would be without you.

A huge thanks to my readers as well, especially the ones who DM or email me with their personal stories about how you relate to the characters. I write because these weird little gays in my head won't shut up, but I also write for you, because you relate to the weird little gays in my head more than I ever could have imagined.

And a final thanks to my partner, who still has not read anything I've written, but still answers all of my questions about experiences I will never fully understand. Like what it's like to be a Capricorn.

The acknowledgements always feel flat, and perhaps that's because I don't often write my own thoughts for others to read. This feels vulnerable. I don't like it. But just know, every ounce of support everyone has shown me over the past few years since I started writing Loving Lee back in 2022 has meant so much, and I would never have come close to the success I've had with a project of this magnitude all on my own. I can't wait for you to see what I've got cooking for the Confession universe, and beyond!

Also by Cozy

If you enjoyed this book (or if you didn't!), please kindly show your support by leaving a review and telling your friends about it. Honest reviews and word-of-mouth recommendations make it possible for indie authors to keep writing. Thank you!

Want to read more by Cozy? Check out their books at cozydubois.com

Confession Series
Book 1: *Loving Lee*
Book 2: *Love on the Sunny Side*
Book 3: *Tempting Tara*
Book 4: *Carte Blanche*
Epilogue: *Finally Phineas* coming soon!

Standalone Novels
Earthly Ties

Summer Weddings in Solberg
Petty Roots
Familiar Faces

Long Nights and Bright Futures
Glimmer in the Dark
Dancing in the Snow coming November 2026

Sleighbell Springs
For Luck's Sake
Happy (Endings) for the Holidays coming December 2026
Searching for Starlight coming November 2027
More Happy (Endings) for the Holidays coming December 2027

Short Stories
"Dad, Are You..." — part of *Bi All Accounts: Volume 1.*

About the Author

Cozy DuBois (they/them) thought writing fiction was a long-lost hobby. A longtime lover of romance novels, Cozy has renewed their love for writing by telling stories for and about LGBTQ+ people. They hope to bring more books into the world that represent the complex and entangled relationships between friends, lovers, and chosen family found in the queer community they love.

Based in Minneapolis, they enjoy life with their partner, two hound dogs, a regal queen of a cat, dozens of houseplants, and a garden that has seen better days. Find them with a beverage in hand on a patio anytime the temp is above freezing or planning their next vacation when it's not.

Connect with Cozy on social media or via email updates at cozydubois.com for announcements about upcoming releases.

www.ingramcontent.com/pod-product-compliance
Lightning Source LLC
Chambersburg PA
CBHW061035310726
48969CB00004B/961